DREAMS OF EVENIN

"Is Danny Lucio's son?"

Erica stared, then burst int
"Lucio's! You think I'd go a ... your brother because I
couldn't have you? Of all the obtuse, stupid ... Can't
you even see what's right under your nose?" She
stopped, fear springing to her eyes. She'd gone too far.

Tonio gasped, then light dawned in his eyes. "You
mean ... Danny is *my* son?"

CROSSFIRE by Naomi Horton

"I guess you decided that being saddled with a wife
and baby didn't fit your plans."

"Like being married to me didn't fit yours?" he
retorted. "Stop kidding yourself about who ran out on
whom, Kailin. You're the one who married Royce
McGuire and let him raise my daughter."

"She's not your daughter!" Kailin shouted.

WISH GIVER by Mary Lynn Baxter

"Todd's a candidate for a transplant, but ... we need a
donor."

His eyes were hard. "So make the hospital find one."

"The ... hospital hasn't tried. You see ... Todd's not Jay's
child."

Blood vessels stood out at the base of his neck. "Then
whose ... ?"

"Yours." Glynnis stood, her lips white. "Todd is your
child, Cort."

KRISTIN JAMES,
a former attorney, is married to a family counselor,
and they have a young daughter. Her family and
her writing keep her busy, but when she does have
free time, she loves to read. In addition to her
contemporary romances, she has written a number
of historicals under the name of Candace Camp.

NAOMI HORTON
was born in northern Alberta, where the winters are
long and the libraries far apart. "When I'd run out
of books," she says, "I'd simply create my own—
entire worlds filled with people, adventure and
romance. I guess it's not surprising that I'm still at
it!" An engineering technologist, she presently lives
in Nanaimo, British Columbia, with her collection of
assorted pets.

MARY LYNN BAXTER
sold hundreds of romances before she ever wrote
one. The D&B Bookstore, right on the main drag in
Lufkin, Texas, is the store she owns and manages.
She and her husband, Leonard, garden in their spare
time. Around five o'clock every evening they can be
found picking butter beans on their small farm just
outside of town.

DADDY'S HOME

**Kristin James
Naomi Horton
Mary Lynn Baxter**

Published by Silhouette Books New York
America's Publisher of Contemporary Romance

SILHOUETTE BOOKS
300 East 42nd St., New York, N.Y. 10017

by Request
Daddy's Home

Copyright © 1993 by Harlequin Enterprises B. V.

DREAMS OF EVENING
Copyright © 1983 by Kristin James

CROSSFIRE
Copyright © 1988 by Susan Horton

WISH GIVER
Copyright © 1989 by Mary Lynn Baxter

ISBN: 0-373-20092-7

Printed in the U.S.A.

CONTENTS

A Note from Kristin James

Dear Reader,

Dreams of Evening is one of my favorites among my own books. Part of the reason is that it represented several firsts for me. It was the first Silhouette novel I had written (indeed the first category romance), and I was a little unsure about whether I could write a book of that length. It was the first in the Intimate Moments line. It was the first time I had worked with Leslie Wainger, my editor at Silhouette, with whom I have since worked on many books and who is one of my most treasured friends in publishing. And, if that wasn't enough, it was the first book I did on a word processor—a real hallmark in my career, since I can't imagine how I ever got along without it before that!

I wrote *Dreams of Evening* in the summer and fall of 1982, and I remember that since I originally wrote it as a full-size book, I had to do quite a few revisions to get it down to the right size—which was why I was so very grateful for my new word processor. I had had the very bare bones of the plot in the back of my mind for a while as an historical. Then, in the summer of 1981, when we went to South Padre Island and the Rio Grande Valley for a vacation, I fell in love with the area, and I became intrigued with the idea of setting a contemporary book there. Then I realized that this was the perfect place and time for the story I had had difficulty developing as an historical.

It dealt with many of the themes that are dear to my heart: family, overcoming prejudice, and the chance to recover from past mistakes, as well as the lasting power of love. I sincerely hope that you find it as meaningful and enjoyable as I did ten years ago when I wrote it.

Kristin James

DREAMS OF EVENING

Kristin James

Chapter 1

Erica Logan stood on the narrow balcony, watching the gentle blue roll of the waves as they washed into shore. This was her one precious moment alone in the whole day, the few minutes she spent sipping her coffee and looking at the Gulf after Danny dashed to catch his school bus and before she went down to face the multitude of problems that were her lot as manager of the Breezes. She lifted her face, delighting in the caress of the warm, moist air. No matter how many customer complaints she had to face or how many crises arose in the hotel, Erica thought it was worth it all to be back on the Island again. When she was a child, she and her parents had often driven from their citrus farm in the Rio Grande Valley to vacation here on South Padre Island, and she had loved splashing in the gentle surf and running down the sandy beach. It had seemed the answer to a prayer when she was offered this job and could return here to live.

With a sigh Erica drained her coffee mug and stepped back inside her living room. She had dawdled long enough and now must start to work. Going to the mirror, she smoothed her hair and checked her simple green pantsuit to make sure that she looked her efficient best. Then, picking up her key, she strode

out the door and down the long hall to the elevator at the far
end.

There was a lush, sensual beauty to Erica, which she managed successfully to restrain. She had learned long ago that
unusual looks or signs of femininity did not help a woman rise
in business. Instead she strove for a neat, pleasant, practical
look. Usually she wore an attractive but businesslike suit, with
a blazer or jacket to hide the lines of her excellent figure. She
pulled her long, rich brown hair, warmed by red highlights, into
a sedate knot at the nape of her neck. And though nothing
could make her oval face with its classic lines and light gray eyes
unlovely, Erica carefully screened from her face the emotions
that made it come alive with beauty. Erica had made up her
mind long ago to be a career woman, and she ruthlessly molded
herself to fit the part.

Downstairs in the lobby Erica walked cautiously across the
rust-colored quarry tile, which was still damp from mopping,
and made her way to the front desk. The clerk behind the chest-
high counter, an attractive but effeminate-looking young man,
smiled at her. Dave, always neat and well-dressed himself, approved of her appearance. Erica knew his dislike of Mrs. Berry,
who ran the coffee shop, stemmed from her teased blond hair
and outdated short skirts.

"Hi, Dave, how's it going?" Erica asked, and he rolled his
eyes heavenward. "That bad, huh?"

"Would you like for me to start chronologically or in order
of importance?" Dave replied.

"Oh, dear." Erica swung open the half-door and stepped
into the area behind the tall counter. Across the back wall of the
small room was the telephone complex. To the left lay the semi-
enclosed desk of Rita Escamilla, who acted as Erica's secretary, assistant to the desk clerk and interpreter for many of the
Mexican nationals and Mexican-Americans who came to stay.
Erica's office was on the right, and she crossed to it to unlock
the door.

"Hi, Rita," Erica greeted the pretty, dark-haired girl with a
smile.

"Hi. Want a cup of coffee?"

"I'd love one. It looks like I'm going to need it." Erica switched on the light and glanced back at Dave Granger. "Okay, Dave, come on in here and dump it on me."

He followed her lazily and stood leaning in the doorway, where he would be able to see the approach of a customer. "Well, first of all, that new clerk on the evening shift apparently has no conception of what a reservation is. She put people staying more than one night in several rooms that are reserved beginning today."

Erica groaned. "How many?"

"About twenty rooms."

"Are we overbooked?"

"No. I think we have enough leaving today to take care of the reservations. But Room 906 is steamed because 908 should be reserved for a party joining them today, but crazy Connie booked 908 last night to someone else who's staying three days."

"Well, explain it to the guy in 908 and move him. Let the reservation have that room. Any more like that?"

"I don't think so. I can move the reservations to other rooms, I think. It's just a pain. Where is that girl's brain?"

"I don't know. I'll help you with it in a minute, and I'll go over our system of reservations with Connie again this afternoon. What else?"

Rita eased through the door with a cup of coffee and answered for him. "Two maids and one of the maintenance men didn't show up for work today."

That didn't surprise Erica. Absences were far too common, particularly on a Friday or Monday. Personnel was always one of her major problems. The minuscule wage the hotel paid its workers did not attract the steadiest of help.

"Rita, call the maid service in Brownsville and see if you can get a woman for today. I think one should be enough, since it's the off-season. Do you have any idea if the absences are permanent or if they'll be coming back?"

Rita shrugged expressively. "Dolores called and said she was sick, but the others—who knows?"

Her secretary left the room, and Erica looked back at Dave. "More?"

"I saved the best for last."

"Terrific."

"Alan Severn called just before you came, and said he's driving out today to talk to you."

Erica stared at him. "Mr. Severn? But why?"

"As Rita said, 'Who knows?'" Dave replied with a sarcastic smile, and moved back to his desk.

Erica sighed and took a sip of her coffee, her eyes narrowing in thought. What reason could Severn have for coming here today? Although he was the owner of the hotel, he did not take a very active part in the management of it. He spent most of his energies on a shopping center and restaurant he owned in Harlingen, where he lived.

She wondered with a leap of hope if he had decided to renovate the hotel, then reluctantly discarded the idea. Severn had made it clear over a month ago how he felt about making any further repairs.

No doubt it was true that he did not have the money to spend on the Breezes. Business had suffered badly the season before because of an oil spill that had polluted the Texas beaches. Poor economic conditions had hurt all the resorts even further. Then in August, a hurricane had ripped through, flooding the narrow spit of land that was South Padre Island and damaging the grounds and lobby of the hotel. Whatever money there was to spare had been spent on cleaning and repairing the damage done by the storm. But the Breezes didn't have the financial cushion of chain hotels or those backed by wealthy conglomerates.

It was a pity, Erica thought, for the Breezes, built twelve years before, was a strong and essentially elegant structure. With a little fixing up, it could have been one of the prettiest hotels on the beach. It was a long, thin, white building with elegant black iron-railed balconies off every room, all cunningly slanted so that each had had a view of the ocean and none looked into another balcony. But the lobby needed to be refurbished and the black paint on the balcony railings was chipped and peeling. Years of use by careless tenants had damaged most of the rooms, and nothing more than spot repairs had ever been done. Less noticeable but worse in the long run, much of the original equipment was in poor condition and continually broke done. The breaks were patched up temporarily, and the machinery managed to hobble along, but it didn't stop the accelerating deterioration of the building.

With an effort Erica put aside her musings on the hotel and Mr. Severn's mission and began to open the stack of letters on her desk. When she had finished, she took the two mailed requests for reservations and Dave managed to straighten out the mess Connie Maldonado had made of the reservations the night before. Just as she finished and was about to turn to go back to her office, the front door swung open and Alan Severn hurried in.

"Why, Mr. Severn," Erica greeted him cheerfully, coming from behind the desk to shake his hand.

Severn smiled faintly and took her hand in his dry grasp. He was a thin man whose financial wheelings and dealings had left him with a nervous stomach and a look of perpetual anxiety.

"Mrs. Logan," he returned soberly. "I hope you got my message."

"Oh, yes. Please come into my office. Would you like a cup of coffee?"

"No, no, thank you." He walked past her into the office, and Erica followed him, closing the door firmly against the interested ears of the secretary and desk clerk.

Erica seated herself behind her desk and waited for the man to begin. Severn sat down, adjusted his coat sleeves and glanced around. Finally, with a sigh, he began.

"Mrs. Logan, I guess you know as well as anyone the financial difficulties the Breezes has been having." Erica nodded, wondering with horror if he was going to demand that she cut back expenses. There simply was not anything left to trim off!

Severn cleared his throat and continued, "I don't have the financial capacity to put this old hotel back on its feet. The Breezes has always been my pride and joy, but I've finally decided that I have to give it up. What I'm saying is that I've sold the hotel."

Erica blinked in astonishment. Whatever she had expected Severn to say, it hadn't been this. "Sold?" she repeated. "But...who—"

"Cross Corporation," he replied. "It's a resort development company out of Houston."

"Yes, I've heard of them. I saw pictures of a lovely condominium complex they built in Florida."

"They work mainly in Texas and the South. I think they're a rather new company, but very aggressive."

"But, Mr. Severn, what do they want with the Breezes? I thought they built new hotels."

"Oh, yes, usually they do. But they wanted our location; it's one of the best on the island. And they liked the basic structure of the hotel. What they intend to do is renovate the Breezes and add two wings of condominiums and another pool, as I understand it."

"I see." She did see, indeed. She saw that her return to the valley might not be very long-lived. The new owners would probably bring in their own manager to run the hotel. They might even let go many of the other employees in favor of people they had trained themselves.

"I signed the papers yesterday in Houston. The Breezes is no longer mine."

"Will the new owner be contacting me?" Erica asked uncertainly.

"Oh, yes, Cross wants to get on it right away. An architect is coming in tomorrow to examine the hotel. I don't believe you were here then, but he came about four months ago, before we started negotiating. Anyway, I plan to meet him at the airport tomorrow and drive him out to introduce him to you. His plane gets in at one, so we should be here around two or two-thirty."

Severn rose, ending the conversation, and Erica stood up too. Still numbed by his news, she followed him out of the office and to the front door of the hotel. When the glass door closed behind him, she turned to face the curious faces of Rita and Dave.

"What happened?" Rita asked, her voice concerned. "You look like you've had a shock."

"I have, rather," Erica admitted. "Rita, tell all the employees that I want to see them in the dining room at ten-thirty. I have an important announcement to make."

"What?" Dave pressed. "Come on, Erica."

"I guess I might as well tell you now. Severn has sold the hotel to Cross Corporation."

"What!" The two of them gasped almost in unison.

"Yeah, that's what I thought," Erica responded with a little laugh. "Cross Corporation is a resort developer, and they're going to renovate and add on to the Breezes."

"Well, now at least this poor old thing will get a facelift," Rita mused.

Dave threw her a dark glance and gibed, "Yeah, and we may be some of the 'old fixtures' that get thrown out."

"I hadn't thought of that," Rita admitted, the new excitement dying on her face. "Will we get fired, Erica?"

"I don't know. A representative from Cross is flying in tomorrow. Maybe he can give us some answers. By the way, Dave, is there anyone in the top-floor suite?"

"I don't think so," he replied, and flipped through his cards. "No. Want me to reserve it for the big shot from Cross?"

"Yeah."

"What's his name?"

Erica's eyes widened and she said in amazement, "I don't know. Severn stunned me so much that I never even asked him. Oh, well, just put down Cross Corporation on the card."

Except for the employee meeting, the rest of the day was the usual mishmash of problems, routine and business decisions. At lunch Glynda Berry tried to pump her for information about the sale, but Erica could tell her very little. All the other employees were obviously worried, too, and Erica wished she could reassure them. However, since she had no idea what the new owners would do, she hated to raise what might turn out to be false hopes.

She tried to appear confident and unworried, going about her usual tasks as if nothing had happened, but worry gnawed at her. Where could she go if they fired her? The economy and gas prices had put most of the resort industry into a slump, and a woman with a small boy was not the most attractive prospect for hiring, anyway.

By the time Danny jumped down from the school bus and ran into the lobby, Erica felt drained and anxious to get away from the hotel. When he catapulted into her office, she smiled and said, "How goes it? How would you like to drive over to Port Isabel tonight and eat shrimp?"

"Okay," he replied, answering both her questions. "Look, Mom. Mrs. Benitez said I should show you this."

He handed a paper to her; written across the top in bold red numbers was 110. Erica's eyebrows shot up, and she exclaimed, "110! How can you make 110? I thought 100 was perfect."

"She said the test was so hard, she gave us a bonus question to raise the scores. But I got them all right and the bonus question too."

Erica grinned and held out her arms to the boy. "Come here, you mathematical genius, and let me give you a hug."

Danny was a warm, affectionate child, and he came readily into her arms. He had never known his father and, as a consequence, had grown doubly close to Erica. She sometimes worried that the boy was too attached to her, that he should have a father figure in his life. But she hadn't fallen in love again after Tonio, and she couldn't bring herself to marry a man she didn't love, just so Danny could have a father. Her own father might have been a substitute, but Erica had never been close to him, and since Danny's birth, his angry disapproval had caused her to visit him rarely.

Erica gave Danny an extra squeeze, then released him, and he stepped back. "Can I play on the beach until we go eat?"

She smiled fondly at the boy and reached out to brush a stray lock of heavy black hair from his eyes. He was small for his age, a wiry bundle of energy, forever collecting shells on the beach or fishing or just racing along the sand in sheer high animal spirits. All boy, he was a joy and yet a constant mystery to her.

Swallowing the sudden lump in her throat, Erica said, "Sure, but come in by five-thirty. No, never mind. I think I'd like a walk along the beach. I'll come get you."

He was gone in a shot, and Erica returned to her work. At five Rita stuck her head in the door to say she was leaving, and Erica set about clearing the rest of the work off her desk. By five-thirty she had managed to get everything squared away, and she slipped up to her room to change into shorts and a T-shirt. Quickly she pulled the pins from her hair and ran a brush through the heavy brown mass that glowed with red highlights, like fine mahogany. What a relief it was to get out of the restrictive mold work imposed on her. It would be heavenly to walk along the sand and let the sea breeze toss her mane of hair about. After all, she had been raised on a farm, and she missed the outdoors and the freedom.

Erica ran lightly down the stairs that opened on to the back of the hotel and emerged from the service door by the pool. She crossed a brick pathway beside the pool to the steps leading to the beach. The soft sand near the steps soon gave way to the closely packed sand that lined the ocean.

Breathing in deeply, Erica drank in the scene before her. The sun sank low on the horizon behind her, spreading a golden glow across the water. Waves crashed in, foaming white, and she ventured out to let the water swirl around her legs. The water was shallow for a long way out, which was one of the Island's major appeals to tourists. Children and adults frolicked in the surf far beyond Erica, and the water still did not reach their waists.

Erica began to stroll slowly along the beach, shading her eyes to look for Danny. At last she saw him, earnestly engaged in building a sand fort with another child. When she called to him, he glanced up, then rose quickly, dusting off his shorts, and ran to meet her.

"Look what I got!" he shouted, coming to a scrambling halt in front of her; then he proceeded to dig two handfuls of shells out of his pockets. When Erica had suitably admired them, he repocketed his collection and took her hand, and they began to walk alongside the ocean, now and then idly dabbling their feet in the water.

"Something happened at work today," Erica began, and Danny lifted his face to her inquiringly. "Mr. Severn—you know, the man who owns the hotel—came to see me this morning. And he told me that he had sold the hotel to a company in Houston."

"How come? Doesn't he want it anymore?" Danny asked.

"Oh, I think he still wants it, but he decided he couldn't afford to keep it. It needs a lot of work, and he doesn't have enough money to do it."

"I see. So the new guys are going to fix it all up?"

"Yes, I imagine so. And they're going to build two more wings on to it too."

"Wow! Then I can watch them building! That'll be fun. When are they going to start?"

"I don't know. A man is arriving tomorrow to look at everything. Then I guess he'll draw the plans for the additions, and after that they could start building."

"That'll be neat. Maybe it will be this summer, when I don't have to go to school." He paused and looked at her again. "You don't look very happy. Don't you want them to build on to the hotel and make it look better?"

"Of course I do. I think it could be a fine place. But I am a little worried. Sometimes when a new company comes in, they want to bring in their own people to operate the hotel. They might not want to keep me."

"You mean they'd fire you?" Danny asked in disbelief.

Erica smiled at his tone. "They might. Not because they don't like me, but because they want someone they trained in the job."

"I see," Danny acceded, although to him it still seemed rather peculiar. "What would we do then? Go to another hotel?"

"I hope so. I would apply to other places here on the Island and in Brownsville and Harlingen. I'd like to stay in the Valley area if we could."

"But what if you couldn't get a job? I mean, here or anywhere else. What would we do?"

"If worse came to worst, we could always go home and live with my father on the farm. How would you like that?"

Danny considered her question. "I'd like to live on the farm, I think. There are all kinds of interesting things to do there. But I'm not sure. We hardly ever go there." He paused. "I don't know if I like Granddaddy."

"Oh, why not?"

"He always looks like this." Danny made a stern face, drawing down the corners of his mouth. "And he talks funny to you, like he's mad about something."

"He probably is. Dad and I never agreed about too many things. I love him, but we don't get along very well." She sighed and looked out at the sea. "He wants us to come home and live and I want to be independent. Sometimes I wonder if I've done the right thing, refusing to go home. Danny, has it been terribly hard on you, living as we've done? I mean, with me work ng, and you having to stay with a sitter, and our moving whenever I got a new job."

Her son looked at her in puzzlement. "What do you mean? Would I rather live someplace else?"

"Yes, like on the farm with Granddaddy. Do you wish that we didn't live in a hotel or that we didn't move so often? Do you get lonely?"

"No. I like the farm, but I like it here too. I get to swim all the time and play on the beach and run around in the hotel. I think it's lots of fun."

She looked down at him, a tiny frown pinching the skin of her forehead, and she wondered, as she so often did, if she had done the right thing for Danny by insisting on raising him on her own. But his open, pleasant face banished the frown and made her smile. Surely she had been right. Danny was so normal, so well adjusted, that it seemed impossible that he should be scarred by his upbringing.

With an affectionate gesture she reached out and ruffled his thick black hair. "Well, that's enough soul-searching for the moment. I think I'm about ready to eat. How about you?"

"Sure. Wanna race home?" he offered hopefully.

With a laugh she agreed, and they set out. Danny was small for a nine-year-old, but quick, and Erica had to run full-tilt to keep up with him. He reached the stairs to the hotel seconds before she arrived, breathless and flushed from the exertion.

"Beat you!" Danny crowed triumphantly. "I'm the fastest boy in my class."

They turned on the outdoor shower head and washed the sand from their feet, then went up to change for dinner. Erica merely exchanged her shorts for a denim skirt and slipped her tanned feet into sandals, for there were few places in this resort town that required anything but casual clothes.

In the blue knit top and with her thick mane of dark hair spreading across her shoulders, Erica attracted several admiring glances as they walked out to their car. However, she paid scant attention to them. She dated occasionally, but between her job and Danny she had little time for, or interest in, men.

They got into her small blue Datsun and drove over the high bridge that connected South Padre Island to the Texas mainland.

Padre Island was a narrow spit of land lying parallel to the
South Texas coastline as it curved south to Mexico. The northern tip of the island was at Corpus Christi, the southern edge
almost at Brownsville. North Padre and South Padre were two
distinct communities without even a highway connecting the
two, and in between them lay the empty beach wilderness of a
protected state park. South Padre, known simply as "the Island" to the nearby mainland residents, possessed a single main
street running lengthwise straight up the middle of the land like
a backbone. Side streets ran off at right angles, none more than
three or four blocks long. Date palms stood at each intersec-
tion and in front of many of the hotels, giving the locale a
tropical flavor, enhanced by the pristine white sand of the
beaches and the glittering blue ocean beyond. The industry of
the island was tourism, and the space was dominated by several tall hotels, with shorter motels, condominiums and a few
beach houses squeezed in between. Except for restaurants,
beachware and supplies stores and realty offices, there was little else on the island. Most of the people who worked on the
island lived across the narrow bay in Port Isabel, which provided the island with the normal appurtenances of a community, such as grocery stores and self-service laundries.

Erica and Danny ate boiled Gulf shrimp at a plain but delicious restaurant in Port Isabel, and after they returned, there
was barely enough time for Danny to do his homework before
he went to bed. They did not speak again about the sale of the
hotel or the possible consequences to themselves.

Erica tucked her son into bed and sat down to pay a few bills,
but her eyelids quickly grew heavy, and she decided to turn in
early. After tying back her hair, she scrubbed her face and put
on a simple white nightgown. Before retiring, she slipped into
Danny's small room for a final look at him.

He lay on his back, fast asleep, his arms flung wide. As she
looked down at him, her eyes misted over, and she smiled.
Asleep, there was no hint of the active, sometimes mischievous boy he was during the day. Lovingly her eyes traced the
outlines of his tanned face. The cheekbones were wide and
high, his mouth firm. His eyebrows were black slashes across
his face. Only his gray eyes were evidence of Erica's parentage.

his facial structure and coloring were very much his father's. With his eyes closed, he looked like Tonio, Erica saw with a sudden pang. The older he got, losing the vague lines of babyhood, the more Tonio surfaced in his face.

A lump formed in Erica's throat, and she swallowed and quickly left the room.

The next day, everyone went about their jobs with their eyes half on the entrance to the lobby. They were nervous about the upcoming meeting with the representative of the new owner— Erica as much as anyone, although she managed to hide her nerves beneath a calm mask. She had carefully chosen for this important meeting her most sedate and expensive suit, a chocolate-brown skirt with a matching brown hip-length jacket buttoned over a plain beige blouse. She wore no ornament except for the small gold studs in her ears and a watch.

At about two-thirty, as she sat reading a letter for the third time, her stomach jumping, Rita stepped into her office. "Mr. Severn's here. I just saw him walking to the door. And you should see the guy with him—absolutely gorgeous!"

Erica smiled tightly. "Good, then maybe we'll leave it to you to win him over."

"I wish," Rita said in a fervent undertone.

Erica stepped past her and walked around the counter into the lobby just as the door swung open and Mr. Severn ushered in his guest. The man was of medium height, dark, with straight black brows and thick black hair. His face was angular, his lips firm, almost chiseled. Dark eyes ringed with thick black lashes glanced about the room and came to rest on her, narrowing with surprise as he came to a sudden halt.

Across the room Erica stood stock-still, staring at him, her mind numb with astonishment and disbelief. She heard faintly, as if he were far away, Mr. Severn speak her name. There was a roaring in her ears, and for a moment she was afraid she might faint. It couldn't be—and yet it was. After all these years the man she had thought she would never see again stood before her: Tonio!

Chapter 2

The roaring in her ears died, and Erica straightened, pulling herself together, as the two men advanced toward her. Wetting her lips, she managed a shaky smile, although her face was paper-white from the shock.

"Mrs. Logan, this is Anthony Cruz, the architect from Cross Corporation," Severn introduced him. "Anthony, this is Erica Logan, the manager of the Breezes."

Cruz, after his initial amazement, had assumed a look of careful indifference. "Yes," he said politely, his glance touching Erica coldly. "I know Erica. We are from the same town."

Erica held out her hand to shake his, trying to match his calm unconcern. "Hello, Antonio. I'm afraid I had no idea it was you who was coming today."

"Well, isn't that remarkable?" Severn commented. "Strange how you'll accidentally meet people you know like that. Well, Anthony, I'll leave you in Mrs. Logan's capable hands. I'm sure she will be able to help you with anything you need to know. It's been a pleasure."

The two men shook hands, and Cruz murmured a polite good-bye. Then he turned back to her, and Erica clasped her hands to hide her nervousness.

"If you would like, I'll take you up to your room now," she offered, although that was the last thing in the world she wanted to do. However, Rita and Dave would think it peculiar and rude if she handed the task over to one of them. She turned toward the desk. "Dave, could I have the key to 1000? Mr. Cruz, allow me to introduce you to my secretary, Rita Escamilla, and our desk clerk, Dave Granger."

Dave handed her the key, and the three strangers exchanged polite greetings. Erica walked to the elevator with Antonio following behind her. She tried desperately to calm her jittering stomach, but the thought of riding up in the elevator with him and walking him to his room was altogether too unsettling. She told herself that no doubt he hardly remembered her. That summer ten years ago had probably been only one in a string of romances to him, even though it had changed her life forever. He would certainly not inject any emotion into this business meeting. There was no reason to feel afraid and sick. It had all happened a long time ago, and she was over the pain as well as the love.

They stepped into the elevator and the door closed behind them. Erica looked down at the floor to avoid his eyes, then forced herself to lift her gaze. She refused to act embarrassed and frightened. She found her companion looking at her expressionlessly, and she braced her shoulders, returning his stare. He was as handsome as ever, she thought, maybe even more so, now that he had matured. However, the sullen, angry good looks had been replaced by a cold hardness. Once he had exuded emotion; now no feeling touched him at all.

"Well, it's been a long time," she commented, to break the oppressive silence, and then cursed herself for sounding so banal. His presence was overwhelming, and she could hardly think or even breathe. Even after all this time, after all he'd done to her, he still set her pulse rolling like a drumbeat and made her nerves quiver.

"Yes," he replied shortly. "I noticed he called you Mrs. Logan."

Her hands turned icy. He must not find out the truth. She gave a brief laugh and said, "Alan Severn isn't known for his memory. For some reason he thinks I'm married. I finally stopped reminding him that it's Miss Logan."

The elevator stopped on his floor, and Erica stepped out gratefully, leading the way down the hall to the large suite at the end. She opened the door and handed the key to Tonio. "If you need anything, just let us know."

"Tomorrow I'd like to inspect the hotel—the lobby, the rooms, the maintenance area, the coffee shop, everything."

"Of course."

"I hope you won't mind taking your free Sunday to show me around."

"Me?" Erica repeated dully, recoiling at the thought of spending the entire day tramping around the hotel with him.

"Of course. You know it better than anyone else."

"Of course," Erica agreed through bloodless lips. "What time shall we start?"

"Nine o'clock?" She nodded, and he continued, "I'll meet you at your office."

"All right."

Erica could feel his eyes on her back as she strode away, and she kept herself stiffly straight. She touched the elevator button, and when the doors slid open, she hurried inside, carefully refraining from glancing around to see if he still watched her. Safe from his gaze, she sagged against the wall, her energy flooding away and leaving her shaking, both inside and out.

Tonio Cruz—after all this time! Why did he have to come here! Why had she accepted this job! She wanted desperately to run upstairs, pull Danny to the car and drive away as quickly as she could. How could she possibly escort that man around the hotel tomorrow as if nothing had ever happened between them?

Once in the lobby Erica walked past the eager, curious faces of the employees and shut herself in her office, where she sat down at her desk and rested her face on her trembling hands. Gradually she calmed down enough to realize that in this state she would not be able to do any of her work. The best thing would be to leave the office and go to her apartment or walk along the beach and think. She had to put her head and her emotions into some semblance of order. Rita stared with surprise when Erica told her she was leaving for the day, but she made no comment. Erica suspected that her face gave away a least some of the turmoil going on inside her. She went to her apartment and changed clothes, glad that Danny was not there but out playing by the pool.

She slipped down the staircase and out the back door, then wandered along the sand for some time, hardly noticing where she was going, her thoughts a jumble. Finally she stopped to glance around her and realized she had walked all the way down the beach.

Erica sighed and sank down to the ground. Pulling her knees up and circling them with her arms, she stared out at the hypnotic waves. Now that she had worked off her nerves, maybe she could begin to think more clearly. Lulled by the beat of the surf, she relaxed, letting her mind drift. Inexorably her thoughts were pulled backward, past all the years and the barriers she had worked so hard to construct...to the time ten years before when she looked out her bedroom window and saw Tonio Cruz in the front yard, talking to her father.

She had been seventeen then, idle, confident and exploding into the full ripeness of her young beauty. Her father was a well-to-do citrus farmer who gave her whatever she wanted in the way of material goods. She spent her summer zipping around in her small sports car or sunning by the pool or gossiping with friends over lunch at the country club. In the evening she flirted with one or another of the boys who pursued her diligently. It was amazing—and a little heady—this new power she held over the boys she had known all her life, and it was fun to exercise it a little. But her basic generosity prevented her from teasing them to the point of cruelty, and her sense of humor kept the whole thing in perspective.

She herself had never felt the ache of teenage love that afflicted her swains. Until she saw Antonio. He stood sideways to her as he talked to her father, and she could see his cleanly etched profile, strong and handsome. His head was bare, and the sun glinted off his crow-black hair. His faded jeans clung to his lean, firm thighs, and the sleeves of his blue work shirt were rolled up to reveal corded muscles that belied his slimness. He was lithe and hard, exciting in a way Erica had never known before. Looking at him, she felt a hot, wild explosion in her chest, a strange sizzling along her nerves, and unconsciously she leaned toward him.

She knew him, of course. The town of Santa Clara was much too small for everyone not to know everyone else. Besides, Tonio had worked for her father when he was a teenager, before he had gone away to college four years before. But she hadn't seen him for four years, and at thirteen she hadn't experienced the same shattering emotion as when she looked at him now.

She watched as he and her father left the yard and disappeared around the corner of the house. No doubt they were going to the side door that led to Grant Logan's study. Without stopping to analyze her motives, knowing only that she had to speak to Tonio, she darted down the stairs, grabbing a magazine from the hall table as she ran, and went onto the wide veranda that surrounded the house on three sides. She hurried to the wooden swing that hung close to the side door, and flopped down on it; then she opened the magazine and fixed her eyes intently on it as she listened for the sound of her father's study door closing inside the house. As she waited, she fluffed her hair and combed through it with her fingers, wishing she had taken the time to brush it and apply a little lipstick. Her clothes were plain and casual, but she knew how well her tanned legs looked emerging from the short cutoff blue jeans and how nicely she filled out the pale pink halter top.

It seemed forever before she heard the closing of the heavy door inside the hall and then the scrape of Tonio's boot heels on the tile floor. The screen door swung open and he stepped out. Involuntarily Erica sucked in her breath. Tonio was even more handsome close up, more wickedly dangerous-looking. The chiseled mouth had a surly, almost defiant set to it, and his shadowed dark eyes burned with a cold flame. He looked wild and fiery, pulsing with energy and life. Erica thought that if she touched him, an electrical jolt might pass through him into her. He didn't see her sitting there in the swing, shaded by a large, purple-blooming jacaranda bush, and he started across the porch.

"Hello, Antonio," she called out quickly to stop him. He whirled, startled, and stared at her for a moment. Even his quick, impersonal glance sent shivers down her spine.

"Ma'am," he replied distantly, and started on.

"Tonio, it's me, Erica!" she exclaimed, jumping up. "Don't you recognize me?"

"Sorry, I didn't at first." He swept her with an impassive gaze. "You're quite a bit older."

His words had none of the leer that usually accompanied remarks about her growing up: He sounded matter-of-fact, almost indifferent. Nor did his eyes light up with interest in the woman's face and figure she now possessed. He said nothing more, and Erica felt awkward and foolish, standing across from him in silence. Tonio obviously had nothing to say to her and was simply waiting politely for her to continue the conversation she had forced.

"Welcome back," she murmured lamely.

Something flared then in his dark brown eyes, and he snapped, "I won't be here long."

Erica sank back onto the cushioned seat and buried her face in the magazine, acutely aware of the sound of his boots on the porch and then on the cement walkway. She blinked back hot tears. His cold, brusque manner had hurt, especially since she felt anything but indifferent when she looked at him. Long after she heard his car leave, she remained in the swing, thinking about Tonio and his reaction to her. For a while she was tempted to try to forget all about him, for her vanity had been wounded. But a "So there!" attitude couldn't stand up for long against the burning desire she had to see him again—and, more than that, to fix his interest.

Looking back on it, Erica wondered at her daring and persistence in pursuing Tonio. Nowadays she would never think of making any effort to capture the heart of a man who appeared indifferent to her. But back then she had never lost, never failed to win over any boy's heart. She couldn't really imagine wanting something and not receiving it. And she had wanted Tonio—more than anything in the world she had wanted Tonio. She was caught in the fiery clutches of youthful love and passion. With her usual confidence she was determined to make him fall for her. She began to seize every opportunity to run into Antonio. And for each "accidental" meeting, she made sure her hair and face were at their loveliest and that she wore clothes that set off her excellent figure. She would ride her horse, Morning Star, down to the citrus groves and wander along the borders between the rows of trees. If she was lucky, she would come across Tonio opening the turnout valves along the irrigation pipe and flooding the rows of grapefruit trees with precious water. If Rafael Escobar, her father's foreman, happened to be there, she could stop to say a few words to him, thus placing herself in Tonio's line of vision for a while longer. But if Tonio was by himself, or with one of the other men, Erica could find no excuse to linger. He would scowl and return her greeting shortly, and Erica would be unable to get any sort of conversation going.

One morning, as she left the house in a smart white tennis skirt and top, on her way to the club to play tennis with Sally Blackburn, she spied Tonio by the barn, working on the engine of the tractor. Quickly Erica tossed her racket into the passenger seat of her car and crossed the yard to the barn.

"Hi!" she called brightly as she drew near, and Tonio glanced at her briefly, then returned to his work. Erica sighed and watched his long, slender fingers turn the wrench. Just the sight of them set up a curious trembling in her stomach. Finally she said, "Tonio, I've been wondering about something. Didn't you graduate from the University of Texas this year?"

"Yeah, got a degree in architecture," he responded laconically.

She went on doggedly, "So why are you back in Santa Clara, working on Daddy's farm? Why aren't you out drawing plans for houses?"

"I plan to design commercial buildings, not residences," he told her gruffly.

"Okay, then, why aren't you drawing big buildings?"

"I've been hired to start work for a firm in September. Until then, I thought I'd come back here and see my mother. Earn a little money."

"I see. Where are you going to work in September?"

He straightened, his brow drawn into a fierce frown. "Don't you have anything better to do with your time than bother me? Aren't you expected somewhere?" He glanced pointedly at her tennis outfit.

A pain pierced her chest at his rough words, and Erica had to force back the tears that sprang into her eyes. "I was just trying to be nice! To be a little friendly! Before you went off to the university, at least you'd stop and talk to me sometimes. At least you were decent. I remember, even if you don't. I remember the time you climbed onto the roof to get the tennis ball I knocked up there. And the time I sprained my ankle out in the groves and you carried me back to the house.''

His dark eyes softened a trifle, and he said, ''You were a good kid. Besides, you'd done me a favor once.''

''A favor?'' Erica stared at him wonderingly for a moment, then understanding dawned on her face. ''Oh! You mean in the school yard when I was in the second grade? When Jim Bob Coulter and Rusty Jansen jumped on you?''

''That's the time.'' He almost smiled. ''You came running over there like a pint-size tornado, kicking and scratching and screaming.''

''Well, they were bigger than you. They were already in junior high. And it wasn't fair, two on one like that.''

''Oh, I'm not complaining. I was rather grateful, as I remember. You brought the teachers running. And gave Rusty a nice bruise on his shin.''

''So if I helped you so much, why do you dislike me now?'' Erica asked bluntly.

His face closed down and he said brusquely, ''You aren't a little girl anymore.''

Something hot and elemental sparked in his eyes as he said it, and Erica felt a fierce leap of hope. ''What does that mean?''

''I think you know.'' He returned to the engine, plainly ignoring her.

Anger spurted through her, and Erica swung away, striding to her car. All right, then, she told herself. Tonio plainly did not want her, and it was time she got used to the fact. Maybe he was in love with someone else, even engaged to a girl back at the university. Or maybe she was too young in his eyes, too immature and inexperienced; he wanted a girl who had been around. There was obviously no hope for her. It had been idiotic, anyway, to try to fix his interest. Tonio was going away at the end of the summer. Besides, Daddy would have a fit if she started dating one of his workers. It had been silly to try to make him desire her merely because she was stung by his indifference. Well, Erica thought grimly, she had learned her lesson now.

One Friday over a week later, late in the afternoon, after the workers had come to the house to get their week's pay, Erica went downstairs and out the side door to the swimming pool. The Logans' house had been built many years before by Erica's grandparents, but the pool was an addition Grant had made a few years earlier for Erica's benefit. Date palm trees and oleander bushes formed a protective wall beyond the pool on two sides, to hide it from the view of the driveway and the front yard. Lounge chairs and a metal table with an umbrella decorated the stone patio beside the rectangular, tile-rimmed pool.

Erica slipped off her terry cover-up and dived cleanly into the water, which glittered in the falling rays of the sun. Quickly she swam laps until her breath was spent, and she had to stop to cling to the side of the pool. The dying sun was warm on her torso, and she slid back into a lazy float.

"Erica." Her father's voice roused her. She brought her feet down and turned toward the house.

Grant Logan exited from the side door and crossed the stone patio to the pool. He was a tall, slender man with a stern, tanned face and fierce blue eyes. His crisp, iron-gray hair was cut short. He loved his daughter, but he disapproved of her generation, and he found it easier to express his disapproval than his love. Erica thought him an unbending man, despite his frequent generosity, and often wondered if he had any real affection for her.

"I'm going to the club to play golf with Fred Barton, and then I'm meeting James Wallace there for dinner. I imagine I'll be gone until fairly late. I sent Cruz over to McAllen for a tractor part, and he hasn't gotten back yet. So when he comes in for his check, you give it to him. It's in my study, in the middle drawer of the desk."

"Okay." Erica's heart began to thud wildly in her chest.

"And for heaven's sake, go upstairs and change into something decent." Logan eyed her turquoise bikini with distaste. "I don't want him seeing you in that."

"Tonio Cruz is the last person you have to worry about," Erica assured him dryly.

Grant gave a snort that indicated his basic distrust of any man, and strode away to the driveway. Erica climbed out and toweled dry, wrapped the white terry-cloth jacket around her, and started for the house to change clothes. Halfway to the door she stopped for a moment, then turned slowly and sauntered back to the patio. Dropping her jacket from her shoulders, she lay down on one of the lounge chairs. She was going to take this one last chance at Tonio. No doubt he would sneer or look right through her with his implacable brown eyes, but she couldn't bear to pass up the opportunity her father had dropped in her lap.

It had been a foolish thing to do, and had Erica been any older or wiser, she would have realized just what her actions might lead to. However, she was young and still rather naive and certain that Tonio's actions had proved his total indifference to her. She wanted something to occur, but she was totally unprepared for what did happen.

Impatiently she waited for Tonio's return, now and then diving into the pool to swim off her excess energy. At last she heard the solid click of his boot heels against the cement walkway, and she forced herself to relax in her chair, her eyes closed, feigning sleep. The steps hesitated as they passed her, then hurried up the steps to the door. He knocked briskly.

Erica opened her eyes and looked at him. Tonio's back was to her, his hands thrust into his back pockets. He wore his usual faded jeans and a white T-shirt. The back of the shirt was damp with sweat, and the short sleeves revealed the bulging muscles of his arms.

"He's not there," Erica called clearly, and rose from the chair.

Tonio swung to face her, turning his head more than his body. The expression on his face was carefully blank, but his eyes flickered over her body involuntarily. Erica felt a warm glow of triumph, no matter how small the victory had been, and she slowly strolled toward the porch.

"Daddy went to play golf and have dinner at the club. He said he wouldn't be back until late and for me to get your check for you."

Tonio stepped away from the door and let Erica pass through before him, then followed her down the hall to her father's study. Erica went to the desk and pulled a white envelope from the middle drawer. The front of the envelope was marked Cruz in Grant's large, precise hand. Erica held the pay envelope out to Tonio and he stretched one arm out to take it from her.

Cruz folded the envelope and stuck it into the back pocket of his trousers as they retraced their steps to the side patio. Erica's hands were cold, despite the summer heat, and the pulse in her throat was throbbing with excitement and hope and fear. She wanted to sit down and let Tonio go his own way, but even more she wanted to make him remain.

"Why don't you stay for a swim?" Erica turned to Tonio and stared him straight in the eyes, a challenge in her unflinching gaze.

Erica could see from Tonio's expression that he was about to refuse, but the dare in her eyes stopped his words. Instead he countered, "I don't have any swimming trunks with me."

Again her eyes flashed a challenge, and an answering flame flared up in his, but she said only, "Oh, Daddy has some extra suits for guests inside. I'm sure we could find one to fit you."

Cruz hesitated for a fraction of a second; then, in one fluid motion, he whipped his T-shirt over his head, revealing a hard, brown chest, smooth and muscled, a small gold medal on a chain bright against his skin. Erica faltered, suddenly shy and amazed at her boldness, fighting the breathless surge of feeling that swelled in her throat. Quickly she skirted Tonio and returned to the house, and Tonio followed her more slowly. The swimsuits were in the downstairs bathroom, and Erica left Tonio there to change. She returned to the pool, a blush staining her cheeks with red.

Erica dived into the pool and swam to the end, then turned, holding on to the rim with one hand, and waited for Tonio to emerge from the house. He came out a few moments later, bright red trunks a slash of color against his tanned skin. His legs were slender but well muscled, his stomach flat and spare. Without glancing at her, Tonio dived into the pool and swam to her end, his strokes smooth and economical. He surfaced in front of her, treading water lazily, the water streaming from his face and thick hair. Impatiently he pushed his hair from his eyes, and his hands sent droplets of water flying.

"You swim well," Erica complimented him.

His smile was thin and bitter. "For a boy who never saw the inside of a country club? Fortunately, U.T. forces you to learn to swim, and I enjoyed it, so I used the pool all the time I was there."

"You don't accept compliments very gracefully," Erica pointed out. "I didn't mean anything nasty by it."

"Sorry. My mistake. I forgot you were the defender of the underprivileged." Suddenly he moved closer, his eyes bright, almost menacing, and grasped the edge of the pool beside her with one sinewy hand. "Tell me, Miss Logan"—his tone mocked her name—"is that why you flaunt yourself in front of your daddy's workers? Riding down to inspect the work in jeans as tight as your skin and a T-shirt that clings to your breasts? Handing out the paychecks in a bikini? What's that for? To give the poor peons a little lift in their day?" His other hand went to the rim of the pool on the other side of her, hemming her in, trapping her between his arms. He sneered as he spoke, white teeth flashing against his tan skin. "Or is it to tantalize them, to give them just the tiniest taste of what they'll never have, what they'd be killed for touching? Damn, you're a little tease, Erica. Doesn't torturing the rich boys down at the club give you enough of a thrill? Isn't their blood hot enough for you?"

"No!" Erica stared at him, her eyes wide with horror. "No, I didn't—I don't do that. I mean, I never intended to—"

"No?" One black eyebrow arched in disbelief.

Wildly Erica searched for something to say to make him believe her, but she couldn't tell him that her actions had been meant to entice only him, to spur him to notice her, want her, ask her out, kiss her.... Erica could only stare at him, unable to defend herself, and shake her head helplessly.

Cruz moved closer to her, and his hands slid along the rim until they touched the bare skin of her shoulders. Erica could hardly breathe or think; Tonio's nearness overwhelmed her senses. His fiery, glittering eyes mesmerized her, held her motionless before him.

Thickly he muttered, "Somebody ought to teach you a lesson, Erica Logan. Not to tease and torment a man until he almost explodes from wanting you." Then his lips were upon hers, pressing fiercely against her mouth, opening her lips to his hot, savage tongue, and one iron arm went around her shoulders, imprisoning her against the tough bone and muscle of his chest. Erica's dismay and resentment fled at his touch, and she was conscious of nothing except the wild roaring in her ears, the sweet delight of his mouth and the hard metal circle of the medallion pressing into the tender flesh of her chest.

Her arms went up to encircle his neck, and her inexperienced lips responded eagerly to his kiss. Erica felt a shudder pass through Tonio's body, and his free hand cupped her breast, gently kneading it through the wet fabric of the swimsuit until the nipple thrust out against the cloth, firm and proud. Tonio lifted Erica, bracing her against the cement edge of the pool, to bury his face against her chest, his tongue and mouth exploring the creamy, quivering tops of her breasts. The rim bit into her back, but Erica hardly noticed the discomfort, so aware was she of the touch of his lips on her skin.

Now his hands were beneath her buttocks, digging hungrily into the soft flesh, pressing her against his lean, hard length. She gasped as a fiery pinwheel burst inside her, a wild and wanton thing she had never experienced before. Suddenly frightened by her own response, she stiffened. No! This was not what she had intended when she had set out to lure Tonio to remain with her by the pool. She had meant only to dazzle him and make him admire her, to sow the seeds of love such as she felt for him. She hadn't meant to bring about this wild, abandoned lovemaking.

Erica reached out behind her and struggled onto the cement that surrounded the pool. He let her go easily, but before she could gather her thoughts enough to wonder about that, Tonio was heaving himself out of the pool with his strong arms, and she realized it had suited him to have them both out of the water. Quickly Tonio stood and pulled her up with him, running his hands over her slick, wet body. His eyes were black and molten with desire, and his fingers trembled slightly on her skin.

He murmured something softly in Spanish, words Erica did not know, but whose meaning was torridly, pulsatingly clear, and his hands fumbled at the thick knot tying her bikini top until it fell from her, revealing her lush breasts, a pale contrast to the rest of her carefully tanned skin. Tonio swallowed hard his eyes hungrily roaming the naked globes, lingering over the soft pink aureoles of the nipples, with their desire-pointed centers. Erica did not move, her body aflame with the fire he had created. Quickly he stood and in one swift motion pulled the swimming trunks off. Erica swallowed, her throat dry, filled with eagerness and yet also touched faintly by fear.

"Tonio," Erica said softly, holding up her arms to him, and the steady flame in his eyes exploded into something more fevered. She meant to ask him to go slowly with her and be gentle, but the words never reached her lips. He covered her with the full weight of his body, pressing her against the cloth slats of the chair, and his knee parted her legs. Erica stiffened at the brief moment of pain, and he paused, his breath searing her neck. Slowly he began to move within her, building to the white-hot pitch of pleasure that shook him and made Erica arch feverishly against him.

"Tonio," she breathed again as he sagged against her, and her arms went around him, clasping him to her fiercely. "Tonio."

Chapter 3

Erica rose from the beach with a sigh, dusted the sand off her bare legs and began to trudge back toward her hotel. It had been ten years, yet she remembered that day by the pool as clearly as if it were only a week ago. She could still feel the dying heat of the sun enveloping them, Tonio's muscled body relaxed against her, his breath warm and uneven on her neck. Tonio had made a funny half groan, half laugh and sat up, plunging his hands into his thick, dark hair. "Well, I guess that cuts it. Of all the stupid things to do . . ."

Erica, awash in the aftermath of passion, frowned faintly and reached up a hand to touch his corded brown back. "What's the matter?"

He swiveled and shot her an unreadable glance. "I—I'm sorry. I didn't know you were a virgin. Oh, hell, I didn't even think about it, any more than I considered the consequences." He looked away, staring at the hot-pink oleander blossoms on the opposite side of the pool. "What do you intend to do now?"

"What do you mean?" His voice chilled her glow, and Erica was suddenly very aware of her nakedness.

"Are you going to send the posse after me for defiling your fresh young Anglo body?"

"No!" She sat up indignantly. "Do you honestly think I would tell anyone?"

"Your father."

"Him least of all." Hurt and embarrassed, Erica turned away to retrieve the pieces of her swimsuit. It was a struggle to get into the wet bikini, and by the time she finished, her face was aflame.

Tonio left his swimming trunks where they lay and pulled on his jeans and T-shirt. Leaning back in the lounge chair, he clasped his hands behind his head and studied her coolly. "So your game isn't to lure the poor dumb Mexican into bed and then claim rape. What is it?"

"Damn you," Erica muttered through clenched teeth. He was destroying all the beauty and warmth of what had happened. "I wasn't playing any game! Why do you have such a chip on your shoulder? You must realize you're devastatingly handsome. You have a degree from U.T. and you're an architect. Why do you insist on pretending you're some poor migrant worker who just sneaked across the border? Why *shouldn't* I be interested in you? Is it a crime?"

"No crime. But hard to believe. I've seen too many like you who love to tease."

"Was that teasing?" Erica gestured toward the chair where they had lain, tears sparkling in her eyes. "Do you think I'd do that with just anyone? For your information, I never—*never*—threw myself at anyone like I did at you. I wasn't trying to show off to the workers. I wanted *you* to notice me, to talk to me. How can you—didn't it mean anything to you? I mean—oh, why did you have to go and ruin it?" With a chocked cry, she broke and ran for the house, slamming the door behind her.

On the patio Tonio Cruz rose and gazed at the still-vibrating screen door, his usually arrogant posture replaced by uncertainty, his dark eyes troubled. Finally he shook his head and whispered to himself, "No. Don't be an idiot, Cruz." Shoving his hands in his pockets, he walked away.

Erica passed the following two days in a haze of misery, shame and remembered delight. She recalled the electric ex-

citement that had flared between her and Tonio. How could he
have gone through that experience and felt nothing? She knew
she would never be the same again. With teenage naiveté she
had thought she had fallen in love with him at first sight,
thought that what she had felt for him up until then was the
most wondrous thing on earth. Now she knew differently. Her
earlier love wasn't a tenth of what she felt for him now. In the
brief moment that they had come together, they had seemed
perfectly united. She understood what people meant when they
said a husband and wife were one. She had been one person
with Tonio and had believed that he shared the feeling. Then
he had shattered her illusion by telling her he believed her to be
a sly, vindictive bitch who had merely been playing a game with
him. Recalling the things he had accused her of, she shriveled
inside with embarrassment. To make it even worse, in her anger and hurt she had exposed her own feelings for him. Had he
dismissed her with contempt? Or had he gone home and
bragged about the easy conquest he had made of his boss's
daughter? Her cheeks flamed at that thought. How could it
have meant so little to Tonio?

Yet, she loved him, wanted him with all her heart. She could
not forget the bursting joy of their lovemaking, and she prayed
he would return and pull her into his arms again to show her all
the hot, yearning mysteries of a man and a woman. Later she
would realize how foolish her hopes were, for the love and pain
she experienced at that time were small compared to what she
would feel for Tonio later.

One evening, when she had all but given up her eager hopes,
she sat at her bedroom window, staring out into the night.
There was movement on the lawn, a shifting of shadows that
drew her attention, and she leaned forward.

The yard was washed in moonlight, the pale gleam shimmering on the leaves of the date palms and turning the century
plants silvery. The tall white oleander bushes along the side of
the yard quivered, and she saw a shadow separate itself from
the bush and stroll to the cover of a palm. Her nerves leaped in
excitement. The man moved quietly, as if he had no desire to be
noticed, but without the furtiveness of someone afraid. His
face turned up and he gazed at her window intently. Erica's
breath caught in her throat. It was Tonio.

Without stopping to think, she darted from her room on tiptoe, carefully edging past her father's room and down the back stairs. Grant was already in bed and probably asleep, although it was barely ten o'clock. He kept farmer's hours, rising and retiring early. Erica silently turned the lock of the kitchen door and slipped out, hurrying across the moonlit lawn to the palm tree where Tonio stood waiting. He did not move from his position, simply watched her, his face betraying none of the tingling that swept him at the sight of Erica in brief denim shorts and a clinging pink top. Erica halted a few steps from him, suddenly uncertain. Why did she act so boldly around him? He already thought her a heartless, brazen vixen. Finally he moved, reaching out to pull her beneath the cover of the palm tree with him. He didn't kiss her or touch anything but her hand, although his smoldering black eyes roamed her body. Finally she whispered, "What are you doing here?"

"Probably risking my neck," he responded dryly. He moved deeper into the shadows, and Erica followed him without a murmur. Soon they were past the oleanders and out of sight on the driveway. They strolled, hands still clasped, the only sound the quiet crunch of the gravel beneath their feet. Tonio broke the silence at last, although his voice was low in the hushed night: "I parked down by the old house."

Erica glanced at him, but did not question his decision. She knew instinctively, as he did, that the less Grant Logan knew about them, the better. He wouldn't take kindly to his daughter slipping out of the house at night to meet one of the Cruz boys, college graduate or not. "I didn't think you'd come back."

His fingers tightened around hers briefly. "You're hard to forget."

"You mean there was something more to last time than punishing a flirt?"

He halted abruptly and pulled her into his arms. His mouth sought hers, lips scorching, tongue flickering and bold. He slipped his hands down her back and dug his fingers into the soft flesh of her buttocks, pressing her into him. Instinctively Erica moved her hips, and he breathed in sharply, his mouth widening as if to consume her. At last Tonio drew away. His voice was shaky when he spoke. "Where can we go?"

Erica didn't hesitate, caution and good sense thrown to the wind as they always were with him. "How about the old house? I know where the key is."

"All right."

They continued along the driveway, his arm around her shoulders, pausing now and then to touch or kiss or hold each other, driving themselves into a frenzy of frustrated desire, knowing how deliciously it would be eased when they reached the house. The "old house" stood near the gate where the driveway met the main road. It was the original structure built by Erica's grandparents when they had settled the land many years before. Her father had grown up in it until he was a teenager, when they had built the "big house" where Grant and Erica now lived. For the first few years of her life, Erica and her parents had lived in the old house. Then her grandparents died when she was six, and the family moved into the larger, newer house, closing up the old one. Now and then it had been opened and rented on her mother's whim until she had died a few years ago. After her death Grant locked it up. It was a sturdily built wooden structure, with three bedrooms, a modernized kitchen, high ceilings and wooden floors.

When they reached the house, Erica slipped around to the side door and found the key in its usual hiding place beneath the tiny stoop. She opened the door and they stepped into utter gloom. The hurricane shutters had been closed to seal the house tightly, and no stray light entered. Erica fumbled in a drawer and drew out candles and a match. She lit one of the candles. Her face shone eerily in the dark. "You seem pretty familiar with this routine," Cruz commented suspiciously, and she giggled.

"I don't meet my boyfriends here, if that's what you mean. But when my friends and I were feeling really daring, we used to sneak over here during a slumber party, to scare ourselves and prove how adventurous we were." She held out a hand and he took it, following her up the stairs to the second floor. What little furniture he could glimpse was shrouded in dustcovers, misshapen and anonymous. "Isn't it spooky?" she whispered, a bit of the thirteen-year-old lingering in her voice. He had to agree.

Erica opened a door on the second floor, and they entered a bedroom. She pulled the covers from the massive four-poster bed, exposing a clean, bare mattress. Suddenly the dim candle and strange surroundings didn't seem strange or frightening, but cozily sealed off from the world for the private use of lovers. Desire flared in Tonio's eyes, and he reached out to slide his hands across the thin pink top, caressing her breasts until the tips thrust boldly against the cloth. "Damn, you're beautiful." His fingertips drifted lower, easing down the taut expanse of her shorts and slipping between her long, tanned legs. Erica closed her eyes, trembling beneath his touch. She stroked the hard muscles of his arms as he explored her body, until finally she could stand it no more and moved away to pull off her clothes.

Tonio watched the pale gleam of her body in the candlelight, desire pounding and swelling in him so that he could hardly breathe. He slipped out of his tight jeans and light shirt and pulled Erica to him, molding her flesh to his and branding her mouth with a deep kiss. They fell quickly into the bed, their hands and mouths wild upon each other, frantically aching for the final sublime moment, but eager, too, to taste each delight along the way. At last they could stand the sensual torture no longer, and they came together, hot and young, soaring swiftly to the heights of love.

Afterward they lay together, her head nestling in the hollow of his shoulder, his thumb lazily, rhythmically, running up and down her arm. Erica tensed, afraid that Tonio would turn sarcastic and hurting, as he had before, but he did not. When at last he spoke, his voice was soft, almost friendly. "What is this old place, anyway?"

"My grandparents' house, the one they built before the main house. We lived in it when I was a little girl. When my grandparents died, we moved into the big house."

"When I started working for your dad, I wondered why he had two houses. Seemed the height of luxury to me."

Erica laughed. "Believe me, this house is hardly luxurious."

"But it's sturdy. I kind of like it." He smiled. "Particularly now." Erica hardly breathed, her hopes rising at his last words. Did he have some feeling for her after all? Besides lust, that was, which he obviously had in plenty. But he did not pursue the subject. "You don't have much family, do you?"

"No. I'm an only child. Mama died five years ago, so there's just Daddy and me."

"No grandparents, no cousins, no aunts and uncles?"

"I have one aunt."

"Yeah? Who?"

"She lives in San Antonio."

"Oh. It must be nice, having everything to yourself."

Erica shrugged. "I guess. I envy people with brothers and sisters. I mean, they fight and everything, but they seem to have more fun. They always have a built-in friend, somebody to stick up for them. Don't you enjoy your brothers?"

"Sure, when I'm not having to get them out of trouble."

Erica didn't have to ask what trouble. Lucio had been in her grade at school, and she knew he'd been expelled or suspended several times. Jorge, the youngest, was said to be even worse. "You don't sound as if you mind too much."

"Oh, Lucio's not a bad kid. His main problem is me."

"You! Why?"

"Because his teachers always ask him why he isn't like me, why he doesn't make good grades. That kind of thing. But that's not Lucio's personality. He's easygoing and fun-loving, like our father. He doesn't feel any drive to get ahead in life. He'd rather flirt or drink beer. Lucio doesn't have anything to prove."

"And you do?"

He shrugged. "Sure. I had to make people realize I was better than they thought. Just because Mama's a maid and Papa's a sometime gardener, I've always been treated like dirt. My father isn't filled with drive. So when he couldn't get a job except gardening, and often not even that, he accepted it. He isn't the kind to beat his head against the wall. So people say he's lazy. Anglos chuckle and shake their heads. 'Typical Mexican,' they say, 'lazy and happy.' He's a smart man. With a little opportunity, a little education, he could have done all kinds of things. But he was trapped in his role."

"You got out of it," Erica pointed out.

"Did I? I'm still a Cruz, still less than nothing."

"That's not true!"

"Then why are we meeting like this? Why not tell your father you have a date with Tonio Cruz?"

Erica bit her lower lip. She didn't have an answer for that. He was right. They both knew Grant wouldn't want her to date him. Finally she countered, "Daddy doesn't want me doing this with any boy."

He shot her a sardonic glance. "Think you can slip out of it that easily?"

"Why not?" she retorted impishly.

He grinned and trailed a hand down her smooth hair. "Pretty clever, aren't you?"

He nipped gently at her earlobe. "You know what happens to girls who are too clever, don't you?" Now his lips were nuzzling her neck, sending pleasant shivers through her.

She laughed. "No, what?"

"I'll show you." He rose up on one elbow beside her, his dark eyes feasting on her body. "They have to pay."

"You're just trying to change the subject."

Tonio bent to take her nipple between his lips, toying with it until Erica shoved her hands into his thick black hair and arched upward, moaning softly. All thoughts of any other subject fled both their minds as his mouth captured hers in a deep kiss.

For the next two or three weeks, they met almost every night. Erica would wait until after ten, when she was sure her father was asleep, then slip out the side door. She hurried across the yard and down the driveway toward the old house, where Tonio sometimes waited for her, seated on the steps of the side stoop, lithely rising when he saw her. Other times he stood just beyond the oleander hedge and swept her into his arms as soon as she passed it, then walked with her to their meeting place. He brought an old oil lamp to provide better light than the flickering candles, which burned out all too soon and left them the option of either being in the dark or parting. Erica went to the old house during the day and cleaned the upstairs bedroom, dispelling the faintly musty smell of the unused room with scented candles. She covered the mattress with fresh, clean sheets, swept the floors, and dusted, even though she and Tonio rarely noticed their surroundings. She wanted the setting of their lovemaking to be as beautiful as the act.

Nightly it became more beautiful. Erica would not have believed such a thing possible, and she had worried that Tonio would soon tire of her and move on to another girl. But each time they came together was better than before. Smiling, he taught her pleasure she had never dreamed existed, new ways to send his own passion spiraling. He couldn't seem to get enough of her body, and he took his time with her, sometimes vaulting Erica to ecstacy several times before he succumbed himself. They no longer met and instantly tumbled into bed, consumed with passion. They talked and joked, before and after, often lying together, content to caress each other and simply be together.

Gradually, as the days passed, Tonio's bitter, suspicious resistance fell. He stopped questioning her motives and accusing her of using him. He accepted her, teased her with laughing eyes, kissed her until she was breathless, murmured endearments in her ears. They talked of their childhoods, their families, of Erica's stiff, uneasy relationship with her father and Tonio's far happier one with his own lackadaisical father.

"Papa was always good to us, willing to listen, to take time to help us with things. Sometimes he drank too much—mostly to soothe his pain over not being able to provide for us as well as he wanted. He had a bad leg from a childhood accident, which made it impossible to work as a picker. He couldn't stand on the ladders for a long time. It was always a sore point with him that he couldn't work in the winter, picking fruit to bring in some extra money. And it hurt his pride that Mama had to work. He kept it all inside, though. He never took it out on us. He was always laughing and loving with us."

Erica smoothed her hand gently over his arm. She knew Tonio's father had died a couple of years earlier, and she would have liked to offer comfort, but she didn't know what to say.

"Sometimes I wish I were more like him—and the others. But I can't let things slide and take whatever comes, without thought or fear, getting by on a sweet disposition, like Olivia, or the face of an angel, like Lucio. I have to take things and make them into something, control my life." He paused and sighed. "Though, God knows, I haven't had any control where you're concerned."

Erica smiled. "No? That's nice."

He studied her, his usually grave mouth curving upward. "So you enjoy that, do you? You like to drive me out of my mind?" She nodded. "Well, you've succeeded. I can hardly work anymore for thinking about you. It was bad enough before, when you'd ride into the groves and flaunt yourself in front of me. God, I'd ache to pull you off your horse and take you right there on the ground."

"Did you honestly think I was merely a flirt? A tease who wanted all the men to desire her?"

"What else could I think? I couldn't believe you did it only for me, that you wanted me to take you. I thought you must do it for your ego, for a cheap thrill, to see me and the others suffer."

"And now?"

"Now I don't know." He ran a hand down her slender arm to her hand, outlining each finger in turn. "Now I work in the groves and wish you'd come out so that I could see you again. Yet, I pray you don't, because I know I couldn't control the way I'd look at you. I'm not sure I could even refrain from touching you and kissing you in front of the men. And I think I'd kill you if you came around the others in your skimpy shorts and tops."

"Don't worry. I won't come. I don't think I could trust myself around you, either, not with other people there." She lifted his hand to her mouth and kissed his palm, softly nibbling at his fingertips.

"What do you get out of this?"

She glanced at him in surprise. His face and tone were serious, open. She saw none of the hostility and suspicion that had been there in the past. "Don't you know? Tonio, it's so obvious—I love you."

He cupped her neck and pulled her head down to kiss her fiercely. His lips burned against hers, and his arms imprisoned her like steel. "Erica, Erica." His words were a hot groan against her neck and cheek. "I love you, too, *querida*. It's insane, but I love you too."

When at last he released her, Tonio reached behind his head
to unfasten the chain of the golden medallion he constantly
wore around his throat. Taking it off, he reached to clasp it at
the nape of her neck. Erica's hand flew upward to touch it.
"Tonio," she whispered, "what are you doing? You always
wear this."

"Now it's yours. It's the only thing I have that I value, not
that it's worth anything in monetary terms. But Olivia, my sister, gave it to me six years ago. She bought it with the first
money she ever made. It's a medal of St. Anthony."

"But it's too precious to you. I can't take it," she protested.

His eyes were warm, glowing coals. "You are a part of me.
If I lost you, it would be like tearing my heart out. This is all I
own that's of any importance to me, that expresses even a
fraction of what you mean to me. I'll never be without it because you will be with me always. It binds you to me, and me
to you."

Erica hugged his avowal to herself in an ecstasy of happiness, just as she pressed the cold medal against her warm skin.
She had no reservations, being young and unused to denial or
failure. Her father was distant but usually indulgent, and she
was accustomed to obtaining whatever she wanted. She
couldn't conceive of not having what she wanted more than
anything else in her life: Tonio Cruz. Grant would balk and be
troublesome, but once Tonio was established as an architect, he
would get used to the idea. After all, Tonio would then be a
young professional with a good life ahead of him, not one of
Grant's workers. And even if her father didn't like it, he would
simply have to accept it. There was the problem of her having
another year in high school, of course, but there would be holidays when she and Tonio could visit one another. And next
year she could go to college in Houston, and they would be together once more. Before, the only real problem had been
whether Tonio cared for her, and now that he had admitted he
loved her, Erica was certain her future was sunny.

She did not see Tonio the next night. There was a big dance
at the country club, one of the two really important, grand affairs for the teenagers that were held there every year. Jeff
Roberts had asked her to it weeks earlier, before she had become involved with Tonio. She would have preferred not to at-

tend, but it would have been unfair and unkind to Jeff to call off the date at the last minute. It didn't mean anything, but it was really a question of good manners. So she told Tonio that she couldn't see him Friday. She saw the small, instantaneous spark of resentment in his eyes, and she thought it wise not to mention that Jeff Roberts would be taking her to a dance. Tonio's jealousy made her warm with pleasure, but she'd just as soon not be treated to a full rendition of it, particularly over something as trifling as a date with Jeff Roberts that she couldn't break.

She and Tonio had agreed to meet again Saturday evening, but when Erica slipped down the hushed driveway to the old house, she did not meet Tonio along the way. His car wasn't parked beside the house, so she sat down on the porch to wait. When time passed and he still didn't come, Erica went to the side door to make sure he hadn't already arrived and entered. The key was in place and the door solidly locked. Sighing, she resumed her vigil on the porch. Soon her eyelids grew heavy, and she leaned against a column and dozed off. She awoke with a start sometime later and stared at her surroundings, at a momentary loss. Then she remembered where she was and why, and she glanced at her watch. It was almost two o'clock! Tonio hadn't come. With an irritated twitch of her lips, she stood up and walked back to the house, strangely frightened in the familiar surroundings without Tonio's presence.

Sunday evening was a repetition of the previous night, and Erica wavered between anger and worry. Had something happened to Tonio? Why hadn't he shown up? Why did he leave her sitting there, waiting for him? He could have called to say he couldn't make it. He wouldn't have wanted to ask for her, of course, but if her father had answered, he could simply have hung up. On Monday she rose early and placed herself conspicuously on the front porch, so that Tonio could innocently stop to say good morning and explain his absence. However, either he had arrived already or he didn't come to work that day. He didn't appear at their meeting place on the following two nights, nor did she see him at work. Sizzling with resentment yet stung by worry, she waited for word from him, debating in her mind whether to go riding in the groves and find him as she had earlier in the summer. One minute she was positive he was being callous and cruel, and her pride would not allow her to seek him out. The next instant, she dreamed up hundreds of dreadful things that had kept him from calling her. He could have been in an accident or caught some awful disease and even now might be lying unconscious, near death, unable to reach out to her. Tears would fill her eyes and she would dash for the stables. But the mood never lasted long enough for her to reach the groves before pride won out and she would turn back.

She visited her friends more than before, hoping to hear some stray bit of gossip that would explain Tonio's absence. She drove around town, hoping to see a sign of him or his car. Once she saw the car, and her heart leaped within her, but then Lucio walked out of a store and hopped into it, and she plunged back into despair. When the local weekly newspaper came out on Wednesday, Erica grabbed it and searched in vain for a story of a wreck or any other event that might make sense of it all. Finally she was driven to question her father.

At supper she began casually, "I haven't seen Tonio Cruz around lately." Her father's only reply was a grunt as he dished peas onto his plate. Suppressing a sigh of irritation, Erica continued. "Doesn't he work for you anymore?"

"No," Grant Logan replied briefly, his attention on the meat he was cutting. "Quit last Saturday."

Erica stared, glad Grant hadn't looked up from his food and seen the shock on her face. She wet her lips and struggled to control her voice. "Why? I thought he was working here all summer."

He shrugged. "I don't know. He told me he'd decided to quit early and go to Houston to find an apartment. His job there begins in a few weeks."

Houston! "You—you mean, he's already left town?"

"That's what I understood him to say. Well, you know the Cruzes. They're a shiftless, unreliable lot."

Erica didn't reply, numbly returning to her food. She took a few more bites, the food as tasteless as cardboard in her mouth. Houston. Tonio had left town without seeing her, without saying good-bye. She swallowed hard to force down the roast, her fingers trembling on her fork. She laid it down and pushed back her chair. She could no longer sit there pretending to eat while the tears beat at the backs of her eyes, no matter what her father might think of her leaving the table early. Let him wonder. She didn't care anymore. Tonio had left her without so much as a farewell.

She stumbled up the stairs to her room and shut the door, collapsing on her bed in tears. False! It had all been false. Tonio hadn't meant what he'd said. He didn't love her. It had been a lie, just as his lovemaking had been. He'd wanted a summer's fling, and once she revealed she was getting serious about him, Tonio had fled. She gripped the medallion and yanked at it furiously. The chain bit into her neck, then snapped. Erica hurled it against the wall. Damn him! Pain knifed through her heart.

The last days of summer passed slowly, and Erica walked through them like a zombie. She had never imagined feeling like this: empty, hurt, churning with anger and yet throbbingly in love. In dismay she realized the full meaning of a broken heart. She knew she loved Tonio even as she hated him for deceiving her. She also knew that it was something she would never get over. The rest of her life would be spent in misery.

School started, and Erica returned to the familiar classrooms and hallways. She was thinner and strangely silent. Her friends found her distracted and morose, uninterested in their conversations and in her normal activities. She quit the cheerleading squad and began to shun club meetings. A new fear welled in her, adding to the turmoil of emotions already battling inside her chest. A first she thought she was off schedule because of her upset state, but after a whole month had gone by, she knew that was not the case. It had been too long. She couldn't continue to pretend to herself that everything was all right. And yet, she couldn't bear to face the implications. She finally gathered up her courage and made an appointment with a doctor in McAllen. The following Monday she drove to his office after school. He examined her and made the necessary test. Erica nervously clasped her hands together, folding her right hand over the telltale emptiness of her left ring finger. Why hadn't she thought to get out her grandmother's old dia-

mond ring? Afterward, she went home, still on pins and needles, anxious yet dreading the answer. The following afternoon
the doctor called and confirmed her worst fears. She was pregnant.

Chapter 4

It took her two more days of soul-shaking fear before she finally told her father. She thought desperately of running away rather than facing him, but she knew of no place to go, nothing she could do to take care of herself and the baby. One of those awful homes for unwed mothers? A backstreet abortionist in McAllen or Harlingen? No, that was unthinkable. She couldn't kill the baby. Tonio's baby. Besides, she had been indoctrinated with Grant Logan's strict moral code. She must face the consequences. She had been silly and headstrong, as always, completely under the control of her desires and Tonio's animal magnetism. The punishment would be facing her stern, puritanical father.

She followed him into the den one evening after supper. He looked up questioningly, surprised at her presence, and Erica swallowed hard. Her father was a difficult man to approach, his gray eyes hard and his square, tanned face unreadable. Clearing her throat and lacing her shaking hands together, Erica bluntly informed him that she was pregnant. Her father's face drained of color as he stared at her. Slowly he rose from his chair and asked her to repeat herself. She did so, her voice barely audible. To her surprise he did not rant and rave, did not

even question her about the identity of the father. Not once did
he tell her that she would have to marry the boy. Later she realized he would have assumed it was one of the local Anglo
boys, the son of a man he probably knew and dealt with all the
time. Grant obviously didn't want to have to face the knowledge of who it was.

Calmly, his face ashen, he began to formulate plans. He decided to send her to his sister Rachel, who lived in San Antonio. They waited until the Christmas break, and Grant arranged
with the school system to allow her to take her semester exams
early, as she planned to move to San Antonio for the rest of the
year. Because she had lost so much weight, the slight thicken-
ing around her middle was not noticed. She felt sure her sudden, mysterious move to her aunt's, as well as her strange
behavior that fall, would cause many to guess what had befallen her. But, her father reassured her, no one would know for
certain. Erica knew the reassurance was more for himself than
for her. Frankly she no longer cared what the people of Santa
Clara thought. She was too deep in her misery.

Her Aunt Rachel, a successful businesswoman and unmarried, welcomed her niece's company, and Erica found her life
much more bearable there than at home, where everything had
seemed to remind her of Tonio. As the time passed, she grew to
despise Antonio Cruz. He had lied to her and abandoned her,
and she built up a fierce hatred of him and all men. They were
either callous, careless creatures like him or self-righteous con-
demners like her father, and she was determined to live without either kind. She made a firm decision to be like her aunt, a
dedicated career woman, able to support herself and her child.

Danny was born late in May, small, squalling and utterly
beautiful to Erica. Whatever she felt for his father, she loved
him completely the moment she saw him—had loved him even
before that. Her father urged her to give up Danny, claiming
she would never have the sort of life a young girl should have
if she were burdened with a child. But Erica was determined to
keep him and she stood fast against her father. Whenever he
visited her in San Antonio, they argued fiercely over the matter and parted in anger. Finally Erica cried at him that she
would never embarrass him by bringing her illegitimate child
home for a visit. Grant left the house in a huff, and though he

continued to send her money, he didn't visit her again for over a year.

Erica finished high school and went on to college, living with her aunt and hiring a baby-sitter to take care of Danny while she was gone. Her aunt doted on both of them, and though Erica was often overworked, her life maintained a steady, pleasant course. She enjoyed school, and Danny was a constant delight to her. She decided to enter the field of hotel management and finished her schooling at the University of Houston. Several times, while she and Danny lived there, she thought of Tonio and wondered whether, in such a huge city, she might ever run into him again. She even looked up his name in the telephone directory, although she never called him. She thought about him and what he might be doing, how he would feel if he knew he had a son, how he might react if one day she ran into him by accident. She wasn't sure whether she dreaded the thought or longed for it to happen. Whatever her feelings, the occasion never arose. After she finished college, she obtained a job as the assistant manager of a motel in Austin, then moved to one in San Antonio. Over the years she learned to tame her vibrant good looks into a sober, genteel attractiveness, striving above all else to appear mature and competent. She worked hard at her job, proving her abilities at every opportunity, and she had done well. She took pride in her work and her achievements, and the rest of her life was her son. There was little left over for other involvements, and though she gradually lost her resentment of men and began to date again, she kept carefully free of any entanglements that might interfere with her career or Danny. It hadn't been difficult, since none of the men she dated inspired the kind of wild, overwhelming love and desire she had once felt with Tonio. Feelings like that, she reasoned, occurred only once in a lifetime, when one was young—and really she was glad she had too much control of herself for it to happen again. It had been as frightening as it was delightful.

She and her father mended their rift to some extent. Though he was obviously never very pleased about Danny, he did come to see her infrequently, and once or twice she went home for a brief visit. In recent years he had begun to urge her to return home and live with him, reasoning that the mother of a young boy should not have to spend her time working. Erica quietly, firmly refused. She wasn't about to live under her father's—or any man's—power again.

She had achieved the independence she sought and even a sort of quiet contentment that she had once thought she would never experience again. In fact, she had been doing very well—at least until Tonio Cruz showed up. Damn him! Why did he have to return to her life? And why did she have to react like a schoolgirl, going shaky in the knees, her stomach twitching, surging with all the old bitterness and pain and—yes, admit it—attraction to his strong male beauty!

Erica shook off the thought. That was crazy. She was no longer an impressionable schoolgirl. Tonio was facing an entirely different woman now. She was calm, mature, and now that she had thought over her past and faced her emotions, she was certain she could face him coolly tomorrow. She would be able to deal with him as one professional to another. Erica lifted her chin determinedly. She refused to be intimidated in any way. She would handle the situation, just as she always handled the tough times in her life: alone.

Erica was at her office well before nine o'clock the next morning. Although she dreaded the meeting, she wasn't about to let Tonio accuse her of inefficiency or tardiness. As she walked through the lobby, she caught sight of Tonio sitting at a small table in the coffee shop. He sipped at a cup of coffee, absorbed in a stack of papers on the table beside his empty plate. Involuntarily Erica stopped and studied him. She had been too nervous really to look at him the day before. He had aged. It showed in the squint lines around his eyes and the sharp creases beside his nose and mouth. How old was he now? Thirty-two? Thirty-three? Tonio was in his prime, and he looked it. The thick, crow-black hair was well cut and shorter, stopping at his ears. The tanned face was sculptured and expressionless, only the full underlip hinting at the sensuality and passion that had once blazed within him. Straight black brows, dark brown eyes ringed with lashes so long and thick it was unfair for a man to have them, prominent cheekbones—the same face, hardened into maturity, the promise of youth fulfilled. He was slender, and the arms below the short sleeves of his shirt bulged with muscle. Erica's eyes followed the line of his arm down the forearm, lightly covered with black hair, to the slender, well-manicured hands. His fingers were sensually long and slender, graceful, but saved from delicacy by the thick sinews running across the back. Erica wondered if his palms and fingertips were still calloused. Color sprang into her cheeks at the thought, and she quickly jerked her mind away, instead noting his clothes. He was dressed informally in brown slacks and a white terry-cloth shirt that opened at a V at his neck, exposing the smooth tanned skin of his throat. No gold medal glinted at his neck now, she noticed, her mind going back for a fleeting moment. Though Tonio's clothes were casual, they were obviously expensive, as were the gold watch on his wrist and the simple gold ring on his right hand. Obviously he had done well for himself.

Erica glanced down at her neat, cream-colored pantsuit. What would Tonio think of her appearance now? Would he wonder how the pretty girl with the thick mane of hair and ripe figure, carefully revealed in halter tops and shorts, had changed into this sober woman of business suits and tight chignon? Had her face aged and bittered in the intervening ten years until it was dry and unappealing? Other men told her she was lovely, but Tonio had known her when she was young and flush with love and life. Erica turned away and strode into her office, telling herself not to be foolish. What did it matter what Tonio thought of her? She had no need to be beautiful for him. Yet, she shrugged out of her suit jacket and tossed it on her desk, knowing guiltily that she did so because the creamy, soft blouse emphasized her swelling breasts and trim waist.

She sat down behind the desk and pulled out a file of correspondence left over from the day before. She didn't want Tonio to find her waiting idly for him. However, she could not keep her mind on the material and kept glancing at her watch. He was ten minutes late; was he purposely being rude to put her in her place? No doubt he enjoyed having the upper hand, just as he had taken pleasure in seducing the daughter of a well-to-do Anglo farmer. Her bitter thoughts were interrupted by a noise at the door, and she forced herself to wait a moment before she looked up.

Tonio stood famed in the doorway, the light from the sunny, glass-walled lobby behind him outlining his figure but leaving his face dark and unreadable. Suddenly Erica's office seemed too small and enclosed, dominated by his masculinity. "I'm late. Sorry," he began curtly. "I hadn't expected you to be on time. You never—" He bit off the words, which Erica knew would have been that she had often been late to their rendezvous spot ten years ago. For an instant the air quivered with an unspoken intimacy.

Erica rose briskly, breaking the moment. "That's quite all right. I managed to catch up on some work." Deftly she shoved the letters back into the file and dropped it on her desk. Unlocking the middle drawer, she pulled out a large ring of keys. "Now, where would you like to begin?"

"Let's take the inner workings first. Pipes, air-conditioning..."

"Of course." Erica left her desk, and he stepped back slightly to let her pass through the doorway. However, she was too close to him for comfort, and had to drop her eyes to avoid making contact. He followed her through the swinging door into the lobby, and she half turned to hold the door open until he took it. As she did so, she saw his eyes upon her, dark and smoldering, sweeping the length of her body and lingering over her hips and thighs. Quickly his eyes went blank, and she wondered if she had imagined the expression.

They turned into the back hallway of the first floor and entered the maintenance men's lair, full of huge pipes and noisy, clattering machines. Erica didn't understand their workings, but she knew enough to understand that everything was in shabby shape, patched but not completely fixed. Tonio examined the area minutely, his mouth tightening with disapproval as he jotted notes on a yellow pad. Next they inspected the lobby, where he poked and pried into every corner, then followed the same routine in the now empty coffee shop. They walked together silently, Tonio busy with his notes and Erica saying no more than was necessary to answer his questions or point out something he had asked to see.

From the coffee shop they went out the front door of the hotel, and Tonio walked to the street for a better view. Slowly his eyes traveled over the face of the building, studying the peeling rails of the balconies and pausing on the iron script sign proclaiming "The Breezes." "It's shabby," he stated, his mouth grim. "How could they let it get into this condition?"

Erica bristled as if he had criticized her, although she had had nothing to do with the hotel's downward slide. "Mr. Severn didn't have the funds to maintain it properly. I understand it was all he could do to repair the hurricane damage last year."

His eyebrows rose lazily, and the corners of his mouth quirked in amusement. Erica knew she had been overly defensive and could have bitten her tongue for her quick retort. "Hotels aren't meant to be hobbies," Cruz said. "Severn should have sold it years ago. He has neither the capital nor the knowledge to run it."

"Hardly any hotel can survive now if it's not part of a chain."

"And that annoys you. Why? Simply the love of the old guard for their fast-dying world?"

"Old guard? I hardly think I qualify. You sound as if I were a Russian aristocrat after the Revolution. I'm simply a modern working woman. You were always more aware of class divisions than I."

"Was I?" His face was cold, his mouth curled in a sneer. Abruptly he turned away and started around the side of the building. Erica grimaced and followed him. He toured the patio and swimming pool, as well as the huge air-conditioning unit hidden behind the building. Afterward they returned to the inside and began a floor-by-floor inspection. Strolling side by side along the halls, it was more awkward maintaining their stiff silence. Finally Tonio commented, "I was surprised to see you yesterday. I didn't think you'd still be single or have a career."

"Oh? And what did you envision for me?" Erica was coolly sarcastic.

"I thought you'd marry somebody like Jeff Roberts, spend your time at the country club."

"And no doubt have two and a half children and drive a station wagon?"

"Something like that."

"You don't know me very well, then, do you?"

He shot her a sideways glance. "No, I guess I never did."

"I, on the other hand, was sure you'd be successful, although I didn't know you were the Cross Corporation architect."

They had reached the end of the hall, and he punched the button for the elevator. His dark eyes swept over her and he added dryly, "And owner."

"What?"

A thin smile stretched his lips. "I take it you couldn't picture me being quite that successful. An architect is one thing, but for a Mexican to be the president of a corporation—that's unheard of, isn't it?"

"I see you still have the same chip on your shoulder," Erica replied heatedly. "Obviously you think I'm prejudiced because I'm surprised a man in his early thirties owns a multimillion-dollar hotel construction company! I'd be amazed at anyone who rose that far that quickly."

"I worked at it. After I left the Valley, it was the only thing that mattered to me."

"Of course. It was all that ever did." For a moment their eyes locked, resentment shimmering between them. Then the elevator arrived, breaking the tension, and Tonio stepped into it. Erica didn't follow. "You won't need me for the rest of the tour, will you? There's nothing to be unlocked or explained on the other floors, as far as I know."

"No, it will be routine, I'm sure," he replied in a clipped voice.

"Then I'll leave you here."

"Yes. Thank you for your help."

"You're welcome."

The doors slid shut, and Erica leaned against the wall, her throat burning with suppressed tears. It had been as awful as she had feared. Tonio was arrogant and hateful, and she had been awash in turbulent emotions the whole time they were together. She hated him. She would have liked to slap his arrogant, handsome face and tell him exactly what she thought of him for leaving a vulnerable seventeen-year-old girl in the lurch. She wanted to scream out the pain she'd suffered from his lies and desertion. It shouldn't have surprised her at all that he owned Cross Corporation. He had all the qualities necessary for a ruthless business tycoon.

Erica turned to walk down the stairwell instead of waiting for the elevator. She needed the extra moments alone to gain control of her emotions. It had been difficult trying to maintain a calm, indifferent mask around Tonio, as if they were no more to each other than casual acquaintances. No doubt that was all she was to him, but he had been an earthquake in her life, tearing open her placid existence and leaving everything broken and changed. However, she had too much pride and hatred to let him know how much he had hurt her, and too much fear to let him learn of Danny's existence. She had had to pretend an indifference to equal his, when all the time she was very aware of the familiar scent of his body mixed with the musky fragrance of his after-shave, aware of the strength of his hard brown arms, aware of the long, sinewy fingers that had once drifted over her body, bringing her untold pleasure. She was anything but indifferent to him, and the playacting had been wearing on her. Thank heavens she wouldn't have to endure him any longer. Whatever else he needed he could obtain on his own, and soon he would leave. Then she would seek another job. She wanted to make sure there was no chance of running into him again. She wanted Tonio out of her life forever.

Erica opened the door of her apartment, and Danny bounced up from the floor, where he had been lying as he watched TV. He launched into his usual set of questions, punctuated periodically by the desperate statement that he was starving to death. Erica made them a quick meal of sandwiches, then escaped to the bathroom, where she took a long, leisurely shower. The steady beat of the hot water on her skin soothed her and helped to take away some of the tensions of the day. Stepping out, she toweled herself dry and put on a short blue terry-cloth robe. Belting the sash, she picked up a comb and combed through her wet, tangled hair. When she returned to the living room, she found that Danny had given up on the television set and had retired to his room to play. He stormed around his room, chasing imaginary monsters, and Erica closed the door against the noise he created. With a sigh she sank down onto the couch and put her feet up casually on the coffee table.

A knock sounded imperiously on the front door, and Erica grimaced. Her employees often brought their work problems to her, even during her free hours. They seemed to think she was always on duty because she lived in the hotel. She rose and went to answer the knock, not bothering to change from her robe, since she expected to find Connie at the door. Instead she opened it to a well-dressed, assured Tonio Cruz. Erica's stomach plummeted to the floor. Dear heaven, she wasn't prepared to deal with him again.

Tonio's eyes flickered over her assessingly, taking in the short robe, its only fastening the casually knotted sash around her slender waist. Erica swallowed, suddenly very conscious of the fact that she wore nothing beneath the robe. Tonio's eyes darkened, and she knew that he, too, realized she was naked underneath the skimpy garment. Erica's hand went instinctively to the neck of her garment and pulled the two sides of the V closer together. She cleared her throat and demanded with as much force as she could muster, "What do you want?"

Unexpectedly a grin slashed his face, and she was reminded heartbreakingly of a younger Tonio. "That's an open-ended question," he commented. "Do you really want me to answer?"

Erica stiffened at the implied sexuality of his remark. Surely, with their past, he couldn't be so at ease as to make lewd jokes! "I beg your pardon," she countered.

His smile vanished and he extended his hand. "I'm returning your keys."

"Oh." Erica looked down stupidly at the key ring in his outstretched palm. Why did she feel this absurd disappointment that he had sought her out only to return the keys? "Thank you."

She didn't want to have to take the keys from his hand, but there was no way she could gracefully keep from doing it, so she reached out and picked them up lightly. Even so, her fingertips grazed his rough, warm skin, and the contact sent a shock up her arm and into her chest. Dear God, how could he still affect her this way? It was impossible. Unfair.

She clutched the keys tightly in her fist, hardly noticing the cruel bite of the metal into her palm as they faced each other, silent and awkward. Finally Erica said, "You didn't have to bring them back to me. You could have left them at the desk."

"I wanted to see you."

"What?" Erica gaped. He couldn't have said anything that surprised her more.

"I wanted to explain to you the changes I plan to make to the hotel. It's always a good idea to clear away any misconceptions the present staff might have about our takeover. I want you and your employees to be fully aware of what Cross Corporation intends to do with the Breezes and to be certain that your jobs aren't endangered."

"I'm sure your word will be sufficient on that score," Erica put in quickly. She couldn't, simply couldn't, spend any time alone with Tonio, casually discussing his plans for the hotel.

"Nevertheless I'd like you to be fully informed. I thought we could discuss it over dinner."

"I've already eaten." Erica felt as if she were suffocating.

"Then let's have a drink together."

"Tonio, really, I don't think it would be a—"

"Look, may I come in?" he interrupted.

"No!" she blurted out in horror, then stopped, blushing. She was behaving like an idiot. Tonio would think she was still in love with him. She wasn't acting at all indifferent or professional. A couple left their room and walked past them toward the elevator, staring at Erica's brief attire. "Really," she continued in a shaky voice, "I must go back inside. People are staring."

"There's a lot to stare at," he remarked genially. "Your robe isn't exactly meant for public display, you know."

"It wouldn't be on public display if you'd leave."

His eyebrows rose questioningly. "Why the coy virgin act, Erica? Don't you think it's a little late for that?"

Tears burned behind Erica's eyes. How could he be so cruel as to remind her of the unrequited love she had felt for him so long ago? "People change."

"It doesn't seem as if you've changed at all," he retorted. "You're just as spoiled and blind as you ever were."

"Well, thank you very much! Just because I don't go along with your plan to ruin my evening off, I'm spoiled. Excuse me, but I'm going back inside now." She swung the door to, but he caught it with his arm and held it back.

"Not quite so fast, Erica. I *have* changed. I am now your employer, in case you've forgotten, and I intend for us to have a little discussion." He grasped her arm firmly and almost shoved her inside the apartment, closing the door behind them.

Erica whirled and tore her arm from his grasp, frustrated anger shaking her voice. "Sorry to disappoint you, *boss,* but I intend to submit my resignation Monday."

"What?" He frowned. "Why?"

"Why?" she echoed. "You can't be serious. Surely even you can see what an awkward situation this would be."

His eyes went to the top of her robe, and she realized suddenly that when she had jerked away from him, the sash had loosened, and the robe gaped open, revealing a wide swath of her bare white skin almost down to her waist. Tonio's eyes were black as night, unreadable, but telltale moisture dotted his upper lip and his hands knotted into fists. "Good Lord, Erica, can't you put on some clothes? Or are you expecting some other male visitor?"

She stared, too insulted by the sneer in his words to even speak. Pulling the top of the robe together, she turned away, retying the sash with shaking hands as she walked toward the balcony door. "Tonio, please go," she said in a low voice. "What's the point of this?"

"I'm sorry for the crack. I had promised myself I'd be civil, but I find it's damned difficult to do that around you."

"I think it's 'damned difficult' for you around anyone."

He smiled faintly. "Oh, you'd be surprised, Erica. I've become downright diplomatic the past few years."

"Then you really *have* changed." She looked through the glass door to the beach and drew a deep breath, then turned. "Tonio, couldn't we talk about this matter tomorrow? I really am very tired tonight." Her eyes flickered toward the closed door to Danny's room. What if he heard a stranger's voice and came out to investigate? Tonio would be certain to guess that Danny was his child the instant he saw him. There was so much of his father in Danny: the dark hair and olive skin, the angular shape of his childish face. Erica didn't know what would happen if Tonio found out—and she didn't want to know. Her pride couldn't bear for him to learn the humiliation and pain he had caused her. Far better for him to think she had sailed through their affair unscarred and uncaring. She would hate to be the object of his casual pity. Even worse, what if he was amused, or even pleased? She refused to swell his masculine ego with the knowledge that he had fathered a child at her expense. And if he happened to be intrigued by Danny, demanded to see him like a father—well, it didn't bear even thinking of. It would be disastrous.

Tonio caught her surreptitious glance at the closed door, and his eyes narrowed. "Is there a lover in your bedroom? Is that the reason for your nervousness? Is that why you didn't want to let me in?"

Erica's eyes widened at his tone. "Of course not! Not that it's any of your business," she added hastily. After all, she didn't have to answer to him.

The spark that had flared momentarily in his eyes died. "Then why the reluctance? It seems a fairly simple request to me."

"Because I'm tired!" she snapped. "Now, would you please get out?" She flinched at the sound of her own raised voice and guiltily clapped her hand over her mouth. Her eyes went involuntarily toward Danny's room. A muscle jumped in Tonio's jaw, and he started purposefully for the door. Erica leaped after him, grabbing his arm frantically. "No! Please don't go in there. I swear—"

The door opened, and Danny peered out, a worried frown on his forehead. "Mama? What's the matter?"

Tonio stopped abruptly, surprise, then relief, chasing across his face. "A child? That's who was in there?"

"Yes, and I didn't want you disturbing him," Erica retorted, amazed to find that she had succeeded in sounding cross rather than fearful. Even more amazing was the fact that Tonio had not recognized Danny as his son. How could he not see it as soon as he set eyes upon him? The thick dark hair, the sharp little face, the creamed coffee skin—wasn't the resemblance obvious to anyone but her? Perhaps it was Danny's size that fooled Tonio. He was smaller than most nine-year-olds and could easily pass for seven or eight. Whatever the reason for his lack of recognition, Tonio was studying Danny now, and unless she got him away quickly, it surely wouldn't be long before he made the connection. She stepped forward, blocking Tonio's view of Danny, and took her son by the shoulder to propel him back to his room. "It's okay, sweetheart. Mr. Cruz and I were discussing something, and I'm afraid we got a little loud. There's nothing wrong. You go back and we'll go upstairs to Mr. Cruz's room to discuss it. You'll be all right by yourself?"

"Sure," Danny replied scornfully. "I'm not a baby."

"I know, I know." Erica had to smile at his indignant tone. She bent and placed a quick peck on his cheek. "If you need me just telephone, okay?"

"Okay."

Erica turned to face Tonio, her face set and expressionless. "Just a second. Let me put on some clothes." She hurried into her bedroom and thrust on underwear, jeans and a top. She didn't want to leave him waiting long, in case Danny decided to return to keep their visitor company. She was back in the living room in seconds. Tonio rose from the couch, surprised at her quick change. His eyes flickered to the softness of her breasts, and Erica blushed. He had noticed that she hadn't slipped on a brassiere. Under his survey, her nipples hardened involuntarily, making it even more obvious that she wore nothing beneath her blouse. Erica wished she had taken the time to don the flimsy bit of lace and satin.

Quickly turning from his gaze, she swept her key from the table and walked to the door. Tonio followed quietly. Why, oh, why had she told Danny they were going to Tonio's room? It had been the first way to get Tonio away from Danny that popped into her head. But she could have agreed to talk to Tonio in the coffee shop downstairs or in her office—anywhere but his room, with the bed looming beside them. That was the last place she wanted to be with Tonio. What did he think about her suggesting his room? Would he decide that she was hinting that she wanted to return to his bed? Her face flushed with embarrassment.

When she reached the elevator, she swung to face Tonio. "Shall we go to the coffee shop or my office instead? Danny can reach me at either of those places too."

He smiled derisively. "Why? Are you afraid the temptation would be too much for me if we were in my room?"

Erica blushed again. Now she felt even more foolish. Of course, there was no danger of his seducing her. That had all ended for him years ago. She was the one who was affected by his proximity, not the other way around. "Of course not. I simply thought it might be more comfortable."

"My room is fine. Your office is a box, and the restaurant is rather public for discussing business. So if you have no objections...?" He trailed off questioningly as the elevator door opened and he stepped inside. Erica shook her head and he punched the button for the top floor. As the elevator climbed, Erica was aware of a sinking feeling in the pit of her stomach that wasn't caused by the ascent of the rather slow elevator. What a mess this was. Why couldn't Tonio have been content to leave things as they were? Why did he insist on talking to her? And why did she have to be so blasted nervous and self-consciously aware of a man she thought she had gotten over years ago?

As they rode up, Tonio watched her, his arms folded across his chest. Finally he said, "Is that why you were so against our talking—because of the child?"

"Yes," Erica replied a little sullenly. What else could she say? She couldn't admit to him that being around him reawakened her senses and reminded her far too vividly of the passion and hurt she had once known with him.

"Why didn't you tell me?" He seemed puzzled. Erica shrugged and made no reply. He went on, "But your name's still Logan. Did you take it back even though you had a child?"

Erica hesitated. She ought to say yes. It would be an unusual thing to do, but he would probably accept it, and that would be the end of his questions about Danny. But even as she opened her mouth to agree, her moment of indecision gave her away. Tonio's face darkened. "Poor little guy."

"Don't you dare say anything about Danny," Erica warned, her voice shaking with anger.

"I wouldn't," he snapped back. "I know how he feels. I've been on the outside too." The elevator opened, and Tonio stepped out. "So you wouldn't marry his father, either," he mused.

Erica, following him, wasn't sure she had heard him correctly. Had he said *either?* What did that mean? Well, whatever he'd said, the best idea was to get him off this subject as quickly as possible before he began to put too much together. "He left me," she stated flatly.

"Left you?" His brows rose slightly. "So someone finally took you down a peg."

Erica swallowed, embarrassed that her lips trembled at the deadly slash of his words. "You're a cruel man."

For an instant his expression softened. "You loved him?" he asked, reaching for her elbow.

Erica averted her face, afraid he would see the truth in her eyes. "Yes."

A faint tremor ran through Tonio's fingers and into her arm. Erica glanced up into his hard, set face. His voice was calm, almost impersonal. "Damn you."

"I seem to choose the wrong kind of guy." She strove for a light cynicism, meeting his eyes defiantly, chin thrust up and out. "What business is it of yours, anyway?"

"None. Obviously." He strode ahead of her and unlocked the door to his suite. Erica followed him hesitantly into the room.

The suite was large and the most luxurious in the hotel. The balcony provided a magnificent view of the Gulf and beach, and there was a sitting area of couch, table and two comfortable chairs set slightly apart from the rest of the room by a waist-high wall topped by a wooden railing. Although it was attractive and afforded some privacy to the sitting area, the wall did not entirely separate the sitting area from the rest of the room. The couch could be reached only by passing the king-size bed. It seemed to fill the room. Erica walked past it, trying to keep her eyes from straying to the bed. Tonio strolled behind her to the table at the far end, where several rolls of paper and his drawing utensils lay. "These are my plans for the Breezes— a rough sketch, of course."

Erica looked down at the table as he unrolled one sketch after another. He stood so close beside her that she could feel the heat of his body, and her heart began to thud in her chest. He extended a hand to point out something on the drawing, and his fingers grazed the skin of her arm like a breath of fire. "As you can see, I intend to add two three-story structures running out in a V from the beach side of the building. They'll be condominiums. Here's a view of the front." He unrolled another drawing and explained the general face-lift the old hotel would receive, then went into his plans for rearranging the top floor to include an elegant dining facility and bar. "We'll enlarge the ground floor, beautify the lobby, maybe put in some small shops. I'll add a couple of tennis courts outside. I'm also considering a second pool. We'll pretty-up the rooms as well, though I haven't yet thought out a floor-by-floor renovation."

"You seem to have done an awful lot already, considering the short amount of time you've been here."

"Oh, I came earlier in the year—before you were here, I guess. These sketches are primarily from what I saw then. I wouldn't have bought the place if I didn't have some notion what to do with it. Now I'm getting into the details. By the time I leave, I hope to have enough concrete ideas that I can draw the final plans." He paused, and when she didn't say anything, he prodded, "Well, what do you think?"

"Very nice. It'll hardly be the same place."

"Which you, naturally, disapprove of."

"I didn't say that!" Erica flared. "You make a lot of erroneous assumptions. As a matter of fact, it's everything I could have wished for the place. I've wanted to fix it up since I started here. I didn't envision anything on such a grand scale, but . . ."

"It'll do? Well, thank you. I'm glad it meets with your approval."

"Why are you so sarcastic? You asked me to look at the plans! You wanted my opinion, didn't you? Are you sorry I like it? Would I have fit your stereotype better if I had hated it?"

"I don't think of you as a stereotype. Believe me, you're one of a kind." His face was drawn and bitter. Strangely, Erica felt a stirring of something akin to pity. Pity Tonio? How absurd. Pity the man who had left her? The man who had clawed his way to the top, using who knew what kind of ruthless means? Who had wealth and status and all the things he'd yearned for? Yet, there was something lonely and sad in his dark eyes, and it was only with effort that she refrained from reaching out to him.

"Tonio . . ." she began hesitantly, but he interrupted her, his voice low and fraught with tension.

"Damn, Erica, how can you be even lovelier? All these years I told myself you'd gotten older, fat, lost the luster in your hair and the color in your cheeks." He raised a hand to run his fingers along her clean jawline, and she felt the little tremor in them. "But I don't have the satisfaction. You still turn my knees to water."

Erica swallowed, unable to move, trapped by his eyes and husky voice. The crazy, tingling excitement she had thought lost forever once again shot through her veins. She struggled to control the fiery pulsation his touch aroused in her. This was the man who had broken her heart, who had left her without a word, not caring whether she was pregnant. He was callous and cruel, and she was not about to be trapped by his honeyed words again. She jerked away. "Did you think I'd wither and die without you? Grow pale and languish away like some tubercular heroine out of an old novel? Sorry to disappoint you, but I think you overrate your importance."

She moved to walk past him, but Tonio's hand lashed out to clamp around her wrist like a steel manacle. "No, I knew exactly how important I am to you. I was good for a roll in the hay. I provided a little hot Chicano passion your Anglo boys couldn't. You didn't care about me, wouldn't have dared to be seen with me, but you enjoyed our stolen moments in the sack. One thing I know you never lied about: your body's response to my touch."

His harsh words stabbed Erica. She ached inside for all her old crushed dreams. There couldn't have been a clearer statement of how little their nights of love had meant to Tonio. Her pride held her straight, formed her lips into a sneer, although she wanted nothing but to break into tears. "You're crude. You always were."

"No more so than you, lady. I just say it straight out. I don't hide it in sweet smiles and silken words. You were always as hot for me as I—"

Erica cut off his words, crying out incoherently in rage at his taunts. Every boastful word he said about her love for him pierced her anew, reminded her of her old pain and humiliation until she couldn't bear it. She lashed out, slapping his cheek with all her strength. His head jerked under the force of her blow, and the mark of her hand flamed red against his tanned skin. Choking back a sob, Erica turned and ran. But, lithe and silent as a panther, Tonio caught up with her before she reached the door. One hand clamped down on her shoulder and spun her around. Tonio pulled her forward against his hard chest, his arm imprisoning her. She twisted her head, but his fingers turned her face to his and forced up her chin. His eyes blazed down at her, hot and black as coal. His mouth was a tight line of fury. Erica quailed before his anger, but she kept her back rigid and faced him defiantly. His hand went behind her head, fingers digging into the nape of her neck. His eyes bored into hers for a moment before the hard mouth swooped down to take her lips in an endless kiss. Erica struggled to escape his burning mouth, to quell her responding surge of passion, but the touch of his lips was an electric shock, sealing her to him as surely as his strong arms.

When at last Tonio lifted his head, she sagged weakly against him, averting her face so he wouldn't see her longing. "No," she groaned softly, tears rising in her throat at the realization of what he could do to her. In ten years she had not responded to any man's kiss this way, had not felt yearning flood through her like molten iron.

"Oh, yes," he murmured, his lips nibbling at her earlobe. Impatiently he tugged at the pins holding up her hair, and when it tumbled free, he sank his hands into the sweet-scented mass and dragged it against his cheek, burying his face in it. "God, your hair. I never forgot the way it smelled. I picked up a girl in a bar one evening because her hair looked like yours. But when we got home I found the scent was wrong. I didn't want her anymore."

He bent and kissed her again, his tongue roaming her mouth, rediscovering the honeyed warmth. A wordless moan sounded deep in his throat, evoking in Erica a feeling equally primitive. She wanted him, wanted nothing in the world *but* him. His touch, his kiss, his searing breath upon her skin, were so familiar she thought she might weep. She knew him as well as if they had parted only yesterday, yet she ached for him with the hunger of over nine years. Like a woman trapped in the desert, she drank him up, the taste all the sweeter for its familiarity.

Tonio kissed her eyes, cheeks and throat, running his lips downward until stopped by her blouse. He tore at the buttons and shoved the garment back from her shoulders, sending it to the floor. The soft flesh of her neck and chest was exposed to his voracious mouth, and he explored eagerly, his tongue

working at one nipple while his fingertips caressed the other.
Like a master musician with his favorite instrument, his mouth
played her breasts, sucking and squeezing, rousing her nipples
into hardened peaks. Erica leaned back in surrender against the
steel band of his arm, awash in her passion, hardly knowing
whether she was in the present or reliving that day at her
swimming pool when she and Tonio had made love for the first
time.

She dug her fingers into his shoulders, almost moaning in
frustration at the cloth of his shirt, which impeded her. Erica
tugged at the top buttons, her fingers clumsy with haste, and his
roaming hands left her body long enough to yank his shirt free
of the waistband of his trousers and undo the remaining buttons. Erica slid her hands beneath the cloth and caressed his
chest, moving over his ribs and up to his shoulders, her fingertips digging into the hard muscle encased by smooth, warm
skin. He bent his head, leaning it against hers as he stood still
under her ministrations. His breath was quick and uneven, his
body rigid and almost quivering. "Erica." Her name seemed
torn from him. "Oh, Erica, it's been so long."

He wrapped his arms around her and pulled her backward
with him and down onto the bed. His legs encircled hers tightly
and he rolled over, pinning her beneath him. Slowly, hypnoti-
cally, he rubbed against her, arousing her breasts to tingling
pointed fullness. A steady, aching throb started low in her abdomen, building and building until she thought she would explode from the force of it. Tonio cupped her breasts and rose
on his elbows to gaze down on her. His eyes were dark fire as
they roamed over her, quickening her desire almost as much as
his hands. Erica moved against the tight prison of his legs,
wordlessly urging him on. A sound that was almost a growl escaped his lips, and Tonio bent to take one nipple in his mouth,
sucking at the dark pink aureole. His tongue laved the engorged peak as the soft suction of his cheeks tugged at it, creating a fierce pleasure in her that was almost painful.

He moved to the other nipple to work the same magic on it,
and his hands slid behind her and down, digging into the soft
flesh of her hips, pressing her even more tightly against him.
Erica felt lost, engulfed, sinking down into a dark, endless
abyss of pleasure and desire. She caressed his arms and chest

and back, her hands moving in a ceaseless pattern of passionate exploration, digging her fingertips into him whenever he caused a spasm of even more intense yearning. Her nails scratched his skin, but he was as heedless of the pain as she was of causing it. She turned her head, kissing the salty, moist skin of his shoulder, just as his tongue started to create a fresh delight, and she nipped him. Tonio shuddered, and suddenly his mouth was wild and frantic over her skin, as if he yearned to consume her. Erica twisted helplessly, caught up in the maelstrom of passion. She sank her fingers into his thick, black hair, kneading, tugging painfully. He tore at the rest of their clothing, almost ripping her slacks from her and undressing himself with equal haste. Then he separated her legs with his knee, and she arched up eagerly to meet him. Clenching his teeth, he battled the force of his desire and moved slowly. Savoring each moment of joyful torment, he drove them higher and further until they were beyond thought or words, aware of nothing but their wild rush to fulfillment, building to their final burst of glory. Together they slid into sleep, exhausted by the earthquake of their lovemaking.

Chapter 5

When Erica awoke, she was at first bewildered by the hard brown body sprawling beside her, one arm and leg thrown intimately over her. Then with a flash of shame she recalled what had just occurred. Tonio had kissed her, and she had yielded to him with disgusting alacrity. For almost ten years she had ha him from the depths of her soul, yet his expert hands and mouth had brought her to abject surrender within minutes. She blushed, recalling the way she had writhed beneath him. She would have begged him to take her if she had been capable of speech.

With a soft moan she sat up, covering her face with her hands. No doubt it would give Tonio a good laugh to know how swiftly he had brought her under his control again. How could she have done this? She seemed to have no pride or control around him. He had boasted of his onetime power over her her eagerness to bed him, and then he had proved that he could handle her just as easily today. Despite all the pain he had given her, despite her hatred for him, despite everything, she had received him willingly, even eagerly. He must think she was a weak, mindless slut, so ruled by her passions that he could trea her like dirt and she would still want him. Never had she felt so humiliated and ashamed of herself.

Shuddering, she reached for her clothes and began to pull them on. Behind her on the bed, she heard Tonio stir and mumble sleepily, "Erica?" He reached out and touched her shoulder with his hand and she pulled away violently.

"Don't you touch me!" she spat, whirling to face him, her self-disgust clear in her eyes. "God, don't you ever touch me again."

His relaxed face went suddenly taut, and the dark eyes, warm before, turned blank and cold as slate. Almost wearily he sighed, "Oh, so now we're going to go into an outraged virgin routine, huh? Don't you think that's a little bit outdated now?"

He was mocking her, just as she had feared, reminding her of the fact that he had taken her virginity long ago and was making fun of her present lack of self-control. Hot tears bit at the back of her eyes, and her voice shook with emotion as she whispered fiercely, "I loathe you!"

There was a moment of pure, still silence. Then Tonio pulled his face into a look of wry mockery. "You have a peculiar way of showing it."

He was right, of course. That was what was so awful about it. As much as she hated him, she had acted as if just the opposite were true. "Damn you." She buttoned her blouse with shaking fingers. "No matter what you think, I will not fall into bed with you whenever you get the urge." She didn't know why he had taken her, what strange titillation he got from proving she still wanted him no matter how he had mistreated her, but from now on she wasn't going to provide his entertainment. He wouldn't get past her guard again, she'd see to that. Tonio might want a weekend's amusement while he was away from home, but she wasn't about to be left bruised and bleeding for a second time. Let some other woman hurt over Tonio Cruz. She was tired of it. "Tonight should never have happened. God knows, I wish it hadn't." Erica summoned up the tough girl smile she had learned years ago when Tonio had first left her. She was determined not to let him know how he had crushed her again. "Just chalk it up to too many months of 'all work and no play.'"

He regarded her woodenly, saying nothing. Erica was sure her pasted-on grin was about to melt into sobs. "Of course, I'd forgotten." When he finally spoke, Tonio's voice was smooth and soft, containing none of her frantic emotion. "You must be well versed in men now. I thought I detected a bit more expertise."

His contemptuous words lacerated her already bruised pride, and she lashed back, "Well, you won't have another chance to test it. I don't want to see you again. I'll type up a letter of resignation tomorrow, and I'll be leaving here in two weeks."

"Don't do it on my account," he retorted icily. "I think I can withstand the temptation of your body next time I'm here."

"I can't bear to have to work for you. I would have resigned anyway."

He shrugged. "Then don't let me stop you. Make your fine gesture."

Erica whirled and stalked away, her back stiff with unspent anger. She hated him, hated him. The words beat like an incantation in her brain all the way to the door. She shut it with a speaking softness. Once outside she ran to the stairway, unable to stand in the hall and wait for the elevator. Tears spilled over onto her cheeks as she clattered down flight after flight of stairs until finally she stopped, exhausted, blinded by tears, and sank onto the cold cement steps. Folding her arms across her knees and sinking her head onto them, she gave way to the sobs storming inside her.

By the time Erica returned to her apartment, Danny was fast asleep, a fact for which she was very grateful. She was able to slip into her darkened bedroom, crawl into bed and go to sleep without suffering the barrage of questions that would have come had Danny seen her blotched face and red-rimmed eyes. She was tired and miserable, and sleep came as a blessed relief.

However, the next morning she had to face the same painful reality she had left the night before. She had gone to bed with Tonio Cruz, a man she had hated for years, and had reawakened feelings she had thought long dead. Once again she was in an emotional turmoil, angry, hurting, yet pulsing with desire for him. No matter how much she regretted what she had done the night before, she was too honest not to admit that she had enjoyed it and that at this very moment she wanted Tonio.

She didn't still love him, of course. How could she? She despised him! She had gotten over her foolish love ten years ago when he had left her. It had been nothing but an adolescent crush. And love didn't survive that long without nurturing except in corny old books and movies. No, love didn't enter into what she felt. But she did desire him. He made exquisite love. No other man's most ardent kisses could melt her like Tonio's mere glance could. And when he stroked her body and rained kisses over her face and neck, when he whispered love words against her skin and patterned her breasts with his tongue, he transported her to a kind of ecstasy she had found in nothing else. Erica thought dismally that she was a slave to her passions. She had believed herself to be controlled and aloof all these years, when in reality it had simply been that she hadn't had to face the temptation of Tonio's lovemaking. It was easy to be calm around other men. Tonio was her weakness. He seemed to be able to make her mindless and shameless.

And that was why she had to get away from here. Tonio was bound to return to the Breezes to work on his plans and then later to check on the construction of the new wings and renovation of the main building. If she was around when he was there and if he put out any effort to get her into his bed...well, she wasn't sure she could resist. She had to quit.

Erica stayed in her office all day, cowardly avoiding any chance of seeing Tonio. Every time her telephone rang her stomach quivered with the fear that it would be Tonio's voice on the other end of the line. Fortunately it was not, and she made it through the day without once seeing or hearing him. Late in the afternoon, Rita casually mentioned that Mr. Cruz had checked out about twelve and taken the hotel's van to the Harlingen airport. Erica breathed a sigh of relief. Good. Surely he wouldn't come back anytime in the next two weeks, and she'd be gone after that. Another shattering episode of her life was over.

That evening she updated her résumé, wrote a form letter of inquiry and began making a list of hotels and motels to which she could apply for work. She had already written her letter of resignation and mailed it to Cross Corporation in Houston.

That had been the first item on her agenda that morning. Now she just had to find another job somewhere to support herself and Danny.

Her list of possibles grew slowly. She found herself reluctant to leave South Padre Island. The view of the blue Gulf from her window grew more inviting daily, the squat date palm trees more appealing, the wide, white beach more beautiful. Resentfully she wished Tonio hadn't thrust himself into her life again. The odds were against her getting another job on the Island. He was forcing her to leave this sunny, balmy place. But however much she might dislike it, she had to do it. So each evening and the weekend were spent typing up letters and sending them out to various hotels, first in the Rio Grande Valley area, then in the San Antonio-Austin area.

Danny noticed her evening occupation and inevitably began to question her about it. Reluctantly she admitted that they would soon be moving again. Although he was obviously disappointed, he stoutly maintained that he would enjoy living somewhere else just as much as he enjoyed it here. Not for the first time, Erica thanked her lucky stars for a son like Danny, then immediately worried that it wasn't good for a child to be so adult. He needed a father. He needed a more normal lifestyle. He shouldn't have to be so responsible and considerate, so grown-up and understanding. Yet, how would she manage if he were not the way he was?

She accepted a date with Joe Westfield on Friday. She had dated him on and off since coming to the Island. A pleasant man in his mid-thirties, he was divorced and had two little girls whom he kept every weekend. Their dates seemed easy and natural, affording them an opportunity to take their children along, with no great commitment or feeling on either side. Nor was there any excitement, Erica thought to herself as she and Danny left Joe at the elevator in the lobby after she had given her date a platonic kiss on the cheek. Nothing could create a safer relationship than three children in the back seat. Everytime they went out, they ate at a fast-food place favored by the children and then went to see a G-rated movie or partook of some other family-type entertainment. It seemed deadly dull, particularly after the fireworks of Tonio's presence the weekend before. But then, she reminded herself, at least it didn't tear her apart. After all, life was a matter of compromise.

Erica told her employees that she had submitted her resignation and would be leaving at the end of the week. Their shock and dismay were gratifying. Rita Escamilla even cried. She reassured them that it was a personal matter and that her resignation had not been forced by Cross Corporation. From her conversation with Mr. Cruz, she was sure Cross would retain the Breezes' present employees. Although they accepted her statement, the rest of the week was spent under a cloud of gloom. Erica expected Cross to send a new manager, but none had arrived by the weekend. Shrugging, she told herself that it wasn't her problem. Rita and Dave could keep the place running smoothly even if the manager didn't show up for another week or so. Anyway, it was no longer her responsibility.

All week, in every spare moment, Danny and Erica were busy packing their belongings. They had done it often enough that they were experts. They had learned to live with a minimum of possessions, which was made easier by the fact that they usually lived in furnished apartments in the motels Erica managed. And what belongings they had were portable and had been packed, unpacked and repacked so often that they could almost go through the process blindfolded. By Saturday they were ready to leave. A couple of the hotel staff helped them load the small rental trailer attached to the rear of Erica's little gas-saving car, and they set off, waving a cheerful good-bye to the employees who gathered to see them off.

Erica had decided to spend some time at her father's house. She had not been to visit him since she had moved to the island a few months ago, and she felt a little guilty about it. She and Grant had never been close, and their distance had been aggravated by his attitude toward Danny. Erica had felt a definite reluctance to take Danny to her father's farm. However, Grant had asked her often in the past two or three years to come back home to live, and she knew he must want to be closer to her as he grew older. When she got the job at the Breezes, she had promised herself that she would go to see Grant more often. However, the problems of settling into a new job, as well as the usual catastrophes that a hotel manager had to deal with, had kept her so busy that she had let the time slip away from her. She realized in dismay that she hadn't seen her father in over six months and had talked to him only once or twice over the phone.

Her quitting had presented her with the perfect opportunity to visit him. She knew it would be awhile before she got a response from any of her letters of inquiry to other hotels. She had little to do and no particular place to go until then. She could go home and let Grant get better acquainted with Danny. Maybe a better father-daughter relationship would grow out of it. After all, she was too old and should be too mature to let the rift of ten years ago still stand between them.

So she drove west through Port Isabel and on to Highway 77 leading from Brownsville to Harlingen. As elsewhere in the Valley, the road was lined on either side by towering Washingtonian palms, bare all the way up their enormously tall trunks to the cluster of leaves at the top. Looking out across the flat land, one could see the various lines of Washingtonians that marked distant roads. The land on either side of the highway was arid, almost a desert, dotted with scrubby mesquite and various other cacti: Spanish dagger, with its sharp, thrusting points; prickly pear; aloe vera; yucca; the wide, spreading century plant. The beautiful flowered plants of the Valley—the royal poinciana, the purple-flowered jacaranda, the bright scarlet and pink bougainvillea, the oleanders ranging from pristine white to pink to deep crimson—grew only where there was water to be lavished on them.

Erica turned right onto oleander-lined Highway 77 to Harlingen, then headed west toward McAllen. She exited from the highway before she reached McAllen and took the county road to the small town of Santa Clara. A warm eagerness crept through her as she drove through the dusty, somnolent town. Santa Clara had changed somewhat in appearance since she had lived there—a new storefront here and there, a new supermarket on the edge of town—but the basic quality of the place was unchanging. There was still the central town square with a squat stone municipal building in the middle. The businesses clustered around the square, and the residential areas ran out from the business center. Old men sat on benches outside City Hall, and shoppers strolled along the sidewalks, mingling with businessmen and teenagers looking for something to do. There was little going on, and the few people who were out moved slowly or not at all, part of the slow, lazy, small-town scene. Erica smiled. There was something about her hometown that brought forth all her sentimentality, no matter how much she had disliked it when she had lived there.

Past Santa Clara she stepped on the accelerator, eager to reach the house. After a few miles she slowed, searching for the gravel driveway of her father's farm. "There it is," she exclaimed, turning off. "Danny, that's the old house where I lived when I was a girl and where my grandparents lived later." Where Tonio and I used to meet, she added silently.

Danny shot her a scornful look. "I know. You showed me when we were here before."

Erica grinned. Clearly Danny had little use for her sudden heart-tugging nostalgia. They drove past the row of date palms, noticing a gap here and there where weather or disease had taken one out of the line. Then she glimpsed the roof of the house and the cascade of crimson bougainvillea down the side. She drove past the sheltering hedge of oleander and pulled to a stop in front, then climbed out of the car and looked around, taking stock. The hedges and bushes had grown shaggy, and the cream-colored house needed a paint job. One of the two lemon trees was clearly dead, but hadn't been removed. Several of the overlapping brick-red Spanish tiles were missing.

Danny raced to the porch, then turned questioningly. "What's the matter, Mom?"

"Nothing," she replied with false brightness, though inside she was dismayed at the changes in her home. "Just looking around."

The front door was locked for the first time she could remember, and she had to ring the doorbell for admittance. The house looked so different, so untended and careworn, that she half expected a stranger to open the door. It was a relief when the heavy wooden door was opened a few moments later by Lupe, the housekeeper who had worked for Grant ever since Erica's mother died. She was a small woman, fragile-looking, although Erica had seen her moving couches single-handedly, and her thin, usually reserved face was quiet, almost sad.

After an initial surprised stare Lupe burst into a wide grin. "Señorita!" she exclaimed, reaching out to pull Erica into the foyer. "*Gracias a Dios!* God has answered my prayers. Come in, come in."

Erica followed her, startled by her unusually enthusiastic greeting. "Lupe? What's the matter?"

Lupe shook her head sorrowfully. "Come into the kitchen with me. I have to talk to you before you see Señor Grant."

Erica frowned and turned to Danny behind her. "Sweetheart, why don't you go outside and play? There are all kinds of interesting things around here."

"Sure," Danny agreed, glad to get out of listening to grownups talk, and took off at a run. Erica strode rapidly down the hall to the spacious kitchen.

"Now, what is all this, Lupe? Is there something wrong with Daddy?"

"Oh, señorita, I wanted to call you, but Señor Grant wouldn't let me. He said I was being a silly old woman, but it's not true. He is very sick."

Erica's heart began to hammer wildly. Her father ill? But that was impossible. Grant was like the rocks, the cactus, the soil—indestructible. Logically she knew that was a silly idea. Grant was human, like everyone else, and he was getting older. It wasn't unlikely that he might be ill. But emotionally she couldn't conceive of it. Erica drew a calming breath. "How sick?"

Lupe looked away. "I think he is dying."

"No!" Unconsciously Erica stepped back. "You're wrong. He never said a word...."

Lupe shrugged. "He wouldn't. You know him. He wouldn't even tell me what is wrong. But he has a death face."

"Lupe!"

"It's true," Lupe assured her with placid acceptance. "My Uncle Emilio looked that way when he came home from the hospital to die in his own bed."

"But what—why—" Erica stammered to a halt, too stunned to think. Slowly she turned, one hand going to her head as if to still the turmoil inside. "I...guess I better see him myself. Where is he?"

"In his room. He's been in bed the past two days, hardly gets up. It's worse than before." She paused, then added, "Just remember, he will not look the same. He is smaller, older. Don't be too shocked.''

Erica nodded and walked slowly to the staircase and up the curving stairs. The upstairs hall floor was made of tile and covered by a runner of Mexican design. Its bright colors had dimmed with age, and it was thinning and worn through in spots. Erica knocked at her father's door and opened it cautiously when she received no response. Her father lay propped on his pillows in bed, half sitting, half lying. His eyes were shut in sleep. Erica drew in her breath sharply, and the fear in her swelled. Grant Logan had aged since she had seen him last. He had lost weight and seemed almost to have shrunk. His face was deeply lined and the texture of his skin was papery and thin. The hands, which lay loosely clasped on the bedcovers, once so strong and sinewy, were an old man's hands, knotted and splotched.

Erica's knees began to tremble, and for one wild moment she wanted to run away—down the stairs and out of the house. But, biting her lip, she waited. Grant seemed to sense her presence, and his eyelids fluttered open. At first his gaze was puzzled, almost unfocused, then his eyes brightened and his lips formed a narrow smile. "Erica? What are you doing here?"

"I came to see you, Daddy," Erica responded, amazed at how normal and cheery she managed to sound. "Business is slacking off, so I was able to take the time off." No point in letting him know she had quit her job. That would worry him needlessly. "How are you?"

"Fine, fine," he lied and pushed himself up straighter against the pillows. Erica pulled a chair to his bedside and sat down. An awkward silence fell upon them. She could not ask the questions which simmered in her. Grant was too private, too reticent a person, for her to intrude upon him with personal questions. It seemed a violation to ask him about his health—and, yes, admit it, she was afraid of his answer. Oh, dear God, what was she to do?

Pasting a weak smile on her face, she began to talk about the hotel and its sale. "You'll never guess who bought it!" she added brightly. "Antonio Cruz! Remember? He used to work for you. He went to the University of Texas and became an architect."

A shadow touched his eyes. "Yes, I remember."

"He's quite a success now, runs a big corporation."

"Did you meet him? Talk to him?"

"Yes." Erica glanced at her father's face, surprised at his interest. "I showed him around the hotel."

"What did he say?"

"Uh...not much. We didn't talk about the past. It was purely business."

"Good." He lay back against the pillows, his face weary and pained.

"I'm tiring you, aren't I?" Erica asked quickly and stood up. "You go back to sleep and have a good nap. I really need to see what Danny's up to, anyway."

"Yes, that's fine," he agreed, his eyes already closing. "We'l talk later. We—need to talk."

"Of course, Daddy." Erica stepped into the hallway and closed his door behind her. Away from his gaze, she stopped and pressed her palms to her temples. Tears swam at the edge of her vision, and she blinked them away, breathing deeply to stem the flood of fear rising in her. Grant was terribly sick. Dying? No, she would not think that way. It was simply that he needed someone to take care of him. Maybe that was why he had been urging her to come home to live the past year or so. She had regarded it as an attempt to control her, but now she wondered. Perhaps he had wanted her with him because he needed her. That possibility had never occurred to her. She realized that for too long now she had continued to look at her father with a child's eyes, not an adult's.

Slowly she made her way downstairs to the kitchen. Lupe turned at her entrance and silently studied her. "Would you like a cup of coffee?"

"Yes, please." Erica sank into one of the heavy wooden chairs around the plain kitchen table.

Lupe poured a cup of coffee and set the steaming black liquid before Erica. She waited for Erica to take a steadying sip then asked, "So? Now you've seen him."

"Yes. Lupe, there's something terribly wrong with him. What is it?"

Lupe shrugged. "I don't know. He won't talk."

"Is he going to Dr. Marsden?"

"No. Old Dr. Marsden's gone. He retired and went to live with his daughter in Brownsville."

"Then where does he go? He has been to a doctor, hasn't he?"

"Sí. My brother Rudi drives him. A few months ago he got sick. In his stomach, you know. He thought it was ulcers or appendicitis or something. He went to McAllen. He was in the hospital a week. After that, he went to the hospital all the time, then once a week for a while. He got Rudi to drive him because he always felt sick when he came back."

Erica ran a shaky hand through her hair. Chemotherapy? Radiation treatment? It sounded as if that could be it. Cancer? Did her father have cancer? "Why didn't he tell me? I could have helped. I could have come home earlier. I didn't know...." But an insistent voice at the back of her brain reminded her that she hadn't asked, hadn't visited even though she lived only a couple of hours away. If she had visited him, she would have known far earlier that something was wrong with him. Erica rose, leaving her half-finished coffee on the table. "I think I'll take a walk around."

Aimlessly she wandered about outside the house, half looking for Danny. She strolled to the barn, her head sunk in thought. The door to the equipment shed stood open, and instinctively Erica went to shut it. It had been engrained in her all her life to keep the equipment protected. Glancing inside the shed, she stopped, shocked. Tools and pipes lay scattered about carelessly, some rusting in pools of water that had collected beneath leaks in the roof. Erica gaped. No self-respecting farmer would allow things to get in this condition. If she had needed any proof that Grant was desperately ill, this was enough. He obviously hadn't inspected the farm in weeks, possibly months, and that would never have happened if he hadn't been extremely sick.

Erica bit her lower lip and turned away from the barn. She couldn't afford to dither around here like a frightened child. Grant needed her help. She had to find out what was the matter with her father and what she could do to heal him. She wouldn't let herself consider the possibility that perhaps healing was not possible. Hurrying toward the house, she saw Danny playing by the swimming pool. Her father had had it drained long ago, and the gaping hole wasn't a very safe place. Her mind registered the danger, but she reminded herself that Danny was a good, cautious boy. Waving a hand, she called, "Be careful!"

"Oh, Mom" was his scornful retort. Erica wondered when a person lost his youthful certainty that all bad things could be held at bay forever.

She strode down the hall to the kitchen, willing her mind to think rationally despite the knotting of her stomach and the pounding of her heart. "Lupe? Do you have any idea of the name of the doctor Grant sees in McAllen?"

Lupe shrugged. "He's at the hospital. I don't know if he sees just one."

"Would Rudi know?"

"Maybe. I'll call him."

Five minutes and several phone calls later, Lupe returned with the triumphant news that her brother had been tracked down at his sister-in-law's house and that he had remembered the name of the doctor. It was Blaisdell. Erica quickly dialed information and obtained his home phone number in Mc-Allen. His wife answered the phone and was reluctant to call him to the phone on business, but finally Erica's persistence won out, and the woman set down the receiver with a sigh. After a moment a man's rich baritone came on the phone. "Yes? This is Dr. Blaisdell."

"Doctor, I'm sorry to disturb you at home. But my father, Grant Logan, is one of your patients, I believe, and I'm rather worried about him."

"Yes?" His voice turned sharp and quick. "What is it?"

"Then he is your patient?"

"Yes, of course. I've been seeing him since June. What's the matter?"

Tears of relief clogged Erica's voice. At least she had found someone who could help her. "I don't know. I didn't know there was *anything* wrong with him until I came for a visit today. He looks awful." Stumblingly she related her story.

When she finally came to a halt, there was a long pause on the other end of the line. "Miss Logan, I don't discuss my patients over the phone, even with close relatives. I think it would be a good idea if you brought him to the hospital and let me look at him. From your description it sounds as if his condition has deteriorated since I saw him last. After that I'll discuss his situation with you. I think it would be better face-to-face. Can you bring him in?"

Erica's fingers clenched around the phone. "Yes, yes, of course." Even after he hung up, she remained staring at the blank kitchen wall, the receiver still clutched in her hand. It couldn't be good if he felt he had to tell her face-to-face. Deteriorated. His condition had deteriorated. Mechanically her hand moved to hang up the phone, and she began the long walk down the hall and up the stairs to her father's room.

This time she did not knock, just walked into the quiet room. Her father's face was waxy, his eyes closed. Erica swallowed and bent down to touch his arm. "Daddy? Daddy? It's time to wake up. I've talked to your doctor, and he—Daddy?" Panic entered her voice. Why wouldn't he wake up? For a moment the thought that he was dead jolted through her like an electric shock. She bent even closer. No. She could hear his shallow breathing. Erica sought the pulse in his wrist and finally found a weak beating. "Daddy!" she demanded more loudly, but received no more response. "Lupe!" Erica took a few swift steps to the open door and called at the top of her voice. "Lupe! Quick! Come here! I need your help."

Within seconds the wiry woman was racing up the stairs to help her. But even Lupe's deceptive strength could not help her get Logan's unconscious weight out of the bed. "There's no way," Erica said, panting from the effort of trying to lift him. Panicky sobs were beginning to rise in her throat. "We could never get him down the stairs, even if we did manage to get him out of bed. I'll—I'll have to call an ambulance." She started for the door, then stopped. "But it'll take ages to get here. Oh, Lupe, he could die by then. What am I going to do?"

Chapter 6

A sleek tobacco-brown Mercedes sedan eased into the town of Santa Clara and pulled to a stop at the town's single red light. Shoving up his sunglasses, the driver rubbed his eyes. Antonio Cruz was tired from more than the long drive from Houston to his hometown in the Rio Grande Valley. He had spent a hard two weeks, working like a driven man on the plans for his new hotel. Today, finished with the preliminary drawings, he had decided to take a break. For some reason he had been drawn to Santa Clara and his family.

He rolled his shoulders to get out the kinks, then on impulse turned right instead of proceeding directly to his mother's house. After two blocks he turned into the parking lot of Cruz Chevrolet. Four years earlier Tonio had bought out the former owner of the town's only car dealership and given it to his brother Lucio to run. To everyone's amazement except Tonio's, his happy-go-lucky younger brother had made a success of the business. The charm that had enabled him to breeze through school without opening a book, coupled with a native shrewdness that he had done his utmost to hide all his life, had enabled Lucio to wheedle almost anyone into buying a new car. Within two years he had offered to buy Tonio out of the deal.

ership, and Tonio had willingly agreed. Nothing could have been more to his liking than his brother's success and ultimate independence.

Tonio slid out of his low car and strode into the glass-fronted building. Since Lucio had taken over he had repainted the fading exterior of the auto dealership and added bank after bank of tinted glass. In business, as in everything, Lucio believed in flaunting it. The showroom was deserted, so Tonio climbed the wrought-iron staircase to the loft offices overlooking the lobby. There were three offices, each with a window on to the showroom below. Lucio's, the largest, was on the end. Lucio glanced up, saw his brother and immediately jumped from his chair to greet him. "Hey, Tonio! *Qué pasa?*"

Tonio's younger brother resembled him in the face, although Lucio's was more delicate, more perfectly handsome, without the sober lines around his mouth and eyes. However, at twenty-seven, there was a slackening in the firm lines of his face, and a small paunch now protruded above his belt. Lucio was beginning to show his years of rich, easy living, but he was still an arresting-looking man in his smart blue pin-striped suit, a diamond ring flashing on one finger.

"I think I'm doing better than you," Tonio retorted, indicating the room below with a flick of his head.

Lucio grimaced and enfolded his brother in an affectionate hug. "Don't rub it in. The car business, *mi hermano,* is not exactly in a boom period."

Tonio began to play an imaginary violin, his mouth drawing down in mocking pity. "Think you'll have to sell out?"

"Naaa . . . who'd be crazy enough to buy it? Come on inside." He motioned toward his office. "Want some coffee? A soft drink?"

"I'd rather have a straight shot of whiskey."

Lucio's brows rose expressively. "Rough day?" He pulled open a door of his low credenza and extracted a black-labeled bottle and two short, heavy glasses. He splashed a healthy portion of liquor into one, handed it to Tonio, then poured himself a drink.

"Rough week," Tonio answered, then amended it. "Rough two weeks." He grinned. "Always trust you executive types to have a bottle hidden away."

Lucio turned his hands palm up. "So what's the problem at the top?"

Tonio rubbed a hand wearily across his brow. "You wouldn't believe me if I told you."

"Try me."

"A woman."

Lucio stared. "You're right, I don't believe you. Antonio Cruz, the celebrated Hispanic without a heart? Come on. Well, at least you've come to the right place with your problems. Who is it? Anyone I've met?"

"Oh, you've met her all right." Tonio's mouth twisted into the semblance of a grin. "Erica Logan."

Lucio's mouth literally fell open as he stared at his older brother. "*Qué!* B-but, Tonio, where? Why?"

Tonio chuckled grimly. "Would you believe she's an employee of mine?"

Lucio laughed. "How rich. A Logan working for a Cruz. That's a switch. So tell me, what happened?"

"It's a long story, longer than you think. Do you remember the summer after I graduated from U.T.? When I came back here to work before I went to Houston?"

"Sure. That was the summer you kept stealing my car and sneaking off someplace, but you'd never tell me where— Wait a minute. You're not telling me—you were meeting Erica back then?"

Tonio nodded, his face etched in grim lines. "Yeah, I was meeting Erica."

"I'll be . . . well, go on."

"It was crazy. She was bored and restless, and I guess I piqued her interest because I didn't fall at her feet like every other guy. I wasn't a total idiot, so I tried to resist her, but let me tell you, it was difficult. Anyway, we started meeting at the old abandoned house on her property. To her I was handy, a safe subject for her sexual experimentation. But I loved her. I really loved her." He paused, swallowing, memories flooding in on him. He remembered the hot sun beating down on his back in the groves, and a vision of Erica pulsing in his brain and body. Every day had been torture until they met at the old house and made wild, sweet love. He had lived for nothing but the taste and smell and feel of her in his arms. Blindly he had entrusted his heart to her keeping, even dreaming she would marry him, making plans to take her away when she finished high school. "I thought she loved me too. She took away all my bitterness. The past didn't matter with her. Who I was didn't matter. I was proud, happy."

"I remember," Lucio put in softly. "I've never seen you like that, before or since."

"Then I discovered I was building castles in the air. She didn't really love me. One night I admitted how much I loved her, and I suppose it was what she'd been aiming at all along. The next day her father came to 'talk' to me. He was really blowing smoke, said he'd found out Erica was sneaking out to meet me. He wanted me to leave town. 'Course, I was really cocky and replied that I'd take Erica with me. He laughed in my face and asked me how I thought he knew about us. Erica had told him and asked him to get rid of me for her. She didn't want to see me again. I said he was lying. Erica loved me. So Logan revealed that all the time Erica was meeting me, she was dating other guys—'boys of her own class,' as he put it. I was okay for a thrill, but not for the public. I knew he was right. It had been too good to be true. But I still tried to pretend I didn't believe it. He told me I could see for myself. Erica had a date that night with Jeff Roberts. I went there that evening and hid by the driveway behind the oleander hedge. Sure enough, about seven-thirty Jeff picked her up." He closed his eyes, seeing her again, her hair swept up in a grown-up hairdo, her lush body wrapped in a floating, pale-green chiffon dress that lay like sea foam against her creamy skin. And again Tonio experienced the piercing ache in his gut that he had felt then. "I watched them drive away, and the next day I left for Houston."

There was a hushed pause. Finally Lucio said, "I'm sorry. I never knew...."

Tonio shrugged. "It was a long time ago. And I have her to thank for my success. When I went to Houston I decided to work my tail off and become somebody, just to spite her." He smiled, minimizing the almost ten years of driven work, the obsessive need to succeed, the sterile, contemptuous relationships with women. It had taken him several years to get over Erica, and every step on his upward climb had been stained by bitterness.

"Well, you certainly managed that," his brother agreed. "And now she's working for you."

"Yeah. She's the manager of the Breezes, an old hotel I bought on the Island. Isn't it ironic? When I stepped through the front door and saw her walking toward me, I thought I'd slipped back in time."

"And?"

"And what?"

"What happened? How'd she act? What did she look like?"

"She hasn't gotten her just rewards, if that's what you mean. I was hoping she'd grown fat and was beginning to age, but no such luck. If anything, she's even prettier." Tonio had once thought he would never see a woman more beautiful than the teenage Erica, bursting with health and life. But now he knew he had been wrong. The mature Erica was far more lovely. The luxuriant mane was tied back in a repressive knot, but the warm color glowed, tantalizing in its restrained lushness. The naive wonder was gone from her face. Time and experience had stamped it, but they had served only to bring out the promise of her youthful countenance, melting the roundness of cheeks and chin and leaving stark, fine-boned beauty. Even the hint of sadness that darkened her eyes made them more mesmerizing. "And she was cool as a cucumber, kept it on a purely business level."

"Uh-huh," Lucio agreed, disbelief tinging his voice. "And you've been upset for two weeks because she was just business to you?"

"Oh, no. I said *she* kept it on a business level. I couldn't. I started telling her some drivel about liking my employees to be aware of the changes I'd be making, so I wanted to take her out to dinner."

"And did you?"

"No. Even worse, we went back to my room to talk. She has a kid. Can you imagine that?"

"I'd heard rumors. No husband, though."

"No. No husband." His eyes turned remote and blank.

"So? What happened? Did you . . . ?" Lucio's voice trailed off delicately.

"Oh, yeah." Tonio laughed shortly. "I made as big a fool of myself as ever. It was— God, there's no other woman like her.

I felt like a green kid again.'' He ran a hand distractedly through his hair and stared at his feet, unable to meet his brother's gaze. ''Oh, Lucio, when am I going to learn? Afterward she looked at me with such disgust, such loathing in her eyes. She told me she hated me and never wanted to see me again. Then she left. The sex is great between us, it always was. But anything more than that—uh-uh, she wouldn't stand for it.''

''Women.'' Lucio shook his head in an eternally male gesture of bewilderment at the opposite sex.

''Especially Anglo women.''

''So what are you going to do?''

''Do? What can I do? She wants nothing to do with me, and believe me, I'm better off without her. She submitted her resignation the next day. I don't know where she's moving. It'll be easier this way.''

''Is that why you've been working so hard for two weeks? To convince yourself of that?''

''I don't care for her anymore!'' Tonio insisted, standing up to pace the thick carpeting. ''There's nothing between us. But that one night haunts me. When I went home I took out a girl I've been dating recently. A knockout. Holly Blakely. Not much for brains, but a gorgeous figure. Young, sexy. I felt about as much desire for her as I do for that chair. Couldn't even touch her.''

''Tonio, Tonio, what am I going to do with you?'' Lucio exclaimed in mock exasperation. ''You're too serious, too involved. Just because you still have the hots for Erica Logan doesn't mean you can't enjoy the rest of the feminine half of this world.''

Tonio shot him an amused glance. ''Not to you, obviously. Like you said, I'm too serious. But I can't get her off my mind.''

Lucio shook his head. ''I am going to have to take you in hand.'' He paused. ''You know, it's strange, your saying all this about the Logans. I have a kid who works for me who's one of Lupe Delgado's innumerable nephews. He told me the other day that Logan's real sick. Dying, in fact.''

''Dying?''

"Yeah, Rudi's been driving him over to McAllen since June to take some kind of treatments. Cancer, I guess."

"Poor Erica," Tonio murmured. The phone rang shrilly and they both jumped.

"Excuse me, I'm the only one here. I have to get this." Lucio punched one of the buttons at the bottom of his phone and raised the receiver. "Cruz Chevrolet." He frowned in silence as a voice rattled off something in Spanish. "Wait, wait, he's not here." There was another spate of words and Lucio covered the mouthpiece, raising his eyebrows expressively. "Speak of the devil," he stage-whispered. "This is Lupe. She's going crazy. I can hardly understand what she's saying." He spoke into the receiver, "No, Lupe, Johnny's not here. Everybody's left for the day. Wait! What's the matter?"

Across from him, Tonio went taut. "What is it?"

Lucio held up a hand. "Look, Lupe, I'll be right out, okay? No problem." He hung up and rose. "Lupe says Erica's there and wants to take Logan into McAllen to the doctor. Apparently he's lapsed into a coma or something. They can't lift him, and she was trying to get her nephew to come help them. I told her I'd go, but you don't have to—"

Tonio was already out the door and running swiftly down the stairs. "Come on!" he called back over his shoulder. "We'll take my car."

"Lucio said Johnny wasn't there, but he would come himself," Lupe announced, rejoining Erica in her father's bedroom. "It'll take awhile, but not as long as an ambulance from the hospital."

Erica clenched her hands tightly together. "Oh, God, Lupe, I feel so helpless. If only I'd come home sooner."

"Shhh. There's no sense to that kind of talk. You didn't know."

"I should have." Erica walked to the window and looked out. "I'd better go tell Danny. Will you stay here with him? I'd hate for him to have to sit and wait for me in a hospital."

"Of course. I can spend the whole night if you need me."

"Thank you." Erica smiled faintly and went downstairs to explain her departure to her son. She found him in the barn, and when he saw her, he began to chatter about all the wonders he had found. Erica nodded absently and took his hand to tell him about her father's illness. When she told him she was taking Grant to the hospital and that Danny would stay here with Lupe, her usually pliable child turned suddenly stubborn, insisting mulishly that he come with her. Erica sighed. Why on earth did he have to choose this moment to be recalcitrant? "It's out of the question, Danny," she began, then looked at his thin face. She saw fear in his wide brown eyes, and she realized that he was afraid to remain with Lupe in this strange house. The move, the new house, the unexpected illness of his grandfather, had combined to throw him out of his usual equanimity. Of course he was unsettled and wanted to remain by her familiar side. "Okay," she reversed herself. "You can come, but I warn you, you'll get tired and bored."

"That's okay."

She took his hand, and they strolled back to the house together. When they reached the front porch Erica turned to glance down the long driveway. Had she heard a car? Moments later an elegant Mercedes came into view. Erica opened the front door and yelled up the stairs, "Lupe, I think Lucio's here." Eagerly she ran down the shallow steps of the porch and across the yard to meet the car.

To her amazement it was Tonio's trim form that slid out of the driver's seat. "Erica? Are you all right? What happened?"

Strangely Erica was swept with relief. Hardly thinking what she was doing, she stepped forward and reached out to take the hand Tonio offered. "Oh, thank God, Tonio! Daddy's so sick. He's dying and I can't wake him. I have to get him to the hospital."

Tonio strode into the house, still holding Erica's hand in his comforting grip. Lucio and Danny followed them, eyeing each other curiously. "Where is he?" Tonio asked, and Erica wordlessly pulled him upstairs to her father's bedroom.

Lupe stared at Tonio's entrance, but wasted no time with questions. She stepped aside and Tonio went to the bed. Erica watched, her hands knotting nervously together, while Tonio pulled her father to a sitting position. With Lucio's help he lifted him from the bed, and the two began the slow, treacherous descent of the stairs with their heavy burden. Lupe followed with a blanket, and Erica and Danny came on her heels. They carried Grant to the back seat of the car and gently laid him inside, where Lupe covered him with the blanket, before they buckled him in. Despite the warmth of the September day Grant's skin was cold and damp.

Erica grabbed her purse from the kitchen table and hurried out to slide into the front seat, Danny jumping in after her. Tonio turned to his brother and said tersely, "I'll take them to McAllen. Can Lupe drive you back?"

"Sure."

Tonio slid behind the wheel, turned the key and took off with a roar. Erica, seated close beside him with Danny on the other side of her, for once was not unnerved by Tonio's presence. Somehow, in the stress and anxiety of the moment, it didn't seem peculiar that he had appeared when she needed help or unnatural that she should turn to him. There was a calm, cool air about Tonio, the air of a man accustomed to taking command. And that was what she wanted. Her mind whirling with fears and guilt, she didn't want to have to make any decisions.

"It'll be okay," Tonio assured her, his free hand sliding with feather softness over her hair. "We'll get him there."

"I know."

The trip seemed endless, although Tonio blatantly outstripped the speed limit in the powerful car. He drove with one hand, the other holding Erica's. Erica clung to it, grateful for the reassurance in his quiet, steel-hard body beside her. When they pulled up outside the emergency entrance, Tonio calmly took charge, going inside to summon two white-clad orderlies to bring Grant Logan inside. Tonio led Erica and Danny to chairs in the small waiting room, then went to the waiting nurse to relay the necessary information.

Erica sat numbly, watching Tonio talk to the nurse as the orderlies whisked her father into a small curtained-off cubicle. Moments later a tall, bearded doctor appeared in the emergency room. After a brief consultation with the nurse and Tonio, he, too, disappeared into the cubicle. The nurse followed, and Tonio came back to sit beside Erica. "That was Dr. Blaisdell," he explained. "He said he'd know more later. We'll just have to wait until he's examined him."

Time dragged by. Tonio offered to bring her coffee or a soda, but she refused both. Danny, however, was quick to accept the offer of a soft drink and went charging off in search of a machine. While he was gone the nurse emerged and told them that the orderlies were taking Mr. Logan to the lab for tests and then up to his room. "Would you like me to show you to his room now?" she asked gently.

"Yes, I—I guess so. Oh—Danny..."

"Don't worry. Go on. I'll stay here and bring him when he gets back," Tonio said quietly.

"All right." Erica didn't spare a second thought for the danger of Tonio spending time with Danny, which had so bothered her two weeks before. Now she had no concern except for her father.

Tonio waited for the boy, his mind on Erica. No matter what had passed between them, he had jumped to help her. One look at her wide gray eyes filled with fright and he had felt as if he would fight dragons to take away that fear. He had no more stopped to think than she had, reacting with the swift, sure movements of a strong man protecting his woman. His woman. Tonio sighed. Did he still love her? Had he been fooling himself all these years? He had thought himself wise and cold, immune to women because he had learned. Could it be that he simply hadn't wanted anyone else because his heart still belonged to Erica?

"Hey, aren't you the man from the hotel?" Danny's return interrupted his thoughts. Tonio looked up at the boy, studying him. He was a good-looking child, Tonio thought. He could see Erica's elegant bone structure in his face, and Danny had her wide eyes, although the color was different. Small, tan and wiry, Tonio judged him to be about seven or eight years old. What man after him had given Erica a son? She had told Tonio that she loved him, then left him so soon for another. His insides twisted at the thought.

"Yeah, I am," he replied calmly, long used to hiding the ache inside him.

"Why're you here?" Danny asked bluntly.

"Lupe, your grandfather's housekeeper, called my brother Lucio, and I happened to be there with him. So I came to help Erica."

"Why?"

Tonio stared at him, puzzled. "Why wouldn't I? She needed help."

"Yeah, but you made her leave the hotel, didn't you? That means you don't like her, doesn't it?"

"Did she tell you that?"

"Naaa," the boy replied. "She'd think I'd worry about it. She told me she wanted to go someplace else, but I know that's not true. She liked living on the island. She'd always wanted to go there. So I know she wouldn't have left unless you forced her to."

"I didn't. I promise you. But, you see, your mother knows me from a long time ago. We grew up in the same town."

"Santa Clara," Danny supplied knowledgeably.

"Yeah. Anyway, your mother has some bad feelings from when we knew each other before. I—uh, she just didn't want to work for me. But I never asked her to leave."

Danny tilted his head, considering. "You seem okay," he admitted finally.

"Well, thank you." A grin flickered across Tonio's face. "You seem okay too. You're pretty protective of your mother, aren't you?"

"What does that mean?"

"You take care of her."

"Sure. I have to. My dad's dead, you see."

"He is?"

"Yeah. He was a real great guy, always helping people and everything. Everybody loved him."

A lump grew in Tonio's throat. "Including your mother?"

Danny flashed him a scornful look. "Sure! Mom loved him most of all. That's why she had me—'cause she loved him so much. I'm part of my dad, see, and that way she'd always have him."

Jealousy pierced Tonio's heart. Erica had loved the man who had gotten her pregnant and not married her. Had he really died and was that the sorrow Erica carried in her eyes? Or was the sadness because he had deserted her?

"I never knew him, but Mom told me all about him," Danny continued, going on to relate a few stories about his father, who seemed to be a kind of hero who rescued people from one misfortune or another. They suspiciously resembled the tales of Robin Hood, which convinced Tonio they were stories learned from Erica rather than boyish imaginings. Obviously what she had told Danny about his father bore no likeness to the truth, but equally obvious she had tried to foster the boy's love for his absent parent. She must have loved the man to picture him so for her child.

Despite his gnawing jealousy of the boy's father, Tonio couldn't help but like Danny. He had a frank, open charm, and an almost adult sense of humor twinkled in his eyes. For the first time Tonio experienced a twinge of regret that he had never loved anyone but Erica. There was something to be said for marriage and children.

Tonio laid a tentative hand on Danny's head, and the boy didn't seem to mind. As he was used to doing with Lucio's and Olivia's children, Tonio ruffled Danny's hair and received a grin in return. "You're quite a boy. I think we'd better go upstairs and join Erica. All right?"

When they stepped off the elevator Tonio guided Danny to the waiting room. It was furnished with a comfortable couch and chairs and had a small television set. Before long Danny was happily ensconced in the room, watching TV and sipping at his soft drink.

When Tonio stepped into Grant's room there was no one in the bed, but Erica was sitting in the lone chair, staring out the window. She turned at his entrance and smiled, her lips trembling. "Hello, Tonio. I'm sorry. I haven't thanked you for helping me."

"Don't worry. There's no need."

"I—somehow didn't seem to be able to cope. This has all been such a shock to me. I didn't know Daddy was even ill. He—I—the doctor came in to talk to me."

"What did he say?"

"A lot of words I didn't understand. Basically what it boils down to is that Daddy is dying. He's been dying for over three months now. He has stomach cancer, and the treatments haven't helped him. He stopped taking them almost a month ago." She stopped and drew a shaky breath. Tonio put his hand on her head, then slid it down to her shoulder. Tears sparkled in her eyes. "I—I'm so glad you're here."

Tonio pulled her up into his arms and held her comfortingly. She leaned her head against his chest and absorbed the hard strength of his body. "I'll be here as long as you need me. I promise." He rubbed his cheek softly against her hair. Funny how after all these years without it, giving could bring as much pleasure as receiving.

Chapter 7

Two attendants wheeled Grant into the room moments later and transferred him to the bed. "He's been regaining consciousness on and off," one of the men told Erica. "He might be able to speak to you."

"All right." Almost timidly Erica approached the side of the metal bed and picked up her father's cool, flaccid hand. "Daddy, can you hear me? It's Erica.'

He made a faint movement, rolling his head on his pillow, but did not open his eyes or speak. Tonio came up behind her. "Would you like me to leave you alone with him? I'll check on Danny."

"Thank you.". Tears stung Erica's eyes. After Tonio left, Erica talked to Grant for a time, speaking of any inconsequential thing that came to her mind. Finally, after receiving no response from him, she abandoned the effort, replacing his limp hand on the bed sheet. She sank down into the large easy chair nearby and watched him. Night crept in through the window, and gradually the room dimmed. Sitting there in the dark, Erica tried to make her peace with the father she had never known well.

Tonio brought her a meal from the cafeteria, but she could hardly touch the food. Around midnight she strolled down the hall to the waiting room to check on Danny. He lay stretched out on the couch, his head in Tonio's lap. A considerate nurse had covered him with a light blanket. Beside him Tonio, too, was asleep, one arm stretched along the top of the couch and his head resting on it. The picture of the two of them together brought unshed tears to Erica's throat, adding to the warm ache there.

She returned silently to Grant's room and continued to sit with him, marking time by the comings and goings of the nurses. Now and then Grant grew restless, twisting his head and moaning. Once he called out Erica's name, but by the time she reached him, he was quiet again. She fell into a shallow sleep, waking often, until Grant's voice disturbed her. "Erica? Erica, is that you?"

"Yes, Daddy." She was on her feet and beside him in an instant. "I'm here."

"For a minute I thought it was your mother. Where is she?"

"Mama?" she repeated, momentarily stunned. "Why—why, I'm not sure, Daddy." Obviously his mind was wandering.

He turned his head away, then back, and asked about his crop. Erica assured him that the crop and farm were in fine condition, though if the state of the house was any measure, she doubted she was speaking the truth. Grant was quiet for a moment, then began, "Tonio Cruz..."

"Yes? He drove us here. Did you see him?"

Grant seemed to have lost interest in whatever he had been about to say about Tonio. He frowned. "Baby, I—I'm sorry. I didn't know."

Didn't know what? Was he still talking about Tonio? Or something else altogether? "It's okay, Daddy, don't worry about it."

He slid into a shallow sleep. About thirty minutes later he awoke and struggled to sit up. "I was wrong." The words burst out of him in short, panting gasps. "I thought you'd be happier without him."

"It's all right," she reassured him earnestly, assuming that he was now referring to his demand that she give up Danny for adoption. "I understand. You wanted what was best for me."

Grant nodded weakly. "That's all any child can ask. I was hurt then, but not anymore. Since I'm a parent, I can understand your concern for me."

"Forgive me."

Tears coursed down Erica's cheeks unheeded. "Of course, of course, I forgive you—if you'll forgive me for the worry I gave you. It must have been hard to raise a daughter alone after Mama died. I didn't think about you, just me and my problems. I'm sorry I didn't come back when you wanted. I never realized." Tears choked her into silence. Grant seemed calmer. He fell into a deeper sleep, no longer moving his head, his breathing shallow and irregular.

Erica sat down and wiped away her tears. She continued her vigil through the night, dozing, then awakening with a start. Grant did not move or speak again as dawn gradually lightened the sky. His breath began to come in fits and starts, sometimes stopping for a moment, then resuming with a long shudder. It reminded her of Danny's breathing when he was a baby. At about eight o'clock Tonio came in, tousled and sleepy-looking. He convinced Erica to go to the cafeteria for breakfast with Danny and him. Erica hated to leave Grant for even a few minutes, but eventually Tonio's reasoning won out. She would feel a little better, she knew, if she escaped from this bleak room for a while.

She picked at breakfast, consuming little but her coffee. It seemed strange that it should be Tonio who sat through this with her. He was the last man she would have dreamed would help her. But it felt too comforting to quibble about it. Her mind and emotions had more than enough to handle trying to deal with what was happening to her father.

When they returned to Grant's floor, they saw Dr. Blaisdell stepping out of Grant's room. Catching sight of Erica, he motioned to her. Erica hurried toward him, a tight band of fear suddenly cinching her heart. His news was bad. She could see it on his face. "Miss Logan," he began gravely, "your father's breathing has slowed considerably. I think he's near the end. Do you want to be with him?"

"Yes." Erica walked past the doctor to Grant's bedside and took his hand in both of hers. He was barely breathing. She stood motionless, her hand as icy as his, as his breath gradually shuddered to a stop. It was a moment before Erica realized what had happened. Then the nurse was beside her, gently opening her hand and releasing Grant's. Numbly, Erica allowed the nurse to propel her into the hall. She glanced around, not knowing what to do. Tonio. Tonio would deal with it.

She walked to the waiting room on leaden feet. Tonio stood against the wall beside the door. When she turned the corner and he saw her, he straightened. She knew Grant's death must be written on her face, for Tonio came forward without a word, his face filled with compassion. He held out his arms to her, saying only "Erica." She went to him, leaning her head against the solidity of his chest. The steady thud of his heartbeat was reassuring, the warmth soothing. She was too numbed to cry and could only stand, clinging to Tonio.

Tonio took care of everything for her. He drove Erica and Danny home and firmly instructed Lupe to put Erica to bed. Lupe, weeping, led her to her old room and guided her into bed. Erica didn't resist. She was too weary to do anything but sleep. It seemed a heavenly comfort at the moment.

It was the middle of the afternoon before Erica awoke. She found that Tonio had notified her Aunt Rachel in San Antonio, who was flying to Harlingen immediately. Tonio would pick her up there. Erica was overwhelmed by his support. He had seen to all the details, so that she was required to do no more than visit the funeral home and pick out a casket for her father. Tonio even helped her do that, a strengthening arm around her waist.

Erica was silent on the drive from the funeral home to the farm, lost in a haze of stunned sorrow. Tonio glanced at her. "Erica, have you looked around your farm?"

Erica shook her head. "No, just the house," she replied absently. "It looks awful. Daddy really let it go. I guess it was too much for him." She left unspoken her next guilty thought: *should have been there to do it for him.*

"Well, the rest of the place is in the same condition. Oh, not quite as bad. Mr. Logan's been letting the house deteriorate for years. He was much more interested in the groves. But he's begun to slip there too. After I brought you home this morning, Danny and I walked in the groves. He wanted to learn about citrus farming. Anyway, I noticed that several of the trees are in bad condition. Some irrigation ditches have caved in, or close to it. There were weeds sprouting around the trunks. There were quite a few dead trees that should have been cleared out and some others with gummosis. They should have been taken away, too, to keep the rest of the groves from getting infected."

Tears welled in Erica's eyes. "Poor Daddy. It must have killed him, knowing he couldn't keep everything going." She paused, then frowned, her brain beginning to function through its haze. "But wait, Rafael wouldn't have let those things happen, even if Daddy wasn't there looking over his shoulder."

"Rafael Escobar is no longer his foreman," Tonio told her grimly. "I wondered about that, too, so I asked Lupe a few questions. Believe me, she was more than eager to tell me what had happened. Apparently your father had been sick for some time before he went to the hospital. He realized he was no longer capable of keeping the farm up, so he hired a manager."

"Daddy? I can't imagine that. He would have hated anyone else having control of his land!"

"I'm sure he must have been feeling pretty desperate. Anyway, he hired a manager named Goodson, whom Lupe described as something barely short of the Devil. He's been careless and incompetent. But more than that, I think he's cheated Mr. Logan. He must have been cutting corners to let the farm go so, and I'm sure the excess money went into his own pocket. No one knows for sure. I called your father's attorney, Bill Matson, and Rafael. Rafael quit because he couldn't continue to work with Goodson, seeing what he was doing to the farm. Matson was very suspicious of Goodson, too, but he could do nothing without dragging Grant into it, and he thought that was out of the question, with Grant being so ill."

Erica sighed. "How awful. How could anyone do that to a dying man? He must have known how sick Daddy was, yet he cheated him and ruined the one thing Daddy loved most. I'm glad Daddy didn't know what was happening. It would have crushed him."

"I agree. It made me furious to see those ruined trees and neglected ditches. I know how your father felt about his land. I was going to confront Goodson, but Lupe told me he took off this morning. Just went into the office and got a few things, then left. He must have known it was close to being over. He was renting a duplex on Lamar Street, but when I checked there, he'd vanished. Cleaned everything out, so I'm sure he's skipped town. If you don't object, Erica, Bill Matson and I want to go over your father's books to find out how badly Goodson was cheating him."

"No, I don't object. Why should I? It's very kind of you to want to help."

He glanced at her again but said nothing. Erica lapsed into her fog again, the distressing facts that Tonio had related sliding away before the onslaught of her grief. When they reached the house, Erica went in to see Danny. Several visitors were waiting in the formal living room to express their condolences, so she straightened her shoulders and went to thank them, although she wanted nothing but to be left alone. Visitors continued to arrive all afternoon and evening. Her father had been a well-known and respected member of the small community. By the time Tonio returned with her aunt, Erica was ragged and worn. Rachel held out her arms in an unusually affectionate gesture, and Erica went to hug her. Then, although it was growing late, Bill Matson arrived. After offering his sympathy, he disappeared with Tonio into Grant's study. Erica left her aunt to greet any guests who might come so late and went upstairs to be alone.

She sat in her room, in the one uncomfortable chair that was there. When she had been living at home, she had never sat in a chair, only on the bed, with her legs folded under her, Indian fashion. Funny how the room she had lived in for so much of her life didn't seem to fit her any longer. She sighed and left the chair to stand by the window, gazing out into the black night. Nothing was the same anymore. Nothing.

The funeral was the next afternoon. Erica moved through it dry-eyed and seemingly calm. Inside she was shaking and scared. What was she to do now? she kept thinking, not quite sure what she meant, but certain that the question terrified her.

Emotion was seeping back in around the block of numbness. Her aunt sat on one side of her and a quiet Danny on the other, and Tonio was never far away. It occurred to Erica that he probably ought to return to Houston, that he must have business he needed to attend to. But she didn't suggest it to him. Nor did she think about the situation between them and the strangely warm relationship that had blossomed over the past two or three days. She needed Tonio too much right then to question it.

After the funeral and the brief ceremony at the cemetery, Tonio drove Erica, Danny and Rachel back to the rambling farmhouse. Erica contemplated how few people the Logan family had shrunk down to in the past few years. Rachel would die childless, and Erica felt certain she would never marry and produce more children. The future of the Logans rested entirely in Danny, a small child to constitute a whole family.

She pulled her mind away from her gloomy thoughts and summoned up a fairly cheerful smile for the others. She offered to throw together a little dinner from the mountains of food that neighbors and friends had brought to them. Rachel helped her, and somehow the familiar routines of the kitchen were soothing. Erica even managed a small joke about the shiny, expensive microwave Grant had bought a couple of years ago, which Lupe refused to operate.

After eating, she even felt strong enough to help Rachel dig through some of the old photographs and memorabilia stored away in a spare bedroom. She smiled over pictures of herself as a child and exclaimed when Rachel found an album from her own childhood. When Rachel left late in the evening to go to bed, Erica continued for a little while, then set aside the box she was exploring and wandered downstairs. The coffeepot was still half-full, and she poured herself a cup before she strolled into the den. Tonio was the only person there. He looked up and smiled at her entrance. "Hi. How are you doing?"

"Okay. Better. At least I was able to get something done instead of just sitting and staring." Erica walked over to sit on the couch beside him. She gazed at her hands. It was hard to describe the process occurring inside her, the gradual thawing of her frozen emotions and consequent realization of the extent of her loss. She was emerging from her foggy state, only to find herself lost and frightened, not knowing what to do. "You've been awfully good to me the past few days," she murmured.

"I wanted to help you."

"I've needed it." The feelings that had been awakening in her during the day suddenly pressed in upon her, filling her heart with a piercing, frightening agony. "Oh, Tonio, I feel so helpless. I couldn't do a thing to help him. He wanted me to come home to live, and I wouldn't. Even after I moved to the island four months ago, I didn't come for a visit. I said I had too much work to do. Can you imagine that? Too much work. I don't remember even a third of what I did. Anyone else could have done it as easily. Yet, I wouldn't let any of it slide in order to see my father. And now I'll never see him again." Her voice turned raspy with tears.

Gently Tonio laid a hand on her head, sliding it down the smooth length of her hair. "Don't think like that. It wasn't your fault. Grant didn't tell you he was sick, and he wouldn't let anyone else tell you, either. How could you have known he was dying? You wanted to do well at your new job, so you put it before a visit home. That's only natural, considering the fact that you thought your father would live for years yet. There's no reason to feel guilty."

"But that's not all there was to it. Daddy and I hadn't gotten along well since—well, for several years. I avoided coming home. I didn't want to face the hassle we usually had. It wasn't only that I had work to do. I didn't want to see him!"

"Erica, please, don't do this to yourself."

"Oh, Tonio." Erica turned to him, huge tears shimmering in her clear gray eyes. She was beautiful, vulnerable, and suddenly he wanted her more than he ever had before, wanted to hold and comfort her, to take away her pain with the balm of his lovemaking and turn her aching sorrow into joy. It was with a great effort that he restrained himself from pulling her close to kiss her. Now was not the time. He must put her before his own desires. "Tonio, I'm so scared." She gave a shaky little laugh. "Isn't that ridiculous? I'm twenty-seven years old and have a son, and I've been supporting us both for years. But suddenly I'm scared to face the world without my daddy. Like a little girl. Oh!" A tremendous sob racked her body. "Oh, what am I going to do? He's gone, and I never even told him I loved him!''

"He knew," Tonio assured her. "He knew."

He pulled her against him, and she laid her head on his firm chest. The tears that had been dammed up in her throughout her father's death and funeral burst their barriers. She wept in loud, painful sobs, pouring out her loss to the man she loved—and hated—more than anyone else in the world. And he accepted it, holding her and rocking her gently as he murmured unintelligible, soothing words.

Erica awoke the next morning with a tremendous headache from crying. She padded to her dresser and peered into the mirror above it. Her hair was wild and tangled, her face puffy, her eyes swollen and red-rimmed. She looked, she thought, like the wrath of God. But she found she couldn't care very much about it. The numbness of the past few days was gone, washed away by the night before in her flood of tears. Her brain had finally begun to accept the awful truth that Grant was dead, and her emotions were coming painfully alive again.

She showered and dressed in drab brown slacks and a plain matching blouse. She had never liked the outfit much, but it was the first thing she found when she reached into the closet where Lupe had hung up her clothes. It really didn't matter what she looked like. Downstairs she poured a cup of coffee from the percolator and sat down at the kitchen table. She sipped at the hot liquid and stared listlessly out the window.

Now that she was beginning to think again, it seemed incredible that she had cried her heart out on Tonio Cruz's chest the previous night. Why was he doing all this—comforting her, protecting her, taking care of all the painful tasks for her? He was acting like her husband, when actually he cared so little for her that he had run out on her years before. On the surface he seemed to be acting out of the purest human kindness, but Erica couldn't help but be suspicious. He had hurt her too badly for her to truly trust him. Perhaps she had wounded his ego a couple of weeks earlier when she told him she would not return to his bed and he was determined to prove he could win her back, no matter what. It was the only thing she could think of to explain his attitude. There couldn't possibly be any monetary benefit to him or his company in helping her.

No, it had to be that she had sparked his desire when he saw her, and he had decided to seduce her all over again. He had done it with humiliating speed, but then she had informed him that she wouldn't hop into bed with him again, had in effect refused him in advance and told him she despised him. Doubtless that had made her quite a challenge to him, and he hoped to lure her back by moving in when she was at her weakest point.

Erica grimaced. Well, she had certainly fallen in with his plans once again. She had been so bruised and stunned that she had turned everything, including herself, over to him, letting him do things for her, be with her, comfort her. Why, she had even left him with Danny for long periods of time, when that was the thing she had feared most! With her father's death she had reverted to a helpless female, clinging to Tonio as if to a rock. It was discouraging to realize that she wanted to continue in the role. She quaked inside, lacerated by guilt and felt vulnerable by the death of the parent who had protected her all her life. Erica remembered that she had felt a similar panic and remorse when her mother had died. But then she had been only twelve years old! And the feeling had not been as strong. She had had her strong father to take care of her. Nor had she been expected to behave as an adult or look after a child of her own, as she did now.

She wondered if everyone felt this way at their parents' deaths, or was it only women who reverted to childhood no matter what their former independent state? Or was it only her?

Erica was awakened from her thoughts by the muffled purr of a car—no, two. She rose and went to the window to peer outside, where she could glimpse the distinctive grill of a Mercedes. Tonio. Firmly she pushed down the instinctive surge of relief. She had to stop behaving like a child and letting Tonio make all her decisions. No matter how frightening the future seemed, she must be a responsible adult. There was no one to help her anymore. She was all alone and she had to take care of Danny. The best way to start was to get Tonio Cruz out of her life. Whatever he wanted from her in return for his help, she was sure she would be foolish to give it. She couldn't let him run her life or pull her back into the seductive circle of his charm. She had to protect Danny and herself. Erica knew she couldn't bear the ultimate pain that would come from falling in love with him all over again.

Straightening her shoulders and wetting her lips, she strode purposefully down the hall toward the front door. She opened it almost immediately after the sharp ring of the bell and stepped back a little in surprise at finding not only Tonio on the front porch but also her father's attorney, Bill Matson. "Oh. Hello, Mr. Matson. Tonio."

Tonio smiled, his dark brown eyes holding hers warmly. She felt as if he had touched her, and something pulled at her; she wanted to step into his arms and abandon all her problems once more. Firmly she turned away from him toward the older man. Matson was slightly younger than her father, a hearty man with a shock of pure white hair that gave him a kind, avuncular air. "Erica, I hope you don't mind our barging in this way, but there are some matters of importance that we need to discuss."

"Of course. Come in." She showed them into the formal living room, which seemed appropriate for a call by the family attorney. They settled into the heavy Spanish-style furniture, and Bill Matson opened his briefcase. Erica could feel Tonio's gaze on her, slightly puzzled by her sudden coldness, but she stubbornly refused to look at him, keeping her eyes fixed on Bill.

"Now, Erica, we have to talk a little business. I know this is an unpleasant time to do so. People think it's mercenary, disrespectful, but with a farm you can't just sit around waiting for a few months until you feel better able to cope with it. Unfortunately *we* have to fit into Nature's timetable, not the other way around. It'll be October in a couple of days. The first shipments of oranges are already going out. Next it'll be the grapefruit. You know as well as I do that the crops from this farm will be growing and maturing from now until April. Somebody has to have the authority to hire and pay workers, oversee the growing and make contracts with the shippers. And since you're the executor named in your father's will, I'm afraid the burden will fall on you."

"Yes, of course." At least the work would give her something to occupy her time and mind.

Matson went on, handing her a copy of Grant's will and explaining the various clauses that left the farm and all his possessions to her, as well as naming her the executor. He also enumerated the duties of an executor, assuring her that he would take care of all the legal work. Erica nodded uninterestedly. What he was saying held very little appeal. At the moment she could summon up no motivation except the drive of duty and responsibility. Someone had to run the farm. Someone had to take care of Danny. Someone had to keep life going on an even keel. On that sort of thing she would move day to day. But she couldn't work up any eagerness.

"The big problem, of course, is money."

"Money?" Erica repeated almost stupidly. "What do you mean?"

"Erica." Tonio leaned forward earnestly, reaching across the gap between their chairs to take one of her hands. His was warm and strong, and she was conscious of a treacherous longing to leave hers there. However, she forced herself to pull it away and folded her hands together in her lap. Tonio frowned, but continued, "Look, I know your father has always had plenty of money. Of course, you know farmers have suffered economically the past few years. There simply hasn't been as much profit. Still, there would be plenty if not for Goodson."

"Who?"

"The manager your father hired. You remember my telling you about it."

"Yes, he was incompetent."

"More like crooked. Mr. Matson and I checked the farm accounts, and it's obvious that he's been robbing your father blind. The ledgers and bank statements show payments for which there are no bills, and many of the bills in the file were for much less than what was recorded in the ledger. Several pieces of equipment were supposedly bought from a nonexistent firm in McAllen. I'm positive Goodson was endorsing and cashing the checks. He's skipped town, of course, but if you're willing, we can bring a criminal charge against him."

"Providing he's caught."

"Yes."

"Does it really matter now?" Erica asked lethargically. "It won't bring Daddy back. It won't restore the farm. I mean, even if he's caught and tried, I'm sure he wouldn't still have the money."

"No," Tonio admitted. "You're probably right. But, sweetheart, you can't just let him get away with that, can you?"

Erica stiffened at his use of an endearment. For the first time she looked at him. His dark eyes gleamed, and his whole body was taut. He wanted vengeance, Erica thought, and wondered why. Was it the successful businessman in him, horrified that another business had been embezzled from? Or was it the compulsive achiever who would never let anything slip from his grasp? Or was it just another way to put her in his debt, to suck her further down into the whirlpool of helplessness and gratitude? Deliberately she turned to Matson. "What do you think? Is it that important?"

"Well, Erica, I'm devoted to upholding the law. You must know that. And I'd hate to see some swindler get away with taking a dying man to the cleaners, wouldn't you?"

"Yes, well, I have no objections, certainly. It just seems a futile exercise, but if the police want to look for him..."

"Good. However, you brought up the salient point when you said it wouldn't help the farm. Grant's estate is not very large, except for the cash value of the farm. Grant's treatment wasn't inexpensive, and with Goodson's skimming and the cash bequest Grant left to your aunt, well, the estate isn't very liquid. We'll know more for sure after we've collected the assets, but I suspect we're looking at selling the farm. No doubt that's what you'd want to do anyway, since you won't be living here. Mr. Cruz has come up with a very generous solution."

Again Tonio took over. "Erica, I want to buy the farm from you. I'll offer you top dollar. I've considered getting a place around Santa Clara for some time now. I have to return to Houston today, and I'll have my lawyers get started on the deal."

"Perfect, isn't it?" Matson chimed in like the other end of a song and dance team.

"Wait!" Erica grated out. "Just a minute. I think I'm the one who's involved in all this, not you two." She rose, her eyes flashing fire. "You've got everything worked out to your satisfaction, haven't you, and of course 'the little woman' will go along with whatever her protectors tell her is best, right? Well, I'm sorry if I've given you the wrong impression the past few days. I was dazed by Daddy's death, but I'm not mindless or incompetent."

"Now, Erica," Matson began soothingly, while Tonio leaned back with a sigh, he dark eyes regarding her impassively.

"Don't you 'Now, Erica' me," she retorted. She swung on Tonio. "Is that the goal you've been after? The Logan farm? I knew you must have some ulterior motive."

Tonio's tanned face tightened, turning as chilly as Erica's voice. "Naturally you'd think of something like that."

Matson blinked at the sudden animosity, finding himself inexplicably in the midst of a fight when he had envisioned nothing but grateful acceptance of his plan. He glanced at Tonio, who returned his gaze with a wry lifting of one eyebrow. Matson swung back to Erica. "Now, honey, I think you're being unfair to Mr. Cruz. He's making a very generous offer, much more than this farm is worth in its present condition, to be quite candid."

"Oh, please, let's do be candid for once," Erica thrust. "Mr. Matson, you knew my father as well as anyone, I think. I'm sure you know that this is not what he would want done with his property."

Matson sighed. "I'll admit Grant had a certain old-fashioned allegiance to his land...."

"He loved it!"

"Yes, but, Erica, it simply isn't feasible for you to operate the farm. Even Grant was aware of that. He knew you'd probably sell."

"Well, I won't. Grant Logan looked upon this land as a sacred trust given him by his parents, something that he would hand down to me and I would someday give to Danny. I've heard him say so many times. He didn't build one of the finest citrus farms in the valley just for his own aggrandizement! He did it for me, for his posterity. It meant something to him, and I can't just throw it all away because keeping it might be a little difficult."

"But, Erica, surely you don't intend to run the farm yourself?" Matson expostulated.

"Why not?" Erica thrust out her chin stubbornly. "I *am* familiar with the business, after all. I've already quit my job, as Mr. Cruz can tell you. So there's nothing to stop me."

"But this is a tough operation, even for a man."

Erica bristled. "You think I'm not capable of doing it because I'm a woman?"

Hastily Matson tried to soothe her ruffled feathers. Tonio made an exasperated noise and stood up. "This is pointless. Erica, you're obviously in too emotional a state to make any rational decision. We'll discuss it some other time."

"My answer will be the same then."

Matson quickly stuffed his papers back into his case, seizing the opportunity to salvage the situation. "Yes, yes, of course. We'll talk again in a few weeks, Erica. I'm sure that once you really get involved in running the farm, you'll see that it would be an impossible task."

Erica escorted them to the door. She and Tonio didn't exchange a word until he opened the door and turned. "Erica, I..."

"Thank you for all your assistance, Tonio. I'm sorry I haven't been properly grateful."

A muscle in his jaw jumped, and he swung away, eating up the distance to his car in lithe, easy strides. Watching him go, the terror of being alone swelled inside Erica, and she longed to call after him, to beg him not to go. But she held still, managing not to give in to her weakness.

Chapter 8

Erica's antagonism to Tonio's offer served to snap her from her lethargy. Running the farm gave her a goal to work for, a purpose. Instead of sitting aimlessly and wallowing in her sorrow, she called Rafael Escobar, her father's foreman before the advent of Mr. Goodson. He was ecstatic to hear from her, although his voice lowered in regret as he told her how sorry he was about Grant's death. When Erica revealed that she planned to run the farm and asked him to return to help her, he agreed quickly.

She and Rafael toured the groves, and he pointed out the weakened irrigation ditches and diseased trees, recommending that she hire a good crew to make repairs and cut down the trees. Everything she saw of what Goodson's crooked management had done to her father's beloved farm made her more and more determined to stay on the farm and build it back into something Grant would have been proud of.

In general Erica knew the process of selling and marketing the citrus crop. The fruit was usually bought by a shipper, who then transported and sold it to grocers or processors, or gift packaged it in boxes for the holiday season. It could also be bought by a processing firm that canned the inferior fruit. The shipper or a buyer for the processor would inspect a farm and offer a cash price for the fruit on the trees. Then the buyer would hire a contractor to furnish a crew to pick the fruit and load it into trucks. However, Erica knew none of the buyers or their reputations, and she was happy to rely on Rafael's recommendations as to what buyers to deal with and what price to accept.

She put Danny into the public school in Santa Clara and plunged into learning her business. Daily she listened to Rafael's advice, and every evening after Danny went to bed she dug out all her father's pamphlets and books from the A & M Agricultural Extension Service, which contained information about raising citrus crops. She hired a crew who, under Rafael's direction, set about getting the groves in order. Lupe volunteered the services of her brother and several nephews to shape up the house and grounds. Erica took pride in the fact that before two weeks had passed, the house and yard, at least, looked decent.

She enjoyed her work. It was challenging and a good release for her energies. It gave her something to concentrate on besides the loss of her father and her brief but painful reinvolvement with Tonio Cruz. She was glad she hadn't yielded to Matson's urgings. This was where she belonged, what she needed to do. It provided the contact with her dead parent that she had not had earlier.

As the days passed she grew more certain that Tonio's kindness had been a ruse to satisfy some selfish motive of his own. She remembered how he had hurt her before and how she hated him. Even if he had been sincere in his efforts to make her father's death easier for her to bear, it couldn't make up for the past. No, she had to get along on her own, as she always had. Maybe Tonio had been there for her this time, but she knew it wouldn't happen again. This farm, Danny and herself: That was all she had in life.

Between the farm and her father's estate, Erica kept very busy. Although she managed to run the farm on the money she received from the buyers of her grapefruit and orange crops, she knew that before long it would not be enough. There were enormous estate taxes to be paid because of the high value of the land, even though there was little cash in the estate. Also, she had to buy new heaters for the trees to replace several of the old ones, which had been damaged by neglect. She needed to buy new seedlings to ensure the future of the groves. Fixing the place up a bit had drained what little cash there was. Any profit would be poured right back into the operation, but Erica soon realized that it wouldn't be enough. She needed more capital.

She was sitting in her study one day, poring over her account books, trying to figure out a way to squeeze extra money out of the farm without having to sell part of the land, when Lupe interrupted her. "Señorita, Señora Miller is here to see you."

"Mrs. Miller?" Erica repeated blankly. "Jess's mother?"

"No, oh, no, I am sorry." Lupe almost smiled. "It is Señor Jess's wife, the one who used to be Judy Barton."

"Judy!" Erica exclaimed at the mention of her high school friend. "Heavens, I haven't seen her in years."

Erica jumped up and strode into the living room. Judy was plumper than she had been, and her blond hair had faded to a light brown, but there was still a merry twinkle in her brown eyes and her face was prettier in a soft way. "My, you look good!" Judy commented as she stepped forward to hug her old friend. "You've hardly changed. If anything, I think you're prettier than ever. It doesn't seem fair."

Erica smiled. "It's nice to see you. I didn't realize you still lived in Santa Clara. So you're married to Jess Miller now?"

"Yeah." Judy laughed. "Who'd have thought it? When we were in high school, I'd have said he was the *last* person I'd ever marry. But you know how it goes."

"Well, bring me up on the gossip of Santa Clara."

"Oh, you know this town. It never changes. Let me see. The bank had a face-lift, and the club needs one, but it can't raise the money. So it's beginning to look seedy. Cat Benavides married a boy she met at college and they're living in Utah, o. all places. Jeff Roberts still lives here. He's running his fa ther's store. He and his wife were divorced about a year ago The scoop was that she was running around with Lucio Cruz."

"Really?"

"Yeah, and you'll never guess what Lucio is doing now. He bought the Chevrolet dealership. Or at least his brother did

Antonio went to Houston and got filthy rich. Had you heard that?''

"Yes," Erica replied shortly, her heart beginning to knock.

"Well, Lucio's made a big success of it. Of course, the youngest one, Jorge, is still always in trouble. He's wild. Antonio could have given him all the money in the world, and it wouldn't have helped him. You should see Tonio. He's better-looking now than Lucio. I saw him in town about a year ago, and he was absolutely yummy—the most beautiful body in the world, and he was wearing tight-fitting jeans and a gorgeous short-sleeved shirt that showed off his muscles. He looked hard, you know, like someone you wouldn't want to tangle with, but handsome. . . ." She trailed off with a sigh. "I told Sylvie Harrison, if ever a man could make you forget husband and family, Antonio Cruz is it!''

Erica dug her fingernails into her palms, trying to maintain an expression of amused interest despite the jealousy surging through her. She could clearly envision Tonio from Judy's description, and she hated the response he evoked in Judy—and every other woman he met. No doubt Tonio had made quite a few women forget everything for him. Erica was sure she wasn't the only woman he had fooled. Somehow that knowledge only made her pain more bitter. She wanted to snap back sarcastically that she was confident Tonio would be glad to oblige Judy, but she realized she would make an idiot of herself and reveal far too much of what she felt. So she forced herself to sit calmly until Judy finally ran out of things to say. After extracting a promise from Erica that she would come to visit soon, Judy left.

Erica decided to take a walk to clear her head. She drifted past the oleander bushes and the spill of bright pink bougainvillea against the side of the house, wandering along the graveled road toward the main highway. Before long she came upon the old house, and for a moment she stood studying it. On impulse she circled around to the side door and felt for the key in its old hiding place. After all these years it was still there, rusty with age. She tried it in the lock. It turned resistingly, and the door creaked open. It was dark inside the house, the curtains and drapes closed. Erica found a candle and lit it, then climbed the stairs to the bedroom she and Tonio had used. She paused

in the doorway, and the pain of a time long past pierced her
She whirled away and scurried down the stairs, but as she
reached the bottom step, she stopped, struck by a thought.

She could make a little extra money by renting this house
Her mother had done it several times. She wavered, reluctan
to allow others into the house she and Tonio had shared. I
seemed an invasion. She squared her shoulders and took firm
hold of her emotions. It was ridiculous to regard the house a
a sanctuary. It wasn't as if a great love affair had taken plac
there. To Tonio it had been nothing but a quick fling, a sordie
little affair. There wasn't anything about it worth saving, and
she refused to pander to her crazy sentimentality. She despised
the man. Why keep any reminder of him?

Quickly she marched to the main house and called the town'
real-estate agent, as though to ensure that she wouldn't break
her resolution to rent. Frank Dolby, the agent, was pleased to
hear from her, although his pleasure was muted somewha
when he realized that the purpose of her call was not to plac
the farm in his hands to sell. However, he assured her heartil
that he would be happy to rent the old house for her, and sug
gested she drop by his office to sign papers designating him a
her rental agent.

Taking Lupe with her, Erica walked back to the old house
While Lupe determined the amount of cleaning it would tak
and how much extra help would be needed, Erica strolle
through it, examining the state of draperies, floors and fur
nishings. It was in surprisingly good shape. Grant had take
excellent care of it through the years, sending Lupe in to clea
it periodically and always making the necessary repairs. Th
roof was good, the foundation firm and the furniture pro
tected by dustcovers. Erica was pleased to discover there wa
little to be done to it besides cleaning. It was a nice house
roomy and comfortable, although not grand. Her mother ha
modernized the kitchen and bathrooms. The quality of th
furniture was good, although the style was several years out o
date. All in all, it seemed to her that it shouldn't be too diff
cult to rent at a decent price.

Lupe and her sister-in-law cleaned it up in three days, an
one of the multitudinous nephews cleared away the weeds an
bushes that had overgrown the yard. By the time they wer

through, it was sparkling clean and rather attractive in a roomy, homespun way. Erica was pleased with her decision to rent it.

Erica stood at the stove, whipping up a quick breakfast of scrambled eggs for Danny. It was so early that the light outside was still muted, washing out the vivid colors of the yard. Danny bounded in and prepared his lunch pail while Erica dished up the eggs and added a slice of toast to his plate. Danny gulped down his breakfast, chattering between bites about the drawing project they were to start that day in school. Erica listened absently, now and then nodding or making an appropriate remark. Her mind was really on the old house. It had been almost three weeks since she had decided to rent it, and there hadn't yet been a nibble. Frank Dolby had pointed out pessimistically that only a large family would want a rambling old house like that, and what parents with a lot of kids could afford it? Erica had thought of lowering the rent to make it more accessible, but when she imagined four or five children and accompanying pets crashing through the place, she decided to keep the price where it was. Maybe there would be someone without a lot of kids who could afford it and just happened to like comfortable old houses.

"Gotta go." Danny jumped up and Erica leaned down so he could plant a kiss on her cheek. Then he grabbed his lunch box and schoolbooks and made a mad dash to the front door. Erica sighed and poured herself a cup of coffee. She sat down at the kitchen table and sipped it, enjoying her time alone before Lupe or the workers arrived, before she had to deal with any of the problems.

It had been almost two months now since her father had died. The work had helped her through her worst period of grief, had given her something to think about and fill up her days with. But now life was beginning to return. She found herself enjoying things—the morning quiet, a lovely sunset, a laughing romp with Danny. Anxiety was starting to weigh on her where once it had been unable to pierce the shell of her loss. What was she going to do? Even if she rented the old house, she still wouldn't have enough money. The other day Rafael had dropped the bad news on her that they needed a new underground drainage system for about forty acres of the groves. The old one was beginning to fail, and without drainage the trees would go bad. Erica sighed. She had to get a substantial loan. There was simply no other way to raise the necessary capital for repairs and improvements except by selling a portion of the land, and *that* she was determined not to do.

Propping her chin on her hand, Erica stared out the window into the side yard with its empty, cracking swimming pool and the high, shading hedge beyond. For Danny's sake she wished she had the money to repair the pool and fill it with water again. However, that was out of the question right now. Maybe in a few years... Erica almost groaned aloud. The farm was going to be a burden on her for the rest of her life. Even if she could get it back on its feet and running smoothly, she didn't know if it would ever make enough profit to allow her to afford a manager for the place, so she could return to the line of work she really loved. Yet, she couldn't sell it. She simply couldn't—not when it had meant so much to her father. She had to keep it, no matter what.

Grimacing, Erica rose and put her half-finished coffee cup in the sink. She couldn't sit around worrying about the future. She had to get to work. As she crossed the hall to her study there was a sharp knock on the side door, which lay at the end of the hall. She glanced at her watch. Who on earth would be here at this hour? Surely not a buyer. The next crop wasn't ready for purchasing yet. She strode down the hall and swung the door wide, then froze.

Slim and handsome in black slacks and a black shirt, he stood framed in the doorway, his thick straight hair as dark as his clothing, heavy, sensual lids drooping down to hide the black gaze. Tonio Cruz.

"What are you doing here?" Erica demanded.

"I can tell you're delighted to see me," he remarked dryly, moving past her through the hall and into the kitchen, where he took up a casual stance against the counter. Erica followed resentfully. Who was he to barge into her house and take over? And why did her mouth and throat go dry and her knees begin to quiver at the mere sight of him?

Tonio folded his arms across his chest, drawing Erica's eye to them. She swallowed, very aware of the hard brown strength of his arms. She knew their touch well, just as she knew the mobility of his long, sinewy fingers, their toughness as well as their incredible gentleness. It took all her willpower to appear calm. "I asked you a question. Why do you keep turning up in my life?"

He shrugged. "I must be the proverbial bad penny."

"I'm not in the mood to stand around trading quips with you."

"I can see. Well, it doesn't matter. I came to talk business, anyway."

"You and I don't have anything to discuss. I am no longer in your employ."

"That isn't the business I'm concerned with at the moment. Erica, I want to buy the farm."

"Absolutely not." She remembered guiltily her earlier regrets that the farm would be a millstone around her neck forever.

"Don't be so stubborn. You won't get as good an offer anywhere else. Money's tight. Few people are interested in or can afford to buy a whole citrus farm. The best you'll get will be local offers to buy a parcel here or there. Even if there is a buyer somewhere, it'll take months of advertising in several newspapers and magazines to find him. This way you'll save time and expense—and make a lot of money."

"I don't care about making a lot of money. What I care about is this farm. Daddy loved it. I was raised here. It meant a lot to him and to me too." She moved farther away. His nearness was overwhelming and made her forget her decision regarding him. Instead of remembering that she hated him for what he'd done to her and that she'd decided his kindness to her had an ulterior motive, she found herself staring at the straight black hairs sprinkling his tanned arms and the slender fingers, with their callused tips.

"If you don't care about making money, you shouldn't be in the business. Erica, being the daughter of a citrus farmer does not automatically qualify you for farming. You have no experience."

"Don't I? Do you think that living here for eighteen years, hearing Daddy talk about nothing but raising and selling a citrus crop, I didn't pick up any knowledge? I'm reasonably intelligent, and I paid attention. I used to ride Morning Star through the groves, watching what was going on. I saw the grafting, the planting, the irrigation, the picking. I even helped out sometimes when Daddy was short of workers."

"Do you think the industry hasn't changed since you left? Tell me quickly, which insecticides have been outlawed and which are still in use?"

Erica set her jaw. "Okay. I can't answer you. But Rafael could, and he's my foreman. And I can find out in the pamphlets from A & M that are in Daddy's study."

"There's more to successful farming than planting the trees and letting the fruit grow. You must manage men. You have to deal with contractors and shippers. You'll be bargaining with some pretty crafty buyers who'll be only too happy to outsmart an inexperienced girl."

"Woman," she corrected coldly. "You forget I'm not seventeen anymore, Tonio. I've had some experience in the business world. I managed a hotel, remember? I had to handle employees, wholesalers and salesmen. None of them were looking out for my interests, either. Besides, it's not your concern. It's mine. And if you're so sure I'm going to fall flat on my face, why not wait to buy the farm from me then? It'll be a lot cheaper."

Tonio made a disgusted sound and turned away. For a few moments there was silence as he stared out the window. Finally he swiveled back to her, his brown eyes boring into hers, hot and beckoning. "Do you really think what I'm concerned about is the farm? Damn it, there are lots of farms around here I could buy, and most of them in much better condition than this one, too."

"But this one is different, isn't it?" she blazed, crossing her arms defensively over her chest. It was so hard to think properly when he looked at her like that, his eyes offering her the whole world, and she hated the fact that he could so easily lead her astray. "You used to work for Grant Logan, and you resented the hell out of him for that. Humbling his daughter wasn't enough, was it? Now you want the satisfaction of owning his property, of knowing that I was forced to sell to you!"

The skin around Tonio's mouth whitened, and for an instant his eyes flamed. "Is that what it was for you? Humbling? What was so humiliating about it, Erica, feeling my dirty hands on your skin or aching to feel them there?'' His nostrils flared. "I ought to have my head examined. For some crazy reason I thought you needed my help. I thought after a while you'd realize that this great crusade of yours to keep Grant Logan's land was only the aftermath of grief, a desire to assuage your guilt by offering yourself up as sacrifice to his land. I hated to see you sweat away your youth and beauty, struggling to make this farm profitable again.''

His voice was raw, persuasive in its pain. Erica wanted to reach out and touch him, to smooth away the anguish. But she reminded herself sternly that there was no reason for him to be hurt. After all, she had every right not to sell her land if she didn't want to. And though he was very good at twisting words to make it sound as if he had been wronged, not she, they both knew the truth. She clenched her hands and sneered, ''Such honorable motives.''

"I don't know why I bother. You'll wrap the shippers around your little finger, and your workers as well. You won't sweat. Some poor dope will do the sweating for you. Where there are men involved, you always come out all right. Sorry I disturbed your morning.'' He whirled and slammed out of the kitchen and through the side door. Erica slumped into the nearest chair, feeling as though her legs wouldn't hold her up another second.

How did he always manage to get to her? He seemed to know exactly which buttons to push. Just seeing him threw her into an emotional state. She wanted to cling to him as she had when her father died. She wanted to move into his arms and let him bring her body alive. Erica was sure he knew exactly how she would respond to him. Then, when she had refused to sell, which was really none of his business anyway, he had looked so hurt that she longed to run after him and give him whatever he wanted.

She groaned and plunged her hands into her hair. Was she wronging Tonio? Did he really mean to be kind? Surely he wasn't that good an actor. Maybe he had a fondness for the girl whom he had made love to so long ago and, being wealthy, found it easy to help her out by buying the land. Or maybe he was sorry for his youthful callousness in leaving her and hoped to ease his conscience. Or maybe he was exactly what she thought he was—cold, scheming and seeking revenge for the Anglo contempt he'd known when he was a child.

Erica drew a long breath and stood up. Well, whatever it was, she wasn't going to waste any time worrying about it. She wouldn't sell him the farm, and that was all there was to it. Nor was she going to try to smooth things over between them. It was better this way, even if she had wronged him. If she let him back in her life for any reason, she would be walking on the edge and could teeter over into love for him at any time. Far wiser to simply stay away.

Two days later Erica returned from a day in the groves and headed immediately for the shower. She needed to wash away the grime before she drove into town to do some errands she had put off for too long already. She was halted by Lupe's voice from the kitchen. "Señorita, that Mr. Dolby called."

Erica started for the phone eagerly. Perhaps he had found a family interested in renting the house. She looked up his number and dialed it, then waited impatiently while his secretary transferred her call to him.

"Erica, I have great news. I can hardly believe it myself. I have a renter for you."

"Fantastic! When do they want to move in?"

"The sooner the better. He only wants the place for six months, but I figured, why look a gift horse in the mouth?"

"My sentiments exactly. Well, the house is ready for occupancy. I have some errands in town this afternoon. I could drop by your office in, say, twenty minutes, and sign. Would that seem too eager?"

"No, oh, no, he's anxious to move in."

"Great. See you in about twenty minutes."

Erica hung up the phone and wondered if she should change clothes. She was dressed for the fields in old jeans and a red and white T-shirt, with one of her father's flannel shirts thrown on like a jacket. She had worn a hat against the sun and had knotted her hair up under it. Not exactly the look of a well-dressed businesswoman.

She sighed. Frank Dolby would have to put up with her as she was. She didn't have time to shower, dry her hair and change into something smart if she hoped to complete her errands before the stores closed. She knotted the ends of the flannel shirt at her waist, ran a quick comb through her hair and tied it at the nape of her neck. Not too bad, particularly if she changed her muddy boots for clean sneakers. Grabbing her purse and keys, Erica bounded out of the house and into her car. The little blue Datsun sped along the main road to town, and Erica surprised herself by flipping on the radio and humming along. It had been several weeks since she had wanted to listen to music. Maybe it was a sign things were getting better.

When she reached Santa Clara she parked on the square and hopped out of the car. She strode briskly down the street, turned the corner and pushed open the door of the Dolby Real Estate offices. Inside she stopped dead still, letting the door go. It eased pneumatically closed behind her. Directly in front of Erica was the receptionist's desk, where an attractive, auburn-haired woman sat smiling up at Tonio Cruz. He lounged against the desk, flirting with her. Tonio Cruz! He turned up wherever she went.

At her entrance Tonio swiveled his head, then gracefully rose, his dark eyes fixed on Erica. The redhead, every hair in place and her makeup perfect, cast a speaking glance at Erica that moved from the bottom of her tennis shoes to the top of her thick, tousled hair, pulled back and held in a simple red yarn bow. Erica bit her lip, acutely aware of the tightness of her faded jeans and the embroidered strawberry adorning one thigh. She wore no makeup except a dab of lipstick, and she could feel the tiny hairs that framed her face curling with dampness. Next to the other woman, she knew she appeared plain and all at loose ends. Tonio looked her up and down, his eyes dancing with amusement.

Erica flushed. "What are you doing here?" she snapped.

The secretary's jaw dropped at the bite in her tone. Dolby, hurrying forward from his glass-enclosed office, boomed merrily, "Miss Logan! I'm so glad you're here. When I told Mr. Cruz you would sign the lease this afternoon, he offered to come in too. I take it you know each other?"

"Yes, I know Mr. Cruz," Erica replied dryly. "Are you telling me *he* is the man who wants to rent the old house?"

"Yes. Isn't it nice it's someone you know?"

"No! I won't let you live there," Erica told Tonio fiercely.

"I'm not allowed to set foot on your sacred property?" Tonio asked, an indulgent smile curving his lips.

"But, Miss Logan, you've already agreed!" Dolby expostulated, his meaty cheeks quivering with the fear of losing a customer.

"I had no idea who wanted the place," Erica retorted. "If you had said it was Tonio Cruz, I wouldn't have consented."

"But Mr. Cruz is ready and willing, even eager, to lease the old house. It could be weeks, months, before another prospect comes along."

"That's true," Tonio added lightly. "Who would want such a rambling old house except a large family—and they don't usually have the money to pay the rent. Face it, Erica, I'm a golden opportunity."

Erica's lips tightened, and she would have liked to snarl her fury at Tonio. It was impossible to explain to Frank Dolby why she didn't want Tonio living there. She couldn't reveal to a stranger the twisted strands of their relationship, couldn't admit that Tonio had once deserted her, much less that she had been fool enough to fall into his arms a second time, making him believe she'd be easy pickings again. No, that was something she could never tell anyone.

"Mr. Cruz has already given me a check for the deposit and the first month's rent." Mr. Dolby gripped her arm to lead her away from the others. Lowering his voice, he muttered, "You better grab this tenant. He didn't quibble about the rent, just paid it quick as a wink. You'll never find anyone else as good. Trust me, he's wealthy. You haven't been home in a long time, but he's—"

"I know, I know," Erica interrupted brusquely. "He's made good."

"Yes, he has. The best chance you'll get has just dropped into your lap. This is perfect, absolutely perfect, and I promise you'll regret it if you don't accept the offer." At Erica's unyielding silence, his voice rose in desperation. "He didn't even ask to see the inside of the place!"

"I used to work for Mr. Logan." Tonio entered their conversation. "I've been inside the old house several times." His eyes challenged Erica with their mutual knowledge of the reason for his visits. Then he turned back to Dolby, his rich voice inviting the others to share his amusement. "I have to confess, Mr. Dolby, that Erica has a long-standing grudge against me. I once made a pass at her when she was a teenager, and she's never forgiven me."

Rage bubbled up inside Erica and she wanted to take a swing at Tonio's smiling, complacent face. He had effectively blocked whatever excuse she might give for refusing his offer. No matter what Erica said, Dolby would believe she was nursing a petty grudge. What excuse could she give, anyway? Not the real one. And nothing else sounded believable or important enough to inspire her adamant dislike of Tonio. She glared at him and saw, beneath the light amusement, a rock-hard promise that he would eventually win their struggle.

Well, then, let him, she thought furiously. Give in and get it over with. Once he'd won, he'd be content and would probably go away. Let Tonio discover that he could force himself into her life, yet not beguile her into his bed again. He could stay at the old house as long as he wanted. She had so much work that she could avoid him for months. So she would hand him the victory and let him bask in self-congratulation. He'd learn soon enough that the house was all he'd won. And she'd be making money from his mistake for six months.

"All right," she spoke up suddenly. "Let's sign the thing and get it over with."

Chapter 9

It took a moment for her words to register on Frank Dolby, but when they did he pounced on his secretary. "Diane, have you finished typing the lease?"

"Yes, I made two copies." She pulled open a drawer and bent over it, the smooth, chin-length cap of auburn hair swinging forward. Erica wondered irritably how anyone managed to tame her hair into such lustrous perfection. She herself had either to let her thick mane tumble free or restrain it in a harsh knot.

Diane found the file she sought and set it on her desk, spreading out the copies of the lease for inspection. Erica picked up a copy and skimmed through it, conscious of the other woman's blue gaze upon her. She was sure Diane was wondering why Tonio had once made a pass at someone who looked such a fright. Diane was assessing the competition—Erica was certain the girl had her eye on Tonio. After all, they had been flirting wildly when Erica had entered the office. Hastily Erica scrawled her signature on both copies and handed the pen to Mr. Dolby, carefully avoiding placing it in Tonio's hand herself. That effort won her a sardonic, knowing smile from Tonio, and she crossed her arms, bottling up her rage.

When Tonio had finished signing and Dolby held out Erica's copy, grinning like the Cheshire cat, she snatched it from his hands.

"Thank you, Mr. Dolby." She folded the copy and stuffed it into her purse, turning on her heel to leave.

"But wait," Dolby protested, "you forgot Mr. Cruz's check."

He bustled to his office and returned with a cream-colored check signed in Tonio's bold, flowing script. As she waited, she was fully aware of Tonio's eyes upon her, and assiduously avoided looking at him. She took the check and wrote one of her own to Dolby for his commission. Still ignoring Tonio, she handed the check to the real-estate agent and stalked out the front door.

She had taken only a few steps along the sidewalk before a firm hand gripped her arm and Tonio's husky voice sounded in her ear. "You must let me buy you a drink to celebrate our signing of the contract, Miss Logan."

Erica jerked her arm away and retorted without bothering to look at him, "I thought you were a pretty bright guy, Tonio. Why haven't you gotten the message? I don't want anything to do with you."

"Then why let me camp on your doorstep for the next six months?"

"You know perfectly well why!" Erica exploded, forgetting her resolution to not look at him or carry on a conversation. "After that idiotic story you made up to explain my not wanting to lease to you, anything I said would have looked foolish."

He shrugged. "What a straight line. But I won't comment—I'm too much of a gentleman."

"Look, I don't know what little game you're playing. But I'm not joining in."

"What game? I'm not in the habit of playing games."

"Leave me alone," she growled through gritted teeth.

"I will if you'll have dinner with me."

"It's too early for dinner."

"A drink, then? Cup of coffee? I understand the Pioneer Cafe is still in operation."

"And after that you'll leave me in peace?"

"Yes."

"All right." Again he gripped her arm and guided her across the square. In the middle of the block hung a familiar white sign lettered in green: Pioneer Cafe. Inside, there were a few renovations. The booths had been reupholstered and the chairs changed, but the Formica counter and tabletops were the same, as was the black-and-white tile on the floor.

"This place always reminded me of a big checkerboard," Tonio commented as his firm hand against the small of her back maneuvered her to one of the green vinyl booths.

Erica had to smile at his apt remark, involuntarily warmed and softened by his confident hand steering her along. She slid into a booth and Tonio sat down opposite her. For a moment she stared at him, but the sight of his molded face and dark, simmering eyes made her far too shaky inside, and she glanced down. "I'm sure you must have some reason for this," she commented.

"Hell if I know what it is."

"Then why do it?"

"Sometimes I like to play my hunches."

"Do your hunches turn out successfully?"

"Not always." He picked up a plastic-backed menu and glanced through it. "What'll you have? Coffee? How about something sweet? They have pecan and apple pies. You look like you could use a little lift."

"Too fattening. Coffee will be fine."

He reached across the narrow table and touched her chin. "Your face is thinner. Have you been eating properly?"

"Yes, Mother," she retorted. "Now, will you kindly forget the pie *and* my weight?"

A grin broke across his face and he leaned back against the seat. "Okay. How's your little boy? Enrolled him in school here?"

"Yes. Why?"

"Don't glare. I'm simply making conversation. I thought your son's school might be a fairly safe topic."

"Sorry."

They lapsed into silence, broken by the waitress's demand for their orders. After the waitress left, Tonio sighed and ran a hand through his thick, dark hair. "Look, Erica, I'm sorry I lashed out at you the other day. I'd had a hard day the day before on the island, working out a structural problem on my design for the Breezes, and I'd gotten up early to drive over here to see you about the farm. I was irritable and sleepy, and I assumed you would have thought it over and decided to sell. So when you were resistant and antagonistic, I just blew up. I realize I was nasty to you and I apologize. Certainly there's no reason why you should sell to me if you want to keep the farm."

Erica, prepared for another attack on the subject of the farm, was thrown off guard by his apology. She stared, and suddenly her previous anger vanished. "Oh, Tonio, me too," she sighed.

He reached out and covered her hand on the table with his own. "Do you honestly believe I stayed with you when your father died because I wanted your land?"

The touch of his hand created a liquid heat in the area of her stomach. She concentrated with difficulty on his question and finally replied, "No, it doesn't really make sense. I was so emotional then that I wasn't thinking clearly. Obviously it would have been an excessive amount of trouble to buy a farm when all you'd have to do is offer the money. And I've looked at the land prices since then. I know you're offering me top dollar, more than it's worth, really. So I have to accept that you're trying to help me."

Again he grinned, and an accompanying sparkle lit his dark brown eyes. "But it's hard, isn't it?" he teased. Erica hardly noticed what he said, for his thumb had started to draw a slow, hypnotic circle on the back of her hand. There seemed to be no feeling anywhere in her body except in that small circle of flesh, and there her sensitivity was almost painfully acute. She imagined she could feel each separate ridge and whorl of his thumb as it rasped over her skin. The area burned with a surface fire, ignited by the friction of flesh against flesh.

Their surly waitress broke the spell, slapping down their cups of coffee so hard that the dark liquid splashed over the sides of the cups and into the saucers. Erica jerked her hand out of Tonio's grasp and folded both her hands in her lap. "But that doesn't mean I trust you!" she blurted out. "I know your kindness must have some purpose."

"Oh, of course," Tonio snapped sarcastically. "Naturally *I* couldn't be honest."

"Well, it's true, isn't it?" Erica pressed. "You want something from me, don't you?"

"Yes!" he grated, frowning. "Yes, I want something." He paused and sighed. "Look, Erica, I don't care about the farm. What happened back at the hotel between us—frankly I don't want to lose it again. All those years since we—since I left Santa Clara, I've been searching for the passion we had. I never found it. Then I walked into the Breezes and saw you, and all the years in between seemed like nothing. I wanted you so badly I was shaking, inside and out. When we made love, it was still the same."

Erica bit her lip and glanced away, unable to bear the warmth in his eyes. Every word he spoke made her quiver inside and long to reach out to touch him. But she knew she must not believe his words. He had lied before, even pretending to love her. She must be cool and firm, or soon he would have her in his grip as surely as before. "Oh, no, Tonio, better." Her voice was sharp and jagged as glass. "You've obviously had a lot of experience since then."

Unexpectedly he chuckled. "Jealous?"

"Hardly. I had my fill of you ten years ago. I'm not going to risk it again. I won't have an affair with you. It's better if we avoid each other entirely."

"Why?"

"I don't have to explain myself to you!" Erica flared. "My life is my business. Can't you accept that and go find yourself some sweet young thing like Dolby's secretary? She's obviously panting to hop into bed with you."

Tonio grinned. "You *are* jealous."

Erica slammed down her cup. "You're insufferable. I'm not jealous. I don't care enough for that."

His mouth tightened. "All right. You're not jealous. But you can't deny what happens when we touch each other." She set her jaw stubbornly and gazed out the window, refusing to meet his eyes. "Go ahead, Erica, ignore me as long as you can. But remember, I want you in my bed again." He rose abruptly and tossed money onto the table for their bill. "And I've changed since the old days. Now I'm used to getting what I want."

Erica continued to stare out the window, ignoring his departure. Her stomach tightened. She believed Tonio. It was obvious that he had become accustomed to winning. Everything around him was the finest, the best, the most expensive. Price didn't matter. And he was stubborn. Whatever rebuff she gave, he soon countered with a new attack. It would be hard enough handling the farm without having to fight Tonio too. What devil made him persist in pursuing her?

"Erica?" A man's voice interrupted her thoughts, and she glanced up, startled.

"Yes?" She stared at the man standing beside her table. He was tall, blond-haired, with a great, drooping mustache across his upper lip. There was something familiar about him—the gray-blue eyes, the blunt fingers, the long legs. "Jeff Roberts!"

He laughed. "Yeah. Gee, it's nice to see you."

"You too. Sit down." She waved toward the empty seat across from her.

"When I walked in and saw you sitting there, it was like jumping back in time. Then I remembered about your father—I'm sorry."

"Thank you."

They began to chat about old times and what each was doing now. Erica revealed that she intended to operate her father's farm and for the first time was met with approval. Jeff laughed at her almost comical surprise and explained that he had encountered the same resistance when he had taken over his father's business after Mr. Roberts's heart attack. They edged into their personal lives a little, Erica telling him that she had a son.

"I don't have any family," Jeff said a little sadly. "I was married, but now I'm divorced. My wife, Diane, was too young when we married. I suppose I was too. She was nineteen and I was twenty-three. We lasted three years and then split."

"Does she still live here?"

"Oh, yeah. She didn't want to leave the area. She thought she had something going with Lucio Cruz. I could have told her differently. He dropped her a few weeks after we separated. Old Lucio isn't interested in long-term relationships." Like his brother, Erica thought bitterly. Jeff paused, then continued, "Anyway, now she's working for Frank Dolby."

"That was your ex-wife!" Erica stared.

"What do you mean?"

"I was just at Frank Dolby's office."

"Red-headed girl? Pretty? Looks like she stepped right out of a fashion magazine?" Erica nodded. "Yeah, that's Diane."

"Small world. I haven't gotten used to being back in a small town."

He smiled. "There's no getting away from anybody in Santa Clara."

Erica returned his smile, hoping grimly that his remark would not hold true where Tonio Cruz was concerned. They lingered for a few more minutes, then Erica rose. "I'm sorry, Jeff, but I have to run. I need to hit the hardware store before it closes. It was great seeing you again."

"Same here. Whenever you're downtown, stop by the store and we'll have a cup of coffee. Maybe sometime we could drive to McAllen for a movie."

"Sure. That sounds nice." Erica grabbed her purse and hurried out the door. It had been nice talking to Jeff, but how flat and pale he seemed in comparison to Tonio. She could be with Jeff for hours and not feel a twinge of anger or desire. She could easily understand why his wife would prefer either of the Cruz brothers to Jeff. Thinking about Diane, Erica could barely suppress a snort. Apparently she would be more than happy to settle for Lucio's brother instead of Lucio. Little did she realize that Tonio was much harder than his younger sibling. He'd been getting out of entanglements with women for a long time now.

Erica got into her car and inserted the key, her movements sharp and irritated. Tonio was so confident of his ability that he planned a repeat performance with her. Well, this time Tonio would find out she wasn't so naive or easy. She'd simply stay far away from him. That way there'd be no chance of danger. Eventually he would be bound to give up and leave her alone.

The days and weeks passed quickly. They were approaching the holidays, the best market time for the grapefruit and or anges, and the picking crews were hard at work. Although Erica had nothing to do with that aspect of the operation, she was very busy. When she wasn't keeping the books, consulting with Rafael or dealing with buyers, she spent her time preparing a financial profile of the farm to present to the bank when she went to get the loan she needed to pay for the new subsurface drainage system.

She was constantly on the run, which made it easy to avoid Tonio. She saw him now and then at a distance as she drove down the driveway, but he kept to his house and didn't venture over to the main house to bother her, as she had been afraid he might. Half relieved, half piqued by his lack of interest, Erica was not as successful in avoiding him in her mind. Ironically the very fact that he stayed away made her think about him more. She was curious about what he did at the old house and where he went when he wasn't there. At first he spent only weekends at the house. During December he remained for longer periods of time, sometimes as much as four days at a stretch. Erica wondered how his business got along with him absent so much. And if he was doing all this to win her over, why did he never come to visit her?

Christmas sneaked up on her, and before Erica realized it, Danny was out of school for the holidays. She scurried around, buying his presents, thinking guiltily that she was hardly making it a merry Christmas for her son. She was too tired and hard-pressed to get into the holiday spirit. She noticed that Tonio came home for an entire week, and she often saw his mother, Lucio or his sister Olivia at his house. As always he made no attempt to speak to her, but the week after Christmas he came to the house to pay his January rent. When Lupe popped into the study and announced excitedly that Tonio wished to see her, Erica clenched her hands, fighting the sudden rapid pounding of her heart. "You can accept the rent for me, Lupe," she told her coolly.

"Oh, but, señorita, he wants to give it directly to you," Lupe protested with rounded eyes, obviously astounded by Erica's lack of interest in Tonio. "He wouldn't give so much money to me."

"Why? Does he think you aren't trustworthy?"

"No, of course not, but it wouldn't be right."

Erica glared at her housekeeper. "Lupe, can't you see I'm busy? Tell Mr. Cruz he'll have to give *you* the check."

"He said he'd come back tomorrow if now wasn't convenient."

Erica grimaced. "Oh, all right." She rose and marched stiffly into the front room, where Tonio stood, gazing out the front windows. He turned at the sound of her heels against the tiles of the hall, his face unsmiling, cool and devastatingly handsome. "Hello, Tonio."

"Erica. How are you?"

"Fine, thank you. I understand you brought the rent check?" Her voice went up on a note of polite inquiry.

"Yes." He extended the check, and Erica pulled it from his fingers without touching them.

"Why didn't you mail it, the way you did last month?"

"I was out of town last month when the rent was due, but it seemed a waste of postage to mail it this time when I could so easily bring it. Besides, I wanted to find out how you're getting along. I haven't seen you drive by the past few days."

"I've been busy," Erica replied shortly, sticking the check into a pocket of her jeans. Tonio was as immaculate as ever in tan corduroy slacks, a pale green shirt and a forest-green pullover sweater. Erica felt at a distinct disadvantage in her casual jeans and navy-blue turtleneck. It didn't seem fair that one man should be so handsome, so at ease. Whenever she saw him she felt as if her bones would melt, while he remained as calm and cool as an autumn day. Of course, he probably found that easy to do around her since she always seemed to be sloppily dressed and lacking makeup whenever he met her. Surreptitiously she wiped an ink-stained hand against her trouser leg and wished she were wearing one of her trim business suits. However, jeans were the only feasible thing to wear when she was constantly in and out of the groves or the dusty barn.

"Thank you for the check," Erica told him coolly. "Now, if you'll excuse me, I must return to work."

"You shouldn't work so hard. Believe me, the farm won't run off. It doesn't all have to be done immediately." He kept his eyes on her, his husky voice making the mundane words warm and special. Erica found herself wanting to tell him all her problems and seek his help, which was ridiculous. He'd used her weakness to get into her bed—or start in again about selling the farm. She wasn't going to rely on his help. She couldn't, not if she wanted to keep any self-respect.

She forced herself to answer calmly, "Irrigation begins in February, and I have to get the drainage system repaired before then. After that we start planting. I won't have time to delay anything." Which was why, she added silently, she was going to talk to a banker on Monday. If she didn't borrow the money soon, it would be too late for the improvements.

"There's something wrong with the drainage system?"

"You needn't concern yourself about it." Erica realized that she had already revealed too much.

His mouth twisted. "Sorry I expressed any interest."

Erica remained silent. She refused to let herself be drawn into any further conversation with Tonio. He lingered for a moment, his eyes steady on her. Then he sighed as if giving up, murmured a polite good-bye and left. Erica followed him to the door and closed it behind him. She stayed at the door, watching Tonio through the etched glass side panel as he walked away. His long stride quickly took him past the oleander hedge and out of her line of vision. Erica turned away, in her mind's eye still seeing his lithe walk and the lean, smooth line of his legs.

Chapter 10

On the first Monday of the new year Erica dressed in one of her most attractive suits, a slim-lined brown skirt and jacket with a shimmering rust blouse beneath. The skirt and jacket were tailored and very businesslike, but the sheen of the blouse and the dainty ruffle around the high neck and cuffs gave the outfit warmth and beauty. Brushing her hair back, she curled it up in a low roll that was smooth and no-nonsense yet possessed an old-fashioned femininity. Her only adornment was an old ivory cameo at the throat of her blouse.

Anxiously she made a final inspection of herself in the mirror, rechecked her file on the farm's financial picture and ventured forth to face the loan officer at the bank in Santa Clara. As she drove past the old house, Erica saw Tonio standing on the porch. Diane Roberts was beside him, her auburn hair gleaming in the sunlight. She gazed up at Tonio, her face glowing, her mouth slightly parted in laughter at his last remark. Tonio raised a casual hand to Erica in greeting.

Erica's lips twitched with irritation. How dare Tonio wave at her as if nothing lay between them, as if they were friends! And what was Diane doing at his house this early in the morning? Why, it wasn't even nine o'clock yet! Was she leaving after spending the night there? Erica knew Diane had been chasing Tonio from the first. Perhaps her chase had been successful. Erica's fingers clenched around the steering wheel. She told herself that whom Tonio slept with meant nothing to her. She was through with Tonio Cruz. Absolutely through.

By the time Erica arrived at the bank, she had managed to smooth the frown from her forehead and put Tonio out of her mind. The loan officer who came forward to greet her was a short, rotund man in his forties. She barely knew him, for he was too young to be in her father's age bracket, yet too old to be a contemporary of hers. Erica wished she could have presented her plea to one of her father's friends. However, the man was friendly and shook her hand warmly as he introduced himself as Jason Smith, then asked if she'd like a cup of coffee. The bank still operated on a small-town basis, one of the centers of the community, where customers as often as not came to sit and chat rather than conduct business.

Erica refused the coffee and laid out her file on Smith's desk. Carefully she explained the sales figures for the last five years and the projected numbers for this year and the next, which she had spent several agonizing hours over. Proud of her handiwork, she sat back, smiling.

"Very nice," he commented. "Yes, very nice work." He paused and cleared his throat, braced his elbows on the desk in front of him and carefully positioned the tips of his fingers together. Watching his hands rather than her, he began, "Miss Logan, these are very tight times in the financial world. It's difficult to obtain a loan these days, as I'm sure you're aware."

"Of course, but not when you have the kind of collateral I do. The farm has only one small existing mortgage."

"Naturally, we don't make a loan solely on the basis of security. Bankers work with money. We aren't in the business of farming or selling farms. Say you don't make your payments and we have to foreclose. The only way we can recover our money is to sell the land. That takes time, money and effort, and all the while we're sitting there with a producing farm on our hands. We want good security, but our first consideration is whether or not you can repay the loan. If it was your father asking, or some other farmer, it would be different, but frankly speaking, Miss Logan, we can't afford to take the risk on you."

"But you can see the figures right there," Erica protested, pointing to the file. "It's obvious I'll be able to meet the payments."

"Yes, if everything goes exactly right. You're cutting it too close. If something unforeseen happens, you won't be able to make the payments. Ma'am, I'm sorry as can be, but it's impossible to lend you the money at the present time. Our holding company wouldn't approve it. They're always on our backs because we lend money on the basis of character without sufficient proof that it will be repaid."

Erica clenched her jaw, anger and frustration surging through her. She managed to thank Smith politely and leave the bank without her rage bursting through, but all the way home she reargued her case with the loan officer in her mind. Imagine not lending her the money with that kind of security backing it up! It was crazy. Fuming, Erica made a sharp turn into her driveway, kicking up gravel. Tonio was still on his porch, although Diane was gone. He sat with his feet up on the banister, lazily leaning back in a chair, a sketch pad on his lap. He glanced up at her loud entry into the driveway and again raised his hand in friendly greeting.

Without thinking Erica slammed on her brakes and skidded to a halt. After cutting off the engine, she jumped out and strode toward the porch, her anger boiling up in her, aching to be released. It seemed that Tonio sitting in cool possession of the old house was the last straw in a terrible morning. "All right, Tonio, this has gone on long enough," she snapped as she mounted the shallow steps. "What do you hope to accomplish by camping on my doorstep?"

His eyebrows sailed upward in reproachful surprise. "Apparently what I've accomplished is to get on your nerves."

"Is that what you want? To know that your presence here makes me furious? That I hate driving past this house? That you annoy me terribly? Why didn't you tell me before? I'd have admitted those things gladly, and you wouldn't have had to rent the house to find out!"

He studied her, an errant grin tugging at the corners of his mouth. Finally he remarked, eyes gleaming, "Damn! You're beautiful." Erica clenched her fists, arms rigid at her side, barely restraining herself from stamping and shrieking with frustration. Tonio rose, laughingly apologetic. "I'm sorry. Did I make the wrong response? Should I have shouted back and given you a chance to display your splendid fury? Go ahead and scream if you want. I won't mind."

"I'm tired of this cat-and-mouse game you're playing!"

"What game?" He opened the door and motioned for her to precede him. "Won't you come in? You might like to inspect what I've done to the place and drink a cup of coffee while you vent your anger."

Erica glared at him and stalked through the open door. Inside, she stopped stock-still and gazed around. The old house had been transformed. The walls had been repainted a soft, creamy white. The wooden floors were waxed until they shone, and were warmed by vivid Navaho rugs. A large Indian sand painting in muted colors adorned one wall. Tonio had imprinted it with his own personality without changing the appeal of the rambling house and old furniture. Erica realized that she would love to throw herself on the large sofa and indulge in a good cry, then snuggle up before the fireplace with a book. Despising the traitorous yearning within herself, Erica swung on Tonio. "You've painted it."

"Yes, the walls needed it. Surely you don't object to my sprucing the place up a bit—I didn't deduct the expenses from my rent."

"You had no right. This is *my* house."

He cocked his head quizzically. "Do you want me to restore the house to its former grandeur? I could paint the walls a dingy beige."

"No. It looks lovely, and you know I wouldn't repaint it to look old and tacky. But you should have asked me first."

"How could I? You wouldn't see me or answer my calls."

"You didn't call me!"

He grinned. "So you've been keeping track."

"This is pointless. I don't know why I stopped." She started for the front door, but Tonio grabbed her arm.

"Wait. You must see the rest of the house. Who knows what other horrors I might have perpetrated? Aren't you afraid I painted a wall somewhere turquoise or purple?"

"I wouldn't put anything past you if you thought it would get under my skin. Why do you try so hard to make me mad?"

"I don't *try*. It comes naturally."

"Why did you rent my house? Why is it so important that you somehow obtain a piece of this farm?"

"The reason isn't quite as dramatic as you believe. I need peace and quiet to draw my designs, and it's hard to find such commodities in Houston. Plus, I've begun construction on the hotel on Padre. I'm close enough here to check on the work often while I clean up my backlog of work. And I can fly to Houston whenever I need to."

"Why not live on South Padre? That's where the construction will actually take place."

"Ah, but there I'd be forced to be constantly involved in the construction. I merely want to check on it periodically. I need time for my plans. Besides, my mother and family live here. I wanted a place near them."

"Why this one? There are lots of other places to stay in Santa Clara."

"Give me an example. The El Sombrero Motel perhaps? Santa Clara is not the rental property capital of the state, you know. Finding a nice, roomy house to rent isn't easy. Yours fitted my needs exactly. I've turned the den, which is sunny, into my workroom. Come look at it." He led her down the hall and into the small den, now dominated by his drafting table. He had covered one wall with corkboard and tacked up several of his sketches. Erica stepped closer, drawn against her will to the drawings of a multistory glass and concrete structure.

"Like it?"

"It looks . . . very elegant."

"Thank you. That's what I was hoping to achieve. It's a hotel on an island off the coast of Georgia. I plan to begin construction this spring. Here's an overview of the whole complex." He pointed to another sketch. "This L-shape is the hotel, and this is the pool. Over here, a small wading pool. See how the pool thins out? I'm going to give it the appearance of a stream, trees branching across it and flowers growing beside it. I'll build a couple of walkways over it as it curves back into the main swimming pool. Then here in the center I'll set the pool bar on an island. There are tennis courts inside and out. It sits, as you can see, on the edge of the golf course. In the future I plan to add a string of condominiums along the perimeter of the course."

"Quite a development."

"Yes, it's one of my biggest projects. The worst problem was obtaining the backing. That's why I'm doing it in stages. The hotel will bring in the cash and prove its potential. Then I'll be able to find the backing for the condos."

"Do you get loans, or do other people buy a piece of it?"

"For this one I obtained a loan—or, rather, several loans. I'm developing it in partnership with a couple of moneymen. Cross will run the development and they'll get a percentage of the profits."

"Is that the way you build all your hotels?"

"No. We design and build some for other corporations for a fee. Others we build and sell to a chain. And then we keep some and run them ourselves."

"How do you decide?"

"In some cases money decides. I need quick cash flow for another project, so I require a short-term money-maker. We'll sell. Longer-term profits mean we keep it. We're more likely to keep condominiums, which involve less management than a hotel."

"Will you keep the Breezes, then?"

"Possibly. Most of the hotels Cross owns and operates are in Texas and Louisiana. I want to keep the chain small and close to home. Operation is not my specialty." Suddenly he grinned. "That's your area."

"My area?"

"Yeah. Isn't that what you're trained for, hotel management, not running a citrus farm?"

"Are we back to that again?" Erica swung away, the friendly mood broken.

"Don't you miss it?"

Erica sighed and leaned back against the wall beside the sketches. Miss it? Oh, yes, she missed it. Particularly after her disappointment with the banker. What was she to do? For a second she was tempted to tell Tonio about her meeting with Jason Smith and his refusal of a loan. Tonio was a far more experienced businessperson than she. Perhaps he could help her, could show her how to draw up a profile that would have a bank jumping to loan her money. He obviously could get people to loan him millions of dollars for his projects. She bit her lip and looked up at him.

He sucked in his breath and came toward her. "God, when you look at me like that, I could..." He stopped before her and placed his hands on either side of her face, forcing her to turn her face up to him. Erica's stomach turned uneasily, as if she were looking into a bottomless black pit. She knew she could fall into the depths of his eyes and be lost forever. "I want you."

She began to tremble violently. Why did she let Tonio do this to her? Where was her cool, her resolve? Why had she stopped to talk to him, after all her vows to keep away? Sternly she tried to control herself, to summon up a sharp comeback. But, embarrassingly, when she spoke, her voice came out tiny, almost pleadingly, "For the moment?"

"For ten years." His hands slid down the wall to her waist, brushing her arms with a feather-light touch that set off shivers along her spine. "Do you know what you look like in that suit? A very expensive, very creamy, very delicious chocolate candy." He pulled her forward, and limply Erica made no resistance. His hand caressed her hair. "You're so tempting with your hair up all prim and proper." Softly, slowly, he kissed first her upper lip, then the lower one, tugging it gently between his lips. One finger moved to trace the convolutions of her ear. His mouth came down fully on hers, and he wrapped his arms around her. The touch of his lips, the velvet of his tongue roaming her mouth, shook Erica to the core. She wanted to give herself up to the magic of his lovemaking, to forget both her cares and the past and drown in the trembling glory of his hands and mouth on her body.

His hands slid under her suit jacket, caressing the satin softness of her blouse, and came to rest on her breasts. Mindlessly Erica responded, molding her body to his, the nipples of her breasts thrusting forward for the touch of his hands. He answered their need, his thumbs circling the hard buds through her blouse, using the material to arouse them further. His mouth ground into hers, the hard nipping of his teeth highlighting the incredible softness of his lips and tongue. His ragged breath seared her cheeks as his mouth sought her earlobe and feasted on it. He fumbled with the buttons of her blouse, opening it to his roaming hands. Expertly he unfastened her brassiere, all the while driving her further and further into mindless passion with the movements of his mouth on her skin. He kissed her throat, his tongue making wet designs and traveling across the thin skin of her chest to the trembling lushness of her breasts. He pulled back and for one long moment gazed at Erica, his hot eyes caressing the blue-veined globes with their eager, swollen tips. When she felt as though she could stand it no longer, he came back, bending to reverently take one nipple into the hot, moist cavern of his mouth. He sucked gently, his teeth barely grazing the tender skin and his tongue slowly stroking the button of her engorged nipple.

Tonio slid his hands down and up, pushing up her skirt as he caressed her silky legs. The lacy panties she wore were little protection against his hard reality as he pulled her ever tighter against him. He groaned deep in his throat, mumbling, "Erica." He raised his head from his delightful work and breathed huskily, "Come to bed with me. Upstairs in our old room." He nuzzled her neck. *"Querida. Mi amada."*

Erica did not hear the gentle love words he murmured. The reminder of their earlier love affair had shattered her haze of mindless pleasure. Tonio desired her as he had before—and he would break her heart again just as carelessly. She wasn't a person to him but a prize. He was determined to win her over. He'd told her so. No doubt it was a challenge to reconquer the woman he'd hurt so badly years before. And how easy she made it for him! Here she was in the middle of the day in his workroom, her blouse gaping open and her skirt pushed up above her hips like some cheap hooker, panting and yearning for his expert touch. Humiliation coursed through her, and she jerked away, tugging down her skirt and pulling her blouse closed, her arms wrapped defensively around her. "No!" Tonio took a step after her, then stopped, his breath harsh and heavy. "No, Tonio, not again. I refuse to be a few weeks entertainment for you."

"Erica, don't—not now—come back." He extended his hands and started toward her. Erica broke and ran, darting out of the room and down the hallway. Tonio didn't try to follow her as she escaped to her car. He crashed a fist into the wall, then turned away, plunging his hands into his thick, black hair and pacing until his breathing slowed. Finally he slumped into a chair. "Cruz, you're insane," he whispered.

Erica carefully avoided Tonio's house after that, although she found it far harder to avoid the shameful memories of how she had almost yielded to him again. She used her work as a shield, driving herself harder than ever. She applied to other banks in the area—McAllen, Harlingen, even as far away as Brownsville—but she received the same negative answer everywhere. Erica hadn't thought she was naive in money matters, but she realized her hopes for getting a loan had been overly sanguine. After the sixth straight refusal in two weeks, Erica dragged herself home disconsolately. It appeared that she would be unable to improve the land unless she sold part of it to some local farmer. She hated to do it, but she couldn't allow the farm to sink into a gradual decline, either. She poured a cup of coffee from the old percolator and ambled into the den. Kicking off her shoes, she plopped into a chair and propped her feet up on the edge of the coffee table. She exhaled wearily and rubbed a hand across her eyes.

Danny spoke up from his reclining position on the floor beyond the coffee table. "What's the matter?"

"Oh!" Erica's eyes flew open. "I'm sorry, honey. I didn't see you when I came in."

"I was reading." He indicated the book spread open on the floor before him.

"The light's not good enough there," Erica lectured automatically. "You ought to sit on the couch and turn on the table lamp. You could see much better."

Danny ignored her warning with the ease of long habit. "What's the matter?"

"Nothing. Why?"

"You went like this when you came in," he retorted, imitating her. "Like you were tired or upset."

"I suppose I'm both. I've been trying to get a loan to improve the farm, but the banks turned me down. I need a new drainage system for a few acres. Plus, I'm having to hire extra help to repair the damage Goodson did."

"Why won't they lend you the money?"

"Because I don't have any experience. They're afraid I won't be able to pay them back."

Danny's forehead creased into a frown. "I could get a job," he offered earnestly.

Erica smiled. "That's very sweet of you, but I'm afraid you're under the legal age to work. Besides, it wouldn't be enough. I need a big chunk of money immediately."

"Maybe Tonio would buy the old house. He likes it a lot. Would that be enough?"

Erica sat up straight, her whole body tensing. "You sound on awfully familiar terms with him. Danny, have you been visiting Tonio? I specifically told you not to bother him."

"But I didn't! I was just playing on the driveway one day and he was sitting on his porch. He asked me how come I never came to see him and I told him you wouldn't let me 'cause I'd bother him. He said he wouldn't mind and I could come anytime I wanted to."

Erica laced her fingers together tightly. She mustn't make a big deal out of his visiting Tonio, or it would seem suspicious. If she refused to permit Danny to visit Tonio after he had given him permission, it might make Tonio curious, even cause him to delve into Danny's background. He obviously hadn't recognized Danny's resemblance to himself. After all, people rarely were aware of how they looked or saw others' similarities to themselves. It was a risk to let Danny visit him, but a worse one to insist on keeping him at home. Reluctantly Erica admitted, "Well, I guess it's all right then, as long as you don't go so often you wear out your welcome."

"I won't. Well, what do you think? Would he buy the old house? He must be rich, 'cause he drives a Mercedes. And I know he likes you."

"What?"

"Well, he asks about you all the time, what you're doing and how you feel and whether you're still upset about Granddaddy."

"He's just curious," Erica protested.

"Nope, I don't think so. You know, when we were all at the hospital, he looked at you funny, like guys do in the movies. You know, right before the big kiss." He jumped up and demonstrated a movie clinch, wrapping his arms around his thin body and smooching an invisible partner.

Erica had to laugh. "You nut. Well, whatever you think about Tonio's liking me, I don't want you to talk to him about buying the house. He doesn't need it, and I won't put him on the spot. I'll handle it, I promise."

Danny shrugged so innocently that Erica would have been suspicious if she hadn't been preoccupied with her own thoughts. "Okay." In his head Danny noted that he hadn't promised not to tell Tonio about the turned-down loans.

Erica's fingers tapped the keys of the calculator, figuring the profits from the last month. The front doorbell rang and she punched up a partial total, sighing. She had to answer the door because Lupe was cleaning the old house, a task Tonio had charmed the dour woman into doing weekly. Erica strode to the door and swung it open briskly. When she saw who stood outside, she gasped, her cheeks flaming with embarrassment. Instinctively she moved to slam the door in his face, but Tonio was quicker than she and caught it with his forearm. "Hello, Erica, it's always nice to receive a warm welcome."

Erica's throat tightened, though whether it was from humiliation or his nearness, she wasn't sure. She looked away. "What do you want? I'm trying to work."

"I'm here on business—and I think my offer will prove more profitable than whatever you're doing at the moment."

"All right." Grudgingly she stood aside to let him enter, then walked down the hall to her office without glancing back at him. In her office she pointed in the general direction of the red leather chair opposite her desk. "Sit down. Now, what do you want?"

"I understand you're in need of a loan."

"How did you know?" She stared, then narrowed her eyes suspiciously. "Has Danny been talking to you?"

"Relax, Erica, I don't usually discuss financial matters with children," he lied, as he had promised Danny he would. "Bankers talk, you know. One hears rumors eventually."

"Okay. You're right. I've been trying to get a loan to fix up the farm. What of it?"

"How much do you need?"

"Fifty thousand, not that it's any of your business."

"But it *is* my business. I intend to loan you the money."

"You're crazy."

"Maybe. But I told you once that I built my business by following hunches."

"*Sound* hunches."

Tonio chuckled, a rich, throaty sound that tickled at her abdomen. "Are you trying to persuade me that you aren't a sound investment? I think you have that backward."

"No, of course not. I'll repay the loan. But I don't understand why you're so anxious to lend to me when no one else thinks I'm a safe bet."

"I'm willing to make a loan based on personal knowledge of your character." His eyes suddenly gleamed, and Erica's cheeks reddened again. "Do I have to beg you to take my money? How about if I promise not to charge interest?"

"No! It's just that I—I don't want to be beholden to you." There was no way to explain her fear of loving him again and being crushed by him. She couldn't tell him that each thing he did for her bound her ever more securely to him, was another strand in the web he was spinning around her.

"Is it so terrible to be in my debt?"

"I don't know what you'll want in return. I'm not for sale, Tonio."

He growled inarticulately and rose, slapping his hands down on her desk and leaning over her. By sheer strength of will he forced her to look up at him. "Do you think I'm going to demand your virtue, like some villain out of a melodrama? Don't worry. I don't enjoy coerced sex. There are plenty of women out there who are willing."

"I'm sure you've sampled a few, too," Erica retorted hotly. "Was Diane Roberts first on your list?"

"That sticks in your craw, doesn't it? What's the deal, Erica? You don't want me, but it wounds your pride to think I might settle for someone else? Would you rather I wasted away with feverish longing?"

"The only thing I'd rather you do is leave town. Whom you choose to sleep with is no concern of mine. Maybe you enjoy sharing women with your brother."

His face paled and he clenched his fists. "What the hell doe‹ that mean?"

Erica stared. Did it bother him so much that Diane had ha‹ an affair with Lucio? Was his feeling for the woman that in‹ tense? An icy pain pierced her chest. "I—I'm sorry. Weren'‹ you aware that Diane and Lucio were once—I mean, that's th‹ rumor."

He rolled his eyes. "I don't give a damn about Diane Rob‹ erts's sex life!" he roared. "For your information I haven'‹ slept with her and I don't intend to." Visibly he forced himsel‹ to speak calmly. "Look, I think we're getting rather far afiel‹ here. As I recall, we were discussing your loan. Now, if ‹ promise not to take my interest out of your delectable body, wi‹ you accept the money?"

"I don't want to have to be grateful to you!" Erica ex‹ claimed honestly.

"Meaning it's easier for you to believe I'm mean through an‹ through? Well, if it will help you any, I'll require a lien on you‹ property. If you can't make a go of it, I'll get the land I want‹ Is that self-interested enough for you?"

"Oh, I see." It made more sense that way. It was still humil‹ iating to take Tonio's money, but with the land as collateral, i‹ wouldn't bind her to him in quite the same way. That made it ‹ business deal, not a personal favor. She couldn't stand to b‹ dependent on him in any way. "If you'll charge interest an‹ accept a lien on the farm, I would . . . appreciate the loan."

"Careful, you might choke on words like that," he teased‹ "You drive a hard bargain. I'll take eight percent. What do yo‹ want, a ten-year loan?"

"Actually I was thinking of five."

He raised his eyebrows. "Sure you can make it? Let me se‹ your figures."

She dug among the files on her desk and handed him th‹ projections. He studied the papers, one finger runnin‹ thoughtfully over his lips. With his attention elsewhere, Eric‹ could study him freely. She took in the smooth fit of his slack‹ and the well-cut navy-blue shirt, the strong line of his jaw, th‹ shadow of his thick, black lashes, the finger sliding across hi‹ chiseled lips. A warm glow started in her abdomen and spread‹ She couldn't tear her eyes away from his hard face, and sh‹

knew she wanted to pull the papers from him, to place her own fingers against his lips and feel their velvet warmth, to know the touch of his hand upon her flesh.

"Let's try a ten-year time period with no prepayment penalty. That way you can pay earlier if you want." He glanced up and his voice trailed off. Erica knew he had read the desire in her eyes. She looked away, blushing. What must he think of her? How humiliating for Tonio to know she had no control, that she hungered for him and would probably leap into his bed if he so much as crooked a finger. "Erica." His low voice was a tangible caress. A shiver snaked through Erica.

Desperately she shoved herself away from the desk and strode to the window. "If that's what you want, it's fine."

"You know that's not what I want," he replied huskily.

"Oh, then what do you want?" she asked bravely, turning to face him. His eyes were dark and smoldering, sinking into her heart and soul and trapping her.

"You—willingly—in my bed."

"Tonight? Or until you tire of me?"

"Tonight and every night . . . until you want to leave."

"Tonio, please, don't."

"Don't what? Don't desire you? Don't tempt you? I haven't touched another woman since I met you again on the island. That's a long time, Erica." His mouth curved sensually. "I've developed a huge hunger."

Erica's mouth went dry as sand, and she forced a swallow. Using all her willpower, she managed to shake her head no. A fire flamed for an instant in the dark eyes, but he lowered his lids, and when he reopened them, his eyes were their usual hazel. Tonio rose and tossed the file onto the desk. "Have your attorney draw up the note and deed of trust. I'll have the money whenever you want."

Trying to maintain a light tone, Erica quipped, "I hope Cross Corporation won't regret the investment."

"It's not from Cross Corporation. It's a private loan from Antonio Cruz."

She stared. "You have that much money lying around?"

"I can get it. I think you ought to raise the amount to sixty thousand. I suspect fifty will be short."

"But I . . . thank you." She flushed and glanced away.

"Hard words for you to say, aren't they?" He crossed to the door. "Oh, by the way, I have one further stipulation. Invite me to supper when the papers are drawn up. I'm tired of my own cooking."

"Yes, of course."

He opened the door, then swung around suddenly and returned to Erica in two swift strides. His sinewy fingers dug into Erica's shoulders and pulled her to him. His lips sank onto hers. For a long moment neither moved, their mouths clinging desperately. His teeth were sharp against her lips, his tongue demanding, possessive. Finally he tore his mouth away, his face contorted with passion and anger. "Damn it, Erica, how long are you going to keep us from what we both want?"

It was a rhetorical question and he didn't wait for an answer, but almost flung her from him and walked rapidly through the door. Erica stared at the empty doorway, her arms wrapped tightly around her to still the shudders coursing through her body. She knew she had done the wrong thing. Why, oh, why, had she let him become involved in her life again? He would suck all the life and love from her and leave her an empty shell, just as he had before.

Chapter 11

The promissory note and deed of trust were standard forms. Bill Matson finished them in two days. After Erica picked up the legal papers, she returned home and dialed Tonio's number. When he answered, her stomach knotted and for a second she couldn't get out a sound.

"Hello?" he repeated impatiently.

"Uh, Tonio, this is Erica."

There was a fractional hesitation. "Yes?"

"I have the note and second lien ready. You do understand that the bank has first lien on the property?"

"Yes. It's negligible. I'm not backing out on that account."

"Would you . . . care to come over this evening? I'll give you the papers."

"All right." His voice turned teasing. "And do I get that dinner?"

"Yes." Erica bitterly regretted agreeing to his dinner deal. The more she saw Tonio, the less she was able to hang on to her good sense. "What would you like?"

"Whatever. It doesn't matter."

"I'll ask Lupe to prepare enchiladas. It's her best dinner."

"No! I don't want Lupe to fix supper for me. I want you to."

"What difference does it make?" Her voice rose in amazement.

Tonio hesitated. He felt stupid, now that he'd said it. She was right. Why should it make any difference? But he wanted to know that Erica had prepared the food for him with her own hands. As if she cared for him. As if she were his wife and Danny his son, a happy family scene. "Indulge me. I want you to cook it."

"Okay," she replied in a tone of someone humoring a crazy man. "But I warn you, it won't be nearly as good. I'm not much of a cook."

"I'll suffer the consequences. I'll be there, say, six?"

"Fine." Erica hung up and began a search of the kitchen. Lupe followed her movements suspiciously. Erica almost giggled. Why, she believed Lupe was actually jealous of her invading the housekeeper's domain. "I thought I'd cook supper tonight, Lupe, if it's all right with you."

"Whatever you want," Lupe replied coldly.

"You see, someone's coming over for supper at six, and if you had it ready before you left at five, it would be either cold or dried out by the time he got here."

Lupe was diverted. "You have a man coming for dinner? Who?"

"Tonio Cruz."

A smile cracked Lupe's dour face. "Mmm. He's a good man for you, that one. Very—I don't know the word, very much a man."

"Virile?" Erica suggested dryly. "Honestly, Lupe, I didn't figure you'd be swayed by his sex appeal."

"You think I'm dead?" Lupe retorted.

"Lucio's handsomer," Erica teased, amused at discovering a weakness in the solemn woman.

Lupe made a face. "A pretty boy. There's not enough man in him. Ever see his children? He's married five years and only two children, both girls. But Antonio—a son every year, just like that." She snapped her fingers three times to emphasize her point.

"I don't want a son every year!" Erica protested, but her insides warmed.

"You wouldn't want him to give you fine sons, brothers for Danny?" Lupe queried. Erica's eyes narrowed. Did Lupe suspect or was her remark meaningless? Lupe shook her head despairingly. "You think I don't know?"

"Know what?"

"That Danny is his son."

Erica glanced around sharply to make sure Danny wasn't within hearing distance. "Lupe, how could you know? No one does, not even Tonio."

"He's a man." Lupe dismissed him. "What man can see what's right in front of his eyes? No, he'd be too blind with jealousy, wondering if this man or that was the father. But I'm not. I see Tonio in Danny's face."

"Lupe, please, don't say anything about this. I don't want Tonio to know. Or Danny."

"Whatever you say. I won't go against you. But it will come out."

"Not if I can help it," Erica replied grimly. "Now, what shall I fix for supper?"

Since she was preparing a dinner for the man of Lupe's choice, Lupe apparently had no objection to Erica's using the kitchen. She reeled off a list of possible dishes.

"No, no," Erica objected. "Nothing fancy. I don't know how to make any of those."

"I will show you."

"No. If Tonio wants me to make supper, he'll have to eat what I know how to cook. Do we have any steaks?"

Sighing, Lupe surrendered and pulled three steaks from the freezer. Erica thawed the meat in the microwave. Giving in to Lupe's pleas, Erica allowed her to dictate instructions for a chocolate cake and then spent the rest of the afternoon putting together the ingredients and baking it. Danny wandered in, drawn by the delicious aroma of the baking cake. He was thrilled to learn that Tonio would be their guest at supper and insisted on helping to ice the cake, anxious to be included in preparing the treat for his friend.

The cake took longer than Erica had expected, and by the time it was iced, it was almost six o'clock. Erica glanced down at her worn jeans and loose red shirt, both splattered by flour and drops of icing, and muttered a terse expletive. She couldn't meet Tonio looking like this, she thought, remembering her sloppy appearance at the real-estate office, the awful contrast to Diane's careful style. But she had little time to change. For a moment she hesitated, wondering defiantly why she should care how she appeared when Tonio came to dine. She hadn't wanted him to eat with them in the first place.

Erica bolted for the stairs, calling to Danny, "Honey, I'm going to bathe and dress. If Tonio arrives before I'm through, stall him."

"Okay," Danny shouted back cheerfully, and took up watch at the living room window.

Pinning up her hair, Erica dumped powdered bubble bath into the tub and ran the water while she searched her meager wardrobe for the proper outfit. Everything she pulled out seemed dreadfully tame or far too suggestive. Finally she compromised on dark purple slacks with a matching jacket, collarless and perfectly plain except for the piping down the front and on the two slanted slash pockets. Underneath the jacket she would wear a thin lavender blouse, very understated and feminine, with a low oval neckline that dropped almost to the tops of her breasts. One large, soft ruffle adorned the neckline. Erica tossed the clothes onto the bed, returned to the bath and quickly stripped to step into the tub. She scrubbed until her skin was rosy from the heat and friction. She would have liked to soak lazily for a while, but there wasn't enough time. Tonio would tease her all night about her feminine tardiness if she wasn't on time; in fact, she wouldn't put it past him to barge right into her room while she dressed.

That thought inspired her to towel-dry at top speed and jump into her waiting clothes. After slipping on earrings that resembled gold lace, she pawed through her jewelry box for the matching necklace. As she searched, her fingers brushed a small, round metal object and halted. Slowly she pulled it from the box. Tonio's medal. Holding it in her palm, she traced the raised figure on the front. She replaced it gently and closed the lid, deciding not to wear the necklace that matched her earrings. Hearing the doorbell ring downstairs, she dabbed on makeup and mascaraed her eyelashes. Then she brushed out her thick hair, pulled it back and caught it on one side with a dainty barrette covered with tiny lavender flowers. A quick splash of perfume was the final touch. She hurried down the stairs to the den, from which came the sound of Tonio's and Danny's voices.

The tableau in the room stopped her in her tracks. Her breath caught harshly in her throat. Danny was instructing Tonio in the use of an electronic game and they were laughing over Tonio's mistakes, their dark heads close together. How could anyone not realize they were father and son? she thought. And how much longer could she keep it from Tonio? Someone would see the resemblance and mention it to Tonio, and then— what? She didn't know, but the idea frightened her. "Hello," she exclaimed brightly, a little too loudly, to break the intimacy before her.

They raised their heads. Danny whistled boyishly and Tonio stood, his face a silent tribute to her looks. "Erica."

"I hope Danny's been keeping you entertained," she continued in a hostessy voice.

"Very," he answered gravely. His hand rested on the boy's head.

"Could I get you a drink?"

He shrugged. "If you like."

Her question had been the first thing that popped into her nervous mind. Erica regretted it immediately. Her liquor cabinet was poorly stocked, as she rarely drank, and so didn't bother to buy any liquor. "What'll you have?"

"Scotch and water," he replied carelessly.

Erica crossed to her father's liquor cabinet and opened it. "Sorry," she apologized, blushing, after a fast search. "No Scotch."

"Bourbon, then."

"None of that, either." Erica bit her lip.

A grin flickered across Tonio's mouth. "Gin and tonic?" Erica shook her head, her face flaming now. Tonio laughed. "I'm sorry. I didn't realize this was a quiz game. I give up. What's the answer?"

Erica turned back to the cabinet. "Well, I have rum and vodka."

"A screwdriver would be fine. A small one." He hesitated, then added with a teasing smile, "I trust you *do* have orange juice."

Erica cast him a fulminating glance and stalked away to the kitchen to fill the ice bucket and get the orange juice. Returning to the den, she mixed the drinks, poured Danny a glass of orange juice and carried the glasses to the coffee table. Then she realized she had no cocktail napkins. She hurried back to the kitchen for coasters. "I'm sorry." She was completely flustered now. "I'm not used to company, I'm afraid. I also forgot to get nuts or mints or anything like that." She brightened a little. "I do have some cheese."

Tonio chuckled and reached out to take her hand. He brought it to his lips, forcing her to move closer, and grazed her knuckles with his soft, warm mouth. Erica's stomach quivered at the velvety touch. "It's all right. I never expect the amenities from citrus farmers." Erica snatched away her hand and took a large gulp of her drink, which she instantly regretted. She had made it far too strong. Tonio grinned at her wry face. "Next time *I'll* make the drinks."

"When do we eat?" Danny questioned, not one to lose sight of the important things in life.

"Right now." Erica rose quickly. "I'll put on the steaks. How do you like yours cooked Tonio?"

"Medium rare." He stood also, slipping out of his tan jacket. Erica couldn't help running her eyes down the smooth line of his body in the eggshell-colored silk shirt and tan slacks. His stomach was flat and hard, flowing into graceful, muscular thighs. Tonio rolled up his sleeves. "I'll grill the steaks. Why don't you get the rest of the meal on the table?"

Erica's mouth thinned irritably. How dare he take over like that! She started to voice her indignation, but he was already gone, Danny on his heels. With a low, wordless growl, she followed them. What an abominable evening this promised to be. She found Danny rummaging through the drawers for the long barbeque tongs while Tonio seasoned the steaks. "I thought you wanted this prepared by my own lily-white hands," she told Tonio sarcastically.

His eyes danced. He nodded toward the oven, in which the foil-wrapped potatoes were visible. "You've made the potatoes. That's adequate taxing of your culinary skills."

"What's culinary?"

"Cooking," Tonio replied, having become used to Danny's style of conversation.

"Oh, she did more than the baked potatoes," Danny assured him with pride. "Look." He skipped to the opposite counter and lifted the lid from the cake plate.

"You made that yourself?" Tonio queried Erica, his eyebrows rising.

"Yes," she retorted. "Don't look so amazed."

"She didn't even get it out of a box. She made it from a recipe," Danny informed him with pride. "And I helped her put on the icing. We fixed it especially for you."

"Danny, why don't you go set the table?" Erica asked through tight lips.

"A chocolate cake especially for me?" Tonio teased after the boy had gone, a flame glowing briefly in his eyes. "Erica, I'm honored. Are you trying to seduce me?"

She whirled to escape his gaze and opened the refrigerator, staring blindly at its contents. His arms stole around her from behind, and Erica jumped. "You won't find it in there."

"What?"

"What you're looking for." His lips feathered across the back of her neck, sending shivers racing down her spine.

"And what is that?" Erica could hardly think. She wanted only to lean back against the steel of his chest and give herself up to his caress.

"This." His hands slid up under the jacket and over the silk of her blouse, crossing to cup her breasts. He nuzzled her neck.

"Tonio," she breathed. Her mind was a swirl of sensory perceptions far removed from thoughts. She trembled beneath his touch, aching for him.

Danny's high voice called from the dining room, piercing the haze of desire. "Mom? Do the spoons go after the knife or before?"

A soft groan of frustration escaped her at the interruption. One of Tonio's hands slipped down between her trousered legs and pressed her to him. She could feel the rigid expression of his desire against her buttocks. "Tonight," Tonio whispered in her ear. "I promise you. Tonight." He dropped a final kiss on her bare neck and released her. "I'll get the steaks going."

"Mom!" Danny repeated impatiently. Erica envied Tonio his escape to the gas grill outside. She could go nowhere to hide her hot cheeks and sparkling eyes.

"Yes, honey, I hear you. The knife goes to the right of the plate and the teaspoon to the right of the knife."

"Okay."

Erica took the salad bowl from the refrigerator and set it on the dining table, added the dressing and condiments, then brewed a pot of coffee. She steamed fresh broccoli, put it in a bowl and sprinkled it with lemon butter while Danny finished setting the table and plunked down the baked potatoes. By the time Tonio returned with the grilled steaks, the rest of the meal was ready. It was absurdly like an ordinary family meal, Erica thought. Unconsciously she had placed Tonio at the head of the table, and she and Danny sat on either side. It was an intimate grouping at the large, formal dining table, and a natural way to arrange them, but it also put Tonio in the position of father to the family, head of the household. He assumed the role with ease, dishing out the sizzling steaks, joking with Danny, reaching over to ruffle the boy's hair. Although his eyes touched Erica with a scorching intensity now and again, reminding her of his promise for the night to come, he kept the conversation on a normal plane. They discussed the weather, which was unusually warm for January, even in the valley, and talked about her crops and the progress she was making on the farm. Danny asked about the renovation of the Breezes, and Tonio described it in detail. "Tell you what, one day soon I'll take you to the island and let you see what they're doing. Would you like that?"

"Oh, yeah!" Danny responded enthusiastically. "That'd be super. When?"

"Danny, don't push," Erica admonished softly.

"It's all right. I don't mind. I'll be going over next week. How about then?"

"Sure!" Danny smiled and turned to his mother. "Can I, Mom?"

"Of course, as long as it isn't on a school day. Now, are you ready for some chocolate cake?"

Danny answered with a wide grin and Erica went into the kitchen to cut the cake and set it onto dessert plates. "Tonio, you want some coffee?" she called.

"Yeah. Black."

She carried in two plates of cake, then returned for the coffee. By the time she set the cups and saucers down and splashed a dollop of cream into hers, Danny was almost through his dessert. "What did you do, inhale it?" she asked, laughing.

"It's good," he replied by way of explanation. "Especially the icing."

"You would say that."

Tonio looked at her. "Aren't you having any cake?"

"Nope. Too fattening."

He grimaced. "You worry too much. You're thin enough. A man wants more in his arms than bones."

A treacherous warmth seeped through her at his words. To cover her reaction, Erica joked, "What do you want, for me to be *gorda?*" She puffed out her cheeks.

Tonio chuckled. "Here, just try a bite." He cut a piece of moist cake dripping with icing and extended it to her on his fork. Somehow he managed to make the gesture intimate, suggestive. Erica clenched her hands beneath the table. How did he manage to be so damn sexy even about offering her a bite of cake? She leaned forward to eat the piece of cake, but it was awkward, and a bit of the gooey icing slid off and landed on her chin. Danny giggled. Erica reached for her napkin, but Tonio was quicker than she. He scraped the icing from her skin with his forefinger and held it to her mouth. With an instinct deeper and faster than thought, Erica opened her lips and caught his finger between them, the tip of her tongue raking the icing from his skin. His eyes smoldered at her sensual action. The roughness of his skin against her sensitive lips and the salty taste of his flesh mingling with the sweet icing stirred her.

"Mom, could I have another piece?" Danny's voice broke the moment and Tonio's hand dropped. Erica dabbed at her lips and chin with her napkin.

"Later, maybe, before you go to bed."

"I'm through, then. Can I go outside and play?"

"Sure." Danny was gone in a flash, the front door banging behind him.

Erica wet her lips and looked around nervously, unable to meet Tonio's eyes. Why did she possess so little control around him? He knew exactly what bells to ring, and she responded like one of Pavlov's dogs, hot and eager. It must give him a lot of amusement to toy with her, to watch her melt wantonly whenever he chose to make her respond. "Erica, look at me." His voice was velvet, husky and caressing.

She jumped up, seizing the first excuse she could think of. "Let me warm your coffee." She almost ran into the kitchen, unplugged the percolator and returned with the pot to refill both their cups. When she started back to the kitchen, Tonio pulled the pot from her hands and set it on the table.

"I've had enough coffee for the evening," he told her firmly. His warm hand clasped one of hers and pulled her closer until she stood right beside him, close enough to feel the heat of his body. Erica stared down at his hand, still avoiding his eyes. He rubbed the back of her hand with his thumb. His voice was low and resonant. "I enjoy having you serve me." He lifted her hand to his mouth, kissing it slowly, softly, then rubbed it against his cheek. He mumbled a string of Spanish words against her skin, his breath searing her.

"What did you say?" she asked shakily.

He raised his eyes and grinned. "Probably nothing you'd like to hear. I was, uh . . . eulogizing your physical attributes."

Erica flushed and jerked her hand from his grasp. She sank into her chair, her knees suddenly turning to water. She began to pleat the tablecloth between her fingers. He placed two fingers beneath her chin and tilted up her face.

"Look at me. I want to see your lovely eyes." She gazed into the black depths of his eyes, bracing herself against their glittering intensity. "I've been sitting here all evening, talking like an idiot, no idea what I'm saying. All I could think about was you. Your hair, your eyes, your mouth. I could have been eating cardboard for all I cared. What I tasted was your skin on my tongue."

"Tonio, please."

"Erica, come here." His tone was soft, but brooked no disobedience. Erica rose, almost without effort, and took two small steps to his side. His arms slid around her waist and he buried his head between her breasts. Erica leaned against him weakly. Tonio tugged her down onto his lap, and her head lolled back against his steely arm. His lips covered her throat, nipping, sucking, massaging the soft flesh. One arm curled around her, supporting her torso, and the hand of that arm cupped her full breast. The other hand roamed freely over her open body, exploring and arousing her through her clothes. Erica's nipples tingled and pressed against the cloth of her blouse, turgid and aching for his touch. She twisted on his lap and he groaned at the movement. His mouth moved to hers and she strained against him eagerly, her tongue sliding out to lock with his in a contest of pleasure. His hand spread into her hair, holding her head immobile, and his lips worked over hers, his breath searing her cheek.

Finally Tonio wrenched away, his fingers digging into Erica's hair and pulling her head back. He closed his eyes and sucked in a chestful of air. "God, I want you," he rasped.

Erica's tongue traced her bruised lips. "Then take me," she whispered.

He shuddered violently. "Don't tempt me." He lifted her onto her feet. "I could use a cold shower about now." Kissing one ear lightly, he stepped away. "Later," he promised huskily. "When Danny goes to bed, we'll have the whole night before us."

Erica swallowed. She would have liked to retort that she wouldn't succumb to him later, but she knew it wasn't true. She would melt as soon as he kissed her, just as she had now. Shakily she picked up the small dessert plates and carried them to the kitchen. Tonio helped her clear the table and stack the dishes in the sink. "I'll do them later," she suggested. "Just leave them there."

He smiled, his eyes twinkling. "I have plans for later. Let's clean up now. I'll help." He began to scrape and rinse the dishes and Erica placed them in the dishwasher. It was odd to stand beside the man who had just swept her away in passion and engage in such a mundane task as cleaning the dishes.

"What's the smile for?"

"Oh, nothing. Just thinking that you aren't exactly dressed for dishwashing."

He glanced down at his immaculate shirt and tailored trousers and shrugged. "My clothes adjust to me, not me to them."

He nodded toward the chocolate cake remaining on the counter. "What inspired the dessert?"

"What makes you think I don't usually do such things?" she inquired loftily. He cast her a speaking glance and she giggled. "Okay. I've never made a cake from scratch in my life. Lupe told me how to do it, then stood over me to be sure I did it correctly. She was absolutely horrified because I was going to cook such a simple dinner."

"So you fixed it to appease Lupe?"

She hesitated. "I'm sorry. That doesn't sound very polite, does it?"

"You're worried about being polite to me? The evil genius who plots to destroy you?" He raised one eyebrow in exaggerated amazement.

Erica flushed and quickly bent to drop a fork into the basket in the dishwasher. She felt unbearably stupid and awkward. She wanted—oh, so desperately—to hate Tonio. Then she wouldn't have to fear loving him again and being broken on the rack of his loveless passion. But it was so *hard* to resist his charm, to continue to believe he was wicked. His constant hounding of her seemed to have had no purpose except to help her despite her rejection. Erica grabbed a dish towel to dry her hands and stood twisting it. "I'm sorry. Have I been an ogre?"

"A very pretty ogre." He brushed a finger along the line of her jaw.

Tears sprang into her eyes. "Tonio, I don't understand you! How can you be so kind, so gentle sometimes, and yet . . . ?"

"And yet what?"

She shook her head, unwilling to reveal her hurt from the past. "Nothing. I'm confused."

His hand slipped behind her neck, massaging the tightness. His voice was soothing, seductive. "Let me help you, Erica. You have too much to bear alone—a son to raise, your father's death, this farm." She raised her head and his face tightened at the sight of her tears. Putting his hands on either side of her face, he wiped away the tears with his thumbs. He wanted to ask her to give herself to him wholly, to put her heart and soul in his safekeeping, to let him shoulder her burdens, but he was afraid she might pop back into the protective shell from which she had been shyly emerging all night. Don't move too fast, an inner voice warned. Tonio forced himself to be content with asking, "Will you let me help you? If you need anything, will you call me?" She nodded mutely, feeling weak but warmed and comforted. "Good." He smiled and released her. "Now, let's join Danny outside. It's a beautiful night."

He closed the dishwasher and turned it on, then led her to the side porch and the old wooden swing. It was a warm night for January, and with her jacket on, Erica was quite comfortable outside. The stars blazed white above them, and the moon was large and round, flooding the yard with a pale light. When he heard them step outside, Danny dashed around from the front yard to greet them, then charged off, returning to his game. They settled into the swing, and Tonio curved his arm around Erica, pulling her close. His hand drifted gently downward, cupping her breast in the dark, his thumb now and then tracing a lazy circle around her nipple.

"Tonio," Erica whispered, unable to raise her voice any louder. "Your hand—Danny."

He smiled faintly. "It's dark. Besides, he's gone back to the front yard. The only harm I'm doing is driving myself wild."

"You're not the only one," she retorted without thinking, then blushed at her admission.

Tonio chuckled. "Don't tell me you're affected too." His free hand slid beneath her jacket, roaming freely in its concealment, stroking the soft curves of her body, slipping lower to caress her thighs, while the first one kept up its slow, steady caress of her nipple. His fingers were adept, creating a pulsating warmth even through her clothes. Finally he traveled up her inner thighs, to the juncture of her legs, and stopped. He held her firmly, not moving, but the heat radiating from him spread insidiously through her. Erica felt heavy and weak, malleable, yet itching, aching, for more.

"Tonio! Please." She wriggled her bottom as though to escape his trapping hand, but the movement served only to create a delicious friction. She almost gasped at the sudden pleasure. Slanting her eyes up at him naughtily, Erica smiled. "Two can play at that game, Mr. Cruz." Slowly, deliberately, her tongue edged out and traced her lips. Tonio's eyes were fixed on her, and though his expression did not change, she could feel the surge of heat in his body.

Erica looked away from him, for all the world as if she were studying the darkened yard, but her hand went to his leg and began to move up and down it, making lazy patterns on the tight cloth of his slacks. She teased with her fingertips, drawing away, then returning. Tonio groaned and took her ear in his mouth, his teeth and tongue fiercely demanding. "Oh, baby," he growled softly. "Stop. I yield. I can't take any more." He removed his hands and she shifted slightly away from him. Tonio grinned at her. "Doesn't that kid ever go to bed?"

Erica glanced at her watch, but it was too dark to read the dial. Tonio's explorations had left her mind in some never-never land of the senses, and she found it difficult to think. It was insane to succumb to him, she knew. It would mean only heartbreak for her. Yet, she wanted him so badly, longed to feel the touch of his hands on her skin. She realized despairingly that she wanted to belong to him, would not be satisfied unless she did. And Tonio? She wouldn't let herself think about what Tonio wanted. Hastily she rose and went to the edge of the porch. "Danny! Honey, it's time for bed."

"Ah, Mom," he responded with automatic disgust, but came without any further fuss. With a smiling good-night to Tonio and an unexpected hug, he bounded through the door and down the hall to the stairs. Erica turned to Tonio a little shyly. "I—uh, have to go tuck him in."

"I'll wait for you in the den," he promised, his voice rasping with suppressed desire.

Erica left without looking back and climbed the stairs to Danny's room. It seemed to take him forever to finish his bath and brush his teeth, which he usually did with lightning speed. Finally, however, wearing his crisp pajamas and smelling delicious, as only a child can, he ran into his bedroom, where Erica waited on the bed. He popped into bed and settled against his pillows for their nightly chat. "I like Tonio," he told her.

"Do you?" Erica sighed. "I do, too, I'm afraid."

"That doesn't make sense."

"Sometimes things don't."

Danny shrugged her comment aside as the vagary of an adult. "He told me he'd take me to see the hotel next weekend. Is that okay?"

"Sure." Erica carefully curbed her impatience as Danny continued to chat until she decided he had reached the stalling point in his dialogue. Then, with a firm "Good night," she rose and left the room, pulling the door to behind her. Her knees were shaking as she went down the stairs and into the den.

Chapter 12

Tonio was slumped on the couch, his hands locked behind his
head, staring up at the ceiling. Lithely he rose, his dark eyes
glowing at her. "I finally gave up trying to read your magazines."

Erica didn't know quite what to do. She didn't want to seem
too bold, but neither did she want to stall. It was time to quit
denying that she wanted him. She was fooling no one, not even
herself. Perhaps it was the absolutely wrong thing to do, but it
was inevitable that she do it. "Shall we—" Her voice squeaked
and she had to stop and try again. "Shall we go upstairs?"

He came forward without a word, extending one hand to
clasp hers. Erica was grateful that he didn't tease or gloat. She
led him up the staircase to her bedroom. He glanced around it
briefly as he closed the door behind them. It was still a teenage
girl's room. Erica had never been the frilly type, so there were
no ruffles or yards of eyelet. But there was a fresh, young
quality to the yellow curtains and patterned bedspread, a confusion and searching for style. The furniture was white French
provincial, too dainty and fussy for the adult Erica. He suspected that now she would choose strong, simple furnishings,
coordinated but not perfect, with subtle tones and shadings.

His eyes returned to Erica, who stood a little uncertainly in the middle of the room. He came forward slowly, luxuriating in the moment. "I've waited a long time for this," he told her in a soft, almost dreamy voice. He grasped the lapels of her jacket and peeled it back and off her arms. "You have no idea how I've lain awake at nights, imagining it." He tossed the jacket on a nearby chair, then started on the buttons of her blouse.

"If I live to be a million years old, I won't understand you. You're tough, brave, hardworking, vulnerable. Beautiful. Callous. Cruel. But a good mother. And a true artist in bed." He placed his hands flat on her chest above her breasts and slid them beneath her open blouse, pushing the material off her shoulders and down her arms until it fell in a crumpled heap of purple silk on the floor.

With the same slow, almost reflective gentleness, he continued to undress her, letting her other clothes join the pile at her feet. At last she stood completely naked before him, and for a long moment he simply viewed her exposed body, taking in the heavy, thrusting breasts, the nipples pointing under his gaze, the slender waist that flowed out into softly curving hips. Erica scarcely breathed, captured by his smoldering eyes. His look was as tangible as teasing fingers, setting her aflame and turning her insides to wax. She raised her hands to him and he caught them between his own, lifting them to his lips. The skin of her fingers was sensitized, alive, vibrating to the barest touch of his moist tongue, the tender nip of his teeth.

"Tonio," she breathed, and he bent to kiss her ear, her cheek, her throat and finally her mouth. His lips fitted hers naturally, satisfying a deep primitive ache within Erica. His tongue entered the moist cave of her mouth, and Erica pressed herself into him, yearning to feel him inside her, to meld into his flesh. He kissed her again and again, ardent, molten kisses that shot sparks along her nerves. Erica moaned and moved against him, pleading wordlessly for the fulfillment only he could provide.

Tonio kissed her throat, his lips sliding to the delicate, pulsing hollow at the base of her neck. Lightly his fingertips caressed the hard line of her collarbone. He bent his head, moving downward to the soft crests of her breasts, making a slow circumnavigation of each with lips and tongue. Erica curved over him, nestling her cheek against his head, nuzzling the thick black hair, kissing it, while her hands played across his back. He smelled faintly of cologne and the pungent sweat of excitement. Erica felt for the hem of his shirt and rolled it up, her fingers seeking his sleek skin.

Tonio groaned and sucked at the peaks of her breasts. The pink-brown flesh darkened with desire under his expert massage, the points swelling and hardening even more. When she thought she couldn't stand it any longer he slipped farther down her white, lustrous body until he knelt before her, his head buried in the flat plane of her abdomen. He rolled his face against her skin, tickling, arousing, demanding. Erica clutched his hair, her fingers digging heedlessly into the thick mass. Gently Tonio parted her legs, and his tongue went to work. She writhed under the delightful torture, and he gripped her buttocks with his firm hands to hold her captive to his masterfully teasing mouth.

Erica quivered, panting mindlessly, as Tonio propelled her body to the heights over and over, drawing back just as she reached the summit so he could catapult her upward yet again. Her legs felt too weak and shaky to stand, but she couldn't break away, could only trust that he wouldn't let her fall, just as she trusted that he wouldn't leave her trembling on the brink, but would at last thrust her into the shattering pleasure she craved.

His tongue was moist, silken fire, rhythmically lashing her to a higher and higher frenzy. Erica sobbed his name and his fingers dug into her hips, pressing her against the hot seal of his mouth. At last he hurled her to the zenith and glory burst in her, sending rippling waves of electric joy throughout her body. Erica twisted and jerked under the onslaught until at last it subsided. She sagged, weak with dreamy satisfaction.

Tonio released her and Erica sank into the bed, filled with sweet lassitude and a swelling tenderness. Tonio had been so kind, so giving. Erica opened her eyes to look at him. He stood beside the bed, watching her, a faint smile playing across his lips. Her eyes were wide and glowing as she studied him, her expression so speaking of love that Tonio's heart flip-flopped in his chest. He wanted to crush Erica to him. He leaned over the bed, bracing himself with his hands on either side of her relaxed form.

"No." Erica smiled, her hands going to his chest to hold him off. "Can't I serve you now?"

"Whatever you want." His voice was husky, throbbing. Erica pushed him up, rising to her feet. Slowly she unbuttoned his shirt and slipped it off his shoulders. Next her hands went to the buckle of his belt, undoing it at the same leisurely pace. She caressed his hard, flat chest, tracing his ribs and the line of hair that crept down his stomach. Her hands slid over the taut material of his slacks, exploring thigh and buttock, floating with feather lightness as she led him ever deeper into desire. She heard his sucked-in breath and smiled, glancing up to watch his face, eyes closed, skin stretched tightly across the bones, nostrils flared.

She opened the snap of his trousers and pulled down the zipper, then tugged them off his hips and down his thighs. They fell at his feet and he stepped out of them, his hands going out to draw her to him. "Not yet," she whispered. "Wouldn't you like a bath first?"

"A bath?" he repeated blankly, and she nodded, a giggle threatening to break through at his frustrated expression. Wrapping a robe around her, she led him out into the hall to the bathroom. Quickly she ran water in the tub and removed his underwear and socks, teasingly massaging and caressing as she did. He swallowed hard, obviously fighting for control, and sat down in the warm water as she instructed him. He rested his head against the rim of the tub, watching Erica as she soaped a cloth and leaned forward to bathe him. Her robe gaped open, revealing the pink-crowned globes of her breasts, her slim waist, and it was somehow more exciting to merely glimpse her riches than if she had knelt beside the tub fully naked.

With the soapy cloth she roamed his body, scrubbing, stroking, slickly arousing him, all the while her breasts jiggling tantalizingly with her movements. She didn't miss an inch of his skin, proceeding at a snail's pace to wash his hair and lather his body all over. Then, with the same precision, she rinsed him clean. By the time she finished, Tonio was flushed and bursting with desire. "Enough," he growled low in his throat. "God, Erica, I'm going to explode." He moved to get out. She pushed him back and he groaned. But before he could protest, Erica dropped her robe and stepped fluidly into the tub, sinking onto her knees astride him. Tonio swallowed, his glittering eyes intent upon her as she began to move. The water vibrated around them, repeating Erica's movements, enveloping them in a warm caress. Tonio's breath was ragged and harsh as he lay acquiescently, luxuriating in the supreme pleasure she gave him. Erica leaned forward and took his mouth and his arms went around her fiercely, his fingers digging into her sweet flesh. Their lips ground together, tongues flickering in imitation of his hard thrusts inside her, and their breath mingled. Tonio's cry was muffled as he arched, his passion engulfing them both. Then he relaxed, gulping for air, and Erica buried her face in his shoulder. It was a long time before either of them could speak. With a shaky chuckle Tonio whispered, "I never knew a bath could be quite so exciting."

She smiled, snuggling against him, eyes closed in lazy contentment. "Just takes a woman's touch," she murmured.

Erica opened her eyes, disoriented for a moment. Her head was pillowed on hard brown flesh. She remembered what had happened and closed her eyes, savoring the memories. After they had left the tub and toweled each other dry, she had massaged his muscles, warming lotion in her hands and then spreading it over his body. When she was through, Tonio had returned the favor. By then they were once again breathless with passion and had retired to bed to make love with the same wild fervor.

Smiling, Erica stretched and slid carefully out from beneath the sheets. Trying to move quietly so as not to wake Tonio, she pulled clothes from her closet and dresser, wrapped her old robe around her and tiptoed out of the room. She knocked on Danny's door to make sure he was up and getting ready for school. Then she went into the bathroom for a quick shower. As the water beat down her in a hot, hypnotic rhythm, Erica tried to put her life into perspective. But it seemed too jumbled up for that. She found that she wanted to think only about Tonio, to daydream like a schoolgirl about his face and voice, to recall everything he had said and done the night before.

She stepped out of the shower and dried off, then dressed in warm oatmeal-colored slacks and a shirt of various colors in a thin pinstripe design. She finished the ensemble with a pink pullover sweater that added a flush of color to her cheeks. After tying her long hair back with a barrette, she applied makeup, mascara and lipstick. Erica knew she was dressing better and spending more time on her makeup than usual because Tonio was there. However, she was too happy to try to fit into the rigid mold she had invented for dealing with him.

She raced lightly down the stairs, then began to make breakfast. She might as well face it, she thought. She still loved Tonio. She had vowed when she met him again not to let him come close. But she couldn't seem to keep from falling for him all over again. Or perhaps her original love had never died, but had simply remained dormant all these years. His handsome, sensitive face, his lithe body, his soul-shattering lovemaking, made her pulse with desire. Despite everything he'd done to her, he continued to hold her heart in his hand. She guessed some people just never learned.

But what if—what if Tonio had changed? He had been a young man then, probably driven by little but his sexual desire, as young men so often were. Maybe now, after years of bachelorhood, after success, maybe he was ready to settle down, ready to love and be loved in return. Certainly she had seen none of his former callousness. Of course, she reminded herself sourly, she hadn't noticed it then, either—until he had left her. Still, she couldn't stifle the bright hope suddenly glowing in her chest.

Danny dashed into the kitchen with his usual vitality and plopped down his schoolbooks and jacket. He went to the refrigerator and pulled out the makings of a sandwich. After carefully building his sandwich, he slid it into a plastic bag and sealed it. Then he returned to the refrigerator and dug in the crisper drawer. "Mom, do you think this apple's okay?" he questioned, holding it up and studying it dubiously. "The last one I got was all brown and icky inside."

"I just got them a couple of days ago," Erica replied absently. "They should be all right."

"I think I'll take a tangerine," he decided, and dropped the apple into the drawer with a solid plunk.

"That's probably the way your last apple got 'all brown and icky inside.'" Tonio commented from the doorway. "From your shooting baskets with it."

Danny whirled to stare at the man lounging gracefully in the doorway, and his mouth dropped open. Erica turned from the stove, a crazy mixture of shyness and excitement boiling inside her. Tonio smiled across the room at her, and her heart set up an idiotic pounding. She loved him so much. Oh, please, she thought prayerfully, this time don't let it end badly.

Her son let out a yelp and rushed to greet Tonio. Tonio swung him up in the air and Danny shrieked with happiness. Watching them, Erica felt a lump form in her throat. They looked so good together, so right. When Tonio set him down, Danny danced excitedly from one foot to the other. "I didn't know you were here!"

Erica flushed and turned back to the stove. It was an awkward situation, to say the least, one she hadn't really considered. How was she to explain Tonio's presence?

"Did you spend the night here so you wouldn't have to walk home?" Danny went on innocently.

"Uh, yeah, something like that." Tonio glanced over at Erica. He wanted to go to her and kiss her, but he didn't know how she'd react to that in front of Danny, particularly after the child's question. He wondered why Danny so easily accepted his sleeping over. Was it simply the natural innocence of a child interpreting a situation according to his world? Or was it because Danny was used to men staying with Erica? Tonio's eyes darkened with jealousy.

"Okay, Danny, you better sit down and eat your food. Would you like something, Tonio?"

His warm glance told her exactly what he'd like, but he answered mundanely, "Eggs and toast are fine, thank you."

Her knees watery, Erica turned back to the stove to cook an omelet. It was one thing she knew how to cook fairly well, and she felt the need to counter the poor impression she had given the night before. Danny chattered as he ate, now and then laughing at some remark of Tonio's. Erica paid little attention, so she didn't see when Tonio, gazing at the boy, suddenly frowned.

There was something familiar about Danny, he thought. It had just occurred to him when Danny smiled. There was something sweet and charming about the way his dimple bounced in and out that looked like . . . Lucio. His heart began to pound in huge thuds. No! Erica's lover couldn't have been his brother.

But why not? Lucio hadn't know about Tonio and Erica until a few weeks ago. He wouldn't have known he was making love to the woman his brother loved. And when Tonio had told him about his affair with Erica, Lucio wouldn't have told him, not wanting to hurt him. No, no, it couldn't be. Lucio wouldn't have been so crazy as to leave a woman like Erica. He pushed the thought away, but it returned, wiping out all the elation he had felt that morning.

"Danny, you better hurry or you'll miss your bus," Erica warned as she set the omelet down in front of Tonio. Danny groaned comically, but picked up his lunch pail and books and hustled out of the house. Erica sat down across the table from Tonio and an awkward silence fell over them.

Tonio found himself suddenly without appetite, and though the cheese and mushroom omelet was delicious, he could only toy with it. The jealous thought of Lucio with Erica was driving everything else from his mind. He cleared his throat, knowing he shouldn't start this conversation, yet somehow unable to stop himself. "Erica, Danny's father . . ."

Erica stiffened. "Yes?"

"Who is he?"

She swallowed, fear and pride battling with her softened feelings for Tonio. She couldn't tell him. At least not yet, when she wasn't sure how he felt about her. "Please, let's not discuss this right now."

"Was he Hispanic too?"

"Why does it matter?" Erica asked fiercely.

"Because I want to know what son of—" he began in a low, explosive voice, then broke off abruptly.

"What? Handled your property?" Erica jumped up, anger surging in her. "God save me from the Latin ego! Or is it simply the male ego?"

Tonio's nostrils flared and color flamed in his cheeks. He rose to face her. "I'm sorry if the 'Latin ego' is such a trial to you. Does it cramp your style that he demands fidelity from his woman?"

"Fidelity! That's a laugh, coming from you. And I am not your woman! I don't have to answer to you."

"You *were* my woman. And last night—" He closed his eyes, visibly controlling his emotions. When he opened them again, his face was cold, expressionless, the fury drained from it. "I'm sorry. I have no rights over you."

"Well, I'm glad to hear you admit it," Erica retorted, feeling no triumph at all.

"Just tell me one thing. I have to know. Once you said something about sharing women with my brother. You said you were speaking of Diane. But—is he Lucio's? Did you sleep with my brother?"

Erica stared, then burst into almost hysterical laughter. "Lucio's! You think I'd go after your brother because I couldn't have you? Of all the obtuse, stupid . . . can't you even see what's right under your nose?" She stopped and sucked in her lower lip, fear springing into her eyes. She'd gone too far.

Tonio gaped, his face going slack; then light dawned in his eyes. "You mean . . . *Dios!* Danny is *my* son?"

Erica's frozen face was answer enough to Tonio's question. She clasped her hands tightly together, frightened of the storm about to burst around her head.

"You bore my son and didn't even tell me? For nine months you carried him in your belly and didn't bother to inform me? My God, what kind of mother are you, that you would allow your own son to be born illegitimate rather than let me know!"

Erica whitened under his attack. His rage was fierce and vicious. She had never seen him like this. She took a cautious step backward. He followed her, his lithe movements fearfully similar to those of a jungle cat. His fingers dug into her shoulders, and she could feel the sizzling current of anger surging through him. He backed her against the wall, his black eyes boring into hers. "It would give me great pleasure to snap that lovely neck of yours. You arrogant, heartless bitch! You kept me from my son, stole his childhood from me—and deprived him of a father. How deep is your selfishness? I'd told myself that the vanity and spoiled behavior were things of the past, yet even now you've refused to reveal his identity to me. Why, Erica? Did it give you some kind of kick to see me with him, unaware of our relationship?''

Erica swallowed and struggled to summon up a false front of bravery. ''I never dreamed you'd care.''

''Not care!'' he thundered. ''My son, and you think I wouldn't want to know? You'll have to come up with something better than that. What's the real reason? Was the idea of marrying me too awful, even to give a name to your boy? No doubt you didn't think Cruz a good enough name for him. Better to have a bastard Logan than a legitimate Cruz.'' He laughed bitterly. ''I knew you were ashamed of me, even when you moaned in my arms and begged me to love you, but I didn't realize you thought that little of me. Even if you wouldn't marry me, at least you could have let me know I had a child. I could have seen him, held him. But then, I suppose I wasn't worth considering, was I?''

''How could I let you know?'' Erica cried, goaded past fear by his unfairness. ''You ran away and I didn't have the slightest idea where you lived! I'd have given anything to keep Danny from being illegitimate, even married you.''

He snorted. ''Then I guess the joke was on you for sending me away.''

''What? How can you say that? What warped reasoning did you use to arrive at that conclusion?''

His lips curled into a sneer. ''Erica, I was there. I remember what happened. I'm not some stranger you can fabricate a romantic story for.''

''No, there really wasn't any romance, was there?'' Erica replied coldly. ''And you're right, I wouldn't have married you. I could have found you if I'd tried. I knew you'd gone to Houston. I even remembered the name of the firm you worked for. But I wasn't about to debase myself that way, to go to you and beg for a wedding ring.''

''Heavens, no,'' he mocked. ''Such degradation, to marry me.''

''You're very good at twisting everything I say. But there's no way to misinterpret this: I didn't come to you because I hated you with every fiber of my being.'' She half turned from him. ''I think you'd better leave.''

There was a moment of silence, then he agreed coldly, "Yes, you're right." His lids fluttered down to mask the pain in his eyes. He strode rapidly along the hall, turned down the intersecting hallway to the front door and walked out, closing the door behind him with a solid click.

Erica wrapped her arms tightly around herself, forcing back the sobs boiling inside. Mechanically she placed one foot in front of the other and walked into the study. Closing the door behind her, she looked around almost blankly. Her mind seemed unable to focus on what she should do. There were so many things that needed her attention. She knew she ought to buckle down and get to them. Personal pain would have to wait. Immersing herself in her work would help ease it. She'd had plenty of experience in that.

She walked over to the desk and sat down, picking up a file with trembling fingers. Then a bleak wave of memory engulfed her. She wouldn't see Tonio again, at least not in a loving way. It was as if her life had ended once more. The only difference between the love she felt for him now and the love she had known as a teenager, she realized, was that now the hurt was even worse. She crossed her arms on her desk and laid her head on them, and no longer fought her tears.

Chapter 13

The next morning, as Erica sat in her study, trying to work on the farm's books, there was a sharp, peremptory knock on the side door. She went to open it and was taken aback to find Tonio outside. She stared, unable to find anything to say after their bitter parting the day before. His face was cold and tight, his eyes hard marbles, and when he spoke, his words were clipped. "Erica, I didn't give you your check yesterday."

He extended a small piece of paper. Erica had a momentary urge to fling it back in his face, but she resisted. No, she was determined not to be emotional. The relationship between them now would be strictly business. She must remember that. She reached out and took it, saying coolly, "I have the note and deed of trust in my office. Let me sign them and give them to you."

For a moment Tonio hesitated, then gave a brief nod and stepped inside. Erica realized with a flash of hurt that he was reluctant to even come under her roof. Resentment helped her walk into the study, pull the papers from her desk drawer and sign them. She handed them to Tonio without a word, and he received them in the same chill silence. Erica's stomach curled and she folded the check nervously.

Tonio started toward the door, then paused. "By the way, I'd like to take Danny to the island with me this Saturday."

He hadn't really asked permission, but Erica gave it anyway. She must not let him assume rights to her son. "Yes, Danny told me. It's all right with me. It'll be good for him to have male companionship."

Tonio's mouth twisted. "It's too bad you didn't think of that nine years ago." He swung and stalked through the door, taking the porch steps in a single stride and hurrying away across the yard. Erica shut the door, her spirits sagging even lower, if that was possible. Returning to her study, she laid the check on the desk and pulled out a deposit slip. Why was it that Tonio was so willing to give her financial help, yet tried so hard to break her emotionally?

Erica saw nothing more of Tonio until he came on Saturday morning to pick up Danny for their trip. Danny had barely been able to contain his excitement, and after breakfast he sat by the front window, watching for Tonio. As Erica was washing the morning dishes, she heard her son shout, "Here he is!"

Erica dried her hands and strolled down the hall, her heart knocking against her ribs. The front door was open. Danny was bounding down the steps and racing across the yard. When he reached Tonio, Tonio swung the boy high in the air, his impassive face suddenly radiant. He continued walking to the front porch, carrying Danny on one hip, Danny's legs twined around his waist. Erica swallowed the tears that sprang to her eyes at the sight of her son's shining face.

"Can I go now, Mom?" Danny asked.

Erica smiled. "Of course. But get a jacket. The sea breeze can be pretty cool."

"Okay," he agreed readily and darted up the stairs.

Erica glanced back at Tonio. He had remained on the porch. He still hated to enter her tainted house, she thought bitterly. "Please don't bring him home too late," Erica said stiffly.

Tonio agreed with an abrupt nod. Erica didn't know what to do. It seemed rude to walk away, yet he obviously hated to be near her. It was a relief when Danny came pounding back down the stairs. Erica bent to give him a kiss. "Have fun."

"I will." Danny skipped out the door and jumped off the porch, his enthusiasm causing him to run around in circles before he ran to the passenger side of the car. Tonio followed him without looking back or speaking to Erica.

She closed the door, biting her lips to repress the tears. She was simply *not* going to cry over Tonio Cruz anymore! Erica returned to the kitchen and finished the dishes without enthusiasm. Somehow she managed to stumble through the lonely day. The hours dragged, and she missed Danny as she hadn't done since he was a baby. She refused to admit that her loneliness was tinged with jealousy that Tonio hadn't asked her along on the outing.

She tried to work, but found she couldn't keep her mind on it, so finally she decided to give herself a treat and take the day off. She started to call Judy Miller, but realized that Saturday would probably be a day she'd prefer to spend with her family. After a few more minutes of restless pacing, Erica decided to drive into town and do some window-shopping. When she passed the furniture store that the Roberts family owned, she recalled Jeff's offer of a cup of coffee and a visit whenever she was in town. Impulsively she decided to take him up on it.

Walking straight back through the store, she found Jeff hunched over a desk in a tiny cubicle. She knocked lightly. He glanced up and a smile spread across his face. "Erica! I was beginning to think you were avoiding me."

Erica smiled and shook her head. "Just too much work."

"Same here. Well, come on in, sit down. I apologize for the surroundings. Could I get you a cup of coffee?"

Erica agreed, glad she had decided to come in. He brought her a cup of bitter coffee and they chatted for a few minutes. He was obviously lonely in this small town, where so few of his friends still lived. And he was just as obviously not interested in her romantically, but merely looking for friendship, living with a postdivorce fear of intimacy. When she rose to leave, he looked disappointed and suggested that they continue their talk later over dinner in McAllen.

Erica hesitated. She had no desire to spend the evening alone, but she didn't want to be away from home when Tonio returned with Danny. "Why don't I fix supper?" she compromised. Jeff agreed readily, pleased at the idea of home-cooking.

She stopped by the aging food store on her way out of town and
strolled along the aisles, her mind running over the problem of
which of her limited repertoire of dishes she should prepare.
She paused at the steak counter. That was easiest, but she was
suddenly seized with the distinct desire not to have Jeff Roberts grilling their steaks. Hastily she grabbed a package of
chicken.

When Jeff arrived, they ate and talked companionably. Jeff
wolfed down the simple chicken-in-wine dish she had cooked,
praising it as if it were the finest cuisine. They ate in the kitchen,
stacked the dishes in the sink and left them there while they retired to the den to talk. Erica did her best to stifle comparisons
to her meal with Tonio, but she met them at every turn. She remembered their shared amusement over her drinks, the quiet
competent way Tonio had taken charge of the meal, the tenderly sensual love play in the kitchen that had left her weak and
molten.

She kept one eye on the clock, a fear so horrifying she
couldn't admit it swelling within her. It was late, and still they
hadn't arrived. Didn't Tonio know that Danny needed his rest?
It was a petty anxiety, unworthy of the fear, but beneath it lay
a larger, more basic terror: What if Tonio didn't bring Danny
home at all? When at last the front door opened, then
slammed, and Danny's familiar steps bounded down the hall,
Erica released a pent-up sigh of relief.

"Mama, you should have seen it," he called, rounding the
corner boisterously. He skidded to a halt at the sight of a
stranger in the den.

Erica smiled and enveloped him in a hug. Danny shrugged
her away boyishly. "Danny, this is an old friend of mine, Jeff
Roberts."

Danny's loud entrance had covered the sound of footsteps
behind him, but now Tonio entered the room, his hair ruffled
from the day spent outdoors. He wore soft denim trousers,
boots and a light-blue T-shirt, with a navy-blue Windbreaker
thrown over it. His face was softer than it had been that morning, his dark eyes content, and he looked so good, so relaxed
that Erica had to fight a sudden urge to go to him and curl her
arms around his neck. Tonio glanced at her; then his gaze
moved across the room to Jeff. His face tightened, the pleas-

ant glow vanishing. "Hello, Erica. Jeff." He nodded briefly at the other man.

Jeff rose, his face as stiff as Tonio's. It occurred to Erica that it must be awkward for Jeff to have to meet Lucio's brother. "Hello, Tonio."

Tonio's obsidian eyes slid back to Erica. "Sorry if I'm interrupting anything." His tone implied the opposite of his words.

"It's all right," Jeff hastened to assure him. "Erica and I were just talking, old-friends kind of stuff."

"Yes, you two go back a long way, don't you?"

"Yeah, since grade school, I guess," Jeff replied, either not hearing or choosing to ignore the underlying sarcasm.

Danny, tired of holding back his story, jumped into the moment of silence. "Mom, you should have seen the hotel. It doesn't look the same at all!" He went on to describe the new construction with great enthusiasm and detail. When he finally wound down a little, Jeff interposed quickly that it was time for him to go.

Erica walked him to the door politely, conscious all the time of Tonio's watchful gaze on her back. He even trailed them into the hall like a stern parent. Erica was tempted to kiss Jeff just to show Tonio, but she didn't want to scare the poor guy. When he had gone, she closed the door and marched purposefully to the den. Tonio had discarded his Windbreaker. He stood waiting for her, arms crossed, his face glowering. Danny had flopped down on the couch on his stomach, chattering away to the oblivious Tonio.

"Danny," Erica began as she walked in, "it's past your bedtime. He's used to going to bed at nine o'clock, Tonio."

"I'll remember that," he returned dryly.

"Run upstairs, brush your teeth and hop into bed," she commanded Danny, and after only a token protest he obeyed her. Erica swung back to Tonio. "Exactly what do you think you're doing, coming in here and glaring at my guest as if he were an intruder? And following me out into the hall to watch us! What's the matter with you? Your relationship to Danny gives you no rights over me, you know."

"I'm fully aware of that. How can I not be, when you're so cozy with me one day and Jeff Roberts a few days later?"

Her cheeks blazed. "How dare you imply that I—that I was sleeping with him!"

He raised one eyebrow. "You're hardly a nun."

"I never professed to be. But neither am I a slut. Even if I were, it's none of *your* business!"

His well-cut nostrils flared. "Perhaps not. But Danny is my business. I want him with me."

"No!" The adrenaline of terror coursed through her. It was happening, what she had feared most; Tonio wanted to take Danny from her. "Absolutely not. You have no rights to him."

"I'm his father! What more do you need?" His brows contracted. "You've kept him from me for nine years, but no longer. I intend to be a father to Danny now."

"He thinks his father is dead. It's better that way. Danny believes him to be a hero, someone larger than life. I won't let you spoil that."

"He needs an actual father a lot more than he needs a bunch of wild dreams. Erica, I want to tell Danny I'm his father."

"No!"

"I deserve at least that much."

"You deserve nothing!" she spat at him. "Nothing! I am not going to tell Danny that you're his father. It would be far too upsetting and to no purpose. You'd probably be interested in him for a few weeks, while it's still a novel experience being a father, but when you got bored you'd drop him too. I won't let my son be hurt that way." Everything inside her screamed that she would protect Danny from him, even though she was incapable of protecting herself. "I won't allow you to see him anymore."

"You won't allow it?" he repeated sarcastically. "I'm sorry, my dear, but you won't have anything to say about it. I'll go to court to get my rights established." His face was as still and cold as a glacier. "He is *my* son and I want to be with him. I'll never drop Danny. You don't know a damn thing about me and never did."

Erica paled. "You aren't serious, are you? Surely you wouldn't expose yourself to the embarrassment of going to court."

"Watch me."

"Well, you can't prove Danny is your son. Only my testimony will do that. I'll say he's not yours. I'd claim a relationship with every man in town before I'd let you take Danny."

His upper lip curled. "I'll recite in detail every time we made love, where we met, what we did. I can describe it all perfectly, right down to the color blouse you wore."

"I'll deny it." Her voice rose hysterically. "I'll say that at the same time I was sleeping with Jeff Roberts or Bill Cunningham. Chuck Wilson. Any- and everybody, whenever you weren't there."

His face was taut and blank, a skull with skin stretched over it. His eyes glittered ferally. "Are you really the kind of mother who would do that to her son? You don't deserve to have him." He turned on his heel and stalked from the room.

Erica raised trembling hands to her face. He was right, of course. She wouldn't do any of the things she had threatened. Of course, a court usually gave custody to a mother. Surely, if the parents weren't married, they would be even more likely to do so. But Tonio had money and could hire a stupendous attorney. He could have all kinds of evidence manufactured so that it would appear that she was having affairs with several men, that she wasn't a fit mother.

She wrapped her arms around her body, choking back the tears. Oh, God, he couldn't do that. But then, she had no idea what Tonio might be capable of in order to get what he wanted. He hated her for not informing him of Danny's birth. As if she should have realized that he would want to see his illegitimate son when he didn't care about the mother. Tears battered at her eyelids. It was all too much: the farm, the work, her father's death, the need to mother Danny, the pressure Tonio had put on her to sleep with him, then his abrupt rejection when he found out about Danny. This was the final straw. What if he managed to take Danny from her? How would she live?

She stared at the dark-blue jacket he had taken off and discarded on the couch, gulping down the sobs tearing at her throat. Tonio... how could he do this to her? How could she stop him? She must. She must. Erica knew she was allowing her fears to run away with her. She was hysterical. She cautioned herself to be calm, but it was as if a violent storm hammered at her, sweeping away all rationality. Fear controlled her, drove her.

Suddenly she grabbed the Windbreaker and ran to the front door. Tonio was out of sight. She pelted down the sidewalk to the drive. Far ahead of her, Erica could see his slim, straight figure, and she ran after him, not daring to call out lest Danny hear and come down to investigate. Her breath was rasping in her throat, joining the unshed tears in ripping it to rawness. Tonio whirled at the sound of her frantic approach, frowning when he saw it was she. She slowed to a halt and approached warily, holding out his jacket as if it were a peace offering. "You left this."

He almost jerked it from her grasp. "You ran after me to give me this?"

"No. I—I—" She drew in a deep breath, fighting for control. In a low voice she continued, "Tonio, I came to ask you—beg you—not to do this. Danny loves me; he's happy with me. He's all I have." The panic was rising now, taking over her voice, cracking it with sobs. "Oh, God, Tonio, don't take him away. Please! Please! I'll do anything, sell you the farm if you want. Anything. But don't take Danny from me. Don't put him through a custody hearing."

Tonio stared at her for a long moment, his face unreadable in the dim light of the half-moon. When he spoke his voice was laced with anger. "Is that what you think of me? That I would jerk my son from the only parent he's known for ten years and force him to live with me? Do you think I'm so cruel, so unfeeling?" He shook his head and ran a hand through his hair, sighing.

"I don't know what you are. I only know what you said."

"I said I want my rights to my son. I want to visit him, to see him, to be able to take him out as I did today. The kind of thing a divorced father does. I never meant to steal him from you. That was your warped idea."

Tears of relief suddenly gushed from her eyes. "I'm sorry. I'm so mixed up. It's all so crazy. You've been so—so *hard* about Danny."

"Lord, Erica, what did you expect me to be? Happy? I was so low in your eyes, you wouldn't even let me know I had a son."

"Well, of course you were low in my eyes!" she lashed back, stung by his words. "What else could you have been after you deserted me? I was only seventeen, Tonio!"

"You have a very convenient memory. If you'll recall, you were the one who gave me my walking papers. I didn't leave you."

Erica stared. "Do you actually believe that? Have you managed to mentally change what really happened in order to justify yourself?"

"Change! What are you talking about? Ten years ago you tricked me into thinking you loved me, then dropped me flat. I wanted to die. Didn't you realize how it would kill me, having Grant tell me you didn't really love me, that you didn't want to see me anymore, not even facing me yourself. Or did you just not care how much pain you caused me?"

"What are you talking about?" Erica almost shrieked, fear suddenly seizing her stomach. "I never asked Daddy to tell you anything. He didn't know about us. I kept it a secret from him. That's why I sneaked out every night to meet you. Do you think after all that I would have told him?"

"But you did," he argued, confused. "You asked him to get rid of me for you. You didn't have the guts to do it yourself."

"I just told you! I never let Daddy know about us. I certainly didn't ask him to talk to you. Where did you get such a crazy idea?"

"He *told* me! He drove to my house one afternoon and called me out to the car. He said you'd informed him about us because you were tired of me. You didn't want to see me again, so he had come to warn me off."

"You're lying."

His eyes flashed. "Damn it, I'm not lying! Why should I lie? Would I make up something like that just to tear my heart out? Believe me, I'm not in the habit of inventing conversations to destroy my world."

"Oh, my God," Erica whispered. Suddenly the world seemed distorted, unfamiliar. Her mind went to her father's words on his deathbed. He had mentioned Tonio, then in fragmented sentences had said that he never knew and that he was sorry. She had assumed that his mind was wandering, that he was talking about Danny. Had he meant he was sorry for lying to Tonio and breaking up their romance?

Tonio watched her, concerned. She had paled, and her eyes were huge and staring, her lips colorless. What was the matter? What was she doing? Why insist she hadn't told her father about them when he knew it wasn't true? He strode to her and gripped her arms firmly. "Erica, for God's sake, tell me what's wrong. Do you swear you didn't send him that afternoon? Did Grant lie to me?"

Tears formed in her eyes. "If he said I'd told him about us and sent him to get rid of you, yes, he lied. I never breathed a word about you, even after I discovered I was pregnant." She uttered a brief, mirthless laugh. "No wonder he didn't question me about the father. He knew all along it was you."

Tonio's hands trembled on her arms. The truth was staring him in the face, but it was too awful to accept. He whirled away violently. "But I went to your house that night, and he was right. He said you were going out with Jeff Roberts, and you did." He faced her, searching her features for the truth. "Grant told me you had been dating Anglo boys all the time you were sleeping with me. He said you were ashamed of me, wouldn't be seen in public with me. You'd never marry me because I was a Mexican. You'd love and marry only an Anglo."

"That's not true!" Erica cried. "How could you believe it? I'd just told you the night before how much I loved you. Didn't you have any faith in me?"

"Oh, yeah, I had faith in you. I told Grant it wasn't true, that he was lying. I was going to ask you to marry me. But he said he could prove it. Jeff Roberts would be there that evening to pick you up for a date. You were going out, as always, with an Anglo. So I went to your house and, sure enough, there was Roberts."

"I had made that date with him weeks and weeks before. I didn't think it was fair to break it at the last minute. It was a big dance at the club, one of those times when it was important to have a date. I'd promised to go with him before anything happened between us. I didn't feel I should back out. That's all. I had no interest in Jeff Roberts. I was bored stiff all evening and kept wishing I was with you. Except for that one time, I didn't date anyone from the moment I saw you. I wasn't ashamed of you. I loved you, and I'd have dated you publicly, but I was underage, and I knew Daddy wouldn't approve. Sneaking out was the only way I could continue to see you until I reached eighteen. I hoped that after you went to Houston and became an architect, Daddy wouldn't object any longer, that he'd regard you as something besides one of his workers. Then we could have brought it out in the open. But you disappeared. I waited and waited for you at the old house. I was worried something had happened to you. Finally I worked up the courage to ask Daddy about you. He said you'd left town. I couldn't believe you didn't love me, that you'd deserted me. But eventually I had to. I couldn't continue to fool myself. Then I found out I was pregnant. Is it any wonder I didn't seek you out in Houston to let you know? I was too proud. And I hated you, despised you, for deserting me.''

Tonio backed away, the full horror of her words creeping through him. "No, Erica. No. I didn't know. I thought—I thought you didn't love me, that you were playing with me. I loved you.''

"Then why did you believe my father?" Erica lashed out. Rage was boiling in her now, rage for all the wasted years, the heartache, the loneliness. "Why did you take his word over mine? I'd said I loved you only the night before, yet when he came to you, you automatically assumed that he was telling the truth and I was lying!''

"I told you, I saw you with Jeff and I thought—''

"The worst, naturally," Erica finished with contempt. "It's what you always thought of me. You must have been so pleased to have your doubts confirmed. You *wanted* to cast me as the villainess.''

"That's not true. I loved you," he retorted.

"Oh, yeah, sure. You loved me," she mocked. "No doubt that's why you assumed I was running around on you. You could have asked me, you know! You could have told me what Daddy said. Why didn't you say, 'Erica, I love you and want to marry you. Will you marry me? Do you love me too? Or is what your father said true?' I could have shown you it was all a lie. But no, you were so anxious to think I was a cruel, conniving bitch, so eager to believe I didn't love you, that you lit out without a word to me. What did you care if I suffered? All you worried about was *you!* Because I was an Anglo, I was constantly under suspicion. I had to prove myself over and over, and it still wasn't enough.''

Tonio sighed and shoved his hands through his thick hair. Erica made a sound of disgust at his silence and whirled away. "You threw away both our lives, I can't forgive that. I'm going home. Don't call me. Don't come by. Just leave me alone!''

Chapter 14

Erica hardly slept that night, tossing and turning in her bed, bombarded by the conflicting emotions. She was swept with incredulous horror and a deep, bitter regret when she thought about the mistake. It seemed such a shattering waste of time, such bleak, unnecessary pain. And she burned with rage that Tonio had condemned her without even hearing her side of the story. He hadn't had a speck of trust. There could never be anything between them if he mistrusted her so.

Then she would stop and ask herself why she would consider anything between them. She didn't know if Tonio loved her now. A lot of time had passed. They were changed people. It wasn't simply a matter of picking up where they had left off. Yet, a thrill raced through her when she thought that Tonio had loved her and hadn't purposely deserted her. He still wanted her. He loved Danny. His love might rekindle easily.

In this manner she passed the middle hours of the night, dropping to sleep just before dawn. She awoke late and dragged herself downstairs. The sleep hadn't improved her mind, she found. She struggled to get some work done and finally gave it up to play with Danny, but she couldn't keep her mind on that, either. She teetered between highs and lows, loving Tonio, filled to bursting with the knowledge of his past love, then furious with him and certain nothing could ever be worked out.

Late in the afternoon Danny decided to visit Tonio. Erica waited impatiently for his return. When he came back a couple of hours later, she tried to maintain a casual air as she asked about Tonio. When Danny told her that Tonio had packed a bag and left for Houston, her breath caught painfully in her throat. Tonio was gone. True, she hadn't wanted to see him. She was in too much turmoil to face him. But a small voice within her cried: She hadn't meant for him to leave completely! What if he didn't return? If he didn't, it was all her fault, because she had sent him away.

His departure jolted Erica from her confused, angry state. She realized how much she loved him and how foolish she had been to lash out at him when she discovered her father's treachery. In the first fraction of an instant when it had dawned on her what had happened, she had been shaken by a hatred of Grant and of herself, hatred that she immediately transferred to Tonio. Tonio had been at fault, certainly, for not talking to her, but she had been to blame too. She had been stupid not to realize that her father had probably found out about her affair with Tonio. The glow of love must have shown plainly in her youthful countenance. Grant's lack of interest in the identity of Danny's father would have given her a clue, if she hadn't been thinking only of herself. But she had been blind and willful and proud.

Looking back on it, Erica could see how her flirtatious pursuit of Tonio would have encouraged him to think her vain and heartless. She hadn't given her love to him freely, but had tried to lure him into extending his love first. And when Tonio had left without a word, she could have written or called him to find out why he had left so abruptly after declaring his love. But her pride had held her back. Her pride, as much as his mistrust, had kept them apart.

Though the events and the years in between had been painful, Erica knew they had been valuable too. She had been too immature at seventeen to handle the problems and responsibilities of love. The heartbreak and her struggle to raise Danny by herself had forced her to grow up, developed her into a thinking, caring person. If she had gotten Tonio as easily as she had everything else in her life, Erica suspected she might have wrecked their marriage with her selfish, willful ways. Now she was mature, and so was Tonio. They had borne their troubles and learned to conquer them. They would be more careful this time to nurture their love. So the pain and years apart had not been merely a devastating waste. It wasn't often a person learned from his or her mistakes and then was given a second chance to try out the new knowledge. She would tell Tonio so and apologize for her anger when he returned—*if* he returned.

But before that she would make a start on correcting the past by talking to her son. On Monday after supper Erica joined Danny in the den. He lay crosswise on an old easy chair, his heels drumming a soft tattoo on the side as he read a children's mystery book. Erica sat down on the couch across from him, her hands placed nervously on her knees. Where did one start with a story like this? "Danny, I—uh, I need to talk to you."

He let the book flop down and raised his eyes to hers, startled by the seriousness of her tone. "About what?"

"Well, about telling stories." His forehead wrinkled in a puzzled frown. "See, I've been telling you stories about your father for years, things that weren't true. I did it with the best intentions. I wanted you to love him, even though you'd never seen him. I wanted you to think he loved you and had been forced to leave you."

Danny cocked his head, hurt beginning to show in his eyes. "And that's not true?"

"Not exactly. He does love you, and I'm sure he would have loved you all these years, but he didn't know you were alive. Now that he knows, he loves you very much. A couple of days ago I found out that my father lied to me because he wanted what he thought was best for me. But it was the worst possible thing he could have done. So I decided that no matter what happens, I need to tell you the truth." She drew a long breath as though about to plunge into cold water. "Danny, Tonio is your father."

For a moment he stared at her, then jumped up to throw himself into her arms and launch into a joyful babble of questions. Erica laughed and hugged him. "If you'll calm down enough to let me get a word in edgewise, I'll tell you." She related the story of her youthful love for Tonio and of Grant's deception. Wide-eyed, Danny took it all in, and at the end let out a shrill yelp.

"I'm glad," he told her earnestly. "It's nice my dad turned out to be Tonio. It'd be terrible if he'd been a real jerk, wouldn't it? Some dads are, you know."

"I know," she agreed, smiling.

"Now he'll be around a lot, won't he? Will he move in with us? Or will we go down to his house? Do you think we'll move to Houston with him?"

Erica tensed. "Danny," she began cautiously, "we might not live with Tonio. Not all fathers and mothers live together."

"I know. They don't when they're divorced," he replied knowledgeably. "But you and Tonio will, won't you? I mean, you still love him, don't you?"

"Yes."

"Then what's the problem?" He backed off, a new thought obviously occurring to him. "He's not already married to somebody else, is he?"

"No, I don't think so." Erica hid a grin. Danny was such a funny, charming mixture of innocence and sophistication. "But, darling, sometimes after such a long separation two people don't click anymore. They don't feel the same way. People change a lot in ten years."

"But Tonio likes you. I can tell," Danny argued.

Erica smiled and teased softly, "Mr. Know-it-all strikes again."

"Well, he does. Besides, even if he didn't, you could get him to," Danny assured her confidently.

"Danny, I can't make Tonio love me. He went to Houston the other day without saying a word to me, and I'm afraid that means he doesn't want to see me anymore."

"Why don't you ask him?"

"I couldn't..." Erica stopped short. She was doing it again: assuming what Tonio thought or felt, interpreting his actions without checking them out. Why shouldn't she call Tonio, as Danny suggested? Better yet, she could visit him and talk it out face-to-face. She'd take off work tomorrow and fly to Houston. The worst that could happen would be that he'd tell her he wasn't interested anymore. It might be embarrassing and painful, but this time she wasn't about to stand back and lose her chance for a happy, loving relationship. Her pride had already cost her too much.

With that firm resolve she made a reservation on a morning flight from Harlingen and went to bed early. Her sleep that night was undisturbed, and she awoke the next morning refreshed and in bubbling spirits. Tackling life head-on was so much better than sitting around, waiting for things to happen to you. She switched on her radio as she dressed, humming merrily along.

A weather announcement came on and the nasal voice of the weather-service spokesman drew her up short. An unexpected cold front was moving toward the valley and a freeze warning was in effect for that night. Erica slumped onto her bed and listened despairingly. A freeze was one of the worst things that could happen to a citrus farm. Although much of her crop for the year was already harvested, the freeze would damage the remaining crop and, far worse, would hurt the trees, affecting future crops. With a sigh Erica stood up and began to skin off the clothes she had just put on and replaced them with worn, warm clothing. There was no question of her going to Tonio now. She had to help prepare the groves for a hard freeze.

After a quick breakfast with Danny, she walked out to the equipment shed, where her foreman and crew were loading heaters onto the backs of several pickup trucks. Rafael called to her, "Did you hear?"

"Yeah," she responded glumly. "They're predicting it will drop to nineteen degrees."

Rafael shook his head sadly. "It could hurt. We don't have enough heaters for the whole grove. We'll have to protect just the best trees." Freezes were rare in the valley, which made it economically unfeasible to provide much cold protection for the trees.

Erica donned thick work gloves to protect her hands and helped the men lift the tall, cylindrical heaters onto the pickup. When they were all loaded, she drove the farm's truck to the groves while Rafael drove his own truck also loaded with heaters. When they reached the groves, they placed the heaters in niches between the trees. The hedgerow planting of the trees would help keep the heat in and protect them. Erica's arms soon ached from pulling the metal heaters and from controlling the steering wheel of the pickup as she sped over the bumpy earth. However, she couldn't stop to rest, for the temperature was dropping fast. By noon a wind had sprung up and the cold sliced through her jeans and flannel shirt and jacket. Inside her boots and heavy gloves her hands and feet were numb.

Shortly after one she drove the truck back to the shed for another load. She parked and leaped out, followed by two workers. Glancing across the yard, she stopped, her heart suddenly pounding. Tonio was loping up the driveway. He was dressed in old jeans, a flannel shirt and down vest, and was pulling on a pair of work gloves as he came. Erica bit her lower lip, her worries about the freeze vanishing at the sight of Tonio. She wondered why he had returned and what she would say to him in front of the men. She turned quickly and disappeared into the shed. Tonio followed and took a firm grip on the heater beside her.

"Thought you could use some help," he told her shortly.

"Yes, thank you." What else could she say? The urgency of the situation overshadowed their personal problems. They worked side-by-side, silently and quickly. By four o'clock Erica was dragging with exhaustion and chilled to the bone. When they returned to the yard, Tonio grasped her firmly by the shoulders and propelled her toward the house.

"You're through for the day."

"I'm not tired. We aren't finished yet," Erica protested.

"*You* are." His voice was firm and final. "No matter what your inflated opinion of yourself, you are not capable of doing a man's share of manual labor." Erica started to argue, but he plowed on. "Isn't it possible for you to simply shut your mouth and do as you're told?"

"You have no right to tell me what to do. It's my farm and I intend to see this through to the bitter end."

"I have every right," he replied, and the look in his eyes warmed her even in the brisk cold. But he explained prosaically, "I loaned you the money and have a lien on your farm, remember? I have a vested interest in it. Besides, I'm more experienced than you. Don't you think Rafael and I are capable of lighting the heaters without your supervision?"

"Of course, but I should be there."

"You haven't a single logical reason. Believe me, no one will think any less of you. Your workers admire you for what you've already done. Please, go home and take a long, hot bath. You're no use any longer. You're too tired. You'll merely slow down the rest of us."

Erica grimaced. He was right, of course. She could barely drag one foot in front of the other. It seemed disloyal, like a captain leaving a sinking ship, but she no longer had the energy to argue. "All right."

She plodded to the house and up the stairs to her room. There she stripped, wrapped an old, dingy bathrobe around herself and ran a hot bath. She soaked for a long time, then climbed out, toweled dry, slipped into the robe again and padded to her bedroom. Sprawling across her bed, she was instantly asleep.

It was dark outside when Erica awoke. There was a light blanket spread over her. She sat up, yawning, and fumbled in the dark for the switch on her bedside lamp. The sudden glow revealed a hunched form in the chair across from the bed, and she jumped, her heart pounding, then let out her breath loudly. It was Tonio sitting there, fast asleep.

The noise she made awakened him and he stared at her blankly for a moment. "Oh." He sat up straighter and rolled his head, massaging his neck. Erica noticed that he held a small gold object in his hand. "You were asleep, so I put that blanket over you. I thought I'd wait for you to awaken, but I guess I fell asleep too." His eyes traveled over her and Erica was acutely aware of the old, unattractive robe she wore, as well as of the way it gaped at the top, revealing a great deal of her white throat and chest. She knew Tonio wouldn't miss a bit of it, either. A warm flush bathed her stomach and she rose nervously, tightening the sash. "I liked your other robe better," Tonio commented, referring to the short terry-cloth robe she had worn at the hotel. "But this one has its advantages."

Erica didn't know what to say. His words were melting, out of place with his businesslike attitude earlier in the day and with the anger of their parting. She wanted to tell him she loved him and ask for another chance, but her throat closed. Tonio rescued her by rising and coming toward her. She saw that the small gold object was a medallion on a chain. Then she recognized it as his St. Anthony medal.

"I found this lying on your dresser beside your jewelry box," he told her, extending the medal toward her. "You kept it all these years."

"Yes."

"Why?"

She chewed at her lip and glanced away. "I—it was special to me."

"I've been asking myself why a woman would keep something like that for so many years if she hated the man who'd given it to her. And why would that same woman tell her child—*his* child—wonderful, loving stories about his father? Erica, I know you said you hated me after my desertion, and the other night you told me to get out of your life."

"Tonio, I—"

"No, let me finish. I got a call from my secretary in Houston on Sunday, and I had to go there for an emergency meeting with the engineers on one of my projects. Otherwise I'd have been back sooner. When I got in this morning I heard about the freeze, so I came to help you. Circumstances seem to keep getting in my way and delaying the talk I planned to have with you."

"Talk?" Her heart was knocking against her ribs. Tonio was so close that she could have reached out to touch him. His clothes were stained with dirt and sweat from the day in the fields. She fixed her eyes on the still-damp cloth in the center of his chest, then realized that was as dangerous a place to look as any. There was no portion of his body that wasn't sexually inviting, from his thick black hair to the open collar of his shirt revealing the strong column of his throat to the glove-tight fit of his faded blue jeans. Unconsciously she clenched her fists and took a small backward step.

"Yes," he continued. "I did a lot of thinking after the other night. You were right, of course. I acted like an idiot. I threw away both our lives for nothing. But it wasn't because I mistrusted you, Erica. It was because of how I felt about myself. I had an inferiority complex, or whatever you want to call it. I'd been treated like dirt all my life because of who and what I was. I expected to get kicked in the teeth, and it became a sort of self-fulfilling prophecy. It didn't take much to convince me you'd used me, because I didn't feel worthy of your love. I was hurt and angry, but I didn't question it."

"I'm sorry."

"It was a long time ago. I'm a different person now. I've made a success of myself and I've shoved it down everyone's throat. Along the way I found out that I always tried a lot harder than was necessary. I told you once that I'm not the same guy you knew before, and it's true. I believe in myself now, Erica. There won't be any more suspicion and distrust." He turned away slightly. "I want to marry you."

"What!" His words stunned her. "Why—what—"

"Danny needs a father. I want to be with my son. I want to be a real father to him, not merely a guy he sees on the weekends who takes him out for hamburgers or to the circus. We could hire a manager for the farm and move to Houston. You could join the operations side of Cross, do the work you really love."

"Are you trying to bribe me with that?" she asked, hurt surging through her. Not once had he said anything about loving her. He wanted to marry her for Danny's sake. "Well, it's not good enough."

"Erica, we could make it work this time, I promise. I'd be a good husband, a good father."

"I'm sure you would, but a good marriage isn't based on giving me a good job or loving Danny or providing us with a nice home. What is this? Do you want to support us because you feel guilty?"

He made a low growling noise. "Why are you thwarting me about this? Damn it, I know you still care. Tonight Danny told me you'd explained that I'm his father. And the stories you told him, your keeping my medal . . ."

"Yes, I still love you!" Erica almost shrieked. "But what about you? One-sided love is no good. Neither is marrying for a child or to make up for some past wrong. I won't marry for anything less than love."

Tonio stared, then began to laugh, a harsh, grating, almost uncontrollable laugh. Thrusting his fingers into his mop of hair, he pivoted and flopped back on the bed. "Oh, God, that's good. That's rich. You don't want to marry me because I don't love you? Why do you think I've been chasing you all these months when anybody with any sense would have been deterred by your constant rebuffs? Why do I live here and run myself ragged commuting to Houston and the island? Why did I give you a loan and try to buy your land for a hell of a lot more than it's worth? I'm not an idiot, Erica. Or at least I'm not with anyone except you." He drew in a shaky breath. "Yes, I love you. I never stopped loving you. No other woman has ever satisfied me. I've never felt the slightest urge to marry, or even to spend two months with the same girl. I wanted you. All the time I hated you, I wanted you. And when I saw you again on the island I knew it had all been wasted effort. I hadn't forgotten you. I loved you as much as ever. More. You're stronger, more beautiful—both inside and out. You're even more desirable." He sighed, resting one arm across his forehead. "Oh, Erica, you manage to make me feel like a bumbling, fumbling sixteen-year-old again. When I try to talk to you, it comes out all wrong." He held out his arms to her. "Come here. I love you and I want to marry you." He grinned. "I also want to kiss you and hold you and make love to you until neither one of us can move. Is that clear enough?"

Joy swelled in Erica and she rushed forward, flinging herself onto the bed so hard that the springs creaked in protest. "Oh, Tonio, Tonio, I love you." She rained kisses all over his face. His evening stubble was rough against her lips, exciting. She breathed in the pungent odor of his male sweat, stirred by a primitive longing. "Yes, yes, I'll marry you. Why did you keep rattling on about all that other stuff? I love you so much. I have for years and years. I was going to fly to Houston and tell you so this morning, but the freeze interfered."

His hands moved to either side of her face to hold her still and he kissed her deeply, lips and tongue claiming her mouth as his. His breath was harsh against her cheek, as hot as his seeking, moist tongue. Erica shivered, her desire shooting to the surface, and she murmured his name. It set up a soft ache within him, but he took her shoulders firmly and pulled her up, rising with her. Puzzled, she blinked at him. "Don't you think I ought to take a bath first?" he asked.

"I don't care." She snuggled against him.

"Ah, but I have a certain fondness for your baths." He grinned, merriment lighting his eyes wickedly.

Erica caught his meaning and chuckled. She leaned against him and kissed him hard, her lips aggressive, sucking and nibbling at his until he groaned. Her fingers worked at his buttons, sliding down his chest until all were undone, and then beginning on the snap of his jeans. Tonio's skin was aflame, and his hands dug into her arms almost painfully. Erica drew away enough to whisper, "Shall I run your bathwater now?"

"Later," he growled. His arms wrapped around her and he pulled her back with him onto the bed. "Later. We have all the rest of our lives."

* * * * *

A Note from Naomi Horton

Dear Reader,

It was Brett Douglas who made me write this book. Right from the instant he turned up on the pages of my Silhouette Desire novel *Pure Chemistry,* he started demanding equal time. And a woman. Oh yes, Brett Douglas definitely wanted a woman.

The problem was finding the *right* woman! Brett needed a serious shaking up. I wanted to bring into his laid-back, smooth-running life-style a woman who could turn it upside down and knock some of the edges off his brash self-confidence. Maybe someone out of his past. Someone he never thought he'd see again— isn't too sure he *wants* to see again. Someone with a secret....

And in that moment, I knew what the secret would be. The first line of the book—"I'm pregnant"—flashed into my mind as though written in neon, and my first (but not my last) "mystery baby" story took life.

Stories of star-crossed lovers have always been a favorite of mine, especially when fate gives them a second chance. And when that love bond has been deepened with a baby—well, it doesn't get much more romantic. Hope you enjoy it!

Naomi Horton

CROSSFIRE

Naomi Horton

Prologue

"**I**'m pregnant."

How she got the words out, Kailin didn't know. She listened to the fading echo of her voice as though it belonged to someone else and watched the tall, bearded young man standing by the window stiffen. Slowly he turned his head to stare at her.

"Pregnant?" His voice was soft with disbelief. "How?"

Kailin had to smile in spite of being nearer tears than laughter. "You're the veterinary student, Brett. And you'll have to agree that we haven't always been as careful as we…we should have been."

The heavy beard did nothing to hide the flush that touched his handsome features. But even as numbed as she was, it took Kailin only a moment to realize that it was anger burning his cheeks, not embarrassment. She stared at him in bewilderment, her initial awkwardness giving way to unease as he made no move toward her. She'd expected him to be surprised, perhaps even momentarily angry at their mutual carelessness, but not once in the past two nightmare weeks had she anticipated such cold remoteness.

The blue eyes that had been filled with love in the past were hard now, and a little cold. "You're lying, Kailin."

It was her turn to stare in disbelief. "What?" Her voice was thin and high.

Brett's smile was humorless. "You're good, Kailin. You're real good." He sauntered across to his ancient brown sofa and dropped onto it, stretching his jean-clad legs out in front of him and draping both arms along the back of the sofa as he gazed coolly across the room at her. "Your old man was here a couple of hours ago."

Kailin blinked, feeling curiously light-headed. "Daddy was here?"

The corner of Brett's mouth tipped up even further, his eyes cutting. "He told me you're not pregnant at all, Kailin." The faint smile might have held a trace of honest humor for a moment. "Your old man doesn't like me much, Kailin. Apparently a troublemaker from the wrong side of the tracks isn't quite what he had in mind for his only daughter."

"Brett!"

"You've been using me." The smile vanished, and in its place was a hardness she'd never seen on that lean, handsome face before. "You've been flaunting me in front of your rich friends like a dog on a leash. And I've been great ammunition in that firefight you've been waging with your father all summer. He told me all about it—how every time you two have an argument you threaten to run off with me. How you've been keeping him 'in line,' as he put it. He also told me that he's tired of it and has called your bluff. He warned me, man-to-man, that I was being used, and not to fall for it too seriously."

Stunned, Kailin shook her head numbly. "Brett," she finally managed to whisper, "that's not what I—"

Brett lunged to his feet. "What game are we playing now, Kailin?" he demanded. "Am I supposed to toss you out into the street so you can run home to Daddy and get his sympathy? Or am I supposed to marry you? God, that would really drive your father nuts, wouldn't it?" He paced to the window, his body taut with anger. "It would be the ultimate act of rebellion, all right. Next to *actually* getting pregnant, that is." He looked around at her, his mouth wrenched in that bitter smile again. "And I wouldn't even put that past you, Kailin. You're as twisted and manipulative as he is. But don't expect me to play this one out to the end, baby, because I'm tired of your games."

"Brett—" The name was no more than a harsh sob torn from her. "You can't believe—!"

"Oh, I believe," he said softly, his eyes shadowed with pain. "There's just one thing I'd like to know, Kailin. Was any of it real? When we were making love and you'd say all those things—did you ever, even just once, mean any of it? Or was it all just part of the game?"

One

One

"This isn't some silly game you're playing! So will you shape up and stop acting like such an idiot?"

Kailin glared at her own reflection in the mirror above the dressing table. God! Half a pound of blusher and twice her usual amount of eye shadow and lipstick and she still looked like a terrified eighteen-year-old on the first day of a new job. Where in hell was the cool, self-possessed businesswoman who was under there *somewhere*?

Cool? Self-possessed? Kailin managed a grim smile. She'd been about as far from self-possessed as it was possible to get ever since she'd stepped off that plane in Fort Myers three days ago. And any remnants of bravery that had survived that far had dissipated completely during the five-mile drive across the causeway to Sanibel Island. She was, in a word, a wreck.

"You should have told them no," she muttered for the umpteenth time that morning. It was the same refrain she'd been repeating for nearly seven weeks, ever since she'd found out the unpleasant little truth behind why her father had *really* recommended her for this job.

"He set me up," she found herself whispering. She glared at the wide-eyed woman in the mirror and took a deep breath. "And you, you idiot! You walked right into it. Why didn't you just stand up to the whole lot of them and tell them no?"

Except that she had. She'd told the Miami bank executives two or three times that she didn't care if the Paradise Point investors *and* their trouble-fraught resort complex was sucked into the vortex of the Bermuda Triangle, she was *not* getting involved. She was an industrial management troubleshooter, not a miracle worker. Her job was to go in and save companies that were sliding toward disaster because of bad management or outdated production methods or faulty quality control—*not* to bail banks out of bad investment choices.

What the bankers hadn't known, of course, was that it wasn't them she was refusing to help, but her father. Quentin Yarbro had gotten himself into serious trouble this time. Trouble that he wasn't going to be able to bluff or bully his way out of, and she'd been looking forward to seeing him brought down by his own greed. A fitting end, all things considered.

Kailin gave a snort of laughter and started brushing her thick, shoulder-length hair furiously. In the end she'd caved in, exactly as he'd known she would. With the fortitude of wet cardboard, she'd capitulated even while swearing she wouldn't and had stalked out of that bank boardroom in a simmering rage at her own spinelessness, contract in hand.

The bankers and their desperate clients, that small group of people—her father among them—who had invested cold, hard cash in the Paradise Point development, were delighted and relieved. Paradise Point was in serious trouble, and with it a hair-raising amount of investors' money. They needed someone to go down to Sanibel Island who was used to salvaging businesses on the verge of bankruptcy. Someone who could go in and pinpoint the trouble spots and plug the holes before the entire ship sank and left everyone—developer and investor alike—floundering around in unfriendly waters.

Someone like Kailin McGuire.

It was her father who had recommended her to the bank and investors; her father who had explained everything to her and had finally pleaded with her to help.

Except he hadn't told her one thing.

He hadn't told her about Brett Douglass.

Kailin's stomach tightened. She closed her eyes and forced herself to relax. So far this morning she'd managed not to think of him. Well, not more than six or seven dozen times, anyway. But every time she *did* think of him, her stomach gave that same sick little twist. As she had a hundred times during the past three days, she looked yearningly at the empty suitcases standing by the door. She could be packed and halfway across the causeway to Fort Myers in an hour; on a plane back to Indiana in another two. The Paradise Point developers could find someone else to bail them out, the Miami bank and the rest of the investors could find someone else to salvage their money, and Brett . . . Brett Douglass wouldn't even have to know she'd been here.

Kailin, Kailin . . . don't go. Don't . . .

It was his own voice, echoing off the walls of his bedroom like a cry from the past. It faded into the darkness, leaving him wide-awake and sweating and cursing softly.

He sat up and stared bleakly into the dark of the room, still breathing fast, his heart racing like a runaway flywheel.

Kailin. Always, the dreams were of Kailin. Bad, wild dreams that left him shaking and sweating in the night, so filled with anger and loss that his very soul ached with it.

This one had been no different from all the others. They'd fought, the bitter, angry words the same as always. Kailin's tears glittering just as they had that night. At the end, when she'd turned away and her eyes had caught his for an instant huge and filled with hurt and betrayal, he'd felt something splinter inside him. That, too, was the way it had happened.

But then the dreams always veered off from reality into a special nightmare of their own. Unlike what had really happened on that night eleven years ago, he went after her in the dreams. He would sprint across the room and snatch the door before it slammed shut, then run out into the street and try to call out to her, to follow. But he would be trapped in that special slow-motion dreamtime, like a fly in amber, unable to move or shout, watching as Kailin disappeared. The woman he'd loved as much as life itself.

And had hated as deeply.

Brett drew in a deep, careful breath, the ache like a hard, bitter stone under his heart. Eleven years. One would almost think that a man should be able to shake free of a woman after eleven years. "Damn you, Kailin," he whispered into the empty darkness, the ache higher now, in the back of his throat. "Damn you, why won't you leave me alone?"

She should have left well enough alone.

Kailin thought suddenly of her father. Right now he was probably sitting in his study up in Greenlake, Indiana, chuckling about how clever he'd been. He had known that Brett was down here. That's *really* why he'd recommended her for this job: not because he believed she was the best person to handle it, or even because of some faint paternal pride, but simply because he thought it would give Paradise Point an advantage, an edge....

Advantages. Edges. Those were the only terms her father understood. Things like fair play and trust and honor were as alien to him as his way of doing business was to her. Yet somehow they were on the same side this time.

In spite of herself, Kailin smiled. It seemed strange, fighting *for* her father instead of simply fighting him. They'd been at each other's throats for so many years that she couldn't remember a time when they'd been anything but bitter opponents. Even as a child, she'd fought and fought: the rules, the reasons, the way things were. She'd called him rigid and authoritarian; he'd called her irresponsible and disobedient. She'd called it growing up, he'd called it rebelliousness, and they'd even fought over the naming of it.

It had gotten worse that last summer. That was the summer she'd fallen in love with Brett Douglass, and the battles between her and her father had escalated into all-out warfare.

Kailin's smile widened. She and Brett had been a study in classic chemistry, the pull between them so strong it had raised sparks. They'd made an eye-catching couple, all right, she blond and rich and very much from the right side of town, he dark and bearded, a born rebel out to change the world. They'd come together like colliding comets, and those sparks had turned incendiary, exploding into a passion that had left them both shaken.

And burned, Kailin reminded herself.

The smile slipped. She drew in a deep breath and was annoyed to feel her eyes sting. She blinked the sudden tears away angrily and pulled the brush through her hair again with long, savage strokes. "Why don't you grow up!" she hissed at her reflection. "So you fell in love and got hurt. So what? It happens all the time. You're not that stupid nineteen-year-old anymore—it's been eleven years. He probably doesn't even remember you!"

The brush hit a knot and she wrenched it free roughly, her eyes filling with tears again at the sharp pain. "It's too late now, anyway," she muttered as she rubbed her scalp with her fingers. "You took on this project and you're stuck with it. So start worrying about how you're going to keep this Paradise Point thing from falling apart, and *stop* worrying about a man you haven't seen in over a decade."

To her relief, the pep talk worked. For a moment or two at least, the nerves-of-steel businesswoman took over. The green eyes that met hers in the mirror were calm now and filled with a steady determination that flirted with outright stubbornness. There was a jut to the square jaw that boded ill for anyone rash enough to underestimate either the mind or the iron will behind it. Becky called it her Wonder Woman look.

Again Kailin had to laugh. She turned away from the mirror with a toss of her head and strode across the room, snatching up her handbag and briefcase from the bed on her way by. Did Wonder Woman ever get a run in her last pair of panty hose or forget to pay her parking tickets or get lost on a Los Angeles freeway and wind up in Santa Barbara when she was supposed to be going to San Diego? And would Wonder Woman ever sit through four consecutive showings of *Top Gun* because her nine-year-old daughter had a world-class crush on Tom Cruise, or cancel a business meeting at the last minute to go kite flying with that same daughter, or still delight in building sand castles?

Probably not. But then, who wanted to be Wonder Woman anyway?

Brett parked his pickup truck in the shade beside the old church that now housed his veterinary practice and turned of the engine, noticing that his hand was trembling slightly. Damn it, what was happening to him? He made no move to get out of the truck, still solidly shaken by what he'd seen. Or by what he *thought* he'd seen.

Kailin . . .

Brett took a deep breath. No. He'd seen *someone*, all right, but it hadn't been Kailin.

All he'd seen was a tantalizing glimpse of wind-tangled hair and honey-gold flesh. God knew, there was hardly a shortage of either on Sanibel this time of year.

He wrenched open the truck door and got out, his footsteps crunching on the crushed coral and shell that made up the driveway. Talcum-powder dust rose in small puffs behind him, hanging languorously in the still, hot air. Besides, he reminded himself as he took the front steps two at a time, she'd probably cut that gorgeous mane of sun-bleached hair by now. She'd worn it loose back then, in a thick torrent that the Indiana sun had turned a hundred shades of silver and gold. He could remember how she would run her fingers through it and scoop it off her face with a toss of her head, then give that quick, flirtatious glance that had half the men in town falling all over themselves.

Damn it, will you stop brooding about her? He wrenched the door to the clinic open and a blast of air hit him, arctic after the tropical heat outside. What the hell was the matter with him, anyway? Kailin Yarbro—Kailin *McGuire* now, he reminded himself bitterly—had walked out of his life eleven years ago. He was eleven years older and wiser now, and surely past the point where an unexpected glimpse of long tanned legs and a cascade of sun-silvered hair could still turn him inside out. Just how long, he found himself speculating ferociously, did it take for a bruised heart to heal?

There was the scamper of small feet and an explosion of delighted barking as Artoo, the tiny mostly-terrier mongrel that had adopted the clinic, came tearing around the corner. He lost traction on the polished floor and went spinning out of control, then scrambled to his feet and tore headlong at Brett's ankles, tongue and ears flying.

Brett laughed and scooped him up in one hand. "Take it easy, youngster."

"How are you with bees?" The cheerful voice of his assistant fluted from the door of the tiny office cum waiting room.

"Bees?" He walked into the office and looked at Kathy Fischer warily, depositing the excited Artoo on her desk. "What kind of bees?"

"Wild bees." She tossed him a clean white lab coat, not even missing a beat as she deftly rescued a telephone bill that was disappearing into Artoo's mouth. "Workers putting in the foundation for that new condo at the end of Island Inn Road unearthed a hive this morning. They've swarmed—the bees, I mean—and the construction crew refuses to go back to work until someone gets rid of them."

"Me," Brett groaned. "Why do they always call me?"

"Because everyone knows you're the best veterinarian in Florida," Kathy said teasingly. "Maybe on the entire East Coast. And everyone knows that veterinarians have a special way with creatures." She laughed at Brett's eloquent look. "The foreman's been calling here every twenty minutes. He says he's losing eight hundred dollars an hour and that you can name your price if you'll move the swarm so his men can get back to work."

"I wouldn't touch them if he named the place after me," Brett muttered as he pulled on the lab coat. "Give old Jonas Merriweather a call. He used to raise bees. I've seen him move a swarm with his bare hands.... The man's nuttier than a fruitcake."

At that moment Artoo stuck his face enthusiastically into a mug on the corner of Kathy's desk. Recoiling with a sneeze that sprayed cold coffee in all directions, he promptly backed off the desk. He landed on the floor with a surprised yelp, paper cascading around him, then snatched one end of a streamer of adding machine tape and raced out the door with it.

"That," Kathy said calmly, nodding toward the door, "was this month's accounts receivable." She smiled as she picked up the scattered mail from the floor. "You've got a visitor."

Brett felt the hair on the back of his neck stir.

He walked to the window, pretending to look out at something with eyes squeezed shut. What was happening to him? First the dream, then—

"Who?" he asked abruptly, not looking around.

If Kathy heard anything unusual in his voice, she didn't let on. "Zac Cheevers. Something about Paradise Point."

Brett hadn't known he was holding his breath until he released it in a *huff* of relief. How long, he wondered, would the impact of last night's dream stay with him? Sometimes it lasted for days.

"I sent him down to your office."

"Thanks, Kath." Brett glanced around to smile at her, finding her gazing at him with a faint frown.

"Is, uh . . . everything all right? You look a little . . . pale."

Silently cursing the intuitive abilities of women in general, and Kathy's in particular, Brett held his smile firmly in place. "Nothing about twelve hours of sleep wouldn't cure," he lied, heading for the door. "I got together with a couple of old friends last night, and we watched the sun come up over a bottle of good Scotch and a lot of reminiscing."

"Oh." Kathy's face cleared, and she laughed. "Hunt and Jill Kincaide, I'll bet. Jill called yesterday to tell me they were on Sanibel again for a few days. What's the baby like?"

"Small and noisy." He grinned at Kathy's look of outrage and stepped into the corridor before she could quiz him further. Jill and Hunter *had* come over the previous night, but they'd left well before midnight.

I don't know what the hell's wrong with you, Douglass, he muttered to himself as he walked down the corridor. It's been eleven years, for crying out loud. Last night was just a dream, and this morning was just . . . what?

A mirage, he told himself brutally. Wishful thinking. It didn't matter. Whoever that woman had been, she hadn't been Kailin McGuire.

Without even wanting to, he found himself thinking of the way she'd looked that first time he'd seen her: tall and cat-lithe, skin burnished by a summer's worth of sailing and tennis, that magnificent mane of silver-gold hair tousled and loose. She'd been one of a bunch of college kids piled into a baby-blue Mercedes convertible, all of them laughing and windblown as they'd cruised slowly by the besieged gates of Yarbro Paint and Chemicals. They'd radiated the lazy arrogance that comes with the right address, the right car, the right college, and it hadn't taken him more than one look to know that she was rich and spoiled and more trouble than any one man needed.

But one look was all it had taken. He hadn't known then that she was the daughter of the very man whose chemical plant he and his environmentalist friends were picketing. He doubted it would have made any difference. The protest had been one of many they'd staged that summer. By then they, Yarbro's security people and the police had had the entire thing down to a well-choreographed ballet: gates picketed, speeches given, fists shaken, everyone lazy and good-natured in the heat of high summer. Every protest had brought out a parade of passersby—some to support, some to jeer, others simply to stare curiously. Then, that late afternoon, along had come the woman who would change his life.

Warned of trouble, Yarbro's men had closed the high chain-link gates barring the only road into the plant, which was exactly what Brett had been counting on. He'd chained himself securely to those same gates, and what had been designed as a barricade to keep troublemakers like him *out* had worked just as effectively to keep the two big tanker trucks filled with chemical waste *in*. It had been a grandstanding gesture, done more for media attention than in any real hope of stopping Yarbro from polluting the river.

But this time it had caught more than just media attention. The blue convertible had slowed as it had passed the gates, and he'd held his breath as eyes the color of new grass had met his, appraising and faintly amused. She'd taken in the tattered Marine camouflage jacket, the beard, the heavy chain around his waist. Then those dark-lashed eyes had settled on his again, filled with challenge and teasing promise and laughter. Unable to stop himself, he'd swept off an imaginary hat and had flourished it in a sweeping, extravagant bow, and when he'd straightened, grinning broadly, he'd been rewarded with a small, private smile that had told him he'd be seeing her again, and that he could count on it.

She'd been true to that unspoken promise. And he'd been right: Kailin Yarbro had been more trouble than any one man needed.

Brett suddenly realized that he was standing at the door to his office—and had been for the past few minutes, unmoving hand on the knob. Mentally he'd been a thousand miles to the north, standing under the blazing Indiana sun, falling madly in love.

Love. Brett gave a derisive snort and opened his office door, shaking off his pensive mood as a dog shakes off water. Whatever he and Kailin had shared during that long, steamy summer in Greenlake, it hadn't been love.

"About time you showed up." The man seated beside Brett's desk tossed aside the magazine he'd been looking through. "I was beginning to wonder if you were coming in at all."

"It's good to see you, too, Zac," Brett told him dryly. "Get you a cup of coffee?"

"Got one," Zac rasped, shifting his dead cigar to the other corner of his mouth. "Your life-style's going to kill you, boy. You look like hell. Hope she was worth losin' a night's sleep for."

"My life-style's just fine," Brett replied with a pointed look at Zac's cigar. "And it wasn't a woman that kept me up half the night." *Not a real one, anyway,* he added silently. "If I did even half the carousing I get accused of doing around here, I'd have died of exhaustion long ago."

The rolls of extra flesh around Zac's ample middle rocked with laughter. Then his expression sobered and he shoved a manila file folder across the desk. "Well, here's something that'll keep you up nights. They've thrown us a curve, Douglass."

"Who?" Brett eased himself into his swivel desk chair and reached across to pick up the folder.

"Paradise Point, what else?" Zac's voice was bitter. "The Land Use Committee got a call last night from that bank in Miami representing the investors backing the resort. They've brought in a mediator as a last-ditch effort to keep the project afloat—an industrial management consultant or some damn thing. Anyway, seems they're going to try to work up some sort of compromise between us—the Land Use Committee, I mean—and Gulf Coast."

"Compromise?" Frowning, Brett flipped the folder open and started perusing the contents. "What kind of compromise?"

"We won't know that until this afternoon. This mediator or whatever called to set up a meeting with us at three."

"And Gulf Coast? Are they going to be there?"

"From what I heard, Gulf Coast isn't very happy about it, but they'll be there. The bank told them to cooperate—or else."

Brett smiled, a trifle grimly. "So the investors are playing hardball, are they?"

"There's a lot of money tied up in Paradise Point. If Gulf Coast folds, that money's gone out with the tide. Guess they're hoping to salvage something." Zac gave a snort. "Damned fools."

"Maybe not," Brett said quietly. "Nobody wants to see Paradise Point fold. Phase One of the development is one of the most successful on Sanibel."

"Old age turnin' you soft, boy?" Zac asked in astonishment. "When you first showed up on Sanibel you were a real fire-eater. I remember watchin' you go a full ten rounds with any developer not toeing the line. Without you we wouldn't even *have* a Land Use Committee." The cigar shifted. "Hell, boy, you were the one hollering the loudest about gettin' Gulf Coast shut down."

"I want Craig Bryant shut down, not the company. Gulf Coast has always done right by us, you know that."

"Craig's daddy's always done right by us, you mean," Zac growled. "That pup of his ain't worth toad spit." He skewered Brett with an assessing look. "You know as well as I do that Phase Two of the Paradise Point project is garbage. Are you sayin' we should go ahead and approve Phase Three anyway?"

"I'm just saying we shouldn't toss the gold out with the dross. If there's a chance we can get Gulf Coast to clean up its act, it would be as much in our favor as theirs to get Paradise Point finished. And that's impossible unless we approve Phase Three." Brett smiled. "It doesn't cost us anything to listen to what they have to say, Zac."

Zac gave a grunt, but then he nodded and stood up. He took the folder when Brett held it out. "Three o'clock sharp. Douglass. Big meeting room in back of my place."

"What does this mediator sound like, anyway?" Brett asked as Zac walked to the door. "Like he knows what he's doing?"

"Sounds like any other three-piece-suiter," Zac muttered darkly. "Talking about profit-loss margins and bottom lines and a bunch of other stuff I only half understood. And it ain't a he, it's a she. Sounds keen, too. Too damned keen for my taste."

"She?" Brett looked up with interest. "Miss or Mrs.?"

Zac's beefy face broke into a broad grin. "That sounds more like the Brett Douglass I know," he said with a chuckle. "Though from the little bit I spent talkin' with her, I'd say you'd be wastin' your time. Ice-cold, and brittle as steel—it's *Ms.*—Ms. McGuire."

"McGuire?" Brett felt himself turn cold, his mouth suddenly dry. Impossible, he told himself numbly.

"Yeah." Zac paused in the doorway. "Kay something, think she said. Could've been Kaitlin."

"Kailin," Brett corrected automatically, hardly aware he'd said anything at all.

Nearly three o'clock.

Kailin dragged her eyes from the big wall clock above the far end of the meeting table, so on edge that she felt like screaming. Premeeting jitters, she told herself firmly. That was all it was. Once everyone was here and they got started, she would be fine.

Unable to stand still, she wandered across to the long, low windows running the full length of the elegantly appointed meeting room. They overlooked a landscaped garden filled with palmettos, giant scarlet hibiscus and a hundred other flowering shrubs and vines. Along one side, two flamboyant Hong Kong orchid trees dripped loose petals across the grass. It was eerily still as though the whole world were holding its breath. Kailin looked at the sky with apprehension.

Sullen cobalt clouds seemed to press earthward, and Kailin thought uneasily of the tropical storm that had come bellowing up through the Keys and into the Gulf the week before. It hadn't quite reached full hurricane status before it had blown itself out, but it had done enough damage to convince her that she didn't want to be down here when another one hit.

Storm warnings. Kailin smiled. They'd been going off in her mind all day, presaging a hurricane of a different sort. Her own reflection stared back at her against the steel-blue sky, and she realized with a jolt that she looked scared to death.

She sighed and reached up to brush her hair back from her forehead, taking a deep breath and trying to compose herself. It was too late to go back now. They would all be here in a few minutes, and she had a job to do. The only thing that should be concerning her right now was Paradise Point.

A mutter of thunder made her glance at the sky again. For some reason the threatening clouds made her think of the last time she'd seen Brett. That night eleven years ago, when it had all come to an end, as everything finally does.

Kailin shook her head, sending the memories scattering. Enough of that. It had all happened a long time ago, to a woman she couldn't even remember being. A lot had happened since: marriage; a baby lost and a baby born; the car accident that had left her widowed; the struggle that had followed. She'd grown up fast. She'd put the past to rest as best she could, had fought herself free—or almost free—of her father's bullying domination, had made a comfortable home for herself and Becky and had become one of the top management troubleshooters in the country. She was on Sanibel Island on business, and there was no way that anything—not past mistakes, not guilt, not even revenge—was going to mess that up.

Something moved behind her. Another reflection joined hers on the storm-darkened glass, and Kailin suddenly went cold.

Even though she'd expected it, she wasn't prepared for the reality of seeing him again. He was standing so close to her that she could feel his heat radiate through the thin silk of her blouse, could feel the intimate warmth of his breath on the back of her neck. He used to kiss her there. Slow, tickling kisses that had made her melt while he'd stroked and caressed her breasts, her stomach, then lower still....

She closed her eyes, grasping the windowsill when her knees threatened to give out. Hesitantly, half expecting the image to have vanished, she looked up.

He smiled. It was a slow, almost mocking smile. "Hello, Kailin."

His voice was the same. Deep and quiet, with that rough-timbred purr to it that had driven every woman she'd ever known wild. He had a voice, a friend of hers had once said, that made love to you while he was just saying hello.

"Brett." The name was still magic in her mouth. Only this time, finally, he was there to answer it, not simply a memory in the night.

He must have heard some of that in the one word, because for an instant the years between them vanished. His gaze burned into hers, as raw and vital and hungry as it had ever been, and he seemed to sway toward her. She held her breath, waiting for his touch.

Two

Two

It never came. As suddenly as the electric awareness had sparked between them it was gone. Something shuttered across his eyes, and although he hadn't moved a muscle, it was as though he were suddenly across the room from her. He stepped away, and Kailin closed her eyes again, took a deep breath and turned around.

Brett was leaning against the far wall, hands shoved in the pockets of his jeans, one long leg bent slightly at the knee. He looked the picture of relaxation, gazing calmly at her across the barricade of the long oak table.

It was disconcerting how little he'd changed. The beard was gone, but she'd expected that. She found herself staring at him, fascinated, and realized suddenly that it was the first time she'd ever seen his bare face. It was straight-featured and lean, with the high, strong Iroquois cheekbones he'd inherited from his great-grandmother. His hair was much shorter than it had been. Tidily and expensively trimmed, it curled around his ears and the back of his neck and, as always, lay across his forehead in beguiling disarray, as though just disturbed by a woman's loving touch. His eyes were the same, that vivid blue that—like a prairie sky—seemed to darken with his mood, warmly azure one moment and storm-indigo the next. They were an odd in-between right now, and curiously flat.

That cool, steady stare unnerved her. She feigned a smile and walked to the head of the table, taking the papers from her slim leather portfolio as though she had absolutely nothing on her mind but this meeting. "I wondered if you'd come."

There was a quiet chuckle, more malevolent than amused. "You couldn't have kept me away, Kailin."

She gave him a quick, nervous glance. He had shrugged away from the wall and was prowling the room, pausing by the windows to stare out into the garden, his back to her. He was wearing jeans and a pale blue denim work shirt, sleeves shoved carelessly past his elbows, and she could see the corded muscles along his tanned forearms tighten as he gripped the windowframe.

Kailin swallowed as she watched him move away from the window and resume his slow circuit of the table, working his way casually yet deliberately toward her. Somehow she'd been hoping that something would have defused that restless tension within him, but it was still there, as volatile as ever. Her heart sank. Time hadn't mellowed Brett Douglass; it had just seasoned him.

A hundred trite phrases ran through her mind. She discarded all of them and simply stood in silence, letting those wary blue eyes search hers, seeking God knew what. *What can I say?* she asked him silently. *Oh, Brett, what can I say that will erase the hurt and anger and suspicion?*

He stopped finally just a few feet from her and stood there with his hands on his hips, letting his eyes wander over her. Kailin could have screamed, but she managed to stand absolutely still. His gaze moved from her high-heeled sandals, up the narrow linen skirt with its expensive leather belt, the silk leopard-print blouse with the simple gold chain at the open throat, the flamboyant wood-and-feather earrings. Not quite the antiestablishment jeans and T-shirts the Kailin Yarbro of the past had favored. His eyes paused on her shoulder-length hair, still casual but less tousled. She nearly smiled in spite of her nervousness. What had he expected? Banker's gray with a dress-for-success bow at the throat? Cashmere and pearls?

"Eleven years older and wiser, Brett," she found herself saying. "Other than that, everything's about the same."

His eyes met hers for an instant. Then they crinkled slightly at the outer corners, and he smiled. "Sorry."

"Don't be." She returned the smile. "You're not quite the young college rebel I remember, either. What happened to the earring and the beard?"

"I grew up."

"So did I." Check and countercheck.

He nodded slowly, that speculative gaze running over her again. Then his eyes focused on hers. "You're looking damned good, Kailin. It's been a long time."

"Yes." *Too long.* The silence pulled taut between them, and finally Kailin couldn't stand it. Decisively she walked the few steps between them. He watched her warily as she put her hands lightly on his forearms for balance and stood on tiptoe, lifting her mouth to his cheek. She could have sworn he flinched as her lips brushed his skin. "I'm glad to see you again, Brett."

He didn't say a word. They stood like that for a long while, so close that she could see the small crescent-shaped scar on his jaw that was a souvenir from a flying bottle during a demonstration against something she couldn't even remember now. She expected him to kiss her back. But he simply stared down at her, eyes cool and expressionless. Then he stepped carefully away, leaving her standing there feeling silly.

A jolt of sudden anger ran through Kailin. In all the hours she'd spent torturing herself over Brett's possible reactions, she'd never once anticipated such remoteness, such...hostility. It was as though he held *her* responsible for everything that had happened. *He* was the one who had spurned her; *he* was the one who had run off without even trying to find out the truth, who had left her to grieve for their lost child among strangers.

Her instinctive reaction was to snap back at him, but she restrained herself and instead said calmly, "Look, Brett, I know my turning up here without any warning is a shock. I should have called you first. Warned you. But—" She caught herself awkwardly. Why *hadn't* she called him? She didn't really know herself, except that she'd been afraid. "We...I... Oh, hell!" She ran her fingers through her hair, combing it back from her face impatiently. "This is all so complicated and...messy."

"Messy?" He shot her a narrow-eyed look, anger etched in every line on his face. "Is that what you think this is, Kailin? Messy?"

Oh, God, she thought despairingly, is this what it's going to be like? "More than messy, I guess," she said quietly, trying to mollify him and hating herself for it. "Awkward was the word I was looking for. I'd accepted this job before I knew you were down here. When I found out, it was too late. I'd already agreed to do it, and I couldn't just back out because of—"

"Because of me?" Bitterness ran through the words, hot as bile.

"Brett—" She caught herself, hearing the anger in her own voice and refusing to give in to it. She took a deep breath and tried again. "Brett, I know I've caught you by surprise. I'm sorry if I...if I've upset you. I'd hoped we could be friends, but if we can't be that much, can we at least be civil to each other? It's going to be very difficult working together if we can't...talk."

"We never *did* talk much," he retorted, eyes and mouth hard and unyielding. "We were always in so much of a hurry to get into bed we never had much time for anything else."

It was the truth, but the way he said it made Kailin wince. "You make it sound so cheap," she whispered. "As though there was nothing more than—"

"Sex?" he shot back. "Sex was all we ever had. Raw and wild and plenty of it. You knew exactly what you wanted, and you took it. We both did. But we're grown-up now. Let's not pretend we ever had anything else."

Kailin stared at him in disbelief. "You can't possibly believe that," she said raggedly. "Brett, how can you—?"

"There's something I've always wondered about, Kailin," he said with a savage smile, settling one solid shoulder against the windowframe as he turned to face her. "How did good old Royce enjoy being second?"

For an instant Kailin felt so light-headed that she wondered if she'd fainted. The room spun gently around her until all she could see was Brett's face looming over her, his eyes hard and cold and bitter. "What?" she finally managed to whisper as the room wobbled to a stop. "What did you say?"

"Royce," he repeated with a sharklike smile. "You remember him, don't you, Kailin? Your husband?"

"I—"

"Did he ever ask you what it had been like with me, Kailin?" His voice was low now, a soft wash of intimate sound that excluded everything but the two of them. "Did he ever ask how he rated? I'll bet it galled the hell out of him, didn't it, knowing I'd been there before him." The savage smile widened. "Did he know I'd been your first, Kailin? Did he know that every damn thing you knew about making love was what I'd taught you?"

"Brett!" It was no more than a cry of pain. Kailin felt herself sway and snatched the edge of the table to keep from falling.

"I used to think about the two of you together," he went on in that low, harsh voice. "I used to lie awake at night wanting you so badly my whole body ached with it, and I used to think of you making love with him."

"Brett, for the love of God!" She spun away from him with a cry of anguish. She squeezed her eyes shut, trying to blot out the memories, trying not to listen.

"When he's making love to you, Kailin, do you ever think of me?" He sounded closer now, his voice a slash of anger. "Do you ever wish it was me there beside you instead of him? Do you ever whisper my name in his ear when you're whispering all those other little things, and at the end is it ever my name you cry instead of his?"

"Stop it!" Kailin clamped her hands over her ears, feeling hot tears well up and not caring.

"Or does he even take you that far, Kailin?" that soft, purring voice went on relentlessly. "Or does he leave you alone with your memories, wanting me even half as badly as I've wanted you all these years?"

"Stop it!" Kailin's voice rose in an anguished sob. "Brett, stop it! Why are you doing this to me?"

"Because I want to see you hurt like I've hurt!"

He said it with such ragged savagery, the words so shocking in their honesty, that Kailin knew they had been torn out of him before he'd even given them thought.

"Tit for tat, lady," he growled, sounding subdued now, as though his own reply had shocked him out of his anger.

"Oh, Brett," she whispered raggedly, turning to look at him. "I never meant to hurt you. I loved you."

"Love!" His face was white and drawn, his eyes dark with some old pain she could only guess at. "You used me, Kailin, but you never loved me. You didn't even know what love was. You used to flaunt me at those parties like I was some damned Gypsy, knowing it was like dropping a spark into gasoline. And you used me to drive your father crazy, because I was the best weapon you had. You loved the excitement I brought into your life, Kailin. You loved the danger and you loved playing at rebellion, but you didn't love me. I wasn't good enough for you, remember? Quentin J. Yarbro's high-society daughter could take a roll in the hay with a country vet's son, but she sure as hell wasn't going to marry him. *That* honor went to one of the local rich boys."

"Brett, that wasn't how it was! Yes, I used you to annoy my father—I was nineteen, and I was rich and spoiled and used to getting my own way. I'm not proud of that, but I can't change what I was. But you used me, too, remember. All you talked about that entire summer was how much it must be driving Quentin J. Yarbro crazy knowing his daughter was dating the man responsible for picketing Yarbro Paint and Chemicals. We used each other, Brett, don't kid yourself about that. But I loved you. And never once during that entire summer did you ever give me one sign that you loved me back."

He was staring at her, a muscle along his jawline throbbing as though he had his teeth clenched. His eyes were dark and disbelieving, and Kailin felt something start to ache within her. "When I went to your apartment that night and told you I was pregnant, you laughed at me. And later, when I got home, my father told me he'd offered you ten thousand dollars if you'd leave me. He said you'd taken it. I knew you needed the money badly for school. I..." She dropped her gaze. "I believed him. After all the things you said, I had no reason not to. I...I was hurting. Can't you understand that?"

"Yeah, I can understand hurt," he said in a ragged voice. "And that's why you married McGuire?"

She nodded, not trusting her voice.

"You weren't lying that night when you came to see me, were you?" he asked suddenly, quietly. "About the baby."

"No." There was a taut silence, broken only by the clatter of palm fronds in the wind.

Did he know what had happened? she wondered. Did he know about the miscarriage that had cost him his unborn child? She had her mouth half-open, wanting to ask, then subsided again with an inward sigh. It didn't matter now. Telling him the truth would only hurt him more than he was already hurting. She frowned as the familiar pain ran through her. Strange how she could grieve so long over a baby she'd never even known. She knew it was because it had been Brett's. It wasn't really the death of her unborn child she was still grieving, it was the death of love.

She looked up to find Brett staring down at her, his eyes dark and wistful. Although he didn't move, he seemed to reach toward her, his gaze caressing her face like the touch of a loving hand. "We could have had it all, Kailin," he whispered. "I loved you so much it hurts just to think about it. But you threw it all away."

"You never told me." She spoke softly. It was such a simple thing when it was said aloud. "You never once said that, Brett. Never once."

Something like pain flickered across his features. He frowned and looked down. "Yeah," he said. "I guess you're right. Somehow I thought that if you loved someone enough you didn't have to say anything."

"We were both such kids." She sighed and scooped her hair off her face again, feeling worn-out and empty. "Too scared to say 'I love you' out loud, in case we made fools of ourselves."

"Are you happy, Kailin?"

The question surprised her so much that she simply stared at him. Then she laughed quietly and nodded. "Yes, Brett. I am. Very happy."

Again, some emotion she couldn't identify flickered across his features. He nodded abruptly, then turned away and walked across the room.

"And you?"

He paused in the process of pulling a chair away from the table and looked up at her. Then he smiled. It was a grim little smile that scarcely moved his lips. "Does it matter?"

"Brett—" Something moved in the corner of her eye. Kailin glanced toward the door, then swallowed what she'd been about to say with an inward sigh, hoping she didn't look even half as rattled as she felt.

"Hi, gorgeous." Craig Bryant sauntered into the room with just the right amount of nonchalance, his hands shoved into the pockets of his fashionably baggy slacks. He grinned winningly at her. "No one else here yet?"

"Mr. Douglass is here," she replied coolly, taking the rest of the papers from her portfolio and setting them on the table.

Craig saw Brett at the precise instant Kailin said it. The smile dropped from his mouth, and he eyed the other man with open dislike. "Thought you'd be out organizing a rally or something, Douglass. I hear your little group's out to ban bug repellent next. If you pull it off, it'll be a great winter—we'll all be too busy swatting mosquitoes to worry about Paradise Point. Or is that the idea?"

The sarcasm didn't seem to faze Brett. He smiled lazily and tilted the chair onto its back legs. "Hadn't thought of that, but now that you mention it..." He grinned, obviously enjoying baiting Craig. "And we'd win, Bryant. They've been spraying Florida wetlands with insecticide for years to cut down on the mosquito problem. All they've managed to do is contaminate the marshes so badly half the bird and gator eggs laid each season don't hatch, and you wouldn't recognize some of the things that come out of the ones that do. And the animals aren't the only things suffering out there—people are fed up with being poisoned, having their kids sick all the time—"

Craig made a noise in his throat. "You guys jump on any bandwagon that comes along. Last year it was nuclear power plants, year before that chemical waste, before *that* whales and seals. Next you'll be trying to fence off the entire state of Florida and turn it into a natural habitat."

"We've thought of that," Brett replied agreeably. "Maybe next year. *This* year we're after you, Bryant—and all the other money-grubbing land developers who think they can break the rules and not get caught." His smile reminded Kailin of a cruising barracuda. "You're not getting away with it, Bryant, old buddy. Not this time."

"Damn you, Douglass, I'll—"

"Excuse me, gentlemen," Kailin said smoothly, "but perhaps we can save the accusations and name-calling for later?" For some reason she found it solidly reassuring to find that Brett hadn't changed that much after all. Still fighting the good fight. She smiled, more to herself than at the two men who were still trading looks across the wide table. "Is anyone else from Gulf Coast Development attending this meeting, Mr. Bryant?"

"I'm here alone." He smiled warmly. "And it's Craig, remember?"

"Break your leash, Bryant?" Brett asked lazily.

"And just what the hell does that mean?"

"Last I heard, you were halfway to being a married man. Or did your fiancée see the light and toss you out?"

Kailin held her breath for an instant, certain that Craig was going to launch himself across the table at Brett, but at the last moment he managed to restrain himself. He flexed his shoulders and sat down, nostrils flared. "Coming from a man who's bedded every single woman and half the married ones within a hundred-mile radius, that doesn't deserve an answer."

Brett's features darkened, but to Kailin's relief, he maintained a hostile silence.

Terrific start, Kailin thought to herself, trying to ignore the little twinge that Craig's accusations sent through her. It wasn't any of her business if Brett *had* slept with every woman in Florida, or if he planned to work his way north, state by state. She slipped Brett a sidelong glance, but he was staring over Craig's shoulder at the window, where the first streaks of rain were hitting.

She was saved from further thoughts of Brett's alleged sexual activities by an explosion of activity at the door. A group of people herded through, flapping wet raincoats and umbrellas in a spray of water, all chattering and exclaiming at once. There was an abrupt silence when they saw her. Then they hastily made their way around the table, glancing curiously at her as they trooped by.

"I'm Kailin McGuire," she said quietly when they'd settled themselves and fallen more or less silent. "And I'm sorry for calling you out in this weather." She glanced at the window as a crash of thunder rattled the frame. "I'm used to blizzards at this time of year, not hurricanes." There was a spate of laughter, and she felt the tension in the room ease.

"This isn't a hurricane, Ms. McGuire," one of the men drawled. He shifted the dead cigar from one corner of his mouth to the other. "A hurricane's when the roof lifts off. This is just a dust-settler."

Another crash of thunder punctuated his sentence, and a deluge of rain hit the window like a blow from a fist. Kailin winced. "I'll take your word for that, Mr. ... Cheevers, isn't it? I spoke with you on the phone yesterday."

"That's right." The cigar shifted again. "And before we get started, ma'am, I'd like to know just what side you're on here."

"I'm not on anyone's side. My job is to mediate an agreement between you—the Barrier Islands Land Use Committee—and Gulf Coast Development on the Paradise Point resort complex. It's true that I was hired by the private investors backing Paradise Point, but I assure you that your best interests and theirs are *not* mutually exclusive."

Cheevers gave a disbelieving grunt. "Frankly, ma'am, I think you're wasting your time. They—" he nodded in Craig's direction "—aren't interested in anything but getting that complex finished, no matter how many laws they have to break getting there."

Craig leaped to his feet, pointing an accusing finger at his opponent. "And you and your committee won't rest until you bankrupt us and turn Paradise Point into a bird preserve!"

"Gentlemen," Kailin interjected smoothly, "this isn't going to get us anywhere. Shall we all sit down?" Calmly, with a firmness born of experience, Kailin waited until Craig sat down. "I've ordered coffee and a selection of pastries, but I'd like to get started. We have a lot of ground to cover this afternoon, and the sooner we get down to it, the sooner we can discover where we all stand." It took an effort, but Kailin looked down the table at Brett. "I know you're chairman of the Land Use Committee, Mr. Douglass, but I haven't met the others yet. Perhaps you could introduce me, then we can get down to work."

He was watching her with an odd expression on his face, and he nodded slowly, leaving Kailin wondering what he'd been thinking. Just what, she mused, did he think of finding her here playing establishment executive when the last time he'd seen her she'd been scathing in her criticism of that same establishment? Of course, she reminded herself with amusement, he'd obviously learned to play the games himself, using home-grown political pressure groups to accomplish what marches and pickets had. Old rebels don't die, she thought with an inward smile, they just grow up, don three-piece suits and gnaw away at the system from the inside.

After the introductions had been made, Brett leaned well back in the chair and laced his hands behind his head. "Okay, Ms. McGuire," he said with a challenging stare. "It's your show now."

She was good, Brett had to admit a few minutes later. She was damned good!

He watched Kailin speculatively and found himself trying to equate this articulate businesswoman with the temperamental teenager he'd known in Greenlake. It didn't seem possible that she could be the same woman, yet there was no mistaking that funny little leap his heart gave every time their eyes met. God, what was the matter with him? Eleven years and a broken heart later, and she could still make his blood race with just a single glance.

You're a damned fool, he told himself bluntly. He thought of the whirlwind of emotion that had torn through him when he'd walked through the door and realized that in that instant he'd nearly thrown away all his best intentions. He'd approached her, absorbed by the reality of her, drawing the warm, oddly erotic scent of her deep into his lungs as a cigarette addict draws in nicotine. Time had gone spinning away and he'd felt caught in a strange mélange of past and present, and for one heartbeat he'd put his hand out to swing her into his arms.

But he hadn't. Strength, he wondered now, or cowardice? They sometimes got as tangled and confused as love and hate, and it was often just as hard to tell one from the other.

Involuntarily he thought of his outburst only moments later. The rage and pain must have been festering inside him for eleven years. Now he found he didn't feel much of anything. He found himself watching Kailin with a dispassionate curiosity. And that, he decided, was almost worse than hating her.

She had them eating out of her hands, Brett realized with surprise. They'd all come in here convinced that she was the enemy, and within ten minutes she'd defused the tension and suspicion with the skill of a seasoned diplomat.

He found himself watching her with growing admiration, drinking in her soft, musical voice as she spoke with authority and self-confidence, the graceful gestures of her slender hands, the intent tilt of her head when she was listening to someone. Framed by softly waving hair, her features seemed stronger and more defined. Her eyes were still vividly green, but when they occasionally, briefly brushed his, he could see a seriousness that had never been there before. Kailin McGuire had grown up.

They both had. Brett eased his breath out in a quiet sigh that felt suspiciously like regret. He frowned. Douglass, he told himself fiercely, don't you get caught in her web again. She might have grown up, but she hasn't changed. No one changes that much.

He realized that she was watching him with an odd expression on her face, as though she knew exactly what he was thinking. For an instant he thought he saw something like sadness brush her features. Then it was gone.

Damn it, why was he tied up in knots while she was as cool as a cucumber? Twenty minutes ago she'd been in tears, and to look at her now you'd think she'd never set eyes on him before. It had always driven him nuts, that ability she had to close out things she didn't want to deal with.

If you think you're going to shut me out that easily, Kailin McGuire, he thought, you're making a big mistake. I don't know why you're down here, but it isn't half as innocent as you'd have us all believe. You're not Quentin J. Yarbro's daughter for nothing. But you're on *my* turf now. So whatever the hell you're up to, I'm going to find out what it is.

"Can we cut through the bull and get to the bottom line, Ms. McGuire?" he heard himself say suddenly. In the startled silence that followed, Brett felt all eyes swing his way. But he was aware only of the pair locked with his, green as grass and narrowed.

Three

"And what bottom line would that be, Mr. Douglass?"

Kailin spoke casually, easily, but her look held a trace of weariness, and Brett felt a sense of satisfaction at having gotten even that small a reaction. "You know the bottom line I mean, Ms. McGuire. The one with the dollars and cents on it."

Her eyes narrowed again, almost imperceptibly. "If you mean the costs involved with canceling the Paradise Point project outright, they're in the report by your left elbow. If you're referring to the estimates to repair the storm damage on Phase Two and the updated figures from Phase Three construction, they're in the one by your *right* elbow." She emphasized the word slightly, just enough to let him know that she was perfectly aware he hadn't been listening to a thing she'd been saying.

"But as I've already said, Mr. Douglass, those figures are all based on projections done by Gulf Coast Development *prior* to my involvement. They're going to be very different once we've established a new plan of attack." She smiled faintly. "But since we have yet to work up such a plan, I have no way of knowing yet what the 'bottom line,' as you put it, will be."

Brett smiled back. "I have a feeling, Ms. McGuire, that you've not only figured out a plan of attack but have the cost worked out to the last penny. All that remains is to convince us that we thought it up ourselves, then cajole us into signing the papers giving Gulf Coast Development approval to start construction on Phase Three of Paradise Point."

A flicker of something—worry, anger, apprehension—darkened Kailin's eyes for an instant, then vanished. She still seemed calm and in control, but she'd gone very still. "Mr. Douglass," she said after a moment, "I'm here at the request of the investors who put up the money for the resort. Obviously it would be in their best interests for the entire resort to be completed and sold out. It would also," she added with a hint of impatience in her voice, "be in Sanibel Island's best interests.

"You depend heavily on tourism down here. The Paradise Point condominiums are top-of-the-line—they'll bring not only solid tax revenue to the community, but the support industries on the island such as restaurants, recreation and so on will also benefit. What we're trying to do here is come up with a workable compromise to attain that end. I'm not trying to *cajole* anyone into anything."

Brett leaned back in his chair and propped his foot on the leg of the table, draping his arm over his upraised knee. "You want us to approve Phase Three," he said flatly, giving her no way out.

"Yes."

It surprised him. He'd expected an argument, or at the very least a circuitous reply designed to sound like one thing while meaning something else altogether. For some reason her honesty irritated him. "The Land Use Committee has withheld approval for start of construction on Phase Three," he said in the slow and elaborately patient voice of a parent explaining something to a small child, "because Gulf Coast made a hash out of Phase Two."

"That's crazy, Douglass," Craig Bryant snapped. "Phase Two had its problems during construction, we've admitted that. But you can't blame that storm last week on us!"

"Blame, hell!" Brett growled. "It was the best thing that's happened to Sanibel in years. If it hadn't blown down most of those cardboard boxes you called condos we'd never have known just *how* badly they'd been built in the first place." He leaned forward slightly. "You're just lucky that no one was living in them when that storm hit, Bryant, or I'd have had you up on murder charges."

"That's getting pretty damned close to libel."

"Sue me."

"Gentlemen, please."

Brett eased his weight back into his chair and swung his gaze onto Kailin. "Six years ago, when we gave Gulf Coast the green light to build Paradise Point, Charlie Bryant was still president of the corporation. Our agreement was with him, and with the way he did business. He was in charge when Phase One was finished a year ago, and it not only met our requirements, it surpassed them."

Brett paused long enough to give Craig a slow stare. "Then Charlie stepped down, and his son took over." He could see a slow flush of anger rise from the throat of Craig's shirt. "In the last year, Gulf Coast Development has gone from being one of the most respected land development firms in this country to a national joke." Brett looked at Kailin again, ignoring an inarticulate sputter from Craig. "Investors have been bailing out like rats off a sinking ship, leaving Gulf Coast so tight for cash they're selling land they don't even own yet just to raise the weekly payroll. Their operating capital's down to nothing. They built Phase Two out of cobwebs and spit, praying it held together long enough for the units to sell so they'd have collateral to finance Phase Three. But Phase Two's nothing but kindling after last week's storm. They're going to have to bulldoze the site clean and start from scratch."

"That," snarled Craig, "is a damned lie! Sure it sustained some storm damage—hell, half the houses on the island were damaged. But not one person who's put down a deposit has asked for his money back. The only thing that's going to keep Phase Two from selling out is this committee's refusal to approve Phase Three. You all know that Phase Three includes the recreation and marina facilities for the whole resort—without the airstrip, the golf course and docking facilities, you've undercut the main selling feature of the whole complex. *That's* why we haven't sold Phase Two out—because of the uncer-

tainty you people have created with all this foot-dragging!
People aren't willing to risk buying a unit in Paradise Point only
to have a bunch of small-town loonies renege on its original
agreement and—''

"Now wait a minute!" Dorothy Enright sat bolt upright,
eyes widening in indignation. "You can't—''

"Ladies and gentlemen! Please!"

"Our original agreement with Gulf Coast granted approval
for Phase Three *if* this committee was satisfied that the terms
of the original agreement were met on Phases One and Two.
And you haven't even come close."

"May I remind you all," Kailin interrupted in a precise voice,
"that this meeting was called to ascertain where both parties
presently stand—*not* to lay blame for past mistakes."

There was a startled silence, and even Brett found himself
wincing slightly at the impatience in her voice.

Kailin let her cool stare move from face to face. "Nobody
wants to see Paradise Point fold. The investors and Gulf Coast
for obvious reasons, the people presently living in Phase One
and those who have purchased units in Phase Two for even
more obvious reasons—and this committee. It's as much in
Sanibel's favor to see this resort built and sold out as it is everyone else's. If Gulf Coast goes bankrupt, you're going to be
stuck with a half-completed resort complex that'll be hung up
in court for years."

Again that steady, appraising gaze moved around the table.
"And I mean *years*. It could be a decade or more before you
can resell the land, and in the meantime Phase One will steadily deteriorate, the owners will dump their units onto the market for whatever they can get, and you're going to have nothing
out there but a ghost town. Land on Sanibel is too precious for
that. I know it, you know it, and Gulf Coast knows it. So instead of trying to outshout each other why don't we discuss how
to best satisfy *everyone's* needs?"

"I'd like to know what Gulf Coast has to say," Dorothy
Enright said. She was a tall, lean woman with short steel-
colored hair and a mind like a bear trap. "Mr. Bryant has been
uncharacteristically quiet so far."

Brett could have sworn that Craig Bryant winced.

"There . . . have been some changes at Gulf Coast," Kailin said quietly. She glanced at Craig as though waiting for him to say something, but he remained sullenly silent, and Brett sat up, suddenly interested. "Mr. Bryant is here in an advisory capacity only," she said quietly. "Until further notice all business transactions will be handled by a board of directors, upon the request of Mr. Charles Bryant."

There was a moment of stunned silence as everyone assessed the implications of Craig's removal. Then the group started talking at once. Kailin held up her hand for silence. "I'm sorry, but I can't tell you any more. However, I will be dealing directly with Charles Bryant—and so will this committee.

"Gulf Coast is *very* serious about reaching a workable solution on Paradise Point," Kailin said into an attentive silence. "This move was made at the recommendation of the investors." She paused delicately. "At my recommendation, actually. Part of Gulf Coast's difficulties seemed to be caused by personality conflicts and certain . . . management practices. Mr. Bryant Senior agreed that the first step lay in alleviating those problems."

Brett felt his grudging admiration for her take another leap. He had no doubt that Charlie's return to the fray was at Kailin's instigation. Replace Bryant junior or face foreclosure, he imagined her saying and smiled. Even though he didn't trust Kailin McGuire, he certainly had to admire her tactics.

"I've spent the past month assessing this situation," Kailin was saying quietly. "For those of you who don't already know, that's what I do for a living. I'm an industrial troubleshooter. Companies that are in serious trouble hire me to come in and figure out why. And, with luck, get them out of it. The Board of Directors has offered me its complete cooperation. That means," she emphasized, looking around the table, "that they are open to negotiation."

"What kind of negotiation?" Dorothy asked. "And how open?"

"Gulf Coast Development is teetering on the edge of bankruptcy," she said bluntly, ignoring the gasps of surprise. "Paradise Point is the only major project that Gulf Coast has under way, and, quite simply, it's going to make or break the company."

"Holy cats," John Grohman muttered, looking mildly horrified. "Do you mean that we're holding the trump card?"

"That's exactly what I mean," Kailin said. "And since I'm confident that no one here wants to see Gulf Coast file for bankruptcy—if for no other reason than the problems it will create for your community—you can see why it's important that we work together."

"You said you'd reviewed the situation," Peter Rylie said suddenly. "Do you have any recommendations?"

"I have a few ideas," Kailin assured him with a smile. "But I'd rather not discuss them until you've all had an opportunity to think over what I've said and to read the material in those two reports. I *am* confident, though, that we can come to some mutually satisfying agreement."

Mutually satisfying. The phrase made Brett smile involuntarily as he found himself thinking of the last time he'd heard her use it. "It's been a most satisfactory afternoon," she'd purred as she'd been leaving. "Satisfying, too. Mutually satisfying, don't you agree?"

Brett's smile widened. He'd agreed, no doubt about it. There hadn't been an afternoon before or since that had come even close to the magic they'd shared that day.

Kailin's eyes happened to meet his just then, and he knew in that instant that she, too, was reminded of that lazy Sunday. They'd spent their time in what had been one deliciously prolonged afternoon of lovemaking—they would fall asleep, his body still a part of hers, then awaken an hour or so later and start over again. It took no effort at all to remember the hot, musky scent of the rumpled sheets, the sensual feel of Kailin's love-damp skin against his, the soft catch in her voice next to his ear as she begged him for *more....*

God! Brett dragged his eyes from hers with a physical effort, feeling his heart racing. He closed his eyes, praying no one else in the room had heard the groan that had escaped. He felt hot and dizzy and realized without surprise that he was vitally and painfully aroused.

He took a deep breath, furious with himself for being so weak. It had been eleven years. Eleven *years!*

Even if he wanted her, he couldn't have her. She belonged to Royce McGuire. She'd always belonged to Royce McGuire.

That summer-long romp with him had been nothing more than a rich girl's whim.

He forced himself to look at Kailin, but she steadfastly refused to meet his eyes. Good, he thought with a flash of uncharacteristically malicious satisfaction. Maybe she wasn't quite as immune to the past as she was letting on. Maybe she hadn't quite forgotten *everything*....

"...meet and go over these reports," a voice at his elbow was saying.

Brett blinked and stared at John Grohman. He looked at the two colored folders in John's hands, then around the room, and realized that the meeting was over.

"You with us at all today, Douglass?" Zac asked testily. He eyed Brett impatiently, gnawing on his dead cigar. "If I didn't know better, I'd say you were in love."

"What?" Brett frowned, then shook his head to dispel the shadows of the past. "Sorry, I was just thinking about Gulf Coast," he lied. "Let's go over those tomorrow, okay? We don't have to waste much time—it's obvious what they want." When the two men stared at him blankly, he dismissed the reports with a flip of his hand. "They want us to green-light Phase Three without even a whimper."

"Now, Brett," John protested, "I didn't get that impression at all. Gulf Coast has its back to the wall; if anyone's going to be giving concessions, it's them. And with old Charlie back in the saddle..."

Zac grunted. "You know I've been dead set against Phase Three right from the beginning, Douglass, but I think John's got a point there. I figure we can get everything we want if we play our hand right."

Brett stood up impatiently. "Take my word for it, you two— Gulf Coast isn't going to give up a damned thing. They want compromises, for sure, but they want *us* to do the compromising."

"But with this mediator sitting—"

"This mediator," Brett interrupted brusquely, "isn't anything more than a pretty smoke screen. She's sitting squarely in Gulf Coast's backyard, and she's going to be pressuring us all the way."

"Brett, I usually agree with you, but this time I think you're wrong." Dorothy Enright's piercing gray gaze held his. "I don't know what this woman has done to get your back up, but you're not thinking straight on this one—not with your brains, anyway." Her mouth twitched in what, by Dorothy, passed for a smile. "Leave your male hormones out of this, Douglass. It's too important." With that she turned on one heel and strode to the door, looking every inch the former sergeant major she was.

"Damn it," Brett breathed, glaring at the other two. "Is that what you think, too?"

Zac grinned. "I think you've changed your tune pretty fast, that's all. Yesterday you were trying to push me into voting for approval, today you're dead set against it." The cigar shifted. "She's a mighty attractive woman, Douglass."

"So was Mata Hari," Brett muttered. He shoved past Zac and headed for the door, still rankled by Dorothy's gibe. It wasn't hormones talking where Kailin was concerned, it was common sense. And experience. Plenty of experience!

Zac Cheevers's law offices were in the top level of a two-story shopping complex surrounded by tropical gardens. A roofed walkway ran the perimeter of the upper level, its protected wooden railing draped with flowering vines.

Kailin paused at the top of the long flight of wooden steps leading down to the parking lot and drew in a deep breath of clean, wet air. The storm had passed. The crushed-coral-and-shell parking lot glinted with puddles of rainwater, and the air held a welcome freshness. She turned her face gratefully to the sun streaming down through a patchwork of puffy clouds and concentrated on relaxing the muscles knotted across her shoulders.

That meeting was step one. It was always the hardest because it required breaking through everyone's suspicion and anger. That was the problem with a job like hers: she was called in only after everything else had failed, when tempers were raw and antagonisms deeply embedded. It was like walking through a mine field.

"That was an impressive bit of work in there, Ms. McGuire."

Kailin wasn't particularly surprised when the quiet male voice broke through her reverie. Perhaps, she thought idly as she turned to look at him, that was why she'd dawdled out here in the first place. "Thank you, Mr. Douglass. You were fairly impressive yourself. Do you and Craig Bryant always get along so well?"

"Bryant's a jerk," Brett retorted flatly. He strolled to the porch railing and sat on it, hitching one leg up. "He's greedy, he's ambitious, and in the year and a half since he's taken over Gulf Coast he's damned near run it into the ground." He smiled and gave her an appraising look. "Of course, you know all that. You were the one who got him turfed out." When she didn't deny it, his eyes narrowed slightly. "You reminded me of your father up there today."

"Somehow I don't think you meant that as a compliment."

"I didn't."

Kailin watched him in frowning silence. He was like a tropical storm himself, all brooding shadows and thunderheads. Just what did he expect from her, anyway?

"How *is* your father?"

"Not...too well." Where was *this* leading? "He had a heart attack about six months ago."

"I didn't think he had one." There was an awkward pause, then Brett sighed and ran his fingers through his hair. "Damn it, that was a stupid thing to say. I'm sorry."

Kailin laughed quietly. "Don't be. It was just as much a shock to everyone who'd ever known him—a bigger shock to him. I think he was disappointed in a way. I know he was furious that his body dared betray him like that. He was like a bear for weeks, making everyone's life more miserable than usual."

Brett looked around at her, a hint of a smile warming his firm mouth. "I can't see Quentin J. Yarbro being an invalid for long. He probably just *ordered* his heart to repair itself and was back to his usual rampaging self in a week."

"What it did was scare him. For the first time in my life I actually saw my father faced with something he couldn't control—and it terrified him. He hasn't been the same since." She frowned and looked out across the shimmering parking lot. A tiny green lizard scampered up one of the railing supports into the sun. It paused there to soak up the warmth, glistening like cut emeralds.

She felt awkward and uneasy, afraid of saying something that would set off another outburst like his earlier one. She'd planned all the the things she would say if she ever saw him again, but they all seemed futile and empty.

She shook off her moodiness and looked up to find Brett watching her. Their eyes met and held, and for a breathless eternity Kailin stood riveted there. One step, something whispered coaxingly. Just one step, and you'll be in his arms again....

She turned away instead, angry and confused at how easily she could still make a fool of herself over this man.

"Gulf Coast is fighting for its life."

The brusque change of topic knocked her off balance for a moment. Then she recovered, wondering if he'd seen a hint of that weakness in her eyes. "Yes." She strolled to the railing and leaned against it, lifting her face to the sun again.

"Are you paid a percentage of future profit if you succeed in pulling it through?"

"I don't get a percentage of anything," she replied quietly. "I'm paid a flat fee, win or lose. But I like to win. Call it old-fashioned pride if you like, but I love catching a failing company at the brink of ruin and helping it struggle back onto its feet."

"And if we don't approve Phase Three?"

"Gulf Coast will go bankrupt, the investors will lose everything they've put into it, and Sanibel Island will be stuck with a white elephant called Paradise Point." She smiled. "It's a classic no-win situation, Mr. Chairman. I'd really suggest you approve Phrase Three."

"That sounds like a threat."

"For God's sake, Brett!" Kailin fought her impatience and lost badly. "I know you, remember—you're a realist. You know as well as I do that sooner or later *someone* is going to develop that land. You've been pushing for approval for the last six months, so you're as aware as I am of the problems you're facing if Gulf Coast fails."

"Sure the Point's going to be developed—but it has to be the right people doing it. That leaves Craig Bryant out. His father did a good job, but Craig's dangerous, Kailin. Phase Two is nothing but rubble after that storm. If we allow him to re-build—and give him approval to start building Phase Three—he's not going to put up anything better. And I'm damned if I'm going to have the lives of innocent people on my con-science when the whole mess blows into the sea!"

"My reports on the storm damage don't indicate anything nearly as bad as you keep telling me."

"*Your* reports? Or Craig Bryant's reports?" When Kailin remained silent, Brett nodded. "I thought so. He's feeding you what he wants you to know, Kailin. Have you been out to the Point yet?"

"No," Kailin admitted. "The road is…apparently closed."

"I'll just bet it is."

"How do you know what the damage is?"

"I went in by boat a couple of days and looked, that's how."

"Well, I'm not going to work up my recommendations until I've seen it, too, so don't worry." She smiled at him dryly. "I'm not supposed to be taking sides here, but I'll give you a piece of free advice— Charlie Bryant wants to save his company. Play your cards right and you can get every concession you've ever wanted out of them."

"And what concessions do *you* want, Kailin?" He looked at her coolly. "That's the real bottom line I'm interested in hear-ing about. Just what is Kailin McGuire getting out of this?"

The bitterness in Brett's voice made Kailin look at him sharply.

"McGuire International is into real estate, isn't it?"

Kailin found herself staring stupidly at him while she men-tally scrambled to follow another unexpected shift in the con-versation. "Yes, I think so. I know they have holdings in the Caribbean and Mexico—hotels, I think."

"You think."

Kailin turned until she was facing him squarely, fighting a little frisson of anger. "Brett, I'm getting damned tired of this. If you're trying to say something, spit it out. I don't like play-ing games."

"No?" He gave a bark of raw laughter. "Hell, Kailin, you *invented* game playing." Then, abruptly, he sobered. "But you're right, let's be frank. McGuire International owns eight major European hotels, two Caribbean resorts and a combined health spa and tennis clinic just outside Mexico City."

She saw where he was headed. "Brett . . ." she started warningly.

"Do you think I can't see what's going on?" he said angrily. "Gulf Coast is on the rocks, a prime takeover target, and McGuire International wants it. But they're not interested in acquiring it while the Paradise Point project is still up in the air. They sent you down here to soften us up—*me* up. You said it yourself—you know me. You know how my mind works. What better person to send down than someone who knows her opponent, right?"

"Don't be absurd!" His accusations were so preposterous that Kailin didn't know whether to laugh or cry. "Listen to yourself Brett, you've turned paranoia into an art form!"

"Did Royce put you up to this, or was it your idea?" he asked belligerently. "How *is* old Royce these days?"

Kailin stared at him. Oh God, she thought, shocked, he doesn't know! "Brett, there's something you—"

"Just what has your husband got riding on this, anyway?"

Without warning, Kailin's patience evaporated. "My husband is dead."

Brett blinked, then stared at her in stunned silence.

"Royce was killed in a car accident nearly six years ago. Which has nothing to do with this, anyway, because I have never had anything to do with *any* aspect of the McGuire business, before *or* after Royce's death."

"Oh, Kailin." Brett drew in a deep, unsteady breath. He'd gone pale and was staring at her, his eyes dark with shock. "I . . . those things I said earlier," he whispered hoarsely. "About the two of you. I . . . damn it!" A flush suffused his face, and he wheeled away from her, swearing softly. "Kailin, I'm sorry. I was trying to hurt you, but I never dreamed . . ."

To her surprise, Kailin felt her sudden hot anger melt away. She gazed at Brett's back, wondering why seeing him squirm gave her no satisfaction at all. She should have been rejoicing at making him pay for the things he'd said, but for some reason she found herself feeling badly for his obvious discomfort. "I don't know why, but it never occurred to me that you wouldn't know. The papers in Indiana were filled with it for days, but I guess down here he wouldn't have gotten more than a passing mention on a back page somewhere."

"Why didn't you tell me?" His voice was still harsh with shock.

In spite of herself, Kailin had to laugh. "You didn't exactly give me an opportunity, Brett."

He flushed again. What must it be like for him, Kailin wondered, finding himself face-to-face with her after all these years with no warning at all? She at least had been given some time to prepare herself, but he was still reeling from the shock, lashing out blindly as he struggled to come to terms with having her in his life again.

"I'm sorry." She blinked, realized he was looking down at her, a frown wedged solidly between his brows. "It's just that seeing you again brought it all back, Kailin. That's not an excuse, it's just a fact. For eleven years I haven't been able to get the image out of my mind of the two of you together, and when I saw you this morning..." He shook his head wearily and stared off into the distance. "Hell, I don't know. It's been eating me up inside, I guess. Knowing he had you and I didn't."

"You were always there between us," she whispered, not having the faintest clue why she was telling him this. It was none of his business, especially after what he'd said this morning, but for some reason it seemed right that he know. "Royce was terrified you'd come riding out of the mists one day and spirit me away. I don't think he ever really believed I'd married him instead of you."

"He wasn't the only one." His voice was rough. He turned to look at her, eyes unreadable.

Kailin's gaze faltered. A light breeze fingered her hair scented by rain and the sea. "I didn't think you cared," she said softly.

"Damn it, Kailin—" He stopped, as though he'd caught himself about to say something he didn't want to.

"You never came after me," she whispered, rubbing her fingers along the railing.

"Oh, I came, all right." His voice was just a breath of sound right behind her. "Kailin, I was after you like a hound on a fox with your old man running interference all the way. But I was too late. When I finally figured out what was going on, you were Mrs. Royce McGuire."

"My father told me you'd left, that I'd turned into more trouble than you were interested in handling."

"You sure as hell were that," he growled. "And you believed him?"

"I didn't know what to believe by then." She looked up at the cloud-quilted sky, feeling suddenly very tired.

"Mo-om!" There was a rush of footsteps, and Becky raced up the steps like a miniature hurricane, all arms and legs and flying golden hair.

Kailin looked around and was just about to say something to her daughter when she caught sight of Brett's face. And froze. He had wheeled around and was staring at the girl as though a bomb had gone off, his expression holding such indescribable expectancy that Kailin's heart literally stopped beating.

Four

Everything was happening all wrong! Kailin whispered in her mind. She'd hoped to warn him about Becky before they met, but now it was too late.

The girl reached the top of the stairs in a burst of energy, radiating exuberance as a stove radiates heat. "Hey, Mom, can we—whoops!" She saw Brett and stopped dead. Then, unabashed, she grinned even wider. "Sorry."

"Becky," Kailin said quietly. "This is—"

"Brett Douglass." Becky's eyes shone. "Oh, wow, this is too much! You look exactly like your pictures. And you look a lot better without that dumb beard."

"This," Kailin said with a dry smile, "is my ever-tactful daughter, Rebecca. She's staying down here with me for a few days over Thanksgiving, then will head back up to Indiana to stay with her grandparents when school starts again."

Becky made a face, then grinned at Brett. "Everyone calls me Becky. Did you really chain yourself to the gates of Grandad Yarbro's plant? Mom says you even went to jail once. She says—"

"Becky, for heaven's sake!" Kailin protested.

"Sorry," Becky said, not looking sorry in the least. "But it's so great actually seeing you. I mean, I've heard so much about you and—" She stopped at a look from Kailin, grinning unrepentantly.

"She can be a little overwhelming at times," Kailin said with a laugh. "But after Royce died I used to dig out all my old picture albums, and I'd tell her about all the crazy things we used to do." Brett gave her such an odd look that she blushed self-consciously. "I guess you—your memory—helped me through some hard times. And you know how kids are fascinated by the things their parents did when *they* were young. Becky could never get enough of it—" Kailin stopped.

Brett's memory *had* helped get her through the nightmare months after Royce had been killed, but that hadn't been the only reason she'd spent long hours going through those albums, reading the letters, daydreaming of what had been—of what might have been. And it wasn't the only reason she regretted having said anything about it now. Showing that hint of her own vulnerability was bad enough, but what was worse—infinitely worse—was that Brett very obviously thought she'd told Becky about him because he was her father....

Entranced, he was staring at the girl in front of him, his expression so filled with wonder that it made Kailin's heart ache. Becky was tall for her age, seemingly consisting of nothing but long, tanned limbs and masses of silver-gold hair exactly the same color as her own. It would be easy to believe she was a year older than her nine years.

She had to tell him the truth. But how? When?

"Kailin! Glad I caught you!"

Kailin turned toward the voice in relief, grateful for the interruption. Linda McAllister was standing just below them, shading her eyes with her hand as she grinned up at Kailin. Her freckled nine-year-old daughter was beside her, and Kailin smiled at them both. "Hi, you two!"

"How about coming to a movie with us tonight?" Linda called up.

"I'd love to, but I'm up to my ears in work!"

"Can Becky come?" Peggy McAllister piped up hopefully.

"That's a great idea," Linda said. "She can stay over tonight, and tomorrow morning I'll take them both over to the craft and art fair down at the community center."

Becky's eyes widened. "Oh, can I, Mom?"

Kailin laughed. "I don't know why not. You're sure it won't be any trouble, Linda?"

"Hardly!" Linda assured her. "It's great having someone Peggy's age around."

"Come on, Becky," Peggy cried, everything settled to her satisfaction. "There's this real neat parrot over by the restaurant that talks and everything!"

Becky started toward the stairs, then paused and gave Kailin a sly sidelong look. "With me out of the way, you can invite Brett over."

"Rebecca . . ." Kailin said, her voice rising warningly.

Becky grinned. "See you tomorrow! And it was nice finally meeting you, Dr. Douglass."

Brett swept off an imaginary hat and bowed deeply, clicking his heels. "Until we meet again, fair maiden."

Becky giggled with delight, then galloped down the stairs, pausing at the bottom to wave.

"Thanks, Linda," Kailin called after the three of them. "I'll call you tomorrow."

"It hasn't taken you long to make friends."

Kailin smiled and turned to look at Brett. "Sheer luck, actually. Linda's husband owns a manufacturing plant in Virginia. I did some troubleshooting there a couple of years ago and Linda and I got to be friends. It's just coincidence that they're down here for a couple of weeks while Becky and I are here, but it's great for the kids."

Brett was still staring after Becky, his expression wistful. "She's beautiful."

"Yes, she is." Kailin hesitated, biting her lower lip as she realized she didn't have an inkling of what to say next. All her worst nightmares about seeing Brett again hadn't prepared her for *this*. It had never occurred to her that he would think Becky was his; after all, he hadn't even believed she was pregnant!

But she'd been wrong about that, too. Kailin took a deep breath, bracing herself. He'd not only finally believed her, he'd gone looking for her—only to find her married to Royce. Oh,

Brett, she whispered silently, how you must have hated me. And
all those years I hated you, thinking you didn't care. "Brett,
there's something I have to—"

"Taking the afternoon off, Douglass?" Kailin glanced
around as Craig Bryant strolled toward them. He grinned at
her, oblivious to her unwelcoming scowl, and slipped his arm
around her waist. "You never gave me an answer about supper tonight, Kailin."

Catching sight of the expression on Brett's face, Kailin
groaned inwardly. Great timing, Craig, she thought savagely.
Her annoyance was intensified by the knowledge that Craig had
done it on purpose, and that Brett, the big oaf, had fallen for
it hook, line and proverbial sinker.

She eased herself from Craig's embrace and picked up her
briefcase. "Something's come up, Craig, I'm sorry."

Craig's face darkened. "Something or someone?"

Brett's face was like granite. "Ease off, Bryant. You're
walking on thin ice."

"Staking a claim, Douglass?" Craig's eyebrow arched. "In
case you hadn't noticed, I was here first."

"In case neither of you Neanderthals had noticed," Kailin
cut in impatiently, "this is the Twentieth Century. If anyone's
claim gets staked, I'll be the one doing the staking."

"Look, Kailin, what's going on here?" Craig glared at her
belligerently. "You and Douglass got something going I don't
know about?"

"Bryant..." Brett took a catlike step toward the other man.

"You stay the hell out of this, Douglass. I'm sick and tired
of you dogging my tracks everywhere I go!"

Kailin didn't even see what started it. One moment Craig and
Brett were standing nose-to-nose like two rutting stags, and in
the next Craig's fist caught Brett squarely on the side of his jaw.
He staggered back with a grunt of pain, then regained his balance, drew his right arm back and threw a punch at Craig's
outthrust chin that had every ounce of his 170-odd pounds behind it.

"Brett!" Kailin gasped as Craig landed flat on his back. He
lay there staring at the overhanging roof, unmoving. "My God,
you've killed him!"

"Killed him, hell!" snarled Brett, shaking his right fist furiously. "I should break his damned neck!"

"Not on my property," came a low growl from behind them. Zac Cheevers strode toward them, teeth clamped down on the ever-present cigar. "Damn it, boy, if you're going to kill a man, don't do it in front of your lawyer's office. Take him out into the swamp somewhere and stuff him under a mangrove root."

Craig sat up slowly, groaning. "I think he broke my nose." He touched it gingerly, then examined his fingers for blood.

"I didn't come anywhere near your nose," Brett growled through gritted teeth. He was still cradling his fist painfully. "But I'd be happy to oblige."

"That's enough." Zac caught Brett's arm and pulled him back roughly. "If you two young bucks want to have it out, fine—it's long overdue. But take it somewhere else. And leave *her*—" he thrust his bull-like head toward Kailin "—out of it. Fighting over a principle is one thing, fighting over a woman is purely stupid." He pulled Craig to his feet. "Now you get the hell off my property."

Craig left, giving Brett a ferocious glare that earned him a muttered curse. "Damn young fools," Zac muttered. He looked at Kailin. "This is the kind of trouble we don't need right now. I suppose you realize that." Then he gave a snort of laughter and turned away, shaking his big gray head in amusement. "Can't blame you, boy," he said to Brett as he walked by him. "If I was about thirty years younger, you'd be fightin' me off, too."

After Zac had disappeared, Kailin took a deep breath and looked at Brett. "That," she said with precision, "was just about the stupidest thing I've ever seen you do."

Brett looked at his hand, wincing. Then he shook his head slowly and prodded his jaw. "I can't believe I did it myself," he muttered sheepishly. "I haven't pulled a stunt like that in years."

"About eleven of them, I suspect." She took his hand in hers and examined the swollen, bruised knuckles. "It's a miracle you didn't break something."

He flexed his fingers experimentally. Then his eyes caught hers and he started to chuckle. The chuckle grew to a deep, lazy laugh, and Kailin, unable to help herself, joined him. The stiffness between them melted, and for a moment they were best friends and lovers again. It had always been like this between them. It had driven their friends crazy when their eyes would catch and they'd burst into laughter for no apparent reason, linked in some special way that transcended spoken words.

Smiling, Kailin put her fingers under his chin and tipped it up, eyeing the bruise that was already starting to discolor his jaw. "Classic Brett Douglass. I'd have thought you'd learned to duck by now."

"It's been a long time since I had to."

"Paradise Point's important to you, isn't it?"

"It's important. But this didn't have anything to do with Paradise Point."

"I know." She touched his bruised hand. "I'd have never accepted Craig's dinner invitation."

"It wouldn't be any of my business if you did."

"I know that, too."

The silence grew taut as wire between them. Kailin could feel his warm breath stir her hair, could smell the leathery cologne he was wearing. It seemed to fold around her, drawing her into him, and without even thinking about what she was doing she lowered her head and kissed his swollen knuckles. She rested her lips on each in turn, then delicately ran the tip of her tongue along them.

She heard him swallow. He cupped her head with his other hand and slowly drew her against him until her forehead rested on his chest. She felt dizzy and had to fight for every breath, aware of nothing but the pressure of his hand, the touch of his mouth against her hair. The deep, regular thud of his heart seemed to vibrate through every atom in her body, and she slowly relaxed against him, not daring to do more than breathe.

Kailin had no idea how long they stood like that, caught in an otherworldly reality that excluded everything but the two of them. She thought she heard him whisper her name and tried to answer, but the breath caught in her throat as his fingers tangled in her hair and he pressed her tightly to him.

Then, slowly, the real world intruded, a bit at a time: the bark of a dog, a woman's laughter, the startled cry of a baby. Kailin opened her eyes, aware of the roughness of Brett's denim shirt against her cheek. The pressure of his fingers in her hair eased and she felt him take a deep, uneven breath, as though waking from sleep.

She stepped away from him unsteadily. "I . . . uh . . . should get going," she whispered, not looking at him.

"Yeah." He sounded as shaken as she felt. "I've got an irate tomcat back at the clinic awaiting the unkindest cut of all."

"Ouch." Kailin laughed, daring to glance up at him. "Doomed to a life of amorous memories."

"And maybe a few regrets, if he's like the rest of us," Brett said very quietly. He reached out and tipped her chin up with his finger, gazing down at her with a frown. Then, without saying another word, he turned and walked away.

"Glad I talked you into coming?" Jill Benedict Kincaide took a large bite out of the end of Brett's hot dog, then handed it back to him with a smile. "I love country fairs. Food always tastes better outside, doesn't it?"

"I haven't had the chance to find out yet," Brett said, surveying the damage to his frankfurter. "I thought you weren't hungry."

"I'm not." Jill took a long swallow from his soft drink, smiling around the straw. "Not now, anyway. Thanks."

"Kincaide not feeding you properly?" Brett sank his teeth into what was left of his meal with enthusiasm.

Jill laughed. "He's feeding me just fine. You still mad because I ran off and married him instead of you?"

"I've thought of eliminating him a couple of times," Brett assured her conversationally. "I'm always in the market for a good-looking woman who knows her way around a lab. Besides, we could use an extra hand tagging water birds over in the conservation area."

"You're always in the market for a good-looking woman, period," Jill teased. "And I had my fill of wading around mangrove swamps counting alligator eggs and banding egrets while I was down here a year ago. I'm quite happy puttering around my research lab and being a wife and mother."

"It shows." Brett slipped his arm around her shoulders. "I'm glad you two worked it out, Jill. I like happy endings."

"With thanks to you." She smiled up at him. "If you'd been less honorable, Brett Douglass, you'd have kept me all to yourself and Hunt and I would never have gotten back together."

"Except he'd always have had your heart. I'd have been second best, and second best in love isn't love at all." He tightened his arm around Jill as he found himself thinking of Kailin. *Was* it possible that she'd really loved him eleven years ago? That she'd married Royce McGuire because she'd felt betrayed and abandoned at a time when she'd needed someone the most? And what was she doing down here now? Was it simple coincidence that had brought her back into his life again, or was there something else going on, something to do with Paradise Point?

Damn it, this was driving him crazy! He'd lain awake half the night trying to unravel all the possibilities and was no closer to an answer this morning. Half of him wanted to believe her, and half of him mistrusted everything she said. He sighed and rubbed his forehead wearily.

"You're brooding." Jill slid her arm around his waist and hugged him. "What's an old bachelor like you doing pondering the intricacies of love, anyway? Something going on in your life I should know about?"

"No. And yes, I *am* glad you talked me into coming down here." His gesture took in the loud, enthusiastic mob surrounding them.

Dozens of colorful booths and exhibit tables had been set up around the small community center, and the overflow had poured into the huge vacant lot across Periwinkle Way. There seemed to be hundreds of people there, all laughing and chattering as they strolled from one craft exhibit to the next or wandered arm in arm, simply enjoying the sunshine. The air was redolent with the tang of mustard and relish and the sweet scent of spun sugar candy. Brett discovered to his surprise that he *was* enjoying himself.

A puff of warm wind curled around them, scented with pine pitch and the sea, and he smiled. "I needed this."

"I know. You've been in another world for days, Brett. I'm worried about you."

"Everything's great," he lied, knowing by Jill's expression that she wasn't taken in. Letting his smile fade, he sighed and gave her shoulder a squeeze as they strolled through the crowd.

"I'll survive. She'll be leaving soon and I'll be back to normal."

"She?" Jill stopped dead. "I knew it! I *told* Hunt you were showing all the classic symptoms of woman trouble. What's going on, Brett? Who is she?"

Cursing himself for not keeping his mouth shut, Brett simply smiled. "Just an old acquaintance." *And some old memories . . .*

Jill eyed him assessingly. "I'll be damned. You *have* been bitten, haven't you?"

Why deny it? Brett asked himself glumly. Last night he'd finally had to admit to himself that he was still halfway in love with Kailin McGuire. Why and how, God alone knew. He'd thought he'd gotten her out of his system long ago, but it must be like malaria, lying dormant for years before something set it off again. All it had taken was one look into those grass-green eyes yesterday and he'd known he wanted her as badly as he ever had.

Like a moth to a candle, he reminded himself grimly.

Again he shook himself free of it. He looked down at Jill and grinned. "How come with all the miracle cures you hotshot scientists are always coming up with you've never found a vaccine against broken hearts?"

Jill gave a snort of laughter. "That bad, huh?"

"That bad."

"Anything I can do?"

"Besides cutting my throat and putting me out of my misery?"

"She married?"

"Not anymore."

"In love with someone else?"

Brett thought of Craig Bryant. "Not that I know of."

"Then I don't see what the problem is."

"It just isn't that easy," he said quietly.

"Does she love you?"

"Jill—" He caught her expression and swallowed the protest. "In her own way, maybe she did once. But now?" He shrugged. "Who knows? Like I said, it isn't that easy."

"Once?" Jill's eyes narrowed. "Just how long have you been suffering this affliction, anyway?"

"About eleven years."

"Eleven *years*?" Jill stopped so suddenly that Brett nearly ran into her. "God, Brett! You've been in love with this woman for eleven years and still don't know how she feels?"

"I never said I loved her," Brett muttered.

"Don't be ridiculous." Jill slipped her arm through his and started walking again. "It's written all over you. And a man doesn't stay in with a woman for eleven years unless it's the real thing."

The real thing? Brett smiled inwardly. Jill was a classic scientist, able to distill anything down to its most basic components. But there were still some things that defied analysis. Love was one of them. Kailin McGuire was another.

"You stealing my wife, Douglass?"

Brett glanced up to find Hunter Kincaide lounging against a nearby hamburger concession stand, his grin lazy and warm. He was cradling a sleeping baby against one shoulder and a large stuffed rabbit against the other, carrying off the apparent contradiction between the hard-boiled investigative reporter and the doting father with élan.

"I've been trying my damnedest," Brett assured him with a slashing grin, "but she won't have me."

Jill laughed and slipped the baby out of Hunt's grasp. "Our fearless bachelor veterinarian here is in love."

"Jill, I am *not* in—"

Hunter gave a snort of laughter and clapped Brett solidly on the shoulder. "Just ignore it, Douglass. It's called postnatal euphoria, and the symptoms include seeing everything through a rosy haze, being convinced the entire world is in love and trying to marry off all your single friends. Everyone in Washington runs when they see her coming."

"Liar." Jill gave Hunter a poke in the ribs with her elbow, then slipped Brett a teasing look. "I expect a wedding invitation within six months, or I'm coming back down here to raise hell, got that?"

"Yes, ma'am," Brett retorted smartly. "Do you bully Kincaide like this?"

"All the time," Hunter said fondly, giving his wife a hug.

Watching the two of them sharing teasing smiles, cradling their child between them, Brett felt a pang of sadness shoot

through him. When he'd first met Jill she'd been numb with
hurt, her career shattered. For nearly seven months she'd wandered around like a victim of shell shock, trying to put the
pieces of her life together, torn between love and hate for the
tall, gray-eyed man now standing beside her. But Hunter Kincaide, thank God, had refused to let her go. He'd followed her
to Sanibel with the tenacity that had earned him the nickname
of Bulldog Kincaide, and he'd hung on until they'd faced the
problems and misunderstandings that had torn them apart.

He watched Kincaide smile down at his sleeping son, Jill
tucked comfortably into the curve of his arm, and felt another
stabbing ache run through him—of regret this time. All those
wasted years, he found himself thinking. All those years when
Royce McGuire had been raising Becky, seeing her first smile,
her first step, listening to her first tentative words.

Damn.

He had to catch his breath at the sense of utter loss that ar-
rowed through him. And Becky? Where did she fit into his life
now, or he into hers?

He shook his head. He could go on trying to rework the past
for the next twenty years, but the bottom line was what was best
for Becky. He'd walked out on Kailin eleven years ago. He
hadn't even believed her when she'd told him she was pregnant. Kailin had done the best she could. He had no right. No
right at all. And yet . . . watching Jill and Hunter, he had the
sudden, impulsive urge to find Kailin, to talk with her, to
plan—

"Are you all right?" Brett blinked, realized Jill was peering
up at him worriedly. "Hunt and I are going sailing this afternoon. Interested in coming with us? You look like you could
use an afternoon with friends. To talk, maybe . . ."

Brett ruffled her tousled hair with his hand, grinning.
"Thanks, but I've got things to do. There's someone here this
afternoon I have to talk to."

Jill's face lighted up, and she gave a soft, knowing laugh.
"Six months at the latest, Douglass. I mean it." Then, before
Brett could say anything, she slipped her arm through Hunter's and tugged him into the crowd, sparing Brett a sly wink
before she disappeared.

Brett found himself laughing at Jill's indefatigable belief in the marvels of love. But how do you recognize it when you find it? he felt like shouting after her. How do you separate reality from wishful thinking, truth from lie? And how do you ever learn to trust again?

"It's a Spanish piece of eight," the jeweler said. "Salvaged off a galleon that went down off the Keys in 1675. We have certificates of authenticity and provide you with a numbered photo of the piece to identify it for insurance purposes."

Kailin turned the old coin in her fingers. It was worn and irregular, but she could still make out the markings on it. It had been mounted in a narrow border of gold. The jeweler slipped a gold chain through the loop, and Kailin held it up to her throat to admire it in a hand mirror. "It's beautiful!"

"If you want an outside opinion, take it." Two tanned hands slipped around her throat and took the chain from her fingers, startling Kailin so badly that she nearly dropped the mirror.

"Brett!"

"Gorgeous." He took his hands away from the clasp and let them rest lightly on the bare skin of her shoulders, his eyes holding hers in the mirror. "And so's the pendant."

The touch of his hands was like fire. It seemed impossible that such an innocent gesture could rattle her, but Kailin found herself tongue-tied and breathless. Feeling herself blush, she tipped the mirror hastily so that it reflected only the coin. It glowed like fire on her sun-burnished skin, and she found herself nodding.

"You're right." To her relief, her voice sounded almost normal. "I'll take it."

To her simultaneous relief and regret, Brett drew his hands from her. Her skin tingled as though she'd gotten too much sun, although she knew that wasn't the reason. You're acting like an idiot, she advised herself calmly. At thirty you're supposed to be immune to all this silliness, not melting into a puddle at the mere touch of a man's hand. Not even *this* man's hands.

Brett stepped around her and leaned one elbow on the display case, looking at the pendant, which was still around her throat. Kailin picked up the mirror and looked at it again, trying to ignore the way his eyes were moving leisurely from the pendant to the bare sweep of her shoulders above the ruffled bodice of her sundress. "No lecture on how I'm contributing to the destruction of offshore archaeological sites?"

"I've mellowed." His teeth flashed in a teasing grin. "Besides, that coin is displayed much more effectively around your throat than in some dusty museum."

"You *have* mellowed." She lifted an eyebrow as she removed the pendant and handed it to the jeweler. "In the past you'd have been picketing this place."

"Then I thought you could fight the battle on all fronts at once and still win. I've learned to focus my firepower on one or two major skirmishes at a time."

"Like Paradise Point?"

"Like Craig Bryant. There's a difference."

Kailin looked at him seriously. "I'm glad you realize that."

"You know this guy?" the jeweler asked Kailin, nodding at Brett.

Brett grinned, his eyes capturing Kailin's. "Oh, yes, she knows me."

There was no mistaking the intimacies that simple statement encompassed, and to Kailin's intense annoyance she felt herself color again.

"Well, in that case..." The jeweler did some rapid calculations, then quoted her a price that was substantially lower than the original one. He grinned sheepishly. "I charge the tourists a little more."

"No kidding! Knowing Brett Douglass takes me out of that unenviable classification, does it?"

"Knowing Brett Douglass makes you practically family," the jeweler assured her with a laugh. "He saved my old dog a couple of years ago after he tangled with a gator." He cupped the pendant in his palm. "Would you like it in a box?"

A few minutes later, pendant tucked in her handbag, Kailin looked up at Brett and smiled. "Thank you. If I'd known being an acquaintance of yours was the key to getting great bargains, I'd have been name-dropping all morning."

Brett's laugh was throaty. "There's still all afternoon, if you'd like some company." He paused, then added very casually, "Unless you're already with someone."

Kailin gave him a tolerant look. "You never used to be this tactful, Douglass. To answer the question you didn't ask, no, I am not here with Craig Bryant."

Brett gazed down at her calmly. "The man's a hustler and a punk, Kailin. Don't fall for his smooth line."

"I wasn't intending to," she assured him dryly. "I'm a good deal older than when you knew me last, Brett. I don't fall for anyone's smooth line anymore."

He gave her a lazy, appraising glance. "That meant for me?"

"It was a general observation."

He nodded and shoved his hands into the back pockets of his jeans, strolling along beside her as relaxed as a cat. It didn't take Kailin long to realize that Brett knew most of the people there. The mob parted before them as the Red Sea had before Moses, and almost everyone had a word to say, a smile, a nod of the head. Everyone from gray-haired matrons to toddlers knew him by name, and he returned the greetings with the relaxed congeniality of a man comfortable in the community.

"Is there anyone here you don't know?" she asked, a trifle testy, as a gorgeous redhead in the tiniest shorts and the skimpiest French-cut T-shirt imaginable drifted across their path.

Brett wrestled his gaze from the redhead's decorative retreat and blinked, looking down at her. "What did you say? Sorry."

"If I'm in the way, Douglass, just say the word."

He grinned lazily and dropped his arm around her shoulders, tugging her gently against him. "I wouldn't detect the merest trace of jealousy, would I?"

"Of course not," she retorted airily. "Why on earth would I be jealous?" *Why indeed*, an inner voice asked with almost gleeful spite. She ignored it and gave him a speculative glance. "You *do* have a certain, reputation...."

"You probably won't believe this, but I haven't had a relationship with a woman—a *serious* relationship—in over two years."

"And what about the nonserious ones?" she asked flippantly.

"Dinner, a drink or two, maybe some dancing. Then home. Alone." He looked down at her, his eyes serious. "Rumor has it I'm living the classic bachelor's life. But the truth is, I spend most of my nights with no one but my old dog for company."

"Most?" Kailin groaned. "I can't believe I just said that! Sorry..."

"I never said I was perfect," Brett said with a teasing laugh. "Once in a long, long while, Kailin. That's all."

"It isn't any of my business."

"No more than your relationship with Bryant was mine."

Why, Kailin asked herself thoughtfully, were they doing this? People usually got things like old lovers out of the way if they were planning on starting something, not simply as afternoon chitchat. "How come you're still on the loose, anyway? I'd have thought some beach goddess would have snapped you up years ago."

"Maybe I'm still in love with you, Kailin."

He said it easily, his grin flashing in the sunlight, and Kailin laughed. "Are you flirting with me, Douglass?"

"Hard to break old habits." His eyes caught hers, aglow with old memories. "Especially enjoyable ones."

The words had a rough, smokey edge to them, and she remembered with sudden clarity the way he'd growled her name while they'd been making love, the husky catch to his voice when he'd whispered those deliciously explicit things....

"Do you—do you think we could get something to eat?" she asked unsteadily, hoping he didn't have any idea of what she'd just been thinking. Damn it, what was the matter with her! It was difficult enough trying to appear calm and in control without having her mind dart off onto these erotic little side trips. She slipped Brett a curious glance, wondering if he was having the same problem. Maybe that was why his mood kept shifting, silently hostile one moment, antagonistic the next, then this gentle, almost wistful teasing. It was like sharing a cage with a tiger and never knowing what to expect. It was keeping her so off balance that she felt dizzy.

"Does a hot dog sound all right?" Brett asked lightly.

"A hot dog sounds fantastic! With relish, mustard and lots of onions?"

"Is there any other way?"

"Not in any civilized universe." She slipped her arm through his. "You always did know the way to my heart."

"I knew two or three ways," Brett murmured with a chuckle. 'Although I don't remember mustard and onions being in-olved." His eyes met hers. "Chocolate sauce, yes. But mus-ard and onions . . . ?"

"Brett!" Kailin sputtered with laughter, her cheeks burning as the memories of that night came flooding back. "I think I'd like just a hot dog, all right?"

"For now."

Kailin threw him a sharp, puzzled glance, and Brett had to mile. Just what the hell he thought he was doing, he didn't know. Flirting with her was one thing, but he was sailing very close to dangerous waters with all these sly little inuendos and reminiscences. It was as though he were deliberately taunting himself, seeing how near he could get to the past before the pain started.

Smiling, he recalled when he'd been a kid and every winter there had been a dare made as to who could bring his tongue nearest the frosted wrought-iron fence around the schoolyard without actually touching it. And every winter they had all miscalculated and wound up glued to the thing. It had been an act of courage, and he could still remember the thrill of excitement that had preceded the agony of getting free. He looked down at Kailin. Was that what he was doing now, testing him-self? Seeing how close he could get without being burned?

If so, he was living proof that boys could grow into men without learning a hell of a lot along the way.

Kailin was frowning and he said, "I don't remember you getting this uptight when I flirted with you before, sweet-heart."

"You just keep me off balance, that's all," she said quietly. "Yesterday you made it plain that even doing business with me was a major irritation, and today . . ." She shrugged.

"Yesterday I was too surprised at seeing you again to feel much of anything. But today . . ." He mimicked her shrug. "You're an attractive woman, Kailin McGuire. It's a beautiful day, in spite of the fact we're going to get a hell of a rainstorm before the afternoon's out, and I don't have any pressing emergency that needs my attention." She nodded, still not looking entirely convinced that his good mood was going to last, and he smiled. "Do I recall a request for a hot dog? Mustard. Relish. Lots of onions.'' She nodded again and he draped his arm comfortably around her shoulder, enjoying the feel of her tucked close against him. Just like old times.

Relax and enjoy it, he told himself as they made their way through the crowd toward a hot dog stand. Common sense said he was asking for trouble, but for the time being, who cared?

Five

Kailin was still quiet when she took the hot dog from his hand
a few minutes later. He bought a couple of soft drinks then
eased her out of the crowd and into the relative quiet beneath
the tall Australian pines bordering the grassy field that made up
the temporary parking lot.

It was about ten degrees cooler in the shade and a salty breeze
whispered through the lacy foliage. Brett turned his face to it
gratefully, sipping the soft drink. Leaning against the trunk of
the nearest tree, he rested his booted foot on the wide bumper
of a pickup truck parked beside them and smiled down at
Kailin. "Better?"

She nodded enthusiastically, her mouth full, and Brett
laughed and reached down to wipe a smear of mustard from her
chin. "I was starved!" she said a moment later, licking at the
mustard and relish trickling between her fingers. "Want a
bite?"

Watching her, Brett shook his head. The muscles in his
stomach pulled tight as she drew the tip of her tongue along her
upper lip, and he forced himself to look away. He stared across
the glittering rows of vehicles parked haphazardly across the

field, letting the soda trickle slowly down his parched throat as the silence folded comfortably around them.

"I've said a lot of things in the last couple of days." He stared at the sky. Storm clouds were gathering to the west, a towering meringue of lead-gray thunderheads, their edges flaring silver where they caught the sun. "And I owe you an apology for most of them."

"Are you sure?" There was a hint of laughter in the words. She took one of the bottles from his hand and perched on the bumper beside his foot. "We could spend the rest of our lives apologizing for all the stupid things we've said to each other, Brett. Or we could see them for what they are and forget it."

"That being?"

"Hurt feelings. A lot of unresolved anger." She swung her foot slowly and looked up at him. "I spent the better part of eleven years believing you'd taken that ten thousand dollars and had walked out of my life without even a backward glance. I found out the truth—about the money, anyway—a couple of years ago. But I didn't know until yesterday that you'd come after me. I thought . . . well, I just figured you thought I was lying about the baby and hadn't wanted any more to do with me."

"I thought you'd had an abortion."

Kailin had the bottle halfway to her mouth when he said it. "You thought *what*?" she whispered.

Brett sighed and leaned forward to rest his arms on his upraised knee. "When I went to your house looking for you, your father told me you were married to Royce. I called him a liar, told him you were pregnant with my baby and that I was going to marry you myself. He—" He paused, the anger and hurt still palpable even after all these years. "He smiled that cold little smile of his and told me I was too late, that it had been 'taken care of.' "

"Taken care—you mean he told you I'd—"

"No." Brett tipped the bottle back and forth, catching the sun on the sparkles of condensation around the neck. "What he meant, I guess, was just that you were married. But all I could think of was that you'd gotten rid of the baby. That after our fight that night you didn't want anything around to remind you of me."

"Oh, Brett," Kailin whispered, her voice uneven. "I never would have— I loved you!" She shuddered. "And all this time you've believed that I—"

"Until yesterday," he said roughly. "Until I saw Becky."

Kailin closed her eyes, so pale that Brett regretted having said anything at all. Why had he even brought it up? To hurt her more than he had already? To justify all his anger and hostility over the past few days? Or had he needed to get it into the open for his own sake, one more bit of the past he was able to discard? Kailin took a deep breath and opened her eyes, the color coming slowly back to her cheeks. "Why?" he asked softly. "If you really loved me, Kailin, why did you marry Royce?"

"Why?" She laughed harshly and raised both hands, then let them drop. "Do you think I haven't asked myself that question every day for the past eleven years?"

"There had to be a reason," he persisted stubbornly. "A woman doesn't walk out on the father of her child and marry another man six days later without a reason."

"There was a reason. One or two, as a matter of fact." She paused, turning the bottle in her fingers, and Brett waited quietly, sensing that this wasn't the time to push her. "After I left your apartment that night I was scared and ashamed and so hurt I couldn't even think straight. I just wanted to run away and hide until I stopped hurting." She smiled bitterly. "Dad was clever enough to take advantage of the situation. He knew if he waited, I'd get over your leaving and...well, who knows? Go tearing after you, perhaps. He wanted me safely and respectably married, and he moved so fast I was Mrs. Royce McGuire before the ink was even dry on the contract he and my new father-in-law had signed."

"Contract?" Brett felt something cold spill through his guts. "What kind of...contract?"

Kailin smiled wearily. "I was never anything more to my father than a commodity, like a string of glass beads: something to be bartered when the price was right. An unmarried daughter is only as valuable as her worth and he could see mine going steadily downhill as the summer progressed." She glanced up at him. "I was also on the verge of becoming a family embarrassment."

Then she looked away, toying with the bottle. "Sterling McGuire had his problems, too—a youngest son who couldn't do anything right. McGuire needed some out-of-the-way job where Royce couldn't do much damage but which was still respectable enough not to embarrass the family." She paused, as though choosing her words carefully. "So they made a deal. McGuire would provide a socially acceptable husband for Yarbro's knocked-up and rebellious young daughter, and Yarbro would in return provide a job for McGuire's inept son. All very tidy, and all very hush-hush." She smiled bitterly. "My father never did believe in that old adage about marriages being made in heaven."

Brett's oath was magnificently and creatively obscene.

"He was terrified I'd do something crazy—like running off with you." She laughed. "I couldn't have come up with a more effective statement against him than to run off with his archenemy, the infamous angry young man himself. But I should have known he'd figure out a way to plug up the escape before I actually did it." Her smile faded, and she looked down. "He . . . he found out about the baby a couple of weeks before I told you. Our family doctor had been his golf partner for twenty years, and a little thing like patient confidentiality doesn't count when your friend's daughter has gotten herself pregnant by a long-haired rebel from the wrong side of town."

Brett swore again, this time in weary resignation. "That's why he came to me that night. He knew if he got to me first and convinced me you weren't pregnant that I'd fall for it. He *knew* how I'd react—just like he knew every move you'd make." He gave a snort of harsh laughter, filled with an empty, hopeless rage. "I wonder if he really thought I'd take that ten grand he offered me. It didn't matter, really, as long as *you* believed I'd taken it. He led us through that whole thing step-by-step."

"If I'd only told you earlier! If I'd gone to you as soon as I found out, maybe . . ."

"Who knows? We had as much chance against an old warrior like your father as a rabbit against a wolf." He glanced up at her, smiling faintly. "Just out of curiosity, why *didn't* you tell me right away?"

"I was afraid to," she said simply. "There was no excuse for my getting pregnant except carelessness. You usually took care of things, but a couple of times when we just got carried away, I told you it was safe even though it wasn't really. I knew better, but..." She smiled suddenly, a faint blush caressing her cheeks. "It's hard to be very logical at times like that."

Brett had to laugh, and Kailin's blush deepened. "I finally started taking birth control pills, but by then it was too late. I wanted the baby, but I didn't know if I should tell you or...just stop seeing you."

"But why, Kailin?" Brett asked hoarsely. "Damn it, I loved you! You say you loved me. Why—?"

"I was afraid you'd think I was trying to pressure you into a commitment you weren't ready to make," she said quietly. "You used to tell me all your plans and dreams, Brett, all the things you wanted to accomplish—but they never included me. You never mentioned love or marriage or the future."

Brett hung his head, shaking it slowly. "When I think of the things I said to you that night..."

"It was like all my nightmares come true," she whispered. "All the way over to your apartment I kept telling myself I was silly to be so nervous. That everything was going to be perfect. Then...you just looked at me with the coldest expression I've ever seen. When you didn't believe me, I felt like my world had been ripped apart."

"Oh, Kailin." He ached with a bone-deep cold, trying to comprehend what she must have felt that night, knowing he'd never be able even to come close. *Kailin, Kailin...what have I done to you?*

"When I got home, Dad took one look at me and knew exactly what had happened. Looking back, it's no surprise, considering he'd planned it all. But at the time he seemed very wise and very sympathetic, and I was in such shock it never occurred to me to wonder why. Common sense says he should have been after you with the 12-gauge and a brace of hounds." Her smile faded almost as quickly as it had blossomed. "Anyway, he told me how lucky I was, that you'd just been using me as a weapon against him, that if I thought you'd ever marry me I was a romantic fool...and so on and so on. He told me you were just a user and that you'd never settle down."

"And six days later you were married."

She just nodded, her head tucked down so that he couldn't see her face. "I started crying halfway through the ceremony and didn't stop for two solid days. Poor Royce must have been ready to kill both my father and me, but he just brought me gallons of hot tea and told me I'd get over you eventually. Then I woke up one morning and realized I wasn't Kailin Yarbro anymore and that I better get on with being my husband's wife."

Kailin looked at him with pain-filled eyes. "I thought you'd taken the money Dad had offered you and had just left town...."

"I worshiped the damned ground you walked on, Kailin." Brett didn't even realize he was going to kiss her until he felt her lips under his. He'd reached out to cup her cheek in his palm, and before he knew what he was doing he'd slipped his hand behind her head and pulled her gently toward him. There was a moment's resistance, then a soft inward sigh of pleasure, and her mouth was there, lips already parting.

She was as sweet as he'd remembered, the moist tip of her tongue reaching hesitantly toward his, touching. He circled it with his and she gave a tiny shudder and melted against him, the slow, liquid thrust of her tongue against his so vibrantly and explicitly sensual that it nearly pushed him over the edge then and there.

He groaned, half in wonder and half in very real agony as his body responded strongly to the so-familiar taste of her. His fingers flexed in her hair, lifting her toward him, and he felt her shiver, tasted the sudden coppery bite of her desire as she kissed him back with the same sudden, unrestrained need.

She whispered something against his mouth, but he didn't hear what it was, didn't care what it was, didn't care about anything but feeling her against him. All his best intentions about resisting dissolved, and in that instant there was absolutely no reality at all but having her in his arms again.

It was Kailin who heard the giggles first. She wrenched her mouth from Brett's and gasped an inarticulate warning, so light-headed she couldn't even remember for a moment where they were. Brett's eyes were inches from hers, the heat in them fading under a faintly puzzled expression. She smiled. "I think," she murmured, "that we've been discovered."

Brett pulled back so suddenly that he sent one of the soft drink bottles flying, and the two girls watching them burst into a deluge of fresh giggles. "Hi, Mom." Becky's grin threatened to take wing.

"Hello, Becky," Kailin said with as much dignity as possible. She smiled at the small, freckled girl standing beside Becky. "How are you, Peggy?"

"Just fine, Mrs. McGuire." Peggy gazed up at Brett. "Hi, Dr. Douglass. Are you enjoying the fair?"

"Very much," Brett assured her dryly. "You two girls having fun?"

"Not as much as *some* people," Becky put in with dancing eyes. "Sorry we . . . umm . . . interrupted."

"Ready to go home?" Kailin asked mildly.

"Actually," Peggy put in, "we wanted to ask if Becky can stay over at my place again tonight. Mom said it would be okay because then the two kittens won't be—" She gave a squeak as Becky buried an elbow in her ribs, then stood gazing innocently at Kailin.

It was then Kailin realized that in spite of the heat Peggy had her cotton jacket zippered to the throat. It was oddly lumpy, and even as Kailin looked at it one of the lumps moved. "What," she asked with growing suspicion, "are you two up to?"

"Nothing," Becky said with wide-eyed innocence. "Except . . ."

"Except?"

"Well . . ." The two girls looked at each other. Then Peggy unzipped her jacket and reached gingerly inside. She withdrew her hand and passed something to Becky.

The black-and-white kitten wailed and peered around nearsightedly. Becky whispered reassuringly to it and cradled it against her chest.

"Rebecca . . ."

"There were only two left," Becky interjected anxiously. "And the lady at the ASPCA booth said if she didn't find homes for them they'd have to be . . . well, *you* know!"

"They had some puppies," Peggy explained cheerfully, extricating the other lump from her jacket. This kitten was all black and wailed just as loudly. "And some rabbits."

Becky handed the bit of fur to Kailin. "It's so cute!"

It was that, Kailin had to admit. She cupped the tiny thing in her palms, feeling its heart racing. It peered up at her with its milky blue kitten eyes, its tiny rosebud ears not even fully unbuttoned yet, and mewed softly in distress.

"Its mother got run over," Becky said. "Peggy's mom said she could keep the other one if . . . well . . ."

"If I said you could keep this one." Kailin looked at Becky assessingly. "I think your grandfather's been giving you lessons in pressure tactics, Rebecca McGuire."

"Mo-oth-er!"

She made three anxious syllables out of the word, and Kailin cradled the kitten against her cheek to hide her smile. Its fur was like watered silk, and she thought she detected the first rough note or two of a hesitant purr. "Don't wheedle. What's your grandmother going to say if you turn up there after the holidays with a kitten in tow?"

"Grandma likes cats," Becky said pleadingly. "Aw, Mom, please? I'll take good care of it, I promise. I'll feed it and brush it and play with it and—"

"And the litter pan?" The kitten was gnawing industriously on her thumb, clearly over its fright. Its face was all black, except for two white patches on either side of its mouth and two small clumps of white over each eye that gave it a raffish, surprised expression.

"I'll clean it every day," Becky assured her, eyes lighting up with hope. "Please, Mom? Oh, please say yes!"

"Let's have a look." Lifting the kitten out of Kailin's hands, Brett examined it with swift competence. "It's healthy and in good shape. Just needs some love and affection."

"See?" Becky put in swiftly. "And besides, we have a moral obligation. People do so much damage to the planet that when we have a chance to do something good, we should do it."

Kailin looked from Becky to Brett and back again. "Are you two in cahoots?"

"Don't look at me!" Brett protested with a laugh as he handed the kitten back to Kailin. "Your daughter has a well-developed sense of global responsibility, that's all."

"My daughter," Kailin said darkly, "is a con artist."

"Please, Mom?"

Kailin sighed. "If it shreds your grandmother's drapes while you two are up there, you're going to have to take the heat."

"I will!" Becky gave her a fierce hug. "Please? It's a known fact that kids grow up to be well-adjusted adults if they have pets to take care of. You wouldn't want me to grow up to be a bank robber or something, would you?"

"From all the signs, you're going to grow up to be a first-class encyclopedia salesman."

"Sales*lady*," Becky corrected, reaching down to stroke the kitten. "Does that mean I can keep him?"

Weakening, Kailin looked down at the kitten. It gazed back at her sleepily, its tiny paws kneading the ball of her thumb, and broke into a halting, unsteady purr. "Oh, good grief," she muttered in defeat, lifting it up to eye level. "Welcome to the family!"

"Oh, Mom, thanks!" Becky gave Kailin a hug, then gently took the kitten from her. "I'm going to call him Maverick."

"We'll have to buy food and litter and—"

"Oh, that's okay, Mrs. McGuire," Peggy put in happily. "My mom said she'd stop at Bailey's on the way home to pick up all that stuff."

"I have the feeling I've been totally conned," Kailin protested with a laugh. She slipped some money from her wallet and handed it to Becky. "This is for the ASPCA, and this is for whatever Maverick needs."

"And your favorite veterinarian will throw in a free exam, shots and an obligatory lecture on how to care for new kittens," Brett added. "Bring them both around to the office tomorrow."

"Oh, wow, thanks, you guys!" Becky paused long enough to plant a kiss on Kailin's cheek, then she and Peggy danced off. "Come on, Mav. Are you hungry?"

Watching the two girls hurry off, Brett laughed. "Maverick?"

"Tom Cruise's call sign in *Top Gun*," Kailin explained. "At the moment it's her favorite movie."

"She into movie-star crushes already?"

Kailin laughed. "She has a crush on Cruise *and* the plane— she wants to be a naval pilot. A while back she was going to become a marine biologist and study whales, then she decided she wanted to be a bicycle courier. That one lasted a week, I think. For a while she was going to be an astronaut, then an archaelogist. At the moment she's torn between being a fighter pilot and an interpretive dancer—she's studying dance at school and adores her teacher."

Kailin paused. Brett was staring after the two girls, a half smile on his lips, his eyes wistful. She had to tell him, Kailin reminded herself. It wasn't fair letting him think that Becky was his. For eleven years he'd believed that she had gotten rid of his baby as quickly as she'd gotten rid of him, and now he was just as certain she hadn't. It was going to be heart-wrenching having to tell him the truth.

For half a moment she toyed with the idea of never telling him. What harm could come of it? Almost as quickly as the idea occurred to her, she felt ashamed of herself. Not only would she be lying to Brett, she'd be passing that lie on to Becky. It wouldn't be fair either to her or to Royce. All things considered, he'd been a good husband and a good father. He deserved better.

Why, she thought with silent glumness, does life have to be so difficult at times? "Brett," she said quietly, "there's something I have to—"

"It's going to have to wait, sweetheart!" he said with a whoop. "Hang on!" He snatched her hand and pulled her to her feet, then took off across the parking area at a fast lope.

"Brett, for heaven's sake," Kailin sputtered, nearly pulled off her feet. "What are you doing?"

In the next instant, she had her answer. A bolt of lightning ripped the sky and thunder cannonaded around them, making the air shudder. As though jarred loose by the noise, huge drops of icy water started pattering around them.

"My truck's over here somewhere." Brett's fingers tightened around hers. "Run!"

Kailin didn't need the encouragement. Another searing fork of lightning lasered the sky just then, and she flinched as the sky opened and they were deluged by a nearly solid torrent of icy water. Half blinded by the blowing rain and her own hair, she gripped Brett's hand fiercely as they sprinted through the pelting rain toward the blurred outlines of his truck, laughing with exhilaration as they splashed through cold, ankle-deep water.

Brett lifted Kailin into the truck, then clambered in behind her and slammed the door.

"I don't believe this!" Breathless with laughter, Kailin combed her soaking hair back with both hands. Her cotton dress was plastered to her like onionskin, and she plucked at it helplessly.

Brett scrubbed his hands furiously through his hair, spraying water. He rummaged through the clutter behind the seat, then drew out a wool blanket and put it around her shoulders. "You don't mind a few dog hairs, do you?"

Laughing, Kailin wrung a handful of water out of her hair, then started rubbing it with the blanket. "I've heard of monsoons, but this is ridiculous." Gingerly she eased her feet out of what were once a pair of white canvas espadrilles. "Even Noah got some warning."

"It'll let up in a few minutes." Brett's teeth flashed in the dim light. He pulled his sweatshirt over his head and hung it across the steering column, where it dripped into the growing puddle under his feet.

It was raining even harder now. Water sluiced down the truck windows in solid sheets, curtaining out the world, and Kailin sighed and tucked one foot under her, relaxing back against the seat. "All we need is the picnic basket."

Brett chuckled. "You remember that, too, do you?"

"How could I forget?" Kailin slipped him a wry glance. "It was our first real date. You'd promised me a romantic, old-fashioned picnic, and you had that huge hamper that must have cost you an entire week's pay full of cheese and game hen and champagne. We were going to row across the lake to the island. I even wore that silly white gauzy dress because I thought it fit the occasion."

Brett grinned, pulled off his sneakers and dumped the water out of them. "But when we got to the lake we discovered half the town had the same idea and there were no rowboats left."

"So we decided to drive up to another lake. Except we had a flat—"

"And no spare."

"And we got out to walk to the nearest town." Kailin's grin widened. "I was wearing a pair of unbelievably expensive Italian sandals, four-inch heels and cobweb straps."

"Yeah, sexy as hell." Brett's laugh was deep and rumbly. "You got mad after half a mile and threw them in the ditch, then remembered how much you'd paid for them and went scrambling after them."

"Caught my dress on a branch and ripped it to shreds. Then it started to rain." She rested her head on the seat back, laughing. "It came down as though it hadn't rained in a month, and there we were on some little dirt side road in the middle of nowhere."

"But then you saw that old barn and we clambered over a fence to get to it."

"And found ourselves face-to-face with the biggest bull I've ever seen in my life."

"And you were so wet and mad you just marched up to him and screamed at him to get out of the way." Brett chuckled. "I don't know who you managed to scare more—the bull or me."

Kailin laughed. "It worked, didn't it?"

"A loft of dry hay never looked so good!"

Kailin turned her head to look at him, smiling. "Everything in the picnic basket was ruined but the grapes and the champagne. I swear I've never eaten a meal since that tasted better."

Brett reached across and stroked her cheek with his thumb, his eyes warm. "And we made love afterward, for the first time. I've always remembered the sound of the rain on the barn roof and how dry and warm we were, curled up in the hay."

"I itched for weeks." Then, growing serious, she turned her head and kissed his fingers. "That was one of the happiest days of my life. We had magic for a little while that summer, didn't we?"

"Yeah, we had magic." He looked down at her for a long, silent while, his fingers still stroking her cheek. "God, I loved you, Kailin," he whispered. "There's been nobody since who's even come close to making me feel the way you used to."

"Oh, Brett." She reached up to touch his cheek, feeling herself drawn irresistibly toward those blue, blue eyes. They filled her universe and she could feel his breath on her cheek, her mouth, the featherlike touch of his fingertips as they moved delicately down the curve of her cheek to rest undemandingly on the back of her neck.

Wonderingly, as though tracing the outline of a dream, Kailin ran her fingers along the rugged contours of his face. She touched the spray of fine white lines at the outer corners of his eyes, etched there by sun and wind, the sharp blades of his cheekbones. The upper half was the same face she'd once known by heart; below that it was as new and uncharted as any stranger's. She explored the planes of his cheeks, the long, strong thrust of his jaw. His mouth was the same, still wide and full and as inviting as it had ever been, his lush lower lip dimpled lightly in the center.

He opened his mouth and turned his head very slightly, capturing her finger gently between his lips, his eyes never leaving hers. His mouth was warm and moist, and he touched her fingertip with his tongue, swirled around it, worked against it in a gentle sucking motion that made Kailin go suddenly and unexpectedly weak. She rested her forehead on his arm, which was lying along the back of the truck seat, and made no protest at all when he lifted it and drew her close against him.

Six

The skin on his shoulders and chest was slick and cold with rain, yet it was blazing just under the surface. She ran her cheek along his arm until it rested on his shoulder. His hair lay plastered to his neck and around his ears, and she delicately licked away a trickle of rainwater from his neck, feeling him catch his breath.

He murmured her name in a thick, low voice and cupped her head with his other hand, his breathing deepening. Slowly he gathered her soaking hair into a rope at the nape of her neck. Then, even more slowly, he slipped the thin straps of her sundress over her wet shoulders.

Even expecting the moist, warm touch of his mouth, Kailin started slightly. She shivered as he ran a path of lingering kisses from her ear to the point of her shoulder, then slowly back again, his tongue laving the rain water from her skin. He whispered her name against her ear, the very tip of his tongue following its inward curl, and gently tugged her soggy skirt out from beneath her. Slipping his hands under her, he lifted her onto his lap.

There was no mistaking his need, even through the heavy fabric of his jeans, and Kailin had to catch her breath at the intimate touch. She felt the muscles in his inner thighs tighten as she drew her leg up high between his and he whispered something and pressed himself against her. Kailin had to bite her lip to keep from crying out at the unbelievably erotic sensation of the rough denim against her smooth skin.

He knew, she thought dizzily. Even after eleven years, he still knew every move and nuance and touch that could set her afire. Dimly she realized she should be protesting this, but even as she thought it, the words died in her throat. His hands were at the elasticized top of her sundress now, tugging it slowly down, and she shivered again in delicious anticipation.

"Do you want me to stop?" he murmured.

"N-no."

Brett murmured something again, a coaxing whisper of sound she couldn't make out. She drew back far enough to look up at him questioningly and he smiled, his eyes hooded and smoky, then took her hands and placed them on his bare, muscled stomach. His eyes said the rest, and he caught his breath as she slowly drew the zipper of his jeans down, deliberately running her fingernails lightly down the dark hair on his stomach. Teasing, drawing the anticipation out for him, she folded the flaps of his open jeans back but didn't touch him. Instead she ran her hands back up his stomach to his chest, then his shoulders and neck, to slip her fingers deeply into his thick, wet hair.

She smiled at him, tracing the curve of his lower lip with the tip of her tongue. "Want me to stop?"

"You know the answer to that," he growled roughly. He bent his head and captured that marauding tongue between his lips, drawing it deeply and fiercely into his mouth.

Any last-minute hesitancy that Kailin might have had vanished. It was insane, she told herself as his mouth possessed hers. It couldn't be happening, couldn't be Brett—*her* Brett—locked so intimately against her after all these years. She'd dreamed of it for so long that she was half-afraid to move in case she awoke and discovered it was nothing but a delicious daydream, that the lean, hard body straining against hers was nothing more than a memory.

"Oh, angel, I don't know where you're taking me," Brett breathed. He tugged her dress down, and then her breasts were free, the nipples already hard and sensitive. He cupped them in his hands and she arched her back, her thighs tightening on his. Responding, he shifted around, and Kailin gave a squeak of surprise as she suddenly found herself lying on the truck seat, Brett pressed lithely against her.

"Brett!" She gave another gasp, this time of laughter, as he smoothly pulled her skirt to her hips and drew one of her legs up so that she was cradling him intimately between her thighs. "Brett, you idiot," she whispered, still laughing. "We're too old for this! Teenagers make out in trucks, not sedate types like us!"

"We're never too old for this," he whispered, nuzzling her breasts lovingly.

"But not here, for heaven's sake," she sputtered, laughing.

"Why not?" he growled breathlessly, twisting around so he could kiss her breasts. "We're facing the woods, at the far edge of the lot, and it's pouring rain. Even if anyone was crazy enough to come out here, he couldn't see a thing." He drew his tongue around and under her breast, nipping the taut nipple.

It was true. The windows were curtained by pelting rain and fog and condensation. They were cocooned in a tiny cave of warmth and need, hidden from the world. It was incredibly erotic being half-naked in Brett's arms while life went on about them unsuspecting.

"This is mad!" Laughing, she set her teeth across his earlobe and nipped him gently. "We can't just fall into each other's arms and start making love without . . . well, without some preliminaries or something."

It was Brett's turn to start laughing. "We're in the middle of preliminaries now, darling. That's what this is...and this." He slipped his large, warm hand under her panties and caressed her bottom, lifting her against him, his touch gently seeking.

Kailin had to catch her breath, clinging to him as his fingers traced a promising filigree on the sensitive skin of her inner thigh. "Brett, I'm serious! How can we just—?"

"Do you feel like we're strangers, Kailin?" He lowered his mouth and brushed his lips across hers again and again. His eyes were glittering slits, and she could feel his heart pounding against her. "If you do, we can stop here and pretend it never happened. If you need time, I'll give you time. If you need wooing, Kailin, I'll woo you. But it's like—"

"Like we've never been apart," she whispered against his mouth. "Oh, Brett, I don't understand any of this, but it's as though the last time we made love was only hours ago."

"I want you, Kailin." The words came out fiercely and sent a melting, honeyed heat through her. "I want to make you mine again. Now. Here. If you want to wait, we will, but—"

"No." She sank her fingers in his hair and pulled his mouth down over hers with the same hot hunger, lifting her hips against him. "No, I don't want to wait. I want you now. I need you now."

Maybe it was the storm, she thought in dazed wonder, or maybe they were simply terrified of losing one another again. But suddenly she knew this was exactly the way it should be, spontaneous and rough and wild. This is the way it had happened the first time, and now they were being given a second chance. It was beyond simple passion and raw need; it was an affirmation of trust, a loving ritual to signify that they were putting the past to rest and committing themselves to starting afresh.

Brett gave a murmur of agreement and slipped his hands under her silky panties, easing them over her bottom. Clammy with rainwater, they resisted his efforts to pull them over her legs until he finally had to sit up and ease them off inch by tantalizing inch.

Kailin sat up, her legs all tangled around his, and slowly ran her palms down his chest and stomach. His eyes narrowed slightly and he swallowed, holding his breath.

"Kailin!" It was almost a cry of pain when she finally, gently touched him. Both fists knotted and he dragged in an unsteady breath as she caressed him sweetly. Then he suddenly grasped her shoulders firmly in both hands. "I'm like a primed powder keg as it is, sweetheart."

Kailin ran her hands around his ribs, up the molded contours of his back. "Brett, this is crazy," she whispered. "We can't make love in here. *No one* can make love in a pickup—it's physically impossible! The cab's too short, the seat's too narrow and—oh!"

With swift, sure competence, he lifted her up and around so that she was lying on her side, then rearranged her legs so she was straddling him, settled himself comfortably against her again. He cradled her in one arm and smiled. "You were saying?" he murmured against her lips, his other hand gliding around the curve of her bottom to press her against him. "Not a lot of room for fancy gymnastics, but plenty of room for the basics." He kissed her, nibbling her lower lip, and slipped his hand further around, his fingers gently seeking. "Like this..."

Kailin sucked her breath in at the first touch, so ready for him that he murmured something in pleasure. "Tell me what you want," he urged. "Tell me how you want it, Kailin. Tell me how much and when." His fingers moved in long, silken caresses that made her feel as though she were spinning off into space, and she moved against him, moaning his name softly. "Don't hold anything back," he whispered. "Go with it as far as it takes you."

There was no intimate, hidden part of her he didn't still know by heart, no special way of loving her he didn't remember. "Make love to me," she murmured against his mouth long minutes later, still trembling with the exquisite magic he'd brought her. "Now, Brett. Make love to me now."

He lay very still for a moment, breathing unsteadily. "Kailin?" he whispered urgently. "Honey, are you...?"

She stared at him, not understanding. Then her eyes widened. "Oh, no!" she moaned. "Oh, Brett!"

"No risks this time, sweetheart," he said through gritted teeth. "I lost eleven years ago because we couldn't keep our hands off each other and got careless."

"I don't believe this," she whispered, nearly sobbing.

"Pray." He reached up and around and opened the glove compartment, rummaging through it.

"What?"

"I said pray. I lend my truck to a neighbour's teenage son now and again, and last time I looked in here it was obvious that *he*, at least, *is* prepared for situations like this." He gave a soft groan of relief and curled around to embrace her again, kissing her with a deep and drugging intensity that left no doubt that he'd found what he was looking for. "That kid deserves to be knighted," he murmured against her throat.

He brought them together with a sure, gentle thrust of his hips and Kailin sighed, knowing that those eleven years had been merely an eye blink of time, and that things were finally the way they should be. How long it lasted, she didn't know. She was so lost to the magic of Brett's lovemaking that time and the world vanished and there was no reality beyond the lean male body locked with hers, the growing tension that sought release. It caught her in a giant upsurge of pleasure so fierce that it made her cry out and she was only dimly aware of Brett's body arching into hers with sudden, fierce urgency. He went motionless, not even breathing, and she cradled him until the tension eased and he relaxed into her arms, panting and wet.

Finally Brett stirred, smiling sleepily down at her. He felt contented and impossibly happy, and wondered how he'd ever thought he could live without this woman. "Still think it's impossible to make love in a pickup truck?"

"You've done this before," she murmured accusingly.

"The trick's not to hit the gearshift and knock it into neutral," he said with a grin. "I had a friend once who parked on a down slope leading to a lake. He fell off the seat at a critical moment and got jammed against the gearshift level. When he tried to get up, he popped it into neutral and they wound up in three feet of water before the truck stopped."

Kailin sputtered with laughter, caressing his back and shoulders lazily. "I don't believe this. I haven't done anything so impetuous and crazy since—"

"The last time we were together," he finished for her, feeling ridiculously pleased with himself. It was intensely satisfying, if a little selfish, to think that there had been no one else in those eleven years who had made her laugh like this, had made her glow with such happiness.

"You're right." She kissed his shoulder. "You're good for me, Brett Douglass. You always were."

"I'm perfect for you. I just wish it hadn't taken us so long to figure it out."

"Maybe we needed that time," Kailin mused, drawing spirals on his back with her finger. "If we'd stayed together back then, who knows how long it would have lasted? We both needed to grow up."

"Who knows?" Brett said with a sigh. "I just know I'm never going to let you get away from me again."

"That sounds all very medieval and proprietary."

"Maybe they had it right all along. There was a time that when a man took a woman's virginity, he owned her." He gazed down at her slyly, waiting for the explosion.

He didn't have to wait long. "Took?" She gave him a poke in the ribs. "Virginity, you barbarian, is a gift a woman *gives* to a man. It's a symbol of her trust and commitment and love."

"There are still plenty of places in the world where it's no more than a commodity," he reminded her. "Just like a cow or a bushel of corn. A father uses his daughter's virginity as collateral to negotiate political or financial alliances. Without that leverage, she's just a liability."

As soon as he'd said it, Brett could have kicked himself. It hit just a little too close to home, and Kailin went quiet and still. Not saying anything, he simply held her tightly, kissing the top of her head.

They lay like that for an eternity, all wrapped up in a tangle of arms and legs and half-discarded clothing, until Kailin drowsily realized that it had stopped raining. The windows were still foggy with condensation, but the gray blur outside was lighter than it had been, a fact that Brett had been trying to ignore.

"I hate to mention this," she murmured, "but I think we'd better get upright and respectable before we shock some innocent passerby and start a major scandal."

"Do we have to?" His arms tightened around her, holding her firmly captive.

"Mmm." She kissed his ear with a regretful sigh. "I'd hate one of your local lovelies to spot your truck and drop by to see if the good doctor is in."

"The good doctor is in," he said with a salacious chuckle, moving his hips lightly. Then he gave a groan of protest and eased himself free of her, sitting up so they could untangle their legs. "These," he said, holding up a sodden lump of pink fabric, "are yours."

Kailin took her wet, cold panties and started wriggling into them.

Brett helpfully tugged up the top of her sundress, then rearranged his jeans and zippered them. He retrieved his sopping sweatshirt from the steering column and eyed it distastefully. "How would you like to spend the rest of the afternoon in front of a fire with a snifter of good brandy?"

"And a hot bath." Kailin ran her fingers through her wet, tangled hair. "I'd kill for a hot bath."

"Becky's staying with the McAllisters."

Kailin's mouth curved with a smile. "That's right."

"So," Brett breathed, wrapping his arms around her and nuzzling her neck, "there's no need for you to go home tonight, is there?"

"Dry clothes would be nice."

"You don't need any clothes for what I had in mind." He bit her earlobe gently. "I want to take you home and peel you out of that sundress and get so deep inside you again that it'll take us a week just to catch our breath. And I want to stay that way until morning."

"My-my car. It's here somewhere."

"We'll pick it up tomorrow."

"Becky. . . I have to tell Becky where I am."

"Call her from my place." Then he looked at her. "Is it going to be a problem? For her, I mean."

Kailin smiled. "No. I've told her about you."

It startled him. "You have?"

"I've told her we used to date."

Kailin frowned, seeming suddenly pensive, and Brett swallowed a sigh, knowing what she was thinking. She hadn't told Becky the truth—that *he* and not Royce was her father. It saddened him slightly, but he could see why she'd done it. She'd had no idea they would ever find each other again. As far as Becky was concerned, Royce *was* her father. He'd been there when she'd been born, he'd watched her grow up.

He wrenched his mind from the thought, concentrating instead on easing the truck through the lines of parked vehicles toward the exit. It was hard to get used to. What did he know about being a father, anyway? He glanced at Kailin, but she was staring out the side window, frowning thoughtfully.

She turned just then and saw him looking at her and smiled. "Besides, kids aren't as naive as we'd like to think. She told me a couple of months ago that she thought I should have a boy-friend."

"She *what*?" Brett nearly ran into the back of a parked van.

"She said she wasn't ready to deal with my getting married again—she didn't want to have to break in a new father just yet was how she put it—but she didn't think it was fair for me to have to limit my social life because of that. She was even ready to help me pick him out."

"Did you take her up on it?" he asked very casually.

Kailin's mouth turned up. "Awfully nosy, aren't you?" Brett gave her a worried look and she laughed, curling up beside him and resting her head on his shoulder. "No, I didn't take her up on it. I think she has her eye on you as a likely candidate though, so don't be surprised if you find yourself targeted for some very determined matchmaking."

"She won't get any argument from me," Brett assured her with a grin, squeezing her thigh gently. "I intend to do some serious work in that direction myself, starting in about half an hour."

"Half an hour?" Kailin's voice caught as his hand moved.

"It takes about half an hour to get up to my place," he said massaging her leg. "Unless we hit a traffic jam."

Kailin let her eyes slide closed and covered his gently questing hand with hers. "Let's not hit any traffic jams," she whispered. "Brett, what are you doing?"

"Preliminaries," he said with a smoky laugh. "Just a few preliminaries."

To his relief they didn't run into any traffic jams until they reached the wide concrete bridge over Blind Pass. The highway crew still had barricades set up on the far end, reducing traffic to one lane, and Brett swore in quiet resignation as the young, sun-bronzed flagman stopped the car just ahead and motioned it to one side. Brett pulled in behind it and cut the engine.

He draped an arm over the steering wheel and gazed at the water spread out on either side of them. To their left lay the Gulf of Mexico, the lightly rippled surface as bright as hot silver in the lowering sun. The sky there was lightly brushed with crimson cloud, the sun itself a swollen red balloon. To their right lay what looked like a river, clear and blue, the banks lined with heavy green brush. Wide sandbars thrust out into the water, rising like smooth, beached whales.

"What are those people doing down there?" Kailin peered down at the handful of adults and children prowling the sand.

"Looking for shells. Sanibel is one of the three best shelling beaches in the world."

"That's what Craig was saying. In fact, they mention that in the brochures on Paradise Point." She turned to look at him. "He also says you're trying to stop the shelling."

"I'm not trying to stop anything," Brett said patiently. "I *am* trying to convince the local businesses to put more effort into educating the tourists about the ecological damage they're doing by taking live shells off the beach. Theoretically you're not allowed to take more than two live specimens per species per person—but I've seen people come off the beach with buckets full of live shells and starfish. They put them in the car and forget about them, and halfway between here and Chicago they wonder what the stink is and dump the rotting shells out onto the roadside. Or they clean them and take them home with great plans of getting into shellcraft, then get interested in something else and the shells get thrown out in a couple of years." He shook his head. "I hate waste."

Kailin smiled and braided her fingers with his, looking back down at the shellers. They were all wandering along in a curious bent-over shuffle, peering at the sand at their feet, and Kailin laughed. "It makes my back ache just watching them."

"It's called the Sanibel Stoop, and our local chiropractor does a booming business in high tourist season." He gestured to the dense greenery beyond the shellers. "That's all mangrove swamp out there. And Paradise Point."

"I know. I asked Craig to drive me out here yesterday after the meeting."

Brett looked at her sharply. "He drove you into the site?"

"We couldn't get in. The storm blew two big trees down across the access road, and they haven't gotten them moved yet." She looked out the other window at the Gulf. "He said there used to be a sandbar across there, but the storm blew it out, too."

He nodded to the far end of the bridge. "Last week's storm took out half the beach and undercut the bridge pilings. That's what the highway people are working on."

The flagman appeared just then. Brett started the truck, and they made their way slowly across. "What happens if a major hurricane hits?" Kailin asked suddenly. "Sanibel is wall-to-wall condominiums, most of them right out on the beach. If last week's storm could do this much damage..."

"It's a risk you take to live in Paradise," Brett replied quietly. "The hurricane of 1926 flooded the entire island and there have been some since that have done a lot of damage." He looked at her, smiling. "Thinking of telling the Paradise Point investors they'd be better off putting their money into pork belly futures?"

"About the same risk as far as I'm concerned," she said with a chuckle, "but my job's mediation, not investment counseling. They can put their money into snake oil for all I care."

"With Craig Bryant as the original snake-oil salesman." Kailin gave him an impatient look, and Brett laughed, squeezing her fingers. "Okay, okay, I'll lay off. Hell, I'm feeling so benevolent maybe I'll even pressure Zac into voting approval for Phase Three."

Even as he said it, Brett felt a twinge of doubt. It was just a fleeting thing, but it left a shadow that dispelled some of his ebullience. He stared thoughtfully at the traffic ahead of them. This wasn't any good, he thought. He'd made a decision this afternoon to let Kailin back into his heart again and he couldn't spend the rest of his life worrying about her motives. She'd made love with him today because she'd felt the same magic he had, not for any ulterior motive regarding Paradise Point. He had to believe that. Because if he ever stopped believing it, he had nothing left.

"Isn't that beautiful?" Kailin was leaning forward, gazing at the setting sun. It had set the cloud-quilted sky aflame, and even the restless Gulf seemed lighted by some inner fire.

The narrow, winding road ran right alongside the water here, flanked on either side with huge Australian pines, their lacy foliage meeting over the road in a delicate filigreed arch. A squadron of big brown pelicans swept low across the water in tight formation, wingtip to wingtip, then settled on the broken pilings of an old dock.

The road finally turned inland and wound into the small community of Captiva. It was so heavily wooded that most of the houses themselves were barely visible. Narrow, unmarked laneways ran off into apparent wilderness on either side, and when Brett finally turned left into what at first glance looked like a solid thicket of trees, Kailin looked at him in surprise.

The lane went through the palms and sprawling sea grape toward the Gulf. When they finally broke through into the clearing on the edge of the beach, Kailin gave a gasp of delight. The house wasn't large, but Brett had loved it from the moment he'd set eyes on it eight years ago. Like most of the homes on the islands, it was built up on pilings, as much for coolness as for protection against high water. The rough wood siding was worn soft and mellow by wind and sun, and it fit into the landscape of sand and tropical foliage as though it had grown there. Beyond it, out past the broad band of sea oats and the white sand beach, the restless Gulf was swallowing the last crescent of sun in a conflagration of color.

"No wonder you never come back to Indiana," Kailin said with a laugh. "If I lived here, I'd never leave the house."

"Take a good look." Brett slipped his arms around her and pulled her close to him, kissing the side of her throat. "Because I'm not letting you out of my bed for the next eighteen hours."

"You *are* turning medieval." Kailin reached up to grab a fistful of his hair and tugged it gently. "You sound like Bluebeard."

"The island of Captiva gets its name from the Spanish word *cautiva*—meaning captive," he murmured against her ear. "Back when pirates like Gasparilla and Black Caesar controlled these islands, if they found the wife or daughter of a wealthy family aboard any ship they plundered, they kept her for ransom. The women were supposedly kept here on Captiva until satisfactory business arrangements could be made . . . or for a few weeks of pleasure, as the case may be. It was known as La Isla de los Cautivas: the Island of Captives."

Kailin gave a muffled gasp of laughter and caught his straying hands. "And you think my father would pay a ransom for my return, do you?"

Brett grinned, reveling in having her in his arms again, heady with the feel and scent and taste of her. He bent down and scooped her up in his arms and started striding toward the house. "Ransom, hell—I wasn't even planning on asking." He smiled down at her, his heart soaring. "It was the plundering part I had in mind, sweet captive. And maybe a touch or two of pillage." Although who was the captive, he found himself wondering dazedly, and who the captor? And as for a ransom . . . well, what price his heart?

Seven

Kailin awoke to find herself alone in Brett's big bed. She smiled and stretched lazily, knowing she should get up but not remotely interested in doing so. In fact, she admitted with a contented smile, she would be perfectly happy to spend the rest of her life here.

Yawning, she nestled down into the tangled nest of bedding again. The evocative scent of their lovemaking still clung to the sheets, and Kailin smiled. She and Brett hadn't been out of this bed for more than a hour since he'd brought her here. They'd made love until they'd been so exhausted they'd fallen asleep in each other's arms, then awakened to make love again.

And again. Kailin's smile widened. They hadn't been able to get enough of each other, each exquisite encounter seeming to fuel rather than quench the fires within. It had been like this eleven years ago, she recalled sleepily. Pure magic!

Yawning again, she crawled out of bed and rummaged around in Brett's closet until she found a thick terry robe. Then, combing her hair with her fingers, she staggered downstairs, still more asleep than awake.

Brett was leaning over the counter in the airy, bright kitchen, sipping a cup of coffee and reading a newspaper. He looked up when she stumbled in and grinned broadly. "I was just thinking of going up to see if you were still breathing."

"Coffee," she croaked. "Please, coffee..."

"Are you still a zombie in the morning until you've had your caffeine?" He patted her gently on the bottom, then poured her a generous mugful and set it in front of her. "Drink."

"Mmm." Kailin locked both hands around the mug and lifted it to her mouth. Brett gave a snort of laughter and shook his head. Then, to her everlasting gratitude, he went back to his own coffee and the paper and left her in peace.

"Thank you," she said a few minutes later, taking a deep breath and looking around her for the first time.

"Anytime. Want another cup?"

She shook her head. "I mean for not talking. I can't stand people who roll out of bed at the crack of dawn all chipper and full of good spirits."

Brett laughed. "I don't think 9:30 is considered the crack of dawn."

"It is when you didn't get any sleep the night before."

"We didn't, did we?" His smile was warm and lazy.

Kailin looked up at him through the steam from her coffee, feeling a familiar little quiver settle low in her stomach. He was lounging lazily against the counter, naked except for a towel wrapped rather haphazardly around his hips, and he looked decidedly and appealingly male. There was something in the way he was looking at her that made her feel sleepy and warm and she smiled, gazing at him through half-lowered lashes. "What are you thinking about?"

He held his hand out, smiling, and Kailin got up and walked across to him. She set the coffee aside and ran her hands across his broad chest, leaned forward to kiss his shoulder, moving her lips lightly to the hollow in his throat.

"This is ridiculous," she whispered, gliding her hands up his smooth, muscled back. "Do you suppose we're normal? I mean, we made love all night long. Then when we got up the first time this morning, all you had to do was look at me and..."

Brett chuckled. "Some people jog every morning, some people do calisthenics, some people—"

"Most people do not make love on the stairs as they're going down to make breakfast," she reminded him with a laugh. "This is crazy, you have to admit it."

"I'm not admitting anything except that I can't get enough of you." He smoothed her hair back and kissed the end of her nose. "I have to go down to the clinic for a while, but I'll try to get away for a couple of hours. Be here for me?"

Kailin smiled. "I'd love to, but I have to get home. I promised Becky that we'd take a boat tour around the islands today. She's dying to go scuba diving."

"I have a sailboat," he whispered coaxingly. "The *Sweet Retreat*, docked near here. I have a friend in Fort Myers Beach who owes me a favor. I could talk him into taking over at the clinic while we spend a week or more exploring all the little coves and inlets and beaches...."

"And I have a job to do, remember?" she reminded him with a laugh. "I've got to work up a list of recommendations regarding Paradise Point before the next meeting, and that means reviewing your committee's report and talking with Craig Bryant again."

"Bryant?" Brett's brows pulled together.

"Yes, Bryant," Kailin said tolerantly. "I'm supposed to be getting both sides of this, remember? Though heaven knows I think I've compromised my impartiality a bit."

"A number of times," Brett purred, eyes glowing. "And I intend to ensure that we compromise it regularly from now on."

Kailin smiled and rested her cheek on Brett's chest, listening to the strong, regular beat of his heart. And when the Paradise Point project was over and she had to go home? They hadn't talked about that last night. They hadn't talked about anything but the present, as though the past and future didn't even exist. Maybe in a way they didn't, Kailin decided thoughtfully. Maybe it was better if they just went on like this for a while, locked in the magic of *now*, letting the past heal and the future wait.

"You going to fix me breakfast?" she asked, smiling up at him. At his assent, she stood on tiptoe to plant a kiss full on his mouth. "Be down in a jiffy."

Kailin heard the angry voices before she was even out of the shower. One was Brett's, the other an indistinct mutter. She toweled herself dry, then slipped on the robe and belted it as she walked back into the bedroom. There was a scuffle just outside the bedroom door, a snarl of profanity, then the door flew inward and two men burst into the room.

"Craig!" Kailin stared at Craig Bryant in astonishment.

He glowered across the rumpled bed at her, breathing heavily. His face was flushed and the front of his shirt crumpled as though someone had grabbed a fistful of the fabric. "I've been looking for you since yesterday afternoon," he said angrily. "I should have guessed you'd be here. Douglass was panting after you like a—"

"One more word out of you, Bryant," Brett said, "and you're going to be missing some teeth."

"Save your breath for your court appearance, Douglass!" Craig waved a handful of papers in the air. "I know why you and your committee have been blocking Phase Three of Paradise Point. It's all here in black and white!"

"What are you talking about?"

"TexAm Construction," Craig stated triumphantly. "You didn't think I'd find out, did you?"

"Where did you get that information?" Brett's eyes glowed dangerously, and he took a step toward Craig.

Craig smiled. "I'm going to crucify you, Douglass. Collusion with intent to defraud, for a start. By the time I'm finished with you, your little committee's going to be facing enough charges to put you—"

"What are you talking about, Craig?" Kailin snapped.

Craig's angry gaze swung around to her. "I'm talking about a sweet little deal lover boy here has cooked up with TexAm Construction to push Gulf Coast into bankruptcy. With us out of the way, TexAm can step in and pick up the property for a song. But I guess you'd know all about that, wouldn't you?" He let his eyes wander over her. "Looks like the good chairman hasn't wasted any time in making sure what side of the fence you're on."

A hot flush spread across Kailin's cheeks, but she tipped her chin up and stared at Craig without flinching. "Mr. Douglass and I have known each other for years. Our relationship doesn't concern you, the Land Use Committee *or* Gulf Coast."

"Like hell. I've never known a woman yet who could take a tumble through a man's bed, then face the guy across a board-room table as though nothing happened. Or is this how you big-city girls do business?"

Brett growled something and took two strides towards Craig. Craig threw up his hands. "Hey, no problem. I'm leaving."

"Damn right you are," Brett grabbed the back of Craig's jacket and shoved him toward the door. "The only question is whether you're leaving in one piece."

Craig paused by the door and turned to look at Kailin. "Just in case he's got you conned, too, baby, read this." He threw the wad of crumpled papers onto the bed. Then, with one last look at Brett, he shrugged his shoulders to settle his jacket and strode out the door and down the stairs.

Kailin looked at Brett angrily. "Thanks. I really enjoyed that." She snatched up her panties and pulled them on, then tossed the robe aside and slipped into her sundress, too an-noyed to even care that Brett was watching. "Next time you hold a meeting in your bedroom, I'd appreciate a bit of warn-ing. My work is difficult enough without everyone discovering I'm sleeping with one of the parties involved."

"Maybe you should have thought of that yesterday after-noon," Brett snapped back, moving his shoulders as though to loosen tight muscles. He prowled the bedroom like something caged, large and angry and restless.

Kailin had her mouth open to fire back an angry retort, then eased her breath out and subsided. "You're right," she said quietly. "I'm sorry. I knew what I was doing." She smiled ten-tatively. "For what it's worth, I'd do it again."

Brett stared at her for a moment, and then his own mouth lifted with a faint, wry smile. "Promise?"

"Is that what you want?" she asked seriously.

"Yes. It's very much what I want."

Kailin sighed and ran her fingers through her tangled hair, tossing it back from her face. "You do realize, don't you, that this—" she gestured toward the bed "—can't have any effect on my job? I'm not going to sleep with you and sell Gulf Coast out because of it."

"What you and I have here," Brett replied softly, "doesn't have a damned thing to do with Gulf Coast. This has got to do with eleven years ago, and a lot of dreams gone wrong. This is our second chance, Kailin." He walked across and folded his arms around her, kissing the top of her head. "I gotta go, kid," he murmured regretfully. "Kathy will be wondering if I've finally made good my threat to toss it all over and become a beach bum if I don't get down there pretty soon. I called a buddy of mine and had him bring your car up—he dropped it off while you were in the shower. And I left your breakfast on the table. There's an extra house key there, too. I'd like to think you'll be here tonight."

"If I can. But I don't want to farm Becky out with the McAllisters every night just so I can stay here. It's the only vacation we've had together in months, and she has to leave for Indiana in another week."

"She can stay here. There's an extra bedroom."

Kailin frowned slightly, shaking her head. "I don't think she's ready for that yet, Brett. And I guess I'm not, either." She toyed with a button on his shirt, not meeting his eyes. "I've dated a bit since Royce died, but I've never... gotten close to anyone. This kind of close." She looked up at him. "I have to be very sure before I bring a man into Becky's life too, Brett."

"I'm not just passing through, Kailin," he said quietly. He ran the back of his hand down her cheek, his eyes searching hers. "Not this time, by God."

Kailin's heart did a slow cartwheel, and she felt something within her pull so tight it almost hurt. She touched his cheek, wondering if he could read the love in her eyes, then smiled and turned her face to kiss his fingers. "Go. You have a veterinary practice to run. I'll call you when Becky and I get back from our boat ride—we can have dinner together, anyway. Becky's quite proud of the fact she doesn't need a baby-sitter anymore, and the people in the next condo are marvelous, so I don't worry about her being alone for a few hours." She laughed. "She'll make a bushel of popcorn and watch *Top Gun* for the umpteenth time and wish I went out more often."

Brett glanced at the clock, then swore under his breath and kissed her swiftly. He picked up his denim jacket, grinning over his shoulder as he headed for the door. "See you tonight, sweetheart. We'll have dinner here—steak, wine and each other. That sound okay?''

"That sounds perfect." Kailin's laughter rose through the spangled sunlight, and as she listened to Brett gallop down the stairs she felt like shouting with sheer happiness. It was going to work out after all, she thought with pleasure. It was really going to work out this time.

"Is he gonna be okay, Dr. Douglass?" The little boy standing at the end of the examining table wiped one grubby fist across his cheek, smearing tears and dirt. His chin wobbled and he swallowed, gazing tearfully up at the small shaggy dog lying quietly under Brett's probing hands.

"He'll be okay," Brett assured him gently, still examining the dog. It whimpered and rolled its eyes to look at him, shivering so badly the tags on its collar tinkled like bells.

"Oh, thank goodness." The young woman standing by the door closed her eyes in relief. "Joey's usually so careful with Hobo. I've told him not to walk along that stretch of highway, but—" She shrugged helplessly, looking down at her son.

"I won't ever take him there again," Joey sobbed. "I promise, Mom. Honest, I won't." He wiped his face with the back of his hand and stepped nearer the table. "I'm sorry, Hobo."

Brett traded a smile with the woman, noticing that she was having trouble keeping her own tears from spilling. He nodded toward the small desk beside her. "Tissues in the top right drawer, Helen."

She gave a wet laugh and pulled out a handful of tissues and dabbed her eyes. "When Joey came running into the house carrying Hobo, both of them covered with blood and howling their heads off, it scared me half to death!"

"Well, he's one lucky pup." Brett lifted the small dog down and put him gently in Joey's outstretched arms.

"Thank you, Dr. Douglass." Joey smiled up at Brett radiantly.

"From the heart!" His mother laughed and dabbed at her eyes again. "You know I'll pay you something just as soon as Jim's arm is better and he can go back to work."

"Don't worry about it, Helen." Brett turned the water on in the small sink and started lathering his hands with soap. "When

Jim's working again, tell him to drop off a pail of shrimp and we'll call it even.''

Her face broke into a smile almost as radiant as her son's. "I'll send Joey around tomorrow with a basket of preserves and a couple of apple pies." Then, before Brett could protest, she turned and hurried after her son.

"Apple pies," Kathy said a few minutes later. She eyed Brett's trim midriff speculatively. "Last week it was Carla Mason's strawberry jam. And before that, Tilly Kuzack's black forest cake."

Brett grinned at her. "It's a hell of a life, but hey—someone's got to do it."

"Right," Kathy drawled. "You've got company, by the way." She smiled again, one eyebrow lifting. "Very pretty, and very mad."

Brett winced. "Now what? Who?"

"Me." They both wheeled around as the door to the surgery slammed open and Kailin strode into the room, practically trailing smoke. "And I want to know just what the *hell* you think you're doing."

Kathy eased herself from between them. "I'll clean up in here later," she said to no one in particular. "I think I hear the phone ringing." And with that she was gone, closing the door softly behind her.

Brett looked at Kailin. The two tall stained-glass windows, the only remnants of the building's previous life, spilled a rainbow of light behind her, turning her golden hair to flame. But it wasn't her hair that caught Brett's attention—it was her eyes, wide and bright and snapping with anger. "Hi. I thought you and Becky were going—"

She strode across the room and threw a sheaf of papers onto the operating table. "Would you like to tell me what's going on?"

Brett looked at the papers, slowly realizing that they were the ones Craig Bryant had been waving around that morning. "It's not all that complicated. TexAm Construction is a land development corporation headquartered in Houston. They came to us a few months ago about buying property on Captiva and Sanibel. What's the problem?"

"The problem," she said evenly, "is that your committee is coming this close—" she held her two fingers so close together that Brett couldn't even see daylight between them "—*this* close, mister, to outright fraud. Craig Bryant was right this morning—he *could* take you to court on a collusion charge. I doubt he'd manage to pull it off, but he could tie you up in court for the next twenty years!" The last two words ricocheted off the walls, and she stopped, breathing heavily. "Damn it, Brett, how could you be so careless?"

"What the hell are you talking about?" Brett threw the papers down, eyeing her impatiently.

"I am talking about a breach of every antitrust regulation in the country, that's what I'm talking about." Her eyes glittered in the rainbowed light from the windows. "Gulf Coast is sitting on land that TexAm wants. The Gulf Coast project is in trouble, but you're committed. *Unless* Gulf Coast goes bankrupt. Then TexAm can step in, buying up Paradise Point at five cents on the dollar, and everyone's happy. Except Gulf Coast."

"It's a tough business," Brett reminded her.

"Yeah, it sure is." Kailin strode across in front of him and back again, cheeks flushed.

"TexAm hasn't made a firm offer on anything. It's no big deal."

"No big deal." She planted herself in front of him, hands on trim hips. "The resort they're proposing is nearly twice the size of Paradise Point, which is odd, considering you forced Gulf Coast to downsize their original projections by a third. But the really interesting part is that TexAm promises to donate a huge tract of wetlands back to Sanibel for a wildlife and bird preserve."

"So?" Brett felt his temper start to rise in spite of his best efforts.

Kailin stared at him as though she didn't believe what she was hearing. "It's bribery, Brett. Simple, old-fashioned bribery."

"What are you talking about?" Brett demanded. "TexAm came to us with that offer after it was apparent Gulf Coast was in trouble. If Gulf Coast *does* go down, we're going to be stuck with a half-finished condo development with enough liens and writs against it to sink the entire islands. There aren't many developers willing to take over a mess like that."

"And even fewer," Kailin said silkily, "who'd be willing to deed half of it back as a conservation area. All the committee has to do to get that tract of land is to stonewall Gulf Coast's attempts to salvage Paradise Point. Once they've gone down the tubes, the bank will be only too happy to sell the Point off at whatever they can get for it." She took a step toward him. "Except TexAm couldn't possibly know how much trouble Gulf Coast is in unless someone told them."

"Are you saying that I—?" Brett yelped.

"I'm saying the whole thing stinks of collusion and bribery. Whether it was intentional or not, I don't know— I'm willing to give you the benefit of the doubt. But no government probe sent down here to investigate would be that generous." She turned and strode across the room from him, heels clicking on the polished floor. "If it's so innocent, why didn't you tell me about it? Why wasn't it tabled at the meeting?"

"I didn't tell you about it because it hasn't got anything to do with you," Brett told her bluntly. "Your job is to negotiate an understanding between us and Gulf Coast. That's all. TexAm hasn't got a damned thing to do with either."

"It's got everything to do with it!" Kailin turned to glare at him. "I *am* trying to do my job, Brett. That's to sort out this mess so everyone comes out a winner—you, the investors, Gulf Coast. But I'm not going to be able to do that job if you and your committee are sneaking around making deals behind my back. It's not just unfair, it's unethical!"

"Unethical?" Brett's bellow made Kailin blink. He pushed himself away from the desk. "If we're going to talk ethics, lady, let's talk about the ethics of using cut-rate building materials to skim a profit during construction."

"What do you mean?"

"Why don't you ask your good friend Craig Bryant?"

"You're making a serious allegation, Brett."

"Which can be proved by an on-site inspection of Phase Two. Or what's left of it."

Kailin stood looking at him for a long while. "Craig's already admitted that Phase Two suffered some damage in last week's storm. That's to be expected, considering the place was still under construction and especially vulnerable. The storm was one step below a full-fledged hurricane."

"Phase Two is—was—over ninety percent complete, and as solid as it was ever going to be. It didn't suffer 'some damage,' it was damned near totaled. Nothing can explain the extent of the destruction but lousy workmanship, substandard materials and a lot of cut corners." Brett let her think about that for a moment, knowing by her expression that she was taking in every word. She was too good at her job *not* to be thinking about the possibilities. "*Someone,*" he added softly, "made a lot of under-the-table money on that project."

Her eyes narrowed. "What you're suggesting isn't just unethical, it's grounds for a criminal action suit. Craig might play close to the line sometimes, but he's not that stupid."

"Don't be so innocent. You know how the game is played. Hell, you were weaned on Monopoly. Anything goes in big business as long as you don't get caught, you know that."

"And you don't?" Kailin's eyebrow arched delicately. "St. Douglass the Pure, my father used to call you. He'd have a fit if he could see you now, playing at big business like an old pro. When you told me you'd mellowed, I didn't realize you meant you'd sold out."

The tenuous hold that Brett had managed to keep on his temper very nearly snapped. "I have *not* sold out!"

"No?" Kailin stared at him defiantly. "Everyone knows how hard you've been fighting to get more wetlands put aside as natural habitat areas, Brett. You've been one of the leaders in the conservation movement down here for years. If Gulf Coast loses Paradise Point and TexAm picks it up, you'll get that tract of swamp—even though it means approving a bigger development than originally planned. Now *I* call that a sellout."

"Give a little, get a little," Brett growled. "I learned years ago that you can't have it all your own way all the time." He caught the anger, swallowed it. "And no one is sneaking around behind your back—no one from *my* side of the table, anyway."

"And just what is *that* supposed to mean?"

"If Gulf Coast goes bankrupt, the Bryant family is going to be hurting—and I can't see Craig Bryant giving it all up without a fight. I wouldn't put it past him to deal from both sides of the deck and work a deal with TexAm—inside information for hard, cold cash."

"Come on, Brett. That makes even less sense than—"

"Than what?" Brett asked angrily. "Than my selling out?"

"Exactly!"

"You think so?" Brett gave a snort of harsh laughter. "Craig Bryant is like an iceberg, Kailin—you only see what he wants you to see. Or maybe the sellout isn't on Bryant's side of the table at all."

Kailin stared at him blankly. "What are you saying?"

"I don't know what I'm saying," he replied with quiet intensity, wishing with every atom that he could shake free of the suspicion. "It's just that I keep asking myself why, of all the people in the world, you're the one looking at me across that meeting table, Kailin. Coincidence? Fate? Or is there more to it?"

"Such as?" She had gone pale, her eyes very wide. "You think that I'm working with Craig Bryant to. . ." She gestured helplessly, as though at a loss for words.

"The two of you seem to know each other pretty well." He hadn't intended to say it, but the words were out before he could stop them, rancid with suspicion. He stared at her, daring her to deny it, something aching deep and cold within him. "I just keep wondering if—"

"If he's using me to manipulate you," she completed. "That possibility didn't seem to bother you much yesterday afternoon. Or last night. Or maybe *you* were using me. Was I picking your brains last night, or were you picking mine? Am I Craig's pawn or yours? Or am I playing both ends against the middle for some devious little purpose of my own?"

Damn it, that wasn't what he'd meant at all! Or was it? Brett rubbed his forehead, trying to ease a dull throb that had settled there in the past few minutes. It was all falling apart, disappearing through his fingers like smoke, and he didn't even know how to stop it. "Kailin . . ."

"You think I'm using you just like you believed I used you before, don't you?" she whispered. "You didn't believe I loved you then. You didn't even believe I was pregnant. I used to lie awake at night trying to convince myself that you hadn't taken that money, that you'd come riding up in that old MGB and we'd go off together."

"I didn't take the money," Brett said angrily.

"No, but you didn't exactly knock yourself out trying to find me, either."

"Your father—!"

"My father was just a man, Brett. He couldn't have kept you away from me if you'd really tried." She gazed at him, a flash of what might have been tears in her eyes. "I guess you decided that being saddled with a wife and baby didn't fit your plans."

"Like being married to me didn't fit yours?" he retorted. Her accusation had stung, and he could feel his temper flaring again. "Stop kidding yourself about who ran out on whom, Kailin. You're the one who married Royce McGuire and let him raise my daughter."

"She's not your daughter!" Kailin shouted, then stared at him as though the words were as great a shock to her as they were to him.

Eight

Eight

—

Brett felt an eerie coolness drift through the room. "What di you say?" he asked very softly.

He thought he heard her sigh. When she slowly turned an looked at him, her face was bleak. "This isn't how I wanted t tell you, Brett, but it's true. Becky is Royce's daughter, no yours. I—I lost yours."

"Lost...it?" Brett heard the words but didn't recognize th voice as his own. He shook his head, as though that coul somehow make all this come clear. "How do you lose a baby Kailin?" he asked very reasonably. "They're not like umbrel las and old shoes. You don't just put them down one day an forget where you left them."

"I had a miscarriage nine days after Royce and I were mar ried."

"You were on your honeymoon nine days after you wer married." It was a ridiculous thing to say, as though a honey moon somehow made a miscarriage impossible, but it was lik a talisman, protecting him, and he clung to it fiercely. "Que bec City, Canada. The Château Frontenac hotel." She wa staring at him with such an odd expression that he added un necessarily, "I didn't believe you'd married him until I...checked." He took a deep breath. "Look, just what kind of game are you playing, Kailin? Becky for Paradise Point, is that it? If I don't swing the committee over to approve Phase Three, I'll never see my daughter again?"

Kailin had gone ghost-white. "My God," she whispered, "what do you think I am?"

"Your father's daughter." He smiled bitterly and walked back to the desk. How could it have gone so wrong? He'd been so sure this morning, so positive that *this* time it was going to be all right, that *this* time they were going to have the happiness they'd only been promised eleven years ago.

She was staring at him with a look of such unutterable hurt on her face that for the briefest moment he wondered if he'd been wrong. But he caught himself as in the next instant that closed, remote mask shuttered over her face again. She gazed at him for a long moment, those moss-green eyes impossible to read, then turned and walked to the door.

"Kailin?" The word was torn from him.

"What?" She paused with her hand on the knob, not turning to look at him.

"Was that the truth...about Becky?" He held his breath, wanting to know and at the same time dreading the answer. Hating her in that moment for making him ask.

Her back straightened. "I've never lied to you in my entire life, Brett. That was always the problem between us—you never even knew me well enough to understand that."

She was gone. Brett stared at the closing door numbly. He swallowed, aching with a soul-deep emptiness that was so bitterly familiar that it took him a moment to understand why.

Then he remembered. Eleven years ago he'd stood and watched a door swing slowly closed like that. And then, as now, he'd felt a part of himself twist free and vanish.

Kailin stood on the huge balcony of her rented apartment and stared unseeingly down at the beach. The unseasonably warm weather had brought the weekend sunseekers out in force, and the beach was a colorful mosaic of oiled bodies. It was an idyllic scene, and for a moment Kailin found herself hating them all.

She smiled. It had been a long while since she'd allowed herself to indulge in a bit of self-pity, and it felt oddly satisfying. Her father had never tolerated it. But then her father had rarely tolerated any sign of weakness. *Don't show them anything* had been his credo, and he'd taught her well. Only with Becky could she be real and spontaneous. Why, she asked herself idly, couldn't she just let go of all the programmed responses and let the real Kailin McGuire out? Was she that insecure and frightened?

Life hurts, her father had told her once. The trick is not to show it.

She'd hurt today.

Kailin closed her eyes for an instant, holding that remembered pain at bay by sheer force of will. Then, without even thinking about it, she relaxed the barriers and let it sweep over her, relishing its sting. Relishing *feeling*.

Pain. Anger. Frustration. They curdled together, and she didn't even bother stopping the tears. She could still hear Brett's voice. See the disbelief and the suspicion in his eyes. "What's the use?" she asked out loud. "Why don't you just go home and tell your father to find someone else to do his dirty work?"

But she couldn't go home. She'd given her word.

She stepped back into the cool bedroom and kicked her shoes off. They hit the closet door with a bang that startled Maverick so badly he wailed and scuttled for the safety of her ankles.

"Sorry, Mav," she whispered contritely, picking the kitten up and tucking him against her shoulder. "It was just a passing tantrum, nothing serious."

She stretched out on her bed and stared at the ceiling. Maverick bumped his head against her chin, then gnawed on the strap of her dress. She couldn't leave the Paradise Point investors high and dry when she'd given her word to sort this mess out; she couldn't leave Charlie Bryant high and dry, either. She'd felt sorry for the old man when she'd talked with him a month or more ago. His dreams of building a dynastic empire were crumbling around him, and it must have taken fantastic courage to tell her that his son was ruining Gulf Coast Developments.

What price an old man's pride? she found herself wondering. What had it cost her father to beg her to take on this job? What, for that matter, was it costing her?

Frowning, she thought of Brett's accusations about Craig and Paradise Point. He wouldn't be the first developer to make deals with his contractors. It was a simple scam, and it was usually impossible to detect. The building codes and blueprints would specify one thing—a certain size lumber to be used for floor supports, for instance, or a specific distance left between wall joists. The supply invoices would reflect what was specified, but in reality floors would be supported with two-by-eights instead of two-by-tens, wall joists would be set an extra two or three inches apart. If the scam was subtle enough, the contractor could get away with it. Only one buyer in ten thousand ever went into the basement and looked at the flooring in a new house; perhaps half of those knew what to look for.

But if the builder was too greedy, if the rip-offs were too flagrant, the structural integrity of the building itself was compromised. Bridges fell down; office towers collapsed halfway through construction; highways dissolved in the first heavy rain. It happened.

Had it happened on Phase Two of Paradise Point?

There was one way to find out. The first step was to go out there and see if the storm damage was as bad as Brett had said. The second was to bring in a building inspector and have him go over the place nail by nail. If everything was as it should be, his report would settle any doubts still harbored by Brett's Land Use Committee. If it *wasn't*....

"Well," she advised the sleeping kitten, "then we see just how good Kailin McGuire really is."

"I'm sorry, ma'am." The security guard shifted the wad of tobacco to his other cheek, then turned his head and spat tidily into the ditch. "But I can't let y'all in there. Rules."

It took Kailin every ounce of willpower to resist telling the man blocking her way precisely what he could do with his rules. Behind him lay the muddy dirt road leading into Phase Two of the Paradise Point resort complex, tantalizing in its nearness. Two massive trees lay across it just at the entrance, blocking it completely. Behind her lay Phase One, serene and quiet in the noonday sun, the picturesque adobe-style buildings and well-cared-for gardens a postcard version of what paradise should look like.

She drew in a deep, calming breath, and tried again. "Look, Craig Bryant is a friend and I'm working with him on the Paradise Point project. He told me I could come in here to look the site over." She was stretching the truth, but who cared?

"Sorry, ma'am." Calm gray eyes met her, as obdurate and unmoved by her pleas as stone. "No pass, no access, them's the rules." He shrugged a meaty shoulder toward the two trees. "Can't get in nohow."

"Look," Kailin snapped, all patience gone, "I know you're just doing your job, but I need to get on that site. Now if you call Craig's office, they'll tell you that I—"

"Can't do that, ma'am. Couldn't let Charlie Bryant hisself in without a pass." The human mountain smiled congenially. "'Sides, I couldn't let y'all in anyways. It's a construction site, and y'all need a hard hat—them's *government* rules."

"Fine." She turned on her heel and marched across to her rental car. Now what? Craig Bryant was out of town and his secretary at the Sanibel office had no idea where he was, when he'd be back, or even *if* he'd be back. Nor was she inclined to give Kailin a pass to get into Phase Two.

The security guard smiled amiably at her as she turned the car around, and she smiled back. I'll be back, she promised him silently. One way or another, I *will* be back.

There had to be another way.

Kailin draped her arms across the top of the steering wheel, then rested her chin on them and sighed heavily, staring out at the old church housing Brett's vet clinic. Except if there was, *she* couldn't think of it.

Asking Brett for help didn't mean he'd do it, though. In fact, he was just as likely to tell her to go to hell. Not that she could blame him. Kailin winced at the memory of his expression when she'd blurted out the truth about Becky. If she had deliberately set out to hurt him, she couldn't have chosen a more brutally effective method.

It was ironic in a way. Eleven years ago they'd argued over a baby he didn't believe existed, and two mornings ago he'd wanted desperately to believe that Becky *was* his.

And yet it was Brett alone who could get her what she needed. She took a deep breath, then pushed open the car door and stepped out.

"Come on in!" The disembodied female voice came from somewhere under the big desk in the waiting room.

The place had Brett Douglass written all over it, from the blue denim jacket tossed carelessly over the back of a chair to the pair of muddy work boots drying in the corner. There were a couple of battered filing cabinets on one side of the desk, the tops littered with paper, plants and old coffee cups.

A mop of curly brown hair popped up from behind the desk, and Kathy Fischer grinned broadly at her. "Hi!"

Kailin smiled. "Hi. I'm looking for Brett again, but no fireworks this time, I promise."

Kathy laughed and stood up, holding a squirming mass of fur. "He's out back." She leaned over and deposited a ferret into Kailin's hands. "Could you take the little pest out to Brett? Three of them got loose last night and we're moving them to an outside cage they'll *never* get open!"

It was as supple as a fur-covered spring, pausing long enough to sniff Kailin's fingers before trying to go in fifteen directions at once. It squeezed under her arm and found her open canvas shoulder bag and promptly disappeared into its depths.

Kailin found the door leading out to the backyard, full of cages and holding pens. Brett was at the far end, stripped to the waist, his broad back gleaming with sweat as he nailed the framework of another set of cages together with quick, competent blows of the hammer.

She stood in the doorway for a long moment until Brett glanced around. The hammering faltered, then stopped, and he stared at her in silence, eyes dark with surprise. But she could also read the wary suspicion of a man hurt once too often. The taut silence lengthened, and then Brett resumed his hammering, pounding the nails in with short, savage blows.

Great start. They hadn't even said anything yet, and he was already angry.

"I . . . um . . . tried to look at Phase Two this morning."
Nothing. Not even a pause. Kailin stared at his strong, sun-bronzed back in frustration. He wasn't going to give an inch,
damn him.

Ill at ease, she looked at the array of wildlife in the pens: two
opossums curled up in a knot, a small heron with its wing in a
splint, a huge turtle sunning itself in a child's plastic wading
pool, ignoring the three-legged alligator in the next cage.

"You've got quite a little menagerie out here," she said.
"Are you taking up zookeeping or expecting a heavy rain?"

The hammering paused. She glanced around and found Brett
watching her carefully, as though undecided about answering
her. "No flood, no ark. Just strays that people bring in."

He spoke as though each word took an effort, and Kailin
sighed. This was going to be tougher than she'd anticipated.
"How did this alligator lose its leg?"

"Fight." The word was punctuated by hammer blows.

"For food?" Kailin managed to keep her growing irritation
out of her voice. She could play this game as long as he could.
Longer, if necessary.

"Sex." Brett straightened, his eyes holding hers challeng-ingly. He wiped the sweat from his forehead with his arm.

"That will do it," Kailin said calmly. "So, did he get the
lady?"

"No." Three sharp hammer blows. "She ran off with someone else while he and his opponent were battling for her favors."

"She'd probably have broken his heart anyway."

"Undoubtedly. Most women do."

Kailin swallowed a sigh and rested her forearms on the top of
the turtle's cage, staring down at it. "Would it help if I said I
was sorry?" she asked quietly.

The hammering faltered and stopped. "For what?" It
sounded torn out of him, as though he were annoyed at himself for giving her even that much.

"For all of it," Kailin turned to look at him. "For letting you
think Becky was your daughter for as long as I did. I never
thought that you'd think she was, because it never occurred to
me that you'd finally believed I was pregnant in the first place.
I should have told you right at the beginning, but there . . . just

didn't seem to be a good time. And I didn't realize it was…well, so important to you."

His eyes held hers, dark with some emotion Kailin couldn't even guess at. Then he turned his attention back to the cage. "Neither did I," he said gruffly, not looking at her.

Watching him, Kailin felt her heart ache. What had that admission cost him? she wondered sadly. What momentary dreams had the truth shattered? He glanced around. Their eyes caught and held, then he frowned fleetingly and looked away. Unrolling a large sheet of wire mesh, he stretched it across the wooden framework. Silently Kailin walked over and held it for him. Brett started nailing it down without saying a thing.

"Where do they all come from? The animals, I mean?"

"People bring them in." He waited for her to unroll more of the wire. "Anything that's injured, we mend it as best we can and turn it loose again." He gave his head an impatient shake. "Some days it's a losing battle."

You're a kind and gentle man, Brett Douglass, Kailin found herself thinking. Always out there standing up for the little guy, battling for good against impossible odds. Why did he find it so easy to love these small furred things yet so difficult to love her?

"What the hell—?"

Brett was staring at something behind her, and Kailin looked around. Her own eyes widened at the sight of her canvas carryall making its way clumsily across the yard, whirring and chattering as it went.

Kailin pounced on it, laughing, and hauled the rumpled ferret out. "I forgot all about you!"

Brett looked at her quizzically, then nodded toward the far set of cages. "Pop him with the others."

Pop wasn't quite the right word. Trying to stuff a ferret through a hole was like trying to stuff a sock full of marbles through the eye of a needle. The other two ferrets weren't helping the effort—they were just as intent on oozing out as Kailin was trying to get the third *in*. She finally managed to get them all more or less on the right side, and she closed the door, trying not to pinch too many toes, feeling like a drunk tank jailer on a Saturday night.

"You do that like a pro."

"Oh, I have talents you haven't even suspected yet." Brett looked at her sharply, but Kailin simply unrolled another length of wire. She stretched it across the cage frame, watching the play of muscle in his back as Brett worked, the bulge of his biceps, the fine peppering of dark hairs along his forearms.

He looked up just then, those blue eyes so close that it was like falling into deep water. The shock left her breathless and she simply stared at him. She could see the tiny beads of sweat on his upper lip, the almost imperceptible tightening of the skin around his eyes, and in that heartbeat eternity she knew he was going to kiss her.

He didn't. He closed his eyes instead and turned his head away, the muscles along his jaw throbbing as though he were clenching his teeth. Then he breathed an oath and stood up, his fingers, trailing fire where they brushed her arm, lingered for the briefest moment on her shoulder.

"You didn't come here to help build these cages," he said tightly.

He sounded resentful, even angry. So he was still fighting her. Fighting *himself*. Fighting everything he knew in his heart to be true but was too angry and stubborn to admit. "No," she said quietly. "I need your help." Silence answered her, fraught with tension. "I said, I—"

"I heard you. I'm just waiting for the catch."

"There is no catch. I've been trying to get into the Phase Two site for two days, but I'm being stonewalled. I'd hoped you could help me."

Surprise flared in his eyes, followed by frank curiosity. "What do you mean, stonewalled?"

"I called Craig Bryant a couple of hours after I . . . left your place." His eyes narrowed fractionally, but they gave Kailin no clue as to what he was thinking. "I told him that either I got an on-site inspection, trees or no trees, or I went straight to the top. He was quite agreeable to my going out there, but very...vague." She smiled humorlessly. "Since then he's been as elusive as a snake. I went out there yesterday, but they've got a security guard at the entrance I swear is a sumo wrestler in his spare time."

"What do you want me to do?"

"You were the one making all the accusations the other day. The least you can do is help me get in there to see for myself."

"Did you see the roots of those trees across the road?"

"No. No, I don't think I did," Kailin said, frowning thoughtfully.

"The only big trees growing along that road are Australian pine. When they go over, they pull up a huge circle of soil and roots. I suspect those trees have been cut and deliberately placed across the road to keep people out. Especially people like you."

"But why would anyone—?"

Her eyes widened, and Brett smiled. "If word gets out about how much damage that storm really did, Bryant's finished. Even he's not enough of a fast-talker to convince people it wasn't the result of substandard materials."

"Get me in there so I can see it."

"Why?" He held her gaze deliberately. "So you can write a report downplaying the damage?"

"So I can write a report detailing exactly what's been going on since Craig took over from his father." She held his stare challengingly. "You've accused me of being unfair, Brett, but you're ready to write Gulf Coast off without giving them a chance just because of your feelings about me. Paradise Point is too important to be held ransom because you and I can't solve our differences. Unless," she added bluntly, "I was right and the committee *is* trying to push Gulf Coast into insolvency so TexAm can move in."

"Do you believe that?"

"No. I think you and your committee were careless and dangerously naive about even talking with TexAm, but I don't believe any of you were being dishonest."

To Kailin's surprise, Brett's strong mouth trembled with a smile. "You don't pull your punches, do you?"

"No." Kailin looked at him evenly. "Brett, I'm very good at my job. I've pulled companies ten times the size of Gulf Coast out of the fire, and there's a good chance I can save Gulf Coast, too. You love this island, and I know you want to do the best for it.... Can't we stop trying to hurt each other long enough to do what's right for Sanibel?"

"Is that what you think we've been trying to do?" he asked quietly. "Hurt each other?"

"Isn't it?" She smiled crookedly, looking down. "I don't know if we're trying to get even or if we're just getting rid of a lot of anger, but I do know it hurts." She glanced up at him. "Funny, I didn't think it would."

"Yeah." His voice was no more than a growl.

Kailin smiled down at the cages, shaking off her sudden pensiveness. The animals were either sleeping peacefully or roughhousing, without a thought to the outside world that had brought them there.

"Six o'clock tomorrow morning."

"What?" Startled, Kailin looked up to find Brett staring down thoughtfully at her.

"I'll pick you up at your apartment at six tomorrow morning. We'll go in by canoe, through the mangroves and marsh to the east. It'll bring us in on the far side, well back of the road."

"You realize that if we get caught in there we can be charged with trespassing."

Brett suddenly grinned the reckless rebel's grin she recognized and loved so well. "Your old man tried often enough and it never stuck. Figure Bryant will have any better luck?"

Kailin laughed. "My father swore he'd see you hanged on that front gate—and police chief Feniak right alongside of you. He was sure you and Feniak had a deal going. Dad would have you arrested and you'd be out an hour later, charges dropped on one technicality or another." She smiled, reminiscing, then drew in a deep breath. "But I didn't come here just to ask you to get me into Paradise Point," she said quietly. "I . . . thought I should tell you about Becky. And about the baby. Your . . . baby."

Nine

"**K**ailin," Brett said softly, "you don't have—"

"Yes," she replied firmly, "I do." She got to her feet and turned to look at him. He was watching her silently, his eyes filled with a thousand questions she knew he would never ask. "For years I blamed myself. The doctors all said that wasn't the case, but I couldn't get over the feeling that perhaps if I'd been more careful, if...oh, I don't know. A thousand different things." She wandered along the row of cages restlessly. "I think of all the things that happened during those weeks, losing the baby was the worst." She swallowed, remembering the aching loss, the loneliness. "Everyone was so matter-of-fact about it," she whispered. "The doctors, my parents. They said no damage had been done and that I'd be able to have other children." She shivered slightly, rubbing her arms. "No damage! I'd lost the most precious thing in the world to me, and they said there'd been no damage!"

Brett was silent and Kailin kept her face turned resolutely away, knowing that if she looked at him she'd burst into tears. "I wanted that baby so much," she whispered. "It was all I had left of you. As long as I had it, there was hope—that you'd come back, that we still had a chance. But when I lost the baby, there was just . . . nothing.''

"Kailin . . .'' Strong hands cupped her shoulders, turned her against his chest. "If I'd only known! I could have—''

"Could have what?'' Kailin asked him gently, glancing up at him. "I was married, remember?'' She laughed quietly and rested her cheek on his chest, relaxing into the warmth and comfort of his arms. "Poor Royce. It was probably the worst honeymoon in history— I spent the first two days crying over losing you, then a week later I had the miscarriage and scared the daylights out of everybody.''

Brett murmured something and tightened his arms comfortingly around her.

"Oh, Brett,'' she whispered, trying not to cry. "Can you ever forgive me?''

"There's nothing to forgive,'' he said softly. "Kailin, it wasn't your fault.''

They stood, holding each other, talking about the eleven years between them, what the two of them had done and thought and felt. It was a healing time, a time of sharing. They were silent for a long time, and finally Kailin laughed, pushing away the past. "Six tomorrow morning, you said?''

Brett blinked, as though just coming back from some distant place. "I—yeah.'' He shook his head as though scattering a few memories of his own. "Six sharp. Wear jeans and a long-sleeved shirt, good walking shoes, socks, the works—the mosquitoes and no-see-ums are going to be as thick as dogs at a tree growers' convention.''

"Just what, exactly,'' Kailin asked in a preoccupied manner, "*are* no-see-ums?''

"What you're looking for and can't find.'' The paddle sliced the still, obsidian surface of the water without a ripple, and Brett leaned into the stroke.

Kailin was sitting in the bow of the canoe, facing him, looking annoyed as she peeled down her sock to scratch furiously at her ankle. "How do they get through my clothes?'' she asked indignantly.

"They can get through just about anything. There's a bottle of repellent in the top pocket of my pack. And don't scratch those bites—it'll only irritate them."

Kailin's look was eloquent, but when she opened the bottle she held it at arm's length and wrinkled her nose. "You can't be serious!"

"*Eau de swamp,*" Brett teased. "Either you put it on and spend the rest of this expedition in relative comfort or get finicky and suffer."

"This stuff is really repulsive," Kailin muttered, but slathered it on everywhere.

"The bugs think so, which is the whole point."

"Look at that! I think it's working already!" She grinned at Brett. "Thank you, Tarzan." She started looking around her with interest, no longer distracted by the clouds of mosquitoes and gnats that in places were so thick that they looked like smoke.

It was still early enough in the morning that the swamp was shrouded with tattered sheets of mist. Clumps of mangroves rose eerily around them, mysterious in the gray half-light. They were more an interwoven knot of branches than individual trees, the tangled, curving roots creating a maze so thick that nothing but the smallest swamp creature could navigate them. Now and again they could make out the crisp white outlines of ibis as they stood like carved ivory statues in the trees, ghostly in the mist.

It was very still and quiet. Occasionally the stillness was shattered as a heron exploded upward in a flurry of wingbeats, then the silence would fold around them again, as tangible as the mist drafting across the black mirrored surface of the water.

"It's beautiful in here, isn't it?" Kailin whispered, staring out at the mangroves in fascination. The sun was starting to burn off the mist and the swamp seemed to take fire, aglow in a ruby haze. Suddenly wave after wave of ibis swirled overhead, followed by low-flying flocks of roseate spoonbills in their blushing plumage. In the distance, like some primordial heartbeat, came the deep, solitary groan of a bull gator.

"It's hard to believe that places like this still exist. It's as though time has gone by without even touching it."

"Oh, it's touched it." Brett dug the paddle into the glassy water, pivoting the bow to avoid a snag as he maneuvered them deftly through the maze of hummocks and tiny islands. "Look more closely and you can see garbage washed up among the mangrove roots, and that's the least of the problems. There's— oh hell!" He laughed good-naturedly. "Don't get me started!"

"Is this the land TexAm promised to turn over to you?"

"Part of it." He swung the canoe gracefully into a passage between two silent, mist-cloaked islands. "We're coming up to Paradise Point now. Look to your right."

Kailin turned her head, and sucked in her breath as they glided out into open water. The sickle shaped curve of sand in the small bay glowed like liquid gold, and in the morning light the long, low point of land looked every inch like paradise.

Brett sent the canoe sweeping into the clear, still water of the tiny bay. "Phase Two is just there—" He pointed north. "Or what's left of it. They built a road down to the bay, but it hasn't been paved yet."

"And Phase Three?"

"The marina's to be just around that spit of land, and they plan to build the helipad out that way." He swung his arm eastward, encompassing open water dotted with small islands. "They're going to fill all that in."

"Fill it in?" Kailin echoed. "You mean join all those little islands together?"

"That's right."

Kailin looked thoughtful. "What happens if a storm hits? Can they anchor the helipad firmly enough to keep it from being washed away?"

"No one will know that until it happens."

Kailin looked at him sharply. "Cut the tour-guide routine, Brett. What's *your* opinion?"

"If they drive pylons through the mud and get down to bedrock, they might be able to hold it together. But as far as I've seen the swamps are designed to take the changing wave action; any rigid man-made structure isn't."

"The helipad and road would run across the direction of the waves and wind instead of with them. They'll take the full force of both," Kailin said, almost to herself.

Brett was surprised to feel a surge of respect at Kailin's immediate grasp of the situation. He found himself wondering what untested strengths lay hidden under her cool and self-possessed exterior. And just how did this new Kailin McGuire fit into his life—if, indeed, she fit there at all?

He beached the canoe on the sand and pulled it well up onto dry land, tucking it under the low-hanging branches of a sea grape tree. Kailin strode up the shelving beach to the grassy meadow above it, and Brett following, enjoyed the tantalizing view she presented. Her soft, faded blue jeans hugged her like a lover's caress. Her waist seemed to disappear while her legs went on forever, and he grinned as he watched her with frank appreciation. He was happy to treat her as an equal in their business dealings, he reminded himself virtuously, but at times like this a man could be forgiven a moment or two of lustful admiration.

She stopped at the top of the slope and looked down at him sharply, as though suddenly aware of the show she was providing. He wiped the grin off his mouth and pretended to be deeply engrossed in something on the horizon. Lustful admiration was one thing; getting caught at it quite another.

"There's a dirt track back here that will lead us into Phase Two," he said innocently, nodding toward the right. "It's about half a mile."

"Half a mile!" She looked up at him. "The Phase Two condos are advertised as being right on the water."

"They are." He smiled, a bit maliciously. "And after the storm last week, some of them are right *in* the water." He took her elbow and guided her down the muddy road. "The area around the bay where we landed is reserved for the luxury condos in Phase Three. Phase One is midrange. It's good, solid housing, nothing too pretentious, but obviously a quality setup. Bryant used them as the lure to sign people up for Phase Two."

"Then built Phase Two sub-standard, according to you."

"You'll see for yourself," he told her calmly. "Watch your footing...."

Kailin sank ankle-deep into mud and water, and she grabbed Brett's hand. "Lovely country," she said dryly, then asked, "What happens to all this wildlife when this complex is finished?"

"Some of it will die," Brett said with brutal honesty. "A lot of good nesting and foraging area will be lost when the helipad and the golf course go in. The birds will probably move down island, but the turtles will have a bad time. The gators, too. They're territorial: as the wilderness area gets smaller they don't take kindly to being crowded closer together. Diminished food supplies lead to scavenging, and that creates a whole new set of problems, but all this is in my report."

"I know. But it's different seeing it." A blue heron sailed by only feet over their heads, and Kailin looked up as the shadow crossed her face, smiling as she watched it flap lazily away.

Why couldn't all their days together be as pleasant as this one? she wondered. There hadn't been a harsh word passed between them since he'd picked her up this morning. Maybe the healing had finally started. Perhaps all the shouting had purged the rest of Brett's anger and they could both put the past behind them.

Brett stopped. They were at the top of a low rise, and as Kailin gazed down at a marshy meadow where a circle of concrete foundations rose from the mud and water like the ruins of some ancient pagan monument. Some of the foundations held the skeletons of buildings, and lumber and brick lay strewn around in untidy piles.

"Welcome to Paradise Point," Brett said quietly.

"But..." Kailin stared down in dismay. "But there's nothing here!"

Brett simply smiled and started down the incline.

"This...this isn't possible," she whispered, gazing at the twisted piles of plywood sheeting. She realized she was looking at what was supposed to be the small four-unit complexes facing the bay. She let her gaze follow the curving line of bare foundations to where they disappeared underwater. "There's got to be some mistake, Brett. No storm could do this!" Suddenly chilled, she strode over to what looked like bulldozed rubble. Slowly, as she stared, it started to take faint but recognizable form. She swallowed, her mind spinning.

"This...is supposed to be the main lodge," she whispered. "There's a pool under there somewhere. Saunas, an exercise club." Numbed, she turned to look at the rest of the complex. "It looks as though it just...exploded."

"It did," Brett said. "That storm hit this place and blew it apart. If it had happened with full occupancy it would have been a slaughter. Most of the people buying these units are seniors—what chance would they have had? They built the access road right along the bay. It was underwater before the storm even hit its peak, cutting off the only escape—and the only access for emergency vehicles. Anyone here would have been trapped."

Kailin drew in a deep, unsteady breath, pulled her small notebook from her canvas shoulder bag and rummaged around for her camera. She handed it and a handful of film to Brett. "I want photos—every angle. I want shots of the layout, the nonexistent beach, the road. I want—" She stopped, narrowed eyes scanning the scene around them. "I want enough to take to an investigations hearing, because I'm going to blow this thing wide-open."

She looked up at Brett angrily. "This couldn't have happened unless someone was paying off the inspectors. They check each stage of construction, and they're not *this* blind. Someone got to them."

"What happens now?"

"I take all this back to Charlie Bryant who—if he knows what's good for him, and he does—will notify the authorities. Heads will roll in Gulf Coast, and when the dust settles I suspect our good friend Craig Bryant won't be around. A new proposal for Phase Two and Three will be assembled. *If* I can convince the bank to carry the loans for another year, and *if* I can convince your committee that Gulf Coast, under new management, is to be trusted, maybe we'll salvage this mess." She smiled suddenly, feeling the familiar surge of adrenaline that she thrived on.

"You love this, don't you?"

Kailin looked up at him in surprise, then laughed. "Does it show?"

"You're giving off enough energy to light up Miami."

Still grinning, Kailin nodded. "Yeah, I love it. I love the wheeling and dealing, the trade-offs. It's like a gigantic game of strategy, and when I finally bring both sides in a dispute like this together, I feel like I've won a war."

Brett stared down at her, his eyes quizzical, almost pensive. Then he nodded and flipped the lens cap off. "Okay, where do you want to start?"

Ten

It was nearly noon by the time they finished. Kailin snapped her notebook closed in relief and stretched luxuriously, working the knots out of her back and shoulders. "I've never been so hungry in my life," she groaned.

"There are probably a few edible roots around here I could dig up, if you like."

"Roots, nothing," she muttered. "I want steak and potatoes."

"How about pâté, Brie, sliced turkey breast, artichoke heart salad, fruit, wine . . . ?"

"Don't be cruel, Douglass. It's a long way home."

"Maybe we don't have to go that far."

Kailin's eyes narrowed. "You're up to something. You brought lunch, didn't you?" Kailin grasped the front of his shirt. "You sneak, you packed a lunch and didn't even tell me! That's what's in that rucksack you hauled along."

Brett grinned down at her, slipping his arms lightly around the small of her back. "Oh, I may have a dry crust or two. . . ."

"I think I'm in love!" Kailin clasped two fistfuls of his thick, wind-tangled hair and pulled his face down to hers. "Some days you're too good to be true, Brett Douglass. Thank you, thank you!" She kissed him lightly on the mouth, then started to step away.

His arms tightened instantly, trapping her. His eyes were so deeply blue they rivaled the tropical sky above them. "I just saved your life, and that's the best you can do?" he murmured.

Kailin smiled slowly. "How do I know this isn't an elaborate scam to get me to kiss you?"

"You don't." His warm breath mingled with hers as he brushed his lips across hers. "You'll just have to trust me."

"My daddy always told me never to trust a man who holds all the aces." Kailin caressed his lower lip lightly with the tip of her tongue as she looked up at him. "But then again, what's life without a bit of risk?"

"No life at all," he murmured agreeably, lowering his mouth to hers. Her lips parted almost of their own will.

Kailin felt a shiver run lazily through her when he finally kissed her and she sighed with satisfaction. Yes, she murmured to herself dizzily, some things were definitely worth the risk.

It was a playful, tender kiss that turned, halfway through, into something else altogether. Kailin could feel the change in Brett at the same instant, could sense the tension in every muscle. The kiss became deeper, slower, the play of his tongue turning to a rhythmic thrust that sent a honeyed warmth spilling through her. Her breath caught as every inch of her seemed suddenly brushed with a static charge, and she knew if he ran his hands over her she would give off sparks. Every part of her responded to the unspoken knowledge in that kiss, every secret, hidden place that knew his touch came awake. She heard someone moan softly and let herself melt against him, felt the hard, responding thrust of his body, the urgency in his hands.

She let her head fall back and murmured in pleasure as Brett assaulted her throat. He cupped her head and lifted it so that her mouth was under his again, and he kissed her with an abandoned hunger that fanned the sparks of want to the full-fledged fires of need.

Brett growled something and splayed his fingers around the taut curve of her bottom. He lifted her hard against him, his physical arousal aggressively, conspicuously male. She pressed against him, every nerve ending in her being crying out for the release that his body was promising, and she moaned his name in soft assent.

His responding moan was torn from him, rough and breathless, and he buried his face in the curve of her throat. Kailin could feel him tremble as though fighting a tension that was near explosion, and she clung to him with the same desperate urgency.

Slowly he eased his grip and she slid down his body until she was standing on solid ground, her legs so weak they would never have held her if he'd let go. He hugged her tightly and Kailin rested her cheek on his chest, eyes closed, letting the thump of his heartbeat vibrate through her. Then he eased his arms from around her and Kailin stepped away unsteadily.

She dared to glance up at him, and his eyes trapped hers in a wordless look so eloquent it made her catch her breath. Silently he took her hand and started walking back the way they'd come. They walked in silence, still linked on a thousand different levels. It was as though they had already made love, she thought wonderingly.

When they reached the beach it was unspeakably hot. Kailin peeled off her filthy sneakers and socks and danced inelegantly across the burning sand to the water. She splashed out into the shallow bay up to her knees and stood there in bliss.

"You," Brett said quietly behind her, "are going to get burned to a crisp."

Kailin turned and smiled at him. He'd rolled up his own jeans past his knees and was happily swishing his feet through the water. He lured her over with a tiny triangular cracker mounded with pâté and then gallantly carried her across the hot sand to the tiny tree-shaded clearing where he'd set out the picnic.

He deposited her on the blanket, and Kailin looked around her in astonishment. "Did all this come out of *that*?" She gestured at the rucksack that he'd tossed into the bottom of the canoe that morning. "You *are* a genius!"

How he'd done it, Kailin had no idea, but the end result was magnificent. He'd covered the rough camping blanket with a blue-and-white gingham tablecloth, and in the center had set out a feast worthy of a five-star restaurant. "You always *did* have a fantastic flair for putting together picnics."

"And we usually got rained out," he reminded her, his eyes catching hers, smoky with memories.

She let her gaze slide from his, filled with a warm lassitude. It wasn't just the heat of the day, she knew. It was the nearness of him, the promise she'd read so unmistakably in his look.

Kailin helped herself to a bit of everything, exclaiming with delight as she tried each dish. They ate leisurely, feeding each other crackers and pâté and sipping wine. The silence surrounding them was absolute in the heat of midday, as though even the cicadas were too somnolent to sing. Sheltered in the tiny meadow, surrounded by lacy-leafed trees and bathed by a light, cooling breeze wafting in from the bay, they could easily have been on their own tropical island, isolated from the rest of the world.

Kailin sighed with contentment and Brett stretched, then pulled off his shirt and unsnapped his jeans. He lay back with a sigh, arms crossed under his head, eyes closed.

Kailin tried very hard not to look at him, but found it impossible. He was deeply tanned, with the flat, hard muscle of someone used to physical labor. She looked at him for a long, admiring while, watching the regular rise and fall of his chest. It was only when she let her gaze meander up to his face that she realized he was watching her through half-closed eyes.

The lassitude flowed through her again, thick as melted butter, and she let her eyes slide closed. She didn't move when she heard Brett stir. Even though she'd expected it, Kailin started slightly at the first touch of his mouth. He ran his wine-cool lips across the back of her neck, just above the collar of her blouse, then brushed the side of her neck to the down-soft hollow under her ear with tiny, feathery kisses.

Kailin's toes curled as he pressed his lips into the curve under her lobe. It was more bite than kiss, his teeth grazing her as he sucked gently on her warm, damp skin. Kailin arched her neck slightly, and Brett nuzzled her shoulder and ran his hands down her arms to braid his fingers with hers. She leaned back against him, eyes still closed, feeling herself starting to slowly slip away from reality.

The tension that had started with that kiss over an hour ago had been between them ever since, and she had known it was only a matter of time before he came to her. There was no use fighting it. No use at all . . .

As though sensing the answer she'd given to a question he'd never asked, Brett started leisurely unbuttoning her blouse. As it fell open, he trailed his fingertips down her skin, then tugged the shirt out of her jeans and drew it off. He started kissing her shoulders, and brushed the straps of her bra down. The lacy fabric was delicately peeled back and tossed aside, then he touched her breasts lightly with his flattened palms.

Kailin sighed at the delicious friction and her nipples, already swelling, blossomed fully at his touch. He cupped her breasts, then ran his palms down across her stomach and drew the zipper of her jeans slowly down.

"Take them off," he murmured against her ear.

As though in a dream, Kailin eased her jeans over her hips, then kicked them off. A breeze licked around her legs, sensuously cool as she stretched out.

"Everything." Brett's voice was no more than a husky whisper. "Take everything off, Kailin. I want you naked for me."

Slowly Kailin slipped off her lacy panties. When she'd tossed them aside as well, she relaxed back against Brett. He ran his hands down her stomach slowly, then to her knees and back again, his thumbs trailing fire along her inner thighs. Gently he slid his hands between her legs. Kailin moaned sharply, and Brett whispered something, pausing to nuzzle and kiss the side of her throat.

"Brett . . ." Kailin arched her back slightly and let her head fall back onto his shoulder, moving restlessly, grasping his arms. "Please, Brett," she breathed, moving her hips toward his teasing hands.

"Not yet," he murmured. "We've got all afternoon."

"Brett!" It was no more than a murmur of regret as he eased himself away from her.

Kailin took a deep unsteady breath and opened her eyes as Brett helped himself to a pineapple spear. He held it up and caught the juice with his tongue, then nibbled from the end of it and held it up to her mouth. She took a bite, then let her head fall back with a smile as he used it like a paintbrush to draw a trail down her chin, then across the taut line of her throat slowly to one breast, where he paused to circle the nipple before continuing his journey. He brushed it lightly across her stomach, then up the inner flesh of one thigh to her knee, where he finally popped it into his own mouth.

Kailin closed her eyes, hardly daring to breathe as Brett started licking the juice, each slow swirl of his tongue like the touch of fire and ice. As he moved up her thigh, Kailin sank back onto the blanket and felt that delicious, aching tension within her pull so tight that she was sure it would break. He kissed her softly just at the juncture of her thighs, moved inward and paused. Then, as delicately as a butterfly, he dipped into the nectar of her.

Kailin felt herself melt and open to his caress. She heard a low groan that she only half realized was her own, and the sliding pressure of his tongue increased, perfectly attuned to the intricacies of her. She called to him as the hurricane he was conjuring up threatened to sweep her away, and he paused at that final, precise instant, letting her sense it, savor it, then gently carried her the final distance into heaven itself.

There was a moment of stopped time, a heartbeat during which everything ceased to exist for Kailin but a starburst of pleasure so intense it made her cry out. She opened her eyes and found him watching her, knew by the expression on his face that the pleasure he got from loving her was almost as great as hers.

She raised her arms above her head and stretched, arching her back lightly, luxuriating in the tingling little aftershocks of pleasure. Her body felt so sensitive that even the touch of the breeze sent little tremors through her.

"Witch," he breathed, easing himself down beside her. "I'm burning up...." His teeth grazed her swollen nipples and Kailin murmured in pleasure, her body catching fire again. She moved against him sensuously, his jeans an erotic barrier between her and the arousal she sought, and she sank her fingers into his hair and raised his mouth to hers. His lips parted greedily and then he was kissing her with a fierce, demanding hunger, easing himself over her and pressing her into the springy mattress of grass beneath the blanket.

"You're driving me crazy," she moaned against his mouth. "Take your jeans off!"

"Do you want me, Kailin?" he whispered coaxingly, sliding one denimed thigh between hers.

"Yes!" It was no more than a sob. "I need you, Brett. I need you now...."

"How much?" he growled. "Show me how much, Kailin."

Panting slightly, she gazed up at him through half-closed eyes and guided his hand until his fingers sank into the buttery heat of her.

He needed no further encouragement, and she had to bite her lip to keep from crying out as he moved slowly, drawing sensations from her she couldn't have believed were possible. "You're like honey," he groaned. "Melting and warm and soft as silk..." His fingers moved deeper, and Kailin moaned softly. "Open for me, Kailin," he whispered huskily. "Oh, baby, just relax and let me take you there again. Feel me, Kailin. Feel me there...."

His voice went on and on, coaxing her into responses beyond anything she'd felt before, and she heard herself crying out again and again in pleasure, lost to the wildfire he'd ignited. She didn't even realize that he'd slipped out of his jeans and briefs until he eased himself between her thighs, naked and so ready for her that she gave a tiny gasp of alarm that made him chuckle.

"We've never had a problem before," he murmured reassuringly, and with a thrust of his hips proved with heart-stopping satisfaction that they weren't going to have a problem this time, either.

Kailin clung to him in wonder, knowing with utter certainty that it couldn't get any better. Except that it did: so much better, in fact, that she was soon moving helplessly under him, crying his name over and over again as each long, strong thrust of his body brought her nearer the edge. He was there with her this time, his breath as hot as flame against her throat as he transported them both, and when Kailin finally arched against him with an indrawn sob, tasting the hot salt of her own tears in her throat, she felt her very soul touch his.

Shaken and crying for no earthly reason she could understand, she clung to him through the slow descent, her face bur-

ied against his shoulder. It was much later that she felt him stir
He kissed the top of her head and rolled onto his side, cradling
her intimately against him, rubbing her back in relaxing circles
until she stopped sobbing.

"You all right?" he finally whispered.

She nodded, sniffling, and managed a sob of laughter. "I'm
sorry. I—I don't know what happened. It's just that it—it's
never been like this before."

Brett slipped his fingers under her chin and tipped her face
up, his gaze searching hers. "Like what, Kailin?"

"Just for a moment it was as though I wasn't even me at all,
as though I'd become part of you, or you'd become part of me
or... or something." She swallowed tears.

"That's what love feels like, Kailin. It's what we talked about
all those years ago but never really had." He gazed down at her
his eyes filled with such tenderness that it made her heart do a
slow cartwheel. "It's what you've never let yourself feel before, Kailin. You've always been so cautious, always holding
that little bit of yourself in reserve." He smiled, kissing her
gently. "Now it's the real thing, baby."

"Oh, Brett," she gulped, "I *do* love you!"

"I know," he said simply, and the unconditional belief in
that simple statement brought tears to her eyes again. "But I
didn't mean to make you cry."

"Is there any of th-that wine left?"

Brett picked the bottle up and tipped it assessingly. "Enough
for a couple of glasses. Do you want to propose a toast?"

"N-no," Kailin said with a laugh, sitting up and dabbing at
her nose with a stray napkin. "I—I've got the hic-hiccups."

"I sunburned my nose," Kailin muttered, peering at herself
in the side mirror of Brett's pickup.

"That's not all you sunburned." Brett grinned, patting her
on the bottom as he urged her into the truck. "You're going to
have a fine pair of rosy cheeks back here, too, sweetheart. The
next time you go skinny-dipping, pick a cloudy day."

"It wasn't *my* idea to go skinny-dipping," she reminded him.
She scooted across to the passenger side, pausing to give a de-
spairing glance in the rearview mirror. Sun-bleached and wet,
her hair hung to her shoulders in a cloud of sticky tangles.

"What a mess! Charlie Bryant and two of his top people are flying in this afternoon to discuss progress. They're going to take one look and *know* I've been rolling around on a deserted beach with the chairman of the Land Use Committee!"

Brett's easy laughter filled the truck. He started the motor and, after checking that the canoe was secure behind, pulled out onto the dirt trail that led to the highway. "What are you going to tell him about this afternoon?" he asked idly. "Craig'll probably have you charged with trespassing if he finds out you've been to Paradise Point."

"He can try," Kailin said with defiance. "But when Charlie Bryant sees these pictures, Craig is not going to have a lot of credibility—especially when he sees the chainsaw marks on those trees barring the access road—the ones that supposedly blew down."

Kailin shook her head slowly, her expression troubled. "Charlie's going to have a fit, Brett. It isn't just his company that Craig's damaged, it's his reputation. He might have forgiven the first, but I doubt he'll ever forgive the second."

"Is he coming out of retirement permanently?"

"I doubt it. I'm hoping to convince him to come back long enough to see the Paradise Point project to completion, but he likes retirement. He says he wants to fish all day, not fight the Brett Douglasses of the world every time he wants to put up a tool shed." She glanced at Brett. "His words, not mine."

"Off the record, Ms. Mediator," Brett said quietly, watching the road, "if you can persuade Charlie Bryant to come out of retirement for this, I can almost guarantee I can convince the committee to okay Phase Three." He looked at her. "But we'll need guarantees, too."

"Such as?"

"Some sort of bond, for one thing. I don't want to approve Phase Three, then have the bank pull the plug on Gulf Coast halfway through. Either the investors stick with Gulf Coast right to the end or they get out right now."

Kailin nodded slowly, eyes narrowed on the road. "It'll take a lot of convincing—banks are pretty skittish when it comes to their own money these days. *They're* going to demand all sorts of guarantees, too."

"Can you do it?"

She turned to give him a challenging look. "Sure."

"Home, or my place first for a shower and . . . whatever?"

"Whatever?" Her mouth curved up in a mischievous smile. "I'd have thought we'd *whatevered* ourselves out by now."

"Not even close," Brett assured her with a reckless grin, mildly surprised to discover it was true.

By rights, it should take him a week to recuperate from this afternoon, yet just looking at her made his body stir. Without a speck of makeup, her nose sunburned, her hair damp and stringy, she was still so damned beautiful it made his breath catch. Her smile was small and self-satisfied, and he laughed quietly.

"I wish I could, but I have to get home," she said quietly, "I was gone this morning before Becky was even up. She had a pretty busy day lined up for herself, but she was expecting me an hour ago and she frets like a little old woman if I'm late." She smiled fondly. "She was barely three when Royce was killed, but it really shakes a child up to lose a parent suddenly. It was a long time before she could let me out of her sight comfortably. She's over it now—in fact, sometimes I feel she's a little too self-reliant—but underneath I think there's still the suspicion that I might go away one day and never come back, like her father did."

"You two seem to have quite an understanding." Brett looked at her.

"We try. I swore when she was born that I wasn't going to have the kind of relationship with her that I had with my mother, which was no relationship at all. My mother was someone who was either going to or coming from some function. At times it was as though she didn't live there at all but just passed through a lot." She smiled faintly. "You ought to see her with Becky. For that matter, you should see Dad with her—you'd think he'd invented grandparenting."

"Making up for lost time?"

Kailin's smile faded. "I guess so." Brett heard the tightness in her voice and looked at her, but she was staring out the truck window. "He's so sweet with Becky that sometimes I want to scream. I know it's childish, but I find myself wishing he'd treat me that way now and again. I'm his daughter, after all...." She let the words wander off into silence.

"Fathers always demand a lot of their own children," Brett reminded her quietly.

"Maybe. But it wouldn't kill him to say something nice once in a while, would it?" Then she laughed quietly and shook her head. "You'd think I'd be used to it by now, wouldn't you? And the truth is that I'm glad they all get along so well. Becky spends an equal amount of time between my parents and Royce's, and they all seem to benefit."

"You're quite a woman, Kailin McGuire," he said softly, reaching over to slip his hand around hers. "Royce was a lucky man to have had you for those five years."

Kailin's smile turned pensive, and she looked down at their braided hands. "He was a good husband to me, Brett. Better, in a lot of ways, than I deserved."

Brett knew he had to ask the next question, and he hated himself for it. "Did you love him?" His voice was tight, and he stared out at the road, not daring to look at her.

Eleven

Kailin was silent for so long that when he finally did glance at her, Brett found her staring out the side window as though fascinated by the vista of mangrove and palm. "Near the end, I think I did. Not the way I love you, but..." She turned her head to look at him.

He nodded, feeling curiously relieved. He'd wanted her to deny ever having loved Royce, but for some reason finding they'd respected and cared for each other didn't hurt as much as he'd expected. He gave her fingers a squeeze and Kailin curled up against him with a little sigh of happiness.

When they arrived at Kailin's rental complex Becky came racing into the kitchen, shirttails flying, calling out, "Hi, Mom! Boy, am I glad you're home!"

"Hi, honey. Sorry I'm late." Kailin gave her daughter a hug and kicked off her mud-caked shoes. "Am I beat!"

"Good! I mean...you probably won't feel like taking me to the movie tonight, right? Peggy and her mom asked me to go on a sundown beach walk with them, but I told them I'd sort of promised you that I'd go to a movie." She gazed hopefully at Kailin.

"A sundown beach walk?"

"Ken Ludowski from the parks department puts them on," Brett said. "He gives a talk on tidal ecology and shoreline wildlife, bird and shell conservation, that sort of thing."

"Yeah," Becky put in excitedly. "And afterward they light a bonfire and roast hot dogs and marshmallows and stuff, and—" She sobered. "That is, if you didn't want to go to the movie."

Kailin laughed and gave Becky a fierce hug. "If you want the truth, I'd really rather just stay home."

"Really?" Becky had a hard time containing her delight.

Brett sauntered toward the door. "If you need a ride I can drive you over while your mother has a shower." He grinned at Kailin over Becky's head. "Then I'll come back and keep her company until you get home."

"Great!" Becky's eyes sparkled with mischief as she looked around at Kailin. "There's a couple of real mushy love stories on TV tonight."

"Thank you, Rebecca," Kailin told her with a good-natured smile. "Have fun tonight. Call if you're going to be late."

"Or early," said a laughing voice from the doorway and Linda McAllister stepped in. "I had to dash out for milk, and when I saw the truck in the parking lot I thought I'd see if Becky's coming with us tonight."

"With bells on," Kailin assured her as Becky hurtled out the door. "Thanks, Linda. Do you know Brett Douglass, by the way?"

"Not officially," Linda said, taking Brett's proffered hand. "But Becky's filled me in on all the relevant details."

"Oh, Lord," Kailin groaned.

Linda's grin broadened. "When Becky's ready to come home, I'll give you a call first—just so we don't catch you at an inconvenient moment."

"Linda!" Kailin was astonished to feel herself blushing.

Linda started out, then paused in the doorway. "You know, I have a feeling that after all the fresh air and excitement, Becky will be pretty tired. I think she should stay over at my place. I'll bring her back in the morning."

"Linda!"

"You can thank me later," she said with a smile. She was back an instant later, grinning even more broadly. "And that's quite a sunburn you have there, Mrs. McGuire."

"Yeah," Brett added with a chuckle as the door closed. "When you blush like that, you sort of glow all the way down to your—"

"I'm going to take a quick shower," Kailin said swiftly.

Brett chuckled. "Want some help?"

"I said a *quick* shower," she reminded him. "Showering with you always takes at least an hour."

Kailin stepped out of the shower ten minutes later to find Brett stretched out on the bed in nothing but his unzipped jeans and a drowsy, enticing smile. He meshed his fingers behind his head and watched her with lazy enjoyment as she walked across to the closet and traded the big bath towel she'd wrapped around her for her robe.

She deliberately took her time, knowing he was watching her, knowing he was thinking the same things she was. Smiling to herself, Kailin belted the robe loosely and strolled across to the bed, her eyes holding Brett's. They were hooded and smoky, and when he held his hand out silently she let him draw her down beside him.

Tucking one foot under her, she started drying her hair with the towel. "What are you smiling about?"

"You." His voice was husky. "I was just thinking about how things have changed and yet how they haven't changed at all." He drew her hand to his mouth and started kissing her fingertips, one at a time, swirling his tongue around each as he might something sweet. "I remember lying on my bed in Greenlake, waiting for you to come out of the shower. The place was a dump, and yet when you were there with me it could have been the Taj Mahal. And today, lying here waiting for you, I felt the same kind of anticipation. You were every man's dream come true, Kailin. And you were with me. I used to lie awake nights trying to figure out why."

"I loved you."

"And now, Kailin?" He reached out with his other hand and touched her cheek with his fingers.

Kailin gazed down at him, realizing there was only one answer, had been only the one answer right from the start. "I don't think, down deep where it counted, that I ever stopped loving you, Brett," she whispered.

Brett's deep blue eyes were almost black in the dim light, and they burned into hers with a fierce intensity. "Kailin," he murmured, reaching for her. "Kailin, I—"

He was interrupted by the shrill ring of the telephone, and he dropped back against the pillow with a whispered oath. Laughing softly, Kailin tossed the towel aside and bent over him, kissing his chest. "My answering machine will pick it up," she murmured, swirling her tongue around one of his nipples.

As though obeying her, the machine cut in on the second ring. Only half hearing her standard message, Kailin started moving damp little kisses down across the flat, muscle-corded expanse of Brett's abdomen, then started moving even lower. She could hear his breathing change when she folded back the flap of his jeans.

"You said you'd call this afternoon, Kailin."

Her father's voice, raspy and querulous, was so clear that Kailin recoiled as though the old man himself had suddenly appeared in the room behind her. Brett jackknifed to a sitting position and then he, too, realized what had happened and dropped back onto the bed.

"You know I hate these damned machines," her father went on. "I know you're there listening to me. Pick up the phone!"

Kailin's hand was already reaching for the receiver when Brett caught it firmly. She felt his anger, knew it was less at the interruption of their lovemaking than at who had done the interrupting, felt her own anger—and her guilt. Guilt at just *being* here, she realized with irritation, as though her father had walked in on them and had caught her half-naked in Brett's arms.

"Damn it," she breathed, sitting up and pulling her robe tightly closed. She glowered at the answering machine.

There was an impatient silence as her father waited for her—no, she corrected, as he *willed* her—to answer the phone. Then he decided she either wasn't there or simply wasn't going to answer. "I want to know what's going on down there. Your reports are too sketchy—either those save-the-ecology lunatics are going to approve the continuation of Paradise Point or they aren't. Which is it?"

Kailin stiffened. She glanced at Brett, praying he wasn't really listening, and felt her heart sink when his eyes met hers, puzzled and alert. She started to lean forward to switch the machine off, but Brett caught her wrist firmly.

"Leave it."

"Brett—"

"Leave it," he bit out, his voice deceptively soft.

"But—" She sat back, knowing there was nothing she could say. The damage had already been done; anything else her father said now would just be the frosting on an already unpalatable cake. Why now? she asked her father in silent fury. For heaven's sake, why couldn't you just wait for my call, why do you always have to push and push and push?

"I called earlier and Rebecca said you were out canoeing with Douglass," he went on to say. "I sent you down there to pull Gulf Coast's irons out of the fire, not to lollygag around in the sun with that troublemaker. Take a vacation on *your* time, not mine!"

Kailin felt Brett stiffen. His fingers tightened around her wrist convulsively and he stared at her, the puzzled expression in his eyes vanishing under a growing awareness. She swallowed, knowing she'd just have to sit out the storm and hope that he loved her enough to listen, to understand. To forgive.

"And if he chains himself to the gates *this* time, Kailin, don't you stop the trucks, hear me? This is our last chance. Mess it up and the whole company's gone. If you don't think you can handle it on your own, swallow that damned pride of yours and admit it— I'll find someone to go down and give you a hand. And call me!"

The receiver on that distant phone went down with a bang, the sound hanging in the air like an exclamation mark. Kailin stared at a point on the bed midway between Brett's elbow and her knee, barely breathing, waiting for him to say something. It didn't take long.

"Just what the hell," he asked with deceptive ease, "is your old man up to now?"

"He's not up to anything," she replied with an equally deceptive ease.

"No?" Brett's stare was hard. "Out with it, Kailin."

"It...I...oh, hell!" She stopped and ran her fingers through her tangled hair to shove it off her face. "I should have told you this up front, but I—" She stopped again, realizing her reasons for not telling him didn't matter. "Dad's one of the investors behind Paradise Point. He has everything on the line—the business, the house. Everything."

The silence between them was so highly charged it nearly gave off sparks. Brett dropped her wrist and rolled off the bed in one lithe, easy movement, standing to stare down at her. "I should have guessed something like this was going on," he said in a soft, taut voice. "It was just too much of a coincidence, having you turn up out of the blue to work on this. Just too damned . . . easy."

"What do you mean, easy?" she whispered, daring to look up at him.

His eyes glowed like a cat's. "Easy. Gulf Coast is on the verge of going belly-up. The only hope to save it is if the Land Use Committee can be persuaded to approve Phase Three—in spite of obvious deficiencies in the project to date. Along comes Kailin McGuire, the woman out of the chairman's past. There's a little sparring, a little flirting—and Douglass falls for the bait and is firmly hooked. The chairman recommends the committee overlooks the problems with the project and approves Phase Three, the bank agrees not to call in its loans, Gulf Coast wins the day—and old man Quentin J. Yarbro comes out of it with his millions intact."

Kailin stared up at him. "You can't possibly believe any of that," she said in astonishment. "I'm recommending a full-scale investigation of the problems on Phase Two, not trying to cover them up. And—"

"Give a little, get a little," Brett said with a hard smile. "You wouldn't hesitate sacrificing Craig Bryant as a show of good faith and to convince the Land Use Committee you mean business."

"I *do* mean business," Kailin said with some annoyance.

Brett gave another harsh laugh, his eyes bitter. "And this afternoon? Was that business, too?"

Kailin sucked in her breath, staring at him in shock. "You can't believe that!"

"Kailin," he said wearily, "I don't know what the hell to believe where you're concerned. I can't read you at all. I get to the point where I think maybe I've seen the real Kailin, then you pull a number like this and I'm back to square one." He stared at her for a silent moment, his face angry and resigned. "I don't even know who you are."

"Brett, how can you say that after we—"

"Why didn't you tell me about your father's involvement earlier?"

"It's confidential, for one thing," Kailin said quietly. "He got suckered in by the promise of easy money. It happens all the time, Brett. Dad wants to retire, and he figured he could make a killing on the Paradise Point project."

"And you want to protect him."

"I want to protect all of them. He's not the only investor who'll lose his shirt if Gulf Coast goes under."

"But I'll bet he's the only investor who sent his daughter down here to save the day." He stared at her, his mouth a hard, angry line. "And he *did* send you down here, didn't he? He's behind it."

"He isn't behind anything," Kailin said wearily. "There is nothing underhanded or suspicious involved with any of this, Brett. When the bank contacted my father about the situation he suggested they use me to investigate. I wasn't interested *because* Dad was one of the investors, but I said I'd at least look into it. When I found out that you were involved, I turned the job down flat. Then...oh, I don't know." She threw her hands up in defeat and stood up wearily, wandering over to the windows and staring down at the beach. "This is what I do, and I'm good at it. Maybe it was vanity that finally got me. Maybe I just wanted to prove something to my father. Maybe..." She didn't bother finishing it, shaking her head. "Who knows?"

"And your father?" Brett asked silkily. "I don't suppose that crack about not stopping if I get in your way means what it sounds like?"

"Of course not!" Kailin looked around at him angrily. "He doesn't have anything to do with my company *or* how I do my job. That's just Dad, being his usual tactful, helpful self." She looked at him evenly. "He won't admit it, Brett, but he's terrified he's going to lose everything. He *is* the reason I'm down here—but not in the way you think. After I told the bank I wouldn't take the job if it came gold-plated, he called me. It nearly killed him, having to ask me for help. Even then there was no admission of fault, no please or thank you. I wanted to rub his nose in it, but for some reason I couldn't.'' She sighed, knowing he'd never understand. ''Underneath he was still my father. And he needed me.'' She smiled faintly.

''And I suppose that reminder that he sent you down here—that you're working on *his* time—doesn't mean anything, either.''

''No.'' Kailin felt very tired. ''Although, knowing Dad, he's probably convinced himself that that's the truth. It would be easier for him to accept my help if he's convinced himself that *he's* in charge. But it just isn't like that, Brett. You have to believe me.''

''Believe you, Kailin?'' He snatched up his shirt from a nearby chair, then rammed his arms into the sleeves. His eyes held hers, hot and angry. ''I'd have trouble believing you if you told me what day of the week it is.''

''Brett!''

''You're a damned fool if you think you're running the show, Kailin. And an even bigger one if you think you've convinced *me*. He's manipulating you now just like he always has.''

''Brett, that isn't true!''

''Then give it up.''

Kailin stared at him in confusion. ''Give . . . what up?''

''Gulf Coast. Paradise Point.'' His gaze narrowed. ''Drop the whole thing, Kailin. Just let it go.''

She blinked at him. ''Brett, this is my job.''

''To hell with your job,'' he growled. ''Turn it over to someone else—you're not the only person in the world who can sort this out.''

''But . . .'' Kailin simply stared at him. ''Do you mean that you're asking me to make a choice between my work . . . and you?''

''I'm asking you to choose between your father and me. As long as he—and this suspicion—is between us, Kailin, we can't have any kind of a relationship.''

"We don't *have* a relationship if you can demand that," she whispered. "Brett, do you have any idea of what you're asking?"

His mouth was hard and stubborn. "I just know that as long as you're being manipulated by your father, we have no future. I can't love a woman I can't trust, Kailin."

If he'd slapped her across the face, Kailin couldn't have been more stunned. "Damn you, Brett Douglass," she said in a furious whisper. "How *dare* you talk about love and trust when you've just tried to blackmail me into turning my back on a group of people I've given my professional word to help. You're right—you can't love someone you don't trust. But it goes deeper than that, Brett. If you love someone, you *do* trust them—it's that simple. You don't ask them for proof. You don't demand that they give up one thing for another."

Brett stared at her for a long, taut moment, then turned and strode toward the door. "I guess that answers my question, Kailin."

"What question? You haven't *asked* me anything, you've just stood there making accusations!"

Brett stopped dead and paused with his hand on the doorknob. Then he turned to look at her, his eyes shadowed and private. "So are you using me?" he demanded bluntly. "Did you come down here hoping to use our relationship to push approval for Phase Three through my committee?"

Kailin felt something twist inside her, twist and splinter and die. "If you don't think you know the answer to that, Brett," she said very softly, "then it doesn't really matter at all, does it?"

An eerie, breath-held silence slid through the room, thick as smoke. Kailin could feel Brett's hot, angry stare burning into her back, but she refused to turn around, refused to allow him the small victory of seeing her cry. Don't go, she urged him silently. Say you love me, say you trust me....

The door closed quietly behind him. A moment later the outer door to the apartment also closed. The bang reverberated through the room like a clap of thunder. Kailin swallowed very carefully, tasting a hot, salty bitterness in her throat. She shut her eyes and clung to the edge of the dressing table until her fingers ached, knowing that if she let go of it she'd also let go of the paper-thin edge of control she was clinging to.

And her father? She forced herself to face Brett's furious accusation: *was* she simply a pawn? It wasn't inconceivable. He'd known about Brett's involvement in Paradise Point, but he hadn't told her, knowing how she would react. Had he also anticipated what would happen if she and Brett were thrown together?

She felt caught in the crossfire between past and present, between the woman she was and the child she'd been. Between Brett and her father. Always between the two men most important in her life.

Damn it! She picked up the small table lamp and flung it against the far wall. Glass exploded like shrapnel and Kailin stared at it, using every ounce of willpower she possessed to keep from bursting into tears. She'd cried enough tears over the past eleven years to last a lifetime, and she would *not* cry now.

Life hurts. The trick is, don't let it show.

But nothing—*nothing*—was supposed to hurt this badly!

"You're wrong, Daddy," she whispered, her voice catching on the tears she no longer tried to stop. "You're wrong! Because if you really care, you can't help but let it show."

Brett stared out across the whitecaps of the Gulf of Mexico, thinking that those troubled, gray waters exactly matched his mood.

There was a storm brewing out there, out beyond the crescent-moon curve of the Keys where the sea ran deep. The air was hot and tense with it, and the sky along the horizon was clotted with clouds the color of an old bruise. Long, low waves pushed toward the shore, dark as lead and curiously heavy. Even the birds seemed affected. A fleet of pelicans bobbed just offshore, rising and falling with the motion of the waves, and the gulls walking the beach seemed stiff and sullen.

He shoved his hands into the pockets of his jeans, then turned and started trudging up the beach again, kicking at a twisted skein of seaweed. As always, Kailin slipped into his mind. Kailin laughing, her head thrown back, her silver-gold hair blowing in the wind, green eyes alight with mischief....

Damn you, Kailin, why are you torturing me like this? What do you want from me?

He rubbed his temples and swore under his breath, no nearer an answer than he'd been when he'd walked out of her apartment two days ago. She was like the mist, there one moment and gone the next, slipping through his fingers just when he thought he had her pinned down.

She'd been like that eleven years ago. Not a day had passed that long, hot summer when he hadn't wondered, at least fleetingly, why she stayed. She had everything—the rich, beautiful girl from the right side of town. And he'd had nothing. Nothing a woman who had everything could possibly want, anyway.

Was that why he'd let her go? he found himself suddenly wondering. Because he'd never really believed she would stay? Had he thought to lessen the pain of losing her by cutting her out of his life first?

And this time?

I loved you, she'd said the other night. *I stayed because I loved you.*

He closed his eyes, swearing softly.

The storm broke later that night, screaming out of the southeast like a banshee. Brett checked the storm shutters and doors, then poured himself a generous glass of brandy and lit a crackling fire in his little-used fireplace. Smiling at his own self-indulgence, he sank into his favorite chair with a mystery. But he found himself staring unseeingly at the pages, listening to every creak and groan of the house. The wind picked at the shutters like something wanting in, and he finally got to his feet, pacing restlessly.

He stood peering through the storm shutters at the spume flying on the Gulf. The palms along the bottom of his lawn were whipping around like bamboo stalks, fronds shredded, and he watched them with an inner sympathy, knowing exactly how they felt.

How he heard the knock over the noise of the storm, he didn't know. Only half believing anyone would be out in this tumult, he inched the door open. There was something standing out there that looked like a small yellow tent. A wet hand inched out of an oversize sleeve and shoved back the hood of the rain slicker.

Brett stared down at Becky in astonishment. She gazed back miserably, teeth chattering, hair plastered to her head. Saying nothing, he held the door open and she stumbled in, shivering so badly she could hardly walk. She stood unprotesting as Brett pulled the slicker over her head, then ushered her into the living room, pausing on the way to grab a bath towel.

He moved the big square hassock in front of the crackling fire with his foot and pointed to it. Becky sat down, not meeting his eyes, her shoulders hunched, then loosened the drawstring on her sweatshirt and pulled Maverick out. The kitten, rumpled and slightly damp, sneezed, obviously unamused by whatever was going on.

Brett handed Becky the towel, then sat on the hearth and picked the kitten up, stroking it. "Where's your mother?"

"Home." The voice was muffled as Becky scrubbed her hair with the towel. "I ran away."

He should have been surprised, but he wasn't. Somehow he'd known exactly what had happened from the instant he'd seen her standing out there tonight. "Terrific," he breathed, rubbing the tightness between his eyes. Then he took a deep breath and looked at her. "How did you get up here?"

"I caught a ride with Mrs. Peabody, the librarian."

Now what? he asked himself wearily. Runaway nine-year-olds weren't exactly his area of expertise. He set Maverick in Becky's lap, then got to his feet. "I'll have to call your mother."

"I'm not going back." She looked up at him with the same stubborn set to her mouth, the same glint of steely determination in her eyes, that he'd seen on Kailin's face more times than he cared to remember. "I *won't* go back."

"Becky—"

"I mean it!" She tossed her head indignantly. "I'm going to stay down here with you. You . . . you can adopt me or something!"

He opened his mouth to argue with her, then realized he'd have no more luck arguing with her than he'd ever had arguing with Kailin. She'd obviously inherited more than just blond hair and green eyes from her mother. "You two hungry?"

Becky glanced up at him suspiciously, then nodded. Brett sighed and made his way to the kitchen.

He'd started dialing Kailin's number before he realized that the line was dead, and he muttered something impolite under his breath and slammed the receiver down. The electricity was the next to go. It plunged him into darkness at the precise instant he was pouring cocoa into a mug, and he said something even more impolite as he slopped the scalding-hot liquid over his hands. The generator kicked in a moment or two later, and the low-voltage lights he'd installed at strategic corners flickered on, banishing the sudden, utter darkness.

Sucking the back of his hand, he carried the mug of cocoa and a dish of warm milk into the living room. Becky smiled a tentative thank-you and placed the dish in front of Maverick, who promptly curled his tail around his feet and shoved his face into the milk, lapping greedily. Becky cradled the mug in her hands and sipped the cocoa, and Brett dug out the candles and lighted them.

He picked up his glass of brandy and sat on the hearth again, watching the kitten eat. "I tried calling your mother, but the lines are down."

"That's okay," Becky muttered.

"Interested in talking about it?"

Becky ran her finger along the rim of the mug, then sighed deeply. "We had a fight. She wants to go back to Indiana tomorrow, but I don't want to go." She glanced at Brett. "I want to stay down here with you."

"She's leaving tomorrow?" It was out before he could stop himself, an arrowlike shaft of pain.

"She said you guys had a . . . disagreement." Becky glanced at him again. "But it was worse than a disagreement, wasn't it?"

"Yeah," he breathed, staring into the brandy. "It was worse."

"Do you love her?"

It was like being hit by a truck. Brett lifted his head to stare at her, fighting to catch his breath. Becky gazed back at him through her mother's clear green eyes, free of guile or trickery, and Brett heard himself whisper *yes* before he'd even realized what had happened.

Becky frowned. "Then I don't understand why she wants to leave."

"It's not that simple, Becky," he said with quiet desolation. "Sometimes loving someone just isn't enough."

"That doesn't make any sense," she said flatly.

Brett smiled humorlessly. "No one's ever been able to make sense out of love, Becky. Love just . . . is."

She was silent as she thought it over. "Can I stay here for good?"

"Becky—" He stopped, temporarily defeated. Now what? He had a sudden vivid image of Kailin having him arrested for kidnapping.

"You can probably adopt me," Becky said calmly. "After all, I was supposed to be your daughter." Brett lifted his head to stare at her uncomprehendingly, and she shrugged. "She told me that she was expecting your baby before she got married to my father. But then she lost that one and had me instead." She smiled a glowing smile that seemed to light up the room. "So you see, I was supposed to have been yours. I *feel* like your daughter, if that means anything."

"Oh, Becky," he breathed, aching with a deep, indefinable sadness. How in God's name had he and Kailin become so inextricably entangled that even this child, born more than a year after he'd left Greenlake, was herself caught? It was as though those intervening years had been no more than a heartbeat. How long, he wondered, would it take for them to finally be free of each other?

And suddenly he knew, with a certainty so deep it chilled him, that eleven or even eleven hundred years would never be long enough. They were parts of a whole, linked in some way they would never be able to understand—or ever be able to break.

Becky yawned, and Brett realized with a shock that it was well past midnight. Maverick had fallen asleep with his nose on the edge of the milk dish, and Brett picked him up and tucked him into Becky's sweatshirt. "Come on, you two. Maybe things will make some sense in the morning."

But after he'd gotten child and kitten tucked into the bed in the spare room, Brett found himself too restless to sleep. He prowled the darkened house, checking windows he'd checked twice before, peering out into the storm-lashed night as though something might have changed in the past two minutes. Lightning flickered incessantly, and the thunder mumbled and roared over the distant boom of breakers.

When the car lights flickered through the shutters on the side window, he thought at first it was just lightning. But then he heard the sound of an engine and eased himself to his feet, smiling grimly as he took a bracing swallow of brandy.

Twelve

Kailin tried to keep the hood of her slicker up as she ran to the house, but the wind tore it out of her hands. It didn't matter anyway, she realized numbly as she fought her way through the stinging wind: she was already soaking wet and chilled to the bone. Brett was waiting for her, standing in the open door. He was silhouetted against the soft light, and he looked very large and solid and calm. And in that instant she knew everything was all right.

"She's here," he said without preamble, pulling the slicker over her head and tossing it on a nearby deck chair.

Kailin nodded and walked in, shivering so badly she had to clench her teeth to keep them from rattling. Rainwater ran into her eyes and she smoothed her soaking hair back, staring around the comfortable living room in wonder. A fire crackled in the hearth, and the room was filled with dozens of candles of all colors and shapes, bathing everything with a soft golden glow that seemed to reach out and gather her into its warmth.

"I knew she'd come here," she whispered. "We had a horrendous fight and she grabbed Maverick and stormed out before I could stop her." A shiver made her teeth rattle, and Brett took her by the arm and led her across to the fireplace. He sat her firmly on the hearth and draped a bath towel around her shoulders, then walked away.

Slowly she started rubbing her hair dry, feeling the heat from the fire start to seep through her. "I tried to call you, but the phones are dead. So I decided to drive up. But the road's underwater in places and it took forever just to get to Blind Pass and the waves were breaking right across the highway on the Captiva side. Then I got lost and—" She had to stop, an unexpected sob threatening to escape.

"She's fine, except for being wet and cold and mad as hell. She's asleep in the spare room."

Kailin nodded. There was an empty mug that looked as though it had once held hot chocolate sitting on the hearth beside her, and a small dish half filled with milk. She had to laugh. "I see you were dispensing sympathy and first aid."

"It seems to be my night for it." He handed her a glass. "You look like you could use some yourself. Drink that."

Kailin cupped the glass between both palms to keep from spilling it and took a swallow. The brandy made her eyes water, but its glowing warmth started to spread through her almost instantly. "I'm sorry about all of this. She's too much like her mother at times—acts first and worries about the consequences later." She paused. "And I suppose she thinks she can bring us together. She wants to see me happy, and she thinks you're part of that." Kailin stared at the glass. "Maybe I thought so, too."

"She says you're leaving." He spoke without inflection, sitting in the big armchair across from her, one foot braced on the edge of the hassock, the glass of brandy balanced on his upraised knee. The firelight played across the strong planes of his face, giving it a hardness that she'd never seen before.

Kailin nodded, turning the glass in her hands. "It was a mistake, coming here," she said after a long while. "I kept telling myself that I was down here because I'd committed myself to this job, but of course that was just an excuse. I was down here because of you." She didn't look at him, terrified of what she might see on his face. "I realize now I'd hoped that we'd just pick up where we'd left off. Somehow I thought it would be that easy...."

She let the sentence trail off, not certain of what she was trying to say. "I thought that loving you was enough. I thought that if I had the chance to tell you, everything would be all right." She took a deep breath, wishing the brandy and fire would warm that icy, empty little spot where her heart had been. "But I was wrong. It takes more than just words. It takes trust. And we just don't... seem to have that."

She did look up at him then, a quick glance that told her nothing. He was simply watching her. The silence between them lengthened, broken only by the soft mutter of the flames. Even the storm seemed to have receded, and Kailin listened absently to the distant moan of the wind. She turned the glass in her hands, waiting, waiting....

"And Paradise Point?" he finally said, his voice rough, as though he hadn't used it in a week. "Are you leaving it, too?"

For some reason, that nearly made Kailin smile. She realized in that instant that she'd been waiting for him to tell her he loved her, that he *did* trust her, that he couldn't live without her. All the things that he was supposed to say to make it better. But in the end it came back down to one thing: Paradise Point.

"Yes." She was surprised to hear her voice so calm. Surprised, too, that she felt so little pain. Maybe letting go was the answer, she thought curiously. Maybe that was all it took. She looked at the glass for a moment, then set it aside and stood up, looking at Brett calmly. "But not because you asked me to. I'm leaving because my involvement with the project is jeopardizing the entire thing.

"It isn't fair to everyone concerned for us to use Paradise Point as ammunition against each other in our private little war, and since you can't seem to separate the two, I'll do it myself. I've worked up an interim report and proposal with the approval of both the bank and Charlie Bryant. It'll be delivered to you tomorrow, and you can present it to the committee. If it doesn't fit your requirements, make a counterproposal and send it to the bank in Miami. They'll assign another mediator to work with you."

It seemed to take him by surprise. He looked at her, then frowned and nodded, staring thoughtfully at the glass in his hand. He drew circles with it on his knee, tipping the brandy this way and that.

Say something, damn it, she nearly screamed at him. Then, as quickly as it had erupted through her, the anger and impatience were gone. In their place was nothing but a bone-deep weariness, and she got to her feet slowly, nearly staggering with exhaustion. She'd worked for two straight days getting that report finished, phone in one hand and a pen in the other, surrounded by cups of cold coffee and a daughter whose patience had finally given out tonight. Whether it had been worth it, time would tell. Right at the moment, all she wanted was a hot bath and about twelve hours of sleep.

Brett looked up at her. She thought for a moment that he was going to say something, then realized it had just been her own wishful thinking. She smiled wryly. "I'd better collect my daughter and leave before the storm gets worse."

"Where the hell have you been, boy?" Zac Cheevers strode into Brett's office with the subtlety of a freight train, the ever-present dead cigar sticking pugnaciously from one corner of his mouth.

It was odd, Brett found himself thinking, but he'd never seen Cheevers actually *smoking* one of the damned things. "What can I do for you, Zac?"

Zac blinked at him, then hooked a chair nearer with his foot and settled his bulk into it. "I'd say you've already done it." He tossed a thick wad of papers onto the desk.

"What is it?" Brett stared at the thing without interest.

Zac gazed contemplatively at Brett, chewing on the cigar. "You all right, boy? You look paler than a frog's belly, and about as low. Should give yourself a dose of tonic, get some color back in you."

Brett smiled faintly. "Start practicing medicine Zac, and I'll start handing out free legal advice."

Zac grunted. "After seeing the fancy footwork you pulled on that proposal, I'd say you could do better 'n' some I know."

Brett looked up blankly. "What proposal?"

Zac looked at Brett in exasperation, pointing to the papers he'd thrown on the desk. "What the hell's wrong with you, Douglass? Old Charlie Bryant's been wanting to meet with us since Tuesday, and I've been putting him off until I could find you."

"Sailing," Brett said tiredly, combing his hair back with his fingers. "I went . . . sailing." Thinking, was what he meant.

"You've just pulled off the coup of the century and you're off sailing." Zac gave an elephantine snort.

It was starting to irritate Brett now, and he almost relished the bite of anger. Any feeling was better than the numbed emptiness he'd been living with. "Zac, I've been out in the middle of nowhere for four days. I have no idea what you're talking about."

Zac glowered at Brett from under beetling, shaggy brows. "I am talking about a proposal put together by your lady friend, *Ms.* McGuire. I don't know how she swung it—I don't know how *you* swung it—but Gulf Coast's fixin' to give you everything you asked for, with a bit besides—starting with that wildlife sanctuary."

He leaned forward and set the proposal on the edge of Brett's desk, his voice holding none of its usual easy drawl. It was the voice of the shrewd courtroom lawyer he was, and Brett settled down to listen. "Leaving out all the double-talk and legalese, it boils down to one thing—if we approve a revised plan for Phase Three, the bank will agree to float Gulf Coast's loans for two years, interest suspended for one of those two, to free up operating capital.

"I'll tell you, Douglass, that little lady of yours knows how to play the game. Give a little, take a little." He shook his head in amused admiration.

"Yeah," Brett said quietly. "She does that." Then he shook off the sudden pensiveness and looked at Zac. "And Phase Three?"

"Well, they scrapped the golf course and helipad for a start." Zac ignored Brett's startled look. "They're going to negotiate a deal with the neighboring resorts for use of their golf courses and use the island pad and chauffeur the guests back and forth with limos. Save a fortune."

And the nesting herons, Brett thought to himself, remembering the expression of delight on Kailin's face as she'd watched the big birds.

"They've cut the total number of units, but the remaining ones will be top-of-the-line luxury. But the best part is that they're going to turn over that whole back wetlands as a wildlife conservation area on the provision that they can offer limited, controlled access for guided nature walks, canoe trips, birding trips and so on."

Brett stared at the proposal in Zac's hands, a feeling of unreality stealing over him. "What about Craig Bryant and the construction problems they're having?" he asked in a tight voice. There had to be a catch. Damn it, there had to be!

"The whole thing is contingent on dumping the existing people and using Charlie's people. And last I heard, Craig was headed west. His daddy kicked him out." Brett gave a low whistle, and Zac chuckled. "Next time you see that lady of yours, you tell her she done real good."

"I will," Brett breathed. He was just starting to comprehend the enormity of what Kailin had done.

Zac raised an eyebrow and got to his feet, shoving the cigar to the other side of his mouth. "Hell, boy, if you don't marry that gal, you're a damned fool. And if you do, bring her back and give her a job. I like her style."

Deep in thought, Brett didn't notice Zac's departure. What had Kailin said that last night? *It takes more than just words. It takes trust. . . .* She must have been working day and night to pull this off. She'd known exactly what it would take to make the Paradise Point project possible, and she'd gone out and put it together. A parting gift, perhaps. Her way of saying goodbye.

God, he loved her!

He closed his eyes, a sudden wave of emptiness and utter loss engulfing him. He felt hollow and sick and so filled with bleak despair it was like a tangible ache.

Guilt. He stared at the proposal lying on his desk. *You're coming down with a bad case of guilt, my friend.* He must have gone a little crazy to think it was a matter of Kailin choosing one thing or another. It didn't have anything to do with Paradise Point or even with her father. It had to do with eleven years of guilt and the knowledge that he'd deserted her when she'd needed him the most. How could he forgive her when he hadn't learned to forgive himself?

He didn't know if he'd said the words aloud or not, but they rang through the silences of his mind like a cry from the heart—"Oh, God, Kailin . . . what have I done?"

It took him nearly three hours. It would have taken a fraction of that had he used some common sense, but it was only after he'd been trying her Indianapolis phone number for two hours and fifty-five minutes that he remembered it was Thanksgiving weekend.

He didn't have to even look the number up, it was still fresh in his mind. It gave him a strange feeling, dialing those numbers after all this time, and he found himself holding his breath as the phone on the other end rang. A woman with a French accent said Kailin was there and went to find her, leaving Brett to listen to the hum of the open line with growing impatience. Then someone picked up that distant receiver, and he smiled in anticipation.

"That you, Douglass?"

The voice was slurred slightly, but Brett had no difficulty recognizing it. The sound slammed him into the past so painfully that it all but knocked the breath out of him. He closed his eyes, his hand aching where he was clutching the receiver.

"I said, is that you, Douglass?"

It was an imperious voice, used to giving orders, used to being obeyed. Brett felt the slow, sour rise of anger, and had to fight the urge to slam the receiver down. "Yes," he said after a moment. "It's me."

There was silence, crackling with distance. "My daughter doesn't want to speak with you, Douglass. And I don't want you talking to her. Don't call here again."

The receiver went down, hard. Again there was a shifting of time as past and present merged like two out-of-focus pictures. He was twenty-six again and full of fire, battling dragons and in love with the most beautiful princess of all.

He wasn't going to let her go.

"Not this time," Brett vowed through gritted teeth as he strode to the door. "You may have run me off once, old man, but this time I'm fighting for her with everything I've got!"

The mansion on River Road was unchanged. Set back in the trees on its three acres of lawns and gardens, it looked out over river and town like a feudal castle, radiating wealth and power. As he drove through the estate gates and up the long, winding drive, Brett felt as though he were traveling back through time.

To his surprise, they let him in.

He'd half expected Yarbro himself to come to the door, had anticipated a showdown and was almost disappointed. He followed the French maid down the corridor, through a tall carved door. She said something in French to a uniformed nurse, whose eyes settled momentarily on Brett, as though sizing him up for possible emergency treatment. Then she and the maid left without a word.

The room was overly warm. A fire sputtered on the hearth, adding what Brett figured was unnecessary heat to the stuffiness. Tall windows looked out over the gardens, and in the distance Brett could see the stables, the tennis courts.

"Well, come over here, damn it. Where I can see you. Quit skulking around in the shadows."

It was only then that Brett realized he wasn't alone. He hadn't seen the old man sitting in the shadows by the hearth, and as he stared across the room at Quentin J. Yarbro, Brett realized that at least here, time hadn't stood still.

He was an old man now. Not frail—Brett couldn't imagine Yarbro ever being frail—but the signs of advancing years and illness were there. He looked smaller than Brett remembered, but perhaps it was just the big chair or the soft lap robe tucked carefully around his legs. He didn't get to his feet as Brett approached, and Brett noticed with a slight shock that there were two walking sticks tucked unobtrusively beside him.

Only the eyes hadn't changed. They were still as hard as agate, and they homed in on Brett's like twin spotlights. "I was wondering if you'd have the guts to come after her this time."

Brett blinked. It was not by any stretch of imagination the greeting he was expecting.

While he was considering his options, the gray head turned toward a nearby doorway. "Roberts!" A tiny white-haired man appeared almost instantly. He carried a tray across to the desk and set it down. Yarbro peered suspiciously at the silver tea pot. "What the hell's that?"

"Herbal tea, sir."

"Tea?" The bellow rattled the china cups. "Bring me some coffee. *Real* coffee, not that decaffeinated garbage they've been trying to get me to drink."

"Sir," Robert said with a weary resignation, as though he'd fought this battle many times before, "you know the doctor—"

"Roberts, do you enjoy working here?"

"Yes, sir."

"Then get me some coffee!" Yarbro waited until Roberts had collected the tray and retreated with it before breaking into a sly chuckle. "Good man, Roberts. You just have to shout at him now and again to keep him in line." He eyed Brett assessingly. "Want a drink?"

"Not particularly."

"Well, I do. Get me one—bottom drawer of that cabinet over there. Have to hide the damned stuff or they throw it out." Brett hesitated, torn between sympathy for the man's doctor and a sudden, unexpected sympathy for Yarbro himself. Yarbro glared at him. "Now don't you start! My family's treating me like a damned invalid. A man has a heart attack and you'd think he was incapacitated, for God's sake. One drink isn't going to kill me, Douglass!"

"If I thought there was a possibility," Brett said dryly as he walked across to the cabinet, "I'd have brought you a bottle."

Yarbro gave a snort of laughter. "Well, well, well. Grown up a bit, have we? You'd have told me to go to hell eleven years ago, Douglass." He took the glass of liquor that Brett held out. Something moved in his lap, and Brett was astonished to see Maverick curled up in a fold of the robe. Yarbro started stroking the kitten absently. "So you think you're going to get my daughter this time, do you?"

Brett didn't say anything. He strolled across to the windows and stared out at the winter-brown gardens, wondering where this was leading.

"The only things in this life worth having are the things worth fighting for, Douglass." He took a swallow of the whiskey, smacking his lips with satisfaction.

"I didn't come here to fight with you. Or to rehash the past." Brett turned and looked at the old man steadily. "I'm going to marry your daughter, Yarbro, like it or not."

Expecting an explosion, Brett was surprised when Yarbro simply nodded, staring speculatively at him. "Are you approving Phase Three of the Paradise Point project?"

To his surprise, Brett discovered he could still laugh. "You never give up, do you?" he asked with a shake of his head. "I won't negotiate a bride price with you, Yarbro. You can't barter human lives, trading a bit of this for a bit of that. Paradise Point—and your investment—has got nothing to do with Kailin and me."

Yarbro's sharp, bright eyes narrowed very slightly. "You never did scare easily, Douglass. That was one thing I always admired about you."

"Oh, you got to me, all right," Brett assured him. "It was because of you that I turned my back on the only woman I've ever loved and I've had to live with that guilt for eleven years."

"It takes a lot of courage to admit when you're wrong." Yarbro stared into the glass in his hand, his expression pensive. "There haven't been many men in my life who've stood up to me, Douglass. Maybe that's why I admire your courage so much. And I'm not talking about physical courage, I'm talking the inside kind—the moral kind."

"Have you ever taken a good look at your own daughter?"

A tiny smile lifted one corner of Yarbro's mouth. "I have."

Brett nodded, looking at the drink he'd poured for himself and hadn't even tasted yet. "I love her," he said quietly.

"So do I."

The admission was spoken so softly that Brett looked up in surprise, scarcely believing he'd even heard it. His eyes met Yarbro's, and in that instant he felt something shift in the room, and the tension was gone. Suddenly they were no longer opponents but simply two men sharing insights and good whiskey on a blustery November afternoon. He smiled and took a sip, feeling the rich, smoky heat curl around his tongue like satin.

Yarbro lifted his glass in what might have been a salute. Then he swallowed the contents and set it aside, that fleeting glimpse of gentleness gone. "Think you're man enough to handle her? She's grown up into one hell of a fine woman, Douglass. Only thing in my life I can honestly say I'm proud of."

There was a movement in the doorway and Brett glanced up, his heart turning over when his eyes met Kailin's. How long had she been standing there, he wondered? Had she heard that quiet admission of love from the old man she'd been battling for so long? Would she believe it if she had? "Have you told *her* that?"

"Hell, no. You can tell a woman she's beautiful, Douglass, because they expect that sort of thing. But never tell a woman she's smart—ruins 'em. You'll never get a word in edgeways from that day on."

Annoyance flitted through Kailin. Then she remembered the gentleness in her father's voice a few moments ago, the love in it, and had to laugh quietly. They were both like actors in some long-running play, mouthing the lines without even thinking about what they meant.

She shoved her hands into the pockets of her gray wool slacks and strolled into the firelight, oddly unsurprised at finding the two men she loved here, face-to-face. "You're a fraud, Daddy," she said with a hint of laughter in her voice. She put her hands on her father's shoulders and planted a kiss on his cheek. "And a disgusting chauvinist. You'd still have women's feet bound if you thought it would work."

"Biggest mistake we men ever made was giving women the vote," Yarbro growled. "How long have you been standing back there spying on me?"

"Long enough." She looked at Brett, smiling. "What brought you all the way up from Florida?"

"You know what brought me up here," he said softly.

Kailin's heart gave a slow somersault.

"He wants to marry you, Kailin," her father said.

"Do I have any choice in the matter, or have the two of you settled it between you over whiskey and a good cigar?"

"Your mother found my cigars and threw them out," Yarbro growled. He got to his feet, putting the robe and Maverick gently in the chair, and reached for the walking sticks. Kailin stepped toward him, but he gave her a ferocious glare and she subsided as he walked toward the door, slowly and with great determination. "For what it's worth, I think you should take him up on the offer," he said gruffly.

"I think I will," Kailin replied with a quiet laugh. "Thank you, Dad."

He looked at her for a long moment, the faintest hint of a smile playing around his mouth. The first breach in the barriers between them had been made; now it would simply be a matter of time.

His sharp gaze flicked away from hers to look at Brett. "I'll have a spare bed made up for you, Douglass. You may as well spend Thanksgiving with us, seeing as you're going to be marrying my daughter. A man should have his family around him on Thanksgiving."

Kailin watched her father leave. When the door had closed, she sank into the chair and cradled Maverick in her lap, looking up at Brett. "I think he's mellowing."

"Like cider vinegar," Brett muttered, walking around the desk. He perched on one corner of it and looked down at her. "Were you serious about marrying me?"

"Were you serious about asking me?"

"I've never been more serious about anything in my life. I let you get away from me eleven years ago, but I'm damned if it's going to happen again." He leaned over and cupped her chin in his hand, lifting her face so he could look into her eyes. "I love you, Kailin McGuire."

"I know," Kailin whispered. "I've known for eleven years. But we just never seemed to be able to tell each other."

"Well, I'm telling you now. I love you. I'll even put it in writing." He slipped a piece of elegant notepaper out of a holder on Yarbro's desk, then in a large but legible scrawl wrote, *I love you, Kailin McGuire*. He signed it with a flourish and handed it to her.

"I love you." She laughed, reaching up to pull him nearer. His mouth was honey-sweet and infinitely inviting, and she kissed him slowly and well.

"Here." He slipped a sheaf of papers out of his shirt pocket and put them in her hand.

Kailin looked at them curiously. "What's this?"

"Paradise Point. The Land Use Committee approved Phase Three last night." He smiled. "Thank you."

"Why are you thanking me? Charlie Bryant was the one who bullied his board members into making all those concessions.

It nearly killed them, but in the end they agreed it was better to go with smaller than not go at all. He was brilliant."

"You were brilliant." He slipped off the desk and lifted her out of the chair before she could protest, then sat down and settled her comfortably in his lap.

Kailin ran her finger along his jawline, staring at him pensively. "I thought I'd lost you for good, Brett. It was almost as though you were fighting me, not letting me get close."

"I was." He smiled down at her. "Admitting I still loved you meant admitting that I'd made a terrible mistake eleven years ago. It was easier to think I'd been victimized, but the truth was that I was too scared to take a risk at loving you."

"Scared?" Kailin asked with a laugh. "You?"

"I was sure about everything in my life, Kailin—everything but you. That's why I believed what your father told me. I was so damned insecure—"

"Insecure?" Kailin looked at him in disbelief. "You were the most secure person I'd ever known!"

"About most things, maybe. But you intimidated the hell out of me. You were so beautiful and rich and...I don't know. Special, I guess. Unattainable. I couldn't figure out why you hung around with me. I didn't have a nice car, I couldn't take you to parties or fancy restaurants—hell, half the time I didn't have two cents to rub together. I kept telling myself that guys like me don't wind up with the fairy princess. Not in real life. I kept waiting for the clock to strike midnight, knowing I was crazy to fall in love with you. That sooner or later the fantasy would end."

"And then when it did..." Kailin touched his cheek.

"Marry me?" Brett whispered.

"With pleasure," Kailin whispered back.

"Good!" snapped a voice behind them. "Now that's settled, go start building me a dynasty. I'm not going to live forever, you know." Yarbro moved into view, eyes glinting. "And get out of my chair. Can't you see I'm crippled?"

Laughing, Brett got to his feet, Kailin still tight in his arms. "You heard the man," he murmured. "Would you like to build a dynasty with me?"

"I'd like nothing more." Kailin slipped her arms around his neck and nestled against him. "In fact," she murmured against his ear, "we could start right now if you've nothing more pressing to do. Mother's out for a while, and it's time for Daddy's medication and nap. No one will bother us for hours and hours."

"I love you."

"I know." She kissed his ear. "I have it in writing, remember?"

* * * * *

A Note from Mary Lynn Baxter

Dear Reader,

Wish Giver is a book that will always be close to my heart. A dear friend and fan lost her son to leukemia. I so admired her faith and attitude in the face of heartbreak that I was inspired to write this book.

Another reason *Wish Giver* is special to me is that it has been in space. Yes, space! An astronaut friend asked if I'd like him to take something I valued on his next mission into space. *Wish Giver* returned to earth autographed with these words: *Flown Aboard Space Shuttle Atlantis, STS-36, February 28th–March 4th, 1990. Mike Mullane, Astronaut.*

Since *Wish Giver,* I have written other books for Silhouette's various lines. My latest ones are a Silhouette novel, *A Day in April; And Baby Makes Perfect* and *Mike's Baby,* both Desire titles; and a Christmas story, ''Joni's Magic.''

This fall, look for *Dancler's Woman,* coming from Silhouette Desire.

Happy reading to you all,

Mary Lynn Baxter

WISH GIVER

Mary Lynn Baxter

To Freddie Ingersoll—
what can I say, dear friend,
except thanks for everything

Chapter 1

She would rather be anywhere other than where she was, but then Glynis Hamilton had learned long ago that choices in one's life were luxuries, not God-given rights. That bit of knowledge had reared its ugly head two years before when her son had been diagnosed as having leukemia.

Even now, just thinking about that day brought chills to her skin and made her shiver with the same feeling of rage and fear that she'd experienced then.

"Glynis."

At the soft-spoken use of her name, she blinked and focused her eyes on the tall, gray-haired man with eyes the color of the sky on a clear day. Dr. Eric Johns had a bedside manner to match his voice: gentle. And though he was just one of the many white-coated specialists who had paraded through her and Todd's life of late, he was the one she thought of as "Todd's doctor," the one who had been instrumental in holding her together through these trying times.

He was watching her intently, with concern etched in his features. "You seem a million miles away, my dear."

Glynis forced a smile. "Sometimes I wish I could pretend this was all a bad dream, and just run away."

They were sitting behind closed doors in Dr. Johns's office at the Texas Children's Hospital in Houston on a lovely spring morning. Glynis had left Todd at the day-care center and driven across town for the appointment. Dr. Johns's receptionist had called and left word that he wanted to talk to her.

Shaking his head, the doctor stood up from behind his massive desk and crossed to the window. He still didn't respond to Glynis's comment for a moment, seemingly content to watch and listen to the traffic below on Fannin Street. Even though his office was on an upper floor, the sounds of the afternoon traffic did not escape them.

After a moment he turned and faced Glynis. "You know you wouldn't run away, but I can understand why you would be driven to say it. Under the circumstances, you've handled Todd's illness with a remarkable strength." His voice was filled with admiration.

Glynis looked skeptical. "I appreciate your saying that, Doctor, but we both know it's not true. I fell apart at the seams."

He smiled in spite of the seriousness of the situation. "But you glued yourself back together, and that's what counts. So many don't." A frown replaced the smile. "The most dreaded or feared word in our society today is cancer."

Glynis leaned back in the cushioned chair and at the same time pushed an unruly strand of strawberry-blond hair behind her ear. "If only it had been me," she whispered, more for her own ears than for his.

"That's a natural reaction, too, my dear, but unfortunately we're not calling the shots. Someone higher up is doing that."

A silence fell over the room, and Glynis took the opportunity to draw a deep breath, to try to get hold of her frayed nerves. She had known what the doctor had wanted to discuss when he'd called, and she'd dreaded this visit. Todd had just recently undergone an updated battery of tests and she had prayed that his leukemia was still in remission.

"Anyway," Dr. Johns was saying, "I didn't call you here to give you bad news, or to let you wallow in self-pity."

"Oh." Glynis felt her pulse leap.

"Quite the opposite, in fact."

Glynis scooted to the edge of her chair and peered up at him. "Then . . . Todd's still in remission." It wasn't a question, and her voice had a croaking sound to it.

The doctor smiled, a genuine smile this time. "That he is, and—"

"Oh, thank God," Glynis cried, cutting him off in midsentence, her eyes raised toward the ceiling.

"You didn't let me finish," Dr. Johns chided, though with long-standing patience.

"There's more?" Glynis spread her hands. "I don't understand. What could possibly be more exhilarating than to learn that my six-year-old son is cured, that—"

This time it was the doctor who interrupted. "Not cured, Glynis, in remission. Remember, there's a difference." He paused and sat back down at his desk and, after leaning forward on both arms, peered at Glynis, a mixture of emotions playing across his face. "However, what we're about to discuss could lead to that cure."

Glynis was only capable of staring at him wide-eyed. Her heart was in her throat. She had prayed that one day she would hear these words, but she had about given up hope. And though she was hearing them now, she couldn't help but wonder if it would turn out to be another false alarm, another in a long line of many.

It had been shortly after her husband, Jay, was killed in a head-on car collision that she had begun to notice that something was wrong with Todd. Her worst fears were realized when the pediatrician, along with a specialist, had diagnosed leukemia. Since then her life had been like a yo-yo, up with hope one day, only to bottom out in despair the next. Dare she hope? Dare she truly hope?

"Please," Glynis whispered at last, wetting her lips, "tell me. Don't keep me in suspense any longer."

Eric Johns peered at the charts in front of him before transferring his gaze to Glynis. "After studying Todd's test at length, we feel he's a prime candidate for a bone marrow transplant." He held up his hands when Glynis would have interrupted. "Hear me out, then you can ask all the questions you like."

Unable to sit still a moment longer, Glynis got up and walked to the window and stood in the same spot that Dr. Johns had recently occupied. She stared outside also, but scarcely noticed the richness of the sun's glare as it bounced off the tall medical buildings across the street.

The doctor's calm voice drew her back around. "If the bone marrow is a success, and we have every reason to believe it will be, Todd should live a normal, healthy life."

A light flashed in Glynis's golden brown eyes, and tears glistened on her long lashes, making her appear suddenly younger than her twenty-seven years and much more vulnerable. "Oh, Dr. Johns, I don't know what to say... or do...." Her voice broke as she rushed toward him. "How to thank you..."

He cleared his throat. "Don't thank me yet, Glynis. While we're extremely fortunate that Todd qualifies for a transplant, there is a problem." For the first time, he seemed to be less than confident.

Fear gripped Glynis. "And what might that be?"

The doctor sighed. "The down side is that you're not a suitable donor. Your HLA, which are you blood antigens, do not match your son's."

"Oh, God," Glynis responded, feeling as if she'd just been kicked in the stomach. With trembling fingers she delved deep into her purse for a Kleenex, then on unsteady legs made her way back to the chair and sat down.

A furrow appeared between the doctor's blue eyes. "Hey, don't fall to pieces on me, especially now that we can see the light at the end of that long, dark tunnel."

Tears clung to Glynis's eyelashes. "I fail to see how you can be so optimistic when... when you just said I wasn't a suitable donor. And I know how hard other donors are to find." Her tone turned bitter as her sense of jubilation turned into utter hopelessness. "It seems like it's every day that the president or some senator is interceding for a family, asking for help in obtaining a suitable donor for a transplant." She knew she was rambling, but she couldn't help it. It just wasn't fair to come so close, only to be turned away.

"True, but it's not impossible. Donors are located all the time, and we'll find the right one for Todd."

"If only he had a brother or sister or..."

"Or father," Dr. Johns added quietly.

Glynis went white. "What...what did you say?"

Eric Johns looked at her oddly. "I said it would be a god-send if Todd's father were still alive." He paused, then went on, still looking at Glynis. "But since he isn't, and since you're not compatible, and since there is no brother or sister, we'll just have to go with what we've got and do the best we can. But I don't want you to worry," he stressed. "Todd will be taken care of."

"Dr. Johns, I..." Again Glynis's voice faded.

"Glynis, for God's sake, what's the matter?" Dr. Johns's voice was rough with concern. "You look like you've just seen a ghost."

Glynis circled her dry lips with her tongue. "Maybe...maybe I have."

The doctor frowned. "You're not making sense."

For another moment Glynis stared straight ahead. She felt as if she were drowning, drowning in the painful memories of her own past.

Pushing himself upright with his arms, Eric Johns came around the desk and stopped in front of Glynis. Leaning down, he took both of her hands in his. They were cold.

"Glynis," he said, "what's wrong? What did I say that upset you?"

Gently withdrawing her hands, Glynis stood and eased past him. It was only after she reached the center of the room that she turned around, digging her heels deep into the plush carpet for support. The dazed look remained on her face, robbing it of its natural color.

"Glynis." Again that gentle tone.

Suddenly Glynis blinked. "I'm...I'm sorry, Dr. Johns," she said at last, her composure once again intact. "I'm not in the habit of freaking out this way."

"Of course you're not. But still you haven't confided in me."

Glynis took a deep breath. "Todd's father is not dead."

Dr. Johns looked stunned, then confused. "Not dead. But I don't understand. I thought..."

"Jay, my husband, is...wasn't Todd's father."

His eyebrows raised, the doctor exhaled loudly. "Oh, I see."

"No, I doubt you do," Glynis countered softly, twisting her hands together. "It's a long and ugly story, one that I'd just as soon forget."

"While I understand and while I certainly respect your right to privacy, I have to know if Todd's father is alive."

"Yes," Glynis said dully, twisting her head back around.

The doctor was silent for a moment, as if he were deciding how best to phrase what had to be said. "You know what you've just told me sheds a whole new light on the situation."

Glynis nodded.

"Is . . . is Todd's father available?"

"I'm . . . not sure. He . . . he works out of the country a lot, and I have no idea where he is. There's been no contact between us since . . . since before Todd was born."

Dr. Johns leaned heavily against his desk and folded his arms across his chest, his forehead wrinkled in concentration. "I know how difficult this must be for you, Glynis, but I have to have some answers. If Todd's father's antigens match, he could be the donor."

"I know."

"So would you be willing to get in touch with him, explain the situation and ask for his help?"

Glynis swallowed against the hot bile that surged up the back of her throat. However, when she spoke, her tone was firm. "That goes without saying."

He was solemnly reading her face. "Even if it's painful for you?"

"I'd do anything short of murder to save my son's life, Doctor."

He let out another deep sigh. "Then I'll expect to hear from you soon."

When Glynis reached the door, she stopped and turned around. "As soon as I know something, I'll call."

"I don't need to remind you to keep your chin up, do I?"

Though weak, Glynis's smile transformed her face. "Thanks. I'll be in touch." Then, with unsteady hands, she opened the door and let herself out.

* * *

Instead of going to the day-care center and picking up Todd, Glynis went instead to her apartment. Her intention was to call her longtime friend in Lufkin, and she wanted to be alone when she did so.

She strode into the living room, tossed her purse on the couch, then switched on the lamp beside the telephone table. But when she sat down in the chair beside it and reached for the receiver, her hand froze. With a groan, she fell back against the cushion and closed her eyes, feeling once again as if her heart would stop beating.

She'd known the minute Dr. Johns had mentioned Todd's father what she would have to do, no matter how much pain it would cause her personally. Her son came first; he always had and he always would. He was the only decent thing that had come out of her life.

But knowing she had no choice did nothing to abate the pain associated with it.

Without wasting another minute, Glynis forced herself upright in the chair and punched out the long-distance number. On the third ring Milly Tatum's high-pitched voice came on the line.

"Milly."

"Well, it's about time I heard from you, Glynis Hamilton! You were about to get on my bad list, and you know what that means."

In spite of herself, Glynis laughed. "Milly, Milly, you wouldn't do that."

"Maybe not, but still you shouldn't go so long without calling me."

"In addition to Todd, it's been a tough year in the classroom."

Milly chuckled. "Your thirty-two fifth graders never settled down, huh?"

"Oh, they settled down, all right, but still—the sheer number of bodies in the room is enough to drive you crazy. You can imagine what it was like trying to teach them something."

Laughter sounded through the line. "Better you than me. I love owning a day-care center and playing with them, but if I had to teach those buggers how to read and write, our country would be in deep trouble.''

''I sometimes wonder if I'm cut out for the job myself.''

''Ha, you were a born teacher, if I ever saw one.''

''Look, Milly,'' Glynis said following a moment of silence, ''as much as I'd love to chat, that's not why I called.''

''I guessed as much. So what's the matter? You sound like you're down. It's not Todd, is it?''

It was uncanny, Glynis thought, how Milly was able to detect her mood without her having to say a word. ''No, at least not directly.''

''What does that mean?''

''I need a favor.''

''Name it.''

''I need to get in touch with Cort.''

Milly was silent a moment, then said, ''Cort McBride?''

''Milly...''

''All right, honey, I'm sorry. But why on earth would you of all people want to get in touch with *him*?''

Glynis sighed. ''Don't ask, Milly. Not right now. It's a long story, and I'll explain when I see you. Do you know where he is?''

''As a matter of fact, I do. He's here, at his ranch.''

Glynis felt her mouth fall open. ''He is.''

Milly laughed. ''Yes, he is.''

''But why, I mean...''

''Are you ready for this?''

''Milly.'' Again Glynis's exasperation showed.

''He's recovering from a gunshot wound.''

Glynis's lips tightened, though not before a harsh sigh had escaped.

''My sentiments exactly,'' Milly said sarcastically.

''Well, I can't say I'm surprised, though that doesn't change a thing.'' When Milly didn't answer, Glynis went on, changing the subject. ''Since I don't know how long I'll be staying in town, would you please have the utilities turned on in Dorothy's house. Todd and I will bunk there.''

''But...but...'' Milly spluttered.

''Just do it, Milly, please. And I won't forget I owe you one.''

Once the receiver was back in place, Glynis sank again into the cushions, fear and uncertainty numbing her. She could say it had started building inside her when Todd was diagnosed. But she knew better. It had started with her marriage to Jay. The marriage that had turned into a living hell.

Besides the fact that Jay couldn't hold a job, he had resented Todd, mostly because the boy wasn't his child. As a result he'd found solace in the bottle. If it hadn't been for Glynis's salary, they wouldn't have made it.

But now Jay was gone and so were her funds. Even though she had hospitalization through the school, it paid only eighty percent, which left twenty percent for her to pay. And twenty percent was a staggering amount in light of Todd's expensive medicines and treatments. The small insurance policy she had kept on Jay's life had been spent long ago.

So, as she'd told Dr. Johns, circumstances left her no choice. She felt tears saturate her cheeks as she looked up toward the ceiling. She had to see Cort.

Yet, how was she going to approach a man she hadn't seen in years and tell him that the child he thought was his best friend's was actually his?

Chapter 2

"Mom, are we really going to move to Lufkin and live in Aunt Dorothy's house?"

Glynis stopped what she was doing and faced her son. Suddenly an indulgent smile broke out across her face, softening her intense features. "I'm seriously thinking about it," she said, peering closely at Todd, thinking again how beautiful he was—"too beautiful to be a boy" was the standard comment from those who came in contact with him.

And he was. He was blessed with the best of both his mother and father. He had Glynis's fair coloring and light hair and Cort's bone structure and cornflower-blue eyes.

In spite of the fact that he was not taking chemotherapy and hadn't for the past two months, Glynis thought he was still too pale, too angelic-looking for his own good. And it was only a few more weeks before he would more than likely start another round of the strong toxicant in order to ready him for the transplant.

Every time she looked at him, her heart skipped a beat. If something happened to him, she knew she wouldn't want to live.

Yet, when he was feeling good, he behaved like any typical, rambunctious six-year-old, chattering nonstop about anything and everything.

"I don't know if I wanna move, Mom."

Glynis sighed. "I'm not sure I do either, son. But the house does belong to us, and we can live in Lufkin more cheaply than we can live here in Houston." She hadn't discussed the idea of moving with Todd, purposely saving it until now for fear of his reaction. He had gone through so many changes and upheavals in his young life that even a small one seemed big to him.

"Well, nothing's set in concrete," Glynis added with what she hoped was a reassuring smile. "Why don't we see how we like it and go from there? And you know how you like to play with Milly's two boys. They're anxiously waiting for you to come."

Todd's eyes lit up. "Can I go see them the minute we get here? Can I Mom?"

"We'll see. But for now, you go get your other pair of tennis shoes and put them in the car, while I check the apartment one last time."

Todd twisted his head to one side and frowned. "Do I have to?"

"Yes, you have to," she mimicked him in the same whiny tone, and then lightly smacked his bottom. "Off with you. We're running late as it is."

The moment she was alone, Glynis took a deep breath and scanned the room. She was leaving things neat and orderly. The apartment, as far as apartments went, had a homey atmosphere. And for the most part she and Todd had been satisfied here.

But for some time now, she had been toying with the idea of returning to Lufkin, getting out of the city with its pollution and traffic problems, not only for Todd's sake but for hers as well. However, unhappy memories haunted both places. Here there was guilt associated with the tragic death of her husband. And back home... Back home there were memories that she couldn't even face.

She felt sure she could get a teaching job without any problem. The main drawback was the two hours it would take to

drive Todd to and from the medical center. But she wouldn'
worry about that at the moment. Aunt Dorothy's house wa:
hers, and even though it was not in the best condition, it wa:
livable. For now that was a blessing in disguise.

"Mom, I'm ready," Todd said, sailing into the room, grin
ning his endearing toothless grin.

"All right. Get in the car. As soon as I lock up, we'll be off.'

As she went to follow Todd out the door, she stopped to gral
the sack of fruit on the bar. In doing so, she caught a glimps
of herself in the mirror above the couch. She stared at her re
flection, looking for outward signs of her inner turmoil. Ther
were none. Her finely drawn features and creamy, ivory ski
were as flawless as ever. On closer observation, however, sh
noticed her eyes, usually as clear as glass, appeared slightl
glazed.

"Mom!"

Shaking her head and smiling, Glynis called, "I'm coming
son."

The drive down Highway 59 toward Lufkin was pleasant
especially during the springtime. Glynis, however, because o
the nonstop chatter of her son, barely had a chance to notic
the patches of bluebonnets scattered on both sides of the high
way or the tall pines and oaks that seemed to reach up to th
sky. But that was fine by her, as it kept her from thinking abou
the awesome task ahead of her. The thought of facing Co
caused her stomach to turn inside out.

What if he refused to help? she asked herself. What if...wh
if...

"Don't, Glynis!" she spat aloud, then cast a swift glance i
Todd's direction. But her fierce reprimand to herself failed t
disturb her son. The thick, curly lashes that reminded her s
much of his father's remained closed.

It wasn't until she reached the city limits and subsequentl
pulled up in front of Milly's day-care center, suitably name
"House of Tots," that she loosened her death grip on th
steering wheel.

After nudging Todd awake and getting out of the car, Glyn
shoved her sunglasses closer to the bridge of her nose an

eered down at her watch. Three o'clock. They had made good me after all.

The air smelled so clean and fresh, as though it had recently ained. She took a whiff, inhaling it deep into her lungs before urning and following her son up the walk.

Just as they reached the first step, the front door flew open nd a short, slightly overweight woman hurried across the hreshold. "Hey, you two, you're a sight for sore eyes."

Even though Milly Tatum had a dark complexion and dark air, she reminded Glynis of a ray of sunshine bursting through dark cloud, especially when she smiled. And she was smiling ow; her pixy features were alive and her green eyes were spar- ling.

Glynis hadn't seen Milly since the day after Glynis had bur- ed her husband, a little more than two years ago. And though ey had kept in contact by phone, it wasn't the same as seeing er friend.

Now, as if starving for the sight of her, Glynis took a closer ok at Milly. She hadn't changed, Glynis thought, except aybe for her weight. The fact that she'd had twins was be- inning to tell on her, but it wasn't enough to detract from her atural beauty.

"Oh, Milly, I've missed you so much," Glynis said after a inute, giving her friend a fierce hug.

"Me, too," Milly responded before stepping away from lynis and turning to Todd. She reached out and mussed his ght-colored hair. "And how's my boy?"

"Okay," Todd mumbled. Then, looking around, he asked, Where are Adam and Kyle?"

Milly mussed his hair again and grinned. "Out back, wait- g for you."

"Can I go see 'em, Mom?" Todd asked anxiously, looking p at Glynis.

Glynis smiled. "Of course, silly, go on. But be careful," she lled to his retreating back, her eyes filled with guarded anx- ty.

Milly flashed her an understanding look. "It's hard to let him it of your sight, isn't it?"

"Sure is," Glynis admitted honestly. "He's . . . he's bee
through so much, been so sick. . . ." Her voice faded, but sh
knew she didn't have to explain further. Millie understood; sh
had two boys of her own.

Without another word, Glynis and Milly locked arms an
walked inside, where Glynis admired the large room wit
brightly decorated walls, a table and chairs, and shelves fille
with toys and books. Her gaze then traveled to a large wi
dow, and through it she could see a yard saturated with chi
dren of all ages and sizes.

When Glynis turned her attention back to the room, Mill
was talking to a round-faced woman who was sitting at one
the tables reading to a little girl.

Introductions were made, and then Glynis commented, '
always get such a warm feeling when I walk in here, Mill
You've done wonders with this old house. The years seem t
make no difference. It's fixed up just precious."

Milly grimaced. "Believe me, it takes every ounce of energ
I have to keep it this way. But I'm proud of it and what I'
accomplished."

"Well, you should be," Glynis said, following Milly into
small but efficient kitchen and sitting down in one of the pa
ded chairs circling an oak table.

Milly crossed to the cabinet, where a Mr. Coffee set steame
and sputtered, and pulled out two cups. "You still take yo
coffee black?"

Glynis nodded and waited silently while Milly filled the cup

"So what's going on?" Milly asked the moment she sat in th
chair across from Glynis. "Why the sudden need after all the:
years to see Cort?" Her eyes were serious, as was her tone
voice.

Glynis expelled a breath and, pointedly ignoring the que
tion, announced, "Todd's a candidate for a bone marro
transplant."

"That's great news, honey." Milly reached across, grabb
Glynis's hand and squeezed it. "That poor child has suffere
enough, and so have you."

"I know," Glynis said. "I'm excited and scared to death
the same time. It's going to be a long, drawn-out process. B

f it works, and the doctors have every reason to believe it will, hen he'll be cured." Her eyes brimmed with hope. "Just think, to more painful needles stuck in his tender veins and no more oxic medicines poisoning his body."

"Praise the Lord," Milly whispered, her smile overshadowing the tears that had sprung in her eyes. Then the smile suddenly disappeared, and a puzzled frown took its place. "But what does that have to do with you coming back here and wanting to talk to Cort, of all people?"

Glynis diverted her eyes for a moment, realizing that Milly was not going to let her get by with being evasive.

"Glynis, I'm your friend, remember."

"I know, and you don't know how much it means to me to have your support, but..." Glynis broke off and shifted in her chair, still unable to meet Milly's direct gaze.

"But you're not ready to confide in me, right?" Milly pointed out softly.

Glynis paled. "It's not that. It's..."

"Never mind," Milly said, pausing to take a sip of her coffee. "I'm just a nosy old busybody anyway. When you get ready to talk, I'm ready to listen." She smiled. "It's just that simple, okay."

"Oh, Milly," Glynis cried, "I don't know what I did to deserve a friend like you."

"Let's not get maudlin, okay?" Then clearing her throat, Milly added, "Why don't you and Todd stay with Buck and me, until you decide what you want to do, that is? You know we have plenty of room at the house."

"You didn't forget to have the utilities turned on in Aunt Dorothy's house, did you?" Glynis sounded distressed.

"No, of course I didn't, but that darn place is so rundown. I hate to think of you and Todd staying there even for one night."

Glynis sipped her coffee, then said, "It's a mess, all right, but I still think it's livable. Anyway, I wouldn't think of imposing n you, not with your hectic schedule. And since it looks like m going to be here awhile, I may as well get settled."

"But you're not at all happy about seeing Cort, are you? ou're smiling with your lips, but your eyes are telling a dif-

ferent story." Then, before Glynis could respond, Milly held up
her hands in mock surrender. "Here I go again, interfering
asking questions that you're not ready to answer."

This time it was Glynis who reached out and squeezed Milly's hand. "Thanks again for everything. But right now I need
to get Todd and let you get this place closed up so you can go
home." She drained the cup and stood.

It was after they were outside again that Milly asked, "Why
don't you let Todd stay here for a while? I have a mother coming late, so I can't leave. I know you have things to do."

Glynis sighed. "That I do." Without it being said, they both
knew that as soon as she stopped by the home place and unloaded, she was going to Cort's ranch. "Sure you don't mind
I mean . . ."

"Just go. And don't worry, Todd'll be fine."

The moment Glynis pulled up in front of the dilapidated
farmhouse nestled among huge oak and pine trees, she felt her
heart plummet to her toes. Milly was right; it was in sorry condition. The wooden frame structure had obviously settled
causing it to sag toward the middle. Besides that, the paint
seemed to have fallen off in chunks.

But on the bright side there appeared to be no broken windows, at least in the front. And it was blessedly beautiful and
peaceful here, she told herself, especially after the grinding
hubbub of the city.

Yes, it definitely had possibilities. It could be made into
showplace, if one had the money. And the desire. But at the
moment, she had only the latter.

With renewed determination, Glynis opened the car door and
got out. Once inside the house, she flipped on the light to her
right and paused on the threshold. Her breath caught in her
throat. Everything was exactly as she'd left it, furniture and all
just as if her aunt still lived here. However, the carpet was tattered, the linoleum was worn and the wallpaper hung in shreds

Feeling the tears well up in her eyes, Glynis walked through
the rooms, memories both good and bad drifting through her
mind. As if in a daze she walked to the kitchen and opened the

back door, letting in the fresh, warm air and feeling it caress her skin.

It was while she was standing there watching two squirrels chase each other around a tree that she suddenly found herself remembering the day her aunt brought her to this house for the first time. She had been nine years old, and a doll had been waiting for her in a chair in the living room. She had grabbed it and hugged it close to her lonely little heart and cried until her aunt had pulled her into her arms and held her.

Her mother had deserted her when she was only a year old, and until she turned nine, she had been shuffled from one foster home to another.

Dorothy Bickman, her mother's widowed sister, had learned of her existence and had gone to court to get guardianship of her. She had treated Glynis like the daughter she never had up until her death when Glynis was in college.

And even though they didn't have much in the way of material benefits, the shabby house was filled with love and kindness.

But her mother's rejection had left scars. As a result, the longing for roots and a family to love and cherish was the force that drove her. And she'd thought she'd found those roots in Cort McBride, the only man she'd ever loved.

She'd been wrong, and now, years later, having to approach him and ask for his help was a challenge she hadn't bargained on, and it was proving to be one of the most difficult things she'd ever had to do.

She wasn't sure when the warm breeze turned chilly. Nor was she certain when she experienced the crazy feeling that she was no longer alone. But she felt it, nonetheless, like a cool breath upon the back of her neck.

Suddenly, she whirled around, her eyes wide.

A man was slouched against the doorjamb, a Stetson pushed back on his head.

"Oh, God," were the only words she was able to get through her paralyzed throat.

Chapter 3

It was as though he had appeared out of nowhere, but Con McBride was no mirage. He was excruciatingly real. His tall rangy frame filled the doorway to capacity and seemed t shrink the room to doll-like proportions.

For an instant they both stopped dead, standing like tongue tied statues as they stared at each other.

Six years. Had it really been six long years since this man ha walked out of her life, since they had shared the most intima of secrets? It didn't seem possible, Glynis thought, her eye greedily taking in his every feature.

He'd changed very little. An overabundance of light brow hair swirled with gray overshadowed a face composed strong, masculine lines, with a strong jaw and a mouth th might seem sullen if it weren't for the fascinating fullness of h bottom lip. He'd always had the long, smooth muscles of a accomplished athlete and unfortunately an ego to match. H skin had the same leathery look as before, as if he spent all h time outside in the sun.

Yet on closer observation, he *was* different, and the diffe ence was in his blue eyes. Where once they had been penetra ing and alive, they were now cold and unyielding, the lin around them etched more clearly than she remembered. His mouth, too, was different. It was drawn tight as if controlled by physical pain.

However, it wasn't his mouth that held her rapt attention; it was the way his worn jeans rode low on his slender belly, molding his lean thighs to perfection, thighs that she had touched and kissed in moments of wild passion.... Glynis shivered, forcing her eyes away.

Her unexpected movement blessedly proved to be the key that unlocked the ominous silence.

"Well, well," Cort drawled, "wonders never cease. Heard you were back, but didn't believe it."

"I'd forgotten how fast news travels in this town." Glynis's voice sounded foreign even to her own ears.

A smirk touched lips that appeared to have forgotten how to smile. "I guess you figured you could just sneak in and right out again without anyone being the wiser." It wasn't a question, and his tone was clearly meant to be insulting.

Determined to control the situation, Glynis began uneasily, "Look, Cort, couldn't...couldn't we simply start over and say...hello?"

Not only was she trembling, but she was stammering as well. It was uncanny what just being in the same room with him could do to her mind and body, not to mention her equilibrium.

"You're unbelievable, you know that?" Cort laughed, but it wasn't pleasant-sounding. "The way I see it, you and I don't have anything to say to each other, not even so much as a hello."

"Cort...please." She spread her hands. "You're being unreasonable."

He laughed again. "Unreasonable, huh? Well, I'll tell you what's unreasonable and that's to think I'd give you the damned time of day in the first place." He lurched away from the door and strode toward her, stopping just short of touching her. "I'll have to hand it to you. Yeah, you were always a pro at turning men's heads, mine included. And poor Jay— well, he had about as much chance as a snowball in hell. The minute I turned my back, you suckered that poor slob into marrying you...."

Hot, boiling fury drove Glynis into raising her hand as if to strike him. "How dare you!"

"I wouldn't if I were you." It wasn't so much what Cort said but the way he said it that made Glynis lower her hand and step back, turning away.

"That's better," Cort said softly, but with no less power.

Facing forward again, Glynis found it difficult to speak. By letting him goad her into saying things that were better left unsaid, she was jeopardizing her mission. But then Cort had always affected her that way. Finally, she said wearily, "I didn't come back to..."

"What? To see me. Was that what you were going to say?"

"No," Glynis said carefully and with extreme patience. "That wasn't what I was going to say."

"Just out of curiosity, why the hell *did* you come back?"

In spite of her efforts to curb her tongue, to keep her cool, Glynis felt herself bristle. And before she knew it, she was saying, "If you'll recall, this also happens to be my home." The sarcasm was free-flowing. "I have as much right to be here as you do."

Her comeback silenced him for a moment, and they glared at each other, the pain of the past pulling on them like quicksand, threatening to suck them both under.

Again it was Cort who broke the silence. "But you're just passing through, checking on the old home place, right?"

She swallowed hard. "No and yes."

"What the hell kind of answer is that?"

She pulled her slender frame straight. "Actually, I'm here for a purpose, Cort."

"Life's full of little surprises, wouldn't you say?"

Ignoring his mocking sarcasm, she said, "I . . . I came to see you."

"Why?" His tone was without mercy now—flat and icy.

She breathed deeply to keep from panicking, then averted her gaze. The moment had finally come, and still she hesitated. But again she asked herself, *How does one go about breaking the news to a man that he has a six-year-old son?* There was simply no easy way.

She closed her eyes and tried to concentrate. Instead she suddenly found herself remembering what it had been like in high school when Cort McBride and his best friend, Jay Hamilton, had taken her under their wing.

Although Cort was six years older than Glynis and two years older than Jay, they were nevertheless a firm threesome. Glynis adored the ground Cort walked on, saw him as her knight in shining armor, while Jay adored Glynis, saw her as the girl of his dreams.

But she hadn't known how to deal with her feelings for Cort, nor he for her. Each had been afraid to make a move at the risk of offending the other.

Glynis had just graduated from college when Cort returned from the Army. Finally, emotions that had been kept under lock and key for years exploded, and they came together with declarations of love. Glynis was certain Cort would ask her to marry him.

Cort, however, had other plans. He told Glynis an Army buddy had offered him a job in his security company and that he was accepting it and was due to leave on an overseas assignment within the week.

Glynis was stunned and hurt, unable to comprehend how Cort could just walk out of her life and leave her, especially after the heady hours of passion they'd spent in each other's arms since his return.

Cort tried to explain that he was *not* walking out of her life, that he was merely planning for their future. He went on to say that he remembered what it meant to be poor, even if she'd forgotten. He wanted better for them. Eventually they would get married, he added.

Eventually was not what Glynis wanted to hear. Harsh words were exchanged, and in the heat of the moment, both said things they didn't mean, damaging their relationship beyond repair.

A few weeks later Glynis discovered she was pregnant....

"Dammit, Glynis, you've got exactly two seconds to tell me what this is all about, or I'm out of here."

Cort's harshly spoken words drew Glynis back to reality with a start. She twisted her head back around, only to clasp her hands tightly in front of her, noticing with dismay that they were trembling.

He was staring at her through narrowed eyes, his hands stuffed into the pockets of his jeans. He appeared at ease, unperturbed. But Glynis knew better. Underneath that cool exterior, he was seething. Cort McBride didn't take too kindly to being played for a fool, and he believed that Glynis had indeed played him for one long ago. In his book that was unforgivable.

"I . . . have . . . there's something I have to tell you," Glynis said at last. "Would you mind if we sat down?" At this point, she wasn't sure her wobbly legs were capable of holding her up much longer. Confronting Cort was becoming more of a nightmare than she'd ever imagined. But she wouldn't fail Todd. Never.

Suddenly the thought of her son gave her the new burst of strength she needed to cross to the old chrome table and chairs in the middle of the kitchen.

"If you don't mind, I'll stand," Cort muttered tautly as she lowered herself into the chair facing him.

A hard glint sparked in Glynis's eyes. "You're not going to make this easy for me, are you?"

"Why should I? You didn't make things easier for me when you married my best friend behind my back."

Glynis felt the blood rush to her head and wanted desperately to defend herself. But rather than risk starting another argument, she controlled her overactive tongue and let his question slide.

"I'm waiting," Cort said, his arms folded across his chest, holding that same easy stance, which again she knew to be deceptive.

Still she didn't speak. She concentrated on the relatively cool breeze stealing through the screen door. Even so, perspiration broke out over her entire body.

"You . . . sure you don't want to sit down?" Glynis asked inanely, continuing to stall for time, while questions with no answers raced through her mind. What would he do when she told him?

"Glynis!"

"I came to ask for your help, Cort," she said at last, knowing that she had pushed him as far as she could.

"Help. What kind of help?" There was a wariness in his tone now.

She lifted her eyes to his. "Todd is . . . sick."

Cort stood a little straighter. "Sick."

"Yes. Very sick. He . . . was diagnosed with leukemia two years ago."

He looked stricken.

"Actually, he took sick only a few months after . . . after Jay died."

Muttering a crude expletive, Cort moved for the first time, striding toward the back door.

With his back to her, Glynis watched the way the muscles in his shoulders bunched together. She knew he was holding on to his temper by a mere thread.

The hostile silence seemed loud as she listened to the birds' delightful chatter outside.

"He's . . . in remission right now, but . . ." She broke off, pushing her sweaty palms down the sides of her jeans. "But he won't be if he doesn't get the kind of help he needs."

"I see."

I wish to God you did see, but you don't. Glynis forced herself to speak again. "Because . . . of his age and other factors that I won't go into right now and that I don't really understand myself, Todd's a good candidate for a bone marrow transplant and . . ."

Cort swung around, cutting her off in midsentence, his eyes blazing. "If it's money you need, why the hell don't you just come right out and ask for it? Why the elaborate charade?"

"Please, Cort, let me finish," she said on a ragged note, trying her best to ignore the contempt she heard in his voice. But it was there, and it hurt like a hot knife piercing her heart.

He shrugged and kept his eyes pinned to hers. Frustration showed in his face.

"As I was saying, Todd's a candidate for a transplant, but...but we need a donor."

His eyes were hard. "So make the hospital find one."

"They...the hospital, I mean, hasn't tried. You see..."

"You needn't go any further." He exhaled loudly. "I know it takes a helluva lot of money to get a donor and have such an operation. Just tell me how much you need, and I'll deposit it in your account."

She began shaking her head. "Cort..."

"Let me finish. But just so there's no confusion, I'm not doing it for you, baby." His eyes were as cutting as blades. "Oh, no. I'm doing it for the kid, for Jay's kid."

"Todd's not Jay's child."

Glynis's softly spoken words had the same effect as a rock splashing into a pool of water. After the initial shock of the noise, the ripples thereafter were all-consuming.

Blood vessels stood out at the base of his neck. "Then whose..."

"Yours." Glynis stood, her lips white.

The long silence took its toll on both of them.

"Todd is your child, Cort."

Another silence, deeper than the one before, fell over the room while Glynis saw a look of naked panic cross his face. Then Cort took a step toward her, his panic now replaced with naked fury.

"That's a damned lie!" His voice was almost a shout.

Glynis fought off waves of nausea. "No, no, it isn't."

Suddenly and without warning, Cort closed the distance between them, knocking one of the chrome chairs over in his haste to reach her. For a second, as he loomed over her, Glynis thought he was going to strike her.

Unconsciously, she swayed out of harm's reach, but she wasn't quick enough. He grabbed her wrist and held firm. "Tell me that's a lie," he said between clenched teeth.

"Please, Cort, you're...hurting me."

"Believe me, this is nothing to what I will do if you don't call a halt to this little game you're playing and tell me the truth."

"It's the truth," she cried, looking up at him, feeling his harsh breath on her face. "I swear Todd is yours."

For another long moment they stared at each other, golden brown eyes clashing with deep blue ones. Then, dropping her arm as though she were contaminated, Cort whirled around, but not before another expletive colored the air.

"Cort, please, hear me out," Glynis whispered to his back, stopping just short of begging. But she would beg, if she had to, if that was what it took to save her son's life. She'd even get down on her knees and grovel. "You have to know it's true. Do you think I'd lie to you about something like this?"

Cort swung around, and her resolve wavered again. His features were a mask of vivid, ugly emotions.

"Yes, damn you, I do!"

Glynis felt another onslaught of nausea hit her, but she rallied. "Believe me, I don't like this any better than you do. I wouldn't be here if I wasn't desperate. Surely you don't think I'd make this up because I want something from you?"

"Why now? Why the hell now?" There was fury in his voice, but there was something else as well. Was it pain? Yes, she believed it was, and in that moment she longed to crawl off in a hole and cover herself.

Instead, she whispered through a maze of tears, "Because I'm not a suitable donor for Todd and . . . and as his . . . father, you could be. In fact," she rushed on, "you more than likely will be."

His head snapped up, but he didn't say a word, which added to Glynis's already mounting apprehension.

She finally broke the silence, her voice taut and unsteady. "You believe me, don't you, Cort?"

The fight seemed to have gone out of him, yet his eyes had not tempered. They were as cold as ever. "If he . . . if Todd hadn't gotten sick, you would never have told me, right?"

She didn't have a ready answer, so she didn't say anything.

"Answer me!"

"No," she said in a dull tone, "I wouldn't have told you. I never meant for you to find out."

The silence in the room was like a wall of ice.

"Damn you, Glynis, damn you to hell." His words were sharp, his tone whiplike. "How could you have done it? How could you have married Jay knowing you were carrying my child, knowing I'd be back?''

"That's just it, I didn't know you'd be back. You wanted your freedom, remember?''

"Like hell, I did. I wanted you. You knew as soon as I got set up in the job, I'd be back.''

Glynis balled her fingers into fists by her side, trying to remain focused on her son, on the matter at hand, not on the man in front of her and the sea of memories in which she felt herself drowning.

"You knew I'd be back," he repeated bitterly.

Sunlight poured through the window in a blinding slant.

Glynis turned away, not bothering to hide the tears streaming down her cheeks. "No, I didn't, not after the way you stalked out of here, furious because I accused you of putting ambition and money before me. And anyway, I . . ." Her voice broke.

"You what?"

"Nothing," she replied in that same dull tone, reaching into her pocket for a Kleenex. Then, after wiping the tears from her face, she added, "I can't . . . won't discuss us anymore.''

"That's where you're wrong. You *can* and you *will* answer my questions. You did this to me, Glynis! I have a right to know what happened.''

"You did this to yourself, Cort.''

"This was your revenge, was it?''

"There was no revenge to it. You wanted to be rid of me, to be freed from your commitment. . . .''

"Dammit, how many times do I have to tell you that I wanted no such thing. Do you think for one instant that if I'd had any inkling you were pregnant I would have let you go?''

Glynis's eyes were lit with fury. "Nothing would have induced me to beg you to marry me.''

"Don't be a fool," he said roughly. "I loved you. You had no right to conceal this. The child was as much mine as yours.''

"Well, it's too late now. Anyway, I told you I don't want to talk about us.''

"I don't care whether you want to or not. It's what I want that counts now, right?"

Recognizing the tone she knew so well, Glynis nodded, feeling the fight drain out of her like water through a sieve.

"So tell me, when you found out you were pregnant, you went running to old Jay, who was bored to death working for his dad in the logging business, and conned him into marrying you. How am I doing so far?"

"Cort..."

Ignoring her, he went on, "Yeah, I guess old Jay fell for your line like a ton of bricks and waited in the wings just to pick up the pieces."

Glynis flinched, but her gaze was unerring. "Damn you, Cort McBride."

"Sure enough, Jay always did have the hots for you, so when he got the chance, he took it, even though you—"

"Stop it!" Glynis cried, her eyes flashing. "Would you rather I'd ended Todd's life before it had even started?"

This time it was Cort who turned visibly white.

"I could have, you know," she hammered on, knowing for the moment she had the upper hand, "but I didn't. To tell the truth, the thought never crossed my mind." She paused and swiped at the new surge of tears with the back of her hand. "But having a child out of wedlock did. It crossed my mind every waking minute of every day."

Suddenly Glynis realized that Cort had moved and was looming over her, so close that she could smell him. Her heart skipped a beat.

"So tell me," he said softly, "how did it feel to have his hands on you? Did you moan for him the way you did for me?"

"You bastard!" she cried, backing up, knowing if she stayed within reach of him, she'd end up slapping his face. "Stop thinking about yourself for once," she spat, "and think about your son."

The silence was heavy.

"I thought you wanted my help."

She stared at him in disbelief. "Are you saying you'll cooperate, do what needs to be done?"

"Both physically and financially."

Glynis let out her pent-up breath. A semblance of a smile broke across her lips.

"But it's going to cost you."

The smile faded. "What? What's it going to cost me?"

"Your son."

Chapter 4

Inside Glynis froze like an icicle. She touched her throat and kept staring at him. Surely, he wouldn't... No, of course he wouldn't, she quickly assured herself. It was impossible. Todd was *her* son. He wouldn't, couldn't take Todd away from her. Could he?

"What...what are you saying?" she asked finally, trying to curb the rising hysteria inside her.

"You figure it out."

Hysteria overcame her. The fear that had been there all the time, just beneath the surface, emerged like a monster to sink its claws into her heart. "Damn you, Cort McBride! There's no way I'm going to let you take Todd away from me, so don't even try."

"Don't threaten me, Glynis. You're way out of your league." His voice held a dangerous undertone that even Glynis in her highly agitated state could not miss.

She ignored it and went right on, her tone as frosty as her eyes. "No lawyer or court in this land will side with you."

"I wouldn't be too sure of that, either, if I were you."

Glynis's throat went dry. "Don't...don't you dare threaten me."

"I want to see my son. Now."

If he so much as tried to take Todd away from her... Oh, Lord, it didn't bear thinking about. "Until you've been tested Todd and I are... are going to stay here, in Aunt Dorothy' house. Then we'll see..."

"Here? Did you say live here?"

"Yes... What's wrong with that?"

His laugh was short, biting. "What's wrong with that? Have you looked around this firetrap?"

"I resent that," Glynis responded coldly. "Just because i doesn't have all the amenities you're used to doesn't mean it': a firetrap."

"Amenities, hell. It doesn't have even the basics. You're no living here, not with my son, that is."

"Well, it'll have to do because I just might decide to stay her permanently. I've thought about applying for a teaching posi tion in the district and..." Suddenly she stopped in midsen tence as it dawned on her what he'd just said. "I beg you pardon?" she asked, blinking.

"You heard me." Irritation darkened his eyes. "No son o mine is going to live in this dilapidated house, now or ever Hell, Glynis, this thing ought to be bulldozed to the ground, i anything."

"You have no say in what I do or where I live." She wa holding her voice steady, but her hands were balled into fists her fingernails digging into her palms. She wouldn't give in t his demands. To do so would be a grave mistake. She knew hin well enough to know that. She'd let him control her life onc before, and look where it got her.

When he didn't readily respond, she went on. "Anyway that's not true." She quickly looked around the premises be fore turning back to focus her eyes on Cort. "Why, it...it jus needs a good cleaning, a paint job and a few other things, an then it'll be just fine."

He snorted. "Just goes to show you how little you knov about houses. For crying out loud, the place doesn't even hav water. The pipes burst this winter and still haven't been re paired, not to mention the roof. It leaks like a waterfall."

"How do you know?" Her voice was toneless.

"Does it matter?"

"Yes, because you could be lying just to get your way."

It was obvious that Cort's temper was on a short fuse. "Trust me," he said cynically, "I don't have to lie to get my way. Now why don't you just simmer down and listen to what I have to say."

"How dare you talk to me like that?"

Cold fury etched his features. "If it'll make you see reason, I'll talk to you any way I damn well please."

"I won't have you trying to take over Todd's life—our life." She was becoming desperate. "You had your chance years ago and threw it away. You made it quite plain when you walked out where your loyalties lay."

"Damn you, Glynis, how can you talk about loyalty when you, pregnant with my child, married another man? Pardon the old adage, but that's like the pot calling the kettle black."

A cry tore loose from her throat. "What about you? All you could think about was the almighty dollar and a career. And not necessarily in that order." Her tone was filled with scorn. "And nothing's changed. Correct me if I'm wrong, but I bet you have a big deal pending right now, one that's going to make you even richer and more powerful than you already are."

"You're right I do. A government deal that I'm proud of."

"That's why I have Todd and you don't."

His sharp intake of breath was the only sound in the room, and for a moment Glynis feared she had gone too far, pushed him over the edge with her sharp tongue.

Suddenly, feeling as if something had ripped apart inside her, she whispered brokenly, "Why are you doing this, Cort? Why are you making things so difficult for me? If it's to get back at me, you're doing it at the expense of your son. Can't you see that?" She was pleading now, but she didn't care.

"It's my son I'm thinking about. That's why I can't, won't, let him live here." Cort paused and snatched the Stetson off his head. "Anyway, I'm afraid my helping . . . Todd might not be as simple as you think."

Glynis bit her lip. "Why? I mean what makes you say that?"

"In case you haven't noticed, I'm not exactly in tip-top shape."

She put a hand to one cheek. "Oh, God, I forgot about your wound."

"You know?"

"Milly told me."

"Ah, Milly. I should've known."

His mocking sarcasm was not lost on Glynis, but she ignored it. "You...you think the doctors might not let you...?" She was looking up at him out of seemingly bottomless eyes.

"Don't panic. It's just that right now I have a hole in my side that seems to be taking its time healing. I'm not sure how it'll affect things, that's all. They may want me to be completely healed."

"How did it happen? The wound, I mean?"

Glynis could tell by his hesitation that he'd rather not talk about it, which didn't surprise her at all.

"Do you really care?" Cort asked after a moment, his voice hard and strident.

Glynis's chin rose a notch. "For myself, no. For Todd, yes."

Another smirk crossed his lips. "Well, then for Todd's sake I'll tell you. I took a bullet meant for a client."

"I'm not surprised. Danger always did turn you on."

"And what turns you on?" he asked silkily.

Color flooded her face, but she wouldn't give him the satisfaction of rising to his bait. Instead she pulled her dignity around her like a shield and steered the subject back to the matter at hand.

"If we have to delay the transplant, I'll have no choice but to accept that," she said stiffly. "But what I don't have to accept is you telling me where to live."

He gave her a long, dark look. "Well, accept it, because that's the way it's going to be."

Glynis scanned the room again, feeling what energy she had left completely desert her. Cort was right. This place *was* a disaster. Oh, it had possibilities, all right. It could be made livable with a lot of money, money that she obviously didn't have. Yet it galled her that Cort was once again pulling the strings of her life. For Todd's sake, she had no choice but to go along with it—for now.

"All right, Cort." She felt drained and tired, but most of all she was angry. "We'll stay with Milly and Buck until I can make other arrangements."

"I have a better idea." His voice was as smooth as plastic.

She jerked her head up, distrust written clearly on her features. "Oh, and what is that?"

"The ranch. You and Todd stay at the ranch, with me."

As before, she should have seen it coming, but she hadn't. For a moment she stared at him, totally stunned, as if she'd just run headlong into a mirrored wall. Glynis's mind was spinning, her breathing erratic. She took a deep breath and tried to calm down.

"I know what you're thinking, and you needn't worry." Cort's words were a sneer. "I have a live-in housekeeper who will serve as a more than adequate chaperon."

There was no sound in the room except her heartbeat, which Glynis thought was thunderous. She shook her head. "No, no, that's impossible."

"Why?"

"You know why." She couldn't look at him. "Because . . . because . . ."

"Because you're afraid I'll jump your bones. Is that it?"

Glynis narrowed her eyes. "You're despicable!"

Cort moved then with lightning speed and didn't stop until he had her pinned against the nearest wall, his hands on either side holding her captive.

Silence blazed between them.

"There was a time when you didn't think so. Remember?" The softly dangerous tone dared her to deny it.

"Please," she protested weakly, her breath coming in shallow gasps.

"Please what!" he whispered, his voice sounding hoarse, almost guttural, while his deep-set eyes shifted from her mouth to her heaving chest.

Glynis tried to ignore the look. But she couldn't, not when she could feel his hard thigh pressing against her leg and her nipples jutting against the fabric of her top.

A tide of heat washed through her even as she moved her head frantically from side to side, trying to downplay the effect his nearness was having on her.

"Cat got your tongue?" he taunted, rubbing his palm across one of the distended tips.

She groaned, his hand lighting a fire inside her, a fire she'd thought could never be rekindled. "Please," she whispered again, shrinking from his seductive touch.

Suddenly, mercifully, he stepped back, but his eyes lingered on her for another heartbeat. "You're not worth it," he spat. Then, muttering a crude expletive, he turned his back and strode once more to the door and looked out.

The still spring air screamed with silence.

When she thought she couldn't stand it another second, he swung back around. What she saw in his eyes again sent her heart rate up a notch higher. "You've had our son for six long years. Can't you at least share him for a while?"

Glynis eased down into a chair and lowered her head. She wanted to cry, to wash away all of the anguish, all the hurt, all the shame. But she couldn't. The tears wouldn't come. They were now locked deep inside her.

"Well?"

Her gaze slid to him. In that moment she knew he had won, in spite of how he had humiliated her. The look on his face, the pain in his voice were the catalyst that completely destroyed her resistance.

"We'll do it your way for now." She ran a hand over her hair. "But when it's all over, you'll let us—Todd go."

"We'll see."

"Cort," she began, fear curling anew in her stomach.

"Not now, Glynis. I want to see Todd. I want to see my son."

"He's . . . he's at Milly's."

"Get him."

"What then?"

"Meet me at the ranch."

She sighed and rubbed her temples. "It's getting late, Cort. I think it would be better if we...uh, spent the night with Milly. Then tomorrow . . ."

"No. I want to see my son today, damn you."

He was doing it to her again, making her feel guilty, making her the guilty party when he'd been the one who had deserted her. But she had given her word, and even though her heart felt like a piece of lead, she was committed. "I'll . . . we'll be there shortly."

For a long moment Cort continued to look at her, a strange expression on his face. It was an expression she couldn't decipher, yet it made her feel uncomfortable.

Then he pivoted and in long, angry strides made his way toward the door, closing it firmly behind him.

It was not until Glynis heard him crank the engine on his Jeep that she relaxed. Sinking against the cushion, she gave in to the throbbing at her temples while her mind raged.

The thought of living under the same roof with Cort for so much as one day, much less several, made her crazy. My God, she thought, did she still care about him? No, absolutely not. Any feelings she had for Cort were dead.

Suddenly she grabbed her stomach, fearing she was going to be sick. Who was she kidding? She had known the moment he'd touched her, stirring passions both old and new inside her, that she hadn't gotten him out of her system. But then she'd known long before that—she'd known it when she'd turned and saw him standing in the doorway.

Feeling anything for Cort was the last thing she wanted. But she needed him. For her son, she needed him.

"Sure you won't take time to have a cup of coffee before you go?" Milly asked anxiously, following Glynis to the car. Todd was already inside the Honda, his seat belt buckled, looking at a comic book.

Glynis stopped at the edge of the sidewalk, out of hearing distance of Todd, and gave her friend a wan smile. "I'd love to, but I want to get to the ranch before it gets any later." She paused and stared at the point beyond Milly's shoulder, her face pensive. "Cort's . . . waiting."

Milly sighed, frowning gently. "I assume you know what you're doing?"

"Well, you assume wrong."

"Then why are you doing such a fool thing as going to his place?" Milly shook her head. "Why don't you and Todd stay with Buck and me? I've already told you we have plenty of room, and we'd love having you."

Impulsively Glynis reached out and hugged her friend. "I know that and I'm grateful for the offer, but..."

"For God's sake, Glynis, what kind of hold has Cort Mc-Bride got over you? I know how crazy you were about him way back, but when he took off and refused to marry you, I thought you had come to your senses, gotten him out of your system. Now, years later, not only do you ask to see him, but agree to move into his house with him." She rolled her eyes. "Talk about crazy."

Glynis's features were pinched. "I know how it looks and how you could misconstrue everything. But trust me, I have my reasons, and as my dearest friend, you certainly deserve an explanation. As soon as I get settled, we'll have a long talk. But not now. Cort is waiting and..."

Milly's eyes suddenly widened and lit up, as if a light had just come on inside her head. "Cort is Todd's father, isn't he?"

Glynis flinched, but she didn't turn away. "Yes."

Milly balled a fist and slapped it into the palm of her other hand. "I should have guessed it a long time ago, should have known when you married Jay in such a hurry. I never thought..."

"That I'd marry one man, while carrying another's child."

Although Milly flushed, she recovered quickly. "Don't get me wrong, I'm not criticizing. It's just that I'm surprised, that's all," she finished lamely.

Glynis knew what Milly was thinking and she didn't blame her, didn't blame her in the least. "It's all right, really it is. I should've told you a long time ago, but I couldn't. I couldn't...couldn't tell anyone. I was so torn up, so mixed up, so vulnerable...." She smiled through the sudden tears that had sprung up in her eyes. "But now I'm glad you know."

Tears also glistened in Milly's eyes as she answered Glynis's smile with one of her own. But it was a fleeting moment. And when it disappeared, Glynis was once again reminded of the sun dipping behind a cloud.

"Cort didn't know, did he?"

"No, he didn't know."

"But he does now?"

"Yes, he knows now."

"I won't ask what his reaction was."

"Don't."

"Did . . . did Jay know?"

Glynis pawed at the concrete with the toe of her shoe. "Yes, but he never accepted it."

"I'm sorry. I know your marriage must've been more of a hell than I ever imagined."

"There were times when I thought I wouldn't make it, but then I'd think of Todd and the world would right itself once again."

"So is . . . Cort going to do his part?"

"Yes, thank goodness," Glynis said, glancing down at her watch and then toward the car, where she noticed Todd squirming restlessly.

"He's going to be the donor, right?"

"Right. Plus he's going to help me financially. But his help is not without a price." She caught her breath sharply. "He . . . wants to spend time with Todd, get to know him. And he feels the only way he can do that is for us to stay at the ranch. And, like you, he thinks Aunt Dorothy's house is unlivable. So, as you can see, I have no choice."

"You're right, you don't, but how do you feel? About Cort, I mean? How's being around him going to affect you?"

"Oh, Milly," Glynis said wearily, "I don't know. At this point I think I'm numb."

"Mommy."

At the sound of Todd's plaintive cry, both women turned in the direction of the car. Todd had rolled down the window on the driver's side, and his head was sticking out of it.

"Mom," he said again before Glynis could respond, "I'm ready to go."

"I'm coming, sweetheart." Then, facing Milly, Glynis added, "Look, I'll call you later and we'll get together and talk some more."

"Take care," Milly whispered, squeezing Glynis's hand. "And if you need me . . ."

"I know, and thanks."

With that, Glynis hurried to the car and, once inside, slammed the door behind her.

Nothing was the same. Yet everything was the same. The land had not changed, Glynis noticed as she brought the Honda to a stop at the beginning of the long road that would eventually take her to the front door of Cort's sprawling ranch-style house.

But of course the house had changed. The small, unsturdy frame structure where Cort and his brother, Barr, had lived with their drunken father had long since disappeared, and in its place was a new, elaborate home on top of the hill, the setting sun reflecting off the windows.

Glynis, feeling her mouth go dry as cotton, gripped the steering wheel until she felt her fingers go numb. How could she do it? How could she share the same space with Cort? See him day after day? No one should have to endure what she was having to endure. But then she'd learned as a young child that life dealt you no special favors, that if you were to survive, you had to be a fighter.

"Mom, what's the matter? You sick or something?"

Glynis loosened her grip on the wheel at the same time as she smiled down at her son. His eyebrows were drawn together in a frown. "No, I'm not sick or something. I was just thinking, that's all."

"Are we really going to stay here in that big house?" He was pointing toward the hill.

"Yes, we're really going to stay here, for a while, anyway."

"All right!"

"It is beautiful, isn't it?" Glynis said, unaware of the wistful note in her voice.

"It's neat."

The minute Glynis had nosed the car onto Highway 69 toward the small community of Pollock, she had explained to Todd the change of plans. Of course he was delighted they were going to be staying on a ranch.

Todd's nose was pressed against the glass. "Wow! Look, Mom, look at all those cows! They're everywhere."

The sloping hills that graced the front and sides of the house were dotted with cattle contentedly munching on the green grass underfoot. The serene beauty of it almost robbed Glynis of her breath.

Cort had come a long way from the struggling, penniless teenager. She'd have to hand him that. From the looks of this place, he'd more than reached his goal. Suddenly, in an indulgent moment, she wondered what it would be like to share a house such as this with a man. With Cort . . .

"I bet Mr. McBride's got horses, too."

Glynis shook her head as if to clear it. "Uh, why don't you call him . . . Uncle Cort."

Todd wrinkled his nose. "Is he my uncle?"

"No, no, not in the true sense. But he's been my . . . friend for a long time." This was going to be harder than even she had imagined. "And I think he'd like it . . . if you called him that."

Todd shrugged. "Okay." Then, changing the subject, he asked, "If he's got horses, do you think he'll let me ride one?"

"More than likely," Glynis responded with a smile. Then, yanking the car back in drive, she drove it up the asphalt road, her heart pounding.

The second she brought the car to a full stop next to the house, the front door opened and Cort walked out. He paused on the porch, as if uncertain for the first time in his life how to proceed.

Todd had no such inhibitions. Without looking at Glynis, he opened the door and scrambled out of the car. But when his feet hit the ground, he stopped and scrutinized the stranger still standing on the porch.

By the time Glynis got out of the car and came around to where her son was standing, the impulse to flee was beating in her veins.

For the longest time, no one spoke. Even Todd seemed to sense the electricity in the air and self-consciously looked toward Glynis.

It was Cort who made the first move. Taking slow, even strides, he walked toward them, his face looking as though it had been chiseled out of granite.

Glynis remained rigid.

He didn't pause until he was within touching distance of them both. Glynis felt the sting of tears behind her eyelids and was doubly thankful for her dark sunglasses as Cort, ignoring her, dropped to one knee in front of Todd.

"Hi," he said, his eyes on the small, thin face in front of him.

"Hi," Todd answered shyly.

"Welcome to the Lazy C Ranch."

Todd eyed him curiously. "Are you my Uncle Cort? My mom said I should call you that."

For the first time, Cort looked at Glynis. Hatred shone in his eyes. Glynis drew in a sharp breath and turned away.

"Er...that's fine," Cort was saying. "I'll answer to anything."

Todd cocked his head sideways. "My friend's dad looks like you."

"Oh, really." Amusement lurked around Cort's mouth now, making him appear younger and more human.

"Yeah, he's..."

"Yes, sir," Glynis interrupted softly.

"Yes, sir, he's tall like you," Todd went on, unruffled, his eyes showing his awe. "And he wears a big cowboy hat, too." He paused thoughtfully for a moment, then added, "I don't have a dad. He died."

"Todd!" Glynis's horrified cry split the air, and for what seemed like an eternity, no one said a word. No one moved.

Finally, when she could bring herself to look at Cort, she wished she hadn't. The hurt mirrored there was so intense, she feared her heart would explode into a million pieces. Her already fragile emotional dam collapsed, and years of heartache and guilt came flooding back to her, threatening to bury her under its impact.

Cort cleared his throat and stood up, resting a hand on Todd's thin shoulder. "I'm sorry about that . . . son."

"Me, too, but Mom says he's in heaven."

"I'm sure he is."

"Do you have any horses?" Todd asked then, changing the subject.

"You bet I do," Cort said, once again clearing his throat. "In fact, they're the best."

"Could we go see 'em? Please?"

Cort bestowed on Todd one of his rare smiles. "You bet."

Without so much as another glance in her direction, father and son headed toward the paddock located behind the house.

Glynis stood as if cemented to the spot and watched, tears trickling down her cheeks. Yet she was smiling a wistful smile as she witnessed her son mimicking Cort's long, graceful stride.

Gradually the smile disappeared, and reality set in. She stood there alone. A woman without a shield.

Chapter 5

Cort sipped on his coffee and flipped through a stack of papers on his desk. He was starting to get behind on his paperwork, but then that wasn't anything new. He was usually behind on his paperwork.

Even though his company, McBride Security was the second-largest security firm in the United States and had numerous employees who were more than capable of doing anything he asked of them, he nevertheless believed in a hands-on approach. He wanted to be involved in the day-to-day workings of his empire, was not happy unless he was doing so.

However, continuing to work in the field was not without its price. If it hadn't been for his active involvement, he wouldn't be nursing a bullet wound. But when an old friend had come to him for help, he hadn't been able to turn him down. The "heavies" who were after him obviously meant business.

After coming out of the service, having been skillfully trained in Army intelligence, Cort had gone into partnership with an Army buddy who thought he wanted to be in the security business. Cort later bought him out and because of his cunning and astute business mind, had become successful far in excess of what he'd ever imagined.

Yet he was not satisfied. His goal was not complete. He very much wanted the big, lucrative contract the government was letting out to a private company and was determined to get it. While the bullet wound in his side might have slowed him down, it had not stopped him or dulled his determination.

There were only three things that meant a damn to him in this life: his brother, McBride Security and his ranch. And he'd thought he was content, if not happy with his lot in life. Until yesterday, that is, when it had all changed with a blink of an eye.

A deep sigh escaped Cort's lips as he lumbered to his feet and walked to the window behind his desk, coffee cup in hand. But he didn't drink any coffee. Instead he simply stood and stared outside at the sun and watched it slowly peep over the horizon, hoping the sight would ease the turmoil raging inside him.

It was early, and he knew he was the only one up. It had been an effort in futility to remain in bed a second longer. He'd tossed and turned the entire night as it was, using the mattress and springs as a battleground for his frustration and anger.

Unfortunately, he found no solace in the stunning beauty of the rich pastureland where the sun made the dewdrops sparkle like millions of tiny diamonds. Always he could stare at this land he loved and come to grips with whatever was troubling him. Not this morning.

"Damn," he muttered, and at the same time shoved an unsteady hand through his thick crop of hair. Then, turning, he set his half-empty cup on the desk with a resounding thud and walked to the center of the room, where he eyed with longing a number of dumbbells lining one corner.

When he wasn't working the land or cattle, his favorite pastime was lifting weights; not that he did it to excess, but rather for the pure enjoyment of feeling his anxiety and stress evaporate as if it had never existed. But there would be no weight lifting today or in the near future, unless he wanted to rip out the stitches in his gut.

Still, he yearned for the relief. In his mind's eye he visualized how he'd look pumping iron, how he'd feel in a few weeks after the doctor released him.

Sweat would darken his hair, trickle down his face, roll onto his chest, saturate the forest of coarse hair and finally stop a his waistline and stain the elastic on his briefs.

He'd flex his biceps by doing a series of arm curls before let ting the free weight hit the floor. Then he'd grimace from th sheer effort of it all and take deep, slow breaths to control hi labored breathing, all the while conscious of the loud musi screeching from the stereo.

Once again he thought it was too damn bad he couldn't pic up one of those bells and work the kinks out of both his min and his body.

Barr and other close friends referred to this sectioned-off pa of the house as Cort's sanctuary. And in a sense they were righ Not only had he entertained countless women on the mattres next to the stereo, but he had exorcised the demons inside hin

But not today. There was nothing that could be said or don that could absorb the confusion, the pain and the anger.

Without thinking about it, he walked back to the windo and once again stared outside into the sunshine. But there w no sunshine in his thoughts; they were blacker than the depth of hell.

He felt like a loose cannonball, and he knew where to strik

A son. He had a son. God, he couldn't believe it, didn't wa to believe it. But he knew it was the truth. Glynis might b many things, but a liar she was not.

Why? he asked himself again. Why hadn't Glynis contacte him when she found out she was pregnant? She had to hav known he'd come back. And how could she have kept Too from him all these years? Well, there was no use crying ov spilled milk, as the old saying went, but one thing was f sure—he would never forgive Glynis for her deception and b trayal.

And to think he had loved her so much, would have given h life for her if he'd had to.

Suddenly, he felt extremely tired. Turning, he made his w toward the mattress and lowered himself down onto it, back against several pillows and stared into the mirror hanging on t wall in front of him. The grooves around his mouth and ey stood out like neon signs where a few years ago he'd had to e

mine his face closely to find them. Scars. His work had put
em there. So had Glynis.

When he probed further, he realized he was not so much tired
s he was exhausted. He felt like a man who had been to war
ith himself—and lost.

He thought about home, about his mother who had died
hen he was a baby, about how his father used to get drunk and
eat him, about how poor they were because the old man
ouldn't hold a steady job.

But most of all he thought about the beautiful blue-eyed boy
ho was his son. He felt a smile soften his lips as he stared at
e patterns created by the sun on the ceiling. But the smile was
ily fleeting as his thoughts centered on Todd's life-threatening
ness. What if he, the father, didn't have what it took to be a
onor? What if the doctors couldn't find a suitable donor?

Just when he'd found his son, there was the possibility that...
o, he wouldn't think like that. If it took every dime he had,
'd use it to save his son's life. Todd would be cured. Cort
ouldn't lose him now.

"Damn you, Glynis, damn you!" he spat aloud. "How
uld you have done this to me?"

Whether she'd believed him or not, he'd planned to come
ck and marry her. He'd told her that, only she hadn't lis-
ned.

He could still remember that fateful day as if it had been
sterday that the bitter words had passed between them. He
d been out of the Army only two weeks, and they had spent
ery waking minute together, much of that making love. He
dn't been able to get enough of her delectable body.

It was after one of those marathon sessions of lovemaking
at he'd told her about his job offer, expecting her to be as
cited about it as he was. They had just returned to her aunt's
use after spending the afternoon on the lake....

"I have something I want to talk to you about," he'd told
r. They had just rid themselves of their picnic gear, plunk-
g it down in the middle of the living room.

Glynis gazed up at him, her golden brown eyes soft and
eamy. "Mmm, and what might that be?"

Grinning broadly, Cort sauntered over and, placing his arm around her, nuzzled her neck, then whispered in her ear, "I go a job."

She pulled back and once again peeked at him from unde long lashes. "A job."

"Yes, my darling, a real job."

"Oh, Cort," she cried, "I'm so glad."

He tweaked her nose, a nose that was slightly sunburned. " knew you would be."

Glynis bit at a finger playfully. "Since I've been assured o a teaching position, and now with your job, we can start to loo] for a house and . . ."

"Whoa, wait a minute," Cort said with a laugh, backing up holding up his hands.

Glynis drew her eyebrows together in a perplexed frown "You don't want a house?"

"Of course I want a house, darling, only not right now." H smiled again, and his tone was teasing. "Hey, don't you thin you're getting ahead of yourself? Don't you think we ought get married before we start shopping for a place to live?" Hi smile broadened into a grin. "Why, what would all these ol biddies around here think if their children's teacher was livin in sin with a man?" He rolled his eyes. "Heaven forbid!"

Glynis punched him playfully in the stomach. "Of cours we'll get married first. That goes without saying. In fact, I wa thinking this weekend would be as good a time as any." Ther was a teasing note in Glynis's tone as well, but her eyes wer serious. "So tell me about your job."

"I think we'd better sit down," Cort said, looking away.

Her eyebrows arched, as if she sensed something was wrong "What's the matter?"

Cort ignored the slight tremor in her voice and instead pr pelled her toward the couch. Once they were seated and facin each other, he said, "Nothing's the matter. Or at least I did think so until now."

"Oh, Cort, you're not making any sense."

"The job I've taken is not here in Lufkin."

She shrugged. "That's no big deal as long as it's with driving distance."

"That's the problem—it's not."

For a moment there was no sound in the room.

Then Glynis asked, "What do you mean?"

She was no longer bothering to hide her panic, and Cort felt his heart constrict. This was going to be much more difficult than he'd thought. He'd had no idea she wouldn't understand....

"Just spit it out, Cort," she was saying.

He expelled a sigh. "You remember Hank Chase, that Army buddy from Houston I wrote you about?" Glynis nodded, and he went on. "Well, his dad recently died and left Hank his small security company."

"So?" Glynis interrupted. "What does that have to do with you?"

"It has everything to do with me."

Glynis's eyes widened incredulously. "Surely that's not the job you've taken."

"Dammit, Glynis, don't look at me like that." Cort lunged to his feet, then stared down at her, his mouth stretched in a grim line. "I'm doing it for both of us. For our future." Suddenly he sat back down and grabbed her hands, folding them into his large, callused ones. "It's a chance of a lifetime for me, or us."

Glynis jerked her hands out of captivity, her face filled with uncertainty. "But that means you won't... can't live in Lufkin." Her chin was beginning to wobble.

A furrow appeared between his eyes. "That's right, but—"

"No, that's not right," Glynis contradicted tightly. "For God's sake, Cort, I've just accepted a job, thinking we were finally going to get... get married and... and settle down."

"We are going to get married and settle down," Cort said patiently, "only not right now."

Glynis's sharp intake of breath was the only sound in the room. "What... are you saying, Cort?"

He moved away from the couch and turned his back. Moments later, when he turned back around, she was standing and watching him as if in a daze.

"Not what you want me to, apparently. Glynis, you're blowing this way out of proportion. Look, this job will enable

us to have a nice house, money in our pockets, a secure fu
ture.''

She set her mouth in a firm line. "I don't care about thos
things.''

He felt something jump in his gut. "You don't mean that."

"Oh, yes I do. All I care about is loving you, marrying you."
Her proclamation ended on a sob.

"Oh, sweetheart . . ." Cort pleaded, closing the distance be
tween them.

"Don't," Glynis cried, just as he was about to haul her int
his arms. "Don't . . . don't touch me.''

"You're being childish," Cort snapped. Then, realizing hi
harsh tone was only making matters worse, he tried a differen
tactic. He tried reasoning. "I thought we felt the same wa
about things. I thought we were in agreement that we don'
want to scrimp and do without like we've always had to all ou
lives.''

"It's you that's always been concerned with money and ma
terial things, Cort, not me.''

He tensed. "You're damn right. I haven't forgotten what i
means to be dirt-poor, to be laughed at because I didn't hav
enough money in my pocket to buy a penny piece of bubbl
gum. But apparently you have.''

"No, I haven't forgotten what it's like." Her eyes hinted a
tears. "Do you think I'll ever forget kids calling me Little Or
phan Annie and making fun of my clothes? Of course not
Those memories are branded into my brain and will never dis
appear. But our past is not the issue here, or rather it's besid
the point, because we wouldn't be dirt-poor, as you put it. I'
have a job, and you could go into the logging business with Ja
and his father.''

Cort's eyes narrowed dangerously. "I've already told you,
have no intention of working for Jay's father.''

"Even knowing how I feel, you won't change your mind?"
she asked dully.

"No, I won't change my mind, not even for you.''

"I see.''

"No, you don't!''

"I see more than you think." She paused and gnawed on her lower lip as if sorting through her thoughts. "Security work. What is that, anyway? What would you do?"

"Everything. Install alarms in people's homes, offer protection for one thing or another, track down missing persons."

"A glorified private detective, is that what you're saying?" His shoulders stiffened. "I guess I am."

"But you aren't qualified for that kind of work."

"I will be once I get my license," he insisted. "Anyway, as you well know, I worked with weapons in the Army. That was my specialty."

Suddenly Glynis placed her hands over her ears and shook her head. "I don't want to hear any more. All this talk of weapons is...crazy. What's happened to you? You're...you're not the same." She shivered. "You've changed."

Cort felt blood rush to his head. "You're wrong about that and you know it. Just because I want us to have a secure future, something better for our children, you accuse me of changing."

She shook her head again. "No, it's more than that. I can't put my finger on it, but it's there."

"Glynis, for God's sake!"

"Are you going ahead with this cockamamy plan?"

He didn't hesitate. "Yes. In fact Hank wants me to go abroad with him on a missing persons case."

Silence filled the room.

"If you go, don't bother to come back." Her words were barely audible.

"You don't mean that," he said roughly, but he knew she did. She had a numbed, desperate look. He longed to hold her close, tell her everything was going to be all right. But he couldn't; he was afraid nothing was ever going to be all right again.

"I mean that with every fiber of my being."

"You mean if I take this job, it's over?"

"That's exactly what I mean."

Cort's anger was barely controllable now. "But why?"

"Because I want a home, children, a husband who comes home to me every night. I want roots. I don't want a man who's more interested in money and adventure than in me."

"Is that your final word?" His gut tightened as if a fist had jabbed him.

"That's my final word."

"Glynis."

"Go away, Cort. Go away and leave me alone."

It was only after he walked out of the house and closed the door behind him that he realized he had tears on his face. But the final blow had come two months later in the form of a letter telling him that she had married Jay Hamilton.

Cort sat upright, and for the longest time he remained perched on the side of the mattress. Then he slowly got to his feet, made his way back to his desk and sat down.

He felt the old, familiar sorrow as he always did when he thought about that terrible time, that terrible year they parted. He'd felt hollow, dead inside, except he'd continued to breathe, to walk, to talk.

It had been only within the past two years that he'd reached a plateau of contentment, if not happiness. And he'd be damned if he was going to let Glynis's unexpected presence change that.

He wouldn't let her get under his skin. Never again would he be vulnerable to a woman. Yet, even as he made this vow, he recalled how it had felt to touch her again, recalled the agony as well as the ecstasy of it. And how she'd looked last night sitting at the dining-room table after Todd had gone to bed, her features fine in the soft light.

Then later, as she'd left the table and walked toward the door, her fragrance wafted around him and the lure of her perfect body had begun to vibrate inside him.

And he could not remember ever seeing a more beautiful woman.

Suddenly a cry tore through his lips as he pounded the desk with a fist. He knew that in spite of what she'd done to him, he still wanted her.

He didn't realize he was no longer alone until he heard a voice say, "What the hell's the matter with you?"

Chapter 6

Cort jerked his head up and around. "Dammit, Barr, you got something against knocking?"

At forty-three, Barr McBride, ten years Cort's senior, strode nonchalantly across the threshold. He was munching on a sweet roll and carrying a cup of coffee, his lips curled in a mocking smile.

He was endowed with the same thick brown hair as his brother, only Barr's was devoid of gray and not nearly as neat. It always needed cutting. His eyes were black and unreadable, hiding scars left by his stint in a Vietcong POW camp. Scars that had deepened when he learned upon release that his fiancée had married someone else.

Barr tried to keep the bitterness under a facade of polite indifference, but at times he was unable to pull it off, especially when a woman got too close to him. He immediately turned cold and hostile, thereby driving her away. He, like Cort, was not interested in ties that bind.

Barr made his money in the horse and cattle business. His ranch, adjoining his brother's, was the main interest in his life. He didn't care about the outside world; as far as he was concerned, it didn't exist.

But even though the brothers were different in temperament and outlook, they were close. In fact Barr had been the only stabilizing force in Cort's youth, and for that Cort felt he owed him.

"My, but aren't we full of good cheer this morning," Barr was saying, his eyes slowly raking over his brother's face. He took another healthy bite out of the roll.

"Didn't get much sleep," Cort snapped, pushing himself up from the desk with his forearms.

"That hole in your gut still bothering you?"

"Yeah, but not the way you mean. It makes me madder than hell when there's so much around the ranch I want to do, plus I can't even lift weights. It's damned inconvenient, that's what it is."

Barr snorted. "The way I see it, you oughta be glad you're still breathing. I don't know whether you realize it, but it was touch and go for a while."

"Believe me, I know. Every time I start to do something, I'm reminded once again that I'm not invincible."

Barr's eyes narrowed. "Well, while we're on the subject, are you any closer to finding out who shot you?"

"No, not as far as I know." Cort released a sigh. "Ridley's been on it hot and heavy, but he's turned up nothing so far. I'm expecting a call from him this morning."

Holding both the roll and the cup in his hand, Barr walked deeper into the room. "So you think it was meant for your client, huh?" He paused, then snapped his free fingers. "What's his name?"

"Boyd Fisher," Cort supplied absently, though his eyes never veered from Barr's. "But you don't."

"Nope, I sure as hell don't," Barr said succinctly. "From what I know of professional killers, they don't make mistakes like that."

Cort's mouth tightened into an exasperated line. "So what are you saying, the bullet was meant for me?"

"It wouldn't be the first time something like that happened."

"I can't argue with that. But in this case you're wrong, big brother, dead wrong." Cort's face was set in hard, impatient lines. "Boyd just got in too deep with his gambling cronies, and someone turned the heavies loose on him, pure and simple."

"Then how do you figure you got the bullet and he didn't?"

"How the hell should I know?" Cort said curtly. "Anyway, that's Ridley's problem. Let him earn that high salary I pay him." He paused and began rubbing the back of his neck with his right hand. "But right now, that's the least of my worries."

Barr was sitting down on the bench next to Cort's desk and had one long leg crossed over the other. Cort came around, hooked a hip on the side of the desk and faced him.

"Kinda figured that," Barr drawled. "Not only do you look like hell, but you're about as tightly wound as a time bomb ready to go off. Something goin' on I need to know about, little brother?"

Cort focused his eyes on the point beyond Barr's shoulder, realizing that having his brother living so close made privacy almost impossible. Barr knew him so well, instinctively knew when something was bothering him. After all, it had been Barr who had comforted him many a night following his father's drunken beatings.

"Glynis is back."

"You mean in Lufkin?" Barr's tone was incredulous.

"That's exactly what I mean."

"Where? I mean where's she staying?"

"Here."

Barr blinked. "Here?"

Cort nodded grimly.

"Dammit, little brother, have you lost your mind?"

Following Barr's stunned rejoinder, both men were silent for a few moments. Barr chewed on the last of his roll while Cort chewed on something much less edible.

"I have my reasons, Barr," Cort said at last. "Give me credit for having a little sense, anyway."

Barr shook his head, reaching down and brushing off a leaf that was stuck to the hem of his jeans on the right leg. "I do, except when it comes to Glynis."

"What do you mean by that?" Cort's voice was oddly flat.

"Don't be an ass. You know what I mean. She had the power to turn you inside out, and you know it."

Cort lurched off the desk and flashed Barr a hard look. "Glad you put that in the past tense, because that's exactly how it is now. What we had between us is long dead and buried."

"Yeah, sure. And I'm going to be the next President of the United States."

"Go to hell."

A smile toyed with Barr's lips. "I'll probably do that, too. Ah, come on, if what you're saying is true, then why the hell is she staying here?"

"She's not alone."

Barr sighed deeply, as if his patience was running out. "So, who's with her?"

"Her...son, who's very sick."

"Sick? I don't get it."

"The kid has leukemia."

"Godalmighty, that's too bad. But I still don't get it. I haven't forgotten, even if you have, how cut up you were when she married Jay and later when that kid was born. Why, you nearly went off the deep end—"

"Give it a rest," Cort ordered tersely.

Suddenly Barr slapped his thigh. "Ah, I get it. She's hitting you up for some money for his treatments. I should've known."

Cort sighed. "That's part of it, true."

"Only part."

"Todd's a prime candidate for a bone marrow transplant...." Cort paused, then, before Barr could respond, he went on. "And the right donor is needed."

"So?"

"So hopefully I'm that donor," Cort said flatly.

"Now, why would you qualify to..." Barr broke off and stared at his brother, his mouth gaping open.

"That's right. The kid's not Jay's. He's mine."

Barr sucked in a short, involuntary breath, as if speech was impossible. He shifted his position on the bench. "Well, I'll be damned, little brother."

"Ditto that," Cort said, grim faced.

"And the kid's got leukemia, huh?"

"Has had for the last two years."

Barr ran a hand over his hair. "Suppose you tell me how you found out all this."

Cort told him in detail. When he finished, the room went silent as the two men sized up the situation, figured out what to say, what *not* to say.

"I hope you know what you're doing," Barr said at last.

Cort averted his gaze and stared out the window, deep in thought. "Me, too, but somehow I doubt I do."

"Well, you didn't have to bring them here."

Cort swung around, his feature drawn. "That's where you're wrong, Barr. I want to get to know my son. If only I'd—"

"But you didn't," Barr interrupted. "There wasn't anything you could have done. I told you that then, and I'm telling you again now. The past never leaves us—it's full of things we'd like to change. But you can't, and neither can I. The past is what it is—history, and nobody can rewrite it. It's dead."

"I'm going to remind you of that the next time you get drunk and start resurrecting your past."

Barr almost smiled. "Sounds good anyway."

"Sure as hell does, only we both know it doesn't work. Some memories just won't die."

Barr stood, looking as though he, too, were in a daze. "When do I get to meet the kid?"

Cort's features relaxed. "Maybe I'll bring him over later."

"Good enough," Barr said, grinning. He then turned and walked toward the outside door. Once there he twisted back around, and there was a deadpan expression on his face. "Please, just tell me the kid doesn't look like you."

"Kiss off."

Barr's deep laugh lingered in the room long after the door closed behind him. But there was no laughter inside Cort as he slumped back into the depths of his chair, ran his hands through his disheveled hair and down his unshaven cheeks and chin.

Glynis stood on a portion of the cedar deck that jutted off her bedroom and breathed in the fresh morning air.

She'd taken a hot shower in the adjoining bathroom and then slipped into a slightly oversized gold cotton blouse, jeans and a pair of multicolored sandals.

Thank goodness the hot, stinging water had helped soothe her frayed nerves. However, it was only after she'd finished applying her makeup and running a comb through her thick hair that she felt as though she could face the day. More important, she'd felt able to face Cort.

In the distance, at the edge of the woods, she could see two squirrels chasing each other, their tails flipping faster than she could blink an eye.

As she watched, fascinated by the way the animals scampered from one tree to another, a small smile softened her lips. She wished Todd could see them; he would think they were "neat." Her smile widened to display a set of even white teeth.

Suddenly thinking she heard her son's footsteps, she swung around. "Todd?" she said, craning her neck.

The room behind her was empty. She shrugged, not surprised that she was hearing things. Nor was she surprised that Todd was still asleep. Yesterday had been a long day for him; he'd been exhausted when she'd put him to bed last night long past his bedtime.

But it had been a long day for her as well. That emotional scene when Cort had met his son for the first time had left her totally drained. And the following few hours had brought no relief.

By the time Cort and Todd had returned from taking a quick tour of the barn, she had made her way into the house and straight into the arms of the housekeeper, Maude Springer. Maude had known she and Todd were coming, of course, and had welcomed her enthusiastically, her twinkling gray eyes a suitable backdrop for a naturally sweet grin.

Chatting nonstop, Maude had taken her through a large living room with a stone fireplace and oak floor. Glynis's heels had echoed as she'd walked by the wall of glass that faced the luscious green pastureland and the woods beyond.

When she had finally reached the two guest bedrooms joined by a door, she had realized just how successful Cort had become and just how far removed he was from her.

Later it had taken every ounce of her fortitude to get through the short, tense dinner that followed. Though Todd had been worn out, he'd wanted to eat at the table with them, and she had let him, purely for selfish reasons. She hadn't wanted to be alone with Cort.

But she had worried needlessly. For the most part, Cort had ignored her. Yet she had been aware of him with every beat of her heart, especially when he'd walked into the room, looking and smelling like he'd just stepped out of the shower. His hair had been still damp, and his cologne had sent her pulse racing.

After answering several polite inquiries as to her comfort, Glynis had made it a point not to glance in his direction for fear of seeing nothing but cold hostility mirrored there.

Todd had been a different matter altogether. Cort had many things to say to his son and plenty of smiles. Then, as soon as Maude served the berry pie, Cort had patted Todd on the shoulder and bid him goodnight, citing work in his office as his excuse for leaving.

Glynis had been relieved that the ordeal was over, having had no idea what to expect from Cort. And now as she filled her lungs one last time with the intoxicating morning air, she turned and walked back into her room, realizing that she still didn't. All she knew was that she faced the first of many days on Cort's turf with him laying down the rules.

"Mommy, where are you?"

"Right here, darling."

Glynis took another deep breath and pushed a strand of breeze-tossed hair behind her ear, wondering if the nightmare would ever end.

"Long time no see, Glynis."

At the sound of the deep masculine voice, both Glynis and Todd looked up, startled. They were sitting at the wicker glass-topped table in the breakfast room, watching a black stallion prance around the paddock.

Maude was in the kitchen, busily and happily preparing breakfast. The smell of bacon crackling in the skillet filled the air with a delicious aroma.

"Hello, Barr," Glynis said, standing, a smile lighting her features. Even though he was years older, Barr had always held a special place in her heart, mainly because he'd been so good to Cort.

"Ah, surely you can do better than that." He smiled, a smile she knew did not come easily. "I'll settle for a small hug."

Glynis laughed and dived into Barr's outstretched arms. Following a crushing hug, he pushed her away and peered down at her from his towering six-foot-three height.

"You haven't changed—you're still as beautiful as ever."

"Ha, you haven't changed either. You're still as full of it as ever."

But he had changed. Like Cort, the shadows that lurked around his eyes were more pronounced. But then she had always known that would never go away, that he'd never escape memories of the untold horrors he'd experienced in Nam. And though he'd never had any permanent use for the opposite sex, for her there had always been warm words and hugs. Today was no exception.

Barr laughed, then switched his gaze to Todd, who was staring up at him with his mouth open. "You must be Todd," he said, walking over and holding out his hand.

Todd hesitantly placed his small one in Barr's large one. "Who are you?"

"Why, big fella, I'm your Uncle Barr."

With a puzzled frown on his face, Todd faced Glynis. "You mean he's my uncle, too?"

Glynis nodded. "That's right. He's...Uncle Cort's brother." She couldn't bring herself to look at Barr. "So you'll be seeing quite a lot of him while we're here," she rushed to add.

"That's right," Barr responded. "I own the ranch next to your...Uncle Cort."

Todd's eyes were round. "Do you have horses and cows, too?"

"Bigger and better the ones here."

Again Todd's eyes sought his mother. "Really Mom? Does he really?"

Glynis's lips twitched, and she shrugged. "Don't ask me."

"Can I come see 'em?" Tod asked, returning his gaze to Barr.

"Anytime you like."

"Gee, Mom, did you hear that?"

"Yes, son, I heard that."

Suddenly Maude came into the room, carrying a steaming bowl of eggs and a plate of bacon. "Mr. Barr, you want some breakfast?"

"Now, Maude, when have you known me to turn down anything you cooked?" He massaged his flat stomach and grinned. "Without you, I'd starve to death."

Maude snorted before turning to Glynis. "The biscuits will be out of the oven shortly, Mrs. Hamilton."

"Please, Maude, call me Glynis."

The housekeeper looked momentarily disconcerted, then smiled. "All right, Glynis. How about some more coffee?"

Glynis glanced down at her empty cup and said, "I'd love some."

The minute Maude left, Glynis picked up Todd's plate and began filling it with the food.

"Aw, Mom, do I have to? I'm not hungry."

"Yes, you have to," she said sternly. "If you want to play outside today, you have to eat."

He sighed. "Okay."

"Your mom's right, son. If you plan to keep up with your Uncle Cort and me, you'd best clean your plate."

"Does that mean I can ride a horse?"

"We'll see," Glynis said, reaching for the cup of fresh coffee Maude had left on the table along with the pan of biscuits.

"Well, well, what have we here? Can anyone join the party?"

The low, rough voice came from directly behind Glynis. Her hand stilled, but her head jerked around almost of its own volition.

Cort was standing just inside the doorway.

Chapter 7

Glynis gripped her coffee cup with icy fingers and for a long moment the room was quiet.

She swept her gaze over him, taking in the faded blue cotton shirt unbuttoned to the coolness of the spring morning. Equally worn jeans hugged slim hips and long legs. Only when she reached his boots, dirty and scuffed with use, did she stop.

Cort moved then, drawing her gaze back to his. He completely unnerved her. Half the time she wanted to disappear when he came anywhere near, and half the time she couldn't resist the urge to needle him into noticing her.

He was scowling now, looking as if he'd bitten into something sour. Then he moved forward, the firm cadence of his boots on the tile effectively breaking the silence.

"Where you been, little brother?" Barr's tone was deep and easy, as if he was oblivious to the tension in the room.

"Working," Cort said gruffly, "the same thing you should've been doing."

Barr raised his eyebrows. "Mmm, I see our disposition hasn't improved."

"My disposition is none of your business."

Both Glynis's and Todd's eyes vacillated between brothers, Todd's wide and confused, Glynis's wide and troubled. For the time being, she knew Cort was taking his anger out on his brother. But she knew that wouldn't last. If Todd hadn't been present, he would more than likely have lashed out at her.

If punishing her was what he wanted, then so be it. She could take whatever he dished out, as long as he helped their son.

"You still want me to come over and look at those cattle?" Cort was saying now, his tone minus the bite of a moment ago.

Barr crossed a booted foot over the opposite leg. "Sure do. In fact I'm counting on it."

While the men continued to exchange words, Glynis lowered her head and forced herself to take several bites of the bacon and eggs she'd put on her plate out of politeness rather than hunger. She hated the reactions Cort stirred in her, loss of appetite being one of them.

Suddenly she felt Cort's gaze swing back to her. At the same time Barr shoved back his chair and got to his feet.

"Glynis, I'd like to take Todd with me," Cort was saying. He twisted his mouth into a cold smile that matched the glacial color of his eyes. "That is, if you don't mind."

A frown crossed her face. "As a matter of fact, I . . ."

Barr chose that moment to cut in. "Hey, gang, I gotta be going." Then, turning to Todd, he added with an uncharacteristic wink, "I'll see you later, Todd."

"Oh, boy," Todd answered enthusiastically, just after he'd put a large forkful of eggs in his mouth.

"Don't talk with your mouth full," Glynis chastised softly.

"See y'all later," Barr announced, but only after he'd whispered something in Maude's ear that brought the color flooding to her face.

The minute the door shut behind him, Maude, whose color was still high, focused her attention on Cort. "Do you want to eat again? I'll be glad to warm the biscuits and eggs in the microwave."

Cort waved his hand, all the while staring at Glynis. "Thanks, Maude, but no thanks. I'm fine."

"How about you, Glynis? Do you care for anything else?"

Trying her best to ignore Cort's hostile gaze, Glynis smiled. "Heavens no, Maude. It was delicious, but I'm not used to eating much for breakfast. Todd and I both ate more than we're accustomed to."

"And it shows," Cort put in harshly, "especially on you. You never used to be as skinny as you are now."

"I never used to be a lot of things I am now," Glynis countered sharply, feeling the spark of battle ignite inside her. But then, when she saw Todd's reaction to her sharp tone, she forced another smile to hide the antagonism Cort aroused. Her son's face went pale, and he frowned up at her.

"Mom, are you mad at Uncle Cort?"

Glynis felt herself flush and hated it. "No, of course not."

Cort didn't say a word. He simply stood there with a smirk on his lips, as if he enjoyed her agitation and discomfort.

"Todd, honey, if you're through, why don't you run along and brush your teeth and change your shoes. Put on your old dirty ones."

"Then can we go see Uncle Barr?" he asked anxiously, directing his questions to Cort. "He told me his cows and horses were better than yours."

"Oh, he did, did he?" The corners of Cort's lips were twitching. "Well, just so you'll know, Barr likes to tease."

"Oh," was all Todd had to say.

His eyes still on the boy, Cort added, "How 'bout if I show you around the Lazy C, you and your mom? Anyway, I have something I want you to see."

"Neato," Todd gushed, scooting out of his chair and running toward the door that led to the hall.

"Hey, slow down, will you," Glynis called to his retreating back.

When she twisted back around, she sought out Cort's gaze. "Did you mean it when you included me?"

Cort had sat down and was leaning back in the chair, his strong, rugged features fully illuminated by the sun's powerful rays pouring through the blinds.

"What makes you think I didn't mean it?"

The unwavering study of his light-colored eyes and the soft mocking tone in which he spoke made Glynis vividly aware o the primitive charm he used to full advantage. Her heartbeat accelerated briefly, telling her to beware.

Pulling herself together in the nick of time, she dipped her head and took a sip of cold coffee, which nearly gagged her. Then, lifting her head once again, she forced her eyes to meet his.

"Because we both know you don't want me here, that's why," she said, her voice low and oddly breathless. "And why you insisted—"

"You know why I insisted." He ground his teeth together in anger. "You're right, I don't want you here. But I want my son, so..."

"If I'm part of the package deal, you'll just have to find a way to tolerate me, right?"

"Right."

Glynis stood up, her hands clenched by her side, and for another full second, speech was denied her. Finally she managed a jerky laugh. "You've turned into a real bastard," she spat.

"I had a good teacher. I..."

"Mr. Cort," Maude interrupted, standing at his elbow, obviously embarrassed if one was to judge from the heightened color in her round face, "you're wanted on the phone. It's... Mr. Ridley."

"Tell him I'll call him back," Cort replied brusquely, his gaze still holding firm on Glynis.

Maude merely nodded and then shuffled through the archway into the kitchen.

Glynis smiled coldly. "Look, since you have to work, Todd and I'll occupy ourselves."

"No."

Glynis blinked. "No?"

"I don't have to work. We'll take the tour together. Anyway, in light of Todd's reaction to our exchange of words, I think we need to put his mind at ease about... us."

"Does that mean you're willing to call a truce?"

He studied her as the uncomfortable silence stretched out. "Maybe."

Swallowing the angry retort that rose to her lips, Glynis spun around and flung over her shoulder, "As soon as I change shoes, I'll meet you outside."

Cort stood and watched until Glynis was out of sight. With a muttered curse, he strode down the opposite hall and into his office where he shut the door with a resounding thud.

He must have been out of his mind to think he could share the same space with Glynis and not let her get under his skin.

Even the way she dressed rubbed him the wrong way. Or was it because she looked so damn good in what she wore that his blood pressure had risen above the danger level? In that gold blouse the outline of her breasts had been as visible as yesterday when he'd run his palm across a hard, tight nipple. And then, the same as now, every nerve in his body had sizzled to life.

If that weren't enough, she'd looked at him with those big brown eyes filled with a shadowed pain, pain he knew hadn't come merely from her verbal skirmish with him. No, it was the pain of seeing her child suffer with a killing disease. As before, he'd found himself wanting to yank her into his arms, crush her against him and tell her that everything was going to be all right.

But he couldn't touch her. Not again. Nor could he let her vulnerability affect his feelings. She had done him a grave injustice, and he must not forget that.

He sighed, recalling how amazed he'd been that a girl of her age could have wielded so much power over him.

Well, all that was in the past. No woman would ever again get her claws into him that deep.

Cort turned his head toward the bar in the far corner of the room and wished it wasn't too early for a stiff drink. A strong shot of Scotch might have soothed his nerves, stamped out that catastrophic desire for revenge that was tearing him apart.

He was so lost in thought that at first he couldn't identify the sound. Then it became glaringly clear. It was the phone, the private line in his office. Knowing that it would be his assistant in Houston, he muttered a sharp curse and reached across the desk for the receiver.

"McBride."

"Got a minute?" Gene Ridley asked.

"Shoot."

"Well, first off, I guess I ought to ask how you're feeling."

"Like hell."

Gene laughed, and Cort pictured his able assistant's face. He was more than likely slumped over the desk, leaning on his elbows, his eyebrows furrowed in concentration.

"I wish I could tell you something to ease your pain," Gene said, breaking into the short silence.

"Nothing yet on who's after Fisher?"

"Oh, I have a hunch, all right, but nothing concrete."

"How's Fisher?"

"A basket case, even though we've got men watching his house twenty-four hours a day."

"Maybe that'll teach him to stay out of the big leagues."

Gene gave an uncharacteristic snort. "I doubt that."

"Me, too," Cort said, grinning into the receiver. "It'll probably take another attempt on his life to make a true believer out of him."

"Oh, I don't know so much about that. He's pretty shook up. He came by the office twice yesterday, determined to talk to you. Said he hired you"—Gene stressed the you "—personally and that he wasn't happy that you had pulled a disappearing act."

"Why, that selfish SOB. Here I took the bullet that was meant for him and he's the one doing the bellyaching."

"Hope you don't mind, but I told him as much, and I also told him to back off and let McBride Security do its job."

"That's fine by me. Just go with your hunch. Something's bound to turn up."

"Will do."

"We both know it's a sure thing that whoever's after him will surface again, especially since Fisher can't come up with the money to pay off his debt."

"And next time they won't get the wrong person."

"Well, let's just make sure there's not a next time. I want the bastard who put that bullet in my gut."

"That goes without saying, boss."

They were both quiet for a second, both listening to the static crackling between the lines.

Then, changing the subject, Gene asked, "Has the doctor by any chance told you how much longer you're going to be out of commission?"

"Hell, no."

Gene laughed again. "I bet you could bite a tenpenny nail in two by now."

Cort chose his next words carefully. "You got that right. However, something's come up that's shed a new light on things."

"Personal, I take it."

"Very," Cort said, and then told him about Glynis and Todd.

There was a short silence.

"Damn, Cort. I mean that's heavy stuff. A son. God."

"I know. I'm still finding it hard to believe. All of it."

"Yeah, and the leukemia. That's bad."

Cort winced. "But he's going to make it," he said, a determined ring to his voice. "He'll have the very best money can buy."

"If there's anything I can do, just say the word."

"For now, see that you keep the business running on smooth wheels."

"No problem, there, especially since we've got the inside track on the government contract."

"That's good news. You know I want that contract about as bad as I've ever wanted anything."

"Yeah, it would be a challenge, wouldn't it, boss? Debugging an American embassy in a communist country doesn't come along every day."

"Nor does following it up with a new security system."

Gene's deep sigh filtered through the line. "Sounds awesome when you think about it. But I know the firm can handle it."

"I agree. So now all we have to do is get the bid. And here I am, can't do a damn thing to help. Some days just pushing a pencil tires me out."

"Hey, look on the bright side. A man who wasn't in your physical condition to begin with would probably be dead by now."

"That's comforting to know."

Gene chuckled, picking up immediately on the sarcasm in Cort's voice. "I'll be in touch in a day or so."

"Talk to you later, then."

"Oh, Cort, I...er...think it's great about...your kid. I mean that you have...one."

Cort put down the receiver and faced the back window. He stood watching the leaves sway in the gentle breeze until another vision filled his eyes.

Glynis rounded the corner of the house and was smiling down at her son scampering beside her. The sun bathed them both in its warm glow, casting an almost enchanted spell over mother and son. For a moment he was mesmerized, compassion stirring within him.

"You're a fool, Cort McBride."

Then, pivoting on the heel of his boots, Cort stamped toward the door, but not before another expletive singed the air.

Glynis saw Cort coming toward her and stopped. His jerky gait alerted her to his mood, and her heart sank. She was hoping they could indeed call a truce for she truly didn't know how much longer she could handle Cort's volatile behavior.

Now, as they had done so often since her arrival at the ranch, his eyes sliced over her as he fell in step beside her, matching his stride to hers.

Glynis tensed, reacting to the gut instinct that warned her to tread lightly.

"Good morning again," she said, forcing an end to the growing silence.

"Is it?" His voice was low and cynical.

A knot twisted in her stomach while her lashes fluttered, forming a dark fringe above deepening brown eyes. "Cort, I...I thought..."

"Hi, Uncle Cort," Todd interrupted, dashing over to Cort's side, bestowing on him his toothless grin.

Cort purposefully slowed even more, matching Todd's grin. "Hi, yourself. Did you sleep okay last night?"

"Guess so."

"Good."

"Did you?" Todd asked with unchildlike candor.

Cort chuckled and simply shook his head. "Smart kid," he said turning to Glynis with the smile still intact.

"He is, isn't he," Glynis agreed weakly, suddenly finding her control being stripped away by his unexpected smile. For an instant the hostility faded. In its place was something more dangerous. Glynis had glimpsed the Cort of old. Suddenly she swallowed and turned away.

"You promised to show me something," Todd was saying to Cort. "'Member?"

"Sure, I remember," Cort said, his voice sounding raw. "In fact we're headed there now."

The barn was directly in front of them. Glynis presumed it was their ultimate destination but she was in no hurry to enter the barn's interior. It was lovely outside in the bright sunshine.

No doubt about it, the Lazy C was a showplace. And in spite of everything, she couldn't help but feel proud of Cort for beating the odds and making good. But she shouldn't have been surprised, she reminded herself; when Cort made up his mind about something, he went after it with a vengeance. That was precisely what scared her. If he ever made up his mind to take Todd . . .

Her son tugged on her hand. "Mom, we're here. Uncle Cort said the surprise is in there, but he won't tell me what it is."

Glynis touched Todd's cheek briefly with the back of her hand. "Well, if you know in advance, it won't be a surprise, right?"

Todd wrinkled his nose.

"Come on, young fella," Cort urged, pointing Todd toward the entrance.

Inside the barn was cool and much lighter than Glynis had anticipated. She stopped and folded her arms across her chest.

"Cold?"

Unwittingly Glynis encountered Cort's mocking expression. "No, I just wasn't expecting it to be this cool, that's all," she said defensively, though she ached to slap the smirk off his face.

"Show me! Show me the surprise," Todd called from in front of them.

Cort turned his gaze from Glynis and upped his pace. "Hold your horses. I'm coming."

Determined not to be left out, Glynis quickened her steps behind Cort, only to pull up short. Cort had already come to a halt and was kneeling to her right along with Todd. All eyes were on a cardboard box with what looked like an old feed sack draped over the top.

"What's under there?" Todd asked in a hushed tone.

Without answering, Cort slowly and carefully lifted the covering off the box. A white mother cat was lying prone, and several tiny kittens were suckling at her breasts, kittens that reminded Glynis of tiny rats.

"Wow!" Todd whispered.

Glynis met Cort's eyes over Todd's bent head. And once again an electric current seemed to flow between them. Cort was the first to break the contact with a cough.

"They're something, aren't they?" he said to Todd.

Glynis's lashes dropped in confusion. However, before she could even think about deciphering the strange light she'd seen in Cort's eyes, Todd said, "Mom, are you looking?"

"I'm looking, son, I'm looking."

No one said a word for the longest time, each content to watch.

Finally Glynis forced herself to look at Cort again. "Can I talk to you a minute?"

Though he looked puzzled, he shrugged and got to his feet.

"Todd, honey," Glynis said, "you stay here with the kittens while I talk to Uncle Cort. But just look—don't touch them."

"Okay."

Glynis followed Cort to the end of the barn and into the sunlight. Once there, she came straight to the point.

"Before we came to meet you, I had a call from Dr. Johns."

Cort's eyes darkened. "Todd's doctor," he guessed quietly.

"Yes." She paused and took a deep breath, her face chalk white.

"So what did he say?" Cort prompted.

"Day after tomorrow you're scheduled to have your bone marrow tested to see if you qualify as a donor."

Chapter 8

Glynis sat with hands clasped tightly together in her lap and stared at Dr. Eric Johns, her eyes so large they seemed to take up her whole face.

She and Cort had only moments before arrived at the Texas Children's Hospital and were now enclosed in the doctor's office along with two other physicians. Hammond Peavy and Burt Dupree were oncologists, the best in their field, or so Dr. Johns had said.

Following introductions, Cort had politely declined to sit and was standing to one side of Glynis, looking like a stranger in gray slacks, navy blazer and light gray ribbed shirt. He had all the markings of a highly successful business executive, Glynis thought, instead of a man who preferred the rugged outdoors.

After leaving an excited Todd in Barr's capable hands a few minutes after seven that morning, they had made the two-hour trip almost in silence. Cort had sat rigidly behind the wheel of his Jaguar and concentrated on the road, while Glynis had stared out the window with little interest in the scenery.

It was bad enough, Glynis had told herself, that they were both nervous about the test results, without having to endure the tension that filled the air.

But there had always been tension between them. The first time she met him, she had felt it and so had he. But it had been years later before Cort had actually put those feelings into words.

"Some relationships are chemical, but ours is electric," he'd said.

And he'd been right. Still, it rankled. She didn't want to feel anything for Cort. All she wanted was for her son to get well. Then she could get on with her life, a life that did not include Cort McBride.

Now, as Dr. Johns's gaze included them both, Glynis tried to pretend that she was in control, that her bloodstream wasn't filled with ice.

"Mr. McBride," Dr. Johns began, "I felt you needed to be brought up to date on exactly what's involved for both you and Todd. And of course to answer any questions you might have before we send you to the lab for the test."

"I assume it's a blood test," Cort said, looking as if he was still sizing up the doctor.

"You assume correctly," the doctor responded. "As soon as we're finished here, someone will accompany you to the lab and they'll take blood from a vein in your arm, providing you followed the instructions I gave Glynis over the phone."

"To the letter. I've had nothing to eat or drink, not even coffee, since before twelve last evening."

"Good. Now that that's settled, we can move on."

"Please," Glynis cut in anxiously, "how . . . how long will it be before we know the results of the test?" Although she spoke directly to Eric Johns, her eyes encompassed the other two doctors.

It was Johns who answered her, his expression kind and his tone gentle. "Two or three hours at the most. During that time I'm sure Mr. McBride would like something to eat. Maybe by the time he's done, we'll know."

Glynis nodded her thanks, though she wanted to shout her relief that they wouldn't have to wait overnight. Stealing a quick glance in Cort's direction, she noticed that he, too, seemed visibly relieved. His features were no longer quite as taut and forbidding.

"What exactly will the test tell us?" Cort was asking.

"Your blood antigens must match those of your son, Mr. McBride."

"Perfectly?"

Shaking his head, Dr. Peavy spoke for the first time. "No, although it would be great if they did."

"But if they don't?" Cort pressed, focusing his entire attention on the broad-faced doctor with thinning blond hair.

"Then we'll still be able to use you, as long as all your antibodies don't cross with your son's."

Cort shoved a hand into his pocket. "So if it's a go, what exactly will take place?"

Dr. Johns turned to his right. "Why don't you answer that, Dr. Dupree? After all, you'll be doing the transplant."

Burt Dupree had dark hair and dark eyes and was not more than five-foot-seven in height. But that was hardly noticeable as his muscles were honed to perfection, making him appear much bigger than he actually was. He was young and seemed confident of his ability.

"If you are our donor, Mr. McBride, and we'll keep the faith that you will be," Dr. Dupree said with confidence, stepping from the window to Dr. Johns's desk, where he perched on the edge of it, "you'll be taken to surgery along with your son."

Cort placed his hand on the back of Glynis's chair. "Go on, doctor."

"We'll be concentrating on the pelvic area, where there is an abundance of bone marrow."

"Will I be under anesthetic?"

"Yes, but not for long." He paused a moment before continuing, as if to let Glynis as well as Cort digest what he was saying. "Then I'll insert needles into that soft area and extract the tissue."

"How . . . many times will you . . . stick him?" Glynis asked, a lump forming in her throat.

"Approximately two hundred."

Glynis sucked in her breath.

Cort merely asked in a calm voice, "What else?"

But Glynis sensed he was anything but calm. She could hear his breath rattling in his chest, and a muscle pulsed in his jaw. Suddenly she felt a twinge of sympathy she didn't want to feel.

"That's all." Dr. Dupree inclined his head. "The entire procedure will take approximately two to three hours."

"And Todd?" Glynis asked, feeling Cort's brooding gaze swing to her. She kept her eyes averted.

Dr. Dupree's face filled with regret. "I wish I could tell you the boy will have it as easy, but I'm afraid I cannot."

"You mean he'll be in a lot of pain?" Glynis asked tremulously.

"No, he'll be sick to his stomach, just as he was when he took those massive doses of chemotherapy in the early stages of the disease," Dr. Dupree explained. "A few days before we do the actual transplant, we'll give him higher doses of radiation and chemo in order to wipe out his bone marrow."

"Oh, God," Glynis whispered, turning her tormented face up to Cort, who had moved closer to her. For an instant she thought he was going to touch her.

"Take it easy," he said instead, staring at her intently while he dropped his arm limply back to his side.

Then Cort dragged his eyes away and looked at Dr. Dupree. "Then what?" he asked, not bothering to hide his own pain.

"Well, once he's free of his own marrow, we'll insert yours intravenously into his right arm."

"And pray," Glynis added under her breath.

Dr. Dupree went on as if she hadn't spoken. "He'll have to be isolated, of course."

Cort frowned. "Isolated?"

"Placed in a sterile environment to prevent him from being infected. Do you remember the youngster called 'David the bubble boy' who was quarantined for years in a sterile bubble? Well, that's the same procedure we'll use with Todd."

"How long before we know if my marrow takes?" Cort's mouth was thin.

Dr. Dupree stood. "The white blood cells should start reproducing within a week. As for the red cells, they sometimes take up to a hundred and twenty days. And during that time he might need some transfusions."

"God Almighty," Cort muttered, glancing sideways at Glynis, his features pale and grim.

But Glynis could offer no comfort. She couldn't stand the thought of Todd having to endure any more pain. It just wasn't fair. In his young life he had already endured more than his fair share, more than any human ought to have to withstand during an entire lifetime. The thought of him suffering again from the poisons in the radiation and chemotherapy made her want to run screaming from the room, even if the means justified the end.

As if able to read Glynis's thoughts, Eric Johns made his way to her side and patted her shoulder. "I know how upset you are, my dear, but remember the outcome can buy your son a lifetime of good health. And without the transplant..." He paused and shook his head.

"I know," Glynis said, feeling the sting of hot tears behind her lashes, "the leukemia will return."

Cort let out his pent-up breath. "How can you know that for sure?"

"Nothing is for sure, of course, Mr. McBride," Dupree said. "However, with the type of leukemia your son has, the chance of it recurring if he doesn't have a transplant is in the ninety-percent range. And that's based on statistics."

"What about rejection?" Glynis asked, rising to her feet, her face a study in misery. "What if he rejects Cort's marrow? Will . . . will my son die?"

That last question alone was heartbreaking, and for a moment no one said a word.

Then Cort spoke, his voice toneless. "Well, doctor, aren't you going to answer her question?"

"The possibility of rejection is there," Dr. Dupree said, by-passing the question of death. "We all know that. But there are drugs that we'll give Todd to try to prevent it, and in the past, the drugs have done their job in most cases."

"That's some comfort anyway," Glynis said from her position by the window, her eyes straying to Cort. His lips were set in a taut line, and an artery pulsed in his temple. For a crazy second she longed to go to him and beg him to take her in his arms, hold her, comfort her as he'd done so often in the past.

But that was then and this was now. And everything had changed.

"There will be several factors to consider before we can proceed, however," Dr. Dupree was saying, his gaze shifting back and forth between Glynis and Cort. "One in particular."

For an instant Glynis just stared at the ceiling. Then in a voice that was barely discernible, she asked, "What?"

Dupree thrust a hand over his thick hair. "Mr. McBride's physical condition."

The words caught Glynis by surprise, though she should have been prepared. Hadn't Cort warned her?

However, before she could say anything, Cort asked, "You're referring to my gunshot wound?" His words were clipped.

"Yes, I am." The doctor spoke quietly.

"It's going to delay it, isn't it?" Glynis's tone was flat.

"Now, Glynis," Dr. Johns put in calmly, "don't get upset. Dr. Dupree is merely pointing out what could happen. We have to cover all the bases. We'll know more, of course, when we get the result of Mr. McBride's blood test."

"What you're saying, doctor, is my blood loss could be a factor in how soon the transplant takes place?"

"Yes, for the simple reason that your hemoglobin count could be low. And the blood transfusions you've had could also be a factor. Two or three weeks won't make any difference," he went on to reassure them, "or at least we hope not. But under the circumstances there's nothing we can do about it."

"I don't understand," Glynis cried, struggling in confusion and shock. "Why would Cort having had a transfusion make a difference?"

"Because," Dr. Dupree said with gentle patience, "it goes back to the antibodies I just mentioned. They'll be foreign and therefore subject to rejection by both father and son."

Glynis glared at Cort, her face bloodless, her lips so stiff she could barely speak. "Oh, God," she whimpered. Then, on legs threatening to cave beneath her, she crossed back to her chair and sank down weakly into it, all the while wanting to lash out at Cort. Once again his eagerness for danger and adventure had become a source of heartache. This time he had inadvertently put his son's life in danger. Damn him.

"Let's just get the test over and done with," Cort said tightly, completely ignoring Glynis.

Dr. Johns punched a button on his intercom. "Anne, please show Mr. McBride to the lab."

Glynis watched Cort as he crossed the room to the door, but when he turned around, she lowered her head. It was only after she heard the door close that she looked up, squeezing her eyelids shut to hold back the tears.

When you wanted time to pass quickly, it never failed to move at a snail's pace, or so Glynis told herself, standing at the window in Dr. Johns's office, her back to Cort. But then, playing the waiting game was never easy.

Cort had gone to the lab and had gotten his test, and as soon as he'd finished, Glynis had met him outside the lab and they had gone to the cafeteria. But neither had eaten much. Although Glynis had chosen chicken salad, which looked palatable enough, and a glass of iced tea, she barely touched it.

Cort, too, had been uninterested in food, taking only several bites of his turkey sandwich, before all but throwing it down on his plate.

After that, they had sat in silence and avoided each other's eyes.

Glynis had known she was being unreasonable to blame Cort, if indeed the transplant had to be postponed. But it was the principle of the matter, she'd told herself. If he'd had a normal job like most men, they wouldn't be in this predicament.

Yet regardless of the unrealistic blame she'd placed squarely on his shoulders and regardless of the contempt she had seen in his eyes, she'd been aware of his menacing strength beside her.

The atmosphere between them had not improved after they had left the cafeteria and trudged heavyhearted back to the doctor's office, where they were now waiting for the result of the test with mounting impatience.

"Everything's going to work out all right," Cort said suddenly, unexpectedly, having stopped his pacing in the middle of the room. His gaze was fixed on Glynis.

"I wish I could be that sure." Her voice sounded strangled.

"It's a cheap shot to blame me, you know."

She didn't pretend to misunderstand him. "Maybe, but that's the way I feel."

"You're determined to exact your pound of flesh, aren't you?"

There was a moment of charged silence as Glynis fought to control her pounding heart. Then, before she could say anything, the door opened, admitting both doctors.

"Well, doctor, what's the verdict?" Cort asked, hardly breathing, hardly moving.

The recessed fluorescent tube in the ceiling flickered. No one paid it the slightest attention.

Dr. Johns smiled. "For reasons we explained to you, Mr. McBride, there will definitely be a postponement. But as far as a match is concerned, you are perfect."

Chapter 9

"Where's Todd?"

Glynis was sitting at the kitchen table, coffee cup in hand, staring into space when she heard the low, brusque voice.

Twisting around, she watched as Cort sauntered into the room, his jeans riding low on his hips. She looked up quickly and was shocked at his appearance. Lines of fatigue were etched deeply about the corners of his bloodshot eyes. And he looked as if he hadn't slept in a week.

But then neither had she. After they had returned from Houston and picked up Todd at Barr's, she had been exhausted, as much from the strain of being in such close contact with Cort as from meeting with the doctors.

Once they had arrived at the ranch, Cort had disappeared in his office, leaving her and Todd to their own devices, which had been fine by her.

Maude had prepared their dinner, and after they had eaten and watched an hour of TV, Glynis had put Todd to bed. A short time later she'd crawled between the covers herself. But again sleep had eluded her, her thoughts centered on the many reasons why she should leave the Lazy C.

The situation was impossible, threatening to become more so by the day. For the moment, however, Cort had the upper hand, and she had no choice but to try to make the best of it.

Cort made his way to the coffeepot and began generously filling a cup. Without turning around, he repeated, "Where's Todd?"

"Sleeping," Glynis said to his back, observing the way his shoulder muscles rippled with each move he made. Abruptly she turned away, irritated with herself for noticing anything personal about him.

Cort faced her. "At this hour?"

"It's only eight o'clock, Cort," Glynis said with controlled patience. "Anyway, he's used to sleeping late, especially after he got sick," she added in defense of her son, sensing that Cort was being critical. "When he's well enough to enter school, he'll have to be up before seven. That time will come faster than we think—I hope."

Cort didn't say anything for a moment, merely drained the bottom out of his cup.

"Why?" Glynis finally asked. "Did you want him for something?"

"As a matter of fact I did."

"Oh." She let out a breath slowly and nodded. They were behaving like polite strangers instead of one-time lovers who had reveled in the touch and feel of each other.

"Thought I'd take him with me and Barr to look at some horses."

Glynis frowned, and at the same time ran her hand through her silky mane, all the while feeling Cort's eyes track her every move.

"I don't know," she said, shifting in her chair.

He let out an impatient sigh. "What do you mean you don't know?"

Glynis rolled her tongue across her top lip. "Well, I'd planned to go into town to visit Milly and let Todd play with her twins."

"Spare me the excuses." He batted the air in disgust. "You just can't stand the thought of me being alone with my son, can you?"

Glynis looked at Cort a second longer than necessary and then got up and walked to the coffeepot, careful to avoid contact with him.

"Answer me!" Cort demanded once she'd refilled her cup.

Glynis let out a rush of air. "That's not true," she said.

"Prove it, then." His tone was soft, too soft.

"All right," she snapped, "take him with you."

He uttered a muffled oath and slammed his cup down on the counter. Glynis jumped, and their gazes collided.

"And that's not all," he said.

Her heart lurched. "What do you mean?"

"Later this evening I want to take him to the carnival that's out at the VFW grounds."

Glynis dug her fingernails into her palms. "I don't know…"

"Damn, here we go again." Clearly exasperated, he stared at the ceiling, a vein in his jaw pulsing. "What's wrong with him going to the carnival?"

Outside the birds chirped in the huge oak tree nearest the house, but neither Cort nor Glynis was aware of the uplifting sound.

Glynis thought desperately. "It's just that carnivals scare me. I'm afraid of the rides…." Again she let her voice trail off.

"I expect you to come along, if that's any consolation."

She flushed at the sarcasm in his tone, but hers was as crisp as ever. "My being there still doesn't alleviate the problem of Todd getting on those rides. He's never been to a—"

"You mean you've never taken him to a carnival?" Cort interrupted harshly.

"No," she shot back defensively. "And I just told you why. It…was…it is too dangerous."

His look was savage. "Does that go for everything else that pertains to fun?"

"I don't have to justify my actions to you!"

"That's where you're wrong." He was looming over her now. "The days of you turning him into a mama's boy are over."

"How dare you tell me how to rear my son."

"Oh, I dare all right, and with good reason."

"He still needs mothering, in spite of what you think."

"Mothering maybe, but not smothering. There's a difference."

"You don't know what you're talking about. For the better part of his life, he's been too sick, too weak to do the things other kids were able to do. And now..."

"And now, when he's feeling good, you're still holding him back, not giving him a chance to be a boy."

"That's ridiculous!"

"No, it isn't."

"Well, there are worse things than being a mama's boy. For starters, the subhuman you've become."

Cort grabbed her upper arm and jerked her against him. She landed with a thud against his rock-hard chest. His breath burned her face with each word he spoke. "You don't know what the meaning of subhuman is yet, Mrs. Hamilton. But I promise you, if you keep pushing, you're sure as hell going to find out!"

His eyes continued to drill into her, and she could feel his fury. "We'll forget the day's activity, but this evening we will go to the carnival."

"Why, you..."

"Am I interrupting anything?"

Cort released her abruptly, and Glynis turned horrified eyes on Barr McBride.

For a moment no one said a word.

Then Cort faced Glynis and in a deceptively soft tone said, "Remember what I said."

She didn't say a word. Instead she flashed him a murderous look and walked through the door with her head held high and her shoulders squared.

The silence lasted.

The sun warmed the ground with its golden rays. The sky was baby blue. The trees were tall and straight and perfectly shaped. The grass was so green it looked artificial.

Cort stood at the window and watched the spectacular show of nature with disinterested eyes. At the same time he ignored his brother.

He had already finished off his second mug of coffee, which had done nothing to cure what ailed him.

"Wanna tell me what that was all about?" Barr asked.

Cort didn't move, listening with half an ear to the scraping sound Barr made when he pulled out a chair and sat down. Then finally, feeling like an idiot, Cort shrugged and turned around. "You want some coffee?"

"Nope. I've already had enough to sink a battleship. Thanks anyway."

"Well, I haven't," Cort responded flatly, stalking to the counter and once again filling his cup to the brim.

"From the looks of things," Barr remarked, not put off in the least by the grim expression on Cort's face, "you screwed up by insisting Glynis stay here."

Cort's scowl deepened. "I had no other choice."

"Sure you did."

"No, I didn't," Cort said with more certainty in his voice than he felt. "It was the only way for me to get acquainted with my son. And even that's turning into a battle royal."

"So that's what the . . . uh . . . disagreement was about?"

"She doesn't want me around him." Cort's words were spoken bitterly. "Actually that's putting it mildly. She loathes the sight of me and cannot bear for me to touch the boy."

Barr sighed and pushed his Stetson farther back on his head. "Maybe if you give her more time."

"Time, hell. She's already robbed me of six years. Isn't that enough?"

"Yes, but . . ."

Cort glowered at his brother. "Whose side are you on, anyway?"

Barr held up his hands in mock surrender. "Hey, calm down. Truth is I'm not on anybody's side."

When Cort didn't say anything, Barr went on, "Just think about it a minute, use your head, dammit. When it comes to the boy, neither of you should be taking sides. Todd's not a bone to be picked over—he's a sick little boy who needs both his mother and his father."

"That's exactly what I tried to tell Glynis, only she won't listen. Hell, man, Todd's under my roof, but for all the good it's doing me, he may as well be living in South Africa."

"It's only natural that she's protective."

"Yeah, too protective to suit me."

"Well, one thing's for sure, you can't keep on like this. Whether you wanna face it or not, Todd's a long way from being well, and the two of you arguing all the time isn't going to help him or the situation."

A nerve in Cort's jaw twitched. "I know."

"So why don't you kiss and make up?"

Cort didn't crack a smile over Barr's attempted humor. His taciturn face remained unchanged. "Funny."

"Hell, Cort, lighten up or you're going to be in worse shape than you are now."

"And just what's that supposed to mean?"

"I've seen the way you look at her."

Cort's jaw instinctively clenched in anger, and his grinding teeth were visible through slightly parted lips. "I don't know what you're talking about."

But he did know, even though admitting it was like the taste of quinine on his tongue. He was having one helluva time looking and not touching. He wanted to kiss her until she begged for mercy. His idea of heaven was falling asleep with the taste of her on his lips and her body hot and pulsating around him, trapping him as he drove deeply into her.

"Don't pull that dumb act with me," Barr was saying.

Cort expelled a ragged breath and forced his attention back on his brother.

"You know very well what I'm talking about. She's working on you just like she used to."

"That's enough," Cort responded.

If Barr heard the steel in Cort's tone, he ignored it. "The way I see it, you've been without a woman too long, little brother. You're like a big bear with a sore paw."

"You're a fine one to be talking. When's the last time a woman warmed your bed?"

Barr raised a heavy eyebrow. "We're not talking about me. We're talking about you and your relationship with Glynis."

"Past relationship, you mean," Cort muttered, tasting bitterness again.

Barr shrugged. "I hope you mean that. I'd hate to have to put Humpty Dumpty back together like I did after she married Jay."

Suddenly Cort felt dead inside. "You won't," he muttered without expression.

"Whatever you say," Barr concluded. "But it all goes back to the fact that if you can't handle the situation, you shouldn't have brought them here."

"What would you have done?" The hard note was back in Cort's voice. "You know the condition Dorothy's house is in. I couldn't let them stay there. Anyway," he added darkly, "I need to be near my son for more reasons than are obvious. She's turning him into a sissy."

"I don't rightly agree with that," Barr drawled, spreading his legs more comfortably under the table. "Under the circumstances, it's only natural that Glynis would tend to be overprotective. At the risk of repeating myself, your son is a very sick little boy."

"Don't you think I know that?"

"Well then, ease up on Glynis."

Cort didn't bother to control his irritation. "Hell, Barr, you make me out to be an insensitive jerk."

A smile flirted with Barr's lips. "Well."

"So I'm an ass."

"You said it. I didn't."

Cort regarded Barr impatiently. "I know the kid's been through hell. Every time I look at him I get sick to my stomach and I want to pound my fist through the first door I come to, because I know his suffering's not over."

Barr nodded with understanding and didn't say anything. There wasn't anything to say.

"That's why I don't want Todd to miss out on being a little boy while he's healthy. Does that make sense?"

"Yeah. Only I'm not the one you need to convince."

"Don't remind me," Cort bit out. "I'd almost rather tangle with a bull."

Barr laughed outright. "Can't say I blame you. She's sure developed one helluva temper. It makes her even more beautiful."

"Knock it off, Barr!" Cort's voice cracked.

"Sorry," Barr said, but he didn't sound sorry, especially as he followed his apology with a broad smile. Then, standing, he reached for the Stetson he'd removed from his head and tossed on the knob of the adjacent chair. Once he'd jammed it back on his head, he added without the smile, "You aren't thinking what I think you're thinking, are you?"

"Depends on what you're thinking."

"You're not by any chance going to try to get custody of Todd, are you?"

"The thought has crossed my mind, yes."

Barr shook his head and let out a sharp breath. "I just hope you know what the hell you're doing."

Cort's face was lined and sober. "So do I, big brother. So do I."

"Mommy, hurry. Uncle Cort's waiting. I know he is."

"I'm hurrying, I'm hurrying," Glynis said from the bathroom. "Believe me, honey, it won't hurt him to wait."

"Will too."

Though Glynis heard the petulant ring in her son's voice, she chose to ignore it this one time, knowing it stemmed more from impatience and excitement. And tiredness, too, she suspected, though he'd just awakened from an hour-long nap. They had spent most of the day at Milly's, and Todd had played nonstop for hours with her boys.

Now, as she pulled on her clothes, Glynis tried not to think of what lay ahead of her.

Following her confrontation with Cort this morning, she had felt restless and uneasy. What did he hope to achieve by harassing her like that, making her play by his rules? And if she didn't, would he really try to take Todd away from her? Or was it another ploy to further punish her, like the times he purposely touched her.

If he knew those unprovoked attacks on her senses had aroused more than disgust inside her, he'd be unbearable. Every time she thought of those moments in his arms, fear swept over her.

"Mom!"

Forcing a lightness into her expression, Glynis glanced in the mirror one last time, giving her loose curls one last pat. "All right, son, all right," she mumbled under her breath, silently cursing the impatience of youth.

Then, closing a fist around the knob, she opened the door, only to come to a sudden standstill.

Cort, freshly showered and shaved, stood just inside the room. Her first thought was how well his ever-present jeans and casual shirt fit his lean body.

His gaze flickered coolly over her apricot jumpsuit, then his eyes narrowed as they came to rest on the sensuous beauty of her hair.

"Don't ever cut your hair," he said unexpectedly, his tone low and brusque.

Her breathing was uneven. "I...I hadn't planned on it," she murmured inanely.

"Uncle Cort, can we go now?" Todd asked in a small voice.

After another moment's hesitation, Cort lowered his gaze to the child and smiled. "You bet we can."

Todd giggled. "I can't wait. I've never been to a carnival before. My friend Jeremy told me they have lots of scary rides. I want to ride them all." His voice gushed with enthusiasm.

"Now, Todd, you know you can't do all the things Jeremy can."

Todd's lower lip began to tremble. "But Mommy, I wanna..."

"Don't start whining or we won't go at all." Glynis rarely reprimanded him, especially in front of other people. This time, however, she had no choice, for not only did she have to impress upon him that he must obey her, she had to get the point across to Cort that she was in charge.

Todd lowered his head while his shoulders drooped. Then looking up, he said, "I need to go to the bathroom."

Cort laid a hand on the boy's shoulder. "It's all right. We'll wait."

Once Todd had closed the bathroom door, Cort stepped closer to her, the corners of his mouth turned down. "I warned you not to hover and I meant it."

She glared up at him, her face bloodless, her lips so stiff she could barely speak. "And I warned you about interfering."

"You'll lose if you try to fight me, so I suggest you don't even try." All was delivered quietly, but with a menace that was unmistakable.

Glynis lifted her arm, but before her hand could make contact with the contours of his cheek, his fingers closed around her wrist like a manacle.

He simply smiled, as though her action had been expected. Shifting his gaze to a point beyond her shoulder, he said, "Ah, Todd, you're ready. Good. Let's go."

How Glynis got her purse and followed them outside to the car, she could never remember. She felt numb, and the evening stretched ahead, long and treacherous. She should never have agreed to this outing, she told herself despairingly when Todd was installed in the back seat and she had joined Cort in the front.

But then she hadn't been given much choice, had she?

Glynis stood alone at the edge of the trees that bordered the carnival grounds, though the sounds of voices and music were close behind her. She had separated herself from Cort and Todd and come to the rest room with the excuse of washing the cotton candy off her hands. In reality she had craved time away from Cort's overpowering presence.

Dusk was fast approaching, bringing a slight chill to the air. However, she knew the bumps that dotted her skin had nothing to do with the weather, though she could safely say the evening had transpired without event.

She had made every step Todd and Cort had made, yet she had felt as though she were on the outside looking in. Despite Cort's threat, he hadn't let Todd on the more sophisticated rides, holding him to the rides geared to his own age, such as the bumper cars and the hobbyhorses.

"See, I'm not the monster you make me out to be," he'd retorted in a mocking tone, which she'd ignored.

But for the most part her aloofness went unnoticed. Todd had eyes only for Cort. Glynis was stunned at the way he chatted with Cort, as if he'd known him always, laughing and joking with him and asking him questions that Glynis herself wouldn't have dared ask. And Cort was equally enthralled with Todd. It made her wonder if indeed there was something special about a blood relationship.

It was a sense of uneasiness that suddenly jolted her back to the moment at hand. She was experiencing the same eerie feeling she'd had when Cort had crept up on her unannounced at her aunt's house.

With her heart palpitating, Glynis swung around, positive she would encounter hostile eyes staring at her. But there was no one lurking in the shadows.

A man's back was visible as he leaned against a hotdog stand, seemingly more interested in wolfing down the hotdog than in her. But long after she'd turned back around, that feeling of unease persisted. She shivered visibly and all but ran headlong into the throng of people with their excited voices and smiling faces.

"Glynis!"

Cort's puzzled exclamation had never been more welcome. He came striding toward her with Todd at his heels. Hardly aware of what she was doing, she ran to him and caught herself just before she would have lunged into his arms.

He grabbed her hands to steady her. "What is it? What the hell happened?"

Chapter 10

"Are you sure that's all?"

Glynis massaged the back of her neck and stared up at Cort. "I'm sure. I just overreacted, that's all."

They were still standing at the edge of the fairgrounds, and as the minutes passed Glynis was feeling more like a fool. What had come over her? What had possessed her to think that someone was watching her with evil intent? She had never lost control like that before over something so insignificant. Her nerves were apparently more frayed than she'd thought. Still, that didn't excuse her weird behavior.

"For it not to have been anything, you're sure pale as hell," Cort was saying. He stood so close she could see his chest heaving.

"Mommy, are you okay?" Todd interjected, his small hand nestled tightly in hers.

Transferring her gaze down to her son, Glynis squeezed his hand and gave him a reassuring smile, realizing that her fear had communicated itself to Todd as well.

"Mommy's fine, son, really I am."

"Good. Can we go back and play some more?" His blue eyes, so like Cort's, darted back and forth between the two adults. "Can we?"

More embarrassed now by her overactive imagination than anything, Glynis was so eager to put the incident behind her that she would have agreed to anything, even Todd's demands.

But Cort had other ideas.

"No more, Todd," Cort said, shaking his head. "Your mother's had a ... slight shock, and you've had enough excitement for one day."

To Glynis's surprise Todd didn't argue, but he did turn with longing back to the rides.

Cort squeezed the shoulder nearest him and smiled. "Maybe we'll get to come back before the carnival leaves."

Todd's eyes lighted. "Can Adam and Kyle come with us?"

"We'll see." Then to Glynis, "You ready to go?"

"If you are," she murmured, avoiding his eyes.

Cort hesitated a second longer, then sighed deeply. "Come on," he said, propelling Todd forward. "Let's go home."

The drive back to the ranch was pleasant. Deliberately keeping the conversation light, Cort was an amusing companion, and Todd appeared delighted that his mother was back to normal and was joining in the nonsensical chatter.

Todd, however, was worn out and soon drifted to sleep in the back seat. Cort turned to make sure Todd was sleeping soundly. Then, his eyes on the road again, he said, "You're right, this wasn't a very good idea."

Glynis glanced sideways at him. "Considering the way it started off, what did you expect?"

"For which I'm to blame, right?"

Glynis concentrated on picking a string off one leg of her jumpsuit. "I didn't say that."

"You don't have to." His voice was flat.

Glynis shook her head helplessly. "It...doesn't matter about me."

"No, I guess it doesn't," he muttered harshly. "All that really matters is *my* son and the fact that he had a good time."

The way he stressed the word *my* was not lost on Glynis. But once again she schooled her features to show no emotion.

"We can't go on like this, you know," Cort said, following a short silence. "We need to talk."

"Isn't that what we've been doing?" She knew she was being deliberately obtuse, but for the moment that was her only defense against him, against the pull of his powerful masculinity. And it wasn't just that he looked so good and smelled so good. It was more, much more.

She didn't want to talk to him, nor did she want to be confined in the car with him. Her attraction was too strong to deny, and Glynis felt a quiver run through her body as she turned away, feeling a sense of incredulity that she had ever defied him.

"No, we haven't been talking," he said, forcing her thoughts back on track. "We've been arguing."

"Oh, Cort, there's nothing else to say. It's all been said. As soon as the transplant is done and Todd is back on his feet, we'll go on with our lives and you'll go on with yours."

"And never the twain shall meet. Is that what you're saying?"

"No... that's not what I'm saying."

"Well, it sure as hell sounded like that to me."

"Why do you persist in making things so difficult? I intend to... to let you see Todd."

"At your whim?"

"No, at the court's."

"No judge is going to dictate to me."

"You won't have a choice."

"Like hell I won't. For God's sake, Glynis, Todd's my son. My flesh and blood. And I'll be damned if I'm going to cater to you in this."

A quick jolt of fear turned her stomach. Now was no time to go off the deep end, she cautioned herself. She fought her paranoia. He didn't mean it. *He couldn't mean it.* He was merely doing what he did best, which was to torment her, extract his pound of flesh in degrees.

Nonetheless, she noticed that when she tried to speak, her breath was coming in short gasps, and it took several steady gulps of air to steady herself. "Cort, you have your career, your ranch. Those are the only two things you've ever wanted."

"Maybe I've changed."

She chewed painfully on her lower lip. "I doubt that. You're still the most selfish person I know."

She heard his sharp intake of breath, and at the same time she felt his hot glance pierce her. "I'd be careful if I were you, Glynis. I'd be very careful, in fact. Just because I was once crazy enough to bury myself deep inside you..."

A choking sob broke from her lips. "You're despicable!"

"But I made my point, right?" His eyes flickered over her. "I used to let you say and do things to me that no woman has since, but that doesn't mean I'm going to now."

Glynis turned her head and stared blindly out the window. "Oh, you made your point, all right," she said bitterly.

Cort cursed softly, and then controlled himself. "Look, I'm prepared to let bygones be bygones. Would you meet me halfway?"

"There's no halfway mark with us, Cort. What you said just now proved it."

"All it proved is that you're not as indifferent to me as you'd like me to believe."

Glynis was glad for the darkness so he couldn't see the color flood into her cheeks. "You're flattering yourself. Besides, we're not discussing us. We're discussing Todd."

"Need I remind you, Todd is *us*. We made him."

Following that sobering rejoinder, Glynis's stomach did an odd little flip, and for a moment she was at a loss for words. Then, recovering, she whispered, "What...what we shared was a lifetime ago."

"Are you sure?" His voice sounded hoarse.

"Yes, I'm sure."

"When I touched you at Dorothy's house, you weren't exactly repulsed."

Glynis swung around to face him. She could hear her heart pounding as if she'd been running a marathon. "Just because you caught me off guard doesn't mean I'm dying to jump in bed with you!" she spat. "Though you may find it hard to believe, I don't want you to touch me."

A stifling silence followed before they heard a movement from the back seat. Suddenly Todd's face appeared between the seats; he was rubbing one eye with the back of his hand, his lower lip extended slightly.

"Mommy, I thought you and Uncle Cort liked each other."

"Oh, Todd," Glynis cried.

"You told me you were friends." His lower lip was trembling.

"We are," Cort put in, the tension draining from his features.

"Then why are you fighting?"

Glynis ran a finger down one of his soft cheeks. "I'm sorry if we woke you up. We . . . didn't mean to."

"But I want you and Uncle Cort to be friends, Mommy," Todd went on with childlike resolve.

"We are, darling, we are."

There was another silence as Todd scrambled over the seat to sit in Glynis's lap. Once he was snuggled against her, she cast a look in Cort's direction. Even though his profile was unclear to her, she sensed his expression was carved in granite. At that moment, he steered the car under a streetlight, and her premonition proved correct. An artery throbbed in his neck, and deep lines pulled at the side of his mouth.

Suddenly she felt her heart constrict. She was crazy to feel sorry for him. He more than deserved her censure after the things he'd said to her, the way he'd treated her. She was a fool to give his feelings a second thought.

"I'm hungry, Mommy," Todd was saying as Cort brought the car to a stop in front of the house.

"Good. When we get inside, I'll fix you something to eat." Even to herself, her voice sounded disjointed, her mind still reeling from her tormenting thoughts.

"Uncle Cort, will you eat with me?"

Glynis and Cort exchanged a brief glance.

"That's up to your mother." His expression seemed to open slightly, revealing a wisp of uncertainty.

A sense of utter futility overwhelmed Glynis. "By all means, eat with him," she said weakly.

By the time they got inside, Todd was scampering ahead, motioning for Cort to follow him. Glynis kept her head lowered, dreading the moment when she would tell Cort her plans, plans that had been on her mind for days, but that had taken on new meaning in light of their verbal skirmish. She knew she could not put it off any longer.

Out of the corner of her eye, Glynis saw that Todd had Cort cornered in the den, showing him some rocks he had collected at Milly's. She, in turn, headed toward the kitchen to see if there were any leftovers in the refrigerator. If not, she would make them all cheese omelets.

But she need not have worried; there was plenty of shaved ham, fresh tomatoes and a pot of Maude's homemade vegetable soup.

In spite of Glynis's trepidation, the meal passed without incident. Glynis concentrated on her food, refusing to dwell on the time when Todd would go to bed and leave her alone with Cort. Sitting at the opposite end of the table, Cort, too, ate with relish, having rolled up the sleeves of his cotton shirt, which exposed his arms, tanned and muscular.

She kept her eyes off him for fear of what she would see reflected in his. However, Cort's attention was focused exclusively on Todd as he encouraged him to eat.

"Mmm, that was delicious," Cort said at last, downing his second cup of coffee, his eyes still on Todd. "How about you and me pitching in and doing the dishes for Mommy?"

Todd frowned. "Aw, gee, Uncle Cort, that's sissy stuff."

"Yeah, Uncle Cort, that's sissy stuff," Glynis chimed in sarcastically.

She knew immediately she had scored with her barb. Color surged into his face, and his mouth flattened into a straight line. "We're talking about apples and oranges, and you know it," he said.

Glynis merely shrugged, while Cort turned back to Todd and forced a smile.

"Who told you boys shouldn't wash dishes?"

"My friend Jeremy."

"Well, your friend Jeremy is wrong." Cort chuckled and tickled him under the chin.

Todd was basking in Cort's undivided attention. "Can I wash 'em?"

"Well, actually I was thinking about putting them in the dishwasher."

Glynis rolled her eyes heavenward, a gesture that was not lost on Cort. He threw her a fulminating glance. She smiled. To her amazement he smiled in return.

And his eyes seemed to search for and hold her own. For a moment they gazed at each other. Glynis's lips parted on a terrified breath; Cort's heart began to pound. She was the first to recover; she averted her eyes and said breathlessly, "It's almost Todd's bedtime."

As if reluctant to do so, Cort shifted his gaze to Todd. "You heard your mother. We'd better get a move on."

Todd giggled. "I'm ready."

Glynis sat anxiously in the den while Cort and Todd were in the kitchen. Todd was obviously enjoying himself, if the splashing of water was any indication. Also, childish laughter rang out in response to Cort's every word. She couldn't help but wonder why Todd had never responded to Jay in that way. She knew the answer. Jay barely acknowledged his existence, much less anything else. Not so with Cort. He seemed to take delight in sharing with his son.

Glynis rose to her feet and paced impatiently around the room. She was overreacting as usual. His interest in Todd was merely a stopgap, a ruse before something else—another big job—diverted his attention. Wasn't that all she had ever been to him?

When they came back into the den a while later, there were circles underneath Todd's eyes.

"It's bedtime for you, young man." Her tone brooked no argument.

"Can Cort read to me in bed?"

Glynis sighed irritably. "No, playtime's over. You're exhausted."

"If Todd . . ." Cort began, only to have Glynis silence him with an angry look.

"Sleep is the only thing he needs," she muttered tersely, reaching for Todd's hand.

Cort winced, his color rising. "Damn you, Glynis." His tone was low and harsh, meant for her ears only.

During the entire time she supervised Todd's bath, including his brushing his teeth and slipping into his pajamas, Glynis realized she had pushed Cort as far as she dared, that by refusing him the right to get to know his son, she was playing with fire.

So when Todd bounded into the den a short time later and went straight to Cort, she bit her tongue.

"Will you come to my room and tuck me in?" Todd asked, his eyes wide and appealing.

Glynis, watching Cort's face, felt her composure snap and the color seep from her face. She put a hand to her heart and tried to pretend she didn't see the stirring emotions that tightened his face, turned it ashen. Maybe if he'd found a woman...

Suddenly terrified, she balled her hands into tight fists. For all she knew, maybe he'd found that woman. If so, that would certainly strengthen his case against her in the event he chose to fight her for custody. And with his money and influence...

"Can he come to my room, Mommy?" Todd was asking, looking at her with a puzzled frown on his face.

Her lashes veiled her eyes as she gazed downward. "All right," she said tightly.

There was a moment's silence as the child turned back to Cort. Cort stood and took Todd's hand. "Let's go," he said with a twisted smile that did not reach his dark, unhappy eyes.

Glynis went with them to the bedroom and looked on as Todd climbed into his bed and peered up at Cort with adoring eyes. "Will you kiss me good-night like Mommy does?"

"You betcha," Cort said huskily, and bent down.

It was when Todd's thin arms circled Cort's neck that Glynis left the room, tears trickling down her cheeks. The empty den offered little comfort as she crossed to the window and stared into the inky blackness, a blackness that matched her heart. It was so quiet that she could hear the crickets chirping.

Glynis sensed, rather than heard, Cort come into the room. For a moment she remained still; then, with a visible effort at control, she turned around. He was propped against the mantel with one booted foot on the hearth, a brooding expression on his face.

"We have to talk," she said at last.

"Ah, so now it's you who wants to talk, huh?"

She bit the inside of her lip. "Please, I don't want to argue. I just want to..."

"What? You just want to what?"

"Leave," she said bluntly. "Move out."

His eyes turned to flecks of glittering steel. "We had a deal."

"I know, and I plan to keep my end of the bargain no matter how much I detest it."

"So, I don't get it."

She took a deep breath. "I guess what I'm trying to say is that I intend to remodel Aunt Dorothy's house, and just as soon as it's ready, I'm going to move into it. By then Todd should be over his surgery...."

"Dammit, Glynis, that house is a shambles." He pinched the bridge of his nose. "Why the hell can't you forget about it?"

"I think that's fairly obvious, don't you?" She didn't bother to hide the tremor in her voice. "Anyway, I want a place of my own, a place... to call home."

For a moment she thought she saw his features soften, but then he asked in a hard tone, "Where do you intend to get the money?"

"From the bank." She raised her chin a good inch. "I'm going to apply for a home-improvement loan."

He gave her a long look. "And just how do you intend to pay it back?"

She flushed and looked away. "If Todd's condition permits, I hope to get a job teaching second-term summer school and then apply for a permanent one for the fall."

"Forget it."

"Pardon me?"

"I don't want you to work this summer." He slipped a hand inside his shirt and massaged his throat. "And if you're determined to redo the old house, I'll give you the money."

"No."

His eyes narrowed. "What do you mean no?"

"Oh, Cort!" Glynis was near tears again. "We can't keep on bickering like this. You don't really care about Todd—or me. Why don't you admit it? You have your work and..." Her voice faded.

"Go on," he demanded, inching toward her, his sun-bronzed face grim.

"And...and women...or a woman," she finished rather incoherently, licking her suddenly parched lips.

"And would you care?" His voice had a ragged edge to it. "Would you care if I had a woman?"

Hot, boiling fury gripped her. "Stop it!" she cried. "Stop trying to seduce me with words! It won't work." For a moment her voice broke. "Why won't you believe me when I tell you that *I* don't need anything from you, that I don't want..."

Before she realized his intentions and before she could utter a cry of protest, he clasped her upper arms and backed her into the wall directly behind her. He didn't stop until his body was pinned hard against hers and his mouth was only a hairbreadth from hers.

"No...Cort," she moaned, twisting her head from side to side. He paid no attention to her muted cry. Instead he spanned her cheek with a hand and held her face steady.

"No," she whimpered again, placing her fists against his muscled chest and pushing desperately against him. But he wouldn't budge. Then something in his eyes suddenly brought her struggles to an end, and the resistance seemed to pour out of her.

"Oh, Glynis," she heard him groan with agony as his mouth, savage and tender at once, came down on hers. His tongue was soft and insistent, parting her lips, stroking the inside of her mouth.

Still she squirmed, determined not to give in. But then the weight of his body, the pressure of his mouth, drove all coherent thought from her mind, and she wanted to be closer, to remember, to feel.

She wrapped her arms around his neck, digging her fingers into his hair, and pressed his head closer as she arched against him. The warmth of his body was a powerful aphrodisiac, and the scent of his skin mingled with the scent of passion was equally powerful.

"You're driving me out of my mind!" he muttered feverishly, his mouth seeking hers again. Her legs were giving out under her. Her body was on fire. She was beyond denying that no other man could make love like Cort. And all that mattered was that it should never stop.

Then just as suddenly as the assault had begun, it was over. He had pulled back and was staring down at her, breathing hard.

"Now, by God," he taunted, "tell me you don't want me!"

Chapter 11

Sleep was impossible. The night stretched out long and lonely. Her body ached, and she admitted the reason why. Some wanton part of her cried silently for the fulfillment that only Cort could bring her. Though she tried, she was unable to purge those forbidden thoughts from her mind.

Cheeks flaming, Glynis turned her head into the pillow, but they wouldn't go away. His sweet savage assault on her body had awakened dormant longings within her, bringing to a feverish pitch desires she thought had been stilled with the lapse of time.

She had excused her participation because it had been so long since she'd felt a man's touch, Cort's touch. But that was no excuse, and she knew it. Though she had tried to keep her distance, her body had betrayed her. Her senses had drawn her toward his potent masculinity. She had basked in his scent, the feel of him against her. The feel of his hands kneading her breasts had fanned the fire in the lower regions of her stomach that, even now, threatened to rage out of control.

She hadn't fooled him, either. He'd felt her response. He had relished her surrender for the sole purpose of showing her that he did indeed did have the upper hand.

If only he had wanted to marry her. But a commitment like that was a mirage with a man like Cort McBride. She knew he wanted her. She also knew she could arouse him as easily as he'd aroused her. But a relationship built on physical attraction was not what she wanted. She had loved Cort—loved him with all the tenderness and passion of which she was capable. And he had taken that love and destroyed it.

She closed her eyes against those unpleasant recollections and let her head fall back against the pillow.

In spite of her mental turmoil, she must have slept. The next thing she knew, sunlight was peeping through the blinds and her son was on the side of the bed, leaning over her and running a finger down the side of her cheek.

Suddenly she trapped that finger in her mouth and gave it a gentle bite with her teeth.

"Ouch, Mommy!" Todd cried, drawing his hand back and stumbling to his feet.

She laughed and kicked the covers back. "That didn't hurt and you know it."

"Did, too."

She laughed again, then looked at the clock. Her laughter died. Eight-thirty. Good Lord, she hadn't slept this late in a long time. Her face flamed. What must Cort be thinking?

Then, remembering the horrendous scene between them last night, she didn't give a damn what he thought. After all, *he* was the cause of her exhaustion.

"Mommy, you gonna get up?"

"Right this minute."

"Good."

"Why the hurry?"

"I wanna go back to the barn and look at the kitties."

"Where's your...Uncle?" Knowing her son, she figured he had already asked Cort to take him. And since he hadn't, it was obvious Cort was unavailable. She hoped so, anyway. She wasn't looking forward to crossing paths with him this morning.

"That lady told—"

"Mrs. Springer."

"She told me Uncle Cort was with his foreman, tending to the cows." His lower lip protruded. "Wish I could've went with him."

"Wish you could have *gone* with him," Glynis corrected absently, getting out of the bed and padding into the bathroom.

"Isn't that what I said, Mommy?"

She merely shook her head before bending over the basin and splashing her face with cold water. When she came out of the bathroom minutes later, Todd was eyeing her carefully.

"Can I go to the barn? I've already had my cereal. That lady—I mean Mrs. Springer—fixed it for me a little while ago."

"How about if I promise to take you to see the kittens when we come back?"

He watched her apply her makeup. "Where're we going?"

"To town. I have some business to take care of at the bank. I thought I'd drop you off at Milly's and let you play with the boys."

"Yippee!"

"Have you brushed your teeth?"

"Yes, ma'am."

"Good. As soon as I finish getting dressed, we'll go."

"Okay, but hurry, Mom."

Following that order, Todd dashed out of the room, slamming the door behind him. Glynis sighed and again shook her head, but there was a smile on her face. He was doing so well and felt so good. It was a shame it was soon all going to come to an end. The thought of him going through the transplant seemed to turn the blood in her veins to ice water. If things didn't turn out right... No, she couldn't think like that, she told herself.

"You promised, Mommy."

Todd's light hair fell across his forehead as he turned it up to her, his blue eyes anxious. "I know, son. And I fully intend to keep my promise. Just give me another second to get out of these clothes." She paused and kicked her shoes off. "In the meantime, you go ask Mrs. Springer for some juice and take your medicine."

"Okay," Todd mumbled reluctantly, and headed toward the door.

"And remember to say please."

"Yes, ma'am," he said with resignation.

Once she was alone, Glynis could barely contain her excitement, nor could she stop from patting herself on the back.

As she tossed her skirt on the bed, she laughed out loud, and it felt good. She had gotten the home-improvement loan and she was ecstatic. Although it wasn't for as much as she would have liked, it was nevertheless enough to get started repairing the house.

From the bank, she'd gone to the school district office and applied for jobs. Luck had followed her there as well. While the summer position was doubtful since there was already a waiting list for the job, the fall looked promising, especially as she was certified in special education.

From there, she'd gone to Milly's to pick up Todd. Over a glass of iced tea, she and Milly had toasted her success.

Now, comfortable in a pair of shorts, cotton shirt and Reeboks, Glynis walked out the door. Minutes later there was a spring in her step as she and Todd headed toward the barn.

"Do you think they're still here?" she asked Todd as they entered the quiet coolness of the barn. Todd was tiptoeing to where they had last seen the kittens.

He turned his head. "Of course, Mommy. Uncle Cort said that if we didn't touch them, the mama cat wouldn't move them."

Glynis sighed. "And do you believe everything your...Cort tells you?"

"Course I do, 'cause he knows everything. He's real smart."

"Whatever you say." Glynis tried to ignore the twitch in her heart. How was it going to affect Todd when Cort was no longer a major part of his life? She shuddered just thinking about it.

"See, Mommy, just like Uncle Cort said, they're still here." Todd's voice had dropped to a whisper as he squatted down in front of the box filled to capacity with the cat and her nursing kittens.

"Oh, aren't they sweet," she said, using the same whisper-like tone as her son.

"I'll be glad when I can play with 'em. Uncle Cort said—"

"For heaven's sake, Todd," Glynis cried, lunging to her feet, "must you talk about Cort as if he's some sort of god?" Then, looking down into her son's troubled, upturned face, she regretted her childish outburst.

"I wish you liked him better," he said, his lower lip beginning to quiver ever so slightly.

For a moment Glynis struggled to come up with the right words. "Oh, Todd, honey, there's so much you don't know, can't understand."

"What I really wish is that he was my daddy."

Suddenly Glynis couldn't swallow, couldn't catch her breath. She felt as though she were choking to death.

"Then I wouldn't ever have to leave here," he added, his eyes brightening. "I could live here—"

"Todd!" This time Glynis almost screamed his name, and Todd stared at her, a stubborn expression on his face. "I like it here. Just 'cause you don't—"

"Todd, stop it!" Glynis jammed her hands down into the pockets of her shorts to control their shaking. Her nerves were stretched to the breaking point. "I don't want to hear any more about you staying here with Cort, do you understand? As soon as we can get Aunt Dorothy's house livable, we'll be moving into it. And then we just might sell it and move back to Houston," she added as an afterthought. "So let's not say any more about living here permanently. Do I make myself clear?"

Todd looked sulky, but he nodded halfheartedly. "Yes, ma'am."

Glynis's breathing eased a bit. "Now, why don't you count the kittens, so you can name them?"

"Can I really name 'em, Mommy?"

They sank to their knees and hovered over the tiny, furry creatures. "I don't see why not," she said, placing an arm around Todd's shoulder and giving it a squeeze.

"I thought I'd find you two here."

For a moment Glynis remained in that same position, as if frozen. Then, along with Todd, she rose to her feet and turned around. Cort filled the narrow doorway.

"Hi, Uncle Cort," Todd said enthusiastically, running toward him, but not before casting a disquieting eye in Glynis's direction.

Dear Lord, Glynis thought, how long had he been standing there? How much of her and Todd's conversation had he heard? She couldn't control her heartbeat as his long stride closed the distance between them.

Their gazes met for a few disturbing moments, then he focused his eyes on Todd, who was now standing in front of him, looking up with a wide grin that emphasized his toothlessness. "Hi yourself, young fellow," Cort said.

Apparently satisfied that he'd gotten Cort's attention, Todd spun around and went back to the kittens, once again kneeling beside the box.

As he turned back to Glynis, Cort's narrowed eyes betrayed nothing, hidden as they were by his thick lashes. But there was a fine line of perspiration dotting his upper lip, and his shoulders were slightly drooped. Both could have been brought on, however, by the fact that he'd been working around the ranch, doing manual labor from the looks of his clothes. His snug-fitting, faded jeans and white shirt were dusty, as were his boots and Stetson. The only thing not dusty were his spurs; their shiny glint was intact.

Glynis cleared her throat, aching to remove her eyes from him, but she simply could not. "Todd was having a fit to see the kittens again," she murmured at last.

A smile relaxed his features. "I'm not surprised."

A long silence followed.

This time it was Cort who cleared his throat. "Did you go into town?"

"How'd you know?" She trailed her tongue nervously over her lower lip. The action focused his attention on her mouth.

He swallowed hard. "Maude told me."

"Oh."

His breathing was labored. "Well, did you get it?"

She blinked. "What?"

"The loan. Did you get the loan?"

A telltale flush reddened her cheeks. She knew she was acting like an imbecile, but all her senses were reacting to his presence with alarming intensity, remembering that moment in his arms. She hated him for putting her on the defensive this way.

"Well?"

She let out an audible sigh. "Yes, I got the loan."

"So you intend to go through with the cockamamy idea of remodeling the house?"

"Yes, and . . ."

Todd let out a delighted squeal. "Mommy, Uncle Cort, come look. Hurry. The mama kitty's licking the babies."

They looked at each other for a moment longer, then broke eye contact and gave their attention to Todd.

"That's how she cleans them, Todd," Cort said, casually dropping an arm around Todd's shoulders.

"You mean she's giving them a bath?"

"Right."

"Wow, that's really neat."

Cort smiled easily. "Yeah, isn't it?"

"Mommy, you looking?" Todd's upturned gaze was now fixed on Glynis's taut features.

"You like that, huh?" she asked, gazing adoringly at her son, relieved by the interruption.

"When can I pick one up?"

"Soon," Cort said, standing up. Glynis and Todd rose with him.

Without looking at Glynis, Cort asked, his voice low and resonant, "How would you like to go for a ride?"

Todd's eyes rounded, and his lips parted. "Now, with you?"

Cort nodded. "Yeah, on Blackjack, my stallion."

"Cort, I don't think . . ." Glynis began.

Her quick objection brought a pout. But that didn't stop Todd from pleading. "Oh, please, Mommy, please?"

"He'll be just fine, Glynis," Cort interjected, his tone testy at best. "I give you my word."

"All right," she said, an edge in her voice, "but you better make sure he holds on tight."

"Thanks, Mommy," Todd said, his eyes dancing. "I promise I'll be good." Then, to Cort he said, "I'm ready."

"I'm not. I want to talk to your mother for a minute."

Todd shifted his feet impatiently. "Can I wait for you outside?"

"Yes, but stay away from Blackjack."

"Todd, did you hear what Uncle Cort told you?"

"Yes, ma'am," Todd answered in a low voice, before turning his back and running out of the barn, as if fearing they would both change their minds.

The departure of their son created a stifling silence.

Glynis's heart was beating much too wildly, no doubt brought on by the disturbing blue eyes watching her with mocking intensity.

Yet she was the first to speak. "Look, Cort, before you say anything else about the house—"

"Barr and I'll do the work," he interrupted. "Or at least Barr will, as this damned hole in my side rather limits my activities."

Her mouth fell open, and she stared up at him incredulously.

The corners of his lips tilted upward. "Close your mouth."

She gestured impatiently. "What kind of game are you playing now?"

"Believe me, it's no game." What could have been mistaken for a smile suddenly disappeared. "Have you thought about a contractor?"

"No, but—"

"Didn't think you had," he said. "And it's not easy to get one, especially one you can trust."

"Because I'm a woman, is that it?"

"Yes, that's it. But don't take it personally, because that's a fact of life everywhere. Reliable help is hard to come by."

"Well, thanks, but I don't think it's wise for you to tax your strength. I want you to get strong so we can get the transplant over with."

"Glynis."

She ignored him. "I'll get Milly's husband to find me someone."

"No. I told you Barr and I would do it."

"And I said no thank you. I told you I don't want..."

The luster in his eyes turned to metallic steel as he reached out and clamped a hand over her mouth, shutting off the tirade with the swiftness of a falling blade. She pulled at his fingers, but her effort was in vain. He crushed her to his chest.

"I thought we settled this *want* business last night." His breathing was harsh and uneven as he removed his hand. "You can scream all you want. But I wouldn't advise it, unless you want to upset Todd."

"Let me go!" she pleaded breathlessly.

Cort continued to hold her prisoner. Then he lowered his mouth toward her; there was no way she could avoid it. Her whimper went unnoticed as he nudged her lips apart and entered the hot cave of her mouth. By increments he caressed, probed, feasted upon the delights found there, setting her on fire.

His breathing harsh, he lifted his lips from hers and nuzzled the throbbing pulse in her neck. "I can have you any time I want, so remember that."

"No, that's not true."

"You want me to prove it?"

"No!" she cried, using what strength she had to break free of his embrace.

But her freedom was short-lived. He reached for her again. She stumbled backward and only by sheer force of will did she maintain her footing.

"You'd...you'd have to take me by force," she said, trembling.

"I don't think so." His tone was soft and confidently mocking. "Right now you're as hot as I am, ready to explode."

"No," she whispered just as he grabbed her again and hauled her close to him.

"Yes," he countered, his half-closed eyes glittering as he slowly unbuttoned her shirt, exposing her creamy breasts to his hungry gaze. When his breath caressed a nipple, a small cry tore loose from the back of her throat. To heighten the exquisite torture, he caressed each warm curve with his lips before he lifted his head and reclaimed her mouth.

When a hoarse groan erupted from him, she responded greedily, grasping handfuls of his thick hair. He stroked her back, her hips and inside her thighs, applying pressure between her legs and not stopping until he rocked against her, hot and full.

He groaned raggedly. "Why do I still want you?"

Glynis was aware she should be asking herself that question. She should be the one repulsed. When had her need for him replaced her fear? Why was she aching to hold him instead of shoving him away?

"Cort, please, Cort," she whispered thinly.

"I can't forget how wet and tight you always were," he rasped against her lips, "how you moaned when I slid deep inside you."

The feeling his words aroused in her were primitive, ancient and eternal. She trembled, not with revulsion but with yearning.

"And in spite of what you did to me, God help me, I still want you."

Those last gut-wrenched words seemed to bring him to his senses, because his hold on her relaxed and she broke free.

For the longest moment they were both breathing so hard, speech was impossible.

Then Glynis found her voice. "Getting even. That's what this is all about, isn't it?" she spat, still gasping for breath.

His silence answered her question.

Glynis felt as though a bucket of cold water had been sloshed in her face, but she didn't intend to let him know that. Stiffening her shoulders, she said, "I'll fight you every step of the way."

His gaze slid slowly down her body. He said nothing until his eyes were level with hers again. Then he whispered, "And you'll lose."

Chapter 12

Following the encounter in the barn, the next week passed without further incident, much to Glynis's relief. But then she had made it a point to stay out of Cort's way as much as possible. Her nerves had been raw and close to the surface, and another emotional bout with Cort would have been the final straw.

For the most part Cort remained either in his office tending to business by phone or milling about the ranch with his foreman. It was obvious that Cort wanted to avoid her as well.

There were times when she would stand at her bedroom window, especially early in the morning, and watch him stride out the side door looking tan and fit. She couldn't imagine him dressing in a suit and tie every morning, confined to an office building. Here he seemed to be the consummate rancher, one with the land, the land he loved so much.

When she would see him like that, her senses never failed to stir, bringing back to her mind in full color those moments in his arms, the feel of his lips against hers, the feel of his hands on her bare flesh.

She would quiver with renewed fragments of passion. The only way she had been able to erase those thoughts from her mind was to put on her jogging gear and run until she couldn't run anymore. She would then return to the house, feeling much better, less edgy, more able to cope.

Yet when their paths did cross, that emotional stability would evaporate like a pail of water in the sun. Cort was affected as well. Subsequently, both walked on eggshells, knowing it would take only one wrong word, one accidental touch to send their emotions skyrocketing out of control.

Neither wanted that.

But during those trying days, Glynis made certain Todd did not bear the brunt of her unrest. They spent hours on end together, time they hadn't had since his illness. She treasured those hours and made the most of them. They took long walks through the woods where Todd often played in the creek, and on several occasions were guests at Barr's ranch.

Shamefully she had enjoyed those long, lazy summer days, and consequently she didn't object when Cort asked to take Todd with him. On those days, she'd simply go into town and visit Milly or help Maude with the cooking and household chores.

However, she knew that while things were progressing as well as could be expected under the circumstances, she definitely had to change her plans. Deep down she'd known it all along, known that she wouldn't be able to live in the same town with Cort. It simply would not work, not only because she would never have peace of mind, but Cort would eventually lure her son away, without a lawyer or a court of law.

Now, as she was finishing up one of her early morning jogging stints, that thought was again uppermost in her mind.

In a graceful move, she climbed the stairs onto the deck at the back of the house and sat down on the top step. She pushed tendrils of wet hair off her face. Then, closing her eyes, she took several deep breaths of the fresh morning air, drawing it deep into her lungs.

When she opened her eyes, Cort was rounding the corner of the barn. Her only clue that he'd seen her was the narrowing of his eyes. He began walking toward her, his gait measured.

Her nerves tensed instinctively. After a skipped heartbeat, Glynis stood and waited, her gaze sweeping coolly over his aloof features. And in that moment she found it hard to believe they had ever shared laughter, or passion, or tears, or anything other than the hate and mistrust that now threatened to consume them.

Glynis was the first to speak. "Good morning," she said for lack of anything better to say, never knowing what to expect from him or what his mood would be. Today was no exception.

He stopped a few feet from her and drawled, "Mornin'."

Their gazes locked for a minute, and time seemed to stand still. His southern drawl cut right through her. With an enormous effort, Glynis looked away, but not before she'd seen that glint in his eyes, a glint she recognized only too well, a look that hinted of smoldering passion and unfulfilled desire.

"How was your run?" he asked, drawing her back around to face him, while continuing his slow appraisal of her.

His blue-eyed gaze stripped her as he inspected the way the damp material of her T-shirt clung to the full curves of her breast, blatantly emphasizing her extended nipples.

She found it difficult to speak. "Fine, thank you," she said after a few awkward moments, and wondered if that was really her talking in a tone as formal and unbending as her stance.

He seemed to sense the irony in their conversation, for his mouth eased into a smile. Or was it a smirk? Glynis couldn't be sure.

"You ought to quit running, you know?"

She was taken aback. "Why?"

His eyes were dark and mesmerizing. "You're already thin enough, except for one place, that is."

She spoke before she thought. "And where is that?"

"Your breasts." There was a husky timbre in his voice. "Since you've had Todd, they're fuller, more perfect than..." He broke off, staring hard.

Glynis simply stood there mute and panic-stricken, feeling a tide of hopelessness wash through her.

Finally she was able to drag enough air through her lungs to speak. "Cort, please, you've no right to talk to me like that."

Holding her stare, Cort muttered harshly, "You're right, I don't."

"Can't we forget the past and . . . and try to be civil to each other? At least until after Todd's surgery?"

Mentioning Todd's name seemed to have a sobering effect on him. His stern expression relented somewhat. But when he spoke, it was in a hoarse whisper. "Do you think that's possible?"

The dryness in her mouth made it difficult to swallow. Her tongue felt swollen. "We...we won't know till we try, will we?"

He looked at her a moment longer with veiled eyes, only to suddenly change the subject.

"I just got back from the doctor."

The blood drained from her face. "And?"

"I'm in good shape."

Glynis's heart lurched. "Good enough to have the surgery?"

"'Fraid not."

She regarded him helplessly. "When, then?"

"Soon. Doc Davis said my blood count is slowly but surely coming back up."

"How soon is soon?" Glynis pressed anxiously.

"Maybe another week. Maybe two at the most."

She fought to hold back her tears. "Well, I guess if that's the best you can do . . ."

"I didn't deliberately get shot, you know." His eyes weren't kind, but there was no anger either.

"I know," she said softly, "but surely you can't blame me for being anxious."

He looked away from Glynis and was silent for a moment. "No," he said at last. "I can't blame you."

"Did the doctor warn you about . . . about taxing your strength?" she asked, striving to keep her voice steady.

"If you're referring to the work on your house, the answer is no."

"I find it hard to believe you're allowed to do exactly as you please."

"Pretty much so."

"Oh."

His lips twitched, but he never actually smiled. "Sorry to disappoint you, but I'm still planning to work on your house, starting this evening."

"This evening?"

"Anything wrong with that?"

"No, it's just that I haven't thought about the materials."

"I took care of that."

"I need to pay you then."

His eyes turned hard. "If you insist."

"I insist."

"Suit yourself," he said, twisting around in the direction of the barn.

"Cort."

He turned back around and waited.

"Do... you think I could help?"

They looked at each other for a long time. Then Cort shoved his Stetson back on his head and said, "I guess it depends on just how good you are with a hammer."

"I'm a fast learner," she said a trifle breathlessly.

He scratched the part of his head that was uncovered and smiled, a smile that went straight to Glynis's heart.

"I guess we'll see, won't we?"

With that he turned and once again sauntered toward the barn.

Unable to stand up on her trembling legs a second longer, Glynis sank back onto the wooden steps, her thoughts more scrambled than ever. He had suddenly become a man of contradictions. She didn't know which Cort was the most dangerous, the moody, unpredictable one, or the sexy, soft-spoken one.

But one thing she did know—both were unhealthy to her peace of mind. As soon as Todd was up and around, they would move back to Houston. For her own good, she had to get away from Cort McBride.

"Mommy, are you having fun?"

Glynis smiled into her son's face as he hunkered down beside her while she was busy ripping a piece of worn linoleum from the floor. "Well, I wouldn't exactly call this fun."

"Why not?" he asked innocently.

"Because it's hard work, that's why." Glynis paused and wiped the sweat from her forehead with the back of her hand.

"It's too bad I can't help you, Mommy."

She smiled. "Why can't you?"

He grinned. " 'Cause Uncle Cort's countin' on me to help him. He told me so." His chest swelled proudly. "It's fun, too. Me and Uncle Cort and Uncle Barr are having fun."

With that he stood and scurried out of the room.

"I'm glad someone's having fun," Glynis mumbled to herself, giving another segment of flooring a savage yank. She must have been out of her mind when she'd volunteered to help. But then she hadn't known she was going to be assigned the worst job in the whole house.

From the moment Cort and Todd had piled into Cort's old pickup truck that he kept in the barn, and had subsequently arrived at the farmhouse, Cort had been working nonstop, though doing nothing strenuous as he had promised. The strenuous jobs had fallen on her and Barr, mostly on Barr.

Barr, for the most part, had worked outside, tearing out the rotten windows that were being replaced with new energy-efficient ones. Cort and Todd, working as a team, had started in her old bedroom, pulling off what was left of the tattered wallpaper.

They had been there only an hour when she had slowly risen to her feet to rest her knees. It was then that she heard a squeal of laughter and had tiptoed down the short hall and stood at the door and looked in.

Cort was entertaining his son with a story while they worked, Todd imitating every move Cort made. Once again she'd experienced that sharp pain in her heart. After watching them undetected for a long moment, she'd turned and made her way back to the kitchen. It was only after she'd knelt and begun working that she noticed her eyes were filled with tears.

But the tears had long since dried; she'd taken her frustrations out on the linoleum floor. Now, an hour later, she was making real progress. And so was Barr; she could hear him hammering loudly and steadily.

"Todd said you were having trouble."

As usual when Cort came anywhere near her, every nerve in her body reacted. Scrambling to her feet, she pushed her hair away from her face. "No, really," she responded, "I think I've finally gotten the hang of it."

He was leaning against the kitchen cabinets, looking good enough to eat in worn cutoff jeans and no shirt. His upper body was tanned and lean, and the hairs curling on his chest were damp and glistening with drops of sweat.

She felt her temperature rise as she swallowed hard and added, "But it's . . . hard work, just the same."

One eyebrow rose. "You didn't expect it to be easy, did you?"

"No, of course not," she said defensively.

As if sensing he'd struck a raw nerve, Cort looked amused. "We're just getting started. Sure you don't want to change your mind?"

"You'd like that, wouldn't you?" she snapped, raising an arm to massage the back of her neck. In doing so, she unconsciously exposed a portion of her bare, upper stomach to Cort's darkening gaze. Like him, she was wearing cutoffs and a cropped top, which just happened to cup her breasts to perfection.

They stared at each other for what seemed like an interminable length of time, then Cort blinked and looked away, a pulse in his neck beating overtime.

"Yes, I would," he finally said in answer to her question, swinging back to face her. "This was a bad idea to begin with. You don't have to live here."

This time it was her temper that rose. "We can't stay with you forever, you know."

"Why not?" His expression was blank.

Hers was disgusted. "You know why not."

"No, not really." His eyes, unblinking and compelling, bored into hers. "It could be an ideal setup. We could share our son, and you wouldn't have to work."

"And just what would you get out of it?" she asked out of curiosity.

"You in my bed every night."

At first she was so stunned, she couldn't speak, then a high-pitched laugh that held no humor pealed from her throat. "Are you suggesting that I become your mistress?"

His face paled. "Only if you choose to look at it in those terms."

She laughed again, her eyes wide. "I don't believe I'm hearing this."

He took a step toward her, his mouth stretched in a thin, straight line. "Why not? It's an established fact that you'd like to crawl in between my sheets just as much as I'd like you to."

"Why, you smug bastard! If you think I'd—"

"Am I interrupting something?" Barr said suddenly, leaning through the kitchen window, his broad shoulders taking up the entire space, a grin on his face. "It seems as if I'm destined to be in the wrong place at the wrong time."

Barr's subtle attempt at humor did little to disperse the growing tension. Glynis and Cort both stared at him, but neither was capable of saying a word.

"Glynis, how 'bout bringing me a glass of that lemonade you brought with you?" Barr drawled when the silence continued. "I'd sure appreciate it. I'll be sitting under that big oak tree out back." After winking at Glynis, he turned and ambled off.

The instant Barr was out of hearing range, Cort faced Glynis. "I'd give my offer some deep thought, if I were you," he said between clenched teeth.

Then he, too, pivoted on his heels and stamped off.

The suffocating tension that had surrounded Glynis seemed to leave the room with him. She hadn't realized just how stiffly she had been holding herself until she drew a free breath.

Yet when she turned and began grabbing glasses out of the cabinet, her hands were shaking uncontrollably. In fact she was shaking all over. How dare he assume she would become his mistress?

With every breath she took, with every move she made, her thoughts churned. *How dare he even ask?*

"You sure you don't want me to go with you?" Barr asked.

"Dammit, do I look like I need a damned keeper?"

"Yeah, as a matter of fact you do."

Cort snorted. "I'm fine."

"Sure."

"Barr, just move your behind."

"I wouldn't turn my back on her if I were you, little brother."

Cort tensed, knowing full well what Barr was getting at, but not liking it just the same.

Barr chuckled. "Yeah, if looks could kill, you'd be deader than a mackerel washed up on the beach."

Cort was gripping the steering wheel so hard, his knuckles were white. "What's the deal, Barr? Do you get off watching Glynis and me fight?"

Barr didn't so much as flinch. "Just curious about what you said that made her so damned mad, that's all."

"Well, for once I'm not going to satisfy your curiosity. You don't find me interfering in your personal business. From now on I'd appreciate it if you returned the favor." Heavy sarcasm punctuated every word Cort spoke.

It was lost on Barr. "See, you're doing it again, gettin' up-tight—"

"You're wrong."

"No, I'm not, not by a long shot. Hey, little brother, it's me you're talking too, remember?" He paused and, rubbing his day-old beard, leaned further into the open window. "You're testy as hell. What you need is a good—"

"Give it a rest." Cort jammed the Jeep in gear.

"I take that back. What you need is Glynis. She's what you've always needed."

"What you need is to mind your own damned business and get the hell out of my way!"

Barr sighed. "All right, Cort, have it your way. But make no mistake, you're a firecracker with a burning fuse. And anytime now you're going to blow sky-high."

"Stand back," Cort bit out furiously. "I'm going to the cattle auction."

Four hours later, Cort was on his way back from the auction in Tyler, having made several much-needed purchases. He would have thought that the successful outing would have sweetened his mood, but he was still as uptight as when he'd driven out the gate.

Barr was right, though it galled Cort to admit it. Cort was horny as hell; he wanted, he needed a woman. But not just any woman would do. God help him, he wanted, he *needed* Glynis, only Glynis.

And while rationally he could be appalled at his raging feeling and his unorthodox behavior, something stronger than his self-respect was prodding him on. Indeed, her nearness was driving him close to the edge, and while love did not enter into the scheme of things, lust did.

In spite of the hell she had put him through, having her close and not being able to touch her was tearing his gut to pieces. And he'd taken enough cold showers lately to last him a lifetime.

Hadn't he known this would happen? Not at first, he hadn't. He had been obsessed with getting to know his son. Thoughts of Glynis were secondary to that urgent need. Anyway, he'd thought he was over her, thought he had gotten her out of his system.

Wrong again. If anything, he wanted her more than he ever had, found her body more desirable. He wanted, ached to touch her. All over. Every inch, as he'd done an eternity ago when he'd felt her grasp him just before he would penetrate her quickly and deeply.

He swore explosively as his hardening flesh pressed against the fly of his jeans. So where did he go from here? Back home? Pretend she wasn't there? Sleep alone? Hardly. Not with this burning pain at the apex of his thighs.

The memory of her sweet, soft lips clinging to his, the ripe fullness of her breasts under his exploring fingers, the scent of her, the enticing sway of her hips tormented him even as the Jeep clicked off the miles.

As he neared a small town, he eased up on the gas pedal. It was only moments later, after he transferred his boot to the brake, that he muttered an expletive.

He had no brakes. Looking up, he saw that the car in front of him was stopping at the red light. A fine line of sweat popped out above his lips. The choices were slim. He could either crash into the Buick's rear or head for the deep ditch to his right. He chose the latter.

Whipping the steering wheel sharply, he braced himself for the crash.

"Son of a bitch!" he hissed before his head slammed against the steering wheel on impact and a deep blackness pulled him under.

Chapter 13

"Is he dead?"

"I don't know. Do you?"

"No. But I can't find a pulse."

"Here, get out of the way and let me check."

"Did you call the sheriff's office?"

"Yeah, and they're on their way. Told 'em to send an ambulance, too."

"I just hope it ain't too late."

Voices. Cort kept hearing voices, but he couldn't open his eyes and respond, no matter how hard he tried.

"He sure as hell looks dead to me. All that blood sure ain't a good sign, either."

For God's sake, stop talking about me as if I were dead, Cort cried silently. *I'm alive. Can't you see that!*

"Think we oughta try to move him?"

"Hell, no. Here comes the sheriff—he'll know what to do."

I'm alive. Can't you idiots see that? Yet he sure didn't feel alive. The one time he'd tried to move, every muscle, every nerve protested in agony. At least he wasn't paralyzed, not from the waist up, anyway.

Cort identified the sirens. Now if he could just open his eyes, he'd have the battle half won, he told himself. However, that task proved impossible.

It was only after he heard a gruff voice bark "You fellows get the hell out of the way and let us through" that his eyelids fluttered.

The instant he felt a hand on his shoulder, his eyes popped open, and he groaned.

"I'll be damned if it isn't Cort McBride!"

Cort was able to focus his eyes now, and Sheriff Daniel Thompson filled his vision. "Hello, Dan," he rasped.

"Damn, Cort, I thought for a minute that I'd have to call the J.P. to pronounce you dead."

Cort raised his head all the way up and reached a hand to his forehead. When he lowered it, his fingers were coated with blood. "Reach behind the seat, will you, Dan, and hand me a rag?"

The sheriff frowned. "Maybe you oughta keep still until the paramedics get here. They're driving up now."

"No, I'll be all right. Just please get me the rag and then help me out."

"You ain't changed a bit. You're still as hardheaded as a damn mule."

"Yeah, yeah," Cort muttered, dabbing at the blood on his face. Once that was done, he turned his body in the seat, though very gingerly, and with Dan's help managed to get out of the Jeep, which was still nose-down in the ditch.

Two paramedics were standing with a stretcher at the top of the embankment.

"Come on, boys, get down here and load your patient."

Cort raised his hand, stalling them. "No, I don't want to be strapped on any stretcher. Just give me a minute, and I'll be fine."

Dan snorted. "If you could see yourself, you wouldn't say that."

Cort winced against a pain that suddenly shot through his side, then cursed. If he'd torn open that wound . . .

"Cort, don't you dare faint on me now," Dan was ordering, "not after you wouldn't let the paramedics help you."

Ignoring him, Cort probed his side with unsteady fingers. Sore, but not unbearably so. And there was no blood.

"Come on," Dan said, "let's get you outa this ditch and into my car. At least you'll be sitting down."

"That sounds good. Give me a hand and let's go."

Once Cort was seated in the passenger seat of the sheriff's car, he leaned his head back and closed his eyes. Although his head still pounded, his vision was clear, and he no longer had that sick feeling in the pit of his stomach.

Feeling strong enough to finally check the damage to his face, he lowered the visor and stared into the mirror. He grimaced. A large goose egg adorned the center of his forehead, and there was a cut on his right cheekbone. The cut had been the source of all the blood.

He couldn't help but wonder what Barr would say when he saw him. It probably wouldn't be repeatable. And Glynis? Cort's heart skipped a beat. What would she think? Would she be as upset?

He'd lived, and for that he was thankful, given the circumstances of the accident and the fact that it could have been much worse. He could be dead. And this time it wasn't even job-related, he thought with a cynical curve of his lips. Or was it? Suddenly he frowned.

"How you feeling, son?"

Cort angled his head sideways. Dan was peering down at him, the open door bearing the brunt of his weight, which was definitely in excess. But then Cort knew Dan did everything wrong. When Dan was on duty he smoked too much; when off, he drank too much. Still he was a crackerjack law officer, and Cort respected him.

"I'm feeling like warmed-over dishwater, now that you ask."

"Figures. Wish now you'd let those medics haul you to the hospital?"

"Hell, no. I'll be sore for a few days, all right. But then I'll be fine."

Dan didn't look convinced. "If you say so." Then, changing the subject, he asked, "What happened, anyway?"

"That's what I'd like to know."

Dan didn't miss the ugly note in Cort's voice. He straightened up, instantly alert. "Suppose you explain that."

"There's not much to explain. I was coming home from the auction, started to slow down for the light—there was a car in front of me—and when I put my foot on the brakes—"

"It was like stepping on air," Dan finished for him.

"Right."

"Had your brakes been giving you trouble?"

"Hell, Dan, you know better than that. If they had, I'd have fixed them immediately."

"Sorry. In your line of work I guess you can't afford to be careless."

"Right again," Cort said, tight-lipped.

"You thinking what I think you're thinking?"

"Maybe." Cort's tone was cautious.

"Well, I'm thinking they might have been tampered with," Dan drawled.

Cort's face took on a sinister sneer, but he didn't say anything.

Dan scratched his chin. "Well, we'll have the Jeep up momentarily, and then we can take a look."

Both men turned and watched the wrecker, which had appeared on the scene shortly after the sheriff and paramedics, haul the Jeep out of the ditch with one strong tug.

The second it hit level ground, Dan backed away from the car and Cort eased out, though not without a price. His head swam, and his stomach churned. But after he took several gulping breaths, the world righted itself.

By the time they reached it, one of Dan's deputies was on the ground sliding under the right wheel. Cort would have liked to crawl under there himself, but knew that was impossible.

"Findin' anything, Toby?" Dan asked, lifting his hat and wiping the sweat off his forehead. "Damn, it's hot."

Cort made no comment. His gaze was pinned to the deputy, his mouth drawn in a tense line.

"Got it," Toby finally said, scooting from under the Jeep, a hose dangling from his hand.

Cort took it and began examining it immediately.

"Well, what's the verdict?" Dan pressed.

Cort muttered a seething oath. "The damn thing's been tampered with."

"How?" Dan grabbed the hose out of Cort's hand.

"Punctured."

"Ah, punctured so the fluid would drain out slow."

"Exactly." Cort's voice was razor sharp.

Dan thrust a hand through his thatch of graying hair. "Whoever did it had a perfect opportunity while you were inside the auction barn."

"That's my guess."

"Have any idea who wants you gone?"

Cort raised his head sharply, only to then let out a cry of pain.

"You oughta be home in bed," Dan said tersely, "instead of standing out here in this heat. Come on, I'll drive you to the ranch."

"Make that Barr's. I'll get him to drive me home."

Dan nodded.

Cort turned to the driver of the wrecker. "Fred, haul the Jeep out to my place, will ya?"

"Sure thing, Cort."

Once Cort and Dan were in the sheriff's car and turning onto the highway, Cort twisted in the seat and stared out the window, his thoughts in chaos. He didn't want to think he had been so wrong about something he had been so sure of. He didn't want to think that the bullet he'd thought was meant for his client was actually meant for him.

But he was beginning to believe that was the case. Suddenly, his mind conjured up a terrible thought. He flinched. *If* the bullet was indeed meant for him, then Glynis and Todd were in danger.

He muttered to himself, knowing he had a decision to make that had all the earmarks of a double-edged sword. Yet if he sent them to Milly's or Barr's, then they would be out from under his protective eye. He'd be damned if he did and damned if he didn't.

"You're awfully quiet."

Cort sighed heavily. "I'm thinking."

"I'm sure you are. By the way, you never answered my question."

"That's because I don't know the answer," Cort hedged.

Dan threw him a sharp glance. "But you intend to find out, right?"

Cort's eyes were like chips of ice as he narrowed them on the sheriff. "You can rest assured of that, my friend."

Glynis knew she should call it an early night. But why bother, she told herself. She wouldn't sleep. The house was quiet, and she was restless, mainly because Todd was running a slight fever and complaining about a stomachache.

After bathing his face with a cold rag, she'd given him several crackers and part of a Coke, then put him to bed. So far he'd slept peacefully. But if he wasn't considerably better in the morning, she would call the doctor. His ailment could be something more than a virus. . . .

Suddenly furious with herself for borrowing trouble, she lunged off the couch, ignoring the papers that scattered to the floor around her. She'd been going through her files, looking for new ideas for bulletin boards so she'd be prepared when the new school term started.

Now that her concentration was broken, she knew it would be fruitless to try to pick it up again.

She wished Maude hadn't gone to her sister's for a visit. At least she would have been company. Crossing to the window, Glynis toyed with the blinds until she could see outside. The sky was as black as her thoughts, she noted. Not one star was in evidence. Suddenly she saw a streak of lightning followed by a menacing rumble of thunder.

She closed her eyes and leaned her head against the frame, but not before a sigh escaped her. While it was true she was concerned about Todd, she also knew her agitation stemmed from another source as well. Cort.

Since their clash at Dorothy's house last evening, she had not seen him. When she and Todd had gotten up this morning, he'd been gone. And now it was nine o'clock, and he still wasn't home. Which was fine by her, she told herself. In fact, she wished she could take Todd and leave and never see him again.

At first she wasn't sure she'd heard anything. Straightening, Glynis twisted her head to one side and listened. This time she identified the sound. The kitchen door had opened, then closed.

"Cort, is that you?" she asked, her voice sounding hyper even to her own ears.

Silence.

Determined to ignore the way her heart raced, Glynis began walking across the room. Before she got halfway, Cort appeared in the doorway.

She stopped in her tracks, her hand flying to her throat. "Oh, dear Lord!" she cried.

"It's not as bad as it looks. I'm fine, really."

"What on earth . . . ?" Her voice cracked, and for a second she couldn't go on.

"I had an accident."

"You . . . you didn't injure your side, did you?"

"No, thank God."

"Shouldn't you . . . be in the hospital?" she stammered, unable to come to terms with this latest turn of events. "You look awful," she added, her stomach feeling as though she were on a roller coaster.

He almost smiled. "That's what Barr said, only worse."

She raised her eyebrows in question. "Barr?"

"Yeah. He brought me home."

"You should be sitting down," she said in a strangled tone, then turned away for fear he would see the tears that were flooding her eyes. To say he looked awful was an understatement. Ghastly was the more appropriate word. The lump on his forehead was a purplish-green color, and the cut above his eye was caked with dried blood and needed attention. Something terrible had happened, and she wasn't sure she wanted to know what it was.

By the time she faced him again, he was sitting down in his chair, his gaze resting broodingly on her.

"You really should be in bed, you know," she said huskily.

"Are you offering to tuck me in?" His voice was low and rough.

For a moment Glynis shut her eyes against the hot tightness that was turning her insides to jelly. Then she stiffened. "You don't give up, do you?" she asked bitterly.

"Glynis, look at me."

She tried to keep her voice natural, but it quivered revealingly. "No. I just want you to tell me what happened."

When he didn't respond, she glanced at him out of the corner of her eye. His eyes were closed, and she saw his jaw turn rigid as a spasm of pain flickered across his face.

Her breath caught sharply. "Do you want me to call the doctor?"

"No," he said, lifting his head. "I'll be fine as soon as I shower and get some sleep."

Glynis dug her teeth into her bottom lip. "I'm . . . not sure. I think I should call your doctor."

"My Jeep took a nosedive into a ditch on 69."

It took a minute for his unexpected words to sink in. "What did you say?"

With uncharacteristic patience, he repeated himself.

"Did you lose control?"

"Only because someone tampered with my brakes."

She stared at him with disbelief while the color slowly deserted her face.

Cort stood, though not without considerable effort. "I knew you'd react like this. That's why I hesitated to tell you."

"It's job-related, isn't it?" Her voice was toneless.

"Yes."

She shot him a look that was suddenly outraged and cold. "Dammit, Cort, if you let anything happen to you before . . ." She broke off, horrified at what she was about to say.

"Would it make you feel better if I promise I won't get blown away until after the transplant?" There was an icy edge to his voice. "Would it, huh? Would it?"

Glynis felt terrible. "Cort, I didn't mean—"

"Like hell you didn't," he snapped, his eyes bleak. "Ah, hell, it doesn't matter anyway. I'm going to bed."

With that he turned and strode out of the room, leaving Glynis standing in the middle of the room as if rooted to the spot. She didn't know how long she stood there, too shocked at her own outburst to move.

Dear Lord, she hadn't meant it. No matter what Cort had done to her, the pain he had brought her, she still didn't want anything to happen to him. While she might hate him, she certainly didn't wish him dead.

Suddenly she knew what she had to do.

"Who is it?"

"It's me," Glynis whispered, barely able to hear her own voice over the pounding of her heart.

"Go away."

"Please, Cort, let me come in." She stopped short of pleading.

Silence.

"Cort, I'm not leaving."

"The door's open," he muttered.

With fingers that were far from steady, Glynis turned the knob and walked in. Cort was sitting on the side of the bed, practically naked, dressed only in his briefs.

Paying no heed to her audible gasp, he went on with what he was doing—dabbing at his cut with a cotton ball soaked with antiseptic.

Leaving the door cracked behind her, she ventured deeper into the room while she stared openly at his body, remembering what it was like to run her hands over his hairy chest, down his stomach to the thick muscle between his thighs.... She shut her eyes and groaned deep in her throat, feeling as if something had broken apart inside her. When her eyes fluttered back open, he was looking at her.

"I think you'd better go," he said thickly.

"I'm . . . sorry," she whispered.

He shrugged. "I told you to forget it."

"It's not that easy."

"Sure it is."

"You're making a mess of that."

He blinked as if the change of subject had thrown him off guard. Then, taking the cotton away from the cut, he shrugged again. "It's not helping, anyway."

Without stopping to think about her actions, Glynis closed the distance between them and sat down on the bed beside him.

"Here, let me do that," she said, and proceeded to take the cotton out of his hand and gently touch the tender area with trembling fingers.

Though she heard his sharp intake of breath, her hand didn't falter. She continued to cleanse the cut.

Then, without warning, he reached up and stilled her hand. Their eyes met and held.

Glynis was so close she could hear the beat of his heart; it was as loud as her own.

"You shouldn't have come," he muttered thickly.

Glynis was trembling all over now. "I had to."

"Oh, Glynis, Glynis." His voice was raw as he slid one hand under the coil of her hair and stroked the sensitive nape of her neck. "What are we going to do?"

She wanted to cry, to weep in shame. But she couldn't. The tears wouldn't come, nor would the words. She simply sat there, trembling, feeling his breath, warm and tantalizing against her lips.

"Why did you do it? Why did you marry Jay? I went through hell. If I'd known you were pregnant as well . . ." He slid his hand over hers, finding her palm with his thumb. "You remember how it always was with us, and that hasn't changed. God, how I want you, have never stopped wanting you. You're beautiful, do you know that? I've never made love to another woman. Sex, yes—but not love!"

Glynis closed her eyes and swayed, reaching out blindly. He grasped her tightly and clamped his mouth to hers. He probed with his tongue quickly, greedily, and she matched him stroke for stroke. It was an intimacy they both longed for, and it struck them both like lightning. Intense. Beautiful.

She was not fool enough to imagine that the emotions they were deliberately arousing in each other were anything more than an instinctive need for gratification.

Yet she doubted she could have dragged herself away if it hadn't been for the sound behind her. With determination she spun around. Her son was standing inside the door.

"Mommy, I threw up all over the bed."

Chapter 14

"Mrs. Hamilton, the job is yours, if you want it."

"Oh, I want it, Mr. Aimsworth. I want it very badly, only..." Her voice faded, and she looked away from the man who was principal of the Lyndon Baines Johnson Elementary School.

He was tall and thin, almost to the point of gauntness, but he had the gentlest, most caring gray eyes she'd ever seen. She had been looking forward to this visit. But that was before her circumstances had changed, before she'd decided not to remain in East Texas.

Yesterday afternoon she had received a call from Ted Aimsworth asking her to stop by the school at her convenience, saying that he'd looked over her application and would very much like to talk to her. Since she had had to bring Todd in to the doctor, anyway, she'd decided to hear what he had to say. She was impressed with Mr. Aimsworth and with the job itself, which was going to make turning it down that much harder.

"I'm not pressing you for a decision, Mrs. Hamilton, you understand," Mr. Aimsworth said, bridging the silence that had fallen between them. "There's still plenty of time to let me know." He paused, tipping his head sideways. When he spoke again, his tone was cautious. "I don't mean to pry, but when the district gave me your application, I was under the impression that you were very interested in the job."

They were in his office now, and Glynis was sitting in front of his desk, closely scrutinizing the shelf behind him. It sagged with curriculum guides and other materials pertinent to the profession.

"Oh, I am," Glynis said enthusiastically. "It's just that right now I can't commit to anything. You . . . see my son is due to have a bone marrow transplant soon, and until that's over . . ." Again Glynis's voice trailed off.

"I can certainly understand that," Aimsworth said, his features softening sympathetically as he rose behind his desk and extended his hand, indicating the interview was over. "I hope everything goes well. You'll let me know."

"Of course, and thank you very much."

The minute she walked out of the school and into the bright sunlight, Glynis stopped and, balancing her purse on a knee, dug inside for her sunglasses.

Once they were perched on her nose, she strode toward her car, noticing how lovely the morning was. The air smelled clean and fresh, thanks to last night's cleansing rain. She took a deep breath before getting behind the wheel of her car.

A short time later she pulled up in front of Milly's day-care center. Milly's figure appeared in the doorway as soon as Glynis got out of her car.

"Is Todd all right?" she asked anxiously, hurrying up the sidewalk, thinking it odd that Milly was waiting for her.

Milly smiled. "He's fine, going strong in fact."

Glynis's face cleared. "Good. He sure wasn't last night, though. He was one sick little boy."

"That's obvious," Milly quipped.

Glynis stopped abruptly. "Now just exactly what is that supposed to mean?"

Milly laughed, but then it faded almost as quickly. "You look like something the dogs dragged up and the cats wouldn't have."

"Gee, some friend you are, Milly Tatum."

"That's where you're wrong. I am your friend, that's why I said what I did." Milly opened the front door then and with a sweep of her hand indicated that Glynis should precede her inside.

Both women were quiet as they made their way past tables and chairs, chairs filled with boys and girls busily and happily working on various projects.

"Ms. Tatum! Come look," a little blond-headed boy shouted as they passed. He reminded Glynis of Todd.

Milly paused only briefly. "Not now, Albert," she told him with a kind smile. "Hold on to it, and I'll look at it later."

It wasn't until they were in Milly's office behind closed doors, coffee cups in hand, that Glynis spoke.

"Is Todd outside?"

"Yes, but like I told you, he's fine. So stop worrying. I just checked on him before you drove up."

"The doctor said the same thing." Glynis took a sip of her coffee, then frowned. "Heavens, that's hot."

"Blow on it."

Glynis rolled her eyes. "Thanks."

"What exactly did the doctor say?" Milly asked, serious once again.

"A twenty-four-hour bug."

"Just as we'd thought."

"Right, but it sure did me in," Glynis said with a sigh. "Of course I slept with him, afraid he'd get sick again and I wouldn't hear him."

"But that's not the only reason you look like you do."

"Come on, Mil, give me a break. I had a rough night, okay. So let's leave it at that."

As if realizing she'd been overly critical, Milly flushed. "Hey, don't get me wrong," she rushed to say in a conciliatory tone. "You're still beautiful, especially in that outfit."

And she was right. Glynis did look stunning in a bright golden yellow skirt and blouse, necklace and earrings.

"Flattery will get you nowhere, my friend. Anyway, you're just saying that in order to get back on my good side."

Milly shook her head. "No, I'm not. It's just that I'm worried about you. It's your eyes. There's a sadness in them that never seems to fade. And I know it's more than worry over Todd, although that in itself is enough to drive you crazy.''

Glynis nodded and ran a finger around the rim of her coffee cup.

When she didn't speak, Milly went on, ''Is it the job? Are you afraid you're not going to get it?''

Glynis shifted in her chair and averted her gaze. ''The job's mine if I want it.''

''What do you mean, if you want it?'' Milly frowned. ''I thought that was exactly what you wanted.''

Glynis focused her attention on the papers strewn across Milly's desk.

''Glynis.''

''You're right,'' Glynis admitted with a sigh. ''I did...do want it, but I'm afraid I'm not going to be able to accept it.''

''Why not?'' Milly was clearly perplexed. ''Is it the working conditions?''

''No. In fact, it would be an ideal job. Ted Aimsworth would be great to work for, and aside from that, I'd be in one of the new temporary buildings.''

''Then why aren't you going to take it? If you stay here, you have to work—''

''That's just it,'' Glynis put in quietly. ''I'm not going to stay here.''

''You're making absolutely no sense,'' Milly said flatly.

Glynis stood and began pacing the floor. ''Don't make it harder than it already is. Do you think I want to go back to Houston, rear Todd there? Well, I don't, but I have no choice. I have to get away from...'' She paused and struggled for breath.

''You have to get away from Cort,'' Milly finished gently.

''That's right.'' Her voice was no more than a whisper.

Milly threw up her hands. ''Stupid me, I should have guessed.''

''No reason why you should have,'' Glynis said wearily, bringing her pacing to a halt in front of the window.

''You still care about him.'' It wasn't a question.

''Oh, Milly,'' Glynis cried, gripping the glass rod on the blinds and squeezing it. ''I don't know what I think anymore.

Sometimes I hate him. Then other times I want him so badly it hurts." *Like last night*, she wanted to add, but didn't. Instead she folded her arms across her chest and rubbed them simultaneously. "But then I hate myself for feeling that way and hate him for making me feel that way. It's a catch-22."

"Is it possible you two might work things out once the surgery is over?" Milly asked hesitantly.

"Absolutely not." She met Milly's gaze unflinchingly.

"Things that bad, huh?"

"He'll never change, Milly. Cort's as involved with his work as he ever was. In fact, he's in so deep, his life's in danger."

"Are you serious?"

Glynis merely looked at her.

"How? I mean where...who?" Milly was spluttering as if she couldn't coordinate her words with her thoughts.

Glynis inhaled. "Someone tampered with his brakes, and his Jeep took a nosedive into a ditch on 69." Just thinking about it, much less talking about it, brought goose bumps to Glynis's skin.

"That's scary."

"So you see, even if we were willing to work things out, which we're not," Glynis added hurriedly, "it would be impossible. Our goals are still not the same. I want a home with a white picket fence around it and more children, and Cort...well, to tell you the truth, I don't know what he wants. I guess I never did. Only he's changed, Milly—he's hard and cynical and there's no reasoning with him."

"He's threatening to fight you for custody of Todd, isn't he?"

Glynis whipped around. "How did you know?"

"I didn't. I just guessed."

Glynis felt tears filling her eyes, warm and stinging, ready to trickle down her cheeks. She blinked them back and squared her shoulders. "Well, he's not going to take Todd away from me. I told him I'd fight him every step of the way."

"And you'll win, too, honey." Milly sighed and pushed herself up to full height. "But maybe it won't come to that. Maybe after the surgery he'll back off, take another overseas job." She shook her head regretfully. "Only the Lord knows about Cort McBride."

"Isn't that the truth," Glynis said with a sudden smile, determined to remove that pinched look from Milly's face. She'd put more of a burden on her friend's shoulders than was fair.

"You're feeling better now, aren't you?" Milly asked hopefully.

"Thanks to you." Glynis smiled. "I don't know what I'd do without you."

Milly adeptly switched the subject. "You want to stay and have lunch?"

Glynis glanced down at her watch. "Goodness, no. I didn't realize it was so late. You need to get back to work, and I need to take Todd home. In spite of what he said, I know he's still weak." She leaned over and kissed Milly on the cheek. "You're a doll."

Milly grinned her thanks. "I just wish I had the answer to your problems with Cort."

"You listened, and that's what's important," Glynis said, taking one last swig of her now-tepid coffee before making her exit.

Minutes later Glynis settled a tired Todd in the passenger seat, then made her way around the hood of the car. Just as she was about to get behind the wheel, she paused, suddenly nervous. It was there again, that same feeling she'd had that night at the carnival, the feeling that someone was watching her.

Frowning, she slowly turned around and scanned the area. She spotted him immediately. He was leaning against a tree across the street, his features hidden by the bill of a cap.

As her gaze settled on him, he pushed himself away from the tree and ambled down the street, acting as though he didn't have a care in the world.

Glynis stood there a moment longer and stared at the retreating figure.

"Mommy, what's the matter? You look kinda funny." Todd had scooted to the driver's side and was peering up at her.

She smiled reassuringly. "Nothing's wrong, darling. I was just thinking."

"Can we go now? I'm hungry."

"Me, too."

Disgusted with herself for letting herself get so rattled over nothing, Glynis got behind the wheel and promptly dismissed the episode from her mind.

When she pulled into the driveway at the ranch, there was a vehicle she didn't recognize sitting behind Cort's—a sleek foreign model. A man was in the process of climbing out of it.

"Wow!" Todd exclaimed. "Look at that car, Mommy."

"Mmm, nice, isn't it?" Glynis commented, but her thoughts were on the stranger, not on the car.

She guessed she'd find out who he was soon enough, as Cort and Barr chose that moment to round the corner of the house. By the time she and Todd walked up, they were shaking hands with the man.

Cort was the first to spot them, and his eyes narrowed. Feeling them on her, Glynis deliberately concentrated on the man, who was now propped against the side of his car.

"Glynis Hamilton, Gene Ridley, my right-hand man," Cort said promptly.

"Ms. Hamilton," Gene acknowledged, standing up and accepting her outstretched hand.

He was of average height and build with a receding hairline, which Glynis knew was deceptive. He was much younger than he looked, much younger in fact than his boss. And she was equally certain that his gray eyes, despite the thick glasses, wouldn't miss a thing. She'd bet, too, that he was as loyal to Cort as a lapdog.

"And this is Todd," Cort was saying, his tone abrupt.

"Hi, Todd," Ridley said with a smile.

"Hi," Todd answered shyly.

"Gene's here to discuss some business," Cort said by way of an explanation, his gaze once again fixed on Glynis.

And she knew what that business was: finding a way to keep Cort alive. Without being aware of it, she shivered, then looked up, straight into Barr's eyes. He winked, then grinned. She couldn't help but smile.

Cort cleared his throat. "Barr, why don't you and Gene go to my office? I want to speak to Glynis a minute. I'll be there shortly."

"Can I go with Uncle Barr, Mommy?" Todd chimed in, pulling on her hand. "I'm hungry."

Glynis lifted inquiring eyes to Barr. "Would you mind asking Maude to feed Todd?"

"Consider it done," Barr replied, throwing another grin in Glynis's direction. Then, placing an arm around the boy, he added, "Come on, let's you and me go rustle up some grub."

When the others were out of range, Cort focused on Glynis once more, his expression grim. More than likely his mind was on last night, as was hers, thinking how close they had come to doing something they would both regret.

"Where have you been?"

Glynis was taken aback by his brusqueness. "At Milly's, but I can't see why that's any concern of—"

"Couldn't you just once not make a damn big deal out of everything I say?" Cort thrust a savage hand through his hair and added, "What the hell! I don't know why I even bother to talk to you."

Glynis gasped, but for once, and for reasons she couldn't justify, she curbed her tongue. Maybe it was because he looked ready to fall on his face. His eye was almost swollen shut next to the cut, and the knot on his head had a yellowish tinge to it.

Suddenly an unreasoning fear gripped her. What if the person who wanted to harm him tried again and this time succeeded? The thought of anything happening to him... No, she wouldn't think about that. Not now. After he'd given Todd his bone marrow, then he could go play his dangerous games and get himself killed if he wanted to.

She didn't mean that, she told herself. She hadn't meant it last night and she didn't mean it now. And that, she feared, was the crux of her whole problem.

"Glynis."

She flinched, then looked directly at him.

"What did the doctor say about Todd?"

She relaxed a bit, feeling on safe ground. "He's fine. Just a virus."

"Thank God."

"How about yourself? How do you feel?"

"Do you really care?" he asked in an odd voice.

She swallowed, determined not to let him rattle her again. "Yes, I care," she said softly.

Deep blue eyes looked into her heavy-lidded ones, and for a moment the silence was charged. Then Cort drew in a ragged breath and seemed to regroup.

"How do I look like I feel?"

"Like you've been run over by a Mack truck."

The corners of his mouth curved into a smile. "I couldn't have said it better myself."

They both smiled, and the moment was electric.

Suddenly Cort cleared his throat. "You wanna work on the house this evening?"

Dumbfounded, Glynis lifted her brows. "You're in no condition to work on anything, much less the house."

"I can do a little, which is better than nothing."

"All ... right."

His eyes searched hers for another moment before he turned and walked toward the house.

Glynis didn't know how long she stood in the sun, transfixed, wondering if she would ever piece together the puzzle that was Cort McBride.

The minute Cort walked into his office and closed the door, he forced thoughts of Glynis to the back of his mind, though he had a hell of a time doing it. Damn, but she'd looked beautiful standing in the sunlight, the wind molding the material of her blouse to the generous curves of her breasts....

With a muttered curse, he tossed his hat on the desk and turned to Barr. "Did you get Todd squared away?"

"Sure did," Barr drawled, easing back in his chair, spreading his long legs out in front of him. "When I left him with Maude, he was eating like a logroller."

"Good," Cort murmured, the scowl on his face easing somewhat. Then to Gene, "You ready to get down to business?" His tone had turned rough and businesslike.

Before Gene could respond, Barr put in, "You mind if I stick round? I'd kinda like to know who's trying to make you a tatistic, little brother."

"That makes two of us."

"Three," Gene interceded quietly, but with the same deadly dge to his voice.

His eyes still on Gene, Cort said, "I guess the first order of he day is to fill you in on what happened."

"That's why I'm here."

Cort told him, and when he finished, the room was quiet.

Gene broke the silence. "Hell, Cort, you're one lucky son-fabitch."

"That's exactly what I told him," Barr added, reaching in his ocket and pulling out a cigarette.

Cort frowned. "I thought you'd quit smoking."

"I only light up when I'm nervous."

Cort snorted, throwing his brother a disgusted look.

"You think you were the target all along, right?" Gene sked, inching forward in his chair.

Cort sat down behind his desk and leaned on his elbows be-ore answering him. "Sure as hell do. The bullet was meant for he, not Boyd Fisher."

Gene loosened the tie around his neck. "And since they idn't get the job done the first time, they tried again." He aused. "And will more than likely try a third time."

"But who?" Cort's tone was low, as if speaking to himself.

"I don't know," Gene said, "but we're going to find out."

"Any ideas?" Barr asked, getting up and stalking to the indow.

Cort's stomach twisted into knots. "No, but I know a good lace to start."

"Me, too," Gene said. "The prison."

"Right. Check their roster to see if anyone's been released tely who might have a grudge against me."

Gene stood. "I'll get on it now."

"At least stay for lunch," Cort said, standing as well.

Gene grabbed his briefcase. "Thanks, but no thanks. If it's l the same to you, I'll head back to the office and make some phone calls." He paused and turned to Barr. "Nice meeting you."

"Same here."

Gene switched his briefcase to his other hand. "I'll be in touch, Cort."

"Me, too," Barr said, joining Gene at the door. "You watch your step, little brother, you hear?"

"Yeah," Cort muttered tersely, his shoulders slumped in despair. "I hear."

Chapter 15

Glynis cocked her head to one side while she slowly perused the kitchen and the adjoining dining room. Not bad, not bad at all, she thought with a giddy sense of excitement. The renovations on the house were progressing much faster and coming together much better than she'd ever thought possible. And with such quaint charm, too.

She'd chosen an off-white color for the walls, and the floors and counters were bright yellow and orange.

For the past week she, Cort and Barr had outdone themselves, working long hours during the day as well as in the evenings. She found herself doing things that until a few weeks ago were foreign to her—hammering, wallpapering and painting.

Still, the majority of the work had fallen on Barr's shoulders, and she knew she would never be able to repay him for the time and energy he had put into her home.

Cort, for the most part, had continued to supervise, along with Todd. "Mommy, me and Uncle Cort are the foremen on this job," her son had announced one morning. The memory brought a smile to her lips.

She thanked God that Cort had adhered to the doctors' orders and hadn't done anything strenuous. But then she'd suspected he hadn't partly because he hadn't felt like it. The wreck had set him back more than he wanted to admit. She had seen the way he grimaced when he turned a certain way or moved too quickly. Every time that happened, she was reminded of the accident and her stomach would knot.

However, with both Cort's and Gene Ridley's expertise, there was no doubt in Glynis's mind that whoever was responsible for the attempts on Cort's life would be caught and dealt with accordingly. She certainly didn't envy the culprit. When provoked, Cort was without mercy.

After all, wasn't she living testimony to that? Suddenly twisting her lips bitterly, she walked out of the kitchen and into the living room where she sank into one of the lawn chairs that Cort had brought from the ranch.

It wouldn't be long now before she and Todd would be able to move in. The time couldn't come soon enough; she honestly didn't know how much longer she could last under such nerve-racking conditions.

The knowledge that she was tangled in a web she'd never intended to weave was enough to keep her awake most nights and upset most days. It forced her to work that much harder to get the house livable.

This morning saw no change. She'd been out of bed at seven o'clock and at the house by eight. She had been working nonstop ever since.

And if her torrid relationship with Cort wasn't enough, she now had another worry to contend with. A much more serious one: Todd. At the beginning of the week, he had developed a low-grade infection. It had scared her so badly that she and Cort had made a fast trip to Houston. While not serious enough to hospitalize him, it was a cause for concern.

Until the infection cleared, Dr. Johns had told them a date for the transplant could not be discussed, even if Cort received a clean bill of health.

Now, after a week of following the doctor's orders, Todd was better. Not well, but definitely better. If only Cort would get a good report, she thought, peering down at her watch. He was due back from the doctor's office any moment now, and she expected him to stop and give her the verdict before going to the ranch.

The air-conditioning unit suddenly clicked on, claiming her attention. She listened to its steady hum for a minute, as if in a trance.

"Get a move on," she said aloud to her weary limbs. She moved quietly toward the bedroom where Todd lay sleeping on a pallet.

Just as she reached the door, he sat up and began rubbing his right eye with the back of his hand.

"Hi, darling," Glynis said, peering at him closely. Beyond looking a little weak, he seemed his same, endearing self.

"Hi, Mommy," he replied.

Glynis crossed to the pallet and sat down beside him. Then, pulling him into the crook of her arm, she whispered, "I love you."

"I love you, too, Mommy."

"How do you feel?"

He snuggled close to her breast for a moment and let her hold him. "I feel okay."

"Are you sure?" Glynis laid her hand to his forehead and was visibly relieved when he felt cool to her touch.

"Uh-huh," he muttered. "I'm thirsty, though."

She kissed him on top of the head and gently pushed him away. "Well, Mommy can take care of that problem right now. I brought you some white grape juice in the ice chest."

"After I drink it, can I help you work?"

She smiled at him and pushed a strand of hair out of his eyes. "I'm sure there's something you can do, but remember Dr. Johns doesn't want you to get too tired."

His bottom lip drooped. "I know," he said sadly.

Glynis sympathized, pulling him to her and giving him another quick squeeze before letting him go and getting to her feet. "But it won't be long and you'll be as good as new." She prayed silently that she spoke the truth.

"Mom."

Todd's low-keyed voice stopped her at the door. She swung around and faced him, her brows raised in question. "What, darling?"

He had reached for one of the many comic books scattered
around him and was holding it. "Are you and me gonna live
here?"

"Yes," she said, though not without a slight hesitation.

He frowned. "What about Uncle Cort?"

Glynis leaned against the door for support. "What . . . what
about him?"

"Won't he be lonesome if we leave him?"

She kept her voice even with effort. "I'm sure he'll miss
you. . . ."

"I know he will, too, 'cause he told me."

Glynis's heart sank. "He told you that?"

Todd nodded his head.

"When?"

"Last night, Mommy. Don't you 'member?"

She felt herself shiver. "That's right. He . . . he brought your
medicine to you at bedtime."

"And that's when he said he'd miss me—a whole bunch."

There was such a mixture of turbulent emotions churning
within her now, she could barely put her thoughts into coherent words. "He'll come see you."

"But it won't be the same," Todd said petulantly.

"No, it won't be the same," Glynis echoed, massaging the
throbbing pulse at her temple.

"Then why do we have to move? Why can't we stay with
Uncle Cort?"

She had known the question was coming. Still, it hurt; the
pain was like a dull knife in the heart. She struggled to hold her
patience and her temper. "We've been over this before, Todd.
And my answer is the same. We are not going to stay at the
ranch. Mommy wants us to have a place of our own. And as
soon as the house is fixed up, we're going to move in."

He didn't say anything; he just looked at her, then turned and
flopped onto his stomach, cradling his chin in his hands.

Her lungs ached from the sheer effort of breathing. *I won't
let him have you!* her mind screamed. *I'll see him in hell first.*
After looking at her son for another long moment, she swung
around and headed toward the kitchen, feeling as if her heart
were lined with lead.

She had just poured Todd's juice and was on her way back to the bedroom with it, along with his medicine, when a cloud of dust rose outside the living-room window. She paused and stared outside.

A Jeep had just pulled up outside the house.

Cort switched off the ignition and then sat back and watched as the dust settled around the Jeep. Damn, but they needed a rain, he thought idly. It wasn't just the farmers, either. The ranchers, himself included, were beginning to feel the pinch. June had been an unusually dry month, and July had started out the same.

But the weather was not what was dominating his thoughts. It was Glynis. Even though he hated to admit it, he was concerned about her.

Maybe what he was about to tell her would restore some of the color to her face that had been missing since Todd had gotten that infection. She'd been worried sick about him, but then so had he.

When they had walked into Dr. Johns's office, it was as if they were both headed for the guillotine. Even though the news had not been traumatic, as expected, Glynis had taken the setback quite hard.

In addition, their situation wasn't helping any. And he knew who was to blame. If he'd known what he knew now, he would never have insisted she stay at the ranch.

"Damn!" he spat aloud, yanking his hat off and slamming it down on the seat beside him.

The need for Glynis had become an ache deep inside him ever since she'd burst through the door at the farmhouse and he'd seen her anxious eyes and heard her scalding tongue.

Suddenly he looked up and saw Glynis standing at the window, staring at the Jeep, probably wondering why he was still sitting there.

He muttered another nasty expletive, then reached for his hat and after plunking it down on his head, he jerked open the door and got out.

When he walked inside, Glynis was coming out of the small bedroom, pulling the door to behind her, looking good in cutoffs that displayed her long limbs to perfection and a T-shirt that did the same for her upturned breasts.

She paused, and while their eyes met and held, he felt the involuntary response of his body.

Glynis was the first to break the eye contact. She walked toward him, not stopping until she was within touching distance. That was when he noticed her eyelashes were clumped together in tiny wet spikes. He frowned inwardly.

He waited, as did she, the silence seeming to tear at both of them.

Cort finally found his voice. "What's wrong?"

"Nothing," she said quickly.

He knew better. "You've been crying."

She looked away, but not before he saw her lower lip tremble. It took every ounce of willpower he possessed not to grab her and haul her into his arms and tell her that everything was going to be all right. But he couldn't, because he didn't know if anything was ever going to be all right again.

"Glynis, is it Todd?" He heard the panic in his own voice.

She ran a tongue over her upper lip without opening her mouth. "No, actually, he's feeling better. He's clear of fever and beginning to get restless."

"Where is he now?"

"On the pallet in the bedroom, looking at his comic books."

"Then why the tears?" he asked carefully.

She looked up at him, her wide-spaced eyes large and confused, and again he went instantly hard. He coughed and averted his gaze.

"I guess I'm just scared and tired of waiting," she finally said.

While he wasn't satisfied with her answer, he knew it would do no good to press any further, not with her chin jutted obstinately. So he said, "That makes two of us, but as far as I'm concerned, the wait is over."

Her cheeks reddened. "You got a good report?"

"Yeah, how 'bout that? My blood count is back to normal, and everything is functioning properly."

She pressed her hand against her forehead. "Thank God for that. Now as soon as Todd gets over this infection, we can get on with it."

"But in the meantime you need a break."

"What?" Caution had crept into her voice.

"A break," he repeated, "a break in your routine."

She shook her head. "No, that's exactly what I don't need. I want to be settled into this house before Todd has his surgery."

Cort's eyes took on a hard glaze. "There's no need to rush, you know."

"I disagree," she replied firmly.

"All right then, I'll take Todd by myself."

He saw fear spring into her eyes, and he cursed himself silently.

"Where?"

"Fishing."

"Fishing?"

"Yeah, fishing. You know, where you take a minnow and attach it to the end of a pole and put the pole..."

The look she gave him spoke louder than words.

"Just answering your question," he said with mock innocence. "Barr and I have a cabin on Lake Rayburn, and I've been looking forward to taking Todd there."

"Todd's not able to go fishing." Her tone was emphatic.

"Who says?"

"I do."

"So, what if I disagree?" His voice had dropped to a dangerous level.

"It doesn't matter."

He struggled desperately to hold on to his temper. "I thought we had all this settled. All I want to do is take the boy fishing." He stared up at the ceiling. "Surely you can't begrudge me that?"

She seemed to wilt right there on the spot, as if she couldn't bear to see the dull hurt reflected in his eyes. "I won't let him go without me."

"If you'll recall, I invited you, too."

"I'll... we'll go only on one condition."

"And what is that?" The blood vessels on his neck stood out.

"Barr. I want Barr to go, too."

For a moment there was silence. Cort took a step closer, his eyes flashing like glittering steel. "All right," he spat, "I'll agree to that, but hear this. . . ." He paused and loomed closer, watching the color drain from her face. "*If* I wanted to crawl in your bed and take what you so dangerously offered the other night, you, Barr or a whole damned army couldn't stop me."

With that he turned and strode toward the door, only to suddenly stop midway and swing back around. Totally ignoring Glynis's open mouth and chalk-white features, he added, "We're leaving in one hour. Be ready."

Chapter 16

"Oh, Mommy, we're gonna have so much fun. I can't wait."

Glynis forced enthusiasm into her voice. "I'm glad you're looking forward to it."

She and Todd were in the Jeep, buckled in and waiting while Cort was on the phone, having received a call just as they were walking out the door. She suspected it was from his office in Houston or he wouldn't have stalked back inside to take it.

Todd squirmed in the seat. "Uncle Cort said there are big fish in the lake and that I'll be able to catch one—one that big, Mommy." He proceeded to stretch his small arms as wide as they would go.

"Now, darling, not everything Uncle Cort tells you is necessarily true," she cautioned, reaching out to push the hair out of his eyes. Although she smiled, there was a seriousness in her tone that he picked up on.

"Why?" he asked, looking slightly crestfallen.

She searched for the right answer. "Well, for one thing Uncle Cort knows how to catch the big ones and you don't."

"He'll help me," Todd said confidently, his smile wide and innocent. "He promised."

Glynis swallowed a sigh. "I'm sure he will."

Before Todd could reply, Cort opened the door on the driver's side and got in.

No one spoke while he jammed the key in the ignition. Then, turning impersonal eyes on Glynis, he asked, "All set?"

"What about . . . Barr?"

Though his lips tightened, his voice remained as calm and impersonal as before. "He'll be down later."

Glynis released her breath slowly and stared straight ahead, trying her best to disregard the way the inside of the vehicle seemed to shrink the moment Cort got inside. She was instantly aware of his cologne, the way his hands moved in a caressing motion around the steering wheel, the same way they had once caressed her. . . .

She blinked and turned her head to gaze outside the window, watching as the city limits of Lufkin disappeared and the highway toward Etoile and Lake Sam Rayburn stretched in front of her.

Beside her, Todd was hanging on to Cort's every word, listening to tales of fishing ventures.

It had crossed her mind earlier to tell Cort she'd changed her plans, that she and Todd weren't going after all. But she hadn't been able to do that to Todd. When she'd told him that Cort was taking him fishing, his pale face had brightened, and he'd gotten so excited that she hadn't the heart to disappoint him.

So she had decided to make the best of the outing, thereby conserving her energy and her wits. Though she was loath to admit it, the break would do her good as well.

How long had it been since she'd laughed, really laughed? She didn't know, but it had been a long time. Too long. And maybe, just maybe, she might even catch a fish herself.

Suddenly she felt a hand on her arm. In a jerking motion, she looked down into her son's upturned face.

"Mommy, what's funny?"

"What makes you think something's funny?"

" 'Cause you're smiling, that's why."

"Mmm, so I was," Glynis said, venturing a glance in Cort's direction.

As if feeling the pull of her eyes, he turned and looked at her.

"Why, Mommy?" Todd was asking again, jerking on the hem of her shorts.

She turned her gaze from Cort to her son. "I was thinking about the time I caught a big fish."

Todd bounced in the seat. "Wow! Really, Mommy? You caught a fish?"

Over her son's display of excitement, she heard Cort's swift intake of breath. Then he looked at her, and for a brief moment his eyes seemed to absorb every part of her face and body. "So you do remember." His voice was rough.

"I remember," she said huskily.

"'Member what, Mommy?" Todd was looking back and forth from her to Cort.

With her heart thumping, Glynis finally focused on Todd. "The fish, son. I remember catching a big fish."

"Just one. That's all you ever catched?"

"Caught," she said gently.

Cort was smiling down at Todd. "Your mommy wasn't the best with a fishing pole, that's for sure."

Todd wrinkled his nose. "Most girls aren't. They don't like crawly worms or little fishes they have to put on the hook."

Cort laughed a deep, hearty laugh, one that sent Glynis's pulse skyrocketing. She eased another glance in his direction, but saw that he had eyes only for Todd.

Suddenly Glynis ached for him to look at her like that again—with tenderness and love instead of raw desire—only to then rebuke herself for her maudlin thoughts, knowing there would never be anything but red, hot desire between them.

Glynis was roused out of her thoughts a short time later when Cort stopped the Jeep in front of a small grocery and bait store.

"Why are we stopping?" she muttered inanely.

"Why do you think?" There was a touch of acid in his tone. "For food and bait."

"Oh."

Cort shook his head and beckoned for Todd to come with him.

Glynis scrambled out the door on her side, feeling foolish. "I'll help," she said unsteadily, upping her pace to catch up with them.

Cort stopped and swung around. "You think you can handle rounding up some sandwich stuff—chips, drinks, et cetera?"

She reacted as if stung. "Yes, of course I can."

Once they were back in the Jeep and on their way, Glynis leaned her head back and closed her eyes, wondering how she was going to get through the next two days.

"Mommy, Mommy, we're here!" Todd was saying, once again bouncing up and down in the seat between them.

"Goodness, darling," Glynis said gently but firmly, "you'd best settle down or you'll be worn out before you ever wet a line."

"Are you gonna go out in the boat right now?" Todd demanded of Cort, while Glynis looked around at her surroundings.

"Yep. Just as soon as we get unloaded. Here, give me a hand, will ya?"

"Sure thing," Todd said in his most grown-up voice.

Glynis had her hand on the door handle, but she couldn't move. "You call this a cabin?" she challenged, her gaze swinging to Cort. "Why, it's nicer than most people's houses."

Sitting on top of a hill, the two-story brick was a replica of a Swiss chalet, made even more spectacular by the terraced yard that didn't stop until it reached the lake.

"I take it you like it." His lips curved into what she thought was a smile.

"Like it? It's beautiful."

"Yeah, it is, isn't it." He sighed. "I just wish I could spend more time here."

"You could—you just won't," she responded without thinking.

His expression changed. "You're right, I could. And I just might remedy that once the transplant is over and Todd gets on his feet."

His meaning was not lost on her, but before she responded in kind, his booted foot hit the ground and, with Todd in tow, they headed for the cabin.

Glynis had no choice but to follow, though she fumed with every step she took.

The inside was every bit as beautiful as the outside, Glynis noted. The downstairs was composed of the kitchen, dining and living area, the latter dominated by a fireplace and book-shelves. But what made the house special was the view from the ceiling-to-floor windows that flanked an entire wall. The lake twinkled in the distant sunlight like millions of tiny diamonds.

However, she didn't have much time to soak up the primitive beauty. By the time she put the groceries away and tossed their overnight bags in the bedrooms upstairs, Cort had the boat loaded and was ready to go.

"I'm coming," she shouted before taking another second to tie her hair back with a ribbon that matched her green shorts and halter top. Then, bounding down the stairs, she made her way outside and down the slope where the boat was moored, feeling excited in spite of herself.

"You gonna bait your own hook, Mommy?" Todd asked twenty minutes later, after the boat was safely anchored in an alcove that Cort promised was loaded with white perch.

She frowned. "Well . . ."

"That's okay, Mommy, I'll do it for you."

"Would you?" Her tone oozed relief. "I'd sure like that."

From his place near the back of the boat, Cort snorted.

Glynis flashed him a look. "I can do it, you know."

"Well, then, do it," he said flatly. Then, directing his gaze to Todd, his expression lightened, and he grinned. "Got to learn the rules up front, Todd, my boy. If you fish, you have to bait your own hook."

Todd giggled. "Mommy, Uncle Cort says you have to stick your hand down in that box and get one of those little fishes and stick that hook through his eye—"

"Todd, that's enough!" She shivered.

This time both Cort and Todd threw back their heads and laughed. Glynis merely glared at both of them. But in the end, and much to the delight of her son, she did indeed bait her own hook as she'd been taught by Cort many years before.

Just as she was about to lower the baited hook on the end of a cane pole into the water, Cort came up beside her. Her hand stilled in mid-action.

"Here," he said, handing her a hat with a sun visor, "you'd better wear this in addition to suntan lotion. You have put on the lotion, haven't you?"

After anchoring the pole on the side of the boat, Glynis looked up at him steadily for a long minute, her head tipped back slightly. "No," she murmured, suddenly thrown into confusion by the way his eyes were targeted on her halter top. "I put some on Todd, but . . . but I didn't use it on myself."

"Well, I suggest you do." His voice sounded rough, like sandpiper. "You know how tender your skin is."

She touched her throat and kept staring at him, the intensity of the moment as burning as the sun bearing down on them.

At last Cort muttered tautly, "Todd and I'll be fishing in the rear."

Her heart was still beating harder than it was supposed to seconds later when she watched him stop beside Todd, lift his rod and cast it into the water.

She was captivated by the way the muscles pulsed in his shoulders and arms every time he flicked the rod. Having discarded his shirt shortly after they arrived, he was skimpily clad in cutoffs and tennis shoes without socks. With his tanned face and body and his head bent in concentration, he reminded Glynis of a Greek god.

Glynis would have stared at him a second longer, only he chose that instant to swing around, as if feeling her hot gaze.

They stared deep into each other's eyes. The connective force of their gaze was palpable.

"Uncle Cort," Todd said, pointing a finger in the opposite direction. "Look, there comes another boat."

The moment was gone. Cort's expression tightened, and he turned around. Yet Glynis was unable to pull her eyes off the father and son who stood side by side eyeing the boat with the skiers trailing behind.

"Oh, no," she whispered, feeling as if she'd suddenly been punched in the stomach. Why hadn't she noticed before how much they actually favored each other, how wonderful, how right they looked together.

Violent and conflicting emotions suddenly charged through Glynis, and in order to squelch them, she grabbed the pole, only to then yelp with pain.

"Damn, damn, damn," she muttered under her breath. At the same time she stared down at the end of her middle finger. The hook that should have been in a fish's mouth was now stuck in her.

"What now?" Cort was beside her, his voice harsh and impatient, as though he resented the interruption.

"It's . . . nothing," she said, clamping her lips together, determined not to bother him.

"Let me see." His voice no longer had that hard edge. His concern seemed genuine. No longer narrowed and filled with hostility, his eyes moved over her searchingly.

Without warning, he reached for her hand. "Don't lie to me," he said between clenched teeth, obviously not wanting to alarm Todd, who was intently watching his rod, unaware that anything out of the ordinary was going on.

A colorful expletive split the air when Cort saw the hook protruding from the end of her finger.

Glynis hadn't wanted to demonstrate any weakness, but she was losing control. Her stomach was beginning to heave sickeningly.

"I . . . I was going to pull it out, but . . ."

The rest of the sentence died on her lips as he took the hook out of her flesh and brought her finger to his lips and sucked on it.

Glynis's heart almost died in her chest, and for a moment the wound was of secondary importance. Their eyes met and locked, and even when he turned sideways and spat the blood into the water, they never broke eye contact.

Her breath came in short, gaspy spurts that drew his eyes down to her breasts. Glynis's eyelids fluttered, while she blushed uncontrollably, knowing that he was watching her nipples turn rigid.

He swallowed and looked at her intently. Her eyes were filled with awe that he cared. His burned with desire.

Then, as if angry with her, or with himself, he dropped her hand and drew back. "I've got some turpentine. If you'll soak your finger in it, it won't be sore."

Following that brusque delivery, he made his way back to his tackle box, and after rummaging through it for a second, came back, holding a bottle in one hand and a small cup in the other.

She forced her eyes on the bottle and watched as he poured its contents into the cup. But in reality that was all she was able to do. Her body felt hot and cold by turns, and tremors were shaking her lower body with want.

"Mommy, Mommy, come quick!" Todd laughed out loud, still unaware that anything was amiss. "Come see what I caught."

"I'm coming." Taking a deep breath, Glynis set the cup aside, stood, and without looking at Cort, slowly made her way to where her son was standing.

In spite of the shaky start, Todd's first catch was the beginning of a successful afternoon. After she had soaked her finger, the pain was gone except for a slight tenderness.

In no time the cooler boxes were filled with nice-sized fish, a mixture of bass and white perch, both native to the fresh waters of East Texas. It had been so long since she had tasted either that her mouth watered.

Thinking about dinner made her suddenly glance at her watch. Six o'clock. How the time had flown. And she suspected Todd was getting tired even though he would never admit it.

"Cort," she called from her seat at the front of the boat, pulling in her pole and shading her eyes, "don't you think it's time we called it quits, got Todd back to the house?"

Cort was busy helping Todd reel in a fish and didn't answer her for a minute. Todd's excited squeal could be heard for miles around.

Once the fish was off the hook and safely in the box, however, Cort turned toward her. "Yeah. It's getting late."

"Aw, Uncle Cort," Todd wailed, "do we have to?"

Cort smiled down at him. "Yes, we have to," he mimicked.

"Can I drive the boat home?" Todd asked eagerly.

Cort swatted him on the rear and grinned. "Thought you'd never ask."

It was only after they had arrived back at the house and put the gear away, and Cort and Todd had cleaned and filleted the fish, that the back door opened.

"Hiya everybody," Barr drawled, breezing in.

Cort paused in his actions and stared at his brother with a smirk on his lips. "I knew you'd show up after all the work was done."

"You mean I missed all the fun?"

Cort snorted. "Yep, you sure did."

Barr ambled deeper into the room and winked at Todd, who rushed up to him. "Meant to get here sooner, but I got busy working on the house and time got away from me."

"Too bad you weren't with us, Uncle Barr," Todd said, grinning broadly. "We catched a lot of fish."

Glynis closed the refrigerator and faced Barr, a frown marring her features. "You mean you worked this afternoon?"

"Yeah. Put the finishing touches on several things. If all goes well, you and Todd should be able to move in next week."

Glynis's eyes brimmed with excitement. "We can? Oh, Barr, that's great."

"Mommy," Todd began, "I told you I don't—"

"Not now, Todd," Glynis cut in quickly. Her tone brooked no argument.

Todd hung his head. "Yes, ma'am."

Cort turned a piercing gaze on Glynis. "Why not let the boy finish?" he said in a soft, dangerous tone.

Glynis raised her chin a notch. But before she could say anything, Barr chimed in, his gaze on Todd.

"Hey, fellow, how 'bout you and me taking a spin in the boat? No fishing, just a ride out on the lake to watch the sun set."

Todd switched his gaze to Glynis. "Mommy, can I?"

Doing her best to regroup, Glynis twisted her head toward her son. "Oh, Todd, honey, I don't think so. You've had a long afternoon...."

"Oh, please, Mom, please. I'm not tired. I cross my heart, I'm not." With childlike movements, he proceeded to do just that, crossing his thin arms over his chest.

Glynis couldn't help but smile, only to have it turn into a quick frown. "He's had a long afternoon, Barr."

"I promise we won't be gone longer than an hour."

Glynis tweaked Todd's ear. "All right, you little con artist. But when you come back, it's dinner and straight to bed."

The second Todd and Barr exited the room, Glynis cut a glance in Cort's direction. He was leaning against the hearth, his arms folded across his chest.

There was a drawn-out silence.

Her skin felt hot under his gaze. Finally, in a halting voice, she said, "I'm . . . going to take a shower."

"You should listen to Todd, you know." His tone was soft, yet its timbre made it sound thunderous in the quiet room.

She didn't pretend to misunderstand him. "Todd's only a child. He'll make adjustments." Then, without giving him a chance to respond, she wheeled around and dashed up the stairs.

Thirty minutes later she was back downstairs with a new resolve. She would not let Cort rattle her or goad her into arguing with him over her and Todd's imminent departure from the ranch.

She found him on the deck, fiddling with the electric fish fryer, the fish and french fries ready for frying on a nearby table.

It was obvious he'd also showered, as his hair was damp. But he hadn't bothered to shave. There was more than a hint of stubble on his face and chin.

She paused in the doorway and swallowed against the rising heat inside her, trying not to notice how the tight, worn jeans did little to minimize the bulge between his thighs. She forced her eyes away, despising the way her body responded, yet unable to control it. She felt like a frayed cable that was stretched too tight. She had to get away from him.

Nervously stepping forward, she said with a forced lightness she was far from feeling, "Need any help?"

He spun around, as if unaware she'd been watching him. "No," he said. His eyes raked over her, before coming once again to rest on her breasts.

Glynis averted her gaze toward the sun setting across the water. Her eyes widened.

"It's something, isn't it?" Cort drawled, following her eyes.

"It's absolutely breathtaking. I can understand why you like to come down here."

"Feel free to use it anytime you like," he said unexpectedly.

"Do you mean that?"

His head came up quickly. "I wouldn't have said it if I didn't."

"Well, er, thanks," she said uneasily, still not trusting his motives. Yet she wasn't about to look a gift horse in the mouth. "I've never seen Todd so happy."

Cort actually laughed. "Yeah, he did have a great time. The little bugger is a damned good fisherman."

"Yes, he is, isn't he? Just think, when he gets well, he can fish every day."

"Only he won't be around to fish, will he?"

"What do you mean?" Her mouth was dry.

"You know exactly what I mean. You don't intend to stay in Lufkin, do you?"

"Who told you that?"

He thrust his face close to hers. "You did."

She backed up and stopped only when she plowed against the brick wall. "You don't know what you're talking about," she hedged.

"Deny it, then."

Her temper flared. "I don't owe you an explanation one way or the other."

"That's where you're wrong. As long as I'm footing Todd's bills, you damn sure do."

"I'll pay back every cent!" Glynis cried, her eyes blazing, her arms outstretched as if to stop him from getting closer.

"I think I'll settle on payment right now."

"Don't." Her voice was little more than a hoarse croak as she struggled to brace herself.

But there was no stopping him. Their lips were only a hair-breadth apart. She shoved at his chest to ward him off.

With little effort, he grasped her arms and pulled her against him.

"Don't fight me," he groaned, burying his mouth in her scented neck. "You want this just as much as I do."

He trailed kisses around her cheek until he reached her lips. He kissed her hard. She tried to wiggle free, still determined not to give in, but he was indisputably in control. He sought entrance into her mouth, and with the tender penetration, he used his mouth as a weapon to skillfully wipe out her resistance. It worked.

Glynis was burning. She had never wanted anything the way she wanted Cort's mouth, his hands, his body. She matched his stroking tongue with hers, tasting him until their lips fused as one breathless, intoxicating unit.

With her hands in his hair, she drank him in, feeling his steely hardness between her legs.

Finally gasping for breath, Cort moved her to arm's length, and for a moment their eyes clung as each remembered how it once had been between them, how it hopefully would be again.

The wind whistled through the trees as the evening's shadow settled around them, creating a cooling balm for their heated skin. But nothing had the power to dissipate their hungry craving for each other.

He lowered his eyes to her breasts, taking in her nipples as they dented her T-shirt. He fingered one, then the other while she touched him, her fingers tracing exquisite patterns.

Cort jerked his head up and groaned as if in mortal pain. Then returning glazed eyes to her, he began tearing at the tiny buttons on her shirt. Finally the last one was undone, and her breasts spilled into his waiting hands.

Groaning again, he dipped his head and took a breast in his mouth; her nipple throbbed, and a long sigh that was his name broke from her at the pleasure his lips were bringing her. He moved to nuzzle her long throat, but her breasts were too close, too tempting, and he bent close to suck them again—first one, then the other, harder.

Still that didn't seem to satisfy him. He nuzzled her neck, massaged his face between her breasts, nipped at her collarbone with his teeth and inhaled the scent of her body like an aphrodisiac.

"Glynis?" he asked softly.

"Yes," she whispered, even as she lowered her hand to caress him.

"Oh, God," he said in a half-strangled cry, before quickly turning her in his arms and propelling her urgently through the open glass door into the living room. Together they sank as one onto the thick carpet.

"This is for all those times I've dreamed of," he whispered, quickly and adeptly peeling their clothes from their bodies.

With nothing between them but the air they breathed, he bent over her and watched with glowing eyes as he trailed his fingers feverishly, urgently across her breasts, down to her stomach, to the insides of her thighs, where he lingered. And while holding her, sealing his lips to hers, he eased his fingers inside her.

"Oh, Cort!" she cried.

He stopped kissing her to whisper, "Did I hurt you? You were so wet. . . ."

"No!" she cried again, moving her hips rhythmically in response to his fingers, feeling that terminal heat inside her.

"Forgive me," he rasped suddenly, "but I can't wait. It's been so long. . . ."

He entered quickly and deeply then, and she grasped him, her arms and legs locking him to her. She heard a deep cry, but she didn't know if it was her own or his. She could only feel him inside her.

She began to shake. Only then did Cort bury his face in her hair and surrender to an explosion of release so intense, so shattering that he lost himself in her.

Chapter 17

They lay on the couch in the living room, fully clothed now, Cort at one end, Glynis at the other. They both had mugs full of hot coffee, and their bare legs were entwined. It seemed for the moment that the feeling of skin against skin was a sensation they both needed.

At least for Glynis, anyway. From under thick eyelashes, she watched Cort as he sipped from his mug as if he was enjoying it. The lines around his eyes and mouth weren't nearly as deeply embedded, nor was he holding himself with such iron control.

She knew their lovemaking was crazy and would likely lead to more heartbreak, especially for her. But she didn't regret it.

Cort had been right. She had wanted, ached for his touch and she could blame no one but herself when it blew up in her face.

And Cort. Well, she had no idea what was going though his mind, but again she didn't care. At this very moment, he was the same man she had fallen in love with. For now that was enough.

With this thought in mind, Glynis slowly and shyly moved her leg against his in a massaging motion.

"Glynis."

"Mmm?"

"Was Jay good to you . . . and Todd?"

Her leg fell still. "What do you mean?"

His eyes were so intent, he forced her to look at him. "You know what I mean. Did he ever . . . hit you?"

"No," she said, her voice trembling. "But he came close to it one time." She turned away.

"When?"

"Shortly . . . after Todd was born. He never could, never did accept him."

"Is that why you never had any more children?"

"Yes."

"Speaking of children. Are you . . . using anything?"

Everything inside her seemed to shut down. "Do you mean, am I on the pill?"

"I guess that's what I'm trying to say."

"I'm not," she said, then added when she saw the color recede from his face, "but you don't have to worry, it's not the right time of the month."

Without responding, he changed the subject. "Jay started drinking shortly after Todd was born, right?"

She bit her lip as she let her breath escape in a slow sigh. "How did you know?"

"Oh, I knew, all right." His tone was low and husky. "I made it my business to know."

"Oh, Cort," she whispered, moisture collecting in her eyes, "we made a mess of things, didn't we?"

"Mess. That's hardly the word. I'd say we screwed up royally."

The tears chose that instant to spill from her eyes.

Cort scowled. "Come here."

Glynis didn't hesitate. She crawled the length of the couch and snuggled into his outstretched arms.

He cupped a breast in his hand and began tugging on the nipple.

"Having a baby hasn't changed you all that much," he said quietly.

"How . . . how do you mean?"

His hold on her tightened. "You're still tight inside, hot . . ."

"Oh, Cort," she groaned, lifting her eyes to his, the sound of his voice, his words, disturbing her almost as much as the glare she saw in his eyes. Her breathing quickened.

"Don't look at me like that," he whispered.

"Like what?"

"Like how good it was when I was inside you—"

"Cort, please," she said, her voice shaking.

"Ah, my darling, my nemesis," he murmured, stroking her as if reveling in the feel of her next to him.

"I didn't mean to be," she said, trying to keep her thoughts on track.

"I know." The thickly spoken words came after he'd set both cups on the coffee table, and after his hard mouth had swooped down on hers, prolonging the embrace until she hung weak and shuddering in his arms.

It was much later when she said his name on a ragged breath. "Cort."

"Uh-huh?"

"Have . . . have there been lots of . . . women?"

For a moment he didn't say anything; he just continued to knead her breast. "There have been some."

"Were . . . any of them important to you? I mean . . . I thought you would . . . have married. . . ." She broke off, feeling like an utter fool. But even if his answer killed her soul, she had to know.

"Well, you thought wrong," he said flatly.

"I didn't mean to pry," she began awkwardly, realizing that she had shattered the fragile moment into a thousand pieces.

He rolled into a sitting position, then stood, offering her his hand. "Come on," he said in a strained voice, "I hear the boat."

"So do I," she whispered, her voice as dry as a rustling leaf.

Though he continued to hold her hand, he looked anywhere but at her. Finally he stared down at her.

Something soft and strange flickered across his face, some emotion she wasn't able to read—maybe pain, maybe something that went beyond pain. "I . . ." he began at last.

Glynis shook her head. "I know what you were going to say, that this doesn't change things between us. . . ."

"No, that wasn't what I was going to say."

She felt hot and cold by turns. "What . . . were you going to say, then?"

Footsteps pounded on the deck. He dropped her hand and stepped back, his face closed, as if a door had slammed shut on it.

Her skin burned where his hand had been.

"Cort?"

His eyes delved into her for a long, static moment. Then he said, "Forget it. It wasn't important anyway."

For the longest moment, Glynis couldn't move, feeling as though she'd been kicked in the stomach.

"Mommy, why do I have to go back to the hospital?"

Todd's face was pale and pinched, and his blue eyes, so like Cort's, locked on Glynis.

"You want to be well, don't you?" she asked softly, patiently.

"But I am well," he countered sullenly.

Glynis's troubled gaze sought Cort, who was standing against the wooden rail of the deck at the ranch, his hands jammed into his pockets. His tightly drawn features told her he was as troubled as she.

They had driven in from Houston only thirty minutes earlier, and after going to their respective rooms to change clothes, had met on the deck, where she and Cort planned to tell Todd about his upcoming surgery and Cort's role as donor.

After examining Todd and finding no traces of infection, Dr. Johns had scheduled the surgery for two weeks from today. It had been Glynis's decision not to tell Todd on the way home, because he had been so hyper after being poked and pulled on for an hour. He had slept in her arms for most of the trip home.

Once they had gathered on the deck, Mrs. Springer brought a tray of cookies and a pitcher of lemonade. And though their plates were piled high with goodies, they had remained untouched.

"Look, Todd," Cort was saying now, having ambled over to where Todd and Glynis sat next to each other, "going into the hospital is never any fun. Your mother and I know that and so do you." Before Todd could answer, Cort sat down in a lounge chair next to them and drew Todd's slight body between his legs.

"Then why do I have to go?" Todd asked again, climbing up on one of Cort's knees.

Without looking at Glynis, Cort went on, "Because like Mommy told you, this time when you get out, you'll be well."

Todd's wide eyes darted to Glynis and then back to Cort. "You mean I won't have to go back ever again?"

Glynis couldn't have answered him if she'd wanted to; there was too big a lump in her throat. All she could do was listen as Cort patiently and tenderly talked to his son.

Already Todd had been to hell, and he was soon to go there again. Sometimes, like now for instance, she didn't think she could stand it. If only she could bear the pain for him.

And she knew Cort was experiencing similar emotions, though he would never allow his emotions to get out of control. Yet a long moment passed before he spoke again.

"Yeah, that's what it means." Cort smiled and goosed him under the chin. "No more of that yucky-tasting mess that you've had to swallow for so long."

Todd angled his head. "Will you be at the hospital with Mommy?"

"You bet."

"Promise."

"I promise."

"Good," Todd said, showing wisdom far beyond his years, "'cause Mommy always cries when they hurt me."

"What if I cry, too?" Cort's voice seemed to come from a long way off.

Suddenly Glynis stood and averted her face, determined they wouldn't see the tears that were coursing down her cheeks. Nonetheless she felt Cort's eyes bore into her for a second, before he turned back to Todd.

Todd was grinning. "You wouldn't do that, Uncle Cort. Only girls cry." Then suddenly the grin disappeared, and his face fell. "But I cry sometimes, too," he admitted, lowering his head, "especially when it hurts."

Cort grabbed Todd then and pulled him close. "That's all right," he muttered roughly. "I know, and I understand. That's why I'm going to give you something from my body that's going to make you well."

Todd squirmed out of his arms and looked at Glynis. "Did you know that, Mommy?"

"Yes, darling."

Todd turned back to Cort. "What are you gonna give me?"

"Maybe we better let your mother explain. She knows more about it than I do."

Glynis did, and when she was through, Todd was quiet for a moment as if deep in thought. Then, wide-eyed, he said to Glynis, "Someday I'll be tall like Uncle Cort, won't I?"

Glynis couldn't bring herself to meet Cort's eyes, even though she felt them on her. "Yes, son," she whispered against the fresh onslaught of tears flooding her eyes. "You'll grow up to be just like . . . Uncle Cort."

Cort stood and cleared his throat. "Todd, how does a surprise sound to you?"

Glynis smiled at her son. "Mmm, sounds like fun to me."

"Me, too!" Todd gushed.

"You two stay put and I'll be right back."

A few minutes later Cort reappeared with a scruffy puppy in his arms that looked no older than six weeks.

"Wow!" Todd cried, running toward Cort, his arms outstretched.

Excitement replacing the tears in Glynis's eyes, she followed.

"Oh, Todd, isn't he cute?" she said, watching as Cort handed the squirming puppy to Todd.

The puppy began licking Todd's face with its tiny wet tongue. Todd giggled wildly while trying his best to control it. "What's it's name, Uncle Cort?"

Cort laughed. "That's for you to decide. You can name him whatever you want. He's yours."

"Mine," Todd whispered in awe.

"All yours, but you have to take care of him, which means feeding him every day."

With the puppy still wriggling in his arms, Todd shifted his gaze to Glynis. "Can I keep him, Mommy?"

Glynis leaned over and rubbed the top of the puppy's head. "Only if you do what Uncle Cort said."

"Oh, I will, I promise."

"Okay, we'll see," Glynis said somewhat sternly, yet with a bright smile on her face.

Suddenly Todd's face clouded. "But who will take care of him while I go to the hospital?" His chin wobbled slightly.

"Oh, I'm sure Mrs. Springer will be glad to do that for you, or maybe Uncle Barr will." Cort's tone was both gentle and reassuring and seemed to satisfy Todd. His features instantly brightened again.

"Have you thought of a name yet?" Glynis asked, glancing down at her son with adoring eyes.

"Not yet, Mommy. Give me time, will ya?"

Glynis laughed along with Cort. "Sorry, son, didn't mean to rush you," she said.

Todd lowered the puppy to the ground. "I'm going to take him for a walk," he announced proudly.

"All right, but remember to walk slowly."

When Todd scampered off, the puppy followed, its short legs pumping madly to keep up with Todd. Glynis raised her eyes to Cort's, which were already centered on her, and she and Cort both smiled.

"That . . . was thoughtful of you," she said, her mouth feeling as dry as cotton. "He's . . . Todd's never had a puppy or any animal of his own."

"Which is a damned shame."

"I know," she whispered, unable to tear her eyes from his.

She knew by the way he watched her mouth when they talked, and by the way his eyes seemed drawn to her body, that he wanted her, had not stopped wanting her since that day at the lake, the day he'd taken her.

And now, she could hear his breathing, could feel condensation forming in the space between them. She reached out to him frantically, only to suddenly stiffen in the arms that were locked around her like a vise.

The sound of an approaching vehicle shattered the moment as swiftly and accurately as an explosion would have done.

Pushing her away, Cort swore loudly and violently. "Who the hell..." he began, only to let his words fade. They both recognized the car that stopped in the drive.

"It's... it's Gene," Glynis said unnecessarily, grappling to regain her composure.

Cort didn't reply.

Nevertheless, his expression wasn't lost on her. "He's here about the... your accident, isn't he?"

"Yeah." Cort's response sounded laconic at best.

"Do you have any leads?" Glynis asked, saying the first thing that came to mind.

Cort kept his eyes on Gene, who was getting out of his car and walking toward them. "I'm about to find out."

"Well, I guess I'll go see how Todd and the puppy are faring," she murmured, feeling as if the ground were still shifting under her feet.

"Yeah, why don't you do that," Cort responded, his tone detached.

Taking him at his word, Glynis turned and headed in Todd's direction, and even though she felt Cort's brooding eyes follow her, she knew his thoughts were not on her.

"Wanna beer, or something?"

Gene Ridley shook his head in response to Cort's offer. "No thanks, not right now."

Cort shrugged. "If you change your mind..."

"I'll holler," Gene said.

They were in Cort's office, and while Gene rummaged through his briefcase, which he'd placed on one edge of Cort's desk, Cort sat in his chair and leaned back, propping his booted feet on the opposite corner.

"What do you have?" Cort asked evenly.

But Gene wasn't fooled. The hard, menacing edge was clearly visible in Cort's tone, and Gene picked up on it instantly.

"Names. I got names."

"Anything else?"

Gene shoved his glasses forward on the bridge of his nose. "Not at the moment."

"Well, the names are a start."

"Oh, before I forget to tell you," Gene said, snapping his briefcase shut, "Boyd Fisher came by this morning. Wanted to know how his case was progressing."

"What did you tell him?"

"I told him that he didn't have a case, that it was you they were after, not him."

Cort threw back his head and laughed. "Bet that rang his bell."

A smile toyed with Gene's rigid mouth. "I don't think he believed me at first, but after I told him about the Jeep, he changed his mind." Gene paused and laid the paper in front of Cort. "Of course, I told him that until we had proof that you are the target and he isn't, we'd still be covering him."

"Good," Cort said, removing his feet from the desk and rolling the chair forward, all in one fluid movement. He then picked up the paper and began scrutinizing it.

After a moment, Cort looked up. "This is the list of recent parolees, right?"

Gene was standing, watching him. He squinted. "Right. Any of those names leap out at you as possible suspects?"

"Yeah, as a matter of fact they do."

"Which ones?"

"John Brodrick, Ames Coleman and Al Sabo."

"As I recall, they each swore to get even with you when they got out of the slammer."

Cort shoved back the chair and stood. "Let's get rolling on this quick. If one of these is our man, I want the son of a bitch stopped. Find where they are and check 'em out."

"It's as good as done."

"Now, about the government contract."

"It's looking good. The papers are underneath the list. Take a good look at them and I'll get back to you in a few days."

"Right."

"By the way, when do you think you'll be back in the office?"

"Not for a while, I'm afraid," Cort answered with a sigh. "Todd's surgery is in a couple of weeks."

Gene gnawed at his lower lip. "I see." Following a moment of silence, Gene added, "You know I hope all goes well."

Cort nodded. "Thanks."

The moment Cort was alone, he sat back down at his desk and picked up the stack of papers, only to suddenly thrust them aside. The day had been long and nerve-racking. He couldn't concentrate on work; it was that simple. He could only think of Glynis and how good it had felt, *how right*, to make love to her once again.

Sighing deeply, he leaned back and stretched his neck from side to side. The muscles in his neck were so tight, he felt they might snap at any moment. And well they should, he thought. It would serve him right for fooling with dynamite on a short fuse.

But now that he'd feasted on the delights of her body once again . . .

Suddenly he heard the door creak behind him. Scowling, he swung around. His scowl deepened.

"Dammit, Barr! That's a good way to get your head blown off."

"Hello to you, too, little brother."

Cort's face cleared somewhat. "Sorry."

"Apology accepted," Barr said, propping himself against the door frame. "Maude told me Gene just left. Did he bring you any names?"

"Yep. Pull up a chair and I'll fill you in."

You can do it, her mind kept telling her. *You can do it.*

But Glynis wasn't so sure. She had been jogging forty-five minutes, but her goal was sixty minutes. It was her only way to combat stress, she kept telling herself, forcing one leg in front of the other.

Sweat glistened in her hair, rolled down her face.

That passionate interlude with Cort at the lake tore at her night and day. Making love to him had done very little to calm the turmoil inside her; it had only made it worse. She should never have let it happen. But there was nothing she could do about it now except condemn herself for her weakness.

Their hot coupling had done nothing but fill a temporary need inside her, a need that was threatening to consume her again with each passing day.

And she knew if Cort hadn't regretted that interlude a week ago, heaven help her, but she would have swallowed her pride and gone to him, much as it shamed her to admit it.

If that wasn't enough of a problem, Todd's upcoming surgery had her nerves stretched as tight as they would go.

Suddenly she couldn't make it any farther. Her heart felt as if it were going to burst from her chest.

Taking deep, shuddering breaths, Glynis slowed to a fast walk and turned up the road that led to the ranch. After going straight to her room, she showered, slipped on a blue shirt and jeans and went into the kitchen.

Maude was busy preparing lunch. She stopped what she was doing and stared at Glynis. "My dear, what on earth? You look exhausted."

"I've been running."

"I thought you were supposed to do that either early in the morning or late in the evening."

"You are," Glynis said, crossing to the refrigerator, getting out a jug of juice and pouring herself a full glass. "I pulled a no-no. Ten o'clock is definitely not the best time to run."

Maude sniffed. "If you're not careful, someone will be picking you up off that dirt road one of these days."

Glynis smiled before taking a drink from her glass. "You're probably right, but my nerves needed it."

Maude's look turned sympathetic. "Mr. Cort told me the surgery's soon."

"It is. And speaking of Todd, do you know where he is? He was sleeping when I left."

"He ate breakfast and told me he was going to take Champ for a walk."

"I guess I'd better go find him. I don't want him getting too hot and tired." She paused at the door. "By the way, where is Cort?"

"He's at Barr's, helping him mend a fence."

Fifteen minutes later Glynis still had not found Todd. She had searched the yard and the barn, checking with the ranch hands, who hadn't seen him, either.

Nobody had seen him or the puppy.

By the time she entered the barn farthest from the house, where the horses were stabled, Glynis felt the stirrings of panic. Where was he?

Willis, one of Cort's most trusted hands, was brushing down a horse.

"Have you seen Todd?" she asked without preamble.

The old man raised himself to full height and rubbed his forehead. "No, ma'am, can't say that I have. Why?"

"I can't find him anywhere," Glynis said, hearing her voice crack.

"I'm sure he's around here somewhere, Miss."

"Look, would you please saddle a horse for me?"

"Sure will."

Minutes later Glynis's concern had tripled. She refused to speculate on the many things that might have befallen her son.

By the time she found Cort hunkered over a broken string of fence, fear had gripped her from head to toe.

The pounding of the horse's hooves brought Cort to his feet. As she jerked the reins to a halt directly in front of him, he frowned.

"What the hell, Glynis?"

"It's . . . Todd. I . . . I can't find him anywhere."

Chapter 18

Cort reached Glynis just as she started to get off the horse. Circling her waist with his hands, he lowered her to the ground.

"What do you mean you can't find him?"

Glynis mopped her brow with the back of her hand and looked up into Cort's pale, taut features. "I came back to the house from jogging and began looking for him. Maude told me he ate breakfast and went to play with Champ."

"Did you check the barns?"

"Yes, I've looked everywhere."

"And no one's seen him?"

Glynis shook her head. "No."

Suddenly he felt his heart slam against his rib cage. Had Todd been kidnapped? Had the man after him taken his son?

Fear made him move quickly. With a murderous glint in his eyes, Cort detached Glynis's clinging hands from the front of his shirt and put her at arm's length. Then, twisting his head, he beckoned for Barr, who was already walking toward them.

"Get the lead out, man!"

"I'm coming, I'm coming," Barr called. "What's up?"

By the time he reached them, Cort's eyes were back on Glynis. She looked as though she might faint. Her face was the color of chalk. He longed to reassure her that Todd would be found unharmed, but the comforting words wouldn't come. Fear and red-hot anger threatened to choke him.

"What's going on?" Barr demanded, when both Glynis and Cort continued to stand mute.

"Glynis can't find Todd," Cort finally said.

If Barr's expression was anything to judge by, Cort knew his brother was thinking the same thing he was. "Damn!" Barr muttered. "What next?"

Glynis's gaze swung between the two men. "Is there something going on I don't know about?" It was obvious from the way her voice rose several octaves that hysteria was very close to the surface.

Cort's eyes softened as he looked at her, and then, ignoring her direct question, he said, "Come on, let's get you back in the saddle. We'll talk later."

Seconds later all three were mounted and ready to go.

"Where to first, little brother?" Barr asked.

"Let's go back by the house. If he's still not there, we'll head for the creek."

"The creek!" Glynis moistened her lips. "Oh, God, I never thought about him striking out there alone."

"Let's go." Cort gently kicked his stallion in the flanks with his boots. The animal reared on his hind legs, then settled on all fours, pawing the ground.

Glynis bit down hard on her lower lip, but not before a whimper escaped. "Yes, oh, please, let's hurry!"

None of them bothered to say anything as they rode hard, pushing their mounts to the limit. Each was filled with hope that when they pulled up at the house, Todd would be outside waiting for them.

He wasn't.

"Oh, Cort," Glynis cried, looking over at him. "What if . . . what if he's fallen into the creek?" Her voice broke, and she couldn't go on.

Cort rode up even with her, and she blindly reached out to him. "Cort?" she whispered again.

He pressed her fingers warmly before letting them go. "Let's don't go borrowing trouble," he said in a low tone. "We'll find him, I promise."

Her only answer was to grip the saddle horn so hard that the veins in her hands looked as though they might burst through her skin.

He glanced away, his face savage.

The trek through the forest behind the house was carried out in much the same manner as the ride back to the house—in total silence. Glynis sat tight-lipped and reed-straight in the saddle, her face a study in misery.

Because of her fragile hold on her emotions, Cort was making an effort to keep calm. No way did he want her to know that he feared Todd might have been kidnapped.

After they had covered three-quarters of a mile, Barr broke the silence, turning to look at Cort. "I find it hard to believe he would've wandered this far by himself."

"Me, too," Cort agreed grimly, "but we have no choice but to check it out."

"Are we . . . we nearly there?" Glynis's voice sounded raspy, as if her throat were sore.

"Another couple of yards," Cort said, swerving his mount to the right to miss a low-slung branch, then holding it up so Glynis and Barr could pass under it.

Before the creek came into view, it was obvious they had reached it. The rushing water had an eerie sound all its own.

It was hard to say who was first to dismount. It seemed as if all three hit the ground simultaneously, plowed through the underbrush and reached the clearing by the creek with clockwork precision.

Todd, however, was nowhere in sight.

"Barr, let's you and me split up," Cort said. "You go downstream. Glynis can come with me. We'll take upstream."

Barr nodded, as did Glynis, though weakly.

Thank God Glynis hadn't argued with him, Cort thought, taking her hand and pulling her with him. But even if she had, he wouldn't have let her go alone. If Todd *had* fallen into the creek, he didn't want Glynis to find him by herself.

Feeling perspiration oozing out of every pore in his body, Cort walked in front, while Glynis clung to his hand as if it were a lifeline. He dared not look at her for fear of what he would see in her eyes. Somehow he knew he'd be blamed for this, too.

"I'm...so scared, Cort," Glynis sobbed, tears running down her cheeks.

He paused, and turning around, met her eyes. "I know, so am I."

It was in that moment that they heard a loud whistle. Barr's whistle.

Glynis's hand froze in Cort's.

"Come on!" Cort ordered, almost jerking her arm out of its socket.

It took them only minutes to reach Barr. He was leaning against a tree, staring a few feet in front of him.

"Did you find him?" Glynis cried, lifting tortured eyes to Barr, as if unable to look elsewhere.

"He sure as hell did," Cort chimed in, grabbing Glynis by the shoulders and spinning her around.

Both Todd and the puppy lay on the grassy embankment, sleeping peacefully.

Glynis gasped, one hand flying to her chest, the other to her lips.

Suddenly, as if sensing he was no longer alone, Todd opened his eyes, then blinked.

"Hi, Mommy," he said with a grin.

Glynis leaned over the bed and once again caressed her son's cheek with the back of her hand. Even though it had been more than an hour since they had found Todd, Glynis still could not stop touching him, nor could she stop shuddering.

It was a miracle, she knew, that he was unharmed.

"Mommy, you still mad at me?" Todd asked, burying his cheek against her hand.

Glynis felt the prick of tears behind her eyes and she was stunned that she had any tears to shed. "No, son, I'm not," she said, sitting down beside him on the bed. "But I want you to promise me again that you won't wander off like that."

"But Mom, I've already promised three times."

Glynis smiled, but it never reached her eyes. "Promise me anyway."

He sighed. "Okay, I promise."

"Oh, darling, I was so afraid that you'd fallen into the creek and drowned. That's why I fussed at you."

"I already told you I didn't mean to go to sleep, but Champy lay down and wouldn't move. So I sat down, too, and fell asleep."

Those were exactly the words he'd used to Glynis in the woods, with Cort and Barr hovering over both of them. But once he'd been hugged amidst tears and cries of joy, he was severely chastised for his conduct, first by Glynis, then by Cort.

But then Cort had not rebounded. The instant she had put her arms around her son, Glynis had felt the color surge back into her face. Not so with Cort. For the longest time thereafter, he had looked drained.

"Mommy."

The solemn use of her name brought her back to the moment at hand. "What, darling?"

"Do you think Uncle Cort and Uncle Barr are still mad at me?"

"No, of course they're not."

Her words of assurance seemed to pacify him enough that his eyes fluttered shut again. Glynis remained beside him, peering down at him for another long moment, feeling her heart swell anew with gratitude for his safety. Now, if he could just get through the transplant...

After kissing him on the cheek, she stood and said, "I love you."

"I love you, too," Todd whispered without opening his eyes.

When Glynis walked into the den a few minutes later, the tears were no longer in evidence, and her composure was back intact. The men dropped their conversation and gave her their full attention.

"Is he still okay?" Cort asked, concern making his voice low and tense.

Glynis smiled. "He's fine, just tired."

"I guess so," Barr added from his position by the door, his hand on the knob. "He and that puppy took many a step."

"He carried the puppy most of the way because Champ wouldn't walk," Glynis said, her smile easing into a grin.

Barr laughed. "Well, do you blame Champ?"

Cort joined in, and they all laughed, then Cort's expression turned serious and he said, "It's funny now, but it damn sure wasn't a while ago. If that little bugger ever does anything like that again, I'll..."

"Oh, I don't think you have to worry about that," Glynis said with conviction.

"Well, guess I'd better be headin' home," Barr said, focusing his eyes on Cort. "I'm gonna try to finish mending that fence before it gets dark."

Glynis smiled at him. "Thanks again, Barr. Thanks for everything."

"Yeah, thanks, big brother," Cort interjected.

Barr waved their thanks away and turned the knob, only to pause and twist back around. "Oh, by the way, Glynis—in all the excitement, I almost forgot to tell you."

Glynis's head came up quickly. "Tell me what?"

"The house is ready."

"You mean as in ready to move in?"

"That's right."

"Oh, Barr," she exclaimed, "it seems like all I do lately is thank you."

"Think nothing of it," Barr said airily, only to then step hurriedly out the door, as if suspecting he had opened Pandora's box.

The room suddenly filled with a strained silence.

"Did you know the house was finished?" Glynis asked, sliding her hands into the pockets of her walking shorts.

"I knew," he said in a curt voice, his face stony.

He hadn't spoken to her in that harsh and uncompromising tone since they'd made love. She felt heartsick.

"You're moving, right?"

"Oh, Cort, please," she began miserably, "let's not fight about this again. Just accept it as something I have to do."

His eyes turned bleak, and he seemed to be struggling with himself. Then he stared intently at her. "You wouldn't, by any chance, consider letting Todd stay with me until after the surgery?"

Glynis caught her breath, but curiously she didn't feel threatened. Heartsick, but not threatened.

"No," she said quietly and honestly.

He turned away. "I didn't think you would."

Glynis studied his profile, which was cast in relief against the muted sunlight streaming into the room. He was tough, no doubt about it. And opinionated. And brooding. And unforgiving.

But as she continued to scrutinize him, there was more. A fleeting expression? Alerted, she even shifted slightly so that his face was in full view again. Loneliness. Cort was lonely. Even though he had his brother, his business, scads of employees, he held himself aloof. There was a sadness about him as well, a sadness that she hadn't noticed until now. But it was there, lurking in the depths of his blue eyes. Was she responsible for the changes in him?

Before she could sort through her own warring emotions, Cort stared at her with angry eyes. Or were they hungry eyes?

"We'll move your things whenever you're ready."

"You mean you're not going to try to stop me?" Glynis's voice reflected her incredulity. His shifts in attitude kept her continually off balance.

His jaw remained set in a rigid line, but he maintained his composure. "No, in fact I think it will be for the best."

With that he stamped out the door, leaving her standing in the middle of the room with her mouth wide open.

He was actually going to let them go. So where was the elation that should be rushing through her? Hadn't she been praying for this moment, obsessed with getting away from him, away from this house?

Why, then, was the thought of leaving such a bleak one?

"Well, do you like?"

"Of course, I do, silly." Milly grinned. "It's absolutely perfect for you and Todd. It reminds me of a dollhouse."

Glynis and Milly were in the kitchen, drinking iced tea, taking a break from lining cabinets with shelf paper and hanging curtains. They had been working all day and still were not through.

It had been two days since that unsettling conversation with Cort, and today was her first full day of independence. Yet she still hadn't experienced that feeling of joy and well-being she had been sure she'd feel.

Glynis took a quick sip of tea, and as she did, she peered at her watch. She bit her lip in annoyance.

"Buck's going to kill me for keeping you here so long."

Milly shook her dark head vigorously. "No, he won't." She grinned. "But even if he did, I wouldn't care. I'm on vacation this week, and it won't hurt him to feed the twins by himself. In fact, it'll do him a world of good."

Glynis chuckled. "You're probably right."

For a minute they sipped their tea in companionable silence. Then, with a frown marring her petite features, Milly asked, "Do you think it was a good idea to let Todd spend the night with Cort?"

Glynis lowered her eyes and plucked at a string on her shorts. "Probably not," she said with a sigh, "but Todd wanted to, and in a weak moment, I gave in."

"But do you think that was wise?"

Glynis pushed away from the table and crossed her feet at the ankles. "No, but then I'm a pro at doing things that are unwise. We both know that." That was especially true since she refused to muddle through her thoughts, to delve into her feelings. She was too afraid of the answer.

"When the surgery's over, do you think he'll battle you for custody?"

Glynis shifted her attention back to Milly. "He hasn't mentioned it lately, but yes, I suspect he will."

"Then surely I don't have to remind you to beware."

"You don't have to worry about that," Glynis assured her emphatically, "only..."

"Only what?" Milly was watching her closely over the rim of her glass.

"Oh, I don't know." Glynis paused, tilting her head to one side. "It's just that when I told him I was leaving, he seemed relieved, where before he had been adamantly against it."

"And that bothered you?"

Glynis flushed. "Yes, and it still does," she said in a small voice.

"Oh, honey, what a mess . . ."

Suddenly the sound of wailing sirens claimed their attention.

Milly shivered. "They sound awfully close, don't they?"

Glynis rose and walked to the window and peered into the darkness. "They sure do. I wonder . . ."

The phone rang.

Their eyes met as neither spoke about their own troubled and vivid thoughts.

"Want me to answer it?" Milly asked.

"No, I will." Glynis crossed to the wall phone and nervously lifted the receiver. She hadn't even said hello before the blood drained from her face.

Milly jumped up and ran toward her. "What's wrong?"

The phone slid out of her hand and bounced on the floor. "Cort . . . Cort's barn is on fire . . . and . . ."

"And what?"

"And . . ." Glynis's voice was little more than a hoarse whisper. "Todd and Cort are trapped inside."

Chapter 19

The short, hair-raising trip from the house to the ranch passed in virtual silence. Glynis couldn't have uttered a word even if she'd wanted to. Fear held her speechless, fear that was so thick in the car that she could taste it. Milly, too, was at a loss for words.

But the second Milly roared to a stop in the drive and cut the engine, she unbuckled her seat belt and turned to Glynis. "Are you all right?"

"No," Glynis whispered, her lips bloodless. "What...what if they...they didn't get out in time?"

"Don't say it! Don't even think it!"

Nausea welled inside Glynis. "Do you see them anywhere?"

"No, but that doesn't mean anything." Milly paused a split second, then added, "Wait here. I'll go find Barr." Following those clipped words, she jerked open the door and jumped out of the car.

Glynis remained inside, she still couldn't move. It was as if she were frozen. She felt detached, as though the mayhem taking place had nothing to do with her.

Two fire trucks were on the scene, their long hoses spraying the blazing fire with heavy doses of water. Still, flaming tongues of fire licked at the sky.

Everyone—the ranch hands, the firemen, the sheriff and several deputies—was shouting at once. And horses were whinnying loud and long. Glynis shivered.

"Over here!" a fireman shouted.

"No, here! It's outta control over here!"

"No dammit, all of you over here! We've got to get into the barn!"

Barr. That was Barr's voice. Frantically, Glynis's eyes sought the face to match the voice. He was only a few yards in front of her, shouting orders to the foreman.

Suddenly Glynis scrambled madly for the door handle. Once she'd wrenched it open, she stumbled out. But when her feet hit the ground, she almost lost her balance. Her knees knocked together ferociously.

Glynis whimpered as she frantically searched past one face, then another.

There were no signs of Cort or Todd.

"Oh, please, God," she prayed, forcing her legs to move toward Barr.

He turned at that moment and saw her. Meeting her halfway, he reached out and grabbed her arms. His hands and face were grimy with soot, and there was not a dry thread on him.

Glynis clutched at the front of his shirt, her features contorted. "Todd . . . and Cort . . . Are they . . . ?"

"Shh, take it easy," Barr ordered softly, trapping her flailing hands against his chest. "They're—"

"They're what?" she panted, unable to let him finish the sentence.

His words were aborted by a loud cry.

"Mommy! Mommy!"

"Todd!" Glynis twisted out of Barr's arms, her eyes searching frantically through the thick smoke for the sight of her son.

"Mommy! Mommy!" Todd cried again, only louder.

"Behind you, Glynis." Barr took her by the shoulders, and treating her as though she were a windup doll, pointed her in the right direction.

"Oh, Todd, my darling boy," Glynis whispered, running to him, arms outstretched, tears streaming down her cheeks. Todd launched against her like a missile.

She bent and hugged him to her, burying his tearstained face in the crook of her neck.

"Mommy, I . . . was so scared," he sobbed.

"Shh, it's all right now," Glynis cooed, one hand caressing him, touching him, loving him. "It's all right."

"Me . . . and Uncle Cort . . ." he began, only to start crying again.

Cort! Oh, God, where was Cort? Surely if Todd was safe, so was Cort. Biting her lower lip to keep from crying and upsetting Todd any more, she stood and grabbed his hand and walked back to Barr.

He would know if Cort . . . Oh, God, she mustn't think that way. Of course Cort was all right. He had to be.

Suddenly, a figure loomed large.

She stopped short. "Cort . . . is that you?"

"Glynis?"

"Oh, thank God." For a moment stinging tears rendered her sightless. She blinked in rapid succession.

Todd raised his head. "Mommy's here, Uncle Cort," he said inanely.

Cort stopped just short of her and gripped her arms, holding her steady. His eyes were like a caress as they roamed over her.

"Are you all right?" he asked huskily.

"I should be the one asking you that question." Glynis didn't even recognize her own voice.

A tiny smile curved his lips. "Why? Do I look like something the dogs dragged up?"

"Worse."

If it hadn't been for Todd in her arms, Glynis was afraid her legs might have caved in under her. Cort's face was smudged with soot as were his hands and arms. He smelled as smoky as the fire itself.

"Are you...hurt?" she stammered breathlessly, fighting off another bout of nausea.

"I'm all right, just madder than hell."

Before she could say anything more, Todd began to swing her hand. "Can I go stand by Uncle Barr and Milly?" he asked. "Over there."

Glynis took her eyes off Cort long enough to follow Todd's pointed finger. The smoke had cleared somewhat, as had the confusion. The blaze, too, seemed to be under control.

Barr, Milly and the sheriff stood deep in conversation, close to the men with the hoses.

Drawing Todd close to her side again, she said, "No, absolutely not. But you can go sit over there against that tree, if you want to, and watch." Though he seemed to have recovered from his scare, Glynis was not prepared to let him out of her sight.

"Okay," he mumbled, and walked off.

Glynis focused her attention back on Cort, who was busy wiping his eyes with a rag. "What happened?"

"Todd and I were in the barn with the vet seeing about one of the horses, when suddenly the whole damn place went up in smoke." He paused, and she saw his eyes glint dangerously. "To save you from the frightening particulars, we had to fight like hell to get out."

Hearing him admit how close they came to being burned alive, hot bile rushed up the back of her throat. "But why?" she whispered in disbelief. "I mean, *who* would do such a thing?"

Cort's eyes narrowed. "The same bastard who put a bullet in my side and tampered with my brakes."

"So you think the fire was set deliberately?"

"No doubt about it. But what I can't figure out is how he did it."

"What...what are you going to do? I mean—this can't keep going on."

"Don't worry, it isn't going to." Cort's voice dripped with determined fury. "I'm going to find the bastard and stop him."

"I hope so, before... before..." She couldn't go on, the thought so horrifying she couldn't put it into words.

Neither said anything for a moment.

Then Cort muttered brusquely, "Why don't you get Milly and go inside and make a pot of coffee."

Glynis nodded. "Todd needs to be in bed, anyhow."

"Here."

"Yes."

"What about you?"

"I'd like to stay, too." Her voice faltered. "If it's all right."

Unexpectedly, he reached out and ran the back of his grimy hand down one side of her cheek. "I'd like that. I'd like that very much."

Then, pivoting on his heels, he strode off.

Sweat oozed from Cort's pores like a cleansing rain. He turned toward the mirror while lifting, then lowering, the dumbell in his left hand, watching as the blood vessels pulsed in his upper arm.

It felt good to be back in his routine. He reveled in the free-flowing sweat. Fifty, fifty-one, he counted. He could feel his muscles expand as he pushed them, pushed himself to the limit.

The sweat ran down his face, over his lips, his chest, his stomach. Out of the corner of his eye he could see the raw place on his cheek, remnants of the night's humiliation. He clamped his jaw and held the weight steady, then slowly lowered it to the mat. He was iron-tough. And iron-willed.

If it was the last thing he did, he'd get that bastard....

Shortly, Cort draped a towel around his neck and went to the refrigerator he kept in the corner of the room, took out a jug of Gatorade and downed half of it without pausing. He walked into the adjoining bath, and after stripping off his shorts, stepped into the shower.

Minutes later, still clad only in briefs, Cort stood at the window staring at the charred remains of what used to be his barn.

He cursed silently, his thoughts splintering into several different directions at once.

He was finding it hard to comprehend that someone had actually broken through security. And he couldn't believe that same someone had guts enough to destroy his property. But both were hard, cold facts. It hadn't taken the fire marshal or the sheriff long to establish that the fire had been deliberately set.

He paused in his thoughts and took in a deep, settling breath, his ear tuned to the sounds of the night. All was quiet, as it should be; it was after midnight. The firemen, sheriff, neighbors, Barr, everyone was gone. And the hands were sleeping, except for those on watch.

Glynis and Todd were both asleep. Before leaving his bedroom and coming to his office, he'd stopped by their rooms to check on them, but hearing no sounds from either, he'd trudged wearily down the hall.

Now, after having worked off some of his frustrations, he should have been too exhausted to do anything other than fall into a deep sleep. He knew better. He still felt useless and more frustrated than ever. His desire for the bastard who had tampered with his brakes and torched his barn was tangible, like lust, and it tingled along his neck and shoulder muscles.

But equally strong was his appetite for Glynis. Forever Glynis.

He bared his teeth, which bore no resemblance to a smile, and stalked to the sofa. Stretching out on it, he tried to forget Glynis, tried not to let her get a stranglehold on him, all the while fighting the impulse to go to her bedroom and lose himself in her body.

No amount of mental flagellation worked. The longer he lay there, the more the turmoil within him grew. The more he mused, the hotter the fires inside.

Suddenly he lunged into a sitting position, and using the excuse that he needed to check on her one more time, he got up and walked out of the room.

He stopped when he reached her door, and after listening a moment, felt certain he heard movement from inside. With his heart pumping overtime, he slowly turned the knob.

Glynis was lying on her side, staring through the window at the moon. She had tried counting sheep, but that hadn't lulled her to sleep. Every time she closed her eyes, the horrors of the last few hours returned like a hideous nightmare.

Flinging the covers off her naked body, she got up and, after slipping into her robe and loosely belting it around her waist, crossed to her purse on the dresser. Maybe a couple of Aspirins would help calm her.

It was when she leaned over and stuck her hand into her purse that she heard the noise. At first she couldn't decide where it had come from, then she turned toward the door.

It was open, and Cort was standing on the threshold. Her hand froze. Adrenaline raced through her.

Moonlight poured into the room, bathing him in its magical glow while they stood mute and looked at each other, wondering what to do, what *not* to say.

"I…heard someone moving around, so I thought…" Cort muttered at last, only to break off and clear his throat roughly. Still his eyes did not waver.

Her gaze tracked his. The top of her robe was gaping, exposing her right breast, full and firm, the nipple and its areola pink and alluring.

Suddenly he drew in his breath. At the same time she saw him go instantly, achingly, erect.

Glynis groaned and snatched the fabric around her, staring at him, stunned. He edged toward her, and she covered her mouth with a trembling hand and watched him approach, unable to move.

She closed her eyes and tried to erase the image of his strong, beautiful body. She shook her head, her shoulders drooping under the heavy weight of her desire.

He gently tilted her chin with his finger.

"Glynis?" he whispered.

The spark in his eyes, the intensity of the heavy brows, formed a silent plea, mesmerizing her. Though her lips parted, no sound escaped.

Her breathing was so quick, so intense, and her heartbeat was so fast, she feared she was having a heart attack. But she couldn't die. Not now. Not with Cort looking at her as if she was his entire world.

"I've never met a woman as beautiful as you," he ground out.

He delved into the velvet brown eyes he had imprisoned, and outlined one side of her cheek with the back of his knuckles, tracing her lips with his thumb. But it was when his fingers touched the fluttering pulse in her neck that she silently pleaded with him.

"Oh, Cort." She struggled for breath, thinking she'd surely lose her mind altogether. He had the power to make her his for the taking.

Abruptly he stopped moving, and his eyes devoured her. "I can't get enough of you."

It was impossible to say who moved first, but it did not matter. What mattered was that they were in each other's arms, where they both longed to be.

Cort covered her mouth with his. She wrapped her arms around his waist. He held her tight until the mounds of her breasts, now completely free of the robe, were like precious gems against his chest.

He thrust his fingers into her hair and gently bit at her neck. She felt her blood race as her heart beat faster beneath his exploring hands and mouth. But then, he knew all her secrets.

"Tell me to leave." He bent his head so that his mouth was nearly upon hers again. "Tell me," he said in a strangled voice.

"No," she breathed, clutching at him. "Don't go. . . ."

He drew her closer into his arms. He stroked her back, then lower. She couldn't get enough air. His kisses smothered her. His tongue invaded her mouth. She pressed her thighs against him and felt his urgent hardness.

"Glynis, you're doing it to me again," he rasped, sliding the robe down her arms, letting it form a puddle at their feet, along with his briefs. He then swung her around and placed her on the bed.

Wordlessly, she reached out and touched his cheek, his neck, his chest with the hot tips of her fingers. Pleased little moans escaped from the back of her throat as she nestled against him, trapping his hard flesh between her legs.

"Ah, Glynis . . . Glynis . . . !"

Suddenly he was on top of her, using his mouth, his hands to render her mindless. It was only after he bent his head and put his mouth on hers and sank his fingers into her again, that she realized she no longer had any control of how much she was willing to give.

Mercifully and finally, clutching her buttocks, he drove deep inside her and spilled into her. And when he sighed and collapsed onto her breasts, she held him, releasing emotions inside her that she had buried so long ago she had forgotten they existed.

When they were through, she lay in his arms, tears running down her cheeks. She could not remember feeling so much physical pleasure laced with so much mental pain.

Chapter 20

She saw him again.

He was standing in the exact same place, across the street from Milly's day care, slouched against the tree with the same hat casting his face in a shadow.

The hairs on the back of Glynis's neck stood out as she stopped swinging Todd and stared at the stranger.

Who was he? The thought of him watching her son made her blood run cold.

Better still, could he be linked to Cort's trouble? Of course he couldn't, she assured herself, positive her imagination was playing tricks on her again.

"Mommy," Todd whined, twisting around in the swing. "Why'd you stop swinging me?"

For a split second she took her eyes off the man to answer Todd. "Hold on a minute, son."

When she whipped back around, the man was gone.

"Todd, honey," she said, "I'm going to talk to Milly, then we'll be leaving."

Glynis sighed as she made her way across the yard where Milly was playing hopscotch with several children. Stopping by the day-care had been an afterthought on her part when she and Todd had left the doctor's office a little while ago.

Todd had gotten a good report, and she'd decided to share the news with Milly. But they had been there for two hours already, and it was time they headed to the house. Her house.

She sighed again, coming to a standstill. She didn't want to dwell on the traumatic night she had spent at the ranch in Cort's arms, though that was all she had thought about. Giving in to his erotic demands yet again had merely added fuel to an already raging fire, a fire that was destined to burn itself out and her with it.

"Hey, Glynis, you about ready for another glass of iced tea?" Milly was asking.

Glynis smiled weakly. "That sounds good, but it's getting late. We need to be going."

"Sure you won't change your mind?"

"Not this time."

"Come on, then," Milly said, locking arms with Glynis, "I'll walk you to the car."

While Todd ran ahead, the two women walked at a slower pace. Facing Milly, Glynis asked, "Have you noticed a man hanging around the nursery?"

Milly stopped abruptly. "No. Have you?"

"Yes." Glynis's eyes were troubled. "Twice, in fact."

"Where, for God's sake?"

Glynis pointed across the street. "There, always against that tree."

"Mmm," Milly mused, shaking her head. "That's strange." She paused and peered closely at Glynis. "Are you trying to tell me you think he's watching you?"

Glynis shrugged. "I don't know, that's the trouble. Ever since this thing with Cort . . ." She let her sentence fade. "Oh, I don't know. It's just a crazy feeling I have." She gestured with a hand. "Chalk it up to paranoia."

"Well, in light of what you've been through, I can understand why you'd be paranoid. But I truly don't think there's anything to worry about."

* * *

Glynis was not so sure of that then, nor was she sure now, hours later, after she'd prepared dinner, cleaned up the brand-new kitchen and put Todd to bed. The man was still very much on her mind.

Doing her best to shake off her morbid thoughts, she went back into the kitchen and brewed three cups of coffee. When that was done, she filled a cup and walked back into the living room. The instant she sat down, the doorbell rang. Hurriedly putting down her cup, she went to the door, fearing the noise would awaken Todd.

"Who's there?" she asked hesitantly, her hand on the night latch.

"Cort."

"Oh," she murmured, her heart pumping wildly.

"Are you going to let me in?"

She slipped the bolt, and without looking directly at Cort, stood aside for him to enter. It had been two days since she'd seen him. However, he'd called both days and talked to Todd on the phone.

Once she'd closed the door behind him, Glynis pressed against it. "Nothing else has happened? I mean . . ." She faltered, disturbed by the intensity of his eyes as they met hers.

"No, thank God." His face relaxed. "I guess Todd's in bed."

"Yes. He . . . he was worn out." Cort smelled fresh, of soap and cologne, and she stared unconsciously at his mouth, remembering its exquisite sweetness on her body.

He cleared his throat. "I . . . er . . . tried to get here earlier, but I've been working like hell on the barn all day."

"You look like it, too," she commented softly, without rancor.

His dark eyebrows lifted. "And what look is that?" he asked with a faint smile.

"Your usual—tired, exhausted, worn out. Take your pick."

"You wouldn't be offering me any tea and sympathy, now, would you?"

The silence was static.

"Would . . . you settle for coffee instead?" she asked unevenly.

Something too fleeting to identify flashed in his eyes. But for one electric second they were soft and quiet and excruciatingly gentle. Then the look was gone, and he stared down at his hat. "Sure, especially since beggars can't be choosers."

Not knowing how to respond to that last statement, Glynis let it slide, uneasily making her way into the kitchen where she clumsily poured another cup of coffee. When she got back into the living room, he was standing by the window.

He turned just as she set the cup down. Their eyes locked and held. "Are you making it all right?" he asked.

She could see his labored breathing. His chest rose and fell heavily, as if he were having a hard time getting air in and out his lungs. She was having the same difficulty. He was too close.

"I'm fine. We're . . . fine."

"Do you need anything?"

"No . . . no, nothing that I can think of."

"Did Todd not get a good report today?"

"Yes, very good." Her voice was barely audible now.

"Are you sure?"

"Of course, I'm sure. Why do you ask?"

He continued to look at her. "Something's bothering you." It wasn't a question; it was a flat-out statement.

She sucked in her breath. For a moment she'd forgotten how adept he was at reading her, how he seemed to cut through to the bone and blood.

Her gaze fell.

"Glynis, look at me."

She raised her eyes to his, finding shadows, secrets in their depths. Her lips parted on a hopeless sigh as she averted her gaze. "It's nothing."

He moved closer. "Why not let me be the judge of that?"

"It's just my overactive imagination."

"Glynis."

"There . . . was a man."

He became instantly alert. "A man. Where?"

"At Milly's day-care."

"Go on."

"I've seen him there twice. And . . . when he'd catch me watching him, he'd just turn and walk off."

Cort's voice was sharp. "Can you describe him?"

Glynis picked up on his concern, his fear. She licked her lips. "No, because he wore a cap that covered his face."

He muttered an explosive expletive and bent over her. "Is there anything you can tell me about him? Anything at all?"

Glynis thought for a moment, then raised large, uneasy eyes to him. "He . . . he could have had a mustache, but I'm not sure."

"That's something, anyway."

"Cort, you're scaring me. Surely you don't think this is the same man who's . . . who's after you?"

He pivoted on his heel and rubbed the back of his neck. "I don't know what the hell to think. But at the same time, I . . . we can't rule out that possibility."

"But why—"

He cut her off. "I want you and Todd to come back to the ranch with me. Now."

"No."

"What do you mean, no?"

"Under the circumstances, I don't think that would be a wise move."

Cort's face grew hard and remote. "What circumstances?"

"You know," she said tautly.

"Damn, woman! My reasons for wanting you back at the ranch have nothing to do with us personally." He paused, his big shoulders rising and falling. "But even if they did, might I remind you that you were just as willing and eager as I was?"

She felt as if he'd socked her in the stomach. "You always have to bring things down to a baser level, don't you?"

"No, I don't. But you asked for that."

She lifted her head defiantly. "Well, Todd and I are not going back to the ranch."

"Even if the SOB is using you to get to me?"

"You don't know that for sure," she argued, knowing that she was being deliberately stubborn, but Cort had no proof to back up his suspicion. And she wasn't going to budge. At this moment facing an unknown enemy was preferable to moving back in with Cort.

His nostrils flared, as if he was reading her mind. "Is that your final word?"

"Yes."

"I could take Todd with me."

Silence.

She didn't flinch. "But you're not, are you?"

The silence multiplied.

"No, I'm not," Cort said tightly.

Glynis released her breath, but was unable to talk.

"Do you still have that gun I gave you years ago?"

The sudden change of subject caught Glynis off guard. She stared at him as if he'd taken leave of his senses. "What?"

"Do you still have the gun?" he repeated harshly and impatiently.

"Yes."

"Then get it and use it if you have to."

Glynis closed her eyes and reached blindly for the arm of the couch, sinking onto the cushions. It was only after she heard the door close that she realized she was alone.

When she opened her eyes, they landed on the two full cups of coffee that hadn't been touched.

"Betcha you wanted to throttle her, didn't you?"

"That's putting it mildly," Cort muttered tersely. "I believe she's more stubborn than she used to be."

"Seriously, you couldn't make her see reason?"

"Hell, no, she wouldn't listen to a damn thing I said."

Cort and Barr were in Cort's office at noon the following day. They were waiting for Gene Ridley to arrive from Houston.

Rain pelted the window behind Cort's desk. For a minute, both he and Barr stared at it as if they'd never seen it before.

Barr broke the silence by snapping his lighter open and lighting a cigarette.

Cort made a face. "Those damn things are gonna kill you."

"Everybody's gotta die for something."

Cort grimaced. "Your attitude stinks, big brother."

"No more than yours of late, little brother."

Making another disgusted sound, Cort got out of his chair and began pacing the floor behind him.

"You didn't leave her alone, did you?" Barr asked, taking a hefty drag on his cigarette.

Cort stopped his pacing and stared at his brother through a cloud of smoke. "No, of course I didn't. I sent Eddie to stand guard all night."

"I'm sure she'd appreciate that," Barr drawled.

"Yeah."

Barr grinned. "What's with you two anyway? You're either snapping at each other like dogs over the same bone or you're looking at each other like you're in heat—"

"Go to hell."

The rain slapped against the window pane, drowning out the growing silence.

Gene Ridley's discreet knock on the door broke it.

"Come in," Cort said from his position by the window. If Ridley felt the tension in the room, he chose to ignore it. After shaking hands with Barr, he gave his full attention to Cort.

"We've hit the jackpot, boss," he said.

"I'm listening."

Ridley swung his briefcase up onto the desk, but didn't bother to unsnap it. "When you called this morning and gave me the description of the man Mrs. Hamilton saw, I knew we were on a roll."

"Which of the three is he?" Cort asked, his mouth stretched into a tense line.

"Al Sabo," Gene announced proudly.

"Who the hell is he?" Barr's tone was gruff.

"Just one of the many scumbags your brother has sent to the joint," Gene said, switching his gaze to Barr.

Cort moved away from the window. "So how do you know Sabo's our man?"

Gene smiled. "I came here via Huntsville. And while I was there I found out the most interesting things about Mr. Al Sabo." His smile broadened into a grin as he focused on Cort. "Yes siree, it seems that our Mr. Sabo had a big mouth, bragged about how when he got out, your *rear*"—he stressed the word—"belonged to him."

Cort's laugh was hollow as he spread both his hands on the top of his desk and leaned heavily on them, his eyes encompassing both men. "So let's find the bastard and see whose rear belongs to whom."

Chapter 21

"Good night, darling. Sleep tight and don't let the bed bugs bite."

Todd giggled. "You're too late, Mommy, they already have."

"I know. That's why I put medicine all over your legs."

"They bit Adam and Kyle, too."

"I'm sure they did. Milly and I shouldn't have let you boys play outside so late."

His eyes lighted. "We had fun. We played robocops and—"

"That's enough," Glynis chided gently. "It's late, past time for you to be asleep."

When she would have switched off the light, Todd spoke again, stopping her.

"Mommy."

"What is it now?"

"When...when can I go back to the ranch to see Uncle Cort?" His face was scrunched into a frown.

The question didn't surprise Glynis. In fact, she had expected it before now. Since the barn fire she hadn't let Todd return to the ranch.

"Soon, I'm sure," she answered evasively.

"When's soon, Mommy?" he pressed.

"Before you go to the hospital. I promise." She smiled at him. "How's that?"

Todd grinned his acquiescence, then closed his eyes.

Once the door was closed behind her, Glynis wandered into the kitchen, where she poured herself a cup of coffee. Noticing that the pot was off, she put the cup in the microwave.

It was ten o'clock, and she knew she should go to bed herself. But since she and Todd had just gotten home from having dinner with Milly and her family, she was too keyed up to sleep.

Todd's transplant surgery was near and very much on her mind. In just a few days he was due to check into the hospital to begin the preliminary work. The thought of what he had to endure before the transplant could even take place was enough to drive her crazy.

With a heavy heart, she trudged into the dimly lit living room, only to stop in her tracks.

A man was standing in the middle of the room, pointing a gun at her head.

She froze, her heart beating in her throat. Horror and disorientation overwhelmed her. He was familiar, yet he wasn't. Then suddenly it hit her. The mustache! He was the man she'd seen around the day care, the one Cort suspected . . . Oh God!

"What . . . what . . . do you want?" she whispered, involuntarily taking a shaky step back.

The short, extremely muscular stranger glared at her, his face pinched and his eyes bright, unusually bright. For an instant the eyes reminded her of someone unbalanced, out of touch with reality. At the same time they gleamed with hatred, instantly filling her with an unknown terror.

"I want a lot, Mrs. Hamilton," he said, his voice low and tense. All the while he waved the gun at her.

Her mouth dried up. Her heart beat so fast, she could feel her muscles jerk with each beat. *Todd! Oh, please don't let him hurt my baby.*

"If . . . if it's money you . . . want . . ." she began, only to find her tongue suddenly thick and her throat dry. But she couldn't lose control. She had to remain calm so as not to disturb Todd. His . . . both their lives would more than likely depend on it.

He crept forward and laughed a cruel, mirthless laugh. "There isn't enough money in the whole damned world that can give me back what that son of a bitch took from me."

She wet her lips. "Who?" she asked shakily. Didn't the experts say it was best to keep a deranged person talking?

"Cort McBride, that's who," he spat. "And I'm going to make him pay." He paused and edged closer. "With his life, no less. And you're going to help me."

No! This couldn't be happening! Her mind raced, hunting for a solution. *Think, Glynis, think!* But what could she do? She couldn't run, and there was no way to divert his attention.

For the moment she was trapped and at his mercy. She sank her teeth into her lower lip to keep from crying out her fear.

"You're going to pick up the phone and call lover boy."

She shook her head frantically. "No."

"Yes." He leaned his head to the side. "Or you'll be sorry, or rather your kid in there will be sorry."

Glynis's face turned porcelain-white, and she tried to speak, but nothing came out.

"Ah, that's better. Now that we understand each other, suppose you pick up that phone and make that call."

Still Glynis did not move, could not move. She continued to stand exactly where she was as if she'd been cemented to the spot.

"Move it, damn you!"

She moved; her limbs jumped as though she'd been zapped with a stun gun.

"All right, I'll...do it," she whispered, "but please don't point that gun—"

"Shut up, lady, and just do as I say."

With hands that were oozing sweat, Glynis jerkily crossed to the phone and lifted the receiver. The entire time she punched out Cort's number, the man pointed the gun unsteadily at her temple. He was so close now, she could feel his hot, foul breath on her face. She breathed deeply to keep from fainting.

Then, mercifully, someone lifted the receiver on the other end. "McBride residence."

Her heart lurched. It was Maude Springer. Oh, God, what if Cort wasn't home? What if...

"Quit stalling, lady," the man warned, cocking the hammer inches from her ear.

Sweat popped out above Glynis's upper lip. "Mrs. Springer...it's Glynis. Is...is Cort there?"

"Is something the matter, dear? You sound...oh, I don't know...funny."

Glynis gripped the receiver until she feared her knuckles would crack. "Please, let me speak to...Cort."

Mrs. Springer paused a moment, then said, "All right. Hang on, dear. I think he's in his office."

"Is he there?" the man asked.

Glynis nodded.

"Good. You tell him something's wrong with the kid and for him to get over here quick." His tone was as cold and menacing as the gun. "You got that, lady?"

She nodded again.

"Screw up and you'll be sorry."

"Glynis, is something wrong?"

When the cool, crisp voice sounded in her ear, Glynis's legs almost buckled beneath her.

"Cort...it's..."

"Glynis, for God's sake, speak up. I can't hear you."

Glynis kept her eyes straight ahead. If she dared look at the gun, she feared she wouldn't be able to go on.

"It's...Todd. Come quick."

"I'll be right there."

When the cold dial tone sounded, the phone slid from her fingers, and she faced her tormenter.

"He's...he's coming."

"So far so good, lady. Follow my next instructions and maybe I'll let you and the kid live."

It seemed to Cort as if he stood by the phone forever, his mind in an uproar, when in reality it was only seconds. Then, with a muttered curse and two long strides, he was in front of his filing cabinet, jerking it open.

Something was wrong. Something was damned wrong. And it wasn't just his paranoia, either. Granted, if something had happened to Todd, it stood to reason that Glynis would be panic-stricken. But there was something else as well, something he couldn't put his finger on, but it was there nevertheless. Terror? Sheer terror? His gut instinct told him he was right.

After grabbing his shoulder holster containing his .357 Magnum, he slammed the drawer shut and tore out of the room. If Al Sabo had gotten to Glynis... Suddenly a picture filled with sights, sounds and smells of terror flooded his consciousness, almost stopping him cold. But no, that couldn't happen. Eddie was on guard.

Maude was standing in his path in the hallway, her face wrinkled in concern. "Is...Glynis all right?"

"Call the sheriff and then call Barr," he flung over his shoulder. "Tell 'em to meet me at her place."

A short time later Cort was on the road that led to Glynis's house. He brought the Jeep to a sudden halt and switched off the lights. Total darkness surrounded him.

He got out and moved quickly but cautiously until the house came into view. Then he stopped. Lights blazed from the living room, but from no other room that he could see.

With exception of his harsh breathing and the occasional sound of a cricket chirping nearby, the night was eerily quiet.

He crept toward the back of the house, trying to reconcile his actions. If Todd had hurt himself or was sick, then caution was not the way to go. On the other hand, if Todd was a ploy to draw him to the house, then he was doing the right thing. Again gut instinct told him the latter was the case.

When he reached the back corner of the house, he flattened himself against the wood and inched his way toward the window. It was then that his foot struck an object. Hoping for the best and fearing the worst, Cort looked down. Sprawled on the ground was a body. Eddie's body. With his heart beating out of sync, Cort knelt and placed two fingers on the pulse in Eddie's neck. The pulse was weak, but steady.

Praying that Eddie would be all right until help came, Cort rose and once again plastered his body against the house. Luck was with him. The blinds were open. Scarcely breathing, he moved closer.

Hesitating only a heartbeat, he then rounded the corner just enough to allow him to see inside the room.

What he saw robbed him of his breath. Glynis was sitting on the edge of the couch. Sabo was standing a few feet from her, a gun aimed at her heart. Todd was nowhere to be seen.

Sweat popped out on Cort's forehead as he withdrew his gun from the holster, contemplating his next move. Sabo was not in control. That in itself was of primary concern. His hand was trembling, which meant the gun could accidentally discharge at any time, whether Sabo wanted it to or not. No doubt about it, Sabo was an extremely dangerous man.

But as long as Sabo kept his back to the door, Cort knew he had a chance, albeit a slim one, but still a chance. Crouching down so that his head was below window level, he ran to the back door. By the time he rose, flush with the house again, his blood was pounding in his skull. If that son of a bitch hurt so much as a hair on Glynis's or Todd's head . . .

Suddenly the puppy barked.

"Damn!" Cort hissed under his breath. Champ was at the door, barking ferociously and loudly.

"McBride, is that you?" Sabo yelled.

"Yeah, it's me."

"Put your gun down and come inside with your hands raised or I'll waste the little lady."

Cort's eyes glittered dangerously in the dark. "Take it easy, Sabo. This is between you and me. Let her and the boy go. Then we'll talk."

"No!" Sabo shouted. "I'm calling the shots. I give the orders, not you. Understand?"

Cort could hear the tremor in his voice, knew he was hovering on the edge. One wrong word, one wrong move could send him hurtling headlong over that edge.

"All right, Sabo. Take it easy," Cort said again.

"Open the door slowly, McBride, and come in with your hands up. And don't try anything foolish, either."

Cort did as he was told.

The instant he stood on the threshold, his eyes took in the scene in front of him. Sabo had his left arm across Glynis's throat, while his right one held the gun to her temple. Glynis's face was chalk-white, and her lower lip was trembling.

A pulse throbbed in Cort's neck.

"Sabo, let her go," Cort demanded with a calmness he was far from feeling. He felt as if a grenade had been planted in his belly. "This is between you and me."

"That's right, McBride," Sabo cried, wild-eyed. "Only I had to use her to get to you."

"So now you've got me. Let her go."

"No. You're going to pay for what you did to me, for ruining my life, for turning my family against me, for making me a laughingstock in my hometown." He was running his sentences together while saliva gathered at the corners of his mouth. "But...but first I'm going to make those you love pay. Do you hear me, McBride? I'm going to make *her* pay!"

Sabo buried the barrel of the gun deeper into Glynis's temple.

She whimpered, her eyes on Cort.

An alarm went off inside Cort's brain. The silence reached a screaming pitch.

"Mommy!" Todd's unexpected cry split the air like a bullet through a plate-glass window.

Sabo flinched, and when he did, he took his eyes off Cort. That was the break Cort had been waiting for.

"Glynis, hit the floor!" he shouted.

She did, but not before she elbowed Sabo in the gut, causing him to lose control of the gun. It hit the carpet with a thud.

A loud grunt was the only sound out of Sabo as he doubled over like a question mark. Cort moved lightning fast. He grabbed Sabo by his thick hair, jerked his head up and blasted him in the nose with his left fist. It rocked Sabo back, and blood spurted. Sabo shook his head and lunged toward Cort.

"I wouldn't if I were you," Cort warned. He then proceeded to pop Sabo's jaw with the back of his hand. But it was the upper cut to the chin that sent the thug spinning backward onto the couch. His legs spread instantly. His arms sagged. He sat stiff as a corpse, then fell onto his side and was still.

* * *

From that moment on, everything seemed to happen at once. Glynis barely had time to answer Cort's tersely muttered, "Are you all right?" before the wail of approaching sirens made further speech impossible.

Instead of waiting to see Al Sabo handcuffed and hauled to the sheriff's car, Glynis had fled down the hall to Todd's room, only to find that he had fallen back to sleep.

She had leaned over and kissed him before dragging herself back into the living room to face what she knew would be a long question-and-answer session.

Now, two hours later, it was all over. She stood by the window and watched as the last of the taillights disappeared down her long drive. It was the ambulance transporting a now conscious Eddie to the hospital.

It was only after Cort came back inside and approached her that she began losing control.

"Glynis," he whispered in a hoarse, uneven voice, lifting his hands as if to hold her, only to let them drop to his side. "It's all over."

Suddenly her shoulders began to shake, and she looked up at him with tear-filled eyes. "Please . . . hold me."

He didn't have to be asked twice.

"Are you awake?" Cort asked in a gravelly whisper several hours later, his lean length against her back and buttocks.

"Uh-huh."

"Are you still scared?"

"No," she said quietly.

"It's Todd and the surgery, isn't it?"

She nodded, blinking back tears.

After she'd collapsed in his arms and begged him to hold her, Cort had taken her into her bedroom and laid her tenderly onto the bed. Then he'd lain beside her. But he hadn't made love to her as she had thought—had hoped—he would.

Instead he had undressed her as if she were a baby, and after impatiently discarding his own clothing, had pulled her onto the bed with him. Wordlessly he had caressed her body with an artist's sensitive touch, without so much as a kiss.

He'd held her against him, his lips buried in her sweet-smelling neck, his burgeoning masculinity hard against her buttocks. Then, with a sigh and one hand softly capturing a breast, they had drifted to sleep, but only after their hearts had finally slowed to a normal beat.

Now, several hours later, they were both awake. And he was probing her heart.

"Day after tomorrow is the day," Glynis whispered.

Cort pulled her closer. "I know."

"Are you scared?"

He turned her onto her back and gazed down at her, pain darkening his eyes.

"Yes, I am, believe it or not," he said. "But more for Todd than for me."

He was breaking apart inside, just as she was. It was in that moment she forced herself to face the truth, a truth that had been haunting her since she'd walked back into his life. She still loved him, had never stopped loving him.

But instead of the insight bringing joy, it brought more pain. No matter whether he hurt her or not, she wanted to be a part of him one last time. Moaning, she clutched at him.

"Everything's going to be all right," he whispered, his breath warm on her lips. At the same instant he lifted her on top of him, easing her gently and quivering onto him, rising hot and hard into the core of her body.

With a muted sob, she buried her face into his chest and held onto him as if she'd never let him go.

Chapter 22

The transplant was over. The long wait had ended.

Seated in Dr. Johns's office, Glynis's eyes rested on Cort, who was on the other side of the room, his features tense and unyielding.

Nervously she fidgeted with the ring on her right hand, struggling to maintain her composure.

Dr. Johns was due to walk through the door any moment now and tell them if Todd could go home.

It had been almost four months to the day that Todd had been placed in isolation, his bone marrow flushed from his body and replaced with Cort's.

New white blood cells had been manufactured with no sign of rejection, although anti-rejection drugs had been administered on a daily basis.

New red blood cells had taken much longer to appear, and Todd had had to have several blood transfusions.

During the time he had been in isolation, Glynis had not left the hospital. She had stayed at the Ronald McDonald House and several times a day had entered Todd's isolation chamber dressed in a sterile robe, gloves and mask.

Cort, on the other hand, had continued to stay at the ranch and commuted back and forth. His presence had puzzled her. She'd been certain that once he had fulfilled his obligation to Todd, he would have returned to his condo in Houston.

She had looked forward to Cort's visits to the hospital, though nothing personal was discussed between them. It had seemed as if everything had been put on hold until Todd's ordeal was over. Yet she'd been aware of him with every nerve in her body. She had sensed he felt the same way, even though he had kept his distance.

Still, there had been moments when it was all she could do not to fling her arms around Cort and beg him to hold her, to love her. But she hadn't because she'd known the time had come for her to begin weaning herself away from him.

With that thought uppermost in her mind, Glynis tore her gaze from him and forced herself to check the room for articles she might have forgotten to pack.

"Where the hell is that doctor?" His muttered words split the lengthening silence.

Glynis drew in a jagged breath. "I don't know," she whispered. "Maybe . . . maybe those last-minute tests they were running on Todd took longer than expected."

"Well, if he doesn't get here soon, I'm afraid I'm going to tear the whole damned hospital apart."

Glynis saw the anguish in his face, heard it in his voice. Suddenly she knew that no matter what Cort had done to her in the past or regardless of how he felt about her now, she could not deprive him of his son. She had to let Cort be a vital part of Todd's life. Otherwise she would not be able to live with herself.

Dear Lord, she cried silently, how was she going to do it? To see Cort and not be able to hold him or to have him hold her was a fate worse than death.

The sound of the door opening cut into her tormenting thoughts.

Her eyes, along with Cort's, sought out Dr. Johns's as he strode into the room, not pausing until he'd reached his desk.

Glynis couldn't have uttered a word even if she'd wanted to; the lump in her throat was much too large.

Cort cleared *his* throat as if he, too, was having the same difficulty. Still, when he spoke, his voice sounded unlike his own. "Well, doctor?"

Dr. Johns grinned broadly. "To date there are still no signs of graft-versus-host disease, which in layman's terms means there are no signs of rejection."

"Go on..." Glynis managed stiffly, watching as Cort crossed the room to stand beside her. She was grateful for his presence.

"As far as we're concerned, the transplant is a success."

"Are you...saying he can go home?" Glynis's voice cracked.

Dr. Johns's grin broadened. "That's exactly what I'm saying."

Without realizing what she was doing, Glynis lifted wide, tear-filled eyes to Cort and whispered, "Did you ... hear what he said? Our son is going to be all right."

Cort reached out and trapped a tear with a finger. Then he grinned. "Yeah, I heard. Isn't that something?"

This time it was the doctor who coughed, effectively shattering the silence.

"Even though we're dismissing him, Todd will have to be monitored closely," Dr. Johns went on. "You both understand that."

"We understand," Cort responded.

"Before you leave, I'll brief you in detail as to his care."

Glynis frowned. "You mean we can't take him now?"

"When I left him, he was sound asleep. Until he wakes up, I suggest you two grab a bite to eat." He paused with a smile. "Celebrate or something."

"I'm not hungry," Glynis said hastily, "but I do need to go back to my room and pack."

"I'll go with you," Cort put in.

Momentarily disconcerted, Glynis shrugged. "All right."

Dr. Johns came from behind his desk and went to the door. "I'll see you later, then."

On the way back to her small room, they had reviewed every word Dr. Johns had told them, trying to convince themselves it was true.

Now, though, words seemed to have dwindled between them, creating a long and tension-filled silence, a silence that showed no signs of ending. It was as if they both realized the same rules that had governed their lives for months would no longer apply.

Swallowing a deep sigh, Glynis forced herself to fold her things neatly and put them into the suitcase, though her mind was not on the task at hand. Far from it. It was on Cort and the fact that he was standing like a statue by the window, ignoring her.

She squeezed her eyelids shut to hold back the tears, refusing to shed them. After all, this was a moment for joy, not tears. Todd was going to be all right.

Cort was free to return to work, traipse to the far-reaching corners of the globe if he so desired. And she—well, she was free to sell the house and move back to Houston and begin teaching.

Only she wasn't free. Her heart and her soul belonged to Cort, had always belonged to Cort, would always belong to him. Yet he was no closer to belonging to her now than he had been six years ago. He was like the wind, a free spirit, unwilling and incapable of being tied down.

Unable to bear the silence another minute, Glynis snapped the lock on her suitcase and said, "Cort...I'm ready when you are."

Though Cort heard her speak, he pretended not to, stalling for time. There was so much he wanted to say, but the words wouldn't come. Fear held him mute, kept him from saying what was on his heart, his mind.

What drove him now had driven him for years, was his all-consuming desire to get even with Glynis. Only it had backfired. The joke was on him. He had fallen in love with her all over again.

He had to stifle the urge to go to her, to take her in his arms and hold her close and tell her how sorry he was for the pain he'd caused her, that he no longer blamed her for the past because he had been the one at fault. She had pegged him with accuracy. He had been filled with a wanderlust he couldn't conquer, had burned with a need to have material things he had never had.

He hadn't meant to hurt her by his selfishness, but he had. The pain in her eyes broke his heart; he wanted to bring joy and laughter back to them. Was it too late? Was there too much in the way?

He didn't know, he honestly didn't know. His gut was splitting in two.

"Cort, I'm ... ready," Glynis repeated haltingly, uncertain of his dark mood, yet wanting desperately to get out of this tiny cramped room that seemed even smaller with him in it.

He turned then and walked toward her, not stopping until he was within touching distance. "Did you mean what you said in Dr. Johns's office?"

Glynis looked confused. "What ... what did I say?"

"You referred to Todd as *our* son."

She dragged in a shuddering breath. "Yes, I meant it."

"Does that mean you're going to let me be a part of Todd's life?"

"Yes."

They stared at each other in silence.

A muscle twitched in his jaw. "I would never have tried to take him away from you. You know that, don't you?"

Her chest almost caved in under the emotional pressure. She bowed her head. "I ... know."

"Glynis," he said huskily, "look at me."

She bit her lip and looked up. Cort was so close now, she felt herself wanting him, needing him. She remembered well that look in his eyes that warmed her, made her feel secure.

But she knew that was not to be again. Cort wanted Todd, not her.

Hurting inside with all the tears she could not shed, and the emptiness of knowing that she had lost him all over again, she committed everything about him to memory.

"What now?" she whispered, feeling tears burn her eyes in spite of her efforts to keep them at bay.

"What do you mean, what now?" he asked.

"Well, I assumed you'd be off to places unknown, to—" She broke off, her voice fading into thin air.

"Is that what you want?"

I want only you! her heart cried. But she said, "Does it matter what I want?"

"It could, you know."

"What . . . what are you saying?"

His gaze did not budge. "We . . . we could get married."

"Yes . . . we could, but it would be for all the wrong reasons."

"I guess you're right," he said dully. "Anyway, it probably wouldn't work."

Glynis felt her heart crumble into a million pieces. For a moment she had thought, she had hoped . . .

"Glynis," he said thickly.

She shook her head. "I'm . . . I'm going to sell the house and move back to Houston," she heard herself say in a small voice.

"No."

Her head jerked up.

"You . . . you needn't worry. You can see Todd whenever you want."

Suddenly, with a cry straight from the gut, Cort clasped her arms and dragged her against him, roughly aligning their bodies. He was shaking; she could feel it. Something snapped inside her. She went limp, losing all desire to fight him.

"Oh, Glynis," he groaned, "don't do this to me. I don't think I could survive if you walked out on me again."

Glynis twisted out of his embrace and stared at him with disbelief. "Cort, do you know what you're saying?"

"No, but I know what I'm trying to say." His eyes caressed her.

"I'll even let you adopt Todd, if you want to," she said desperately, still certain she was misinterpreting his words.

"You've missed the point," he muttered, grasping her shoulders and pressing her back against him as if he couldn't bear any distance between them. "Sure I'd love to adopt Todd, but only after you marry me."

"Oh, Cort," she cried, nestling against him and feeling his instant response to her closeness. "I...thought it was only Todd you wanted."

"Oh, Glynis, Glynis, I want you both. Surely you know that?"

She started to cry.

"I love you more than it's possible to say."

"And I love you," she whispered.

Groaning, he covered her mouth with his own and didn't pull away until they lay side by side on the narrow bed behind them.

"Oh, Cort," she whispered again.

His kiss cut off her words. Suddenly all the anger and bitterness and regrets vanished, and they were two people deeply in love in a world all their own.

They made love urgently, hurriedly, as if their time together was still a dream. When he thrust deep within her, she cried out with a sweet pain so intense she thought she'd surely die.

Sated, they remained entwined, their clothes strewn around them.

"I never stopped loving you," Cort said huskily, cradling his head in the palm of one hand and bending over her.

Glynis turned slightly so she could peer up at him. "Nor I you."

"Does that mean you're going to marry me?"

She smiled with lazy happiness. "Just try to stop me."

It was quiet in the room while he kissed her soundly.

"I can't believe all those years we wasted nursing our pride."

Glynis expelled a breath. "Me, neither."

He busily caressed a nipple with the tips of his fingers.

"C...Cort..."

"Mmm?"

"I called you to tell you about the baby."

Cort went completely still. "What?"

"You really didn't know, did you? Your partner back then didn't tell you?"

Cort drew in a harsh breath and let it out slowly, painfully. "No, he didn't tell me."

There was a long moment of silence.

"Can you ever forgive me?" he asked, his features tormented, "for that and so much more? For being pig-headed . . ."

She placed a finger across his lips. "There's nothing to forgive, my darling. I was just as stubborn as you. I should have trusted you."

He captured her hand and turned her palm against his lips. That erotic touch set her on fire, driving her closer against him.

"Do you want to live at the ranch?" he asked rather incoherently as she was busy moving her knee up and down his leg.

She frowned and stilled. "I . . . don't understand. I assumed we'd live in Houston, close to your work."

"You assumed wrong, my darling," he said with an indulgent smile. "I'm going to turn the day-to-day running of the business over to Gene. He's shown me he can handle it. I want to ranch, but more than that I want to be a husband and father."

"Oh, Cort," she said, reaching up and touching his face lovingly. "Are you sure that's what you want? Because it no longer matters to me what you do. I can come to terms with a part-time husband, as long as you're happy."

"Well, I don't want to be a part-time husband or part-time father. I want to be with you and my son."

She smiled. "And speaking of our son, don't you think we'd better go get him?"

"Soon, my love, soon."

"And soon we'll tell him that you're his daddy, the daddy he's always wanted."

Cort's eyes were brilliant. "Have I told you that I love you?"

"Yes, but you can tell me again."

"I love you."

She lifted trembling lips to his. "And I love you."

"Forever this time?"

Her eyes glowed. "Forever."

* * * * * *